Beautifully expressed—ANG Newspapers

"Eveline discovers herself and the importance behind the choices she makes as a human being. Told from the perspective of the young girl's mind, Eveline's thoughts are beautifully expressed in a very evolving self-awareness kind of way. The story of one of her love interests, Rourke, an older man who captures her heart, is the central leaping point from girlhood into womanhood. As Eveline becomes transfixed by his attraction to her, she processes the meaning of their personal connection on levels far beyond the surface."

"Notable Fiction," 2003 Book Awards—Writers Notes Magazine

Poetry and brilliant descriptions throughout—It seems as if you are reading a painting
—Beyond Chron, San Francisco

"This beautifully written, poetic novel is leaps and bounds ahead of the typical coming-of-age novels that crowd reading lists. Written as a first-person account of a young woman's experiences in her last year of high school and through her years at college, the book is a throwback to the days when the joy from reading came from the quality of writing as opposed to simply the plot. It is all too rare today to see a novel targeted to a below-30 audience that avoids the usual stereotypes and seeks greater meaning from the characters' relationships with family, friends, and lovers. The book is in the style of a confessional, but it laces poetry and brilliant descriptions throughout, so that it sometimes seems as if you are reading a painting. Hamann is offering a book you will savor—I was in no rush to complete it as I did not want it to end. The book is set in the Hamptons and New York City, though the main character is far from wealthy. Hamann includes many jibes against the Reagan Administration, though the book's politics are more targeted toward the larger question of our values and whether one's desire to pursue art and love should be sacrificed to money and practicality."

The language immersion that takes place while reading this novel is mesmerizing
—The East Hampton Star

"By all accounts, Ms. Hamann loves words. The language immersion that takes place while reading this novel is mesmerizing. A detached, otherworldly aura surrounds Eveline's observations and analyses as she describes East Hampton and its high school crowd in the late '70s. The view we get is tightly focused, like looking in from the opposite end of a telescope. Much contemporary fiction set in East Hampton has more of a broad-scoped, outside-in point of view, and it is to Ms. Hamann's credit that the East End of the novel bears no resemblance to the East End of media hype."

J.D. Salinger meets Edith Wharton—Suicide Girls

"With the cultured style of J. D. Salinger meets Edith Wharton, Hilary Hamann's *Anthropology of an American Girl* gives a fresh perspective on young girls."

V.

ANTHROPOLOGY
OF AN
AMERICAN GIRL

a novel by
H. T. HAMANN

VERNACULAR PRESS

VERNACULAR PRESS
SECOND EDITION — DECEMBER 2004

V.

Library of Congress Catalog Number: 2003107842 (Hardcover Edition)
ISBN: 0-9740266-5-4

Manufactured in the United States of America

10 9 8 7 6 5 4 3 2

Author's acknowledgements, including those for previously published material,
can be found at close of book.

VERNACULAR PRESS
560 BROADWAY, SUITE 509
NEW YORK, NY 10012

www.anthropologyofanamericangirl.com
www.vernacularpress.com

Through his unwavering faith in me, James Benard has made this book—and all my work—his own.

We shall not cease from exploration
And the end of all our exploring will be to arrive where we started
And know that place for the first time.

—T. S. Eliot

CONTENTS

FOREWORD

NOTES

ONE
CROCUS

TWO
OPAL

THREE
TRACKS

FOUR
MONTAUK

FIVE
TROPICS

SIX
CITATION

SEVEN
TREES

EIGHT
RIVER

HILARY THAYER HAMANN'S *ANTHROPOLOGY OF AN AMERICAN GIRL* IS A RARE book. In an age when "chick-lit" reigns because short attention spans and the lure of trashiness skew publishers' bottom lines, *Anthropology* stands out as exquisitely retro. It is a long, seriously pleasurable read, a book one happily carries around for as long as it takes, enriching the hour before bed, or making the wait at a doctor's office fly by. One is taken so deeply into the sensibilities of a community of characters that one feels changed, as if from traveling to another region or country—feeling sharper perceptions about one's self because of the differences and similarities seen so clearly in the hearts and minds of others.

Hamann's skillful uncovering of a particular time, place, and generation in American life impresses for its layers of story. It's about a girl; it's about Long Island and Manhattan and New Jersey. It's about the kids who grew into edgy awareness along with Kurt Cobain. It's about defining the self, the disorientations of divorce, the abuses and resurrections of lust, the varieties of friendship and love, the losses that spur independence, the ways art can heal a soul. And it's about language—because Hamann is a poet at heart, whose sensual sense of words turns meditative moments into vivid, living thought. Her years as a filmmaker trained in anthropological analysis make her scenes richly visual, culturally specific, and psychologically nuanced all at once. Hamann's vision is a throwback to an earlier age, when novels were *the* source for engaging, instructive cultural analysis, often through the stories of women and men as they negotiated the rules and betrayals of their era's values. Such grand stories set the tone for a culture's self-awareness. Now Hamann has given our era a quintessential icon like Jane Austen's *Emma*, George Elliot's *Middlemarch*, Theodore Dreiser's *Sister Carrie*, and Edith Wharton's *The Age of Innocence*.

A few talk show producers, slick magazines, and even reputable newspapers judged *Anthropology of an American Girl* as "too long," not "trashy" enough, or for an audience "too smart." The implications of such judgments are sobering, but clarifying. Hamann's novel is not meant to be a temporary media event. It is a work of art, meant to outlive the fads of an era and to be rediscovered off and on, over time, just like *Emma* or *The Age of Innocence*. As a book reviewer, years ago I saw that book review pages were often filled with male authors, reviewed by male writers, covering public policy, history, or mysteries and thrillers. Worthy subjects all. But only half the story of life. And not the preferred subjects of the majority of book-buyers—women. So I looked for the women writers on the book editor's shelf. And those men writing from life where we live—not just in our intellects, but in our hearts. I avoided the pop-culture made-for-TV books and looked for the prose poets. Some showed uneven talent. Some, like Andrea Barrett, Madeleine Thien, Dan Chaon, and now H. T. Hamann, affirmed that serious, domestic visions and voices are still being published, despite apparent industry prejudices toward the esoteric or the tabloid.

Truth be told, despite the statistics that dictate who gets reviewed on the *Today Show* or in the *New York Times Book Review*, most readers are hungry for a story with which they can actually fall in love—a narrative so well-wrought, it can catch their breath, characters so familiar and complicated, they can irritate, seduce, and change one's thinking. *Anthropology of An American Girl* stands out as a novel which satisfies this need for real, artful storytelling. It is philosophically stimulating without being dryly intellectual and it has characters who wrestle with loneliness, ambition, and sexuality in ways that aren't caricatured, but complex and rich with emotions both terrifying and lovely.

We need more such novels, to counterbalance the polemics and the fluff that we are likely to forget in a day. We want to think and be moved, we want to be swept sensually into someone else's world, so we can be surprised by and reassured about our own lives. Recently, a woman I know said, "I'm bored with TV; it's like those drugstore novels." She had fallen out of the habit of truly reading, she said, and longed for the pleasure of a good book. She wanted something she wouldn't be able to put down, something that would make her long to get home to at the end of the day. I told her, Hamann's *Anthropology* was her girl.

Dr. Beth Taylor
Department of English
Brown University, 2004

I remember turning. I remember exactly what it was to turn.
I remember turning. / (I remember exactly what it was to turn.)

IT HAS BEEN ONE YEAR SINCE THE FIRST EDITION OF *ANTHROPOLOGY OF AN American Girl* went to print, and though much has happened since then, the most tangible marker of the passing time for me has been my distance from the book itself—not only from the characters and the world they inhabit, but from the orderliness of the process, the ritual of engagement. I recently reentered the live document in order to make editorial corrections, and I felt an overwhelming sense of relief to be back. The open file was so familiar and reassuring, so me and mine, that going back in after months away was like returning home from a deeply unsettling journey. It was clean and orderly inside, cool and complete, a place to go, to escape, like walking through white. One year indeed—one year since I had last traveled its corridors— companions to the darkest, tenderest corridors in my mind. And though it was good to be back, there was no hope of remaining. The briefest of visits was all that could be allowed. I suppose it is only fitting that this study of loss—loss of love, youth, faith, life, home, voice, and most significantly, of the will to live meaningfully—would itself be lost to me.

Because it would be unwise for me to attempt to historicize a project that is as new to the world as it is near to me, I will speak in this space only of the things I did, and did differently. I relied on autobiographical and anthropological modes to describe my culture from a position deep within it, thinking more of reaching readers than of conforming to contemporary visions of the marketplace. My objective is to encourage others to write reflexively, and, if necessary, independently, and to respectfully remind those who need reminding that the basic practice of writing—as a means of self-expression, as a method of inner-listening and of outer-recording, as an aid to memory and an heirloom to family and friends, as a reputable and essential art form—falls entirely outside the jurisdiction of industry. While I do not think that literature should shun commercial viability, I do believe that writing as a form should precede the commodification of content. Whether or not a work of literature has the potential to become profitable should be a consequence of its quality or an accident of its fortune as opposed to the result of a well-executed marketing plan.

Obviously, there is much at stake in the production of commercial literature, particularly in the manufacture of titles "big" enough to capitalize on the cross-platform capacities of media giants and to fuel the engines of large— usually publicly-held—publishing houses. In order to "make" a best-seller, these organizations spend a great deal of money to get the book reviewed, ordered, and purchased. Insofar as businesses need revenue to remain viable, and there are only so many books the public can be expected to buy, it would be pointless to challenge the legitimacy of established methods. However, concerned citizens should consider themselves obligated to think critically about the business of art and its implications on local and global culture. Among the inquiries we might make of publishing systems in particular are the following: *How many fine writers are silenced in advance by an industry they perceive as closed to the value of their voices? How many books are published because they are deemed middling enough to be marketable? How has it come to pass that the market prefers brevity in literature? To what degree do industry relationships determine the success of a title before it reaches the buying public? How do systems of literary appraisal—reviews, best-seller lists, awards, media coverage—operate? Do these systems benefit writing as an individual and collective practice? In a commodity marketplace, can literature ever be conceived of as space in which writer and reader engage in a culturally active, meaningful examination of the self and the human condition?*

Anthropology of an American Girl is precisely what it claims to be: the story of a young woman and her culture that strives for a measure of narrative depth, detail, and objectivity. It does not deal in broad strokes because it would not have been reasonable for me to render a reductive view of life while attempting to show the importance of maintaining an expansive one. And so, *Anthropology* is a long book—not about Einstein, Franklin, Lincoln, war, disease, finance, or any other topic typically considered worthy of length, but about a girl. Because there was little chance that a mainstream publisher would have been interested in an unapologetically long novel (about a girl) that defies simple categorization and refuses to appeal to the deficits of its audience, I chose to remain independent. In so choosing, I forfeited the level of exposure I might have received if I had been affiliated with a larger entity, but subsequently, I was able to retain the artistic self-determination that many are expected to sacrifice. Since the length of this novel is bound to its meaning and to its potential effectiveness, it would not have been possible to alter the book to satisfy current publishing standards for page count and degree of difficulty without degrading the evolution of character, disrupting the purity of voice, and betraying the trust I hoped to establish with the reader. I am pleased with the critical and popular response to *Anthropology of an American Girl*, and I would like to thank those reviewers and readers who were, themselves, independent enough to select an independent title. The fact that it sold through its first printing in a matter of months without the benefit of an advertising budget or advice from marketing or public relations experts provides evidence not only that there is an audience for this book, but that there is an audience for similarly unadulterated material.

While earning a masters degree in Cinema Studies from New York University's Graduate School of Arts and Sciences and a post-graduate certificate in Visual Anthropology from NYU's Program in Culture and Media, I was made aware of the problems inherent in representations of gender and identity, and my writing was influenced by virtue of that introduction. I am grateful for the insights I received from my former professors Robert Stam, Robert Sklar, Antonia Lant, Richard Allen, William Simon, J. Hoberman, George Stoney, and, in particular, for the warm encouragement of Red Burns of the Interactive Telecommunications Program and Faye Ginsburg of the Anthropology Department. I am thankful as well to fellow students who seemed at times to take on the critical and ethical thinking of an entire generation. I was enriched by their commitment to approach creative material from the perspective of fairness, and by their resolve to articulate their concerns. During that time I began to consider my own place and position and to analyze the social constructs that had shaped my understanding of the world. Though I am not an anthropologist, and *Anthropology of an American Girl* is primarily a work of fiction, I felt compelled to share what I had learned in the classroom with others, and I tried to embed in my story some essential questions about the politics of identity.

In *Ethnographic Film*, author Karl G. Heider lays out what he considers to be the criteria for responsible ethnography. According to Heider, the portrayal of a person or an event should be based on "long-term observational study" that relates "specific observed behavior to cultural norms." If the data from an anthropological analysis of human behavior is going to be put into a cultural context, ethnographers should strive for *holism*; that is to say, "whole bodies," "whole people," "whole acts." Ideally, the goal of an observationally-based study of character is to overcome problems of interpretation and selection on the part of the maker. As a fiction writer, I did not have the burden of scientific or social "accuracy"; nonetheless, in order to conduct a first-person study of persona that was more holistic than lurid, I chose to remain mindful of basic observational guidelines and of the historical trajectory of ethnographic practices and standards. By intertwining my own experiences as a citizen with those of the main character, I hoped to articulate very large concerns about American society in a very personal way: *Where did I begin? What have I become? Who are my people? What are my rituals? What are my contributions? Where is home? How do I classify myself? How are my freedoms applied/misapplied? What is my debt to feminists? How would I describe the feeling of discrimination? How does my description compare to those of others? What is at stake in speaking/not speaking? What are the consequences of conformism? Am I rich? Am I poor? Am I happy? What have I lost?*

I began with the biggest thing I could imagine in relation to my topic—America itself—and the smallest thing—a single voice. The voice was to provide a thread to follow through the tapestry of components that contribute to an American "ideology," including notions of privilege, prejudice, greed, consumption, and lack of accountability, as well as conflicting ideas of honor, community, autonomy, liberty, justice, and equality. I was assisted in my work by a central figure, Eveline, who is a competent judge of situation and character but whose asymmetric perception of life and wavering estimation of self lead to gaps in narrative detail and obfuscation of personal motive. The possibility for inconsistencies in Eveline's interpretations and selections as the "maker" of *her* story was intended to emphasize the potential artifice of *any* account (including mine) and to encourage readers to assess the genesis of their own expectations and preconceptions.

I could hardly reflect upon my experiences without referring to the changes in American culture that had occurred in my youth as the nation rocked from liberalism in the 1960s to conservatism in the 1980s. Although I made no attempt in my writing to disguise my bias against the political opacity and promotion of private interests characteristic of Republican leadership, I labored at every conceivable turn to move beyond polemics and to tread the subtle and mysterious fields that bind opposing points of view. It would have been too narrow, for instance, to claim that the *language of diplomacy* favored by President Carter was replaced by the *rhetoric of war-mongering* preferred by President Reagan. Instead, I asked myself *to whom was Reagan speaking* when he referred to the Soviet Union as the "evil empire?" *From where had his constituency come? What had happened to the poetic power and radical reach of the 1960s? What could have motivated such a psychic regression? Could it be that the visionary struggle for racial and gender justice had constituted enough of a moral upheaval to buoy the populace for decades to come? Or was it that Americans had become weary of the strenuous demands of public purpose?*

The era of the 1980s is most frequently characterized as one of great greed, but beneath the greed lay the enormous specter of despair. The unconscionable promotion of public fear and paranoia by politicians as fuel to fire imperialist objectives crippled the nation's imagination and esteem. People were terrified of Russia, terrified of nuclear war, terrified of environmental devastation, and terrified of the government's not-so-hidden agenda to drive down the Soviets and to increase military spending via the use of hysteria and blatant exaggeration of facts. Sound familiar? Since volumes have been written about Reaganomics, or "Corporate Darwinism," as it is called, and volumes more will follow, I hardly needed to provide data concerning such things as unsustainable corporate growth and consolidation, or excessive deregulation of trucking, media, banking, savings and loans, telephone, and airline industries. Nor did I need to detail the short and long-term consequences of these policies as companies did everything they could to cut costs and maximize profits (e.g. layoff of workers, elimination of smaller companies, reduction of environmental safeguards, growth of cable monopolies and related decline in programming quality, increased road and air hazards, costly taxpayer bailouts, loss of manufacturing, proliferation of malls, death of the downtown, etc.). I had only to testify informally to the *feeling* of the time, and the feeling was that we were slipping away from a potent but brief period of unification of the disenfranchised toward *yet another* one of unification of the enfranchised.

It is my hope that the characters of *Anthropology of an American Girl* give voice to the emotional and psychological texture of those years. I wanted to describe the overwhelming sense that something precious had been lost— not only to those who did not agree with the administration's claims or policies or its particular vision of utopia, or to those who perceived peace as something other than the end result of war, or to those who understood community as consisting of something other than shared business and leisure interests, but to *the entire nation*. America experienced a dark conservative revival—people turned cynical, selfish, and misanthropic as visionariness turned to graspingness. More than the loss of integrity and idealism, *we had lost the right to dream*. In as early as 1982, with the television sitcom "Family Ties," the rise of the new right (the youthful Michael J. Fox) and the floundering of the pacifist, idealistic left (his aging hippie parents) had entered into American iconography. Whether or not you identified with Alex P. Keaton, the message was clear: it was not stylish to be anti-establishment. The more insidious message pertained to the new nature of the game—*either you were in or you were out*. Those who tightened their focus and conformed stood to gain from the new economy, while those who did not comply would be left behind, relegated to the sorry status of *consumer* (someone had to buy all the stuff those conglomerations were selling).

Eveline's earliest descriptions of the world are vivid and impressionistic but observationally pure. They are as detail-driven as a field guide or a physician's log, and yet, they are not neutral, but intimate and emotionally charged. As the story progresses through the bleak manifestations of her college years, she begins to withdraw from the contemptible noise of living and blind herself to compromise. After having shared herself unconditionally with the reader, her voice turns evasive and her tone matter-of-fact. *She begins to shut down.* This is generally considered to be a difficult part of the book, and indeed, it was difficult to write. I missed her, just as in life I missed many of my own friends who, for all intents and purposes, had vanished. More significantly, I could not reach her: she had fallen from my sphere of influence. I tried to convey through Eveline what I consider to be the moral obligation for people to remain impressionable and accessible—open to the possibility and promise of renewal through friendships and through nature.

The love affair between Eveline and Harrison Rourke, which lies at the center of *Anthropology*, represents an invitation to conscious living, an invitation that both easily accept. It is the *assimilation* of this invitation in the face of alluring moral concessions and in the unfortunate absence of each other that constitutes the main challenge to these characters. I wanted to describe— and through describing, to understand—an *awakening*. What Eveline experiences with Rourke (and he with her) is an animating force, a prophesy of the self, a foreknowledge of devotion, of faith outside reason. The introduction marks the start of a mutual undertaking—the beginning of the work of the soul. Initially, I understood the two to be victims of the time, and I regretted the idea of their relinquished potential—not simply the potential of individuals, but the broader recuperative potential of love and kinship. But, even as I write this introduction, I see ever more clearly the science of their enterprise. Many people fall in love, but Eveline and Rourke's love is about courage *and* vulnerability, resistance *and* receptivity—but exactly what were they resisting? The answer to this question can be found in another: *What did it feel like to resist?* I know now that it felt like sanctuary, like they were a society of two, like they were *ungovernable*. Together they took refuge against mediocrity and the politics of existence—*they preserved the right to dream*.

If through Rourke she is transformed, Eveline is restored—as I myself was— by the unconditionality of that transformation, by the realization that the epiphany is more valuable than its motivator. The function of the epiphany is to induce us to see that there is a living, breathing world beyond our skin, that we are not alone. Such a disclosure has the power to open our hearts and minds exactly as it closes the gap between *being* and *becoming*, and barring a whole new reliance on self-delusion and insularity, its impact should outlast circumstance. Eventually, Eveline has to make the choice (as everyone must) to incorporate all that has moved her—morally, intellectually, politically, romantically—or to become impermeable to life (*this* is the lesson of the moral detonation of the 1960s). It is no accident that she faces this choice in a city where every day citizens pass the tests of tolerance. Like sea creatures of varying proportions, capacities, and incandescence, joined *first* by virtue of their ability to survive underwater, people in a city are related by leniency and latitude, by a willingness to share space, time, and destiny.

I would be remiss if in a discussion of intangible loss I did not mention Jack Fleming. Many readers have expressed a deep connection to Jack, and they have asked whether Jack is based on Kurt Cobain. The resemblance, if any, might have to do with the fact that Cobain and I would have been the same age had he lived, so everyone I knew in high school and college looked and acted that way. Also, Cobain died when I started writing, so I could not help but be moved by a profound sense of grief. Part of Jack's appeal is nostalgic— like Cobain, he belongs to an archetype of American that seems hardly to exist anymore. These were the boys who were ambivalent about following in the footsteps of the previous generation of American men—"their fathers"— because they did not want to engage in behaviors that oppressed others. Through their refusal to accept entitlements, they represented a visible and vital engine of counterculture integrity that is all but absent from contemporary culture. While writing, I kept a note posted over my desk that read, *Jack is dead,* because I wanted to remember all the things one ought never to forget—the reach of the machine, the potential for inequity, the delicacy of ideals, the beauty of non-conformism, the virtues of dissidence and individualism. In the beginning, Evie cannot imagine Jack as a soldier willing to die in defense of America. But by the end, he has done exactly that.

In part, the inspiration for Jack was taken from a boy I once loved, and many of the details of Evie and Jack's relationship have their basis in fact— besides my own journals, I have boxes filled with his letters and drawings. Although he has had an adult life quite unlike that of Jack's, the loss of his companionship was rather like a death for me, so it felt natural to think in those terms. The story of Jack's troubled childhood and his decline into self-destruction was influenced by the stories of friends who died prematurely— two during the writing of *Anthropology* and one after its completion. These were fine, intelligent young men whose lives had been damaged by a mystifying combination of disposition and circumstance. We lose many such people to drug abuse and suicide in this country, and it is a subject that deserves serious attention from a range of perspectives. I conducted research into case histories and endorsed methods of prevention from the 1970s and 1980s, hoping to hit upon a cohesive strategy that the Fleming family might have employed so that I could put it into historical perspective and discuss it sensitively. Regrettably, the family accounts were marked by an astonishing uniformity of detail and the descriptions of therapy contained disturbing sweeps of rhetoric. I discovered nothing that Jack would not have ridiculed. Like many who commit suicide, Jack was too clever for rhetoric; he wanted the talkers to fail, he wanted to be proven right, even if the "proof" meant that no one could save him. I did my best to write responsibly *and* realistically, situating my discussion of suicide along philosophical lines of meaning between people—shared meaning, implied and borrowed meaning, imminent meaning. I let myself be guided as much by the complexity of Evie's love and loss as by the naked honesty of Jack's voice, the sweetness of his mistruths, and the deadliness of his miscalculations. I tried to strike a balance between loving life with an intensity that eludes others, and yet, being repulsed by the sensation of the life force. Though it was not my intention to find solutions, it is worth mentioning that the only relief I felt was when in the funeral scene Eveline says of her mother, who is based in part on my own mother, that if Irene had known about Jack's proximity to suicide, "*She would have thrown herself on him, like he was on fire.*"

In his remarkable book, *The Gift*, Lewis Hyde undertakes an anthropological investigation of gift-giving and gift-receiving to determine what a gift is and what a gift does. Hyde describes the ways in which a creative work can be an agent of change, a bearer of new life. I cannot say whether or not my novel has achieved or will ever achieve such worthy status, but I can honestly say that I endeavored to write for the reader, not for the marketplace, and *no*, I do not consider the two to be synonymous. To me, the reader is the reader—human and humane and as unique as a fingerprint—whereas the marketplace is a fully-integrated, cooperative, rule-based corporate construct, which conceives of people as end-users of products, not as generators of organic needs and original trends. I made every effort to establish and maintain a directness of dialogue and to remain devoted to the expression of common interests and principles. By describing the experiences that moved me, and that move me still, I hoped to motivate readers to reflect upon their own lives as Americans, and to realize that the politics of personhood and nationhood are not mutually exclusive. What is at stake in defining yourself is that you do not allow yourself to be defined.

As Eveline says, *everywhere there are angels*. And so, I close with an expression of gratitude to those who have helped me to accomplish this undertaking—the journalists who reviewed the book, the radio producers and hosts who invited me to be a guest on their shows, the book store managers who helped arrange readings, the websites that provided coverage, and to the readers who have contacted me, making me feel confirmed. A few important people and places I neglected to thank in the first edition include: the beautiful New York Society Library, where much of this book was written; Patisserie Lanciani, formerly of West 4th Street, where the remainder was written; Titus Kana, for the wonderful hardcover jacket photo; and Gleason's Gym of Brooklyn, for the important information on boxing. My appreciation to Julia Homes for proofreading this version, and to my friend and fellow writer, Hillery Hugg, for her precious time and invaluable editorial and critical remarks. My love to my children, whose devotion inspires and restores me, and to Matt Colabraro, Deborah Silva, Jovan Mastrofilippo, and Christine Vecoli, upon whose charm and cheer, diligence and loyalty, integrity and intelligence I have happily come to depend. Finally, my gratitude to my mother and father—complete political opposites, though neither any less American—for impressing upon me the virtue of independence and helping me develop the skill to claim it.

And of the giants in the mind, we shall not speak.

New York City, November 2004

ONE

CROCUS

If a mercenary dies for money and a martyr dies for a cause,
what am I if I die for you?

JUNE 1984

I.

THAT NIGHT WE ARE AT A PARTY. I CANNOT LOOK AT THE PEOPLE, ALL THE
people are like stand-up pigs, like pigs in suits. The eyes are dead and round in
faces that are not real faces but compilations of parts—teeth and noses and
millions of hairs blown and combed and lips that liberate opinions through
tangles of smoke, sideways disclosures about mentions in *Variety* and the
luminescence of diamonds. I stay by my seat. I know it is mine because there
is a card with my name. The card is the color of spoiled cream or curdled
cream, and the ink is a sort of ochre.

Behind my upholstered dining chair is a wall that is a window and through
the diaphanous barrier the city churns, catastrophe and chance, bits and bits
in unison beneath one vascular radiance, one arc or bridge or monotone rainbow that astronauts can detect from space. We are high up, but we cannot
escape the violence of the streets; it clings like ivy to the walls that protect us.
We content ourselves not to see—it is not the fact of indigence that distresses
us, just the spectacle. A red light windmills across the treetops of Central
Park, swiping the towers as an ambulance delivers a body to the aid of
strangers. Red lights are a sign. They refer to a person and to pain, possibly to
death. Every night is the worst night of someone's life. It's easy to forget that.

It is time to turn, so I turn. Arms come together like branches of a star
over the center of the table. Jeweled fingers and gold-cuffed wrists grip clear
tulips. Candlelight inhabits the champagne, making effervescent caramel.

"Hear, hear," they say and we drink—to Mark, his promotion, his
engagement. His success.

There is epic meaning in the erect and stately circle we form, in the alliance of ready arms, in the fists clutching brittle glass. It is a ritual aside, a communal departure, a cooperative meditation, a type of prayer. We step out of time because we have vanquished it. We are superior to the things of which we speak. I think of valorous knights and courageous kings, of fugitive powers expired, notable deeds forgotten, great heroes discalled. Yes, it's true, congratulations are in order—quickly.

Mark claims the ensuing interlude. "A second toast," he says, his voice fashioning tenderness. "To Eveline." He gestures to me, and they gesture to me, and I bow to straighten my perfect dress, which hangs against me perfectly. In the glimmering moon of my china plate, I discover a watery likeness of my face. Mindful of the way I hang my head, I right myself to confront the sea of eyes. "May the rest of our lives be as happy as these three years have been."

"*Salud*," they murmur kindly, though they are not kind. To them I begin with Mark. He is my origin and objective. To them I am what I appear to be. They go to lengths to keep me in the prison of their view.

"Hurry up and drink," Alicia says. "Dinner in twenty minutes."

Bodies cleave from the table, forming genial clusters. There is no opening. I wait for an opening, which is like waiting to be picked for a team. "Three years," a voice thunders from behind my back. I know the voice. It belongs to Mark's friend, his friend Brett. "A long time. A damn long time."

I'm uncertain whether this is true. Sometimes a year is lavish and profuse, riotous as a gale. Sometimes it goes breath by breath by breath, in tiny, tiny sighs. Minutes can be critical, decades without meaning or contour, and so I might say, but he is done with me. My reticence is proof to him of my stupidity. To him I am useless unless seen. He scans the crowd hoping we've been noticed. He feels manly when he stands with me, just as some people feel learned when they carry books. His gaze returns to my body, pouring over.

I am intrepid in this regard. I probe his as well, careful not to conceal my disappointment. His eyes are mean and his skin prematurely wrinkled, and the shock of brittle hair that marks the center of his skull is girdled by hairless prongs. His nails are manicured, and beneath his cashmere turtleneck his breasts droop. The proposition he makes with his eyes is stealthy and simple— money and power for sex. I wonder by what error of nature has he come to feel so virile. And yet his audacity is not without weight. Brett is a man of business, of wealth and renown. No opportunity is to be left unexplored, no friend is so dear that he cannot be betrayed. Maybe I will take him with me into the kitchen. In the kitchen, appliances gleam harshly, sending back warped ideas of yourself. In the light I will let him touch me—he would like that, to touch me. His greedy fingers will knead my flesh, cramming into scars—scars are everywhere, no matter where you touch, you cannot miss.

"Yes," I will say to Brett, through the kitchenish glare. Kitchens are always bright, like car tunnels. "Three years is a very long time."

MY GLASS IS EMPTY. I twirl it by its stem like a baton, sorry for the delicacy of the marks I make. They are specific and very small, like baby bridges. I think of fossils, fishy and particular, weary cadavers in khaki rock—proving, proving something.

Brett and I are joined by Swoosey Schicks, whose name sounds like a drunk with castanets. They discuss treasury bonds and cycling in Bali and the price of Brett's 14-carat-gold octagon Rolex—$1,950. Across the room Mark begins to dance with Amy, a redhead who appeared in *Amadeus*. Or *A Passage to India*. I always get those movies mixed up. Amy wears a green satin blouse. Redheads like green; they think it becomes them.

"Uh oh," Brett says. "Things are beginning to get interesting."

I excuse myself, leaving. I do not go unnoticed. There is a tinny, zincy pressure—all eyes on me. I go to the bathroom. I always go to the bathroom. It is the one place to hide. Men want to know what women do in bathrooms. They *hide*.

I sit on the edge of the bathtub. It is a good tub, a round-edged, pre-war New York tub. I don't need to pee, but anyway I lift my dress and lower my stockings to my knees. The division is strange, black to white—I don't know why we blacken our legs. I touch the division over and over, jumping the line, my finger popping—*nylon to skin, skin to nylon*. From the elastic of my bra, I remove a pen, and on my thigh I draw some fossils, not just any fossils but rose fossils, which are petrified rose remains. Last time I saw my dad we ate *gelato* and he told me that rose fossils have been found dating back 32 million years. He gave me a newspaper article. Also I write of time, of whether it is long or short, and then my name. And a word, *vinca*, which is short for *vincapervinca*, which is Latin, I think, for periwinkle. Periwinkle is an herb and an ivy and a snail, all of which share the color that is the color of my dress—light purple blue pink. Snails are not lucky for much, but they're lucky for their color. My dad—I haven't seen him in a long time. *Gelato* means summer.

Behind the shower curtain above the tub is a tall window set deep in a tiled rectangular cubby the size of two ice blocks stacked. It looks onto a sheet of brick, which is the neighboring building. Outside is music from an adjacent apartment. It's not an old song, but old is the way it feels because it comes from a time when music had no picture, when music used to say who you were instead of how to look, and life was a dream you dreamt streaking by like you're staring out of a speeding vehicle. Nights were dark back then, nights were mother of coal.

I climb into the tub. I push the shampoo bottles to one side of the sill and crank the window open. Some dust blows in, a little ash.

> *Do you say your prayers little darlin',*
> *Do you go to bed at night*
> *Prayin' that tomorrow, everything will be alright.*

The song curls in the airshaft between buildings before getting drawn back through the duct into vastness. I follow its route. Sometimes you see a balloon going that way, bobbing in jerks against nothing, and that is mysterious and that is beautiful, and always will be, forever throughout eternity, even when the earth is reduced in the end to shredded metal and desert. A balloon yanked up like a toy retracted by God makes you nostalgic, and nostalgia is human and humane and hopeful despite the frequently gory conditions of reality. It is seeing the child you once were and conceding that more are coming—you are not the last.

Quiet now. Not quiet but the whimper and rumor of voices skulking through the fissure between door and floor like irreversible rodents. I try to think though thinking without thought to resolution is a waste—the dividend is the same as multiplying by zero.

At the sink I wash the ink from my hands. I touch near my eyes. Eyes are truly glass. Within them the soul appears, inexact and enigmatic, rippling like a likeness on a lake. I unravel a strip of toilet paper to wipe my footprints from the bottom of the tub. It's not that I am neat, it's just that I have so much time to kill.

MARK'S BODY APPROACHES MINE. His hands tow across my skin like damp mitts or squirrels. I feel without feeling, which is nothing, which is easy, like sterile mechanics, like being sensorial with your palms when washing your face. I am thankful he does not insist upon cognizance. There are certain things a girl cannot tolerate.

There is a place to go, a place no one can access. When I am there I do not think of a man, nothing so practical as a man. If I long for a man, it is for an abstract of a man, the way a native shore is a coastline when viewed from the deck of a ship. I go to a barrier; I do not know what it blocks, but I move to it, journeying, further and deeper, to reach the place where—I don't know, just a place.

"You okay?" Mark asks. He always asks. If only he would not ask, I might like him better.

"I'm okay," I say as I stand to leave, "just thirsty."

This is not a lie. The thirst is supreme, as though inside I have shriveled. I stand at the refrigerator, drinking everything, one container at a time, moving left to right so I can keep track of those that I have emptied. I am afraid to raise an empty container as if it is full, the way your hand flies up, deceived.

Against the bedroom window is the Hudson River. It is shallow like a decal or a holiday transparency. I can't see past the glass, only in it. I see my arms and face, white from blue moonlight or blue from white moonlight. My arms look like dead arms, clipped to my shoulders by pins, dangling. I stare into indigo deadness as my image detaches from my silhouette, stepping away.

She touches her cheek. My arm remains hanging. She pivots, winding one-quarter around, though I am still. Her hands draw behind her back and rest airily on the rise beneath it, which is square, which is round, she is a girl. I know this girl, I think. She may be the one I once was. In my throat I taste the extract of her desire, in the slope of my waist to the billow of my hip I see the same petition for seduction. She is driven. I was driven.

I wish to speak, to say something. But things that are legible to the senses are often captive to language, such as the dizzying faraway feeling you get from the way daylight pools on the kitchen floor, mesmerizing you in the midst of sudden misfortune, making you think of the frailty of life—and the beauty. Or the shimmery persistence of a perfume that lingers in the air, filling you with longing when you pass through. Possibly it is the fragrance a teacher wore, or your mother. No words can describe what it means to lose someone you love, or tell what it is to grieve.

And loneliness. I should say something of loneliness. The panic, the sweeping hysteria that comes not when you are without others, but when you are without yourself, adrift. I should describe the filthy province of mind, the blighted district inside, the place so crowded you cannot raise the lids of your eyes. Your shoulders are drawn and your head has fallen and your chest is bruised by the constant assault of your heart. No air, no air, nothing but your own sticky breath, panting wet and sticky. I want to convey the burden of despair, the ruin of compromise. *Be brave*, I should say, the way brave used to be—desperate to live and to love. I want her to prepare for the curse of perseverance. She may not know about resiliency. That she will last.

My belly still hums from coming—that is electricity I think. I wonder—can she see me. I hope she cannot see me. I don't want her to know that sex here is loveless, that here I achieve a goal, an end, like reaching for a ring. But no—she sees nothing. She recedes, losing edge, losing center. She slips back to the chamber of my heart where I reserve like liquor the essence of her—and of him. Secretly I keep us, a rustling quilt of madness unfolding like pealing chapel bells that go gradually softer and farther, twining in and twining around, extending beneath and beyond anything anyone can perceive. I cannot say that I loved him—it wouldn't be right. I can say that I've watched myself die, and that I've seen my lips form his name with my final breath.

TWO

OPAL

*High School is closer to the core of the American experience
than anything I can think of.*
—Kurt Vonnegut, Jr.

AUTUMN 1979

I.

KATE DIPPED GRACEFULLY BACK. KATE WAS SO GRACEFUL, THE WHITE ARC OF
her throat coiling long like the neck of a preening swan. The mansions on Lily
Pond Lane surged then vanished on either side of us, coming and going like
aromas uncapped and recapped, and the sky set down, resting its gravid belly
against the earth's veneer. In my mind I was a ship, breaking through a storm's
center. I was a trawler, a cruiser, skimming an ocean metropolis, pounding,
peak to peak.

"Rain's coming," she called through the clack of spokes.

I didn't mind rain. I was a ship, I was seabound. When you are seabound
you welcome change because nothing is worse than the mixture of boredom
and anticipation, the way the two braid malcontentedly like smelted metal
rods. Kate pedaled faster. I watched her turn small, and I swallowed some air,
trapping in my mouth the suspended drops of water. Unfallen rain makes a
mosaic or a type of hanging tapestry. You can't see it, but you can feel the
membranes pop as you pass, which is sad. It's like breaking a spider's web, all
the fibrous work of nature. Sometimes you can't help but destroy the more
intricate things.

At Georgica Beach we huddled on the concrete step of the empty lifeguard building, taking shelter from the rain beneath the lip of the roof. The
bicycles lay collapsed at our ankles, the rear wheels lightly spinning. Kate lit a
joint and passed it to me. I drew from it slowly. It burned my throat somewhat, cauterizing it, shrinking the veil, searing and disinfecting it, making me
think of animal skins tanned to make teepees, making me think how people

call it *weed* because that's what it tastes like. Indians used to get high, and when they did they felt high just the same as me.

"Still *do* get high," I corrected myself. Indians aren't extinct.

"What did you say?" Kate asked.

"Nothing," I said. "Just thinking of Indians."

Her left foot and my right foot were touching. They were the same size and we shared shoes. I leaned forward on my knees and played with the plastic-coated tip of her sneaker lace, poking it into the rivet holes of my Tretorns. Around us the rain descended halfheartedly, filling up all you could see, making a medial field of staggered streaks. In my knapsack I found some paper and a piece of broken charcoal, and I began to sketch Kate. The herringbone fabric of the atmosphere conformed to her bones the way a pillow meets a sleeping head. I tried to recall the story of the cloth of St. Veronica—something about Christ leaving his portrait in blood or sweat on a woman's handkerchief.

"Know what I mean?" Kate asked musically, freeing from her turtleneck a frail charm. A letter *C* for Catherine. A lavishly scripted *C*, a *C* ready to complete itself, like a golden ear.

"Yes," I said. "I do." I wasn't really sure what she'd said, but I sensed I knew what she meant. My mind had not entered her mind exactly, but the two had sort of come together, little threads of topaz, a tiny Persian byway.

We were close. Nothing was visible beyond her face. The peak of her right cheekbone was the seam where sea joins sky, and the crest nearest me was sloping sand. My hand sawed across the damp paper, moving mechanically, because that is the way to move hands when you're stoned—mechanically—and I wondered what makes a summer rain different from a winter one. When I was seven there were lots of summer rains. When I was seven it rained all the time. Maybe not. Maybe seven is just the age to become conscious of rain. That's when I learned that when it rains in one place, it doesn't rain all over the world. My dad and I were driving through a shower, and we reached a line where the water ended. Sunrays windmilled down, and our faces and arms turned gilded pink, the color of flamingos—or flamencos.

"Flamingos," Kate said. "Flamenco is a type of dance."

I spun around in the seat to see water continuing to fall on cars behind us. There was this linear division. That was 1969, the same year I learned that everyone gets eyeglasses eventually and that there's no beginning to traffic. The last thing bothered me a lot. Whenever I got into a car, I used to think, *Today might be the day we reach the front.*

"Let's go to the water," I said, giving Kate my hand. She stood and wiped her backside, half-turning to check it, stretching one leg out at a five o'clock angle, the way girls do, seeing if it was wet. I brushed some pebbly dirt away, and we walked our bikes to the edge of the asphalt lot, leaning them against a dented green trash can. The sea was bloated beyond the swell of the afternoon tide. A hurricane was stirring off the coast of Cuba, and Cuba isn't far from the South Shore of Long Island, not in terms of weather. Kate and I had heard about the storm on the radio, so we'd come to look. Surfers in black rubber sat slope-backed on boards near the jetty, waiting for waves, steady as insects feeding off a deeply breathing beast, lifting and dropping with each wheeze of their massive host.

I left my jeans and my t-shirt in a pile. The sand closest to the shore was inscribed with drop marks, and the water was purplish and rough. It knocked against me, setting me off balance. Sometimes it's good to succumb—you get tired, always having to be so strong in yourself. Springy bits of iodine plants gyrated in the malicious chalky foam. I could not see my calves though I knew they were there. Dad told me that in Normandy soldiers had to climb from ships into the sea and then onto shore. They waded through the ocean with packs on their backs and guns in their arms. He hadn't fought in Normandy; he just knew about it because he knows lots of things and he is always reading. He said the men had to get up on the beach and kill or be killed. I wondered whether those soldiers had eaten scrambled eggs for breakfast—all the boys lining two sides of a galley's gangling table, hanging their heads and taking dismal forkfuls. Maybe they felt bad about how the boat was safe and dry. Maybe in their lockers they kept pictures of their families, or of their girls, or maybe just Betty Grable pin-ups.

It's insane to think of war. It's one thing to say you're willing to die for your ideals or your country, but it's another thing to have to do so when the moment actually presents itself. I could not have imagined Jack or Denny or anyone from my class dying to defend America, though everyone said it was a possibility. *The Russians are crazy*, people said. *This time it's going to be nuclear. This time we're all going to go in one atomic blush.*

Kate came alongside me. "God, this water is black."

My mother refuses to go into the ocean. She respects it, which is the same as saying she's afraid. I go in *because* it scares me, because certain fears are natural and you have to inure yourself. The ocean can kill you just like a bomb can kill you, but at least the ocean is not awful like bombs or surreal like overgrown greenhouses or scary like the barking sounds that flushing toilets make.

In elementary school there used to be emergency drills when the lights would go out, and we would rise in synchronized silence, obeying hushed orders and furtive hand signals, rustling like herds of petrified mice—if in fact it can be said that mice manifest in herds rather than as random runners. No one ever told us which particular emergency we were drilling to avoid. Probably Russians then too. The thought of Russians attacking Eastern Long Island is not so unlikely, when you think that East Hampton has beaches like the ones in Normandy. Beaches are a threshold.

I asked Kate if she remembered yellow alerts.

Sure she did. "And red ones."

"Didn't we have to kneel under our desks for one kind, like this?" I put my head to my chest and locked my fingers around my neck.

"Yeah, and with the other type," Kate said, "we had to do the same thing, only in the hall."

"Right," I said. "That is so fucked up."

She cupped her mouth and imitated an implausibly tranquil public address warning. It was like a European airport voice, like the one we heard at Charles de Gaulle Airport when we went to Paris with the French Club— maidenly, sterile and cybernetic, glassy and opaque, like rocks at the bottom of a fish bowl.

> *This is a yellow alert. This is a yellow alert.*
> *Remain calm and follow the instructions of your teacher.*

"Which is which?" I asked. "Like, what do the colors mean?"

"Bombs, probably," she said. "Different styles, I guess."

"But a bomb is a bomb. We wouldn't have been any safer in the hallway than in the classrooms. Why not just stay at our desks?"

There was a rush of water. Kate lost her footing.

I continued to speculate. "They must have moved us because the rooms had something the halls didn't have. Like, *windows*. And the only reason they would have wanted us away from windows was if something was outside, like, coming in."

Kate said, "*Christ*, Evie!"

"A land attack. Gunfire. Grenades. A *red* alert. Death by blood. Yellow was above. Yellow meant gas."

The rain had nearly cleared; all that remained was a series of garnet streaks. The sea slapped ominously, confessing its strategic impartiality. The sea is an international sea, and the sky is a universal sky. Often we forget that. Often we think that what is contingent upon us is ours alone. Kate and I waded quickly back. As soon as we broke free of the backwards pull of the waves we started running, yanking our pants over wet legs. All this sand got in, sticking awfully.

"Shit," she said as we scaled the dune to the lot. "I'm never getting high with you again."

AT MILL HILL LANE she leaned her bike to cut left across Main Street, and I followed. The lane was steep and tree-lined. As we rounded the bend onto Meadow Way, Kate's ankle lifted from the pedal, and her leg swung straight over the seat, parallel to the ground, making me think of fancy skaters. She stopped at a low brown house. It looked like a softly sleeping thing beneath a cover of tree branches that were first horizontal and then upraised like candelabra arms. A small sign marked the rim of the lawn. *For Sale. Lamb Agency.* Kate began collecting twigs, which looked like a lonely project, so I thought to help. My bike made a thumping sound when I dropped it, and my feet kicked at the broken slate walkway.

When we were nine, Kate swore she had the distances between the slate pieces memorized. I called her a liar, not because she was one, but because that's the sort of thing to say in summer when you're nine. Kate skipped to the first tile, closed her eyes, and walked along with the path, never missing a step.

"Hey, Kate," I called into the wind. My words dispersed, scattering like coins, taking long to land.

"Hey, what?" she called back, turning. A sheet of yellow hair preceded her angel's face, which tilted at a slender bevel into the half-light. Kate's eyes were like deer eyes staring out. One hand swiped the panel of hair back over the top of her head. It felt lucky that she answered. It had never felt lucky before.

"Remember walking on the slate with your eyes closed?"

"Sure," she said. "I can still do it." She set down the sticks she'd collected and she did it like it was nothing. When she was done, she said, "You try."

I couldn't exactly say no since it was my idea in the first place, so I walked to the beginning and closed my eyes, trying to imagine the path I'd taken hundreds of times before. It's disorienting, closing your eyes and keeping them that way. It made my neck feel vulnerable, as though some famished thing might come and bite it.

"No grass," I heard her say. I wished she hadn't mentioned grass. Grass at twilight is sinister and blue. I raised my right leg, and while considering where to step, my foot fell, landing inches ahead, slightly to one side. "*Whoa*," she said. "You just made it."

I only had to decide where my foot was going to go before I lifted it. I had to take time to imagine the next step. Generally I took my steps for granted. Perhaps it's a cliché thing to notice about blindness, but I could hear so many sounds. When your eyes are open, it's hard to discern between what you feel and what you perceive—within you *is* you, and beyond lies all that *is not*. Yet when your eyes are closed, you are unable to select and discard. You cannot see the world but only sense it, as you sense rather than see your very self. I stepped again and everything moved to greet me. I was particulate. I was pieces matching pieces. There was the benign crinkle of the trees as the wind vaulted into the beds of leaves, spiraling graciously before retiring. There was the music of the birds, never fuller, never sweeter—they sounded so happy to sing unseen. Ten pieces of slate had gone by, four more remained, veering hard to the porch. I half-swung my right leg right, then lowered it. My heel left a pulpy impression.

"Grass!" Kate shouted. "I win!"

My eyes opened. All that endured of what I had not seen was a languid glow, a nostalgic radiance, like when you shut off a television and the picture shrinks to a mysterious pit, which is the gleam of screen innards, the residue of light, and the skeleton of drama. The static fizz and crackle. There is a new focus, a new field, featherweight and new—the wide, wide world.

Together we sat on the front step, and we watched the orphan moon elude the embrace of the trees. She was silent. I wondered if she was waiting, as I was, for the yellow porch light to click on and for the screen door to creak open from inside, tapping our backs.

THE LAST TIME IT opened on us, Maman did not smile. The last time was May. Her birthday is May—*was* May, I'm not sure how it goes with birthdays, whether they die when you do. Her arm unbended with difficulty to prop the door, and when it compressed back on her, I caught it.

"Bon soir, Eveline," she murmured.

When Kate's mother said my name, she did not say *Ev-a-line*, the way many people did, but *E-vleen*, the first part coming from her mouth, the last part escaping from the cage of her throat. We embraced. Her back and shoulders floated waifishly within the vigorous circle of my arms. I could feel the broken *O* of her hip bones against the flat of my belly. I wondered, *When did she get so small?* Kate and I followed her from room to room and the pine floorboards grunted, marking with painful accuracy our creeping march. In the dining room, her fingers skimmed the keys of her husband's piano. He'd died one year before. Maybe she and he would die in a pair, like doves, if, in fact, doves die in pairs, which possibly they don't, but perhaps they ought to.

"I did have this piano tuned yesterday, Catherine," Maman said in hobbled English, "in case you do ever wish to play again." *Ca-trine.*

I helped her into the armchair Kate and I had moved to the kitchen weeks before, lowering her down by the armpits, the way you bring a toddler to a stand, only in reverse. I tucked the chair under the table, inching her closer until she sighed, "*Ah bien.*"

Kate prepared dinner and the room came to life with daunting pops and sizzles. It's shocking sometimes, the grief-stricken noises of food. I drew a chair alongside Maman's. I hoped it was a happy birthday with us there and all her treasures from France—linen and glass and those plates with painted peasants. I wondered what I would keep when I got older. No one in East Hampton really made anything. Maybe an antique map of the bay or a jar of sand. Kate and I once bought these clamshell dolls in Sag Harbor, an undersea barbershop quartet, but they were not exactly keepsakes. They had clipped feathers for eyebrows and plaid highwater pants and mussel shell shoes. In their crab-claw hands were balsa instruments. They were funny for about a minute, but then they got really depressing.

On a slender strip of wall near the window to Maman's left was a tiny oil painting, my first. She kept it in an elaborately carved frame without glass, with just a hole on top for a nail and masking tape in back to hold the canvas. The painting looked nice that way. I liked to nail the things I made into the beams in the barn behind my mother's house or else thumbtack them to the shelves around her desk. Dad would always stick the stuff I gave him into the sun visor of his car or into some book he happened to be reading. "Pretty good," he'd say whenever I gave him something, "but off-center." According to him, everything I did was *pretty good but off-center*. Unless it was a photograph, in which case, he would say, "Pretty good, but you cropped the head. *And* it's off-center."

For my junior year art show, we were told to mat and frame our work. The exhibit was held at Ashwagh Hall in Springs, as opposed to just the school lobby or cafeteria, because Alicia Ross's mother sponsored the reception since the art department had no budget. At the opening, a D.J. played Bach and I wore pantyhose. Streaks of light made important buzzing moons on the Sheetrock walls. My charcoals looked like woolly tombstones.

"What's wrong?" my mother asked as we passed my section.

"They look bristly," I said, "like tongues."

Francis Holland wanted to know what was wrong.

"She says they look bristly," Mom repeated to her friend in a loud whisper, "like tongues." She turned back to me. "They do *not*."

"What does she mean, *bristly tongues?*" Francis asked.

Mom shook her head. "I'm not even sure."

The painting I'd given to Kate's mother was an oil of a white rose, overblown and beginning to withdraw. Maman had the same captivating quality of a flower receding. There was something eloquent about her admission of resign, something august about the inalterability of her position. I squinted to make her young again. If she could no longer be called beautiful, she possessed something more fascinating—a knowledge of beauty, its inflated value, its inevitable loss. By then I knew she was dying. I could see it, but I was not afraid. People think of death as catastrophic, but with her, it was the tender way she treated her body, as though everything inside was feverish and pink. Maybe all we do is dry up, not in the evaporating sense, but into ourselves. This might help explain the phenomenon of ghosts.

She criticized the way Kate sautéed the asparagus while speaking to me of the sea. In her velvety drone, she described coming by ship to America. Her voice was a black sonata; her voice defied time. The sound was flat, it brought to mind a light, a triangle of light, plunging and triangular. Though it was May, I could think only of autumn, of the universe choked and churned, fading and foul. In my throat was the memory of flavor—ash and amber winds, and salt, as we had been by the sea, that is, my own mother and me. I was young.

Leaves circled our feet and we were walking. I was hungry. My stomach was a drum, and there were bird cries, lone and unevolved, giant caws of giant birds, dinosaur birds because all birds once were dinosaurs.

"We're going to school," my mother had said, "a new school."

There were leaves and I was memorizing the way home. We'd just moved from Manhattan, and I couldn't remember where home was—behind us to the side or around the woods towards the water. I fell behind and my mother took my hand, our arms forming a diagonal. Sunlight spilled across the pumpkin earth, saturating her, causing her to vanish somewhat on top. She was singing.

'Twas grace that taught my heart to fear, and grace my fears relieved.

Though my mother had hoped to soothe me, her voice did not soothe me. Maman's voice rolled like currents beneath the sea. You were diving, you were rising. You knew that at the surface was a wafer sheath of glass that could not be broken. To penetrate you had to become. Maman described the water. "It is a woman," she was saying. By her words I could see a female figure unfolding from the voluptuous tumult of the waves—the arm that ascended icily, the whalish nape of a neck, the prosperous swell of a belly.

She said to me, "*Ecoute: La mer, et la mére. Eh?*"

I HEARD KATE SAY something. I looked across the kitchen, but Kate was not there, the kitchen was not there, not the food, not Maman. Everything had vanished, the sweet castle of my hallucination had dissolved, gone down, and with it, her. She had gone down too, spreading fatter and wider to become at last a dubious puddle, a mess to step around. Kate must have seen the puddle because her knee knocked against mine and her hair rushed about me in modest whips. Our shoulders were touching and our legs and the fingers of our opposing hands, which pressed against the cement porch, but our eyes resisted communion. They scanned the new jet sky, contemplating the fossilized black, wondering whether heavens, whether angels.

BIG JOHN'S COMING TONIGHT, MY MOTHER SAID. IT WAS THE LAST NIGHT OF summer before my senior year. She was wiping the kitchen counters. Her arms made fast sweeping circles on the blade and burn-scarred Formica. "Did I tell you that he's an expert birder?"

I was eating from a can of spinach. When I tried to answer, green juice dribbled onto my shirt. She rubbed at it with the sponge. "Hold still, honey," she said, which I did in form, though in fact my spirit lunged, speechlessly crying out, *Jack!* "Be sure to ask John about his duck decoys," my mother said.

Later that night, Big John's voice permeated the walls and spilled into the neighborhood. If you'd put your hands on our window screens, you would have felt them vibrate. I was moving my summer things from the barn back to the house for the school year, and even in the yard, I couldn't help but hear about *ducks* this and *ducks* that—*coots, broadbills, ringnecks, widgeons.* "I just picked up a couple of mudhens," he said.

People who amplify are scary, especially when they do so at the beach or on a payphone or in your kitchen late at night. Loudness is anti-social, which is practically the same as sociopathic, and killers are sociopathic. Sometimes you hear the neighbors of some mass murderer say, *He seemed like a nice guy.* Was he nice actually, or did they miss the warning signs?

I ventured into the kitchen at eleven o'clock. Mom perked up when she saw me. "Hi, babe!"

I said hey.

Big John waved. He was a beefy black-bearded man. Everything he did was loud. He even sat loud. His chair creaked and moaned as gross spurts of wind shot out his nose before getting recalled through his teeth.

"Big John's telling me about—" My mother faltered elegantly. She turned back to him. "What is it that you're telling me about?"

"ATVs," he said, and he sniffed.

"*All Terrain Vehicles*," she said experimentally. "Fascinating." She drew up a chair for me. "Join us."

I went to the sink for a glass of water. "School starts tomorrow." My back was turned, but I could hear a match burst to life.

She sucked back a tight drag. She said, "Oh, right."

"My brother runs a Harley dealership in Hauppauge," John shouted to no one in particular. "He's got ATVs, dirt bikes, mopeds, bicycles, skateboards— the whole gamut, basically."

"Let's just say your brother is *into wheels*," Mom said.

"Basically," he repeated.

"Well, Kate gets up at six," I said. "I'd better turn off the stereo."

"*Six?*" Mom said. "We're a ten-minute walk from the building!"

"I guess she has to do stuff."

"What kind of stuff?"

"I don't know—hair, ironing."

"*Ironing*? I don't even know if we have an iron."

"She brought her own," I said.

My mother nodded. She seemed blue. Maybe she was blue about Kate not having a home except for ours. Maybe she was blue about the prospect of hearing Big John's voice without the accompaniment of the stereo. I took the electric fan from the top of the refrigerator.

"Hot?" John inquired.

"Not at all. It cuts down on noise."

"Goodnight," he offered, waving again. His hand knocked the edge of the glass table. There was a nasty crack.

Mom leapt across. "Is it broken?"

"Nah," he said, referring to a glow-blue school ring throttling his pinky finger. "It's fine."

"I meant the table," she said.

He inspected it. "Oh. Just a small scratch."

THE FAN CLACKED TO a noisy start, then settled into a benign electric hum. Big John's voice was overtaken by the chop and cuff. I lowered myself into my desk chair, and when I closed my eyes, I felt an asymmetric sting, ovate and sort of orange. I breathed deeply. To relax I imagined a place, an apartment in a borough—Brooklyn maybe, or the Bronx—adjacent to an elevated train. It was not a memory since I'd never actually been there, though I could feel myself having been there, and at that moment in my mind I *was* there, one of two bodies drenched in sweat and neon. The other person is a guy, a hustler or a gambler, like Robert Redford in *The Sting*. From the foot of the feeble bed we share comes the metallic whirr of an atavistic fan. There is music, outside music, listless and corpulent, trapped like smoke beneath the lid of night. The world we occupy is ruined, nothing remains. Slack telephone wires look like rigidified ocean spray making waves from post to post above buildings that are menial and diffuse, like those in empty towns between borders. Empty because nature has been killed, nature kills us in kind—it does not disappear, it retreats beneath the membranes, it exerts itself in crimes of sex and betrayal and brutality, in the minds of the bereft and dispossessed, the losers who remain. Losers like us, like me. I do not fear anonymity or decay, or desperation without dialogue, or independence that is actual. If there is no one to trust, no one is trustworthy anyway—and it's so much easier not to pretend. I am naked here; there is nothing left to confess. A subway passes within reach of our window, creaking, sparking, tipping. It is a viper that cries like a mynah, a cat that growls like a wolf. It threatens to churn to bits the filth of me. It augurs the end. Everyone knows the end. The end is when the animals combine.

THE LONG ISLAND RAILROAD runs fifty feet from the side of my mother's house. The windows rattle and the furnishings skid and the pictures cock sideways when it passes, but it is a quaint intrusion, a topic of conversation, not exactly threatening. The LIRR commutes between the sandy farmland of the East End through the projects and industry and sprawling cemeteries of Queens and into the center of Manhattan, which is a rock. In the middle of the ride there are identical houses with identical yards. Each lawn indicates nature. Each box indicates home.

"It's not dying that scares me," Jack would say whenever we went to visit my father in the city. "It's Levittown." He planned to live in the mountains with guns. "The Rockies probably. You coming?"

"Yes," I would lie. I could never live on the toothy tip of anything, but it wasn't good to make Jack sad. When Jack felt sad, he hung his head very low and you could not lift it if you tried.

I preferred the apocalyptic terrain of cities—the melting asphalt, the artificial illumination. Giant car washes and junior trees and aluminum folding chairs that open onto double-wide boulevards. When things are as bad as things can get, there's nothing to lose. I looked forward to the future. The future would be untouchable and hyper-visual, microbial and intuitive. A movable port where logic and progress have been played out to such absurd extremes that survival no longer requires the application of either. In the future, technology loses influence through its own swarmingness and tonnage.

"Notice how all it takes is *The Force* to blow up The Death Star?" I would tell Jack. "The future won't be jet packs and space stations, it'll be an aboriginal domicile beneath the dilating ceiling of the stratosphere. Silica and chimes and solar ladders will lead to a Saharan paradise where there are no numbers and the rivers are gold. The language of the physical will atrophy. The mind will coil inward, and the eyes will grow large to see beyond the seeable. No one dies in the future. We'll all save ourselves to be reconstituted."

"That's the whole fucking problem," Jack would say. "I don't *want* to live forever. I'm having trouble with the idea of Tuesday."

THE BLOWING AIR GRAZED my face. In the mirror, I watched my hair float up. It is chestnut-colored and my eyes are green and ellipsoidal—delicately pointed at the ends like cartoon flames or the acuminate tips of certain leaves.

"They are the color of absinthe," my father likes to say, which is strange as a compliment since absinthe is a drink of bitter wormwood oil—whatever that is. Beneath the green are smoldering circles. They mark the place my skin is thinnest, and so my soul the closest.

Mom's boyfriend Powell says that the soul is contained in the body. He says if instruments are made from your bones when you die, the music tells your story. Powell got his master's degree in engineering from Columbia University after the Navy, then he went on to manage oil rigs. He goes away for months at a time to places like Alaska, where he reads meters and plays harmonica. Powell can play "This Land is Your Land" on harmonica better than anyone.

One disorienting fact about staring in a mirror is that the person you see is the opposite of what you truly look like. Whenever I see someone looking in a mirror I feel like saying, *That's not you!*

I tried to explain it once to Kate, but she could be reluctant to explore topics that require a detachment from vanity. She was at Maman's dressing table, playing with her hair, changing the part from left to right.

"Forget it," she said, "it looks better on the left."

"Actually," I said, "though your hair is parted on the left of your true head, it's parted on the *right* of your mirror head. What you mean is, *It looks better on the right.*"

"That's *not* what I mean." She probed her scalp with her fingers. "It's on the left of my head *here*," she said, holding the spot, "and it doesn't switch places *there*." Kate tapped the mirror.

"That's because you have to *inhabit* the image. If you inhabit the image, the part is on the right." I went to show her. "Now if we were in the world, looking at the girl in the mirror—"

"We *are* in the world," she interrupted.

I sat back on the edge of Maman's bed, careful not to wrinkle the linens. Maman had a special way of folding down the blanket, and I didn't want to mess it up. She'd done it herself the morning she went to the hospital. She'd been admitted for just over a week at the time. "Anyway," I told Kate, "what you see is the opposite of what everyone else sees."

Kate brushed steadily. "No, Eveline. What *you* see is the opposite of what everyone else sees."

Once Kate tried make-up on me—coverstick and frosted eye shadow and face powder and Bonnie Bell lip gloss. She spun me to see myself. "*Ta da!*"

I looked rubbery, sort of embalmed. My cheekbones were gone and my lips glittered like a chintzy brooch. My eyes burned like there was suntan lotion inside them and my skin felt itchy. I smelled like cherry gum. I made my way to the sink, groping walls, because to have a false face is to have a mask. By limiting what is seen of yourself, you restrict what you yourself see, which as a formula eludes most people. Masks are blinding from the inside because as your behavior gets bigger, your performance outstrips your ability to perceive. I rinsed and in the mirror watched myself—anyway, the *opposite* of myself—reappear. Kate's reflection buoyed and skulked to the upper right of my own. She seemed upset. I felt bad about that. Something felt different, I thought I felt something coming, not obvious like a wave but sneaky like a drip, like a subtle sort of rising.

MY PARENTS ARE EXTREMELY good-natured. They remained best friends even after they got divorced. My father always says he married the prettiest Irish girl in New York, and my mother says she married the one funny German. It's true my father is funny and true as well that my mother is pretty like her sister, Lowie, even if Lowie walks with a cane. Lowie had a fever when she was little. Maybe not a fever. Maybe *fever* is just what everyone says. As for me, I arrived dark and detached and though everyone waited, I became nothing like anyone in my family. Even my birth was hard for my mother. I was breech, she tore, she vomited, she got more stitches than there are states. When the nurse handed me over, she was terrified. "I'm supposed to take care of *that?*" Mom says whenever she tells the story. "She looked like an owl."

Since my mother probably does not intend to hurt me, I console myself with the knowledge that it is a true story. Of course, the idea of being consoled by truth is a cliché. The fact that details are true does not make wretchedness any easier to accept. People often say, *For Chrissakes, just tell me the truth!* As a rule, they're being disingenuous.

Lowie is a midwife, so I've seen three childbirth films. When babies come out, they wear a bewildered grimace as though they have arrived by train, and they are peeping about the platform for the friend who promised to pick them up. It's not nice to think of myself as having been left at the station. I know my mother loves me; frequently she says she does. But it's one thing to be the recipient of an affection that is conscious of its lack and another to know fervent devotion, to be a blessing in the flush and the sweat of loving arms.

You cannot recover from a bad birth. The stigma lingers for a lifetime the way bad luck really does last for seven years after a mirror breaks. The special gravity of a mother's first disappointed glance saws itself with surgical accuracy into the infant's waxy blue skin, leaving an impression on the secret underside of its forehead. On my forehead is just such a notch, slightly off center, to the left—that is to say, to *my* left. Beneath the skin is a recess; you can't actually see it, but you can *sense* the mark is there by the distraught cast to my eyes. There is a certain prohibitive aspect to my looks, just as some rivers run too wild for a person to dare cross.

In the beginning of that summer, before Maman died, Dad and his girlfriend Marilyn took me to see an Italian movie, *L'Avventura*, which is about disillusionment and other sixties stuff. It was directed by Michelangelo Antonioni, which surprised me. I'd always figured there was just one *Michelangelo*. Afterwards Dad stopped to reset his watch. He's constantly resetting his watches; none of them keep time. "Funny," he'll say, "I just got this one adjusted." Then he'll shake his wrist by his inclined ear, who knows why, because if that's all it takes to restart a watch, it's certainly not a very good watch. "Must be something electrical in me," he'll surmise.

As we stood there, he asked what I thought of the film. I told him that I liked Monica Vitti. Monica Vitti has this mesmerizing way of leaning against walls and staring out to view nothing, as though the horizon is millimeters away, as though the great distance we all dream into is bearing pestilently upon her skin. As though there is no better place than the shitty place she is in.

"She's my favorite actress."

Marilyn tapped Dad's arm. "See?"

Dad nodded. "I'm impressed."

"You remind me of Monica Vitti," Marilyn said.

Did I really look so sad? Monica Vitti looks sad. She gives the impression of having lived a better past, of having returned to the present to discover the pointless way things have become. She is untouchable, unsaveable, a personal goddess: she too has *the mark*.

"You guys want to catch a cab?" Dad asked.

It was drizzling on Second Avenue. The sidewalk was not yet completely wet, but there was already the dusty smell of rain on cement. I felt the earth cling to sky. I felt the beauty of ruin. There was one moment coming, one single moment at which every inch of the city would be coated in rainwater.

"Mind if we walk?" I said.

Later that night, when my father was reading, Marilyn and I went into their bedroom. The room was lit from the street, so the furniture did not seem like furniture but interpretations of furniture. I could scarcely make out the walnut armoire with the pewter-finish grill of bamboo shoots, or the matching bureau loaded with bargain books from the Strand and old jewels in tortoise shell boxes and the terra cotta bowl of photographs, mostly of me. Or the over-low bed that was mushy but neatly dressed in one of those grand-motherly white spreads with nubby protuberances that form threaded arches and cameo medallions. But I could *sense* them, skimming my legs in tentative portions as we navigated tippingly the channels they created. We knelt at the window, reaching out to feel the rain, and the furniture defended our backs like phantoms or ghosts, like a choir of things I have known for long and loved.

Cars swished dreamily up Elizabeth Street. Tangerine strands of hair broke free from Marilyn's braid then fluttered in the breeze like tails of a kite. Her skin was powdered. It's always nice to kiss her cheek; it brings to mind the gentler things.

"Do you think I'm pretty?" I asked.

She turned to face me. "Of course I do."

My hand stretched out. "But not like Kate." Everyone in school said how pretty Kate was, even though no one ever stared at her the way they stared at me. Girls looked at me like I'd stolen something, and my encounters with boys were uncomfortably direct. They'd get this lost look, as if seeing not a person but a place, somewhere they preferred to be, somewhere they believed I could possibly take them.

"No, not like Kate," Marilyn said, adjusting her elbows on the sill. "You're far more beautiful."

"How come my parents never tell me that?"

She turned back out. "Maybe they're afraid of the way you look."

I never felt myself to be the person envisioned by others. I felt nothing, really, other than a sense that inside I was very small. Maybe all that others saw in me was their inability to inspire my trust. I asked Jack if getting older means you can't trust anyone.

In the mirror, my burning eyes became his burning eyes with the hue changing from bottle green to bright Wedgwood blue. "You never can trust anyone," he answered. "But when you get old, you finally figure it out."

Possibly he was right. You're old when you learn that needs are to be eclipsed behind civility. You're old when you join the sticky, stenchy morass of concealed neediness that is society. You're old when you give up trying to change each other because then people might want to change you back. But when you are young, needs are explicit and possibilities are endless and proofs of allegiance direct.

"Jack," I whispered. "Remember how easy it was to cut ourselves and to share blood?"

THE SUN WAS A MEAN WALL BEHIND US, SHOVING UP AGAINST OUR BACKS LIKE a windless wind. The tar that coated the railroad ties was slick and sticky. A resin smell filled the air. I could feel it creeping the way molasses drips, only upwards, burning the inside of my nose, high against the sides. Kate didn't like the tar to mess up her shoes, so she stayed on the gravel between the ties, stepping with perfect strides. Whenever I tried stepping on the ties or between them, I would get agitated and short of breath. I took the rail instead.

We reached Newtown Lane. I hesitated, teetering on the strip of steel. "I'm gonna grab a cup of coffee."

Her face screwed up into daylight. "We'll be late."

"I'll go fast." I jogged into the street, dodging minor morning traffic, turning back to shout.

Three bells on a crooked wire tinked and jangled against the deli's glass door. Bucket's was full of guys in shorts and Timberlands and t-shirts waiting patiently for egg sandwiches. Patiently because all the city people had gone. When city people go, they go fast as they come, like in speeded up films of Japanese train commuters. I made my way to the counter and ordered. Joe filled one of those jumbo styrofoam cups with ice cubes and cold coffee from a glass container. The radio near the meat slicer played a song by Genesis that reminded me of summertime, either that summertime or the summertime before. Summer songs get connected in my head.

I will follow you, will you follow me.

"School starts today, eh?" Joe said.

"I guess."

"C'mon now," he said. He threw back his head to one side with a smile. When he smiled, I noticed a gap between his teeth. I'd never noticed a gap there before. As a facial characteristic, a gap could not be new, not in the manner of a tic or a sore. I turned away. Outside looked hot, hotter than when I'd come in. It's hard to start school when the weather is still like summer. Sometimes a time ends or a person dies and you have to move on, though reminders are everywhere. Sometimes someone is dead, and you convince yourself that they're still alive, only you haven't seen them in a while. Deep near the back of your skull there's a place similar to a sideways crayon that helps you think that way. Sometimes you go on like that for a long time. I paid for the coffee real slow, knocking the coins around with one finger.

Joe started ringing up the guy behind me. "Forget about it."

"It's okay, I've got it." I funneled the change into one of his hands.

He advised me to at least *try* to have a good day and I told him thanks. I stepped back into the sluggish heat that tipped against the glass door like a chair you use for a lock.

"Took you long enough," Kate said as I climbed the grass embankment onto the sidewalk and unwrapped the straw, popping it through the lid and mashing the wrapper. She extended her hand and took the paper from me, putting it in her pocket, and we started walking. I wondered if straws are named after real straw, the kind animals eat. Maybe some farmer chewed a piece that accidentally you could suck through and then the idea caught on until eventually McDonald's and Burger King made special dispensers just for straws, and now everyone gets mad when a cashier forgets to include one with your drink. What did people do before liquids became portable? Without a straw, I wouldn't have been able to drink and walk. I would have had to stay in the deli, which actually might not have been a bad thing. Maybe straws are social evils, responsible in part for the breakdown of community, similar to highways. You know, just with everyone getting up, going.

I pulled at my shirt. "I'm suffocating."

Kate ignored me and kept stepping eagerly. I thought to copy her. I thought to try to feel eager too, but eagerness is hard to simulate. I drew in the last mouthful of coffee. The straw probed the empty avenues between the cubes, hunting profitlessly for more liquid. Anyway, I kept trying, swallowing only air—the saddest sound in the world, my mother always says her father used to say.

We turned onto the high school driveway. The building appeared exceptionally horizontal, lower and longer than usual, like a flatland, hardly higher than dirt. The parking lot was full, though the main entrance was vacant because no one ever hangs out on school steps and sings the way they do in movies like *Gidget* and *Grease*. As soon as kids arrive, they go inside, stop at their lockers, then just walk around in circles.

At the entrance to the language and math wing, Jodie Palumbo and Dee Dee Barnes were smoking. Jodie had a tan from summer. Her freckles looked three-dimensional, like popped boxes.

Kate offered a bright hello. I edged past.

Dee Dee stretched her lips. "How ya doin'?"

Jodie flapped the tops of her fingers but said nothing since she had just inhaled. It must not have gone down right because she lurched forward and began to cough. It was the rolling, mucousy kind that sounds totally contagious. Jodie was probably short for Joanne, or Josephine possibly. Dee Dee might have been for Donna Danielle or Dina Doreen.

Through the double doors behind them was the school corridor, rank with color. I took a breath and entered directly because nothing is worse than being on the verge of doing something, teetering like a jackass. Packs of bodies lodged like tumors against walls and lockers and doorways, the rest pulsed in fits about the halls.

It had been a long time since I'd been around so many eyes. In schools eyes are everywhere, static eyes in shifting heads, twice as many eyes as bodies, and in our school there were a thousand bodies. The disproportionate ratio between objects to be seen and objects through which to see is chilling and mysterious, like decent science fiction. Schools provide nothing of substance for those eyes to regard. There is no vista to behold other than the panoramas of each others' bodies, which is sort of the entire problem.

Madame Murat filled the doorway to her classroom, blocking the light from the windows at her back, forming a shadow lagoon in the hallway. She was not fat, just inexplicably large. In profile she seemed to be carrying a basket of laundry.

"Bonjour Mademoiselle Auerbach, Mademoiselle Cassirer."

"Bonjour Madame Murat," we recited in unison. Jack called her *Madman* Murat, which Mom said sounded like a Turkish assassin.

"Je comprends que je ne vous verrai pas en classe cette année, Ca-trine, c'est vrai?" Madame said to Kate.

"Oui, c'est vrai," Kate responded, and Madame nodded from top to bottom and over to the left, ushering us along. "Oh, great," Kate whispered, "now she hates me."

"Maybe," I said. It was hard to know for sure. It could have been that Madame felt sorry for Kate, but it was equally possible that she felt offended. French people are funny that way.

Kate craned her neck. "Denny's up there with Alicia and Sara Eden. Want me to get them?"

I said no thanks. Having to talk to people was one thing, but soliciting conversation was something else entirely. If I acted squirmy or didn't make eye contact, they would want to know what was wrong, and I would have to say "nothing," since nothing really *was* wrong. Nothing is an easy thing to feel but a difficult thing to express. It's impossible to describe nothing without seeming sneaky.

I wished I could act normal like everyone else. Sometimes you want to have a good time, but you have a stomach virus, and all you can do is lie on the couch, stiff and limbless as a mammoth slab of ice, dripping imperceptibly, in a filmy layer on the surface. You despise the exquisiteness of human consciousness, and you try with all your mental might to prevent the room from reeling. You stare fixedly, with the furrowed brows of a psychic who bends spoons. You count the minutes until it's over. You say things like, "In eight and a half hours, I will almost be better."

By the time the bell was about to ring, we had made it three times around. You could tell when the bell was about to ring because everything accelerates. Personal time draws to a close and everyone gets bigger. I prepared myself for the change, the way vision adjusts prudently to darkness. My shoulders drew inward. My face dipped down as though to dodge a blow. At the top of the science hall, we heard a group of girls shrieking. They were all the way down by the music studios.

Oh, my God, you are totally tan! That is the cutest t-shirt! You look, like, soooo unbelievably skinny!

Coco Hale saw us coming, and she called Kate over. Something flashed between Kate and me, nothing you could name, not really. Above our heads, the fluorescent lights made a frosty ceiling carpet.

"Do you mind?" Kate asked politely.

"Not at all," I replied, politely. We were like those cartoon chipmunks, those polite ones.

She double-checked. "You're not just saying that, are you?"

I filled my cheeks and expelled the air slowly, who knows why. It's just a thing people do. "No, I'm not."

ONE TIME JACK MADE me explain why I disliked Coco.

I said, "She's, like, witchy, or something."

He was picking at his guitar. "Be specific." We were sitting on the farm table in the barn, and his head was collapsed over the strings.

"Okay," I said, "her teeth." She had a phony smile and beneath her lips lay two rows of miniature teeth, undifferentiated, same-size squares that appeared glossy even in the dark. They were like those miniature corn cobs. "They're witchy."

Jack considered that. "Good one," he agreed.

"Next," I listed, "her eyes." Her eyes shuddered in their sockets when she was being insincere, as if resisting affiliation with her body. "Do you know those earthquake monitors, the rolling graphs with attached pens that measure tremors?"

He looked up with part of his face. "Seismographs."

"She has eyes like that, only they measure lies."

"Seismographic eyes," he said contemplatively. He pulled a felt tip from his pocket and wrote the phrase on the sole of his blue suede Puma. Suddenly out of nowhere, the mirror near the door fell off the wall and into the center of the room, shattering. "Holy shit!" Jack lifted one of the curved triangular shards. "She *is* a witch."

AS KATE WAS ABOUT to break away to Coco, the bell rang. *Bwoop!*

"See you," I said, and I turned down the English hall. I was drawn instantly into the belly of the crowd. Kate's voice trailed me—*Evie! Eveline!* My name from her lips sounded pining and bare. It fell slimmishly, like a willow sailing down. It hit the floor with a diminutive thud and a flowery quiver. Once alone, I felt a mixture of relief and release. I wasn't necessarily eager, but in any event, my body lightened, and when people said hello to me, I answered, *Hello*.

In my head was an image of a horse freed from a hitching post—the feeble rope relaxes, the beast wriggles loose, and wasting no time on thoughts of its own good fortune, it leans into a crooked turn and begins a wobbly gait. Soon it achieves its maximal speed and thunders hugely into parallel planes of earth and sky. The packed dirt convulses beneath the stress of the thumping hooves, echoing back to where you are. The straps of its leather harness, thinner than ever before, slap the rippling wine-colored back in vain. There is the place that the horse holds, there is the thing that the horse is. Such things are nameless. I wasn't sure what it meant except to say that I felt all that I was. I felt agreeably stripped of relationship.

Kate and Coco were cleaning their flutes probably, sitting with mingling meringue hair and four hands polishing buttons and spitty levers. Perhaps they were discussing me, with Coco saying how I seemed envious. It was not hard to envy Coco. Her family lived on David's Lane in a house with a corrugated roof like in picture books of Spain. She wore La Coste shirts and cloth-covered headbands from Mark, Fore, and Strike, and she rode a kiwi-colored Motobecan bicycle to Main Beach after private tennis lessons. She had a collection of those Pappagallo purses with the wood handles and the button-on fabric covers. According to Kate, Coco paid forty-five dollars for a style and a blow dry at that salon by O'Mally's. Mrs. Hale drove a new Mercedes with basketballs and bags of groceries in back, and unlike my mother she never had beer breath or wore hip-huggers with peace-sign patches or hung around with merchant marines and lab technicians. Mrs. Hale did not belong to Mensa.

Once we saw Mrs. Hale running the ticket booth for the Ladies Village Improvement Society Fair. She was wearing straw bonnet with paper peonies that she had made herself.

"Who has time for such nonsense?" my mother demanded. "Doesn't that woman ever *read?*"

In summer, Mr. Hale would take his family on long trips in their sleek cabin cruiser to Block Island or Nantucket or Martha's Vineyard where Coco and her boating friends would meet prep school boys. Every September, the photos would make the rounds—Coco and Breanne Engel or Pip Harriman—honey brown and curly blonde—hugging boys in Duke University sweatshirts, beige docksiders, and puka shell necklaces. Coco never had to go to Gettysburg, West Point, Old Sturbridge Village, or those World War I air shows up in Rhinebeck like I always had to with Dad and Marilyn. All my family photographs are of me overdressed in saggy clothes and bad kneesocks leaning on cannons or lost among acres of headstones in Civil War cemeteries. My mother had never taken a vacation; she did not even own a camera.

It was easy to feel meager compared to Coco. I consoled myself by saying it was a lot like doing math. She was *quantifiable*. I was not. To hate her for the things she had would be as pathetic as liking her for those things, when I didn't care what she had. I just hated her. Everyone always says you shouldn't feel hate or say the word.

"*Bullshit!*" Jack once barked. "Who told you that?"

"People." I couldn't think of anyone at the time.

"Words are constructs, like houses. Say whatever you want. Besides," he added lovingly, "you are incapable of true hatred."

Jack was right. Some feelings just occur and giving them nicer names does not make them go away. If what I termed *hate* could be more accurately described as *an aversion to the witchy way that Coco acted*, it would have changed nothing inside of me.

Then one day, I was overtaken by an enormous boredom with Coco. A soaking, drenching, summer rain type of boredom, liberating and complete, touching down everywhere in equal amounts. And from that moment I was done with envy. Envy is an awful thing to feel. It's a dark presence, a painful connectedness, real or imagined. It's constant and filthy, there until it's done, until something clicks to make it go away. It's a panicky, high-speed search for the thing to trigger the click.

I ENTERED THE FIRST class of my senior year early, which meant I was one step closer to getting out, for the day and also for life. After Kate's mother died, life became very mechanical. I would eat dinner right after lunch and get ready for bed before the sun went down. I marked time. I would think of the task at hand until it was completed, then I would think of the next, never giving my mind a minute to scramble in the circuits of its cage. There is something to be said for automatic living. It makes looking forward to things seem unreasonable. When you stop looking forward to things, you get used to low expectations and you start to think, *What's the big deal about success anyway?* If we're all to attain everything we've been conditioned to desire—wealth, fame, education, prestige, security—then those things will become so prevalent that they'll be meaningless anyway. It would be a very callous world, a very doomed world. Someone somewhere would be paying for all that success.

According to Jack, the only way to maintain dignity is to give up wishes before they don't come true. Maybe that's too extreme. Maybe the best you can do is to refrain from wishing for wishes that are not your own, such as for ranch houses and nice cars, for Capri pants and lamb chop dinners and husbands with good haircuts. Sometimes you have no choice; you inherit your parents' wishes. Some parents work hard to guarantee their children's progress. They don't want any slipping back. They want to maintain balance between the status of the generations. That's why every now and then you meet some poor kid whose life is controlled as if by committee.

My particular future was not so vigilantly guarded. I was to start from scratch. The best thing about my family's indifference was that I had the freedom to fail miserably.

I wouldn't mind living out my life in a fourth story walk-up on Mott Street in Little Italy, with an upright bathtub and cracked plaster walls like Tony Abbruscato's. Tony is my dad's partner in the sign shop, and he can always tell you where to get a better price. "Lemme ask you something," he'll say, fingering a scarf or eyeballing a paint job or running his hands across a gate-leg table. "How much did you pay for this?"

In my little apartment, I would listen to opera on a transistor radio late at night, *Aida* or *Madame Butterfly*. I would eat a dinner of fried eggs and tomatoes while looking through the gated kitchen window, past the dilapidated fire escape and onto the scenic brick of a neighboring building. I'd soak my bras and stockings in the bathroom sink and hang them on string. By day I'd work in a bakery. Ferrara's is air-conditioned in summer when people come for *gelato*, and at Christmas everything smells of anisette. If Jack died early like he planned, I figured I'd marry a cop. Probably there would be a cop who stopped in every night to see me. Some cop named Andy.

I stepped behind the teacher's desk to reach the blackboard, and I pulled down the map of Europe. It's good to pull down a map, by the weight you can tell they are expensive. Kate always said that when she made a lot of money she was going to buy one for me, the kind with lots of sheets. I took a seat in the corner of the room, alone by the window, wondering what Kate was going to do to earn all that money.

Annie McCabe, Breanne Engel, and Darlene Nappa slipped through the door all at once and assembled in an L-shaped cluster by the teacher's desk. Annie began to whisper, and the three heads probed forward rigidly like construction cranes. I looked at the clock—two minutes to eight. They were all so, so *done*. Annie was wearing stockings and a long straight skirt of pumpkin silk. Base make-up covered her from forehead to chest. A stringy ring of mocha stained the collar of her white blouse.

"Wow," I said to myself, "and on such a hot morning!" Girls are game as soldiers with the brave things they do to their bodies and the harsh conditions they are able to tolerate.

Darlene looked jaundiced, like a past-due celery stalk, concave and glassine green with bushy stuff on top, and Breanne was beige and emaciated with a kind of polymer quality to her complexion, like food through Tupperware. Her frosted hair was dry and frazzled at the ends and tied in such a way as to be neither up nor down. Her eyes were wide and shaking. Kate said she takes Dexatrim.

A WEEK AFTER THE funeral, Kate and I saw those girls at Main Beach. It must have been Labor Day weekend because there was litter and guys with cigars. Litter and guys with cigars usually show up around Labor Day. Breanne Engel was so thin her skin appeared to have been shucked off and reglued. She looked like a collage of parts. There was this candy Dad always got for us in Chinatown, the kind with a translucent wrapper that isn't paper, but it's like paper, only you eat it, and it melts in your mouth.

I said, "She looks like one of those Chinese candies Dad gets."

Kate tilted her head furtively into the shady spot between our shoulders, going, *Sshhh!* We were on our stomachs facing the water. It was late afternoon, and the beach was changing strangely, the way beaches do in the late afternoon—young people go and older ones come, and suddenly there are dogs. A yellow lab was making wide and dripping circles around an abandoned sandcastle, and an elderly couple in matching hats sat alongside us, facing their chairs to the west. Their skin was the color of carnations.

"She makes herself throw up," Kate whispered.

I wasn't sure I heard right. I said, "I'm sorry?"

"After she eats, she throws up."

"How do you do that?"

"You put your finger in your mouth. And it comes out. I guess."

"You're kidding."

"I wouldn't kid about a thing like that."

Breanne really must have despised her parents in order to deprive their baby girl of sustenance. It was impossible to know for sure, but her mom probably clapped at her first steps and dressed her in eyelet rompers and kissed her shampooed curls over and over. Some mothers blow air bubbles on their baby's neck and play games with their toes. How pathetic Breanne must have looked, leaning over the turquoise toilet in the Engel's immaculate bathroom, feet and knees sinking minimally into the plush of the matching turquoise carpet, breathing in the gladiola aroma of those gooey obelisk air freshener things, the kind where if you look up through the exposed base, you can see the gel sinking down the shaft into its own neon green hip. The whole thing is kind of like graffiti—the streaky waste spewing from a stiff canister through a ligular tube, the jetting bile and resentment, the profitless attempt by the individual to deface the aggregate of institutional authority. Graffiti is just a means of declaring you exist when there are those who would have you believe otherwise.

"It's suicide," Kate informed me, "only prolonged."

It made sense that Breanne would have such an acidic condition. How sour and superior to spit back all she'd taken in. I thought of Dorothy Becker from school and the cragged seams on her wrists that her polyester sleeves could not cover. The low-class business of bases—blood, water, metal. Actually metal is not basic, metal is nothing, and water is neutral. Yes, that's it, Dorothy—basic, neutral, nothing. I rolled over, trying not to see. It's hard sometimes not to see.

Kate returned to *Seventeen*. "You're so selfish."

If by *selfish* Kate meant conceited or concerned excessively with my own advantage, I did not feel selfish. But if by *selfish* she meant narrow-minded or non-capitulating in matters of self-mutilation, she was right. Of course, it was possible she did not think I was selfish at all, but simply *called* me selfish because selfish was the opposite of what she imagined herself to be.

I scooped up sand. I wondered how many grains were in my hands, which is not an unusual thing to wonder at the beach, but stupefying nonetheless. Kate kept licking the tip of her finger, then flipping the pages of her magazine—*snap, snap, snap*. It occurred to me that she had thrown up too.

I felt a little breathless. There was this stuffy swell in my chest, this incendiary stuffiness that swelled and made it hard to breathe. I felt as though a thing belonging to me had been shattered and beneath my feet were the chipped and chalky remains. I could not put them back together, but I could not leave them where I'd found them, and I could not take a single step without crushing them more. I felt mannish sort of, and inept.

I stood. She sat. "Where're you going?" she asked.

"To the water," I said.

I followed the rim of the shore. I entered the sunless east. Though the day had almost passed, occidental light poured across to make a pink and pious vault. Jack would describe the inside of a wave. "You're groundless. You drop in and you're groundless."

I faced the ocean and stepped down, once, twice. Water radiated as far as my eyes could see. Maman was there, all over, unifying and undulating, liquid and luster, blank and black and melancholy. "Be a friend to Catherine," she'd said to me. And although I was superstitious about things such as last wishes, Kate was beginning to require a type of friendship that was weird.

Pip Harriman pulled up on a banana yellow moped and beeped. The horn made a pinched vituline sound that choked on itself before it concluded, like the last bleat of a dying lamb. Breanne and those girls ran to the parking lot— and Kate, Kate ran too. It didn't bother me that they'd waited until I was gone to extend an invitation, but I did wonder what it was that Kate wanted from them and what it was that they wanted from Kate, and whether either party stood the remotest chance of satisfaction.

THE BELL RANG AGAIN—8:00 A.M. and still no teacher.

Stephen Auchard stepped cautiously past the boys who punched and swatted at each other around the doorway. He chose a desk alongside mine and nodded uncomfortably. Last time he saw me I was crying, which when you're in high school, is sort of like seeing someone naked.

At the funeral he'd worn pressed khakis and a blue jacket with anchor buttons. His mother had glasses with gold rectangular frames and her auburn hair was drawn into a sublime twist. She conferred with her son in ethereal French, leaning close, calling him *Etienne*. Kate's mother was related to Stephen's father and that was how the Cassirers found East Hampton. Outside Williams Funeral Home, Mrs. Auchard held my shoulders and kissed my cheeks, kisses like accidental butterflies. Her skin was dewy and fragrant, cold as packed talc. "Claire did love you," she said to me. *Deed luffed.*

"What's your locker number?" Stephen asked. Our last names were letters apart, Auchard and Auerbach.

"591," I said. "What's yours?"

"590," he answered.

I nodded and he nodded again and we both nodded. It's hard to think thoughts of death in the eggshell airiness of school. Death resides near the ground, magnetic and unavoidable, swinging in time kind of, like a hatchet from a rope.

Nico Gerardi and Billy Martinson sauntered in. I wasn't surprised to see them in an Advanced Placement class, even though they were so stupid.

Essentially jocks are exempt from the standards that bind everyone else. Teachers and administrators humor them because it's in everyone's interests to coax them through school and get them out of the building. Since it's unethical to turn them loose on society, they get sent to college to be kept out of the mix until their frontal lobes develop more fully. As enticement they are given sports scholarships which will later amount to nothing, not even good health. And adults never challenge the popular jock notion that college is *the* place to get laid and to party.

Stephen fingered the corner of his notebook over and over. Stephen was going to be the valedictorian. I wondered if he was irritated by Nico and Billy, by the way they filled the classroom, altering its nature, establishing with their bodies a right of place that their brains could not. The contrast between their physical proportions and their intellectual status made me think of men in small clothes. They were happy enough. They'd been given the basics—food, shelter, girls, trouble to cause. But in the strings and strands of their beings, you got the feeling they were on to the game.

Nico had changed over vacation. His football jersey hung closer to his waist than to his legs, his butt was more muscular, his crotch had thickened— I could not help but notice the way the denim of his Levi's was rounded and slightly whiter there. I knew I should despise him as Jack did, the way he and his friends flirted with female teachers and played buddy with the males, the way they gave congenial grabs to girls in hallways and relied on family ties to get them out of trouble. Once Nico got caught stealing tennis rackets from summer houses, but Judge Baby only made him return the goods and apologize. When Nico was released to his parents, Judge Baby said he was especially disappointed in a boy of such great promise. The boys called him Judge Baby because of the way he talked. Every day they played Judge Baby, cracking themselves up.

"I *cew-tin-weey* hope you've gotten the boyish *pwanks* out of your system, *wittle* man. You have *gweat pwomise*."

Billy had never been in trouble with the police, not that anyone knew of, except he did go through a bay window at his house once when he rode his mother's spare wheelchair down the staircase, and at several parties he'd swallowed goldfish.

Boys will be boys, that's what people say. No one ever mentions how girls have to be something other than themselves altogether. We are to stifle the same feelings that boys are encouraged to display. We are to use gossip as a means of policing ourselves—this way those who do succumb to sex but are not damaged by it are damaged instead by peer malice. Girls demand a covenant because if one gives in, others will be expected to do the same. We are to remain united in cruelty, ignorance, and aversion. Or we are to starve the flesh from our bones, penalizing the body for its nature, castigating ourselves for advances we are powerless to prevent. We are to make false promises then resist the attentions solicited. Basically we are to become expert liars.

Nico and Billy were talking to Annie McCabe. Her voice was inaudible except for the random coo and peep, and the edges of her fine brown hair came forward like crepe curtains to hide her face. I wondered if she had ever masturbated. Probably not. I couldn't imagine her manicured hands reaching to touch such a damp and pulpy place. Did she have the urge but resist? Or could the situation be as it appeared—that she longed for nothing? I started a sketch on the jacket of my book. Mostly I couldn't wait to be alone in my room at night.

THE FIRST TIME I ever had an orgasm was in the third grade. I was making up a math test after school. It was a very panicky and reactive time for me in general, and Mrs. Steckowski was the only teacher I ever had who did not like me best of all. I didn't realize until much later that it was actually my mother the teacher hated, my mother and her braless ways.

Mom and I were called in that year for a conference with the principal because I'd been seen hitchhiking on Route 27 in Southampton. Gwen Curley's car had broken down at Burger King. Gwen was one of Mom's students at the college and also a babysitter. Whenever Mom had a night class, I would wait with Gwen.

"We thought you'd like to know," Principal D'Andrea said. "It was a school night. Naturally, we're concerned for her safety."

"How can you be sure it was Eveline?" my mother asked.

"Because it was *I* who passed them," Mrs. Steckowski stated.

My mother smiled thinly. "If you care so much for my daughter's safety, Mrs. Steckowski, why didn't you pick them up?"

Afterwards whenever my mother related the story, she would describe Mrs. Steckowski as *something out of Poe*.

Later that year on a trip to the bathroom, I had the misfortune of running into two older girls who were smoking cigarettes and chucking bundles of wet paper towels onto the ceiling. I did not see their faces, and they did not see mine because the sinks were on the far side of the bank of toilets. I slipped into the first stall, slid the bolt through the latch, and pulled down my tights to pee. Nothing came out. I was afraid they would make fun of the tinkling sound. But of course, the silence was worse.

"What's the matter," they taunted, "your hole stitched shut?" Just when I thought they might grab at my ankles through the gaps beneath the walls, they became still, discerning before I did the distinctive clatter of the janitor's keys coming from the hallway. "Shit," they said, and deftly they exited.

I flushed the clear bowl and tugged clumsily at my underwear, feeling at last the urge to urinate, but instead I rushed toward the bathroom door. Unfortunately, I was as unskilled in escaping trouble as I was in detecting it, and the decrepit Mrs. Ruggerio proved just agile enough to catch me. She hauled me by the upper arm back into the smoke-filled room, and as she surveyed the sinks, which were littered with smoldering cigarettes, and the ceilings, which were pimpled with dozens of dripping mouse-sized wads, she began to swear in Italian. I knew it was Italian because my father lived in Little Italy, and I knew all the curses. The janitress grabbed my wooden bathroom pass, read Mrs. Steckowski's name, then dragged me behind her limping frame across the hall to my classroom. Mrs. Ruggerio wore a special shoe. It was shiny and tawny with a squared and perforated *U* around the toe.

We barged in on a "Capitals of the States" recitation, and Mrs. Ruggerio began to shout. As I stood there, desperate by now to pee, Mrs. Steckowski took her time piecing the story together, nodding thoughtfully and translating from broken Italian several key phrases, such as *filled with smoke* and *dripping from the ceiling*. Though she knew by my character that I could not possibly have been involved, she refused to defend me and acted as though she had expected as much all along. She apologized to Mrs. Ruggerio and to me she said, "Well, Little Miss, I suppose I'll have to send an escort with you to the bathroom from now on."

Joey Babula threw his arm into the air. "Oh me, me!" And everyone laughed, even Jolene Kent who suffered from chronic head lice. I walked as if through water to the blackboard to replace the wooden pass on the brushed aluminum chalk tray, three pieces wide, and then made my way back to my seat. I never once used the school bathroom again. Sometimes if my mother was late to pick me up, I would have an accident. In fourth grade, after we moved closer to the village and I could walk home, I often made it as far as the front door before losing control while fumbling for the keys.

On the day of the make-up math test, Mrs. Steckowski paced in the hallway. I sat at my desk, petrified, doodling in the columns of an otherwise unmarked test form. After about twenty minutes of my sitting and her shuffling, she sighed volubly, and waddled past the doorway once more. I dropped my face to regard the long columns of numbers, the hundreds of thousands of numbers in portly rows awaiting calculation, but my eyes kept blurring over, the way eyes often do. My legs began to shake, and my hips clenched to lift my body a bit off the chair, and I felt this suffusion in a ring around the inside of my vagina and then in another further concentric ring and then a tingling—upward and outward—as nerves I never knew I had began to contract, slowly, then quickly, bursting in bunches like miniature explosives or several knots coming untied. It was strange because although I was conscious of Mrs. Steckowski's presence in the hallway, I was unconscious of her too. I was in that room, but I was not *really* in that room, and not much mattered beyond the feeling I was feeling. You can sort of lose yourself there. When it was over, I wondered how long it had lasted. It had not occurred to me to check the clock. I felt scared that maybe I'd broken something, so I left the blank test on the teacher's desk, and I ran home.

NICO'S SIMIAN EYES SCANNED for a target and rested on me. He moved and the school room became lush like territory. He swaggered strategically into my aisle, and Billy followed. I curled over my notebook to draw. I probably should have regretted the obviousness of my body, the look of me which corresponded so precisely to the look of them, but in fact I did not.

"Hey, Steve," Nico said in his weedy voice, "you got the hot seat."

"Guess so," Stephen replied.

Nico sat sideways in the chair in front of mine with his knees poking into the aisle, and he put his right elbow on my desk. He leaned close, his breath coming in humid strokes. "Hey, baby."

I said hi and returned to my sketch. My pen moved boldly. It swirled to wobbly heights, making me think of *Irises* or *Starry Night*. Billy settled his lanky frame into the seat in front of Stephen, the four of us carving out a strange chunk in the back of the room.

Breanne said something to Darlene, probably about me.

"What's that, Breanne?" Billy leaned diagonally to shake her seat.

Nico said, "No whispering. Speak up or forever hold your peace."

"That's right," Billy growled. "Speak up or forever hold my *piece*."

Everyone laughed except Breanne, who whined, "Stop it, Billy," in a voice that vibrated because her chair was shaking.

"*St-o-o-p i-it B-il-ly*," Billy imitated, and the late bell rang. Mr. Shepard drifted in, coffee mug in hand. He lingered by the door, talking about golf with the A.V. teacher.

Nico dug deep into his pocket and removed a fistful of stuff—coins, bills, gum, and erasers, those awful ones that fit on top of pencils. He extracted the erasers and laid them on the desk. Other boys did the same, except for Stephen. "This is gonna be great," Nico said.

From his seat in the front row, Marcus Payne addressed everyone with a series of panoramic nods. Marcus had a consoling effect on me. Whenever I saw him, I felt consoled. Consoled that the world had not denied him shelter. "Now listen up, people." His top teeth gnawed at the air. His head cocked to one side, and his arms came out from his shoulders at a preacherly incline. "Watch out for my head with those things."

"Shut up, Marcus," Bobby Tabor said. Bobby's parents owned the liquor store and every night at dinner they all got drunk on good wine. Bobby got invited to all the parties. "*Pouilly-Foussé*," he would say, rotating a bottle lovingly in his hands to feature the label. "*1974*."

"Yeah, Carcus, if you don't wanna get hit, *move*," Mike Stern warned as he emptied a snack bag full of erasers onto his desktop.

"It doesn't matter where you sit, Payne," Billy said. "We're gonna hit you anyway."

Mr. Shepard closed the door behind him. I asked Nico what was going on. "Everyone's gonna toss erasers at Shep when he makes a bad joke," Nico said. "It's tradition," he stated defensively, "I didn't invent it."

I regarded the erasers. It was tradition; they would not be punished. It wasn't *girl* tradition, girls had no traditions—anyway, none that teachers and boys would share. It was *boy* tradition—a test of gender loyalty, part of the male experience—next comes fraternities, bachelor parties, firefighters, war, politics, the police.

"Relax, baby," Nico patted my hand and leaned his face to mine, "we're just gonna have a little fun."

THERE WAS A LINE I LIKED TO WALK, A SINGLE DISCOLORED PLANK THAT stretched from the east wall to the west wall of the barn behind my house. It was not really a barn; I just called it a barn because it was shaped like one, like a cedar box emerging from a hatch in the wildflowers. In fact it was a shed, twenty-by-twelve, with no plumbing, no heat, no insulation, and floors with missing boards. The light inside was gauzy, like light in a tent. It was my favorite place. Every day I went there to paint or study or just to think.

During finals sophomore year, I'd fallen asleep on the floor. When Mom couldn't find me in the morning, she checked the barn and saw me looking pretty destitute. That afternoon, her Plymouth Scamp was parked out in the school driveway. The car was old but anxious to please. It leaned forward like a pollen-yellow rhombus.

"Maybe she got fired," Kate said as we exited the building.

"Maybe she has cancer like your mother," I said.

Mom waved. "Hop in! We're going to Sears!"

The wheels cheeped timidly as we pulled out and headed toward Amagansett on Pantigo Road. At Sears, Mom ordered a piece of foam from a catalog. "A mattress," she said. "Now you can crash in the barn whenever you're working late. It'll be your studio." She tore a plain blue check from her wallet. On top was her name, Irene Ruane, and our post office box number, and East Hampton, New York, 11937. The amount was forty dollars.

"I wrote it on the bottom, Laura," she told Kiki Hauser's mom, who worked behind the counter. Mrs. Hauser had asked for our phone number even though she knew us. As we waited for processing, Mom brushed my cheek with her hand. "Isn't this exciting? You can sleep there all summer long if you want."

Afterwards we were feeling giddy, so we stopped at A&B Snowflake for ice cream. Mom left the car running and the doors open so we could hear "Rhiannon" from our picnic table. She and Kate sang soprano and I hummed along in my burlapy alto, drumming with two plastic spoons, which made mild clacks and didn't sound much like drums at all. Bees swarmed us, so we left, dropping Kate off at her house on Mill Hill Lane. When we pulled away we waved and I felt sad. It's sad to leave a friend, especially at four-fifteen in the afternoon, especially when their mother is dying but yours is not—but, then again, everything is sad at four-fifteen in the afternoon.

My mother continued to sing for the remainder of our errands and the remainder of the ride, her voice wafting out windows and mingling with the whorling lavender and orange sky, all three threading together in a perfect ornamental spiral.

In the barn I always walked that same line—pacing along the strip of windows with French blue panes to the enamel brown door that opened onto no place in particular, just a stall with a potting bench. When I reached the wooden ladder to the sleeping loft, I turned, keeping every inch of my body centered and upright. In some places, steadiness is a requirement. In some places, women carry baskets on their heads. Mom calls those women *sisters*, though they are far away. In America, you don't really need balance, except in athletics.

PIP HARRIMAN'S HAIR WAS steady as a helmet when she climbed the ropes for the Presidential Physical Fitness Exam in gym that day. It wasn't the *actual* Presidential Fitness Test but a simulated version to determine our "health entry points," from which we were expected to improve by the year's end.

Pip's hands went fast, fist over fist, with her legs crossed like wishful fingers, pinching to maintain counterbalance. Despite the ubiquitous gymnasium fluorescence, her hair gleamed handsomely, like a length of satin ribbon.

Coach Slater took advantage of Pip's example by making a speech. "Rope-climbing is noncompetitive, okay, ladies?" she shouted didactically in a stirring bit of showmanship. Her voice bounced through the mid-morning hollowness and echoed from the polyurethaned floors to the soaring metal rafters. "A climb is a personal challenge, okay? It's an opportunity for you to top your own best performance."

It seemed pretty competitive nonetheless, with Pip effortlessly mounting the one available rope while the rest of us sat slumped and cross-legged, averting our eyes and praying like mad for time to run out before Coach got around to calling our names. If they wanted it to be noncompetitive, they should have added up the total number of inches climbed and given us a prize for good numbers. Like a day of kickball or scooter basketball or something. Then at least we'd all root for each other to go higher. I wasn't sure what it all has to do with fitness anyway since the entire gym class was spent waiting and shirking. Obviously the ropes weren't important enough to practice on a regular basis since they only got dropped from the ceiling for tests. It's not exactly a useable life skill, except maybe in the circus or the army. It was funny to think of Pip in the circus.

"Can you imagine?" I whispered to Kate. "Pip under the Big Top?"

Kate shushed me. She didn't want me to draw attention to us. I would tell her later, at dinner, and we would laugh. My mother liked to laugh about Pip.

Once we were all standing in Kate's parents' driveway—it must have been freshman year, because the Cassirers were both alive.

"What is it with these names?" Mom asked. She was leaning onto the inside of the opened driver's door, elbows against the roof. "Claire, have you heard them?"

"Oui," Maman replied in her turbid accent, "Pip." *Peep.*

"What are the others?" Mom asked.

Kate made a list. "Coco and Kiki, Bobum, Winn."

"Skip," I added, "Colt, Duff, and Leaf. Oh, and Fick."

"*Fick!*" my mother said, laughing until she became asthmatic.

Maman didn't think it was funny. "It is very sad, Irene," she scolded, "this American custom of calling a child by the name of a dog."

Pip hopped off, triumphant and breathless, and when Coach made a check mark on the fitness report form, her dimpled forearm jerked and her flabby wrist flew. She called Elie Palmer. "*Palmer*, Elie!"

The worst thing about the ropes was not the physical strain but the sickening panic you felt when you stood up, knowing everyone was staring. Even though I sympathized with whomever was up there, I would stare anyway since there was nothing better to do, and you were wise to feign interest. Elie rose reluctantly, yanked her oversized Abba t-shirt down around her ass, lumbered over to the swinging rope, tilted her head to one side as if wondering how to begin, then looked pathetically to Coach for some kind of break. But coaches never give breaks. They take their jobs seriously—you can tell by the way they wedge their clipboards into their bulging bellies, blow silver whistles up close and indoors, and wear neat-looking Adidas sweatsuits, though they never break a sweat.

Coach Slater did not like it that Alice Lee brought a note from her doctor saying to please excuse her from the fitness exams because it was that time of the month. Coach especially did not like it when Alice asked if she could sit in the locker room or the nurse's office because we were sharing the gym with the boys. "Are you enrolled in this class?" Coach shouted. She must have been upset about Alice not being able to top her best performance.

"What do you mean?" Alice asked suspiciously.

Coach shook her head. "I *mean*, are you enrolled in this class?"

"I *guess*." Alice's head sank meekly, but her eyes lit up with hatred.

"Then *you* go where the *class* goes."

Coach turned from Alice and blasted her whistle harshly, commanding the rest of us to *Get out there and do three laps*. The boys had already started, so we sort of ran in place in the corner until they reached the far side of the room, then we moved ahead in a unanimous bubble. Every time the boys passed Alice, who was on the floor under the water fountains, hugging her knees to her chest, they would yell mean things. The coaches did nothing to stop the boys—two women, two men, four whistles. They seemed to be using Alice as a lesson. They seemed to say that the gym is a realm unburdened by sloughing wombs and engorged breasts. It was frankly sort of confusing, the way everyone stared at our bodies exactly as they tried to erase the ideas of our bodies from our minds. We were supposed to get over ourselves, but no one was supposed to get over us. The female body was our worst handicap and our best advantage—the surest means to success, the surest course to failure.

"It's her own fault," Jodie Palumbo exhaled.

"God, it's *so* gross," Annie McCabe shuddered.

Pip said something, which I couldn't hear, and they laughed. They didn't like Alice, though they didn't know her. They were cataloging. Cataloging is easy—anyone dressed funny is the enemy, especially if they reject your supremacy or do not acknowledge school as entertainment. If the enemy tries to look like you and act like you, only in more affordable clothes, that person is *still* the enemy, only a more contemptible, less terrifying variety—the sort you can be seen with *if absolutely necessary*, for instance if you are soliciting float-making help for Homecoming or votes for yourself in the class election.

I passed the girls, though it brought me to the rear of the boys. Actually the rear of the boys was a nicer class of people than the front of the girls, and that is a carry-over fact for life. I mixed in with Roy Field, who rebuilt radios and ate seven bowls of Trix a day, and Tommy Gardner, who had chronic impetigo and a heart murmur, and Daryl Sackler, who was six-foot four but refused to play basketball because he had a job mowing lawns after school. Daryl Sackler *buries cats and mows their heads off*, that's what everybody said.

"Actually," Jack said of Daryl, "I like him. Most freaks like that would kill for hero status. But he *chooses* to remain a loser. Either he's a total retard or a complete man of honor. Besides, you know how I feel about cats."

I ran hard, really hard, until my body elevated, until I rose and flipped in my mind, insular and elastic and deaf as a sea mammal, spiraling and swimming. I sprinted to the wall and bent over my legs, catching my breath. Others finished after me, forming a docile line at the water fountain. Alice shifted miserably away, as though protecting herself from us, like we might kick her or spit, but she didn't shift too far, since her predicament was legitimate. I felt a strange feeling, an epiphanous feeling. I felt I was with her, though my body stood apart and my voice was silent. In *Jules and Jim*, Jim blows Catherine an invisible kiss when she jumps into the Seine after Jules insults all women, and Jim says, "I admired her. I was swimming with her in my mind."

My eyes wanted to meet Alice's eyes, but I didn't know what message mine were to convey. Pity wasn't right, pity implied disconnection. The rich feel pity for the poor because the rich do not need to become poor, but I was as impoverished as Alice. I considered sitting next to her, but I would have gotten detention and that would have embarrassed Kate. It's very shifty how teachers belong to a union and they teach about revolutions and labor strikes, but they discourage solidarity among students. I twisted the knob and sucked back the water, which was icy cold because I had this trick of letting everyone else cut in front of me. Some went up my nose, and I coughed. I wiped my mouth on my shoulder and looked back to Alice. I didn't know what she'd endured beyond the school walls, but her look was very knowing.

Kate and I saw her doctor's note on Coach's desk when we were sent to return the relay cones to the equipment room. It was halfway unfolded, retreating modestly into the series of squares in which it had been delivered. We could only make out parts.

> *Please excuse Alice Lee, due to severe menstrual*—the second
> paragraph fell into a crease. Something, something—
> *requires medication.*

In the hallway Kate said, "How awful." By that she meant Alice. Kate thought Alice was a poor thing. I thought the awful part was the note. It was written by the sure hand of an expert, by someone who believed what he or she was writing, then it was dispatched into the atmosphere, only to be casually disregarded by some *other* expert. It's hard to believe in anything anyone says with the way experts constantly contradict each other.

Pip was as sure in gym as I was in art, but Alice was also sure about something, and so was Coach, and Alice's doctor too. It's strange that certain things matter so much when *you* are the one they matter to, but in the grand scheme, no one else cares, not really. I wondered who thinks rope climbing matters to girls but periods don't.

IT HAD BECOME DARK. In the dark I could hear. I stayed in place and allowed my senses to arc up as though one end of a rainbow. My mind burst forth on a translucent highway, reaching out blindly for a secure place to touch down, the boneless way inchworms do. First my footsteps echoed off the barn walls like falling pearls, like water beading up on dust. Next my mother's laughter ascended the hill from the front house, traveling on the platform of a breeze. I could smell the wine on her breath and the wintergreen that pirouetted off her coat like fairies escaping. I could see her perform the wonder of her day for her friends—bodies wedged in half-darkness, denim legs jutting from veiled corners, drowsy hands passing a joint, passing a bottle, wrists exposed, voices going, "What happened next, Rene?" *Reen*, short for Irene.

Friends were always there. If ever it looked like they might leave, someone would stagger to a stretch and use the toilet, tuck in a loose shirt and inquire as to who felt like making a run for more beer. If ever I passed through a crowded room, they would confer with me congenially, dipping close to my eyes with cigarettes and tarnished goblets, with natted hair and saliva-caked lips and home-sewn clothes wetted with patchouli and musk. If I ran into them alone, they were mainly quiet. A man might curtsy or a woman drop a tissue. It's not easy to drop a tissue.

If my upbringing made me sensitive to affectations of tolerance and to the irony of that particular hypocrisy, I could hardly be blamed. All I ever heard as a child was how *everything is cool* and *everyone should be cool,* and yet there were never people so quick to judge new shoes or a clean car or to cogitate over the dementia behind matching furniture or monogrammed stationery. I couldn't help but despise the epoxied stench of incense and the smut of overfilled ashtrays and the sticky liquor rings on tables that we cleaned Sunday mornings in March when the clouds were like metal shedding rain in fine needles. I never liked listening to last night's albums, raising the entire stack and letting them drop again. In my room at bedtime, I would drink my dinner of chocolate milk and bury myself beneath stuffed animals, paired with rescued ribbon and bits of yarn, one neck fastened to another neck, belly to belly, buddied up in case of fire, in case they would have to be tossed from the window. My feet rubbing together to drown the noise, the singing, the laughter, the music—Joplin, Dylan, Hendrix.

"I love you," she would say. My mother, popping her head in.

WHEN I WAS CLEAR and when I was able, I lowered myself to the barn floor and, with charcoal and torn paper, I drew three books and a stopped watch. I'd been waiting the whole time for Jack to come, only he didn't. Kneeling before my paper, I looked deep into the space he might have occupied, and I smiled. He smiled also, a fair angel's smile. I could see his watery features transmitting a regard so strong as to defy the inconvenience of his factual absence. I loved my invention, I loved the way it loved me back. It was powerless to make me do the things that Jack could make me do. Had he been there actually, he would have persuaded me to join the party in the house. Jack hated to miss a party. Though I longed for him with all my heart, a part of me was thankful to be beyond the influence of his flesh, the electric tissue that could coerce me down the garden path, the lips that could nudge me with an inflexible kiss through the door of my own home.

"Mom's home, you know." Not Jack, just Kate, sitting on the wooden bench under the windows.

Yes, I knew. The laughter and the wintergreen. Sweet wine and music. In her pocketbook would be a half-eaten tuna sandwich on Arnold's white in soggy butcher's paper and an opened bag of peanut M&M's, spilling out into the linty creases. I scraped the palette knife on the edge of a bucket and then on my jeans. Linseed oil smells like fruity poison.

"Feel like eating?" Kate asked. Her leg jiggling.

I wasn't sure what I felt like, being alone or being with people. Neither seemed very good. I wondered what was expected of me; if I had known what was expected of me, I might have done it. I tried to think, but at the same time there was something I needed to forget, something of which an answer to her question would have reminded me. "No thanks," I said.

Kate popped off the bench. Her feet clocked down the three wooden steps outside the barn. In a few seconds the screen door in the back of the house squeaked open and slapped shut. Then nothing. No, not nothing—silence. Not silence so much as the absence of sounds affiliated with me. There was the loose, careless clank of silverware hitting plates and cabinet doors smacking and the thud of the plumbing every time the kitchen faucet was shut off and a distant muffle of voices—Kate rejoining the party. Mom asking if I was coming. Maybe not. Maybe she did not ask about me at all.

WHEN I CAME HOME FROM THE A&P SATURDAY, HE WAS THERE, AT MOM'S desk, swiveling belligerently in her chair, the way you do at ice cream counters, like at the Candy Kitchen in Bridgehampton. It was as if he'd always been there, always all summer, occupying that very chair, swiveling and invisible.

A scratchy copper beard dusted his chin and scaled the front portion of his jaw up and around the space beneath his nose, making a wafery and sparkling layer like penny-colored frost on a window pane. His hair touched the base of his neck. It was the color of gleaming wheat, his skin the shade of baked marigolds. Jack might have looked healthy except beneath his pastel blue eyes were velvety pouches, and his cheeks were raw and drawn very far in, like a pair of inside out parentheses. It was possible he had not eaten or slept in days.

It's strange to realize you have sustained yourself on a memory of a person that has become untrue. The phantom face of my summer was not the face before me. And, yet, and still, it was Jack, stirring gradually, coming undeniably. Like the haughty, aromatic smell of earth in spring, his arrival reminded me of my need exactly as it satisfied it. I stood at the stairs, holding on.

"Your hair grew," he said. His voice was a beautiful voice.

I lowered the groceries and touched the balustrade. "I hate it."

"Cut it," he said, and he lifted me and we spun.

Beyond his back the chair continued to twist without him. Maybe not, maybe that was my imagination. I tested his existence; my hands felt for the body beneath the shell of his clothes. I measured the way his jeans dangled around the back of his thighs. I confirmed the feathery pressure of his hair on my cheeks. The solid wall of his slender chest, the subtle protrusion of his right shoulder blade, the way his bones were living bones covered by flesh that was warm. He was real with a smell that was real and a slightly sticky gleam to his skin. I rested my head in the bony basin between his ear and his shoulder.

"Are you crying?" he asked.

"I'm sorry," I said.

He tightened his grip. "What's wrong?"

"It's just, you kept coming, like a ghost, like, floating. The angles of your face were flat from light and your hair was platinum and flared at the sides, like this." I lifted the edges of his hair and calculated with my fingertips the minute and mortal thickness of each strand. For a long while I could not speak. "Sometimes I would feel that you were with me, and you seemed so real. Now you're here, but I'm not sure. You seem less real than before."

His eyes studied mine, scanning cautiously. Jack breathed deeply, taking some of me down with the air.

"Have I changed too?" I asked.

"You have." He drew back my hair one side at a time, trailing with his gaze the path of his fingers. Adding gravely, "But it's okay."

THE GRASS IN THE backyard pushed through the skinny flame-shaped gaps left by our bodies. Jack's hand in mine was like a mineral, and he tasted like black licorice, like anise.

"My mom told me," he said, "about Kate's mother." He touched my cheek over and over with a finger that was chapped and parched with pieces of skin sticking up. His crystalline eyes worked in earnest to bait my heartache.

In the sky the clouds were sugary tiers, and my own eyes opened wide, admitting light. If you don't want to cry, by looking into the light you can stop yourself. It's possible to keep grief inside. Grief inside works like bees or ants, building curious and perfect structures, complicating you. Grief outside means you want something from someone, and chances are usually good you won't get it.

"Anise would be a pretty name," I said, "for a girl with purple ringlets."

LATER WE WERE SITTING on opposite ends of the couch, and we were drinking black coffee. Our legs were interlocking and it felt safe to rub my feet together beneath the brittle heft of his pelvic bones. I used to rub my cold feet behind my dad's back when he was reading or when he and Marilyn were watching *Mannix* or that crazy Dean Martin show, the one with the spiral staircase. My father's apartment was always freezing.

"They're like a little machine!" Jack said of my feet, and right then WPLR played "Maybe I'm Amazed." It'd played the first time we met, and by coincidence we often heard it play, which sort of made it *our* song, even though everyone said it was queer to like Wings. Jack left my feet momentarily exposed while he stood to raise the volume, then he plopped back down.

"I'm thinking of doing a cover with the band," he said. He and his best friend, Dan Lewis, had a band—Atomic Tangerine. In a moderate shriek, Jack sang along. "*Der ner ne ner ner ner ne ne.*"

When the song was over, applause erupted. We tilted our heads back over the couch arms. Kate was at the front door. "Katie!" Jack called out.

They teetered awkwardly as though they might hug, only they did not. Jack probably wanted to say that he was sorry about her mother dying, or something similar, but Kate was smiling, which probably made it hard for him to know what to do. He went to the stereo and lowered the volume, then he lingered there discreetly, poking through albums.

Kate removed her sweater. One hand moved deftly down the length of coral cotton, unfastening buttons, and for a while we were quiet. She dropped the sweater playfully on top of me, then craned her neck to regard herself in the mirror over the fireplace. Jack changed the record and Neil Young's *Harvest* started.

"How'd it go?" I asked.

"Good," she said brightly. "Great!"

"How did what go?" Jack wanted to know.

Kate said, "Drama Club."

"On a *Saturday*?" Jack asked. "Is it a *Communist* club?"

Kate sighed like she was exasperated. "We got a donation this year. We get to have the play at Guild Hall." She turned and bolted upstairs to her room. The door slammed and her stereo switched on. *Hers*, as opposed to *ours*.

Jack returned to the couch and sat on the edge facing me, absorbing the way things had become. He plucked Kate's sweater from my chest, pinching it between two fingers, draping it across the coffee table. He looked off to the stairs and said, "This whole thing is very fucking weird."

IT WAS ALMOST SEVEN. We had only a half hour left to be alone at Jack's house. His parents had a six o'clock reservation at Gordon's. At seven-fifteen his mother would deliver his father to the Jitney, and by seven-thirty, she would be home. Mr. Fleming would be back in Manhattan two-and-a-half hours after that. They had an apartment on Madison Avenue and Eighty-seventh Street.

"How come he's going back on a Saturday?" I asked as we walked.

"*I* came home today," Jack said. "He can't get away fast enough."

At the Fleming house, Jack's sister's dog Mariah barked, so he gave it a kick. Not really a kick, just a kind of dragging push to one side with the top of his foot. Inside, the air was heavy with the scent of cologne. It spooked me a little to think of Mr. Fleming's barrel-chested shadow appearing suddenly to block a doorway.

"What perfume does he wear?" I wrinkled my nose. "Lagerfeld?"

"*Cat Piss*," Jack said. He yanked open the refrigerator door. It smacked the counter and glass bottles clanked. A pie-shaped wedge of light unfolded onto one-half of the otherwise dark kitchen, making steel things faintly glow. "He must think he's gonna get laid on the bus." Jack grabbed a yogurt, tore off the lid and flung it into the sink like a Frisbee. He tilted his head back and drank from the cup. Halfway through he paused. "Want some?"

"What flavor is it?"

"I don't know," he said. "I haven't hit fruit yet." He swallowed a little more. "Not the kind you like. It tastes purple."

"Blueberry," I said. "Forget it."

Mariah skulked past our ankles as we moved to the hallway; I extended a hand. She sniffed miserably. "Keep away from that beast," Jack warned. "It's an operative." I asked what's an operative. He said like a spy.

He started up the stairs, his sneakers knocking into the shallow depths. There was something wretched about the sight. "I'll wait here," I said. Mr. and Mrs. Fleming didn't like us to go upstairs when they were out.

He reached for my hand. "C'mon, Evie. I swear, we'll just be a minute."

ON THE SOUTHWEST SIDE of the attic, Jack had constructed for himself a retreat. He liked to say it was the only room in the house uncontaminated by damask and deodorizer. The windows were shuttered and the floors were bare wood because, three months after we'd met, Jack had torn out the curtains and rug. It was Labor Day Sunday, 1978, the day before he was supposed to leave for boarding school. He'd intended to destroy the whole room and after that, the whole house, including the carport.

"*Especially the carport,*" he declared. I had no doubt that he meant it. Unlike most people who say they hate their parents, Jack really did.

He'd tried in all sincerity to talk to them, to apologize for certain things, to reason with them about his feelings, to ask them to please let him spend his junior and senior years in East Hampton, to not send him away. I'd gone with him for moral support—not quite all the way, in case things got bad. I waited at the end of the street, on the porch of the Presbyterian Church. I brought a book, figuring it might take a while. But Jack reappeared in ten minutes.

"That was fast," I said. "What happened?"

"What happened," Jack repeated. "Hmmm, let's see." He took my book and began to play with it, swatting it from his palm to his thigh. "I try to reconcile. I swear to conform. I sit there, totally fucking humiliating myself. I tell them that I don't want to lose you."

"And," I prodded softly.

"And, my mother's sure we'll *stay friends.* She says, *You can write.*"

I hated to hear his voice sound the way it sounded, desperate and alone when it did not have to be. When I was right there.

"Then," Jack said, "the fat bastard goes to the barbecue grill, totally ignoring me, and says, *C'mon Susan, I don't want those ribs to char.*"

"*Char,*" I said. "Who uses a word like *char?*"

"Fat bastards," Jack stated. "Ad agency homos. That's who."

At dawn the following morning, he took a knife to his room. After cutting the curtains and shredding the carpet, the plan was to start on the walls, except far beneath the rug he'd discovered a greeting card, an old Christmas card with stained edges. Inside, in childish handwriting, it said, *Eveline.*

He jammed the opened card into my hands. I was in my underwear and a t-shirt, and we were standing in the driveway by the garage because it was early and that was the back way to my bedroom if you didn't want to wake up other people. I'd heard the aluminum wheels creaking in their tracks as the garage door glided into the pocketed ceiling over my bed. A minute later Jack started pounding the inside door. "*Evie, open up, God damn it.*"

I found him winded from running and covered in the fine white matter of demolition. He yanked me into the sunlight, handed over the card, then he set his hands on his thighs and bent to catch his breath.

I looked from the card to his face. "I don't understand."

"I found it! In my room. I was pulling out the carpet."

I asked was he sure.

He said, "Of course I'm sure!"

"Maybe someone put it there," I said. "Like, planted it."

"That rug's been there for years," he said. "Besides, no one we know is that interesting. What would be the point?"

He dropped to the dew-soaked grass. I dropped too.

"Listen," he instructed. "I'm tearing out the rug, I'm cutting and tearing and throwing the pieces down the stairs, and I'm raising all kinds of dust and shit to really piss them off, and just when I'm about to bust the windows or pry off the molding, I see this paper on the floor." Jack gestured with his hands as he spoke, which he almost never did. "I go to the paper, I lift it. It's a Christmas card. There are angels on front. Did you see the angels?" he asked.

"I saw them," I said.

"*Look at the fucking angels*," he insisted, pushing the card back at me.

"Yes," I swore. "I see."

"And this, did you see this?" Jack opened it again and tapped at my name. It was scrawled in loopy script that dipped to the right, in obsolete penmanship—*Eveline*. "I might have killed him," he said. "I might have done it this time, if he came up those stairs, I might have." He looked at the ground in a way that was numb. "You had to see me, stalled like a gasless piece of machinery in the middle of that chaos. I had a knife in one hand, and in the other hand I had the card."

He left for boarding school in Kent, Connecticut later that same morning without much of a fight. He took the card with him and in the Fleming driveway where we said goodbye he vowed to me privately, but before God and whomever else, to take it with him everywhere he went for the rest of his sorry fucking life, as a mystic but tangible reminder that no matter how far apart he and I might grow, at the core we were one, that we were meant to be, that things would always work out okay no matter what because we were connected—*spiritually*. "Understand?" he said, as his sister Elizabeth tapped on the horn of the family's New Yorker.

"I understand," I said, because truly I did, and to seal the vow we kissed. He popped the passenger door and, before getting in, he gave one final wave of the middle finger to his parents, who were behind the living room drapes. Then he left, and he stayed away all the way until he dropped out at Thanksgiving, which, though just three months, felt more like seven years.

JACK WAS EMPTYING HIS knapsack. It smelled like heath and wax and mold from camping in the mountains. He pulled the card from deep inside and laid it on the desktop. I touched it, the inside part with my name, just for luck, then I sat on the bed. Jack's bed was wedged square and high into the corner. When you sat, your feet did not touch ground. Attached to the long wall above it was a shelf for shells, fossils, field guides, and bottled things such as butterflies and also bones and books. *A World of Fungi*, *The Stranger*, *Demian*. In *Demian*, Jack had found Abraxas.

"Just like the Santana album," he'd said at the time. "Do you think Carlos reads Hesse?"

Near the bed was a brand new Technics stereo, three guitars, and twelve Schwenk milk crates filled with albums—some rock, some punk, but mostly jazz and blues. Near his pillow was a stuffed mouse I'd made in seventh grade home economics, the only thing I'd ever sewn.

"I can't believe you still have this mouse," I said. I was terrible at sewing. "Do you really like it or do you just feel sorry for me?"

"I really like it. Though I also happen to feel sorry for you." He kissed my eyelids and lowered himself on top of me.

"C'mon, Jack," I said, pushing him off. "Let's get out of here."

WE STOPPED AT THE trees across from the Huntting Inn.

"I went straight to your house," Jack explained. "I didn't get a chance to check the trees." He lay in the grass, his head hanging off the curb into the gutter. I watched the car tires whizzing past his extended neck, wondering if he would be decapitated. His untucked Jethro Tull t-shirt crept up his chest and his jeans slid to reveal the waistband of a pair of boxer shorts. The design on them was of red go-go dancers. The shorts were mine, anyway my father's, from the fifties. The shallow pool of Jack's apricot belly was marked by a *V* of muscle low in the center that dropped in ledged recesses along either side and a narrow ladder of hair that mounted the middle. The base of his skinny ribs arched like the frame of a bandshell. I crawled through the grass and got next to him, facing up also. "This one's awesome," he said. "The branch over Main Street is like an arm bent at the elbow."

The streets of the village were full of fog. Along the way to the pizza place, I kept putting up my hands as if to part curtains. Jack was saying how in Wyoming juniper trees have round blue cones like grapes and how Rick Ruddle said if you inhale labdanum, it tranquilizes the mind. Rick Ruddle was Jack's hike leader and a sound engineer from Portland.

Brothers Four Pizzeria was crowded. Troy Resnick was there with Min Kessler, the eye doctor's daughter. Jack and Troy slapped loose hands. "How was the trip, man?" Troy asked.

Jack said, "Outrageous, man."

Troy examined the watermelon-colored Kryps on Jack's skateboard, and Jack informed Troy that his haircut was *butt ugly*. I lifted a copy of *Dan's Papers* from a stack on the floor and took the front table. Through the gauzy ribbon of mist that divided Newtown Lane, the red neon sign from Sam's Restaurant seemed woolly and winterish, making me think of blood mixed with milk and single-bullet shootings. A pop, a body, some footsteps, a detective.

"Catch you later man," I heard Jack say.

Troy slurped something back, hopefully cheese. "Meet us at Wiborg's later."

Jack said he would consider it. Others starting calling out to Jack, and he transmitted a series of apathetic hellos then declared with annoyance, "Listen, people, I gotta get some food."

At the counter he begrudgingly ordered two slices and stared down Dino and Vinny while he waited. They irritated Jack, the way they thought they were masculine. He liked to say that they must have some very big hairy dicks beneath those egg-stained pizza aprons. For his part, Jack astounded them, the way he was puny and unkempt but had a girl like me. He personified for them the trouble with America. Dino would shake his head, which pleased Jack infinitely. Jack liked to take me there; we went about three times a week.

He deposited two paper plates on the table, and they swirled a bit from grease coming through. Jack lowered his chin to the plane of the table and bit a folded slice. "Mooks," he said through his food.

He didn't know what a *Mook* was, he just heard it in *Mean Streets*, which my dad took us to see. Ever since then, everybody was a mook, especially Jack's physics teacher, Mr. Bertrand, who was *Queen Mook*.

I tore the crust from a piece and chewed. Jack wanted to know if the pizza guys had given me a hard time while he was gone.

"This is the first time I've been here since you left," I said.

He knocked his head back to suck the soda from his can. His hair fanned out against his shoulders, and I could see his Adam's apple dip and rise. I don't like to see them, not ever, Adam's apples. I turned away; Dino was staring.

"Let's go, Jack," I said, standing and flinging my sweater around my shoulders, buttoning one button at the neck. "The movie starts in five minutes. We're going to miss the oil globs."

"Right," he said. He grabbed his skateboard and stood also, and when I tossed the remainder of my pizza into the garbage, he caught it before it hit the can and crammed it into his mouth.

As we started for the theater, he jumped onto his skateboard and whizzed by me in the street. Jack was handsome, in a seedy and purposeful way, the way a red barn in disrepair looks good in the middle of a green field. It was true he had changed over the summer, or maybe I had. I said, "I can't believe we're finally seniors."

"I was just thinking the same thing," he said as he rode up the curb then popped back off in front of Tony's Sporting Goods.

"Troy's doing whippets tonight. He wants to meet later."

"Isn't it like breathing into a paper bag?"

"It's so fucking stupid. That's what makes it fun." He approached Newtown and Main and at the corner he twirled smoothly on the rear wheels. His arms were bent at the elbows, his right leg extended, his left leg flexed. His hair windmilled lightly. Then he leapt off, flipping the front end of his board into his ready hand, waiting for me to catch up. We met at the light.

"Your leg ever bother you?" I asked.

"Nah," he said. "Sometimes."

JACK WAS WEARING A cast when we met. "The summer of 1978 is a study in bitter irony," he liked to say. "In the midst of the worst period of a particularly shitty life, I met you."

Because of his broken leg Jack had to cancel his annual Outward Bound trip that year, which meant he was stuck at home with his family. For days he wasn't even able to climb the three flights to his room, so he had to sleep in the den, or, as he said, in the *transverse colon* of the house, where all the shit sits and ferments before moving through. Jack was forced to endure the petty mechanics of family life—every dinner and phone conversation, every key jingle and cabinet slam.

Once he and his dad fought so bad that his dad called the police.

"What did you do?" I asked.

"I threatened him with a weapon."

"A gun?"

"No," he confided, "I couldn't reach the gun. A knife."

"A *knife*? Your leg is broken! He couldn't have been scared."

Jack shrugged. "What can I say? I have excellent aim."

I knew Jack from high school, everyone did because of Atomic Tangerine. Prior to that he and Kate had the same piano teacher, Laura Lipton. Laura was a songwriter from Sag Harbor whose dog Miles was a television actor—Ken-L-Ration, Chuck Wagon, and so on. Occasionally Kate's lesson would encroach upon Jack's, and she would play with Miles just to stick around and listen. She would call me after to say how well Jack Fleming played.

We never actually spoke until the day he came with his parents to the Lobster Roll, where his older sister Elizabeth was a waitress and I was a busgirl. I watched him from across the room. I'd never seen anyone so uncomfortable in my life. As his father talked without pause, Jack stared onto Napeague Highway, clanking his spoon against his cast, keeping an invisible rhythm. He would lower his face to the table to sip his water. His broken leg was propped onto a second chair from which the remainder of his body jutted off in a dramatic curve, coming up like the short hook of a prostrate letter *J*.

Elizabeth asked me to carry over a tray of drinks. "Please," she begged. "I cannot deal with them."

The cocktail tray rested on the flat of my left forearm, and I bent to deposit each drink carefully. I could not help but notice the way the afternoon sun encountered Jack's face, the glassine glow to his eyes. When you looked into them, you could not look away. They became all that was before you—a beautiful horizon, dominions of clouds and winds of ice and insinuations of birds. I considered sadly the world he perceived through those eyes. Nothing actual could possibly match the purity of vision they must have generated.

Mr. Fleming asked my name.

I set down his plastic cup of Chardonnay and said, "Eveline."

"Eveline? *Fan-tas-tic!*" He began to sing. "*Eveline, Evangeline.*"

I delivered Jack's Coke, and my breast accidentally grazed his right arm, a little beneath his shoulder. We both kind of froze.

"Which of your parents reads Longfellow?" Mr. Fleming bellowed. Jack shifted protectively.

"My mother," I replied, "teaches poetry. And Shakespeare. But I think the name is from *Dubliners*."

"Joyce, eh?" Mr. Fleming muttered dismissively. "Let's see, let's see now, *Longfellow*. It's been quite some time."

"Where does she teach, dear?" Mrs. Fleming nervously interrupted.

"Southampton College," I said as he cleared his throat and begin to recite.

> *Gentle Evangeline*—something, something—*When she had passed it seemed like the ceasing of exquisite music.*

"Well, now, Eveline-Evangeline. What do you intend to do with the great fortune you will have amassed by the end of August?"

"Probably I'll buy paints and stuff. You know, art stuff," I said.

He was silent—they all were—stunned no doubt by the humorless sincerity of my reply. As I delivered damp straws and cleared away soiled appetizer plates, I felt for the first of many times the intensity of Jack's gaze and the blood that pooled darkly in my cheeks.

At the waitress station, Elizabeth garnished tall glasses of iced tea with lemon wheels, and she spoke of Jack. I listened from the far side of the lattice divider. It was funny to see her face after seeing his—his was so much prettier. Her parents had tried everything, she said. She said that Jack had seen dozens of psychiatrists since he was seven, that he had been on more medications than she could remember, that he was very talented in music, and that he had just been enrolled in boarding school near their grandparents' house in Connecticut. He was leaving that September. "He tried to kill my father, you know," Elizabeth whispered to Sue and Renata.

Renata admitted she'd read about it in the *East Hampton Star*.

"He should be grateful that he's going to school instead of prison." She hoisted a tray onto her arm. "He's such an asshole"

Since I'd never spoken to Jack, I could not really rise to his defense. But I figured that at least I ought to tell him how I felt about what I'd heard. You sort of have an obligation to tell someone that he can trust you more than he can trust his own sister.

No one offered Jack a hand as they prepared to leave. I held his chair for him and followed him to the door.

"Good luck, Lady Evangeline," Mr. Fleming thundered above his wife's head as she crossed the vestibule to join him. "Though I don't expect you'll need it."

Jack swung past with his body hanging far over his crutches. "Thanks," he mumbled, and I went with him into the corridor, which seemed to confuse everyone, including me.

Mr. Fleming winked knowingly. "Meet you outside, son."

"Sorry about that," Jack said when they left. "He's a dick."

"It's okay," I assured him, feeling shy to be the object of his eyes. Inside the enamel blue rings were specks, little stars twinkling like miracles in day. "So when do you get your cast off?"

"Thursday," he said caustically, dragging the word out, giving each letter new meaning. He looked to the ground. Without lifting his head, his eyes returned to mine. To say he was handsome was not quite right, not quite enough. The starry look in his eyes was transcendent. On the restaurant stereo was "Maybe I'm Amazed."

I glanced out to the cars. "You should come over sometime."

Jack glanced out too. "What time do you get off?"

I said at five.

"All right," he said, moving off, "see you at six."

"Wait," I called. "You don't know where I live."

He paused at the door. "By the tracks," he said. Then he left, his compact frame ticking gracefully between shiny pale crutches.

People always asked why I went out with him. I just liked him better than anyone else. He didn't have that ballooned chest or stiff-shouldered look other boys had. Jack was skinny, but fluid, loose in the legs, and the chances he took were real. One night when he and Dan Lewis, and Dan's cousin Marvin, also known as Smokey Cologne, were out of pot, they smoked oregano leaves and drank codeine cough syrup. On a dare, Smokey did a shot of Downey Fabric Softener and had to get his stomach pumped. After the hospital, they came to my house and dove kamikaze style off the back of the couch until they got bored. Jack had tried peyote in Taos, New Mexico, and LSD at the Roxy during a George Thorogood concert—*a rockabilly nightmare,* he'd said. He'd snorted speed and done cocaine. He hated coke. "I end up smiling all fucking night," Jack would complain.

It didn't really bother me if he got high. I always figured his was like a body without skin, and he had to sort of desensitize himself. I didn't mind the way he predicted his own disappointment, calling everything pointless and existence senseless. I just figured it was a way to protect himself, to build, like, a shell. The only truly threatening thing I ever noticed about Jack was his surplus of confidence—a tremendous ego is a dangerous thing in someone so gloomy. He could not be persuaded away from his blackest convictions, and anyone who disagreed with him was part of the whole fucking problem to begin with. Though I would never ever tell him so, Jack was very much the son of his father.

"WE WERE SLEEPING IN an open field," Jack said as we stepped forward with the movie line. "In Montana. After dawn we heard a weird whooshing sound.

"A UFO!" I said. Jack and I had seen one at Albert's Landing once. It looked like a salt circle pinched at the center.

"A hot air balloon," he said. "Hovering. Like a rubber rainbow. We jumped out of our sleeping bags and ran after it, all of us naked."

Jack would have made a good Indian. He could make fire with a magnifying glass and sleep naked on mountains in the cold. He could tie knots you could not escape from. "Girls too?" I asked.

"Two for *Amityville Horror*," Jack told LizBeth Bennett. She tore two pink tickets off a spool. "Yeah, girls too."

It didn't bother me that he had seen the girls naked and maybe had sex with them. I was envious of all the places he'd visited. I'd only been to eight states—always with my father. Jack had been to twenty-six—always alone.

He shoved a messy wad of change in his pocket. "I wrote a song about it."

"About the balloon?" I asked.

"About how you weren't there to see it," he said.

We sat in the third row and followed the wafting oil globs because that was the thing to do when you were early for the movies, especially if you were high, which, as it happened, we were not. Jack removed his black journal from his coat to show me the stuff he'd collected and recorded and all the songs he'd written for me during his trip. His drawings were compact and obsessively detailed, mathematical almost, like Da Vinci's. Most pages had variations of the same landscape—upside down and tilted. Like a vortex, like water down a bathtub drain.

"That's in the Tetons," he explained solemnly. His group had to cross a ridge with tremendous drops on each side, and there was this yellow plastic tag nailed to the point where some guy had fallen off. "It would have been so easy, Evie." Jack used my name for emphasis, and I listened with care. We were low in our seats, so low that people behind probably couldn't see our heads, only our knees propped on the chairs in front of us. I held his bicep with two hands, my hands just wrapped around his red windbreaker. "The free fall. I would have shattered and spread." His hands pushed out in two opposing directions, "Like, distributed."

"*Re*-distributed," I said. Back to raw matter.

"*Re*-distributed," he said, "*exactly*, yeah."

I liked the idea of marking the place where a life leaves off as opposed to the place a corpse is buried. And the idea of no one collecting your remains. It's bad enough *being* dead, but it's worse to have people *see* you dead, to have living hands feel a dead you, jostle and dress you, push your stiffening arms into clean sleeves and cry over your blood-drained frame. People say the dead are at rest, but actually, they're working. They assist the living, they stop time. They postpone the reality of loss. That's why veins get emptied and refilled with toxic solution, a preservative to cure the corpse. It's hard to know which is worse, never seeing a loved one again or seeing them again packed with fixative and formaldehyde, with plastic and whey and alkalis and binders, and hearing people mutter, *She looks so peaceful*, when what they really mean is *stuffed like a glycerol scarecrow*. Probably that mountain climber's spirit was drifting motionlessly like an eagle soaring in place. Flags flap that way, blowing grandly to nowhere.

"I missed you," Jack said.

I'd missed him too. Truly I did. I took a handful of popcorn, then brought my fist to his mouth, pushing some kernels gently in. He ate until he reached my hand, which he bit lightly. The projector jolted on, and his face flashed to blue snow.

First the Snack Canyon clip started, and Jack shouted, "Yeah! Snack Canyon! Cool!" But when Will Rogers Institute came on, he said, "Fuck these Will Rogers beggars."

Two acne-scarred ushers tripped up the aisle like zombies in red polyester jackets. Jack spit his chewing gum onto the top of the papered can when it came to us. I flicked the wad off and directed the jar back to the usher, Mike Morris. *Mike Morris loves his dog*, that was what everyone said.

"That death marker thing is cool," I whispered to cheer him. Jack could be quick to turn. "They ought to do it instead of cemeteries."

"Ah forget it. There'd be bodies everywhere."

"Not bodies. *Markers*. Bodies get cremated."

"That's true," he said with renewed interest. "Highways would be littered." We hated highways.

"I'd want my marker to be suspended in mid-air, like that guy, only not hitting the mountainside, just like if I died of shock during a fall from a peak. Or projected upwards like the Batman logo, if that's even possible."

"Sure it is," Jack speculated, "if you got shot out of a cannon."

"But you'd have to be a clown to die like that."

"That would blow," Jack said. "Dying as a clown."

I asked him where he would like his marker to be.

Jack said, "Right here." He touched the inside of my elbow.

ONE NIGHT AFTER JACK and I met, I mentioned him to Denny. It was June, and Denny and I were on the steps outside the barn. The door behind us was open, and light from inside seeped out to form a pale pond around our reclining bodies. We were like seals on an iceberg.

"Seals are fat," Denny said. He was breaking pieces off of sticks and throwing them at fireflies. "Let's be shipwrecked. On an atoll."

When I had to pee, I went around to the side of the barn. It was easier than going to the house, and besides, Denny was always on to something new. I didn't like to leave him in case he had some bright idea and took off while I was gone. I leaned under the windows and hoisted my dress up. It was a three-quarter sleeve vintage pink linen dress with a corded seam around the fabric beneath my breasts. Marilyn bought it for me at Reminiscence in the Village.

"Hey Den," I called, "what do you think of Jack?"

"Jack who? Fleming? He's okay, I guess. Why?"

"I saw him at the restaurant."

"He doesn't work there, I hope," Denny called back. "He's a little hostile for the service industry."

I came back and lay against Denny's belly, straightening my arms into the universe while he played with my hair. "It's like white stuff in corn," he said. "Those limp fibers inside."

"That's so depressing," I said. "That's like sad doll hair."

"Have you ever heard him sing?" Denny asked, ignoring me, going back to Jack. "I was at a party and Atomic Tangerine was playing. The band sucked, but then he sang alone. He's really good."

"What did he play?"

"Normal stuff—covers, I guess."

"I mean, what instrument."

Denny said, "Oh, he played the guitar."

A WEEK LATER, JACK and I had sex. We were almost sixteen and we drank rum. It started out when Jack came to find me in the barn. Instead of talking, he stood. He leaned against the water heater in the corner and watched me draw. An orange glow warmed his face; I looked to see where it came from. I wiped my hands on my legs and pushed the loose hair from my eyes with the back of my wrist. When I stood, Jack pulled my face to his face, giving me a kiss.

The Fourth of July fireworks ruptured over Main Beach as we made our way across town from my house to his. When you walk at night through East Hampton, the sidewalk goes black before you, and the world pitches left.

"You okay?" he kept asking, and I kept saying, "Yes."

David's Lane is stately and over-broad. I'd passed the Fleming house on my bicycle about a thousand times, but it looked brand new knowing that Jack lived there. An open plaza of grass led to a beige colonial facade. Inside was beige as well, sort of pastry-colored and spiritless, with furnishings that were obviously unbeloved.

Things were the opposite at my house. My mother would pick up a putrid set of armchairs or a fusty old wall-mount ironing board at the dump and haul it home. I would find her on the front porch, bewitched by some oddity or relic. "I practically had to wrestle Dump Keith out of his wheelchair for this one," she'd say excitedly.

Mom and I would maneuver moldering armoires up staircases and enormous iron fireplace benches through doorways. "You and I can move furniture better than any two men," she would tell me.

Somehow we were always alone on those nights, the house everywhere activated, every corner eligible for overhaul. Phones would be moved, drawer contents rotated, bedrooms swapped, bulb wattages finessed, and chairs re-covered. We would pick at TV dinners of meat loaf and apple cobbler and revivified mashed potatoes, which you will never ever forget the flavor of, no matter how hard you try, or else we would just have coffee and frozen Entenmann's chocolate doughnuts. Surrounded by staple guns and fabric remnants and tools given to her by my father, we would rewire old lamps, paint the beveled edges of dressers, antique all the woodwork, anchor mirrors into brick, outfit tables with perfectly plied fabric skirts, or paper cabinet shelves.

Once we moved the couch to the second story and her bed to the living room. "It's so much closer to the coffee pot," she'd tell people.

To make space for a new piece, she would give others away. Her friend Nargis Lata took the electric couch, and Ari the landlord got the hassock embroidered with black leprechauns. Dad and Marilyn got the Balinese creche, and for Christmas, Walter the mailman got the orange barrister bookshelves and the miniature copper cannon. Walter came to collect on a Sunday in his sagging blue station wagon. Out of postal uniform, he looked laid bare and brought to the light of day. His Rotweiller wouldn't let us near his car.

"Now there's a fine bit of irony, Walter," my mother said.

I navigated the Fleming house, listening to the pressurized pops of holiday rockets exploding, counting thuds—*sixteen, seventeen, twenty*. On the kitchen counter, beneath a fawn Princess phone, there was a tall, brown prescription bottle with his mother's name on it: *Susan Fleming, 500 mg, BID. Refill 3*. Three refills seemed like a lot. Three seemed like a condition. Next to a list for Rita the maid was a neat stack of envelopes. A pair of leather strap sandals for men had been laid alongside the back door on a straw mat, and hanging from a hook on the white laundry room wall was a keychain with a shiny BMW tag—for his Dad's car.

The dryer bounced confidently. I wondered how it felt to be rich, or at least to have money. I was pretty sure that the Flemings never had checks returned and never put locks on the telephone dial and never walked around collecting all the lightbulbs in a straw basket and putting them in the car trunk whenever the Lilco bill got too high. The last time Mom did that, someone rear-ended the Scamp and all the bulbs broke.

And yet, despite the obvious benefits, it did not seem wrong to say that Jack's had been a life of deprivation. All the items that belonged to Mr. and Mrs. Fleming belonged exclusively to them. Since Jack owned nothing, he was responsible for nothing. When we were at my house or in town, it was easy to disimagine his attachments—he was just Jack. But the more familiar I became with his home, the more inextricably bound to those people I found him to be. It seemed like an impossible legacy to overcome, such a sterile, businesslike attachment to family.

Jack patted the kitchen counter, gesturing for me to sit. He reached into a cabinet above the wall oven and got the rum. "One-hundred-eighty-one proof," he informed me. "My old man picked it up in Jamaica. On a *golf trip*."

He hopped up next to me and breathed in through clenched teeth because his leg was still sore. We took a few belts from the bottle. Jack drank expertly, but I would take a mouthful, clench my teeth, and knock the liquid down like screwing a cap on an overstuffed jar with the heel of my hand. The rum scraped my throat and sat like a flaming dessert in my belly.

As we mounted the first and second flights of stairs to his room, I felt like a criminal or trespasser, excitable and without real rights. But the third set was thinner and steeper. It had a curious turn at the top and a feeble light at the end, giving it the feeling of a tunnel leading from one world to another. With each step we detached ourselves further from the living, until at last we reached a cushiony plateau, and everything and everyone we had ever known vanished into inconsequence. The privacy we felt was unlike any other, coming as it did when we needed it most. Ours was a very lucky privacy.

I was not particularly conscious of Jack, of his thoughts or mood, except to say that I sensed I was safe. He was before me, we were near the bed, we were kissing, we were lying back, descending. The smell of his bed was the smell of him, only multiplied. It confused me to be initiated into his aloneness; it confused me to know such a place existed, such a repository of untried masculinity and pathetic virility, such a site of self-love and self-abuse. The quilt bubbled around my body and the weight of Jack was good, reminding me of the times I have been buried in sand. I pressed my hips into his because it seemed like the right thing to do, although the part that longed for pressure was farther down and deeper in. My muscles raised me, uncertainly at first, in a practicing way, each time squeezing more expertly, each time tightening an invisible tube inside.

I thought we might have been waiting for something. I thought maybe it was me. My hand journeyed from his shoulder, drifting fitfully down, and he lifted himself so I could reach where he seemed to know I was going. He was leaning and supporting his body on his left knee, making room, admitting a spine of air and light on just one side. Jack's head hung to watch, his hair cascading around my face like a paper waterfall. With my finger I traced the teeth of his zipper upwards from its base to its flap, and as I started to draw it down, it sort of pushed itself open from pressure, which was cool. Everyone knows about the parts of women, but you never hear about the parts of men, not in any specific regard. Even in great artwork, men's genitals are under-realized, scribbled or shadowy, as if the artist wanted to be courageous, but only *sort of*. As if there were some incentive to keeping men mythic, as if the part and the man were the same, and preserving the mystique of one meant preserving the mystique of the other.

But in my hand was a contradiction of skin and muscle, something solid but fragile, potent but meager, something majestic and vile. Jack seemed helpless to the way it stood parallel to his belly. It occurred to me that grown-up men such as teachers and coaches know but keep secret the way erections make boys defenseless. Maybe women know, but maybe it's late already when they find out. It seems like something girls should know too, and earlier, the way boys are capable of such delicate reversals.

On our way out, we passed the piano. Jack faltered, touching it. Though he used to perform for his parents, now he only played when they were out. He said he tried to deprive them of pleasure whenever possible, but really they made him feel hateful, and he didn't like to touch with hating hands something he loved so much. He swirled onto the ebony bench. He looked like something small going to the ground, like a leaf. Just when I thought he'd forgotten I was there, he reached to pull me to his side. We faced opposite directions, back to back, shoulder to shoulder, the way you face on a love seat, but soon I turned halfway. His hands on the keys seemed long and white and the look of them was defined, like there was nothing much to separate his bones from his skin—no fluid, no flesh, no blood.

"Eric Satie," he said of the music, "*Trois Gymnopedies,* Number 2." Then he played something melodic and easy, something you'd hear on the radio. Over and over he tried the same few bars with a single hand.

"Whose is that?" I asked. "It's pretty."

"No one's," he answered. "I just made it up."

6.

OUR BODIES LAY ENTWINED IN A SLEEPING BAG THAT WAS NAVY BLUE AND musty. The bag had a rodeo pattern on the flannel interior with tiny cowboys on bucking chocolate horses, swinging golden ropes against a wan west-blue sky. I wondered if it's true that such places exist. If it's true that they exist, someday I might like to go. My head rested in the space between Jack's arm and chest. Above us, night was black, an absorbent black, like felt.

"You haven't told me anything," he said. "It's been three weeks."

Though I didn't feel like discussing it at the time, he seemed to *want* me to discuss it, or *need* me to discuss it, and part of living is conceding to the ways of others, even if you don't agree or understand, so I told him what I remembered. Part of *harmonious* living. I tried my best to live harmoniously.

"First you left, then I went to my dad's, then Kate called, saying, *Come home*. After that all the days merged into one hazy, humid streak."

Kate and I witnessed the moody stillness of summer as if from the back seat of a speeding car, catching only partial glimpses of flowered sundresses in pink and lime, and straw beach bags. Jeep roofs with canopies of scuffed surfboards, aqueous forms at the achromatic shore. Crickets in morning, the solitary hum of a mower pulsing through grass, the piggish squeal of a distant table saw, the menacing banter of gulls, the whoosh and patter of flapping things at the beach. Kites and towels. It was like a memory of all the summers I've ever had, chopped up and stuck together.

Jack said, "A montage," and his chest vibrated.

"Yes," I said. "Exactly."

ON THE TRAIN FROM Manhattan back to East Hampton, I placed my head against the mottled glass. A pinching grime smell from the vent that ran along the lower edge of the window came up into my nose, like a climbing thing. I replayed Kate's phone call in my head until it was like meditation.

> *Is it you?*
> *Yes, it's me.*
> *I took my mother to the hospital.*
> *Oh. Is your brother there?*
> *Not until the weekend.*
> *Do you want me to come?*
> *Yes. There's a train at nine.*

The train lumbered side to side, jostling me to a half-sleep. I had a dream of forearms wrapping things in paper, lovingly, like folding babies into blankets. It was a field of arms like a factory, a paradisal factory. In my dream I wondered if my mother had ever wrapped me or wrapped anything and whether I myself could ever wrap, and I felt sad over my ineptitude. Sad because wrapping is a tender undertaking. Few people think of the tenderness it takes to wrap. I asked who had stolen the soul from white women. "Pioneer women were strong," I said. "Ten women strong."

There was the fierce backwards crack of the door between cars gusting open and shut. The conductor called out "*Speonk!*"

I awakened to find neighboring passengers staring at me. A middle-aged woman diagonally across from me shuffled through her tote bag, and a black man in a pink shirt and an ice-blue paisley tie righted his *New York Times* and smiled. Travel is strange—you close your eyes in one place and open them in another, and in the middle all propriety is suspended. People can just stare if they want. Speonk rolled away. I wondered why the train even stops in Speonk, when no one ever gets on or off there. Maybe I'm wrong about that. Maybe there's a special Speonk hatch or chute. A horizontal oval on the window marked where my head had touched, kind of like a giant fingerprint, which was unpleasant, and I tried not to think about it.

It was hot when we ambled into the station, hot and preternaturally still. I stood on the jiggling plates between cars and leaned out, my hair lifting stiffly, my face meeting a wall of air into which all things important and unimportant had been embedded—history and nature and the white stripe down the center of the street and the wild roses in the stockade fence along the foot path. East Hampton was like a portrait of itself, a collapsed likeness. I thought of a stanza of poetry—not any particular content, just the quadrangular shape, the belabored number of lines. What I saw was a landscape of merest components—a station house, a deli, a dry cleaners, a pick-up truck, trees in tight rows, a mailbox resting squarely on sloped grass.

The crossing bells rang slowly as the train hobbled past and landed on its chin like an exhausted bovine. Four people stepped out from under the awning; everyone else was probably at the ocean. There were two parked cars and one taxi. Rising from the hoods and roofs were watery streaks of heat.

The man in pink inquired as to the exact time. He lifted his hand, preparing to synchronize.

"Sorry," I said, referring to my bare wrist. I might have said that the train was scheduled to arrive at 12:10 P.M., that the sun was overhead, that the air was almost flammable, that I was hungry. Surely he was as well. But talk of time seemed an extravagance; it seemed unfair that beyond the problematic stillness of the day, there was an evening ahead for him and for me—when in fact people everywhere were dying without the luxury of precision.

The serrated metal steps were more vertical than usual; my legs stretched indefinitely down. I moved along the platform, dizzy and vaguely lost, uncertain as to destination, though my house was just a few hundred yards away.

"I called home," I told Jack. " I kept making mistakes."

When I saw my reflection in the pay phone, there were stains beneath my eyes. I realized I must have cried in my sleep, and my dime popped out of the slot as I was inserting it. I tried again, but then I couldn't dial right.

My fingers kept slipping from the holes. Finally there were two funny rings and a hiss and an operator asking what number was I trying to dial. I have recurring nightmares about that, about incomplete dialing and incorrect dialing, also about running in place, and one having to do with drinking fountains and lights off in school hallways.

Jack played with the earring in my right ear. "The only recurring nightmare I have is the one about my teeth, where my father is cracking the teeth out of my mouth and putting them in a jelly jar."

"What about the starfish?" I asked.

"Oh, yeah," Jack shuddered. "The starfish."

My mother answered the phone, which was good. It could have been anyone. "Hello!"

I said, "Hi, it's me."

"Hi, you!" she said. "Where are you?"

"At the train station."

"Well," she prodded gently, "come home."

I scraped gum off the coin gully. "Have you heard from Kate?"

"Yes. Kate took Claire in to the hospital this morning."

I wondered what was the difference between taking someone *to* the hospital and taking someone *into* the hospital and taking someone *in to* the hospital. If there was a difference, she was referring to it.

The walk home was brief, unremarkable but for the prismatic and ambulatory brightness of the sunlight and the way in which my body rejoined the lonesome earth. I felt a great and scalding heaviness, an urging into ground. With each step forward, I took two down, entering at a diagonal into dirt, weary like a miner, filthy already before the day.

"THE SCARIEST PART WAS the drip," I explained to Jack, "the knowledge that her body was dehydrated and unable to retain fluid."

Nurses would inject needles into the bag instead of into her arm. The bag was buxom and capable, but Maman's arm was like a broken-off branch you drag to the shoulder of the road after a storm, and the under-skin was loose like folds in drapery.

It was hard to tell if her eyes were open or closed because of her position in bed. Every now and then I'd be watching bubbles cascade down the intravenous tube and into her, and suddenly she'd speak, though I'd thought she was sleeping. Eventually I could not bear the thought of deserts and droughts or anything having to do with a shortage of water. I didn't like Mom to mention her blind friend, Freeman, who'd just moved to Phoenix, which I imagined to be a continent of sand.

"It's Phoenix," my mother said, "not the Sahara."

Once we were watching Maman sleep, and I asked Kate if she remembered the *Little Audrey* cartoon about drought, when Little Audrey's garden dries up in the heat and only three drops escape from the hose spigot.

"Kate kept saying she did not remember," I told Jack. "I kept saying, 'Yes you do, remember the way the flowers had drooping heads and limp leaves and crying faces? Remember how they were broken-hearted to wilt?' She just kept saying 'No, no, I don't remember, no.' But I know we saw it together."

Jack kissed my head, pulling me closer in.

MORNINGS ARE BEST FOR hospital visits. Uniforms are neat, halls are clean, moods are generally blithe. Pain loses some of its drama in day. In the morning celebrity doctors with abstruse test results and breezy manners make you think of all the golf you're missing even if you don't like golf. In the morning the newspaper cart comes around and the sunshine plays nicely against the walls, like bouncing balls. There is a collective feeling of hope.

"In the evening," I told Jack, "there's only waiting for day."

And the drone of the television, and uncollected dinner trays lying awry on radiators, and the loosely crocheted sweaters that nurses wear, and fluorescent bar lamps over the bed that compete with the pumpkin hues of the setting sun. There is the feeling that something has run down in the world like a tank out of gas and that the great machine is winding into crisis. Beneath you, in the emergency room, tragedies of gross dimension transpire, night tragedies that tow in wickedness and set it free. At night you can feel the hallways blacken. And when you leave, you leave your friend alone with their illness, like leaving a child to sleep with a monster in the closet.

"KATE LOST A MOTHER," I said, "but I lost a nothing."

"Kate doesn't feel that way," Jack assured me.

"But what about everybody else besides Kate? How can I ever explain to anyone what she was when she and I had no name? People need names for everything. I wasn't a relative or a friend, I was just an object of her kindness."

He wiped my cheeks, saying *Ssshh*. I buried my face in his shoulder.

"True kindness is stabilizing," I went on. "When you feel it and when you express it, it becomes the whole meaning of things. Like all there is to achieve. It's life, demystified. A place out of self, a network of simple pleasures, not a waltz, but like whirls within a waltz."

"You're the one now," Jack said definitively. "That's why you met her. She had something she had to pass on."

ONE DAY I TIPTOED past the woman in the first bed and set my things on the chair. It was one of those toffee vinyl, hospital-style easy chairs that gives you a funny feeling, kind of like germs and bad luck. Usually I leaned against the window ledge or sat on the bed.

"Your mother's not here, dear," the woman called over. "They took her down to radiology."

I'd noticed the new name on the doorway was Krieger. There was always a new name—someone coming in, someone transferring to another hospital, someone getting well and going home. We kept getting passed over. Things kept happening. The last thing was pneumonia. "She's not my mother, Mrs. Krieger. But thank you anyway."

"Not your mother? An aunt?"

"My friend's mother."

She examined me, one eye half-closed. "Your parents dead?"

"No," I said. I peeled newspaper off the wildflowers I'd brought from my garden. "I guess I'd better get these in water."

She waved her hand. "Go ahead. Pull the drape open for me, will you?" I eased the curtain softly, and Mrs. Krieger rolled to her side. "These doctors. They expect you to recover in the dark."

At the nurse's station, a brown arm reached automatically over the counter with scissors. It was Denise Jordan—Annie Jordan's mom, and the scissors were the special kind with the angled arms and rounded tip, the kind used for cutting adhesives, sutures, and flaps of skin. The nurses did not lend them out, but they always made an exception for me. "You're starting to read my mind, Mrs. Jordan."

"Maybe not your mind," she said, as she continued to tend to business. "But certainly your footsteps."

Nurses have a lot of business to tend to. That's why they do not always get to you right away unless you are irrefutably dying. Marilyn is a surgical nurse at Einstein in the Bronx. She calls paperwork *lawsuit avoidance detail*.

I dumped the old flowers in the bathroom. The water was gray like sodden cardboard with a putrid ripe smell. I hadn't changed it for two days. A lot can happen in two days, in the organic sense.

"My daughter's bringing bagels Saturday," Mrs. Krieger called.

I poked my head around. "Are you allowed to do that?"

"Well, you know what it's like when you're dying for a bagel."

"Actually I've never had one."

"*Never had a bagel?* How do you read the Sunday papers?"

"Usually I eat toast."

"Sunday papers," Jack laughed. "Toast."

"But think about it," I told him. "Coming this far in life without a bagel. Bagels aren't even sold out here. *Are* they?"

Jack didn't think so. His father brings them from the city.

"When my brother worked in Geneva," Mrs. Krieger said, "my late husband and I would pack fresh bagels on dry ice and ship them to my niece in Paris, who would take them when she visited him."

I placed the vase on the food tray between the beds and stood by her. She studied the edge of the sheet, threading it through both sets of fingers the way you eat corn on the cob.

"We called it *The Bagel Connection*," she said, and when she spoke again, she spoke quietly, as though the disease might hear. "It's in my lymph nodes, you know."

In her voice was the gravest echo. In her voice I heard death. I wondered were there footsteps or long shadows. I could hear the place her soul could see. I could hear her diffusing into regions pathless and pristine, trickling through to the alien and the legendary. I felt sorry to have to leave her there, detached like a balloon adrift, unbefriended and surely sort of homesick.

"Do you know what lymph nodes are?" she asked.

She looked beautiful to me, wide-eyed and shiny, like a ladybug. "Yes," I said, looking to the ground. "Like glands."

"Oh, so you know about lymph nodes but not bagels," she said. "What a world I'm leaving."

I DESCRIBED THE BATHROOM. It had a fat, brushed chrome bar attached to the wall alongside the toilet, a cracked plastic box like a doorbell to hit in case of emergency, a plastic mustard bucket to catch revolting stuff, and a giant squirt bottle filled with iodine-looking liquid that did not fit exactly into the indentation for soap on the sink. I always felt dirtier leaving than I did going in. And squares everywhere.

"Did you ever notice how overused squares are in bathrooms?"

"Triangles would be worse," Jack speculated. "Too spacey."

"Once I saw myself in the towel dispenser, and I felt bad about looking healthy. I don't know. It just seemed unfair to face dying people that way."

Jack covered my mouth with his wrist. The arm that had been my pillow curled up, and he turned my body to face his. "Five minutes," he said, his breath hitting my jaw. "Okay?"

I CALLED KATE ONE day near the end. I didn't know it was near the end, it just worked out that way. I said I couldn't make it.

"Okay," she said, not bothering to ask why.

If she'd asked, I might have said that I needed time to think or something. But she didn't ask. It was as if she'd been expecting me to defect, like *she* thought *I* thought I needed a break. Like I might fall apart. Like she had discussed it already with her brother Laurent or my mother. For some reason, I ended up telling a lie.

A lie you volunteer is no different from one you're forced to tell. Forthcomingness does not erase the fact that you intend to deceive, especially since the illusion of candor works to your advantage. The truth was I didn't want her to think I was abandoning her, when in fact I *was* abandoning her, though I did not know why I was doing that. It's madness, of course, to lie to preserve the perception of your good character.

"I'm filling in for someone," I said. "I just got home and now I have to go back. I still smell like beer and fries."

"*Yuck*," Kate said, "didn't you shower?"

"Nah." I took a bite of an apple. "Too beat." I would have continued, but I didn't because I've noticed that when people lie, they commonly say too much as a way to compensate for all they're *not* saying. That's why it's a good rule to eat when you lie. Whenever someone tells me something while they're eating, I suspect a lie.

"My sister does that shit all the time," Jack said.

When I hung up with Kate, I realized that I had to go out from afternoon until midnight, in case she stopped by on her way home from the hospital to see my mother or borrow clothes or eat dinner or shower. She didn't like to shower in an empty house. Some lady was staying with her, but just at night.

"The only place I could think to hide," I told Jack, "was Montauk."

"*Montauk?*" Jack asked. "How was it?"

"Okay," I told him.

"That's it?"

"That's it," I said.

TWENTY MINUTES BEFORE THE train left for Montauk, I called my dad at work and started talking to him about things—his job and politics and all these people in my family. He kept saying that everyone was fine, and then he'd ask again how I was doing.

I'd say, "Good, good. How's Marilyn?"

"Fine, fine, she's fine. And you? What are you up to today?"

"Not much. Whatever happened with Watergate anyway?"

It occurred to me that there was a chance he might talk to Kate. He might call back that evening, particularly since I was being so weird, and if she stopped by, she might answer the phone. I considered covering myself. I thought it would be good to tell him the same lie I told Kate, or even better— *approximately* the same lie. I could use the opportunity of a conversation with my father to undo the lie to Kate. I could have told him that I was *supposed* to fill in for someone at the restaurant but that she called and said she decided to go in after all. That way if he talked to Kate, and Kate found out I hadn't worked, my whole story would sound super authentic. But I'd never lied to my father, or to my mother for that matter. There had never been a reason to lie. I hated to break a record.

Lying is hard. If you want to do it right, you have to visualize the lie, conjure the graphics, tone, and sequence of action, then relate it meaningfully in the midst of seemingly spontaneous dialogue. You have to love or loathe your object so much that you want to protect them from truth or protect the truth from them. In either case, you figure yourself as superior and others as incapable of deduction. And the more actual the lie becomes to the listener, the more actual it becomes to the teller, which is scariest of all. Some people really get to believing their own lies.

IN THE FUNERAL PARLOR it was air-conditioned and minty. I felt guilty to be relieved to be out of the heat. The walls of the parlor were papered with tilting, robust bouquets that burst into the room, triumphant yet ephemeral.

I asked Jack if he ever noticed how arrogant flowers can be.

"As a matter of fact, yes," he said, on his parents' dining room table they could be very arrogant.

My mother and father, Marilyn, Aunt Lowie, and I signed the guest book, then we took our seats. I walked unsteadily. I was a little sick from the flower fragrance. Mom informed me that the intention of funerary flowers is to mask the scent of the dead. "When Uncle Billy died," Lowie said, "he was waked on a board in the living room. The board was really a door off its hinges propped on a table and a borrowed saw horse."

"In those days," Mom said, "children had to kiss the corpse."

In the room emotions were congested, with the promise to pop, like spring snakes in a can. From my position behind Kate, I was forced to abide a surreal procession of crying faces, many faces crying and advancing for meaningful embraces and European kisses. I felt bad for Kate, sitting and standing, standing and sitting, each time smoothing out the back of her midnight crepe skirt. If there were rules, she seemed to know them. I wondered how she knew them. Together with her brother, she acknowledged each person's nearness to the dead and helped the group in its struggle for order—who grieved most, whose pain was most real—because in life there is always hierarchy, and it is frankly not profitable to remain modest and anonymous, not even at a funeral. Kate set aside her own despondency to render gratitude for sympathy received. She gave away pieces of herself until at the end there was nothing. You could tell she hit the end by her shocked and hollowly aspect.

There was a lyrical aria, Parisian and melancholy, a woman softly singing. Over and over, the song played to hypnotic effect. My eyes fixed resolutely on the casket. I became dazzled by its gleam and workmanship. In the crushingly tiny window of my view, people would pass as they came upon the body, looking as if looking was nothing, as if her remains were naturally laid out, naturally speechless. I stood and moved forward. At each end of the radiant coffin were thick candles in amber glass, massive pekoe sentinels stationed on twining iron holders. Behind them, on a swathe of pea green silk, was a framed photograph of Claire with her late husband and their two children. It was a picture I had taken.

Her face was like limestone. Though she lay so still in her pleats of fluted silk, she had also been still in the hospital. Physically, in fact, little had changed in the days since we'd last spoken. And yet, something so profound had occurred that it touched upon the essence of aliveness—*death had made her wiser*. All her earthly needs had been met, and she was enjoying her immunity from those who were so foolish as to endure. Sometimes people say how peaceful a dead person looks, and by that they mean the look of self-possession, of detachment from the relationships that continue to bind survivors to the grind of existence. What they see there is what they never see elsewhere— the look of being done. Maman would give a neat swipe of her arm whenever she'd had enough of whatever, of dinner, of an argument, saying, "*Fin.*"

She looked well, I thought, with the slenderest of smiles and the heaviest of hearts. I kissed my fingers and touched her cheek and left her to rest in kingdom and cradle.

THE LAST TIME WE spoke, it was a Friday. When I die, it will also be a Friday.

Kate had gone outside to talk to the doctor with Laurent and his wife, Simone. I sat at the bed and held Maman's hand. It felt like a live hand, not fleshy but not a bundle of veins and bones like my father's mother's hand had been when she was dying. It's confusing when things die out of time. In childhood we make gains by moving away from birth, and in adulthood we make gains as well—we are made ready for death. It's unfair of death to take someone who has not yet been made ready.

Her lips were dry; I wet them.

She whispered to me, calling me Babe. *Beb.*

I leaned closer. "Please," she entreated, "she is your mother."

Though we had not been discussing my mother, Maman spoke as if we were concluding a long conversation, which in a way we were. It was a deficit she'd perceived in me from the start because we were a match—what I lacked fit exactly with what she was able to give. Of course I knew my mother loved me. She thought highly of me, automatically, intellectually, by virtue of genetic proximity. Yet every time we met was like meeting again, with all I felt compelled to explain and withhold, with all she had forgotten.

Maman's childhood had been far more difficult than mine. She used to tell us stories of France during the war, when German soldiers patrolled the streets after curfew, when behind locked doors people gathered quietly by the light of a single candle. Once, when she mistakenly spoke out during dinner, her father removed his cap and threw it at her, forgetting the knot of chewing tobacco he'd stored inside. The hat flew across the table and the wad fell into the tureen of soup and it broke apart like tea leaves, spoiling the meal. Her mother was angry. " '*Stup-eed girl,*' *elle dit,*" Maman would relate, mixing languages.

Kate's father would nod, corroborating—he'd known his wife since they were children. Maman would sip her Bordeaux and smile, saying of herself, *pauvre petite.* But I would not smile. I did not like anyone to throw a hat at her. She would reach for my hands, comforting me.

And so it was for us—or, so it had been. I was hugged and held by her, fed and kissed. She believed in me as a woman separate from herself. She took pride in our friendship, which made me feel worthy. I loved her with gratitude, though she did not ever expect or request thankfulness.

Her hand shifted slightly into the hospital mattress, trying to draw me back. It was a signal, a warning—there was no time to drift. She needed something, a type of relief. In speaking to me, I had the feeling she spoke to herself. "*Tu comprends?*"

"*Oui,*" I said, glad to give something, anything. "*Je comprend.*"

I took her hand. It was light as new petals. Her eyes were clear and wet and crooked somewhat, lustrous and smooth like the inquisitive lapis eyes of a Siamese cat, and she was present, more present than I could remember her having been in a long time, as if unleashed momentarily from her seclusion, disentangled from the chilling occupations of her soul. For some reason, I was permitted the honor of joining her there.

I felt myself approach; I felt myself move several steps in, unforgettable steps—they were to be our last. I felt us walking as we'd always walked, with the inside of my arm supporting the nook of her elbow, with the sound of her good brown shoes rapping, with the sweet region of her powdered cheek grazing mine, with the afflicted melody of her voice, provoking, initiating. My power until then had been a child's power—the power to withhold forgiveness. But the power to bestow it is a woman's. You do it, she seemed to want me to know, because one day you will expect to be forgiven.

"*D'accord, ma petite?*" she asked. I laid my face on her bed. She touched it. "*Je t'aime.*" That was the last thing she said to me. That and, "Be a friend to Catherine." *Ca-trine.*

THERE WERE THREE RINGS, despondent and shrill, leaping into the August night like lemmings. "It's me," Kate said, "are you alone?"

I dragged the phone by its cord into the upstairs bathroom. It was like a tiny body hauled by the hair, slaggard and obedient. I sat on the tub. "Okay," I said, "I'm alone."

"She's dead." Kate said, just like that.

I raced down the stairs, flying around the corner of the living room, passing all the objects of home, blue and brown over blue, books and books and tatters of glass, misshapen pottery, portraits painted on dinner plates and unopened mail in baskets, hats in a lobster trap, a whole livid blue chamber like a memory of twilight, like a memory of a café down a cobblestone alley never actually visited, and at the end my eyes met a flare of light—the kitchen. My mother was doing the dishes. Her reflection in the window over the sink formed a matrix of humid angles. Her form was coordinated and alive. Her body moved, I could see that it did, and it was true that I had come to life in the carriage of her belly. I heard myself say, "Mom."

"Yes," she answered.

"The phone," I said. "It was Kate."

She rinsed the last dish and placed it carefully in the rack. Taking a towel to dry her hands, she crossed to the table, and she sat. I could see a change in her eyes, in the green, a fleck of clearness, then nothing. Not nothing, but grief that was mute. In the nascent dark of deep wedded pines there's infinite detail you cannot make out, there's sabotage and forfeiture and richness of misery. Where, by surprise, you are made never again the same. For some reason I was thinking of pines. I was thinking if Kate would be inseminated by the same hard seed that had planted itself in my mother when she was young and her own mother died. *Hard* because it takes unyieldingness to substitute sorrow with cheer. Some people exist quite well in injury. It's like having gills to breathe underwater. Some people are clever about not drawing others into their affliction. You could hardly tell by looking at my mother that she was a stranger to the laws of Providence.

She laid her hand upon my shoulder, and, in an instant, the weight of her arm fell away. She was moving—something big, something eloquent, some business with dash and rush, some state, any state, opposed to quiet. There was the sound of dialing. She was calling the hospital, calling Kate, calling her brother. I heard the spinning sound, oh, the sound of infinity, the way you can draw the number eight over and over, your hand just going around.

Kate would live with us and finish her senior year in East Hampton rather than go to Canada with Laurent. We often had people stay—Magnus Ove, the Swedish exchange student, known to us as *The Great Egg,* and *Washington,* the guy from Washington who slept on our couch for six months. There was always some teenager in transition or pregnant college student or wayworn Navy sonarman in need of a bed for a week or two.

My father tells the story of the New York City power outage in 1964. "I was on my way home from the A&P on 14th Street, when the city stopped. There was no transit service. Everybody was stranded. Your mother got you dressed and went out to help people find places to stay for the night. I guess you were two. She came home with a black lady. This was during the civil rights movement. The woman sat in the corner on this yellow chair we had, clutching her pocketbook. Irene offered a blanket, some tea, but the woman kept saying *no, no thanks.* She used the bathroom but not our towels. I remember because she kept coming out with wet hands. In the morning she was gone. One week later, a bone china tea service was delivered to the apartment."

"We love Kate," I heard my mother saying to Laurent. "She'll be with Eveline. Your mother would have wanted this."

AFTER THE CEMETERY WAS lunch. Laurent invited me and my mother, but Mom respectfully declined saying classes begin next week and she had to head over to the college if she wanted to be home early tonight. And I could not bear to think of food.

Kate said, "See you," and when she and her brother crossed the street, you couldn't tell the difference between them with the way their bodies were lean and black and their heads were hunched. They appeared headless. Probably they didn't want to admit anything new. But you can't keep out messages that way. The brain is not the only passageway. There are others.

"You going to be okay?" Mom asked as she stepped into her car. "Want me to drive you home?"

I rested my arms on the roof and looked in the window, the casual way people do, except I was dizzy, not casual. "No thanks. I'll walk."

I moved as slow as possible down Cooper Lane, then along Newtown to Osborne, staring at the houses, fascinated into a practical stupor by sudden gusts of charcoal smoke emerging from behind garages and by Big Wheels abandoned at the edges of driveways and by the shy twinkling of televisions prematurely on. Everyone was oblivious to the untimely death of Claire Cassirer, leaving me to ponder such imponderable things as fairness and loss.

At home I undressed carefully, antiseptically, making little contact with fabric. I constructed a pile of clothes, which I shoved with the side of one foot to the distant bottom of my bedroom closet. I slid the door shut and then reopened it to push the heap further back, again with my foot. Every time I tried to walk away, I would remember it was there, a funny cluster, conspicuously hidden. Finally I gave up and crawled in, pulling out the clothes and adding them to my mother's dry cleaning sack. It would be months before she took the contents in and months again before she picked them up.

Mom always joked with Mrs. Burns, the dry cleaner, when we saw her in town. "I'd get my clothes, Rose, but your building might tip."

When the garments eventually did come back, the funeral things would be on hangers mixed in with normal things, all connected through the hooks with string, and Mom would stick the chain of plastic in her closet, forgetting about them until she needed to wear something nice. Altogether, the process could take six months.

In the barn I climbed to the loft and lay there, hands on my chest. I was a body lying, and Maman was a body lying, both on the same day, three streets apart. Above me was the roof. Above her, the coppery cold earth pressed sizably, like a sulfur quilt. She was still so close, only a few blocks away, as unaccustomed to death as newborns are to the breezy world beyond the womb. I wondered were there nursing hands to help her and sing-song voices. I hoped that there were.

When the mourners tossed down dirt and said good-bye, turning away for the last time, it was her flesh beneath our feet, her body communing with the earth, soaking in and down as does the rain.

The sheets on my mattress were mulish and invincible. I kicked the covers off because my legs itched from the stockings I'd worn. I was hot, so I switched on the fan and moved it close to me, but then I was cold, so I moved it back again. A pain divided the halves of my face, making each eye regent of its own orbiculate domain—that is a terrifying ailment, an eye on a sideways eye. I rubbed at my temples. I wished the lawn needed cutting. I wished we had a television. I wished a phone would ring, but there was no phone where I was. I didn't feel well. When I thought of Kate, I felt worse.

Outside the sunlight struck the westerly wall of the barn at a sunken bevel. That was where I went, where the light was brightest and the heat the hottest. I lowered myself onto the bench, and soon Kate was there, next to me, supporting me on one side.

"Simone's having a baby," she said. "It comes in February."

I could not tell if she was happy. Usually I could tell. I wondered if the baby had persuaded Maman to the grave, in the generational sense. I had the uncomfortable feeling that some work had been done, immense and evolutionary.

"They asked me again to go," Kate said. "They're leaving tomorrow."

"Tomorrow," I said, "wow." Tomorrow seemed sooner than usual.

"But I'm not going," she assured me, and we came in closer.

"I decided I'm going to be cremated," I said.

"Me, too," Kate agreed. "I was thinking that all day."

I recalled the gutless thud and the pebbly, spreading sound the dirt made as it slipped and got trapped in the casket's fittings. "It's tough. The whole thing is tough."

Kate said nothing. Her eyes were fixed on the horizon, on the dampening flame of her mother's final sunset.

"Things keep happening," I went on. "Every day, new things, awful things. It's hard to think about them, *really* think. But, it's like, they're the *only* things. You know what I mean?"

Kate nodded. "After this, there's nothing."

"Yeah," I said, "it makes you wish there was a little awful left."

WE COULD HEAR THE driveway gravel popping, a car door, a gentle whistle. My mother was home, calling the cats. At the sound, Kate covered her face with her hands and crumpled to a heap. She was crying, so I patted her on the back, which was hard for me, comforting a person in that patting way. Mom brushed apart the hedges.

"I thought I'd find you two back here." She squeezed between us, and instantly our sorrow relented. Despite her small stature and unconventional habits, my mother was a superhero—arriving infrequently, often late, but repairing chaos nonetheless with her colossal energy and charisma. Frankly I was glad to be relieved of the burden of consoling Kate. At least my mother had lost a mother when she was a child, so she had some idea of how to be. When you lose a mother as a child, you are indoctrinated into a club, you are taken into life's severest confidence. You are undeceived.

"Has everybody eaten?" Kate had. I had not. The idea repulsed me. Little piles and little balls, laid out, waiting fearfully. "I understand," my mother said, and she patted my knee, "but you're alive."

SOMETIMES YOUR MIND WANDERS. SOMETIMES YOU CAN BE IN A PLACE BUT not really be there. You feel yourself among others, you know you're among them, yet you see yourself from above as well. It's confusing to wonder in which of the two places you actually reside. Is your position within or without? Are you matter bound in skin, or are you—whatever constitutes *you*—a non-thing—spraylike and atmospheric, atomized and externalized, thrust into surrogate dimensions, projected like a movie, to be scanned and interpreted by others? Are you something that can be realized only approximately at best?

I struggle with aspects of vision. Often what occurs to my eyes is not simply real but uncommonly real. At close range my mind has the habit of animating inanimate articles, such as coats on hangers and ceramic statuettes. Things that appear suddenly from edges or ones aimed accidentally at my face seem possessed of intention—J-hooks in hardware stores and wire hairbrushes and pencil erasers. Faraway things look sad and oversmall, destined for defeat. I am not responsible with things on the horizon. I always feel like I'm watching the very last bison on the very last prairie. Either way, near or far, it helps me to squint. Squinting minimizes peripheral excess and imposes a pastoral sort of elegance upon things, preserving in them the gothic might of coincidence.

Denny has a theory about squinting. He says eyes are evolving to become egg-like and that these mutations will be universally evident by the year 2075. "You are on the forefront of the transformation. A pioneer of the eye! Squinting is chic! It's *au courant!*"

Periodically Aunt Lowie would give me homeopathic belladonna, and Kate would lecture me about premature wrinkling. My parents would send me to the optometrist for an examination.

Dr. Kessler would look askance as I rubbed my fists into my eye sockets. "Headache?" he would ask, one eyebrow raised.

Behind him, menacing machinery sat perched in the violet lizard-tank darkness, like stalled robots or expectant marionettes. It seemed crazy, the idea of two jelly-wet eyeballs requiring all that cumbersome equipment—rolling carts with boxes that blow gusts of air into your cornea, pen flashlights, oily chin straps, slide machines for alphabet projections, and those glass goggles suspended on the metal arm that pivots to your face, and which, unlike the periscopes at the top of the Empire State Building, do not magnify the view but, rather, your eyes.

"No," I would say, "not at all."

As I read the charts, Dr. Kessler would lean over my knees to flip the various lenses around, adjusting magnification, checking for some tangible change—I could not imagine what. The rim of each ring would inch sluggishly past the twin windows, *click click*, threatening to snag my lashes and rip my lids off with champagne-cork pops.

"Twenty-twenty," the doctor would firmly conclude, peering at me over the top of his own glasses, which were not regular glasses, but fancy ones like a Viewmaster. "Why, then, do you squint?"

"I don't know," I'd say. "To see better."

"But there's no physiological reason for you to have to see better!"

I always felt sorry for him, sorry as I felt for myself, the two of us stranded in that medieval torture den without hope of resolution. I supposed it was counter-intuitive to regard squinting as a way to see better, especially when I had no apparent need to see better. But it was true, I did have that need, whether he could see it—*diagnose it*—or not. It was all very confusing, and words made it so. Maybe he should have asked a better question. Maybe I should have used the word *differently*. I needed to see *differently*.

MARTY KOCH WAS SLUMPED into one of those shiny beige desk-and-chair units. As he spoke to us of *yearbook objectives* and *yearbook projections*, a lock of unwashed hair drooped persistently over one eye. I tried to follow what he was saying through the action of his hair, but it was like looking into a murky pond to watch a swimming frog.

From my seat on the windowsill, I grabbed a chair with my legs. It squawked lamely as I dragged it over to use as a footrest. I stretched through the half-open window at my back and touched the exterior bricks of the building, which were corrugated and misty rose. Outside the football players were practicing tackles against those padded metal rows that are supposed to be the opposing team. The movement of the boys was gear-like, like wheels within wheels. If I squinted, it all turned balletic, like rows of rushing swans.

"That's it for booster saturation," Marty said. Boosters are those cryptic sentences in the backs of yearbooks—*P.G. dontcha love 2Ramy!!* and *Berry Boy gotta get some tidy shirt?* Marty ran his highlighter across the third line down of a full legal pad. "Let's move on to folio flow."

I scanned the faces of the yearbook staff, thinking there was not one guy I would've slept with if we were trapped. When you're bored you can pretend you're trapped, like hostages. You ask yourself where would everyone sleep and go to the bathroom. Who would hold hands in the dark? Who would be the *real* heroes? Real heroes are the ones you don't expect. That's the lesson of *Superman* and *Underdog*, the lesson of being patient and finding out. That is also the lesson of soap operas. In soap operas a bad person will turn good, or a good one will turn bad, or actors will switch roles altogether, becoming neighbors or relatives of themselves.

People mock soap operas, but soap operas are just serials and serials are reassuring. Everyone is entitled to reassurance. The Bible is a serial and so is the news. With serials you come to know personalities and situations. You predict outcomes and refine judgment skills. You procure a long-term body of knowledge, which is the opposite of stereotype. You become conscious of formula and convention—a critical life skill.

Marilyn reads Agatha Christie over and over, and my father devours accounts of war as though he doesn't know what happens at the end. Boys turn professional sports into dramas of clannish supremacy and revenge, and they accept without question the histrionics of professional wrestling. Jack and Dan could argue for hours about whether Juggernaut first appeared in *X-Men 12* or *X-Men 13*, and though they loved to laugh at a fake hospital set, they were somehow unaffected by the flimsy scenery of *Star Trek*.

High school was actually a lot like *Star Trek*. The building resembled a space station. It was like an ultra-modern vessel creaking through a galaxy of tiny cedar-shake homes. Within its impermeable walls, there was a network of corridors, private cells, and public control rooms through which crew members conducted seemingly unrelated business. The layout was contemporary-naïve, as though inspired by a prehistoric vision of a future aesthetic. Beyond the parking lot lay farmland—intergallactic space. And school had its own vain, self-sustaining logic that ended at the close of each day. The lights went out; the show was over.

The setting sun formed a mountain of light over the football field. I would have liked to be there with my camera, directing the lens upwards onto a wall of staggered bodies, onto the simmering orange black sky, onto the hood of infinity. Athletes make the perfect subjects. They cock their heads and cram their helmets into their armpits and listen like faithful pets to the coaches. They ignore the camera; they are stars.

Adults are always pushing kids to become sports stars. For coaches, the incentive is job security. For parents, it's the possibility of financial assistance. Colleges need to recruit away from other colleges and to sell stuff. Professional clubs need to insure the ongoing chain of new talent and *also* to sell stuff, only slightly bigger stuff, like television rights. For society at large, local systems feed the exceedingly profitable American sports machine—the money isn't in tickets, it's in ad sales, upon which the economy depends. But very few high school players meet with the success they dream of. Most just get teased out of a valid education. When people complain about how the Chinese are beating us in science and math, you have to wonder whether kids in China spend three or four hours a day on sports. No one ever talks about the extreme shortage of time for kids or the logic of how a choice *for* sports is a choice *away* from everything else. If it didn't feel so good to be them, those boys might think about things. Maybe immunity lifts a weight; maybe heaviness returns.

My feet bounced against the radiator; my palms drummed my thighs. Perhaps lines would form on my face because I was mean. Lines are only measurements and measurements mark distance and distance is good. I considered a song about that, but the only rhyme I could think of for *distance* was *his pants*, which is not so much the material of a song as a limerick. Jack can write songs like *that*. I snapped my fingers. It wasn't even true—it often took him months to write four lines. I just felt like snapping my fingers about something.

Possibly I wasn't mean. Possibly I was bored to the point of hysteria with vapid sports rhetoric. In high school you're forced to endure vapid sports rhetoric. *It's not whether you win or lose, just don't lose! A tie is like kissing your sister!*

Unlike with the Marching Band or the Spanish Language Society, you *had* to support the sports teams even if you didn't like sports or else you didn't have school spirit—you were unAmerican. Who knows how it happened, but somewhere along the way from pilgrim times to modern times, school spirit and sports spirit and American spirit got mixed up.

Naturally coaches enlist metaphors in gym classes to motivate students, but metaphors are also helpful in board meetings to defend salaries, budgets, and the allocation of public lands for playing fields. Sportsmanship and teamwork are hailed to taxpayers as critical life skills. Yet these lessons frequently escape the players, many of whom extract from the games little about honor or gracious conduct. Most fail to grasp that teams are *symbolic* units, or to comprehend that boundaries in life are not always as *obvious* as a uniform, or that a peer may be someone *visually* unlike you but to whom you may be otherwise bound—by goals, ideals, or geography. Most consider the team to be a closed club, local and exclusive, conspicuous and indisputable. A *peer* is someone who behaves as disreputably as you do and, therefore, has incentive to keep your secrets. An *equal* is someone with dangling genitals, someone to whom you can toss a ball, or someone to sit next to on a bus ride to an away game.

IN JUNIOR YEAR OUR school was put on an "austerity" budget, and team sports were cut. Student energies were diverted to politics and mutual interest societies—theater clubs, chess meets, charity leagues, beach clean-up patrols, and interfaith discussion groups, all of which were funded by flea markets, car washes, and bake sales. We were constantly at school working for causes—there was nothing better to do. People who had never previously spoken were thrust together because needs were great and entry policies liberal. The school motto changed from *We are the Champions!* to *Beggars can't be choosers!*

That spring, we entered a state-wide competition sponsored by Care*Free Sugarless Gum in which the winning school was the one whose students had written the gum's brand name on the most index cards. All four grades vied against each other, for no particular reason other than boredom and surplus vitality. We held writing vigils. That self-imposed rivalry allowed us to take the state by a titanic margin.

As a prize, Hall and Oates gave a concert in the auditorium. Jack and his friends, irate over the auricular offense, took to the aisles during "Rich Girl" and protested by hopping up and down like pistons or gears, screaming, *Sid Vicious! Sid Vicious!* Afterwards I asked Jack never to do that again.

Surprising new heroes emerged that year, mostly from our class. Cathy Benjamin, who'd made it through only three grades in four and a half years, organized the biggest money maker, a 24-hour Dance Marathon, and Ginny Warwick, who once cried inconsolably during an argument with the biology teacher about creationism, won Best Costume Design in the class play competition. And Denny got *everyone* to contribute to his Old-Fashioned Christmas for the holiday hall decorating week. The home economics department sewed antique-style costumes for baby dolls he borrowed from cheerleaders, the shop department rigged Marcus Payne's miniature mechanical railway, the mammoth Parson twins found and chopped down the perfect "pastoral" tree, the typing students created scrolled gift lists, and the art department pieced it all together.

The night before the start of the contest, twenty-three kids gathered at my house, people like Pip Harriman and Gwen Akers and John Esposito and Sara Eden, people who'd never been there before, all of us wrapping empty boxes, painting ornaments, making soap-flake snow. Alicia Ross came over with platters of cookies made by her housekeeper, Consuela, and Powell ordered six pizzas with extra cheese. Coco Hale and I shared scissors.

"Your snow country landscape collage is nice," she said to me.

I said, "I like your felt sleigh."

Jack and Dan came late, wearing gold paper crowns, and I was happy, the happiest I'd ever really been. Jack had just dropped out of boarding school in Kent, and his parents had agreed to let him finish junior year in East Hampton. He made his way over the hunched bodies, saying, "It's a fucking sweatshop in here!"

He moved piles of fabric and Styrofoam globes from the top of the stereo. As he leaned to insert the cassette he and Dan had made for the contest, his key chain swung loosely from his belt loop. It had a leather strap and a seamed jingle bell, the type you find on cat collars and toddler shoes.

"Hey Evie," Dan said as he leaned against the banister and chewed on a cherry tart. "What would you think of us changing the name of the band to *The Jesters?*"

When the music began, work came to a halt. First, Dan played "O Holy Night" on piano; next came Jack on guitar, singing "Little Town of Bethlehem." If you had seen the faces, you would never forget them—normal faces of normal kids, faces stripped of rank and status. For one brief moment, I loved them. Later when I told that to Jack, he said he was glad the moment had been brief.

Last on the tape was Kate and Coco doing a rendition of "Amazing Grace" on their flutes. The twin whistles wavered bashfully. Everyone clapped and cried, and my mother cheered, "Well all right!"

"Oh, man," Rocky Santiago said as he returned to his sparkles and glue. "That tape is the *clencher.*"

One week later at the holiday assembly, immediately after the choral concert, in the fevered final moments before the start of Christmas vacation, Principal Laughlin ventured to the microphone, awards in hand. After commending the entire student body for its unprecedented display of *esprit* despite the harsh reality of the austerity year, and after thanking Mrs.

Quivers and her janitorial staff in advance for the task of dismantling the hall displays, he explained that the day's winners would receive two hundred and fifty Spirit Points to add to their Spirit Point account. Spirit Points would one day be transferred into dollars—one day, when there was money. So far the junior class, our class at the time, held the distant lead in most points collected—1,750 as compared to 175 for the sophomores, 50 for the freshmen, and none for the seniors.

Laughlin waited for complete silence, then he cleared his throat. "And now, according to a unanimous decision by our distinguished panel of judges composed of administrators, faculty, parents, and local business leaders, *the junior class has won!*"

We flew out of our seats and rushed the aisles, jumping and hugging and screaming so loudly that no one heard the dismissal bell. Mike Stern and L.B. Strickland and Peter Palumbo raised Denny onto their shoulders and carried him around in wild, tipping circles.

In May, a budget was approved for the following year. Sports programs were to be restored; austerity was over. But cuts for humanities persisted—the arts had done perfectly well without financial support. To some, the end of austerity meant the potential recovery of former glories and an opportunity to enhance college applications. To others, it meant a return to chronic disappointment and systemic inequity—no more oneness, no more euphoria, no more spirit.

MARTY WAS FINISHING HIS address. Hands slapped flatly, lightly, like damp fins. Marty was okay. Maybe he wouldn't win baseball trophies or volunteer for the Air Force or anything, but he seemed very mannishly determined about his ambivalence, and that counted for something. It takes courage to remain on the deserted periphery, and you had to admire Marty for that, even if you couldn't conceive of having sex with him.

I'd joined the yearbook by accident when I was a freshman. I'd intended to go to a newspaper meeting, but I got lost. By the time I figured out I was in the wrong place at the wrong time, I'd already been put in charge of Faculty Fun Facts. I was soon moved into the photo department. At first I was kind of embarrassed, since the yearbook was a club for losers, but by the end of that year, when the book came out, and a fragrant June wind swept through the open school doors, and everyone lounged around on the hallway floors clutching each other's books, flipping through the pages to see what had been written, I felt okay.

People would rap on my arm. "Evie, I can't believe you put that picture of me in there."

When asked for my signature, I always chose the yearbook staff page because there was a rule that the place you selected had to have meaning, either factual or invented. You could sign the picture of someone you had a crush on, or you could sign near Mr. Schwab if you hated trigonometry. Jack always signed Troy's book on the page with Miss Herbst because once Troy got food poisoning and busted out of typing class with a massive diarrhea attack.

The staff page was in back. We looked like night crawlers—slack-jawed, slope-backed, and freakishly symmetrical, with shaggy hair parted in the middle, bangs growing out and kinking back up, and polyester-blend oxford shirts hanging loose over cowl-neck sweaters and flare-bottomed, rust-colored corduroy slacks. It was not good to see myself there. My fingers would trace my image as if seeking a tab to pull. But I could not extract my likeness. I'd been there when the shutter snapped—and that was that. I'd write something nice, sign my name, and carefully close the book. Yearbooks shut dryly—*Poof!* Blowing a little inky air up.

Suddenly I belonged to a group, which was weird. Though I'd agreed to join the yearbook, I had not agreed to befriend the staff, yet that's what ended up happening. You couldn't help getting to know people when you worked with them under deadline, when you were stuck together all winter, pasting up copy and developing photos, listening to "Muskrat Love" and "Copacabana," going, *Do you know how much we could be getting paid for this shit?* I would only become cognizant of a person's acne or excessive weight or hair oil or hand-me-downs when I happened to be talking to someone in the hallway and "normal" kids would pass and stare. This put me in a difficult predicament, because I was fourteen at the time. When you're fourteen, everything puts you in a difficult predicament.

It's hard at any age to come to terms with the difference between the label you give yourself and the one others give you. On my birth certificate, the hospital listed my mother's occupation as *housewife*. It didn't matter that she did not consider herself to be one, or that there had never been a woman more indifferent to the challenge of homemaking—it was 1962, she was unemployed, married, and a mother, so she was a *housewife*. When she and Dad divorced, she became a *single welfare mother/college student*, and, with this designation, she was far better satisfied.

A world view is a busy view, engrossed and industrious. To the world you are no more than you appear to be at the moment of appearance, which is a wearisome truth. Few are fortunate enough to experience a confluence of inner interpretation and outer projection, especially when you consider the infinite subtleties of identity—that is to say, there is the way that you are, which is the sum of the way you are *becoming* and the way you *have been*, and which does not take into account the way you *secretly wish to be*. Nargis calls herself a psychic, though she earns her living as an accountant. Is she an *accountant* because that's how she spends her days, or a *mystic* because that's what she feels inside?

"You have tremendous earning potential," she often told me.

Perhaps it's too easy and unofficial to state what you are and to expect people to embrace strictly personal claims. However it seems equally unfair to be categorized as X simply because you *do X* or *look like X*. I like to think that whenever Nargis figures percentages or adds columns, she applies telepathic powers to divine the outcome of the calculations.

MARTY GESTURED FOR ME to join him. "Evie will come up with an assignment breakdown for those of you interested in photography," he said.

I moved to the front of the room, conscious of the fact that people were staring. I sat on the edge of his desk and folded my body into thirds. The body is supposed to be irrelevant, but frankly it's not.

"Just for the record," he added, "though austerity is over, we will not reinstate former habits by using up our entire film allotment on sports. Last year's book was the most pictorially inclusive in school history and, also, the most profitable. Sales were up by more than a third." He looked up to me. "Anything you'd like to add?"

I shrugged. "Not really." Marty had made me photo editor. I wondered if anyone was even going to do what I said.

When the meeting ended, everyone said goodbye like there was not going to be a tomorrow. *Goodbye! See you! Yearbook Club rocks!*

Outside, the parking lot had become mostly empty, and also the fields. No one was in the driveway or on the front steps. There was no movement, not anywhere, no bodies walking, no one laughing, no one lost in thought. There was just light, the last complete light of day. I had the feeling there wasn't much time left. I did not *think* that feeling, my body just presented it to me, with a new sense of urgency. There was much to do, my body seemed to remind me, though for the life of me, my brain could not conceive of what.

8.

I OPENED MY EYES. KATE WAS THERE, SLEEPING, AND HER FACE WAS CLOSE TO mine. I did not know where we were in space and time, years prior or years beyond. Not until Kate's eyes opened did I remember the time, the time of our lives, and the reason my mind chose to disrecall it. People say the passage of time is the cure for sorrow, but even when you trudge obediently through the hours, nothing changes, not really. What good is waiting anyway, if pain is only gone when things no longer hurt? There ought to be a way to get over grief when it is still purple like dahlias and alive.

The cat crossed the lawn and curled into the corner of the quilt Kate and I shared. I stretched to pet its belly, blending my hair into its fur, making a mixture, thinking how grass is a forest when you lie so low. "We're so lazy," I said with a stretch. "Aren't we lazy?"

"Yes," Kate agreed. "But *you* are especially lazy."

In the kitchen, we flanked the opened refrigerator door, splitting a bottle of Perrier. The ceramic floor tiles were cool, and the light was sympathetic and gray, somewhat like rhinoceros skin.

"It's so nice in here," I said, "like a wine cellar," though I'd never been in one. I must have gotten the idea from a movie. *Notorious.*

"Let's go to Sag Harbor tonight," Kate said.

"No, too ghosty," I said. Sag Harbor was ghosty, especially in October. Around the piers and up on the widows' walks. The ghosts of whalers and the women they'd loved. Babies they'd forsaken.

"We'll just go to Corner Bar," she said, "I'll go shower."

LATER THERE WAS A knock, a stranger. Friends never knocked at my mother's house. Through the screen was a guy, slightly older than me, well-built, not tall. He was wearing shorts and an Eagles concert jersey.

"Hi. Is this Irene's house?"

"Yes. But she's not home."

"Yeah, well, okay," he said, embarking on an explanation. "I was hitchhiking a couple weeks ago at the college, you know, by the gymnasium, by the tracks, right before Route 27." His voice was slightly croaking. I got the feeling he was smart. Croaking voices like that frequently belong to smart people.

"Anyway, Rene picked me up, and we got to talking. She told me to stop by next time I came through East Hampton."

"So here you are."

"So here I am," he concurred, throwing his arms to each side, grinning. A faint mustache drew out like taffy to cap his lips. I snapped the latch and the door sprang. He caught it. "Nice place," he said to my back as we walked through. "Unusual."

I cleared the kitchen table, asking did he want anything to drink.

"Got any beer?" he asked.

I peered into the refrigerator, moving stuff for effect, thinking about saying *no*, but changing my mind. He seemed okay. I lobbed a can over the door, then lifted myself onto the counter. My feet rested on the edge of the base cabinet door, and I pushed it open and closed.

"I'm from California," he informed me after a long sip.

"Oh," I said. Three tomatoes lined the windowtop, radiant at the edges. I reached for one and took a bite. "California's far."

He nodded. "Rene your sister?"

"Mother."

"*Mother?*"

"She's thirty-six," I said, anticipating his question. It's always the same question.

Kate came around the hall corner right about then in a curious half-walk, drying her hair with a towel. "Who are you talking to?" she asked.

The guy smiled brightly. "Hello there!"

She peeked out from under her towel. "Hi!"

"This is Kate," I said, locating a single tomato seed and chewing it. And I told Kate, "This is some guy Mom picked up hitchhiking."

"Hello *Some Guy*. Do you have a name?"

"*Some Guy* is fine," he said. "Nice to meet you, Kate."

Kate traveled as if by raft to the refrigerator. She opened the door smoothly and bent at the knees, very excessively conscious of poise, without tipping her head and neck. She looked like one of those old Ziegfeld girls, the kind that shimmies down scenery steps in treacherous heels and sequined breeches, balancing an oafish feather hat. She eased out another Perrier, then closed the door gently.

"*Mom?*" the hitchhiker said. "You two aren't sisters, are you?"

"God, *no*," Kate laughed and sat across from him. "We're just friends. Since second grade. I'm staying here for a few months. My parents passed away."

"Oh," he said. "Sorry." Then he said something else, which I missed. Birds were visiting the feeder outside, pecking discreetly. There was one cardinal. I like cardinals best. They're so decisively red, unimpeachably red.

"What's your birth sign?" the hitchhiker asked.

Kate said, "Aquarius."

"I'm surprised you two are such good friends." He took another swig of beer. "Aquarians and Scorpios usually don't get along."

"Oh, *my* God," Kate said. "Evie, did you tell him your sign?"

"She didn't have to. Scorpios are intense. They're ruthless and self-contained. Like no one's worthy of their trust. Aquarians are like silver rainbows." His thick fingers danced in air. "They're dreamers. Are you a dreamer?"

"Totally," she said. "I'm a total dreamer."

"There you go."

"It is so weird that you knew that."

The hitchhiker apologized to me. "No offense or anything. My ex-girl-friend's rising sign was Scorpio," he said, as if stating his credentials.

I lowered my head into the sink and sprayed my hair.

"Aren't you going to shower?" Kate asked.

"No," I said. My voice inside the sink made a hum. I felt like being dirty. I felt like smelling my own sweat. Water streamed down my neck when I righted myself, and around my shoulders, and onto my t-shirt before I could reach a dishtowel. I fastened my hair into a ponytail on top of my head and held it in place while I hunted for a rubber band. There were no rubber bands where they were supposed to be, which was in the drawer for rubber bands and half-burnt candles and paper clips and other weird stuff such as broken sneaker laces and sticky batteries and lamp wicks, so I used a garbage twisty instead. Every kitchen has a drawer like that, a chaos drawer, filled with every-thing except the one thing you need. *Chaos*, because chaos is a lot like having everything but the one thing you need.

The front screen door smacked against the frame. My mother called out, "*Gir-rls.*" Instantly there was lightness among us. In some houses, where bills are paid and dinner is made from scratch and you get one of those fancy water-melon basket cut-outs filled with fruit balls on your birthday, parents walk in and everyone gets sick to their stomach.

She came through the kitchen threshold, struggling dramatically under the weight of her bags. "*Hello!*" she said, in a mock British accent, referring to the visitor. "What have we here?"

"Some Guy," Kate said.

I said, "A hitchhiker friend of yours."

"Oh, yes," she said. "Let's see, don't tell me." She closed her eyes, stroking her forehead. "Riff. Rug. Bop."

"Biff," he said with a quasi-grin and a backwards jerk of the head. That is the grinning laugh men make when they're not sure whether to be insulted. *Biff.* No wonder he preferred *Some Guy*.

"Of course," she said as she sat, "Biff. From Santa Monica."

"San Diego," he replied. "Good memory."

Beyond the window, daylight languished, and their skin darkened meas-urably. I looked to the lawn. It was etched in shade shaped like the house because the sun was setting on the other side. Shade really does advance the way an army does. I reminded myself it was Saturday. I had a Sunday feeling, a sad and lonely feeling. I wished Jack would come, but he wouldn't. He was in the city, he was going to a concert at CBGB's with Smokey. He would show up in the morning, after the train whistle, smelling stale like smoke and rum.

"Where you going?" Mom asked.

"To mow the lawn."

"Don't be silly. It's October. Sit down."

"Yeah," Biff said. "C'mon, sit." He pulled out a chair.

Kate said nothing. I wondered if she wanted me to stay or to go.

I PUSHED THE SKY blue mower in diagonal lines over the lawn. Powell spray-painted it blue because he didn't want me to be outside looking down, seeing nothing of Heaven. Our neighbor Ernie Lever was mowing also. Ernie rode his tractor mower on his postage stamp yard like he was a bumper car cowboy, jerking back and forth, snapping his neck. He'd chopped down every tree on his property to make for easy driving. I waved—I had to, it was a family rule.

"He's a Republican with a colostomy bag," Powell told me. "That makes him twice as eligible for Christian kindness."

The last tree Ernie cut was a giant maple. I'd cried that day. Everyone gathered around me in a sloppy semi-circle, patting my knees and rubbing my shoulders, offering icy rags. "It's not about me," I told them. Whenever you're upset, people always think it's about you. "It's about the tree."

No one disputed that what had happened was a tragedy, yet they defended Ernie's right to tend to his own house. This was no surprise. I'd heard such logic before. Adults accept unacceptable behavior because they don't want anyone criticizing their own actions. It's a sneaky standard. They encourage you to tell the truth like it's so easy, then they save all the sneaky standards for themselves.

My mom tried to cheer me. "Think of the saplings it sired! What good biological work it did!"

"Ernie *mowed* all the saplings," I stated bleakly. "Besides, the size was the thing." Trees corroborate the past. Years are chronicled in the rings. The hurricane of 1938 pummeled Long Island, but that tree survived, only to be sawed to shreds on an innocuous spring day by Ernie, a retired machinist from Astoria. Not even Ernie, but a crew he'd hired. I wondered how far it might have grown. Maybe it would have broken right through his house, then cut clear across town, making an idle sort of getaway.

"Not possible," Denny said. "There's a critical mass for trees."

But what about those ones out West with trunks so thick you can take a car through—sequoias, I think, or are the sequoias Indians, and the big trees redwoods? There's a photo of Dad's cousin Irna driving a '56 Buick through one. She's wearing a golf hat.

"People deconstruct what they can't understand," Lieutenant Carter Dixon said, as he offered me a mug of grapefruit juice. Carter was Powell's friend from Georgia, where trees are like folks you know, blooming with peaches and magnolias, and it's a crime like murder to kill them.

"Like time and space," Powell contributed thoughtfully.

My mother added, "Like women."

"Be reasonable, babe," Powell said, taking my hand. "We can't save every one." His wolf-gray eyes leveled to convey the gravity of his point. His hair was also gray. It swept back around his ears, and his voice was kind. When he came home after months away, he would have a bushy mustache. When he came home, it was always a three-day party with everyone participating, even me.

"But we *knew* this one," I said.

The night it was cut, I went outside and found the stump, stubbornly attached to the arc of the earth, right where the tree used to be. Of course there was no better or more logical place, but the sight of it surprised me nonetheless. There was something sad about its untimely tenacity, about its belated show of force. I thought of the cover of *Le Petit Prince*, of the boy standing soundly on the rim of his own homely asteroid with nothing to buffer him from the enormity of the universe. I caressed the surface, thinking with an empty sort of pride that it hadn't come down easily. I imagined the first shock to its flesh and the pain it had endured as each limb fell with a leafy thud. No, a leafy whoosh, then a final, defeated thud. And the demonic persistence of the chain saw. And before the stump, the torso, ravaged and disgraced, tall and cruciform, as it was shorn to the ground, disemboweled, section by meaty section.

I saw the pieces scattered. They were near Ernie's shed, like a pile of gigantic wooden lozenges, waiting for the chipper.

MOM, BIFF, AND KATE were still talking, their three voices folding together like wet ingredients from a recipe. I listened from the porch as the voices leaked past the kitchen window, then stopped, perching in air like an umbrella to sit beneath. The brick steps scraped my legs and the feeling was grainy and cold. I was waiting for night. When you wait, you can see it really does fall.

The front door opened, gentle to my back. It was the hitchhiker, coming out. "Like a pretzel," he said, referring to a piece of folded privet in my hands.

"Yeah," I said. "Like a pretzel."

"Biff says he's a rugby player," Mom said. She was there too, leaning against the screen from inside, Kate as well.

"I'm actually on my way to a practice now. At Herrick."

My mother told Biff that I go there all the time.

"Is that so?" he asked me. "What do you do, run?"

"No, she plays on the swings," Kate said.

"You know," Biff speculated, scrunching his face on just one side. "I thought you looked familiar."

I like rugby. It's lawless and alive, as if rules are being made on the spot. Players run kind of like isolated entities in a pack until some strange divination occurs, some message only they seem to receive, causing them to collapse into a knot of unified movement. It's strange to watch, like on the field there is this gravity bias. They hang on, and go in circles.

"Come by next Saturday. Around one. Your mom says you're a photographer. Bring your camera."

I said thanks. "Maybe I will."

KATE AND I DID not get out of the car in Sag Harbor. We just drove through the yarnlike streets in the red Camero Laurent had given her for her birthday, listening over and over to *The Low Spark of High-Heeled Boys*.

If I gave you everything that I owned
And asked for nothing in return
Would you do the same for me as I would for you?

"I forgot to tell you," Kate said, the sound of her no more than a whisper. "The most embarrassing thing happened today. I thought Miss Lawton was talking about *Youth in Asia*, and I took all these notes. Then I saw Lisa's paper, which said *euthanasia*. Like killing stuff."

I said, "That's really dumb, Kate."

"Stephen Auchard leaned over and totally made fun of me. He said, 'What do you expect, Catherine, this is biology, not social studies.' "

9.

AFTER FIRST PERIOD HISTORY WAS HOMEROOM. MRS. KENNEDY STOOD AT THE door to her room, ushering kids through. Between me and her the floors were like marble playing cards. They had metal rims and gray-green flecks.

"Terrazzo," Dad told me and Denny once when he came to help us build sets for a play. "In Friuli, people used to take stones from the riverbeds and make paths. They would grind down the high stones with a hard rock attached to a wood pole, you know, two people on either side of an alley, sawing back and forth. Palladio adapted the style in country houses. Remember I told you about the villas?"

We always tried to remember everything my father told us. Even the most obscure information—such as the movable rudder assembly of radio-guided World War II Azon bombs or the warts under the tail of the true descendants of the 18th-century Carthusian stallion *Escalvo*—had a knack of turning up in conversation or on tests.

"Lose something, sweetheart?" Mrs. Kennedy asked.

"Oh no, Mrs. Kennedy. I'm just looking at the floors."

She looked down and smiled, which was nice. Smiles suited her. Mine is not a smiling face. Its muscles do not naturally move to that position. Strangers on the street always say, *Smile!*

Stephen was reading *The New York Review of Books*. Kate was thumbing through *Glamour*. We said nothing, which was correct. No one speaks in homeroom. Homeroom is an alphabetic grouping, having nothing to do with compatibility and everything to do with chance. It's a civic assignment, like jury duty or the army.

The P.A. system squawked, and the assistant principal started the garbled announcements. Everything Mr. Martin said was garbled because he chewed on tongue depressors to help quit smoking.

I ped a-e-gance to the fwag of the Uni-ed S-ates of A-erica

The Pledge and the flag always stir some intense memory from childhood, some intensely gummy memory, like the inside of cheeks, that I cannot name but which I know is related to *Romper Room* and the flag that stood in the corner of the studio set. Before senior year everyone would stand and recite the Pledge. Those were optimistic times. Optimism is when you're not sure where life is going to take you, so naturally you anticipate the best possible outcome. But if you have a hint already of what your life is going to be like and that hint is not so wonderful, you might as well just stretch across radiators and desk tops and ignore the announcements, halfway thinking about the night before, halfway thinking about the day ahead.

Karen Baker usually slept through the Pledge. Karen was a cashier at Brooks Discount. Every afternoon she wore a name tag pinned droopily onto a strawberry red overshirt, the kind with snaps that ladies in Little Italy call a *housecoat*. When Jack and I took Windmill Lane to the nature trail, we would see her behind Brooks by the dumpster, on cigarette break. She smoked Parliament Lights, which Jack liked to say aren't so much cigarettes as they are expensive toothpicks.

Eddie Anderson worked at Texaco on North Main Street. Eddie definitely could not be bothered with the Pledge. He wore pressed Bad Company t-shirts, though his fingers were purple from motor oil. The ratty hair on his head was neatly parted and tamed in such a way as to have the effect of a giant letter *M*. Every day after homeroom he took the bus to Riverhead because he wanted to be a boat mechanic. He went to *BOCES*—Board of Cooperative Educational Services, a trade school. Jack always said Eddie would end up the richest guy in the class. "Better nail him now, Katie," Jack would tease.

Cheryl Bromley, who used homeroom to file her nails, was going to be a hairdresser and a make-up artist, so she went to BOCES for training in— something, I wasn't exactly sure what—hair and make-up probably, though that seemed inconceivable as a course of study.

If certain people could not be blamed for a lack of enthusiasm in regard to the Pledge, it didn't feel right for the rest of us to leap up and swear allegiance to a nation that was already working out to be more liberal and more just for some than for others. Though I respected the fact that some people had it tough, I didn't necessarily like them better than anyone else, nor did I dislike them any less. Frankly, I didn't want to be associated with anyone from school. I didn't even enjoy being different among them. It depressed me to think that if we were all on the front lawn for a fire drill and a helicopter flew by, the pilot would not be able to single me out from the giant mealy mass.

I was making a drawing for Jack. *Big Wednesday* was playing at the Old Post Office Theater, and we were going to go see it Saturday for the fifth time. It was about surfers, so I drew the interior of a wave with a little body riding it—the little body being Jack's. I was about to write a funny caption about Jan-Michael Vincent when an object fell to the floor. It sounded like a pen. I checked around my ankles, thinking maybe it'd been mine, though of course mine was in my hand.

A voice said, "Sorry."

It was Dorothy Becker. Her gelatin-soft body was tucked into the seat diagonally across from mine, one row over and up. She hung back to reach the pen but didn't turn. Her arm flopped, and her moist fingers pinched at the air. She had those white, kind of noodley fingers without defined nail beds.

"I got it," I offered, lowering myself to grab it. I slid the pen into her hand, and I saw the mark on her wrist. I followed with my eyes the path of the ridge. It was crooked and pale scarlet, a rouge or primrose crest longer than an inch, shorter than when the incision had been fresh. Her palm clamped limply on the pen. I kept myself suspended in case she dropped it again. She thanked me, and I straightened, saying, *No problem*, which was true.

Scars help you get the point. There's a difference between hearing that someone has tried to commit suicide and then seeing the evidence of work done to achieve that aim. I had a sort of scar. It ran under my left eye and almost parallel to it, only it could hardly be seen. It was not self-inflicted, so it passed on no practical information about me, other than that once I was unlucky and got a burn. My mom called me Apache Princess.

I examined Dorothy's back, her hair and her clothes. She used shampoo and soap and toothpaste, just like me. The main difference between us was that when she woke up, she knew that a shitty day lay ahead, whereas I could never be sure.

When you're in high school, you're no stranger to death, especially if you live where kids drive. In tenth grade, two couples from school got killed when they hit a telephone pole on Route 114, and the school planted fig trees by the driveway. It was sad, but I was confused by the way certain people got hysterical, girls like Coco and Pip and Breanne who had never once been nice to those kids.

Coco kept saying, "Oh my God, oh my God, oh my God!"

Though she did not elaborate, I thought I knew what she meant. I thought she meant, *It could have been us*. She definitely did *not* mean, *I wish I'd had the chance to know them better. I never got to tell them how I really felt.* If those people had popped back to life right in front of her, she would have ignored them, same as always.

It's confusing how you're supposed to weep over people who die recklessly, and you're supposed to be disgusted by Dorothy. But actually, a calculated decision to die is less irreverent than putting yourself in a position to depart accidentally. Was Dorothy really weak, or brave like crazy, to have sliced herself, to have presented resistance as a blade punctured her skin and veins and divided the meaty beneath? And then to survive the damage and return to school because anything was better than staying home? It was that double failure that moved me the most—the failure of her life and the failure of her attempt to part from it.

I wondered if her early end was inevitable but temporarily postponed. Maybe you cannot stop death from coming to the dying. Maybe a suicidal person is like a lame animal in a healthy pack, dragging a limb, trailing blood, luring unseasonable death with queer scents and marks. Maybe there's a moment, a reversal of instinct, that leads to the judgment that living is worse than dying. It must require a massive exertion of consciousness to reach a conclusion that is in such direct opposition to nature.

Unless of course, that conclusion is not oppositional at all. For who can be certain that suicide is not just one particular doorway to death—death being in and of itself irrefutably natural? Why should those who take their lives at once be any more criminal than those who do it tediously, with noxious living, with dope and vodka and nicotine, junk food and idle regrets, with behavior that hurts people other than themselves over and over again?

And yet, there are those who endure agony to live. Trapped for days in wells or buried beneath collapsed buildings or imprisoned in filthy flooded cells, they sing or pray or write microscopic poetry on scraps of paper to sustain themselves. When the will to survive is present, it is so sure, so clear—what if that determination is *not present, not clear*? What if a person has been made weary before their time?

I ASKED JACK ABOUT it. We were at Indian Wells Beach. "Do you think suicide is a tragedy?"

"No," he stated. "It's *your* life."

"Aren't you obligated to people who love you?"

"If you love out of obligation, it's not love." He was carving ridges and craters with a stick. "Besides, you're alone from birth."

"But you're born to your parents. To your mother."

"You don't enter the bond with your mother when you're born, you leave it. Birth is the point of departure from the only real communion you'll ever know. Everything else is invention. Your happiness depends on how well your parents handle that. You know, the fact of separation, the fiction of attachment. *Re*-attachment, whatever."

"So you owe your parents nothing?"

"I don't," he shrugged. "Maybe you do." He scraped a platform in the sand. "Most parents don't want the kid or each other. They're just carrying out some brain-dead social functions. They marry because it's time, start a family because it's time. They do it for fear of becoming outcasts, fear of acting on an original fucking thought." My name materialized in large loopy letters. He drew a heart around it. "If abortion had been legal seventeen years ago, I wouldn't exist. That's what my old man told me."

"I can't believe he said that."

Jack said, "Well, believe it."

"You could have jumped when you were climbing," I said.

"But I didn't."

"Because of me, you said."

"Because of you."

"So you're not alone." I said. "You owe me something."

"*You*—that's right. By choice, not by obligation. And if that ever changes," he posed gravely, "I'll do whatever I feel like."

"Would that be my fault?"

"*No*," he drilled. "It would be my choice."

Though I knew he meant what he said, I also wondered if it was possible to isolate a final choice from all the choices that preceded it. Romeo made a choice when he killed himself, but his choice was made meaningful by *prior* choices—Juliet died first, or so he thought.

"How about lost potential?" I said. "The art Van Gogh could have continued to make."

Jack shook his head. "Lost potential is irrelevant. How can anyone feel cheated out of something they were never entitled to in the first place? The loneliness Van Gogh felt was the loneliness he felt, whether it led to paintings or to suicide. Life may be sacred, but maybe his wasn't sacred. In fact, it's well-documented that his life sucked. If people didn't know how to care for him or his art when he was alive, or convey to him the *sacred* sensation of *sacred* living, fuck them after he's dead."

I suppose it *is* narrow to wish someone had lived longer in order to enrich your life. Jack had a point—the irony of mourning people who kill themselves is that the love felt for the dead is insufficient to have prevented them from dying in the first place. It's a special agony to feel feelings that are acute but belated. If suicides result from a longing to be understood, or touched, or reached, maybe it's not inappropriate for those who remain to feel forsaken, to be forced to endure a somber feast of years. If they feel like failures, maybe it's because in essence or in fact they failed. They didn't mind time, connect in time, communicate in time. Somehow time is most seriously implicated, and of all things, that idea made me saddest—*makes* me saddest.

Jack launched his stick into the ocean. It was not a stick; it was a broken piece of snow fence that migrated irresolutely.

Moonlight seemed to seek him out. The most distant darkness beckoned to him, engaging him in intimate address, encouraging him to establish residency. He curled and crouched beneath the altar of the night, like a praying egg implanted in the wombish wall of the universe. My eye trailed from sand to sea to sky, admiring the way Jack's luminescent form touched down upon the flatness of each, making me think of the obviousness of the relationship between solitude and infinity. My body crawled to his body, my face met his shoulder. I wanted to remind him of something—but what? I knew only that at that moment, when he was there and I was there, I loved him.

The waves clapped hypnotically without crescendo. I could hear them. Also, I heard nothing. Jack had given me his curious numbness. He had taken me to the aperture between worlds to acquaint me with the safe way he felt when thus dispatched. In my body there was a quiescent dizziness, a melting together of independent organs, a chiasma of consciousness and unconsciousness. In my body I felt night. It permeated my frame. I felt myself revert back from molecule to atom and then dissipate like dust. I felt suffused with life, true life, which was the aliveness of me and the aliveness of beyond me, and me being entinctured, a liquid in a liquid.

I tried hard to acknowledge the breadth of his despair without judgment as to basis. I tried to be moved by the enormity of his vision without positioning myself in relation to it. If I could not accompany him, at least I could honor him, because what Jack said was so, *is* so—love is born of choice. He reminded me of that choice and asked me to make it again, despite the risk I took, which was the risk of losing him, and the risk I presented, which was the risk of his losing me. And I chose, like he chose.

THE POM POM GIRLS CHANGED THEIR NAME TO THE CHEERLEADERS, AND THE Cheerleaders were not to be confused with the Twirlers, who marched at the front of the band. "It's about time!" declared Cathy Benjamin, who sat next to me in figure drawing. "Can you imagine? Having to call yourself a *Pom Pom Girl*? I mean, it's 1979!"

The first time I photographed them for the yearbook, they made a body pyramid. It took an hour to use half a roll of film because it was raining outside, and there wasn't enough room in the hall to achieve proper launch. Ultimately they settled on a *finishing pose*, a bewildering conglomerate of kneeling, standing, half-kneeling, half-standing, and a little systematic reclining. The pose had to follow an actual cheer. Otherwise it would not appear *natural*. This proved technically arduous since each time they tried it, they would land in a new place. "Did you get it?" they would huff, cheerfully.

"I think so," I would say. "Let's do a few more just to be safe."

I ended up using a wide-angle lens, which had the unfortunate effect of distorting the image and making the faces look fishy and squished, as if they'd been photographed off a doorknob. The cheerleaders didn't complain when the book came out, in fact they were good sports in general, always inviting me to join them at their lunch table, telling me how great my hair looked or what a nice sweater.

In the hall they chanted through lips that were pink and glossy. And with slightly open-fisted hands resting on the square of their hips, they took turns shouting a player's name.

> *2, 4, 6, 8, who do we ap-prec-i-ate?*
> *Kevin! Eddie! Nico! Billy! Mike!*

One rule, either official or good manners, was that each girl got to shout the name of her boyfriend or someone she had a crush on, which was the same as a boyfriend according to the code of girls. If you liked someone, you *called* him, the way you called the front seat of the car when you were a kid. When we were little, we loved The Monkees. Kate called Davy Jones, so I got Mike Nesmith. Boys have codes also, but the punishment for breaking them is severe. If you hit on someone's girl you could get beaten or killed. With girls, things are never so straightforward.

I once asked Kate why it's considered betrayal on the part of an innocent girl if a boy someone else is interested in approaches *her* instead of the girl who called him. "Or take a steady couple," I said, fortifying my point, "if the boyfriend asks another girl out, why does the girlfriend blame the new girl rather than the boyfriend?"

"Because," Kate said, "the new girl shouldn't have done that."

"But the guy was the one who *did* it," I said.

As each cheerleader called a name, she jumped in the air, making an *X* with her body while the others clapped twice for punctuation. Something about them intrigued me, something brave and paradoxical. They dressed the way girls are *supposed* to dress, in earrings and ruffles, with blue eyeshadow and permanent waves. Yet they were not so ladylike, and the things they did with their bodies were insane. They were powerful and athletic and built, not like the tennis players whose bodies were of perfectly middling proportions. They were confident, loyal, and optimistic. You have to be that way to fly through air, believing someone will catch you. The flying part really made me blue. Just how far they would go for their team. How there are no teams in the real world for women like that.

I watched them through my camera lens. Annie Jordan and Elizabeth Hill had just joined the club. Having black girls in the group gave it a visual allure that formerly it had lacked. When the cheer was over I whistled. They turned and waved, *Hey Evie!,* and I snapped a picture, which was actually very nice, how they were all standing, modest and tasteful and caught by surprise, pretty, pretty, in girlish disarray. I waved too, then walked to the auditorium. There was a sign on the door.

> *October 22, 1979, 3:00-5:00 P.M.*
> *Final Auditions—EHHS Drama Club*

I pushed it open and a round of cheers rushed in with me. All the heads in the first few rows turned, as the drama advisor, who was also a guidance counselor, made the announcement that auditions were officially closed.

"That is, unless Miss Auerbach has decided to sacrifice camera and canvas for the stage," Mr. McGintee said to me.

I drew the door closed and moved to a seat in the top row.

"I'm just waiting," I said, "for someone." I didn't have to say *Kate* since everyone knew. Mr. McGintee knew also.

"Do you have one moment?" Mr. McGintee inquired, as Kate and I passed the main office on the first day back from vacation. "Just for a chat." He had high wiry hair and wiry glasses and he looked dry as an old cattail. Like he could use a stiff drink. "Please come in."

While he spoke in private to Kate, I waited on the sofa in the guidance lounge, listening to the secretary's clock radio play *Fernando*. I kept crossing and uncrossing my legs. It was one of those awful vinyl sofas that you find in the basements of ranch houses. The rear of the seat went low, making an arrowhead-shaped crevice that I kept slipping into. There was a name for the upholstery—not melamine, not cellophane, naugahyde, maybe. Like plastic pachyderm skin.

The door to Mr. McGintee's glass cube whooshed open, and he asked me to join them. He perched on the edge of his desk and asked questions that were not exactly questions. "So, have you two had an opportunity to review the events of the summer?"

Kate said, "Yes. Yes, we have."

"Yes," I said, "we review a lot."

"Very good," said Mr. McGintee, slapping his knee. "Ter-*rif*-ic."

It's not always a crime to lie. Sometimes it's easier to give people the answer they expect than to explain what you really think or feel. No one likes to admit it, but conversation is never truly spontaneous. Everyone works toward a goal, and few people like to be surprised. You can prevent a lot of mutual embarrassment and tedious negotiation simply by pinpointing your partner's aim at the outset.

Mr. McGintee had spent a lot of time and money earning his degree in educational psychology, and you couldn't blame him for trying to get some use out of it. He didn't want honest answers about how Kate was doing, just some key phrases that would allow him to classify her feelings as normal and call her case closed. It's somewhat like asking someone, *How was your summer?* You don't really want details. You're just checking in. But certain kinds of pain are not easily measured or swiftly eradicated. Kate could not possibly speak of her suffering because words could never convey her feelings. I'd *seen* her sorrow. It came in the way she sat motionlessly in her room in our house watching the day skulk from orange to blue. Time passed twice as slowly for her and *around* her. We would sit for what felt like hours.

"What time is it?" I'd ask with a yawn.

She'd say, "Ten minutes past the last time you asked."

Invariably she overdressed. And when she cooked, she leaned against the counter with her legs tightly wrapped around each other. Her sorrow expressed itself in trepidation. She was afraid to move, as though movement might draw her irrevocably from the sphere in which her mother had resided.

"Why did you drop French, Catherine?" Mr. McGintee asked the top of her head. Her hands played with the fabric of the chair, which was beady like dehydrated oatmeal.

"She's fluent," I said. "How much better is she supposed to speak it?"

"The point is, French Five would have raised her class rank," he said, and his eyelids fluttered, then his gaze resituated itself on Kate's skull. "*The point is,*" he counseled, "we need to consider Kate's future. She doesn't have the luxury of family to fall back on."

He nodded meaningfully to me, as though I'd had any experience with the *luxury* of family outside of what I'd known from Kate's. The past for Kate was not like the past for anyone else. She'd lost an entire way of being—red wine in her water glass, pounded veal for dinner, a platter of soft cheese and fruit for dessert, strolls around Town Pond with Maman's skirt crinkling stiffly like tissue paper. On Saturdays there was dancing, Yves Montand or Jacques Brel, and when the song ended, Maman would spin, clapping twice by your eyes like a joyful, brazen someone—*Ha! Ha!*

We were eight when they taught us to dance. We practiced in the living room where there were grooves in the rug. If you followed the grooves, the steps were easier. In dancing school advertisements you see black plastic cutouts shaped like shoes. A week after the funeral when we cleared Kate's belongings from the house, I was given the job of catching her cat Mindy. After running through every yard in the neighborhood, Mindy finally darted under the couch. The white tip of her tail poked out right by those dance patches. I knelt soberly. The space was almost alive. The absence of fabric indicated friction, and friction signifies heat. Friction and heat come from the meeting of bodies. The air above the carpet was imprinted with that memory, of friction, of heat—of them.

How could I possibly help Kate? The Kate I had known passed when her parents passed. She no longer had proof of herself. She had become a nothing. Not a nothing, but a former something, which is infinitely more complicated.

IN THE AUDITORIUM, I sat on the upright edge of a seat, dropped my knapsack onto the floor beneath my feet, and squinted to find Kate. You could find her by her hair, which in mythology would have been called *a golden mane*. She was second row center. Mr. McGintee was complimenting the group on the turn-out—*forty-three students!* He launched into a speech about how so few popular dramatic works could accommodate that many people, and he ominously extracted a sheet of paper from his briefcase, telling everyone to write down their names and interests, in case they didn't make the cast. "It's important to remember that the backstage volunteers, the costume designers, the lighting technicians, and the sales crew are as important as the performers." He shouted up the aisle, again to me. "Isn't that right, Eveline?"

"Sure," I said. "I mean, I guess." It wasn't really right, not if you wanted to act. I happen to like doing the sets, but Kate would have died if they made her property mistress or something.

When Kate asked me whether she should join the drama club, I said no. She was pretty, and her hair was long, but that didn't make her a stage actress. Carol Channing was a stage actress. Ethel Merman. Helen Hayes. Gwen Verdon. I told her my opinion, just not in those words. I said, "I don't think it would be good."

Kate would have been fine on film, playing herself or a type of fairy—an equestrian fairy. By that I did not mean a fairy that assumed the form of a horse so much as a normal-looking fairy that flitted *about* horses. You know, lounging on horse foreheads and sending wand-loads of sparkles into horse ears. Once when we were in the city, Dad sent us to Theater 80 because Marilyn was on duty and he had to work on a vertical sign installation at Wo Hop's in Chinatown. Kate and I saw a film called *The Smiling Madame Beudet*, which was made in the 1920s by Germaine Dulac. I asked Kate about *Dulac*.

"Does it mean *some* lake, or, *of the* lake?"

"Of the lake, I guess."

"That's nice," I said, and she agreed that it was.

The movie had lots of gauzy close-ups of a housewife who sat around looking at magazines and dreaming about being someone other than herself. It reminded me of Kate, not because it was French, which you couldn't tell since the picture had no sound, but because of the part about flipping through magazines. Kate was constantly flipping through magazines. It was unlikely that the drama club would select *The Smiling Madame Beudet*. One thing about drama clubs is that the plays they pick have to be vehicles for three talented kids and an incompetent mob. If I were in charge, I would've had them act out the newspaper.

"Let's see, *Fiddler on the Roof* was last year," I said as I ate a chicken leg and fell back on the couch. "And *Harvey* was the year before. It'll be *Guys and Dolls* or *South Pacific*."

"C'mon, Evie, be nice."

"Five bucks," I said. "*The Mikado*. I bet you. *Damn Yankees*."

Kate felt I was making fun of her hobby, which I was. She wanted to act because she was beautiful, and beautiful people feel entitled to attention. It was the same thing with everyone saying Daryl Sackler should play basketball. It didn't mean he had the necessary stamina or agility or dedication or wits, it just meant he was tall, that his figure would have made sense on the court. People like things to appear to make sense, even if that visual logic comes at the expense of factual excellence.

There were boys all over the auditorium, sitting against the edges of things. Boys like to sit against edges or crawl along edges, like lab mice. I saw Jack. It was weird to see him there. He was on the floor against the wall at the far right with Dan Lewis and Troy Resnick, and he was glaring at me as though I were encased behind glass. I relaxed into the gaze, my head relaxed and my neck relaxed.

I wasn't surprised that he remembered the date. It said it right on the auditorium door—*October 22nd*.

"ARE THE RUMORS TRUE?" he'd asked.

Twigs were caught on his red plaid lumberjack coat, and the morning light heated his back, making me think of sunnyside eggs. He'd just returned from boarding school for Thanksgiving. His duffle bag was on the front step. I could see one nylon end of the lazy cylinder through the storm door. It was 1978, five months after we'd met.

It was a very uncharacteristic sentence for him to speak. I was confused not so much by the words but by the tone, the swiftness of delivery. It was as if there was a piece of me he'd lost, and he was frantic to retrieve it, like scrambling to collect a stack of bills that had blown away in a vigorous wind. He was leaning forward. I couldn't see his eyes. If I could've seen his eyes, I might not have spoken.

"It depends," I said, "on what the rumors say."

"That they slept with you," he countered fearlessly. One thing—Jack could be fearless. He did not ever hesitate to ensure that we were both speaking of the same thing. We were sitting on the couch in the living room. His knees brushed the coffee table.

I looked at the ceiling. "Well, no one really slept."

"You know what I mean."

"It makes a difference, the words you use."

"Did you have *sex* with them?"

"I wouldn't say that either."

Jack took a breath. "What *would* you say?"

"I would say it was the other way around."

"That they had sex with you?"

"Right," I said. That's right.

Jack looked at his shoes. He looked at his shoes for a long time. He became so still I thought maybe he'd fallen asleep. I tried to think what it would be like to be him, hearing such news for the first time, but that was hard to do when I'd known already for a while. It was possible that he might like to do something about what happened. Unfortunately, it happened a long time ago. It's not hard to get emotional about the past. It's just hard to apply those emotions effectively. In movies people say, *Don't show your face in this town again* or *You'll live to regret this*, but Jack was sixteen, he couldn't say such things with any sort of conviction.

Did the rumor happen to mention the way they came into the upstairs bathroom of Maria Brierly's house while I was peeing, the way they hoisted me against the wall before I could pull my pants up, the way L.B. Strickland covered my mouth with his mouth while Nico twisted the faucet on the sink very hard. Water splattered up from the basin onto my belly in piercing and icy slivers. I do not like water to fly up, not ever.

Would Jack feel better or worse knowing that because the back of my neck was pressed against the wall, I could hear but not see Nico's zipper coming undone with one sharp shot. Worse probably. Jack would not have liked the idea of me being blinded and silenced while my mind raged on, memorizing the feel of my two wrists fitting into someone's one hand, the feel of drunken gasps on my neck, going in time with strokes that tear me open, the steel wool feel against my very velvet skin.

"Rapture" by Blondie played. It played exponentially, with each next verse multiplying out. Surely no one had described that to Jack or the part about Maria banging on the bathroom door and pushing it open onto the mass of the three of us, shrieking, *Get out of my house!* and *You tramp!* Did people include in the notes they passed a description of her nails going into my arms when she dragged me into the hallway with my pants around my ankles. How when I reached down to dress, there were streams running down my inner thighs. How I stumbled down the stairs, how I ran out the front door, how I had hoped against hope that no one noticed.

The night was moonless but not entirely unkind. Three bodies appeared. Rocky Santiago and his younger brother, Manny, and some underclassman whose name I could not recall. Rocky eased me into the passenger seat of his dented Chevy. My bike fit into his trunk. He drove cautiously toward East Hampton, and Manny followed in his friend's car, cautiously also.

Rocky asked was I okay.

I felt bad not to answer. He seemed concerned. I could not get past this feeling, this after-feeling, this harrowing after-feeling, a feeling beyond grasp or intelligence—beyond any obvious comparison to having been robbed or cheated, inside I *felt* robbed and cheated. Inside, I felt the *physics* of injustice, which, as it turns out, has little or nothing to do with the *dialectics* of injustice. I felt cruelty on a level that was cellular, electrical, nervous in nature. The indisputable wrongness of someone's having taken something that did not belong to them, filthied something that I'd kept clean, made their mark on property that was mine, and contemptibly crossed over into my intimacy in defiance of my desire was all distant conjecture compared to the pragmatics of my impressions. The pulled muscle in my neck, the cut on my mouth possibly from a watch, the moisture in my underwear not made by me, the surface abrasions and internal hairline splits that I could not mention to Rocky despite his kind interest because it is hard for people to understand the inside of a girl, the way it is shaped like a conch with filigreed avenues that are spectacular and ornamental. People tend to think it's just a hole.

I asked him to pull over and he did and I leaned out to vomit. Manny turned off the headlights on the second car to give me privacy.

When we arrived at my house, Rocky shifted the arm of the car into park and asked was I all right to go in on my own. I said that I was. Maybe I was in shock, but I didn't feel embarrassed with him. I had the feeling he'd seen enough of the world to understand the random brutality of instinct and to know I was not to blame. He came from Colombia in 1976. His real name was Raúl. I would have liked to know about his home, about what had made his family leave it, but I didn't want to make him nervous with talk. We both knew that it would have made the story of my assault far more plausible if I blamed *him* for what the others had done. It would have made me a more credible victim. It was good of him to take a chance on me.

"Thanks, Raúl," I said, waving my hand weakly.

He ran his fingers through his hair, scratching at the back of his scalp. "No problem, Evie," he said. "Anything for you."

When he walked to the rear of the car, he did so deliberately, not really tiptoeing but padding noiselessly, as though stepping from a sleeping child. He lifted the bike out of the trunk and waited for me to join him, then he stood watchfully as I moved down the driveway. The dimmed headlights of the two idling cars poured onto the ground. They were waiting headlights, fraternal and discreet. When I reached the garage door, I turned back and waved again, not realizing then that the timing of Rocky's benevolence, the gentlemanly readiness of his heart, had reversed in one elegant gesture the violence I'd experienced. In fact, it saved me. It was poetry really—the random enmity, the random good.

Jack was saying that I should have done something. That reporting it to the police would have been cathartic. "You know," he said, "like, helpful."

It was a funny suggestion, the part about the police, coming from him. I was sorry for my involvement in an incident that would cause him to betray the basic principles of his thinking.

Even if he was right, it was easy to say in retrospect that something would have been the sensible thing to do, when at the time, I did not feel sensible. At the time I was too busy thinking. Should I slice off the top layer of my skin. Should I scrape the purpuric lip marks from my neck. Would I use a knife for that, and with that knife should I create a pocket in my belly wide enough for a hand. Should I reach in and remove the contaminated organs, scrubbing each fleshy gelatin piece in acid, my arms moving like washer-woman arms, mechanical, blistered, and bright. Periodically throughout the night I would tell myself to get over it, to act practically, to take a shower. Instantly after, I would drop back to the floor of my room, made sick by the thought of my own body, afraid to glimpse even the smallest portion of my undressed self. It was not impossible that they'd had ink on their fingers. That underneath I looked splotchy like a zebra. Not a zebra, but one of the spotted kinds of animals. I just thought of zebras because of the sorrowful way they hang their heads.

"Have you seen those cops?" I asked Jack, trying to bolster his mood with complaints. My hands made circle motions around my eyes. "Those mirrored aviator glasses they wear?"

"Yeah," Jack muttered. "Fucking assholes."

Maybe the image of me talking to my own bloated reflection in gleaming Ray Bans would make him understand how pointless it would've been to file a report. Still, if I could have guessed that telling the police would have profited Jack, I might have done it. He seemed to need to know that some manner of justice had occurred. It was like sticking a pin into a bruise to hear him wish so naïvely for equity.

Jack's body had not yet moved. He was like a jetty rock, obstinate and motionless against the savage force of the sea. I wasn't sure whether I was supposed to comfort him so I waited, passing the time by thinking of the things I knew about him. I knew that he loved me desperately, never more so than at that moment. I knew that he was ready, aroused for once by the honorableness of his emotions, and yet the anger that moved him had no means of expression. How betrayed he must have felt by his belligerent pacifism, by the ambivalence that he constantly displayed. He was thinking that the attack had not been arbitrary, that it had happened to me for a reason. He was thinking the reason was him.

"Don't you see," I said. "It's like trying to catch a flying bird." Time does not move backwards, nor does it rest. Nothing could have changed what happened. There are no authorities in matters of savagery. No cop or court would have had the jurisdiction to do what was fair—to vacuum the grizzling glue from my insides and cram it back into the pinhole openings of their penises. All the way back to the testicles with some sort of wire, the kind used in plumbing, the stuff called *flux*. No expert could say why it happened to me.

"It was unavoidable," I said, "like a choice I made."

"*To get raped?*"

"No—I just mean—I don't know." A bleak shaft of carrot-colored light grazed his left eye and a round patch beneath it, making Jack seem one-eyed and invincible like a cyclops. I wondered if it was three o'clock. Usually things get carroty and bleak and Homeric at three. I tried to think. "Something made me choose to go out that night," I said, pausing lightly, "and something made them—*them.*"

"Say the rest," he demanded.

He wanted to hear the part about him—that he should have been different than he was, that he should have been an obedient son who would not have taken a knife to his father and would not have been shipped to boarding school, that he should have been a typical male who walked with his arm around my waist and his hand crammed in my back pocket, who should have bragged about fucking me to guys he despised, who should have played a sport and not an instrument. He wanted me to connect it to him.

I shrugged. "There is no rest."

I accepted that it had to happen the way it did when I came home that night and found the house still smelling like food from dinner. It seemed intensely meaningful that I could not draw back in time. The dishes in the drainboard were not yet dry, and the radio by the stove that I had turned on earlier was still playing. The time was one-thirty. It was Sunday, October 22nd. Hours before, it had been the 21st, Powell's thirty-eighth birthday. On Saturday at six, Kate had called to say she couldn't make it to the birthday dinner or to the party, that her mother was sick. They were leaving Sunday for Sloan-Kettering in Manhattan.

I lifted the phone and listened for Kate. There was no Kate, no reverberation, no mellow rumble, just a dial tone. Dial tones can be hellish and unpleasant, like continual burping.

I rested my knee on the chair I'd used at dinner. While we were eating cake, Mom had told the story of a new student who'd ordered a soda at a fast food place but was given a cup of lye instead. He drank it and permanently lost his voice, but he won four hundred thousand dollars in a lawsuit. He applied the winnings in part to the expense of an education, which he would not otherwise have been able to afford. "See that," she'd said, slapping the tabletop lightly with two palms. Powell brushed down his mustache with his napkin and considered the dark peculiarities of fate.

"I think I'll go to that party," I'd said as I cleared the dishes.

"Need a ride?" Powell had asked.

"No thanks. I'll take my bike." I didn't want to bother him on his birthday. The bike affected my destiny; I arrived late and everyone was drunk. Like the guy who ordered a soda but got lye instead—had his day transpired differently, he might have gotten a Coke after all.

I circled the empty kitchen. Around me lay the gruesome evidence of a seemingly inconsequential chain of events, which, as it turned out, had not been inconsequential after all, and there was a lesson in that, in remembering to seek meaning where you least expect it. I was feeling hysterical. I wanted to laugh, but instinct would not have it. I wanted to move, but there was no place to go. Beyond the windows the world was ferocious with life. How was it that I had not noticed before leaving the inauspicious snap to the wind, the drunken flop of the trees?

I threw my ruined underwear into the garbage, then sat in bed and watched the clock. I watched the numbers flap. I timed my headaches. The headaches were very bad. Like ant hills, they were busy places and numerous.

At 4:09 A.M. it occurred to me that someone might see my underwear in the trash and pull them out, thinking I'd made some kind of stupid mistake. I returned to the kitchen and cut them with scissors then shoved them into a cereal box, a Rice Krispies box I emptied. I wished that it had been a kind of cereal I didn't like—Total or Wheaties. I crammed the package down to the bottom of the can and covered it with other garbage. When I pulled my hands out, they had jiggling flecks of congealed chicken grease on them. I lifted the bag from the can, tied it, and dragged it into my room. Then I returned and put a clean liner in, wondering, how do people conceal murder? What do they do with their consciousnesses? I could do nothing with my consciousness.

Morning hummed when it came, like a choir of light, and in the whiteness I showered. I could not select clothes. I kept trying things and trying things until the contents of my dresser had been emptied onto the floor, and my skin was itching, and there were hives like violet ivy. Since I couldn't pick one thing, I wore several. In the mirror I looked homely, like a straw corn doll with stick-out hair and no neck and skin colored with the juice from berries. I looked like the product of impoverished child artisans.

It was very cold in Powell's car while I waited for the 6:17 to pass. As soon as the train rumbled by, I started the engine and pulled out of the driveway, stopping first at the nature trail, where I fed the leftover Rice Krispies to the ducks, and then at the dump, where I had the distinction of being the first customer, if in fact dump users can be considered customers. In Paris, some women are the first customers at the *boulangerie*, waiting on the dim and blue glistening cobblestone street for the doors to open to buy bread. I wanted to be one of those women.

I stood in the grand vacuum of sand like a slave in the Coliseum, with the wind above like the speech of angels and the sweeping gulls a wild opus. Though I moved in autonomy on the plane of earth, I'd never felt more engrafted. I felt shorn at the head and face and seized at the foundation, somewhat like the stump in my neighbor's yard. I teetered on the precipice of the sandy mound and swung my arm back to hurl the bag into the abyss. Vulture seagulls swarmed down. I wondered whether they would pick so far through the bag that they would arrive at the cereal box and my underpants, and then would they fly about with shreds of stained cotton hanging from their beaks. That would be ironic, if a strip of familiar underwear dropped onto the windshield when my mother and Powell drove to the Paradise in Sag Harbor for breakfast. I unbuttoned one of the several sweaters I was wearing and stayed listening to the repetitive caws of the gulls.

Jesus, I thought, *they never fucking stop.* And when they die, more come. They are the rats of the sky. Skyrats. If it surprised the old people who had begun to pull in alongside me to see a girl in poor clothes crying on the hood of a car at the dump, it should not have. I was just like them—victimized by my own bad luck, turning my hatred toward the birds.

At home, Mom and Powell were in the kitchen. I considered telling them what had happened, but I couldn't bear for the proud way they looked at me to change. I didn't want their faces to change into new faces that looked at me in a new way. Besides, Powell would have ended up going over to everyone's houses, and there would have been confrontations and arrests, more than likely of him. The telephone rang, awfully. *Bllwanngg!*

"Whoa!" My mother shouted.

"I'll get it," I yelled, diving to prevent a second ring.

Nico Gerardi's voice cracked through the wire. "Hello?"

I took the phone to the staircase, nearly to the top, where I sat, facing upwards. The carpet felt especially synthetic. Sometimes it hits you, the way a carpet is just weird fake stuff.

He asked was I okay.

"I guess," I said, wondering what would he have done if I'd said no. Wondering who'd told him to call—his father, his brother? How many people knew already when I'd told no one.

He kept talking, saying things, stupid things, and I kept trying to stay in the present, to keep my mind from receding into recall. Anyway he wasn't saying anything I wanted to know—such as, did it have to be me, or could it have been anyone, and did his partiality for violence have to do with genetics or environment.

"I think it's gonna rain today," he said. "Do you?"

"Do I—what?"

"Think it's going to rain. Or not rain. You know, get sunny."

Nico and L.B. had families who denied them nothing. Their parents bought them their favorite foods, gave them new cars and nice clothes, intended to pay in full for their college tuition, and dispensed generous allowances without expecting responsibility in return. Such parents are wrong to shelter children so completely, to condone immaturity, to exempt boys from basic social requirements of fair exchange. People can get hurt that way.

"Sun, I think," I said. "Or rain. I'm not sure."

In the end, Nico said nothing of the remotest relevance to me. The only thing I learned, I learned by supposition—if the event had been intended, it had not been intended to change him or L.B. They were clean. They had no bruises or hives or sore flesh. They had no opaque coat to their insides. They had no remorse. There was no larger lesson for them. To them, it was just a night, a *lucky* night. As for me, I'd been critically altered.

And so if the rumor was that I had sex with them, the rumor was only partly true. "It was that," I said to Jack, "and much more." I went on, taking care. "I mean, I didn't get hurt, not *really*. Some people get injured, you know—badly. I don't want to diminish what happens to them. It's hard to know what rape even is, exactly."

"*Shame*," he interrupted, "is a good way to know you've been raped." Jack examined every inch of my face as if it were unfamiliar to him and also very familiar. "You were wrong to keep it to yourself. You let your shame silence you. It's exactly what they were counting on. You protected them."

It was an interesting point, to think that shame can take your voice away. Maybe it was so. Maybe I thought that if I kept my humiliation to myself, it would go away faster. And if I shared it, then I would have had to wait for everyone else to forget also, and them plus me could take a very long time. I tried to think what is the half-life of uranium-238. Whatever it is, that seemed about right.

The living room was entirely bereft of radiance; the day was gone. A black shroud covered Jack's head and angel's hair. He seemed to be in mourning. His anger had been replaced by his customary, self-analytical brooding, and that was, in fact, progress for the worse. I knew I had to speak to prevent him from venturing to a very bad place, but I could think of nothing in particular to say. My voice cracked through the dismal inertia of the November evening then croaked meekly like damp fireworks. I longed to lean on his shoulder; instead I lowered my head to my own lap.

Once I had a long conversation with a deaf woman, one of Mom's students named Monica, for two and a half hours. Afterwards I needed a nap. I only knew the ASL alphabet and very few signs—*dead* and *hungry* and *uncle*—which were not sufficient to convey with any specificity the content of my thoughts. Jack and I were having similar problems. I possessed all this information, but, for whatever reason—survival or shame—my vocabulary was quite limited. Jack was handicapped as well; his predicament made him uncommonly fluent. He had more space inside than things to fill it. He could only reach forth with his cerebral might to claim my reluctant impressions.

He stood, and the movement of his body upwards signified the end of the conversation. Jack went to the window and leaned against its frame. I could not see what he saw from where I sat, yet I knew precisely what was there. Directly before him was a tabletop plane of hedgerow that extended four feet from the base of the picture window into the flat and liverish late autumn yard, in the center of which stood a leafless mimosa with molasses-colored scars that were vertical. Beyond the tree was a fort-like wall of Russian olives, bare almost as well, which protected us from infiltration on three sides. He beheld a landscape stripped of vigor and hue. He beheld energy reined in. In the winter, suppleness is secreted away. In summer it returns, all the things formerly impacted break apart with sounds and smells and everything blooming.

Jack was going to take off for a while, he said, then he left. Although I saw him every day for the remainder of Thanksgiving week, those were the last words he spoke until five o'clock on the very same afternoon his mother took him back to boarding school. A Sunday. We received a collect phone call.

The operator said, "From Jack, for anyone."

My mother said, "Yes, of course, we'll accept," and she handed the receiver to me. She did not go away.

"Where are you?" I asked. Car horns were in the background and the hum of a P.A. system.

"Port Authority," he said. "I just got off a Greyhound."

"What about school?" I asked.

"I quit," he said. "Fuck it."

The next day Jack was back at East Hampton High School, where he remained for the next year and a half, until we graduated. Once he returned, life for me changed dramatically, though I did not dare tell him. To say things were better would have been to imply that at some point they had been worse. Where would he have gone with his malice if I confessed how much more painful the public humiliation had been than the private. How might he have treated himself upon learning that it was easier for people to think poorly of me than to think of two football players as rapists?

I did not tell Jack that for weeks I'd gone to Denny's car at lunch. That I'd carried all my books all the time so I wouldn't have to stop at my locker. That boys in the hall would cram their hands in the pockets of their Levi's and laugh or sigh over-loudly, blocking my way if I wanted to pass. That girls would turn their backs. That people jumped on an opportunity to denigrate me, as if they'd been waiting. Not everyone. Not Marty or Denny or Dan. Not the yearbook people. Not Kate. Only the popular ones, which is a customary but nevertheless confounding fact of social science—that is to say, the most liked people behaving the least likeably.

The only good thing about Maman's illness is that Kate ended up in New York for the week after the incident. When she returned, she was too despondent over the latest diagnosis to have been included in any gossip. Possibly I was incorrect; people can be quite heartless.

"It's your breasts," Denny said. "People obsess on such things."

With Jack there, and with us together as a couple, it dawned on people that I had not agreed to sex with Nico and L.B., or tried to trap them into dating me, as some girls had suggested, that, actually I had no interest in them whatsoever. Suddenly, not only did I possess the practical knowledge of their astounding sexual ineptitude, but my situation showed that they had to steal sex because no one was giving it to them voluntarily.

The boys treated me from then on with a bizarre sort of deference and civility. Possibly they felt bad for me, possibly they felt guilty about having been mean. Possibly they were awed by the fact that I hadn't told on Nico and L.B. I wasn't proud of this, nor was I ashamed, things just happened to unfold this way, and daily life became easier for me, just having allies, which happens to be survival—snatching every minor advantage, immodestly taking help wherever you can find it. The part that bothered me was the girls—nothing was ever forgotten or forgiven with the girls. That is to say, them forgiving me.

Or with Jack. Jack never recovered. Periodically he would go into a tirade about how the sacredness of sex had been ruined. He would sink into a penetrating wretchedness marked by a prolonged and seething silence. I never asked what went on in the sulfurous corridors of his mind, but he was to be forgiven. God knows we all have fantasies of retribution.

"You don't understand, Eveline," he would say as soon as he could speak. "I can't clear it from my mind."

I moved on because I *had* to, because pain gets heavy when you carry it far from its source, like a bucket of water hauled miles from a stream—it acquires a whole new value, which is the sum of its essence and your investment, and there is no way to look at it straight anymore. It becomes a story of itself. It was no good for me to ruminate over details. If I thought too much, I would forget things, such as meals and homework and the names of friends. Once I found blood on my leg and on my hands, and I saw that I had been scratching. Once I found myself walking; I did not know to where.

I told myself that it was enough to pity Nico and L.B.'s criminal lack of kindness and to feel sorry for all the lies they had been told—about women and themselves—and for the way they went very fast, like midget rabbits, when they had sex. Maybe the cruelest revenge was to say nothing, to inform no one, to satisfy myself with the fact that they had already hit the limits of their dubious potential, that for them, only stinking crisis lay ahead.

I wasn't sure what was the right way to think. I just tried to do my level best with the little I had.

"Whom you all know by now," Mr. McGintee was saying, and everyone clapped as a figure leaning against the lower left wall gave an abbreviated wave.

I squinted to see Jack, on the opposite side of the room, squinting back at me. I wondered if we were going to argue; he looked ready to argue.

Mr. McGintee shouted a few closing remarks as everyone rose. *Roles will be posted, rehearsals start next Wednesday, don't forget to sign the paper going around.* Kate lingered near the base of the stage, and Jack idly ascended the aisle to my left. The lanky muscles of his thighs expressed themselves beneath the paper-thin denim of his jeans. Beneath a white oxford shirt was a blue Columbia University t-shirt that corresponded in pale hue to his eyes.

"Nice entrance," he said. He sat on the arm of the seat by mine, facing away. He gnawed at his cuticle then kicked a loose piece of carpet strip.

"What are you doing here?" I asked him.

"I'm like you," he said. "Just waiting for someone."

The group at the base of the auditorium began to thin, passing by us on the way out. Tim Storey charged up after Troy. *Give it to me, you little shit.*

Kate arrived. "You owe me five bucks, Evie."

"Don't tell me—*Oklahoma*." I'd totally forgotten *Oklahoma*.

"No, *Our Town*."

"*Our Town?*" I said. "Shit."

Jack grabbed my knapsack, and he followed Kate out, and I followed also, first unzipping my jeans and tucking in my shirt. As I moved to the door, I glanced over my shoulder. A handful of people were at the bottom. No one I knew, though I felt—I don't know—some trigger into possibility.

"We had a bet," Kate was saying as she held the auditorium door for us. "About the play. She wasn't very nice."

"She's not a nice girl, Kate," Jack said as we spilled into the lobby. "You ought to know that."

He tossed my knapsack to me, thrusting it, as you would a medicine ball. Medicine balls are bizarre. The concept, the name, the whole inside-out look of them. "I'm going to Dan's. See you later."

"What's wrong with *him*?" Kate asked. I just shrugged.

WE WALKED DOWN THE south hall. She was combing her hair when we got to her locker, so I opened it. 10-24-8. My tongue was pressing against the inside of my mouth, and as I triggered the latch, she poked my cheek with one finger, forcing my tongue back. I leaned onto the locker alongside hers and rubbed my eyes with the heels of my palms. I remember feeling sort of hungover—sort of tired, sort of free, electric-like and sexy. Like I just didn't care. Like there was nothing to bind me. Like the components of my life had gone down to the thickness of thread. Like I was not hospitable. And I could fly.

Kate was getting her stuff, smiling to herself and humming. I remember thinking, *Something's coming.* I could feel it coming.

Though the school was uninhabited, there was influence to its stillness. It was not simply a place, but a place evacuated, a place dispossessed of prior standing. To this day, I feel that I could render it, the *feeling* of it—the shining, the glowing, the empty.

Our shoulders grazed as we walked, her shoulders and my shoulders, though no signal was transmitted in touch. It was five o'clock. And there was wind, helical and shallow, making things appear to blow down as we passed, like peasant heads for royalty. One long, low ribbon of sunlight slipped through the parted doors at the far end of the hall, making visible dust trestles, and the rich, ripe aroma of cut grass infected the early autumn air.

She breathed in. She said, "I think I'm in love."

Kate pointed to her chest. She blushed, and the hollows of her cheeks filled with pink, like light warming rubies, coming up through them. Her eyes were girlish and pleading. She seemed to be calling upon me to join her somehow. I remember turning. I remember exactly what it was to turn.

I saw a figure, a man, walking also. He was several paces behind us along the wall, closer to the side than the center. His presence seemed to consume the entire width of the corridor, cleaving the air like an angry black slash, like some fanatical, godless intrusion. Never in my life had I seen anything so profoundly extrinsic, so exotic, so mystifying.

His eyes were not on Kate, they were on me.

He knew me, as I knew him. We entered instantly into confidence. It was as if he'd caught me committing some crime that rendered me eligible for his persuasion. He smiled, one swift and contemptuous smile, and I felt the accuracy of my instinct. I felt I had accepted his terms, that nothing could conceal the perversion in me that was manifest to his eyes. I turned back. And the unfavorable face of that day lifted, altogether and instantly, and the catastrophe it marked turned ancient and irrelevant. Whoever he was, he was inside—like a bullet, lodged.

THE CLOCK ON KATE'S dresser said 9:05. She climbed over me to the spot by the wall, and the bed rocked like a motorless boat. Her breath passed delicately through her nose. Kate had a delicate way of breathing that reminded me of those puckered white flowers, the kind that hang upside down like sad bells. I was reading a magazine. I tilted it for her to see.

"It's cold," she said, huddling down. She was wrapped in a towel.

"Yes," I said, "it is."

In *Seventeen,* Mariel Hemingway demonstrated her favorite exercises. You had to hang over crossed legs and lay both palms on the floor while straightening your knees. I tore out the page for us to try them. Magazine pages come out with a therapeutic feel that is milky beneath your wrist.

"So, what do you think?" she asked, as the railroad crossing bells began to clank. Beyond the window the night blinked red. Within seconds, the whistle blew and the house began to shake, buoyantly then furiously, then less and less as the train moved west. After a brief buzzing silence, the second set of chimes rang and the gates lifted. I could feel the lacy gust of her lashes; it was 9:08.

"Think of what?"

"Of Harrison," she said.

In the magazine was a picture of a model with a short haircut. I thought I might like to have that haircut. Kate was waiting.

"Is that his name?" I asked.

"Harrison Rourke," she replied.

"He's kind of old." Old wasn't right. Old was the only thing I could think of. That and the idea of him filling the hall behind us, a terrifying miracle of engineering, like a jet rolling into an alley.

"He's not *old*," she said.

I had the feeling I should say something. If I didn't say something then, I never could, because Kate would want to know why I hadn't said anything from the start. But often what feels implicitly true seems less true when you put it to words. Often things sound crazy. I didn't want to sound crazy.

"Is he a teacher?" I asked. Obviously he did not belong in a school, but it was hard to imagine him belonging anywhere. "Or an outside guy coming in?"

"An outside guy."

"For drama?"

"Uh huh."

"An actor?"

"I think so. The people who gave money for drama hired him. Once they visited with Alicia Ross's parents. They had a driver for their car."

Kate got up to put on a record. After the spongy opening lull came the crisp pops of the shiny black ring at the song's outer edge, then, magically, a guitar. It was Blind Faith, my favorite, one of them anyway. I thought she was trying to make me happy.

> *You are the reason I've been waiting all these years—*
> *Somebody holds the key*
> *Well, I'm near the end and I just ain't got the time*
> *And I'm wasted and I can't find my way home*

She sang along in her confectionery soprano and stood at the doors of her closet before a wall of meticulously folded garments coordinated in blocks of evolving color—cobalt to turquoise, coral to red, mocha to black. Kate could hunt for clothes with a transfixing resolve, making you think of Hollywood starlets. The bath towel slipped down the slope of her chest, scraping her nipples before dropping to the floor. I observed her talcum-coated body—the secure set of her neck upon the balanced outline of her spine, the milky skin.

Had she said that she *was* in love or that she *thought* she was? Somehow it made a difference. "Hey, Kate," I said. "Can you do this?"

She returned to the bed. She was buttoning a big shirt with one of those Mandarin collars like the Beatles used to wear. I pointed to the short haircut and she frowned. "It's totally layered, you know."

My eyes were closed and she was cutting. My head was connected to my shoulders and chest, so when she drew a comb-full of hair towards her, the rest of me went swayingly with it, which was hypnotic, which took me to the place of dreams, the place where they are manufactured, which in my mind is shaped like a tiny seahorse.

In grade school I had the prettiest hair and the longest. Girls would take turns braiding it during films about electricity or refracted light. While the teacher caught up on paperwork, we would sit on the cold grubby floor, awash in a sepia haze, listening to the methodic rattle and chop of the projector, our necks extended screen-ward to view the nonsense mechanics of current and charge and defracted rays. Scientific hands would tap dry cells and arrows would pulse through prisms. There would be hovering plus and minus signs and also the tingling feeling in my scalp. Nothing is so nice as being desired for a quality you irrefutably possess.

"It's not so sudden," she said, meaning Rourke. "It's been weeks."

I opened my eyes. In the bathroom mirror my eyes looked scared. Sometimes a thinking brain scares me.

"Is that enough," she asked, "or do you want to take off more?"

My hair came to my jaw like a swing bob. "More."

Her fingers kept capturing new sections, faster and faster. She would hold them with one hand and with the other she would snip, her head tilting affectedly, professionally. Her father had been a barber, and her aunt and uncle own a salon in France, in a city called Grasse. I closed my eyes again. Kate said hair is dead, but I could feel the scissors cutting. Maybe I only felt the sound.

"Any shorter and you might as well shave it," I heard her say.

She tossed her father's scissors into the sink, and they bridged the drain catch. I didn't like to see them that bridging way, so I moved them, and my arm looked lithe and muscular, beautiful as a tentacle. On the floor was my hair, a collection of pitiful commas. My hands moved to touch my head; no strand of hair was longer than three inches.

Kate sat on the toilet. "Oh my God. You look like a war prisoner."

I looked in the mirror. I liked how I looked—all eyes, all bones, my skin very, very fair. I looked as though I had survived something catastrophic. For the first time, I thought I could see myself.

She was crying. "I can't believe it," she kept saying. "I can't believe it."

I was probably supposed to tell her not to cry, that it was not her fault. But I could not come forward. I was not catatonic, just mildly insensate, as though the me to whom she addressed her regret was not me but a facade of me, something printed with a rendition of my features—and the essential me, the me I had just become, was out of her reach. I felt myself shrink back. I felt my vitality fly in reverse. I felt it obey some nameless command. I felt my soul abandon the cage of body and the prison of time to travel back through a tunnel of corpulent pulp, as if the point of greatest gravity was not my feet but my cerebellum.

I could see us from another place. I could perceive the shadowy contours of Kate and myself incarcerated at the elliptical mouth of that passage. I could perceive the boundaries of our gentle one-two configuration and, as well, the shimmering edges of her tears, but something colossal was guiding me back, insisting upon my withdrawal into its own indefinite space. I could not help her because I was already halfway to vanishing. I turned to the mirror with new eyes staring out like liquid dishes from hair that hid nothing.

THERE WAS THE ROLL of the garage door, then two quick raps. It was late. I came out from deep beneath my quilt and unlocked the lock.

"The living room lights are out," Jack said, brushing past. "I didn't want to wake Irene." He threw his jacket on the floor, then he turned and saw me. "Holy shit!" He dropped on the high end of my bed near the pillow. I dropped beside him. A long time passed, during which we mostly breathed. Jack snatched the spoon from a teacup on the bed table and he whacked it in his hand over and over. Then he began to slap it on his forehead instead. He asked me, "Did it leave a mark?"

"I think you have to do it harder for that. With the other side."

"Fuck it." He tossed the spoon back into the cup and looked to the floor. "It's pretty fucking short."

"You said to cut it. You said, '*Cut it short.*' "

"Yeah, well, I wasn't counting on short being so incredibly short."

"Let's not say *short* anymore." It sounded weird—*short.* The horsey way you have to drop your jaw. I crawled behind his back, drawing up the covers. I rubbed my legs together.

"Cold?" he asked.

I said that I was.

His eyes remained averted, though he moved closer. His hands reached for the collar of my sweater and he fussed with the top button, then he fastened it, fastening every next one all the way down, jerking me forward each time.

"I—don't—like—people—looking—at—you."

I didn't bother to argue. It only made things worse to argue with Jack. Furniture would break, or terra cotta pots would shatter, or he would disappear. Once he took off for days, and when he returned he had a huge gash on his left forearm. When my mother asked how it happened, he said, *fishing*.

I didn't even ask what he meant because I knew what he meant. It had been a strange day—a beginning, an ending, a measure of distance, impending and in reverse. None of us had been immune to the sweep of its effects, not me, not Kate, not Jack. I felt somewhat like a pet, a little bird, blinking dumbly at the just opened door of my cage. There was no point in reassuring them, in promising to go nowhere. Evidently they believed otherwise. They seemed to feel it would be asking a lot of me to defy my nature.

"I'm sorry," I said, kissing him. "Sorry for making you angry."

He raised his head, saying, "Okay, so let's see the new face."

Cᴀꜰᴇᴛᴇʀɪᴀ ᴛᴀʙʟᴇꜱ ᴀʀᴇ ʟᴀɪᴅ ɪɴ ꜱᴛʀᴀᴛᴇɢɪᴄ ʀᴏᴡꜱ ʟɪᴋᴇ ᴛʀᴇɴᴄʜᴇꜱ. ᴛʜᴀᴛ'ꜱ ɪɴ case they have to get *to* you fast, or get you *out* fast, or get away *from* you fast. Such are the dark inferences you learn to live with in high school. Madame Murat and Pat Egan, the one-armed shop teacher, circled the room, acting superior as prison guards. I wondered why they acted superior, since they were there just like we were there, only they'd been there longer and we were getting out first.

Jack and I were sitting by the windows in the northern corner. He was doing calculus, I was studying. Not exactly studying so much as staring at the patterns of text on the page, which were coming together and apart before my eyes like color pieces at the bottom of a kaleidoscope. At the table to our left, Peter Palumbo and Daryl Sackler lunged emphatically, playing that football game boys play with the triangular folded paper. To our right, girls with tipped-in shoulders and nodding breasts huddled together over brown bag lunches. Kip Madington flicked her mousey hair and took a bite from her sandwich. The compliant white bread flopped outward. Kip said, "I told him, 'Don't bother lying. I saw your car there. *Twice.*' "

Jack pulled at his lower lip. He leaned back in his chair, crossing one foot over the other knee like an Italian movie star, like when their jacket folds open and their tie splits apart and the fabric of their pants makes wrinkled keys on the inner thighs. Jack was not Italian, and the only tie he owned had flames painted on it, but he looked sexy nonetheless. I arched my back and reached behind my head and rotated my hands at the wrists, then I wriggled my hips down into my chair, into my jeans, and around.

Outside was raining like crazy. Sheets of water pounded the roof, going straight over the gutters, past the windows, and onto the saturated ground. I could see through the ashiness, past the parking lot, and into the sober queues of the potato fields on the opposite side of Long Lane. When it does not rain, the dust the fields produce is the color of sable and fine as talc.

The storm had started the night before at one-thirty in the morning. Twelve hours is a long time for a hard rain. It must have been a special rain, a monumental rain. I wanted to go into it with fanned-out arms, to bow and stomp and dance something similar to an Indian dance. I wanted to be touched by it and changed. It was rain to pray into, rain to save the world.

Jᴀᴄᴋ ᴀɴᴅ ɪ ʜᴀᴅ witnessed the very first drops. The water tapped like rat teeth at my bedroom window. Jack said, *Listen.* His head tilted curiously, like an animal's head. The beads of rain stuck to the glass as though pitched by arms. They grabbed hold from the side, beached and lonely. We stared in the manner of zombies.

"What time is it?" he asked.

I said, "One-thirty."

"I don't even feel tired. You feel tired?"

My head hurt and my eyes burned. My throat was sore. "A little tired, I guess, yeah." We'd been arguing for hours, though Jack refused to call it that.

"Disagreeing," he said, "is sufficient." Adding, "Strenuously."

"Are we *at odds?*"

"Yes," Jack nodded once. "We are at odds."

I did not like to be at odds with Jack. It was like being in a rowboat with only one person rowing. My oar would be raised, skimming the glassy lake, and Jack's would flail—digging too deep, flying too high, ticking spastically. It would take us forever to go nowhere.

I had certain feelings, I'd told him. "Inside. They need relief."

He peered through me as if to a minuscule spot on the wall.

I asked if he knew what I meant.

"Of course I know what you mean," he snapped. Then he reminded me emphatically that I was not an animal. "You are separated from depravity by a conscience."

Even if it was crazy to consider the activity of a few witless nerve endings as depraved, I did not take exception. Other girls hadn't mentioned such feelings, so I knew that I was at the very least abnormal. It was common knowledge that if a girl was assertive in regard to sex, it was because she wanted to keep a boyfriend or steal a boyfriend or act out against her parents. Possibly she craved togetherness. But I'd never heard of a girl who wished to alleviate the tingling sensations along the walls of her vagina, or at the posterior rim of its base, or in a third place, sort of an alcove where the seam of low underwear hits, only on the inside. No one ever spoke of seeing a boy or seeing a man and thinking thoughts.

"The job of the conscience," Jack was saying, "is to marshal urges. Otherwise, any object in your field of vision is eligible for fucking."

I thought he was missing the point.

"I'm not missing the point," he shouted. "It's not a particularly sophisticated point to miss."

Jack stood and did something he never did, which was to tuck in his shirt. His scaly hands crammed the fabric down in bunches as he began to pace. "Your problem is that you haven't read enough. If you'd done more reading, you'd realize that desire which moves from origin to fulfillment but circumvents the intellect is corrupted by compulsion. It's immoral and untrue—it's *feral.*" Feral was his new favorite word; he used it cleverly, sometimes three or four times a day without sounding repetitive. "Understand what I'm saying?"

I said, "Sort of."

"Be specific. What *don't* you understand?" He lifted a scallop shell from my desk and bit at its edge, gnawing at the corrugated reservoir of pink, dragging his lips across the veins that spread in a fan from the squared cap to the sheerest, translucent edge.

"I'm sorry," I said. I couldn't remember.

He cast the shell aside. It made a solitary clink when it hit the table, like a fork ringing out on glass. "You were saying you *sort of* understood."

"Oh. I was saying, even if longings are immoral, why are they untrue?"

"Because one *arrives* at truth, one cultivates it. Truth doesn't materialize instantaneously. So, how can it be true to go around satisfying impulses?"

"Imagine you're walking," I said, "and you get the urge to run."

"*Urge* is the operative word," Jack interrupted.

"Okay, fine. It's a *physical* urge or a *feral* urge—whatever. But instead of running, you think of all the things that running entails, like, whether you're wearing the right shoes, and what the neighbors might say, and what if you trip, and so on. If after all that thinking, you decide *not* to run, that decision would be impure. It would have come from fear—fear of judgment or failure. And if, after thinking, you decide *to* run, that choice would also be impure, coming from a wish to defy convention or to take a personal risk. So, you could say that the *first* feeling, the *truest* feeling, the physical, feral urge, is contaminated by secondary things, things coming from thought."

"Yeah," he said. "*So?*"

"I'm just saying, maybe urges start out okay, but it's the thinking afterwards that contorts everything."

"Wrong," Jack said. "*Circumstance* contorts everything. Urges are not needs, they are perversions of needs and are inseparable from circumstance. You can't discuss the urge to drive fast without presupposing the circumstance of a car. Or jumping from a plane without presupposing being in air. Or overeating if there's no food. An urge is like not being hungry but anyway you eat. It's like eating cake because cake is there. What if, instead of cake, there's celery sticks. Would your body manufacture the desire to eat celery sticks?"

"I don't know," I said. "Maybe." I happened to like celery.

"To the point that you would actually gorge on it?"

"Probably not."

"So is your urge to eat celery a *true* urge?"

I picked at the carpet. It was weird to argue about celery.

"Of course not," Jack answered for me. "An *urge* is relevant only in regard to *urge impetus*. The reason urges are untrue is because they change when circumstances change." He joined me on the floor.

I wasn't sure what it all had to do with sex anyway.

"Simple," he said. "You can't go out fucking every time you get the urge."

"Why do you keep saying *go out*? This is a conversation about you and me."

"No, this is a conversation about *you*." Jack gestured with somber hands. "Don't you see? Orgasm is secondary to intimacy. True bliss comes from the union of soul to soul. If you are driven strictly by the will to copulate, you are no more than a beast—unrefined, spiritually bankrupt, devoid of the capacity for distinction. You are *feral*," he concluded triumphantly.

I frowned and exhaled. I was thinking of church, of one type of church in particular, the old type we saw in France, where there are planes beyond your plane, where angels are glass and exquisite. In those churches the air is cold, and the floors and the walls are cold, and like a hive around your head is a musk that intoxicates. Your eyes cannot stray past imbricated walls and racks of tiny fires and vitreous cellophane mosaics that strain the sweat from the sun, that filter down the hugeness of the cosmos to a single flat emission. Light through a prism is oblique and dazzling—you are persuaded. You suspend disbelief. You accept the divine drama.

And yet, the moment you leave, all things ambrosial and supreme simply dissolve, and you are returned to the poise and counterpoise of repulsion and attraction. There are tulips—cherry reds and Dutch yellows, and music—an accordion. You turn back to the building sitting frozen still like a rabbit in the grass, winkingly watching you back, and you wonder, *What could I have been thinking?*

"Okay?" Jack asked, caressing my head. "Silly girl."

THE FALLING WATER FORMED a lead-like curtain on the outside of the cafeteria glass. Birds fluttered behind it, sheltered by the soffit beneath the roof. Birds are God's creatures, neither innocent nor profane. Their songs are not conscious or known, they're physical songs that come from the joy of being.

I leaned back and looked around. I let my chair drop. The metal legs and capped feet cracked against the floor, sending up a shock. "I'm gonna take a walk," I said. 'See you later."

"Later," he mumbled, going back to his books.

It's always a risk to stand when other people are sitting. Standing when other people are sitting makes you an object of gossip, especially if you are a gossip-worthy person, which I happen to be, and there is no sense trying to change the fact. Some people try to change the fact by being extra nice or helpful. Some people depress me.

I was fifteen when Tony Abbruscato taught me how to ward off the evil eye. "See that?" he said, one day when we were walking through Washington Square Park. "That bitch is giving you the evil eye. Quick, do this." He took my hand and curled all the fingers except the pointer and the pinky. "She don't have to see it," Tony advised. "You don't gotta point it at her—unless of course you want to. Just let your arm hang down, nice and casual, this way you protect yourself." As we passed the woman, he laughed in her face. "*Ha!*" he said, "comin' right back at ya, babe!"

I moved through a maze of tables, with each group going silent as I approached then snapping to action again as I passed, like a baseball wave. I held my hand the way Tony taught me. When I reached the table with Kiki and Pip and Coco, there was an outburst of laughter, probably about my hair. Not everyone liked my hair.

Dad said I looked like Mia Farrow in *Rosemary's Baby*. "Sort of big-eyed and eerie."

"*Eerie?*" Marilyn said defensively. "As in what?"

"I don't know, as in supernatural, as in ghostly."

"Like she's a ghost?"

Dad shrugged. "Anyway, like she can attract them."

THE DOORS OF THE gym were open. I could see the boys in the pine tar light, their bodies skidding like litter in a drunken wind. I made my way down the right side of the courts, through a corridor of idling forms waiting for the next game or recovering from the last. They nodded. I didn't mind the way they were, and they didn't mind me. What we meant was all that we were and all that we needed to be.

I sat on the last set of bleachers. The staccato back and forth of feet trampling the court shook the wooden stands. It must feel good to trample and to run undressed without fear of scrutiny, to be the legitimate heirs to such a definitive space as a gym. Sometimes you can feel sorry to be a woman, or at least you can forget why you're supposed to be so glad about it.

I leaned forward. My eyes blurred the margins of the bodies, factoring out details, homogenizing. The movement began to loop back on itself and to fuse amiably in pulses like plasma in biology films. I pushed my sleeves up because it was very hot. The veins in my arms were swollen and blue, salt was on my lips. Drops of sweat collected tentatively beneath my breasts and charged down my ribcage one at a time like street urchins through hydrant spray.

There was the piercing squelch of rubber. *Do it! Go! Go!*

The boys signaled with clapping hands or twitching heads, and when the guy with the ball was blocked, you figured he would hand off, but instead his jaw would relax, and his eyes would go stony, and he would pivot very low to cut past the rangy gate of arms that sought to obstruct him, and he would try the shot anyway. You had to admire the break-away risk. Break-away risk is the law of the sperm. They unify, but only to a point. That's why coaches enforce consolidation, to beat back the ego—*Keep your eyes on the prize!*

The wooden plank depressed alongside me—slowly creaking down, slowly easing up. I looked back and saw the man Kate had pointed to in the hallway. He came to sit behind me, knees on either side. He was wet and his chest was heaving. He must have come from running in the rain. There was a track out past the football fields, probably he had been on the track. Through his drenched shirt I could see the outline of his stomach. It was a square; it was several squares, linked. I thought I would like to touch it. I thought I already had. Didn't my hands possess the memory of his skin, hadn't my palms felt the heavy plan of his arms—beautiful rises, beautiful hollows?

His legs bounced. His soul was not quiet. He'd come to give me that message. He'd come because he felt entitled. I knew because I felt similarly entitled. He'd come because he had no choice; there was nowhere else to go. I knew that too. I also had nowhere.

The light cotton of his smoke-gray shorts revealed what I had never seen made so legible, a region of tenderness, and that made me proud and made me sad, which was strange, to feel proud that way, as if I were connected to him, as if I had some place in his supremacy. Sad because of course I did not. I looked to his face. It was king-like and balanced like the face of a large animal. The cheekbones were so prominent as nearly to hide the eyes, which were small, dark as carbon, but glassy, like lights were shining on them. His hair was black and dripping. Kate had said his name was Harrison, Harrison Rourke.

Someone screamed, *Let's go asshole, let's go!*

I did not turn back to the court. His nearness was miraculous. If I looked away, he would vanish. It was nothing I could explain; it was an old knowledge, a former proficiency. He seemed so familiar. Images of him and images of me hurled forth in florid gushes, whorling like cylinders of ash like dormant things revivifed, regaining dimension, spinning to life. And the world turned alive. Like an infusion of pink into a bloodless, bloodless blue.

I stayed very still, letting him regard me. He did not seem to be disgusted by what he saw. I closed my eyes and against the lids came a sorcerer's pageant—crescents and esses and batons, jubilant cubes wheeling on corners, helixes spiraling, spheres dropping in sure tugs like spiders coming down, and dewdrops in rows ascending like ladders to the clouds. To be near him, I felt truly, deeply happy.

When I was able, I went down cautiously into the empty gym. Reaching the end by the doors, I turned back. He had not moved. His elbows were on his knees, his head hanging down, his face turned to me. He was smiling.

12

It was the day before november. In november the sun draws back, sick of us, and the wind turns odious and overbold. Acorn casings batter skinny cement paths, and there is noise, woeful and inharmonious—the music of decay. November is fearless and volatile, with all the warrior objects of the world flexing to prove their might, with everything revealing its cryptic underside. I was born in November. I am of the month and of the battle.

I searched for myself among the birthdays I'd known. I could not connect all the versions of me when the link between those versions, in fact, was me at the particular moment of my thinking. Nothing was more whole or real than the attendant swerving of my mind. Yet, with the passage of each new second, the refuge of the present slipped from my reach to couple mordantly with the past. My soul kept shifting up, inching up, moving forth with the minutes, shunning cruel illusions of constancy.

Each of the sixteen days had the segregated, irrelevant quality of a bead sprung from a chain. Beyond some pathetic irreducibility, some unmovable glueish oneness, which had simply to do with my having been present when those days transpired, I could find nothing more than an attachment to the month itself, to November. It, above all things, had sheltered me. Though images of my mother and my father belonged to each province of my life, I could not recall the sensation of being held, not once, nor of being kissed. In my memories, my parents were twin figurines—simply man, simply woman.

At seventeen, I was bereft of skill and endowment. I knew no instrument, no sport, no language—none, other than the vernacular of art. All that was mine for me was some vague excellence at manufacturing and expressing feelings—great feelings of autonomy as ordained by my culture versus conflicting inside ones of loneliness, ambivalence, and confusion. I suppose that inside each of us there are primal emblems of better things and better ways, deep-seated intimations of real love. I suppose it is for these that we search.

Friends kept asking, "What do you want for your birthday?"

"Nothing," I would say. It would have made me a liar to receive courtesies that I could not in good conscience return. My appreciation for their generosity would be mixed with a type of pity, and gratitude plus pity is toxic. It would be wrong of me to invite others to commemorate the anniversary of my birth and to celebrate the fact of my existence as if there were some clarity to my character, some obvious overlap between the child I'd been and the woman I was to become, as if I were not on the verge of apostasy.

When I was four, I hid beneath the table during the singing and candles part because I wasn't sure what was expected of me. They seemed to expect something. My grandmother's head tilted when she looked under to call me out and all the fluid pooled to one side of her hanging face, blowing it up and turning it blue, proving for certain that beneath the skin is nothing, just loose stuff. She wore cat's eye glasses, black with rhinestones around the screws.

At seven, my birthday meant a new ski jacket and some games like *Hands Down* or *Mouse Trap*. When I was nine, my mother gave me a party, the only one she ever gave me, though I made the invitations and the cake myself. It was 1971 and I played freeze tag with school friends near an acorn tree on the neighbor's lawn. Acorns make me think of my birthday. Those spiny acorns with hooked stems that look like toy weapons, and if you fall on one you can really get hurt.

My mother's gift to me that ninth year was a stuffed whale that was gray with bells in its belly and a red corduroy tongue you could pull all the way out. After my friends left I sat on the front porch and held the whale. The bells made a plunking nursery rumble; possibly it was a baby toy. There is a sound I can remember, a birthday sound, which is the sound of those plunky bells being lifted by a November gust, skating high and away into the stippled pale between the trees, into the milk glass offing of Heaven.

I stood in the school foyer leaning onto the front door, waiting for the pep rally to begin. My camera swung, hitting the glass, which was wrong, but I couldn't bring myself to stop. Sometimes you get to feeling melancholy. You get to feeling you are very small crawling through tunnels that are big. Inside them you can only half-hear yourself think.

A BLUE MUSTANG REELED expertly into the school parking lot. Ray Trent and Mike Reynolds got out, their doors closing simultaneously—*boom-boom*. Ray and Mike were from Montauk. They had nice clothes and nice cars. Everyone said they sold drugs.

Troy Resnick disagreed. "I never bought drugs from them. They must run guns."

Jack said to shut up. "Why would they would blow their cover dealing to a douche bag like you?"

I didn't care what they did—they were always nice to me and to everyone and you could have a good time with them without getting molested. I knew because Ray had taken me to the Junior Prom.

He asked me on Valentine's Day, 1979. Jack and I were at lunch, working our way through a bag of cookies Denny had made for us. Denny was an awful cook. He always added ingredients off the recipe—spices, oils, herbs, whatever happened to be around.

"Perfect timing," Jack said when Ray arrived. "Dig in before we puke."

Ray dug into the bag and checked with Jack about asking me to the Prom. "Because I know *you're* not going, man."

Jack gnawed at a cookie. "Actually, Ray," he stated, "I'd love to go to the Prom, but I can't afford it. Lobotomies are expensive."

"What do you think, Evie?" Ray asked. "You up for it?"

I shrugged. "Okay."

"Cool," Ray nodded, then he took a bite. Instantly he gagged. "What the fuck is in these things?"

"*Nutmeg*," we said in unison as Denny came up the aisle with a loaded cafeteria tray.

"Ray's here?" Denny said. "Thank God I got six milks!"

Ray and I ended up having a great Prom night, dancing and mingling and driving around in the Mustang, which he'd just bought. I talked about my dad's sign shop and gypsy moth infestation, and he spoke of his sister Kerrie, who was a competitive gymnast, and the giant television set he and Mike had just picked up in Smithtown for Mike's eighty-two year old grandmother. Ray did offer me cocaine, but the proposal seemed more or less a courtesy, just in case I had certain expectations in regard to the evening. He didn't do any himself, not that I could see, nor did I once observe him exchanging packets for cash. After the breakfast party, he returned me safely to my house and kissed me goodbye, giving me his copy of *Terrapin Station*.

"Thanks for coming out with me," Ray said, "and thanks for not being afraid. Most girls in school are," he rattled his arms at hip height like he was pretend-spooked, "*whoa*, like, weird."

"Yeah," I said. Most girls in school were *whoa, like, weird*.

"You see the beauty in people, so people feel beautiful around you. You don't have any fears or hang-ups," he said. "You're all right."

Tempting as it was to contradict him, particularly in regard to fears and hang-ups, I said nothing. It's impolite to refute a compliment. When people need to be nice, you must let them. You must force yourself. Practice.

I hid behind a square brick pillar on the school steps. Through my telephoto, I followed Ray and Mike as they eased around fenders and hoods, swiveling their narrow hips. They were wearing business suits. Halloween costumes probably. Mike banged on the fender of a muddy Dodge Dart and a girl in an aggregate of shredded purple rayon bounded from the passenger side, Instamatic in hand. It was Laura Migliore, also from Montauk, dressed as Stevie Nicks. Laura passed her half-spent cigarette back through the open window to the invisible driver and she waved one witchy arm, directing Ray and Mike to come together for a photo. I got a shot of her taking a shot of them and a few more of Ray leaning on the car, bending furtively to talk to the driver, with Mike flanking him protectively, staring into the fields. Mr. Cuneo, the algebra teacher, called the fields *lots*. He was always talking about having grown up in the potato *lots*.

The boys came up the school steps handsomely, ignoring the leafy particles that whipped their ankles and halfway mounted the lengths of their legs.

"Hey, hey, it's the beach bunny," Mike said, referring to a day I'd spent in Montauk, the day I lied to Kate and took a break from going to the hospital to see her mom.

Ray and Mike had found me at the beach seeming sad, so they tried to cheer me. They bought me espadrilles and a sundress at the Surf Shop since I'd come by train in my bathing suit and shorts. We went to Ray's boat for sunset, the Yacht Club for dinner, and to Tipperary for darts. Ray and I spent the night on the boat and in the morning had brunch at the Royale Fish in Amagansett. We ate challah bread French toast covered with powdered sugar. I didn't feel guilty since it ended up being a good time when I needed one, and I was grateful to the someone somewhere who had taken pity on me and sent relief in the form of friends and fun. *Someone Somewhere*—people like to say that as though it means something other than God.

Ray held the door for me. "Where's your costume, Evie?"

"Don't tell me," Mike said. "You're a private detective."

"You better go easy on the eye-spy stuff," Ray teased. "I don't want to have to buy you a new camera when Mike busts that one."

A crowd of kids was cramming into the gymnasium, and we joined them. I didn't want to, but I didn't have a choice. I felt depressed about that, about the paucity of choices and the depressing state of things in general. I walked on witlessly and cultishly, like a member of some lunatic woodsy society. When we passed through the arch into the packed gym, I ducked, though the ceiling was far away.

Ray threw one arm around me and with the other tousled my hair. "That's some chop job," he said over the shouting. "Very sexy."

"You working," Mike shouted too. "Or you wanna sit?"

"Working," I yelled, though that was not entirely true.

There was never a shortage of Halloween pictures, but I'd assigned myself anyway because it gave me an excuse to wear regular clothes and skip classes. I spent the day reading *Pride and Prejudice* in the bathrooms and drinking coffee with the cafeteria workers and cleaning the inside of Kate's car. Kate's car was always filthy. I could not deal with Coneheads playing the trumpet and life-sized pairs of dice taking trigonometry tests and strangled ogres browsing through the Dewey Decimal catalog. Halloween makes me nervous—the way customarily nondescript people use the opportunity to dress up and act badly. All the office ladies had fake fangs. Even Mr. Hartman, the nicest of all the janitors, was wearing a tousled blue-black wig.

Denny said he was supposed to be Joey Ramone.

"But he's black," I said.

"Yeah," Denny said, "so what?"

"Well, do black people even listen to the Ramones?" I figured they had better taste than that.

As Ray and Mike waved and walked off, I called out, "What are you guys supposed to be, anyway?"

"Ourselves," Mike hollered, "in a couple years."

After taking photographs of the teacher heads staring unflinchingly into the maniacal teenage horde, I withdrew to the wall beneath the basketball hoops, climbing onto a stack of folded exercise mats. Each grade filled its own section of bleachers, then the cheerleaders emerged to lead the competition for school spirit, which was another way of saying who could make the most noise. The girls burst into the center of the gym, flipping and shaking and triple high-kicking. They performed their two best cheers with incomparable gusto, then came that Queen chant—*We will, we will, rock you*.

Everyone joined in, stomping their feet, one, then the other, ending with a clap—one-two, *three*, one-two, *three*. I searched for Ray and Mike through my telephoto lens. They were at the base of the senior section, talking nonchalantly, as if they happened to have met on the street in Lisbon. I didn't know why Lisbon, except to say there was something Portuguese about the interaction, something streetwise and baroque. It relieved me to see them, like there was nothing in the world to be afraid of. I wondered why I chose Jack instead of Ray, when Ray was good-looking and polite and much better to sleep with than Jack, and he had a car instead of a bike.

One by one, football players were jogging out in full uniform and grease paint, coming together in bungling formation before the screeching multitude. After one final gargantuan roar, everyone began to descend to the gym floor, and the whole frenetic assembly urged itself to the doors, eager for an early dismissal, eager to go home and sit around and sneak booze and wait for night, when the business of the street would begin. In drug stores and delis, there would be a run on shaving cream and eggs. Directly beneath me was an elliptical band of teachers and assorted grown-ups moving first through the doors, and then, behind them, in the immense center of the room, a breathing plane of faces and balloons, a colored cloud, kind of percolating.

Suddenly it all went white—the flash from a camera blinded me. By the time everything turned normal again, whoever had taken the picture was gone. My back cascaded down the wall, I jumped off the mats, and joined the crowd, allowing myself to be transported in a swilling back and forth motion, until I was ejected into the wide lobby.

Kate appeared, running up to me. "Did you see him?" Her massive hoop earrings clanked. Kate was a gypsy. Not a gypsy, a *bohemian*.

"See who?"

"Harrison. C'mon!" She took off down the hallway, dragging me. "Let's see if he posted the roles. Hurry!" Once the auditorium doors were in sight, Kate squealed. The list was there. She spun and buried her face on me. "Oh my God, Evie, I think I got it."

I hugged her. Her eyes were closed, screwed up tight in their sockets, like lavender bottle caps. We were like finalists in a beauty pageant—Kate's breath on my face, the cushiony weight of her breasts against my breasts, the rosewater fragrance of her hair.

"Wait a minute," I said. "I'll go check."

On the door was a sheet of yellow legal paper carelessly taped. It hung tilted to the right as though it had come in forcefully from the left. The letters were blocky and sure, the ink was red. As I dragged my free hand down the page, I was overcome by an inexplicable fascination with the architecture of the handwriting, with its reservoirs and alcoves, with the straked indentations made by the salient pressure of Rourke's pen.

"Did you find it?" Kate asked.

"Not yet," I murmured, reaching again for the top, mesmerized.

"Come on," she stomped.

"Oh," I said, "here it is." I traced the grain of the letters. Rourke had pressed so hard, I didn't need my eyes to read. "Ready?" I asked, stalling once more. "Emily Webb...Kate Cassirer."

Her eyes popped open. "Told you," she whispered.

She leaned back against the wall. I observed her from across the portal; I was thinking what to say. I was probably supposed to say something. It was weird, but I didn't feel as glad for her as I had at first, when we were hugging. All I could think was that he had written her name.

"Well," I said, "you worked hard. You deserve it."

Then I nodded for no reason, the way people do, when they pull their lips slightly into their mouths and set aside the magnitude of their own very exceptional feelings. My left fingers remained on the paper, feeling every crease and notch for the pressure of his hand, the breadth of his wrist, the bulk of his forearm, as if I could detect within the pooling contours and crested impressions of Kate's name a message to myself.

13

SEVERAL THINGS HAPPENED AT ONCE. JACK SLID THE BARN DOOR OPEN. HIS arm in a scarlet windbreaker jerked right, two times, like a madman reloading a rifle. I led the way into darkness, darkness changed to light, and light came down, and, suddenly, all the faces.

A chorus of voices screamed, *Surprise!* A chorus is a lot; I would not have thought I knew a chorus. A beer landed in my hand. There was music, that birthday song by the Beatles. Damp lips grazed my face and many hands held me. Aromatic gusts in my mouth, personal gusts. *Happy Birthday Evie! Congratulations!*

Kate steered me into the lurching pack. "Surprised?"

I reached back for Jack; he was gone. Others filled the spot alongside me, the spot that belonged to him, and through their otherish bodies, I could see him receding. He was going back out through the barn door. Troy was with him. I felt a bad feeling in my stomach. Like a metal marble at the high valve. Like Jack would come back stoned or tripping.

On the top of the stack of gifts was something from my mother. It was wrapped in the same paper she'd used on other things she'd given me. I picked it up because I did not like to see it stranded there. A paper heart was on top. She'd cut it herself, which depressed me.

> *For my Eveline. Have fun at your party.*
> *I love you, Mommy.*

Inside was a pair of flower barrettes from the drug store. When I was a little girl, she would bring barrettes whenever she'd been to fill a prescription.

"Which hand?" she would ask, keeping both behind her back. I would point dutifully to one side, and she would smile, bringing the hand I'd chosen around and playfully exposing its emptiness. No matter which hand I chose, the gift was in the other. It was a game she liked to play. I liked when she played that game.

"Hey!" Lisa Tobias snatched the barrettes, lifting them like a dead fox over her head. "Look at this! She can't even wait until cake!"

Denny lunged for the clips and gave them back to me. "Leave her alone, you barbarian."

"They're barrettes, Denny," Kate said. "Lisa won't *break* them."

Denny ignored Kate. "*I'll* take you around. Okay, honey?"

Lots of people were there—Jack's friends and Kate's and Denny's, and a few who could possibly be classified as mine, like Ray and Mike and Marty from the yearbook and several cheerleaders. Part of my brain, the thinking part, which is a revolving metal cone angled out like an observatory telescope, appreciated everyone's excellent intentions. But the remainder, the loose piles of random brain shavings and brain bits, feared the lazy swag of streamers and the humiliated balloons and the smell of spilled beer on the buckling barn floor. By the time Denny and I reached the back, I had a headache. It felt like a yellow corn-cob holder was jammed into the bone above my eyebrow, sticking out like a dart.

When Jack returned, he didn't seem high, he seemed okay. I burrowed under his jacket, hiding there. He handed me a beer.

"It's okay," I said. "I still have one."

"Well," he said, "now you have two."

We were interrupted by a loud laser beat—*zung, zung, zung*. Then plunging whistles, tripping bweeps, manufactured claps, aboriginal whoops, and the deep fishy vociferousness of disco. Jack threw his palms over his ears. His ears were sensitive to disco and also to polka.

Denny had changed the album. "*Let's go!*" he called.

"What *is* this?" Dan Lewis asked. He raised his tousled head and furrowed his brows as though trying to discern one particular ingredient in a complex stew. He was on the ladder to the loft, rewiring a broken light. He shoved his glasses up with his wrist.

"It's the fucking Sal Soul Orchestra!" Jack complained bitterly.

"Actually," I said, "I think it's Parliament."

"Whatever," Jack said, "it's gotta go."

I grabbed him as he walked off, telling him to wait. "Maybe it will keep them, you know, occupied."

Jack relented—partly because it was my birthday, partly because it pleased him when I was intolerant of others. He wrapped his arms about me from behind and together we gazed at the shocking and incongruous sight of disco dancers in the barn, which was somewhat like watching your house burn to the ground from the opposite side of the street. Aunt Lowie always says the two biggest concerns about throwing a party are worrying that no one will come, then worrying that they'll never leave.

Denny wanted me to dance. He loved to show off what we'd learned from Uncle Archer. Denny's uncle was a retired Broadway choreographer. We'd been taking regular lessons ever since *Saturday Night Fever*.

"Maybe later," I said.

"Go ahead," Jack insisted, though he didn't mean it. He hated to see me dance in public. He'd only gone to a disco with me once. When he saw me and Mike Stern dancing to "Brickhouse" on the platform at Mellowmouth, he had some kind of an optic seizure. His left eye stayed bloodshot for days.

"What's an *optic seizure?*" Kate had asked afterwards.

"I guess your blood pressure goes up and your veins pop."

"That's a stroke!" she'd exclaimed.

"Yeah," I'd said, "I guess it is."

Through the writhing trunks and ticking heads, I noticed what appeared to be a cardboard playhouse. "What's that?" I asked Jack, and I wiggled past the loose gate of his arms.

"What's what?" he volleyed apathetically, and he leaned down to light a cigarette. I crossed the room. The dancers retreated to create a moving aisle. Against the wall near the door was a refrigerator box with a window cut into the center of its face. Painted above the hole was a brief message in cuneiform letters: *To Evie from Jack.* The writing looked like spilled nails, magnetized.

There was clapping. Voices calling, *Open it, open it.*

I lifted the flap. Hanging from a pink ribbon, the ribbed kind you can curl with the edge of a scissors, in the dead center of the overcast box was a limp balloon—not limp, unblown. The path back to Jack was meaningfully unobstructed. He stood as I'd left him, leaning to his right, smoking his cigarette. I touched the balloon tentatively. Inside was something resistant.

"Pull it off," Denny yelled.

I didn't want to. It seemed content to dangle within the cavernous safety of its house. I hated to be the one to introduce it to chaos. I closed my fist around the string.

"Don't just stand there," Kate said, "*open it.* Aren't you curious?"

I shook my head. I was not curious. I knew exactly what it was.

"HEY LISTEN," JACK SAID, "a warbler."

We reclined in the sun on a wooden footbridge in back of the nature trail. We hung by our backs from the belly of the earth. We weighed a flawless weight, a liquid and consequent weight like cylinders half-filled and lying on sides. We were essence and anima, inchoate and divine, complementary and dilute. We were shapes fitting shapes in a universe that was a soft-side maze.

If ever you were outside with Jack, you would know the feeling—your heart would be stable and your body could spring if you wished and you could drop back in space and be caught. You would feel yourself perfectly composed and fundamentally necessary, respectful to laws long forgotten, native laws. You would feel like a column beneath the natural entablature.

My eyes were closed. I imagined he was walking—*Listen*, he said as he came, impeded only slightly by the thick gel of my imagination. One leg hitting down, then the other, crashing dully, *a warbler.*

How beautiful he was, how striking and direct. How good it must have felt to be him, so free in the frame, so intellectually capable and morally sure. The way his pronunciation was clear, the way his ideas were clever, the way his indignity switched over into language. To know Jack was to wonder at his integrity and to know there would never again be anyone like him. I love him, I thought. I will always love him.

"There it is Evie, look."

I opened my eyes. Jack's hand was thrust into the air, bobbing wretchedly to chase the able bird. The minute and mortal reach of his limb depressed me awfully. We did not levitate against the arc of the planet as I'd thought—we were mired in circumstance. There was something about the love that did not transfer well from the mind.

"Jack," I said, but before I could say more, he stopped me.

He pressed his forehead to mine. "The way you say my name. I hear myself in it."

Though I should have felt happy, instead I felt impeded by my influence. I remember wanting to say something but not wanting to hurt him. Of course, saying nothing constituted the worst sort of betrayal. Oh my God, I thought—Jack, me—the tragedy of us.

We returned to town through a sudden early darkness, with my hand in his coat pocket and the seam of the pouch cutting against my wrist. Main Street seemed particularly immense that night. The casements of dormant stores were indistinguishable, and they were flat, like screens of stores or projections of stores parted by slender alleys and wandlike stripes of paint.

The architecture of East Hampton is colonial; *colonial* is like *colony*. We study colonies in science and history. Colonies are systems of incestuous interdependency. A beehive is a colony. Bees like the hive to be a certain way, so it becomes impractical for a bee to live elsewhere. Bees need the bees to stay and work for the whole of the hive. A colony is a team, like villages and bees and cancer. *The breast cancer has colonized in her lungs*, Dr. Richter said of Maman.

In front of Rose Jeweler's I stopped. In the window I saw one of Jack's eyes—an iridescent egg-shaped opal framed by a brocade of gold and attached to a chain-like thread. The necklace rested securely in the cinched center of a plush sapphirine cushion, like a bug in your palm, like one of Jack's eyes.

"What is it?" he asked, turning back. His eyes joining the jewel in the glass, all three swimming.

I couldn't help myself. I was confused by love, and I began to cry.

"What is it?" he asked again.

"Don't you see," I said, "I couldn't go by."

I PULLED OUT THE necklace, and Jack was there. He was placing his cigarette in his mouth, he was removing the chain from my hands, unclasping it, hanging it about my neck, arranging it on my collarbone. I felt its frail burden. I did not like the bubbling sputters the people made. I did not like the thoughts they were likely thinking. They felt they knew things when really they knew nothing, not about the warbler or the eye, not about Rourke.

Speech, speech!

I said nothing, and I looked out like I didn't know them as much as they didn't know me. Jack's lips met mine. His kiss was dispossessed of dimension.

"Here," he said, handing me something small. I swallowed it.

When quiet came, it came loudly, like an explosion of quiet and an avalanche of nothingness, which is strange when you think about quiet that way. The ambient noise of the party flattened down like a stone into the bed of a brook and the quiet was like water running around the stone on either side, fast like antlers or the horns of the bull and the stone was the head. I was thinking of sand, soaked and black, and shallow fast water.

Denny was laying gifts on my lap and all the people were gone. Okay, okay, he kept saying to no one, to no one in particular, hold on, and, I'm not ready, or I'm coming.

Kate was there on the floor, me on the bench, and Jack across the room leaning against a broken dresser. Jack was watching me with the living dead look of a portrait. I wondered what it was in me that always interested him so.

Denny collapsed next to Kate. He was so exhausted. I thought maybe he should sleep. Maybe he should lie and I would lie too and I would pull the threads from the hem of his dress shirt and say all the things I never said. That I loved him. That my love for him was a tactile love like things everywhere blossomed, like a field of flowers. That it didn't matter to me that he was gay, which I'd never said, which of course I did not have to say, but I wanted to say because life is complicated and clarity is rare. I wanted to tell him he did not need to hide himself from me. I wanted to name the love we shared before it was lost— I was afraid, I don't know, just afraid, and that fear brought a dilating grief. I wanted to know that I thought he was chivalrous and handsome. That he was the best friend I would ever have and I knew it.

Save the ribbon, Denny said with a wink. I'll make you a hat.

I pushed my back against the wall and bit at the rubber tag of my tongue. It was time to open gifts. Everything felt a little imperious, a little rigid but also floaty, like a Japanese tea ceremony though of course I'd never been to one or been to Japan. I wondered would I ever get to Japan. Denny and Kate were at my feet, Jack remained at the dresser. Packages were coming apart, their innards passing off to the right and the left before I could see. I couldn't see.

Don't worry, Kate said, I'm making a list.

Open the heavy one, Denny said. It's from me.

It was a *Janson History of Art*. Between the gray twill covers, the lustrous sheets proclaimed a distance between the art and my body. The distance was a snobbish distance because scholarship is a privilege. Newspapers are cheap with leaking ink because they are supposedly local and economical and insurgent, as if they have been made in basements by the thinking people you know. My palms swirled over and over on the pages—cool and superior. Repellent.

I thanked Denny, I thought I did, I definitely did because he nodded several times, and he blew a kind of kiss. He was eating a baked potato. I did not know where it'd come from. When he lifted it, it sagged in the center and curled at the edges like a canoe.

Now mine, Kate said, handing me a box with silver wrap and inside was a rust-red cashmere sweater—Maman's. I drew it to my skin, breathing deeply. I was not trying to recall Claire's smell or how it had felt to hold her. It did not even sicken me to consider that I could no longer remember. I just liked the shield the sweater made, the way I could hide behind the barrier with no one seeing me. Maybe that was incorrect. Maybe they were seeing, but I was not seeing, which was a scary thought and I dropped the sweater down. Denny and Kate still had not moved, their faces were moons at my knees. Jack was in the same place too, though surely hours had passed. Did Jack feel what I felt when what I felt was so very high. Did he feel he wanted to move but could not, that his legs were sponge. But no I was wrong, they were moving, I could see them rise up like puppets being lifted by hands that were not there, and me going too.

Denny surrounded me with bear arms. *Oh, honey.* Kate's hand light on my shoulder. I thanked them, me thanking them both, for everything.

We were alone. I told Jack I wanted to dance.

He said, "Oh shit."

I careened to the stereo like a skidding vehicle and shuffled through the horizontal strip of records, lined up long like a coffin, a child's coffin. I was flicking them *left, left, left.* Going fast to find the perfect album. I wanted it *instantly.* Not instantly, *previously.* Instantly was too late. Drugs make you crazy about time. Drug time is a window between the moment you feel high and the moment you feel *less* high. I flung unwanted records into a pile that swirled like cocktail napkins on a bar, like a dodecahedron.

Not a dodecahedron, Jack said. That's a twelve-sided polygon.

A Chinese lantern. I meant to say Chinese lantern.

You meant to say a conical spiraling thing.

I found a record. I pulled it from its jacket.

What did you pick? Bee Gees?

Etta James, I said.

Cool. Play Plum Nuts.

I dropped the arm over the turntable. The needle slipped, making a choking parrot sound. Jesus, Jack said, take it easy.

The atmosphere was watery. As I danced, I felt the wiggly pressurized feeling of diving to the bottom of a pool, then swimming rapidly to the top. The feeling when your hair sweeps back from your skull and your arms are limp like fins that trail the central chesty force of your movement. I felt elastic and wet like a cheerful dolphin. In the water you don't worry about the action of your hands, hands always feel engaged in water. I was dancing, making figure eights, using all my muscles, going ever so slightly up and down. I felt engaged.

> *Well I'm plum, plum, plum, plu-u-m—*
> *You know I'm plum nuts over you.*

Jack sat on the table, his feet propped on a chair. He was carving a candle with a cake knife. Evil hips, he murmured. You didn't learn that from me.

Later we were lying in the center of the room, overlapping. I could not tell where I ended and Jack began. We were two halves of something same, each of us companionless—for all that we were, we were nothing that we were not. I wished Denny had stayed, his stomach made a nice pillow. I sighed sadly.

Jack asked what happened to the cheerful dolphin.

I miss Dennis, I said.

To make me happy Jack put on the *White Album*. I'd left it on the dashboard in summer and the vinyl had warped into wide scalloped waves that bubbled hypnotically off the turntable. The record circled lazily, up and down, up and down, making benign boatish heaves. It was like listening to a Hawaiian flower. My head was on Jack's shoulder. If I closed one eye, the zipper tag dangling from the neck of his sweater became a skyscraper in the tiny, tiny room. Pigs were snorting, that meant next came Rocky Raccoon.

I asked him please to sing. He said to wait for Julia.

He fed me a piece of my birthday cake, breaking up humid stuff and pressing bits into my mouth. It tasted like box cake with crackled tricks inside; they could have been anything, since Denny made it. Once he filled a cake with Barbie shoes. Also the cake was cold. Maybe it was cold because the barn was unheated. Maybe I was cold as well, only I could not feel cold. I did not like being numb like cake. Like a comestible. I spit out the stuff in my mouth. It landed on the floor and I looked at it. My mouth had transformed the food from black into trenchy brown, and the depiction of that internal operation nauseated me.

Don't leave, I said to Jack as I dropped back.

Never, he promised.

The floor near my legs creaked eerily. Jack was kneeling over my belly to make a bridge with his groin, and his hunched body cast a huge shadow. When Julia came he did not sing. I tried to say this, but nothing came out. I rattled my head all the way from one side to another in gross spastic sweeps, I was not sure why, except to say that my head was my only mobile part.

What's that, baby, Jack asked without really asking.

I couldn't remember, though I knew it had been important. I did not like him to call me baby. Something, I said.

I thought I felt him undressing me. I thought I felt the rimy wind pass through the tunnel made by the small of my back arching off the filthy plank floor. I thought I felt his fingertips touch the recesses beneath my hipbones. He may have had sex with me. I thought he did, I wasn't sure.

THREE

TRACKS

*His face reveals what any face should reveal—the non-existence of banality
in human beings—those eyes, those cheekbones, those lips.*
—Julie Kristeva

*I know another's secret but do not reveal it and he knows that I know, but
does not acknowledge it: the intensity between us is simply this secret about the secret.*
—Jean Baudrillard

WINTER & SPRING 1980

I.

*I AM IN A ROOM, HIGH, NEAR BEAMS THAT ARE EXPOSED. THE BACK OF MY HEAD
smacks the ceiling and hair that is not my hair hangs around my face like screwed straw
or blindworms or tails of chameleons unfurling and coiling just partially back. There is
no motion, no time—no—there is time, time fallen off its continuum, like gears that have
skipped intervals and forged down to a mangled silence. I am kept up, pushed up, by
what I do not know. On one beam there is writing, code writing, a wicked code, legible
to me. And so I am wicked, I think; yes, I think I must be wicked.*

MY EYES OPENED FROM the dream precisely as day gave way to dark. The twilight seemed robust when I felt feeble, so I lay in bed and waited for people
to come home and switch on appliances. I wanted all the machines to be on.
I did not like the way equipment was sitting out, arrogant and fat and proving through muteness that everyone was elsewhere, involved with other
things, personal things, things separate from me. They were wrong to lea
me on my own, negligent and careless with the way trouble seemed to seek
me out. I switched on the lamp and retrieved a note from Jack that wa
beneath it. The crumpled paper circled in my palms, chasing it's way open.
Faded penciled letters were wedged between the blue rules, strung together
and nearly indecipherable. There were words, certain words—*love* and *me* and
mystery, also *key* and *sleep*. Yellow lamplight soaked the gray page. I did not like
the combination of yellow and gray, the way it is timid like carnival elephants.
    I fell back onto the mattress, sideways and down, dropping Jack's note on
the floor. My quilt felt fleecy around my neck, and I nestled into the pillow.

Clams and mussels burrow into the floor of the bay, and they listen from their beds of sand to the clamoring of the sea above, the way it clamors like rolling potent clouds.

THAT MORNING I SAW him in town. Through the picture window of Long Island Sound, I saw him. He must have been shopping for something; I was shopping too.

There was no reason to turn from what I'd been doing, I was not sure how I knew to turn, but I did, and when I did, Rourke was there, staring incautiously. He seemed bewildered by me or provoked. He was wearing a navy blue down jacket that yielded obediently to his body, and his right hand was crammed halfway inside his jeans pocket. Beneath his open coat was a dark green shirt with several unfastened buttons, and the waist of his pants came low around his hips. His black hair was wavy, tousled.

I smiled. He did not smile back. He reached for the front door, which whooshed open, then clattered to a positive close. I returned to the wall of albums, feeling a futile feeling of waiting, like when there's no avoiding the thing you're waiting for. If I tried to leave the store, he would watch my body on the way out, the way my legs and my ass were bound in my jeans. I slipped behind a display rack.

He struck up an incidental conversation with Eddie, the record store guy. As they spoke, Rourke kept taking pieces of something from his hand, nuts maybe or candy, and eating them. His jaw moved in even claps and the muscles at the base of his hollow cheeks flexed into knots. He had not shaved.

"It's definitely inferior," Eddie was saying.

"Yeah, it's crap," Rourke agreed, and from his coat pocket he withdrew a bottle of lime-green Gatorade, raised it to his lips and drank. There was something especially sexy about the random way he was dressed, making it easy to imagine him in bed that morning, thinking thoughts as I had, jerking off probably, then deciding to alleviate a morning's boredom by going into town for a while. I flipped mechanically through the section of albums marked *S* and allowed myself to imagine that I'd been home with him, wherever it was that his home may have been.

Eddie had mottled red facial hair that could not be called a mustache and could not be called a beard, yet it was undeniably a little of both. He was much scrawnier next to Rourke than Jack, practically like a voodoo doll. His badly scarred skin and arched eyebrows were visible to me just above the albums in the wooden aisle dividers as he led Rourke down the row by mine. When Rourke walked, his chest inclined casually back and his legs stretched forward and his stride was smooth but resolute, expressing direction and also resistance of direction. They drifted to a halt at the *P*'s, facing me. I lowered my head over the record well and pretended to read.

"These guys are strongly influenced by McGuinn," Eddie said. Eddie had an incomparable aptitude for music. The store had an *Ask Eddie* lockbox for questions. Answers got posted on a white board by the register. Everyone took the process very seriously, especially Jack, who regarded the system as something along the lines of *Ask God.*

"Yeah," Rourke said, his voice slipping away from Eddie, moving sinuously, calling to me, calling inaudibly.

His eyes held new worlds. All the fractions and features of the ghetto about me disintegrated, leaving me alone, with him alone, and between us a circle, not a circle, a fragment of a circle, a modest vault or treasury that seemed to possess the full meaning of pretty much everything. My heart began to beat rapidly and irregularly, hitting the underwire beneath my left breast. I adjusted my bra because I did not like to feel the beat of my heart, the way the blurps were so miniature, the way the organ strived but failed to be timely. Weeks had elapsed since I'd seen him last, and, though I'd thought of him, those weeks had not hurt my mood or disposition. Yet having him before me, I knew I'd been deprived.

I recalled the way he'd watched me through the store window—I too was provoked by the sight of him. I was irritated by his interest and confused by my desire and sobered by our impotence in respect to circumstance. It's hard to describe what happened in those moments except to say that we stepped out equally, we confessed equally, we were rendered equally weak, and as weakened equals we met, victoriously, at some median of daring and possibility.

I was thinking, *I must, oh you know, say something.*

Eddie handed a Tom Petty album to Rourke. Rourke's eyes left mine, and right away the two men returned to the front. I realized I'd been looking at the Supertramp section. I moved on.

Rourke paid and while he waited for change, he held his wallet between his teeth and yanked his pants up by the belt loops. Eddie inquired about Rourke's New Year's plans. I could not hear the answer as the music was very loud. Probably his plans involved a girl.

You're all I've got tonight. You're all I've got tonight.

When he left, he just left, with his head high and his eyes steady on their course, causing me to wonder if he didn't pity me for my naïve infatuation.

FIRST SHE KNOCKED, THEN she just came in and her coat was still on. I was in bed. I would be there forever, forever in bed.

"I'm sorry," Kate said. "Were you napping?"

I asked her to put the radio on, and she said okay and in a minute the radio burst to life. It had been broadcasting all afternoon, transmitting to moving bodies, bodies in kitchens and cars. I'd missed so much. My wrists rubbed my face. Impure stuff blew through my opened door and settled on my skin—dust maybe, cat hair or cigarette smoke or mold. Possibly something rotten in the refrigerator, a lemon or some ham.

"I was at the movies," she said. "With Harrison."

I was surprised. I couldn't help it. Sometimes Kate surprised me.

"Actually, he was in the middle of the theater, so we asked if we could sit with him. Not the middle, but up a bit, by the aisle."

"Who's *we*," I asked.

"Michelle. Michelle was with me." She played with the zipper on her parka. "He said he saw you in the record store. Did you see him?"

"It was pretty crowded."

"He said you never say hello."

"I don't really know him."

"Well, he knows you," she said. "You should try to be nice."

There is a way to become invisible. Nargis taught me how. There is a river of electrical energy in your frame, and you have only to locate its orbit with your mind's eye then trail it precisely as you decline into it. I situated my entire awareness on a single blunt and probing lead, like a divining rod or one of those trick dog leashes. Directly I was leaving, I was leaving, descending and inverting in broad and buttery swipes, pulses in white pulses, feet over face, my voice saying *Ssshh, ssshh,* blocking with sound each aspect of Rourke that threatened to present itself.

The memory of him proved too powerful to erase. I thought of the effortless way he'd been dressed, the lazy curl of his hair, the hidden influence of his body beneath his partly unfastened shirt. I felt a rubbery kind of ache, an internal exertion like a solitary light, like a beacon cast from a miner's helmet, a light swinging in an indolent arc back and forth across the cavernous flesh of my underbelly. The muscles between my legs squeezed to hold nothing, and I felt a preliminary shiver in my groin, a stiff rise in my hips, a begging pull that crawled up the alley of my back, elbow to elbow, like a grimy legless soldier squirming for cover.

"Listen," I said, trying to think of her name. "Kate. Let's just drop it."

"My God," she said, "what did he ever do to you?"

We sat and sat for a long time. I wondered was she sweating beneath the bulk of her coat. She looked like she might be sweating. I toyed with Jack's letter. The letter had made it to my house, my bedroom, my hand. He did not write to communicate. He wrote to exercise privilege, to stake territory. The letter was proof of intimacy. Symbols make abstracts real—rings prove love and deeds prove ownership and certificates prove you were born. Autographs prove you know a celebrity. "A stand-up guy," Dad and Tony will say of Paul Newman. They'd waited behind him on line once in a Chelsea deli. In the sign shop a framed napkin hung next to the first fifty they'd made—*To Tony and Anton at A & A Signs, the best signs of the times—Paul Newman.* "Drinks Bud," Dad says, "none of that imported shit."

Kate said Rourke said he saw me; he told her I never say hello. Rourke did not exactly lie to her, but he did not exactly tell the truth either. He spoke in code to reach me, or so I thought. I had no proof.

"You coming to Coco's New Year's party?" she asked. "Please." Her voice was girlish, breathy and pleading. "I don't want to go alone."

I gestured to my throat. "I'm a little sick. Thanks anyway."

"Come upstairs then and help me get dressed."

BETWEEN THE TWIN CLOSETS in her room, there was an alcove and, squarely in its center, a window. I sat and propped my feet against the sill and looked into the sky, which was a gray hollow, caving with snow. Kate dressed and the sound she made was a gurgling noise, like kittens in your lap. There was the crinkle of paper-covered hangers, the slippery whisper of plastic bags, the smooth oaky snap of drawers, the miniature clank of miniature buckles, the thin thud of pointed heels. Her secret zone gathered up as she practiced herself, pre-greeting everyone she expected to meet. I would be home, safe in the ease of my solitude, but Kate would be out, which was strange. Strange that when you set forth, things really do happen.

"What do you think?" she asked. She was wearing black rayon pants and a silk blouse, ivory and sleeveless. People who normally have strict rules about seasonal dressing, such as no linen or short sleeves in winter, are the first to suspend those rules for New Year's Eve, the one night they really ought to dress practically.

I pointed to a teal-colored sweater. "Try this."

She extracted it from a meticulous strip of blues, held it to her chest, and pirouetted before the mirror. "It's not too *juvenile*?"

Flurries were falling. In the distance they fell fast, pattering relentlessly, but near the house they scrolled and slowly scrambled and acquired alarming new dimension, which had to do either with perspective or aerodynamics, with the way the structure impeded the wind. There was the Christmas poem that I loved.

> *As dry leaves that before the wild hurricane fly,*
> *When they meet with an obstacle, mount to the sky.*

Jack hated that I loved that poem. He thought it was an inferior poem. He was always trying to get me to read Rilke. The snow on the tree branches was like panther tails, leaning to reveal the origin of the storm, and also like cotton balls gathering on brown crooks and twiggy edges. The wind advanced from the east, from the northeast. East at night in snow is lavender, especially when there is wind, and that is like being a child—lavender and snow and wind, of course, the worldly sound of it.

"WHOSE NAME DO YOU want?" my mother had asked.

I was playing with her things on the floor of what had been her bedroom and my father's bedroom on East 9th Street. I must have been three. This is not my earliest memory. My earliest memory is a nightmare about a clown. I would lie in my bed and on the ceiling would be a projection of the face of a bad clown. Maybe it was Bozo. Yes, I think it was Bozo.

My mother had dropped the phone in the living room, and I knew by the *clip-clop* way she'd come down the hall that she was feeling not nice. My mother had a certain not nice walk. She was dressed in heels and a full slip. And her hair was in wide curlers. Not curlers, rollers. Behind her head, a bare bulb peered out from a ceiling socket.

"Mine or Daddy's?"

The light burned my eyes. "Daddy's."

"Fine," she said, going back to the phone. *Clip-clop* down the hallway, which was thin and bare. It was a railroad apartment, scary like a glass cutter, like a little letter *f*.

There was the sound of her dressing. And the feeling of me willing her to come but not calling, of me preferring her to be wrong. And me moving from her room to my own. Three posters hung on the wall there—children's posters in cellophane, frameless posters of Beatrix Potter characters—a rabbit, a duck, and a frog, I think, in a snug pink jacket. The memory leaves off with those posters, with the world tipping and towering but me not feeling small. Me feeling complete with everything inside, sealed like a drum. Feeling the divide between being and knowing, as though I'd witnessed myself, as though I'd been incorporated into my society.

Alongside the posters was a window facing east and through that window a lavender snow had begun to fall.

"You're right," Kate was saying. "This is better."

Flakes were coming harder, toppling like butterflies shot from the sky. How fast it happens—no snow, snow. Snow is a special event, unlike rain, which goes away. There's a difference between weather that stays and weather that disappears.

Kate applied make-up, her implements fanning out on the table—sharpener, tweezers, Vaseline, cotton balls, powder, lip gloss. I felt us synchronize with the people and the objects of the night, with everything achieving celebratory speed, coming together like clocks in a shop, counting out a chorus to twelve. Our house joined the rest. It joined the beyond.

The stairs creaked past the half-opened bedroom door, which was my mother climbing to join us. It depressed me to hear the floors creak. We did not create the creaks, many feet had preceded ours, many would follow. I thought of juggling, of balls fleetingly suspended. Of us, touching down. Mom came in. She wore a crushed velvet bodysuit the color of pomegranates. "Kate, you look beautiful."

Kate giggled in the self-effacing style of someone who knows she is beautiful, who is always told that she is beautiful, but who, deep down, does not feel very beautiful. She brushed her hair. It was winning hair, populous and blonde like thatch or animal ruff.

"And you," my mother said to me, "Miss Appalachia." She touched my cheek and the pink polish of her thumbnail passed the edge of my eye once, twice. "Remember I used to call you that?"

I remembered. I said yes, that I did.

She turned. "Kate, did you telephone your brother yet?"

"Not yet," Kate said. "I will before I leave."

"Be careful tonight," my mother said as she returned to the door. "Don't get in any cars. If it keeps snowing, I'll stay at Lowie's." She waved goodbye, then the squeaking steps again, then the front door popping, then her tread vanishing, dimming and dulling into the snowcapped path. The car engine coughed to a dubious start, and she was gone.

JACK PHONED FROM DAN'S house. "You coming, or not?"

I answered but he did not hear. The music was deafening.

"What?" he shouted. "Christ, hold on. *Daniel, turn that shit off!*" The music vanished with a flushing *zzzt* sound. "What did you say?"

"I said, I'm not feeling so well."

"Smokey's a master chemist. He'll make you Irish coffee."

"I think I'd better stay home."

There was a pause. "See you later," he mumbled.

"Bye, Jack," I said, and I thanked him then hung up. I wasn't sure why I thanked him, except to say that he seemed to be doing me a favor. I untangled the knotted phone cord and poked around my mother's desk, reading a few lines from a half-graded paper.

> ### Christianity and Salvation in the Works of Flannery O'Connor
> #### by Jeanette Hickson
> *In her short story, "The Geranium," Flannery O'Connor vividly depicts the inner state of a sickly old man who has moved from the country to live with his daughter in New York. Through the apartment window that has become his horizon, the man becomes involved with the comings and goings of a neighbor's geranium plant. His bitter regard—*

Kate was coming down. The zealous stench of rosewater anticipated her. It grabbed me from behind. Like claws. "Was that Jack?"

"Yeah," I said. "He's at Dan's."

"You'd better not go there. I bet they're getting wasted."

I pulled at my bottom lip. It was not a good day. Not a secure day. Some days are not secure, and you feel a stretching pain. I wanted to go out. I asked Kate if I could walk her to Coco's. She said sure.

OUTSIDE THE SNOW LACED the treetops, spreading like a web of mercury into ground, and upon the ground we walked. Snow makes everything so connected, so intensely one, the way we walk the earth, returning to it, the way the world is a genteel host. I said, "It's a miracle, isn't it?"

"What is?" Kate asked.

"The snow." I said, "The way it touches everything, changing it."

Main Street was silent and lonesome. Lonesome because when there is no noise, there is no implied source of noise, no inference to faraway, and so the place you are becomes center. I thought of the Headless Horseman. I tried to recall if the story has a moral. I remembered only that it takes place in Sleepy Hollow and that there is a character called Ichabod Crane, which is a frightening name, evocative of cracked and bloody feet and half-lit lanterns and leaves that twist inward at the prongs like a witch's fingernails.

I photographed Kate near the blue-lighted Christmas trees outside the shops, which was nice, but at the Church on David's Lane we paused awkwardly. She did not want me to go any farther.

"What if someone saw you," she said, "after telling Coco you felt sick. We might seem like liars."

I waved, and she slipped away.

The empty A&P parking lot was like a coconut plateau, like the uplands of a coconut layer cake. Coconut things are agitatingly white. I find myself wishing to touch them with a desire that is inexplicable. I cut through the lot, walking without raising my feet, just propelling them through, carving tracks. Under the snow was asphalt and under that, smothered things. I wondered whether the record store was the last time I'd ever see Rourke. The time before that was the last for quite a while. One day would be the last, I informed myself, perhaps today. The way he looked at me through the window was strange, as though I'd caused a dramatic impasse in his day, as though he'd been delayed by a building on fire or an impending suicide. Inside he examined me as if for flaws, as if looking for a way to release himself.

It was odd that we'd never spoken, but we understood each other. Sometimes you work hard to understand someone, sometimes you don't work at all. Some people are advocates of shrewd choices. They choose partners more carefully than careers. My mother's friend Nonnie is a sleep lab technician who ran a classified ad to find a husband. After studying the resumes and photographs of dozens of applicants, she dated seven men from the A-pile before choosing Brian from the middle of the B's. Within six years they'd had four children.

"You can never be too careful," Nonnie would say. "Never."

Mom would smile and say, "Nonnie, you're a brave woman."

A second dream I'd had that afternoon was that I was going to have a baby. I was excited to feel the satiny folds of its skin with my hands and to hear the stiff crinkle of its diaper. But during the dream, a place in my brain the size and shape of an almond moved like lips to announce: *This is a dream. This is a dream.* The almond shape alerted me to the fact that I was not pregnant, that I would not get to touch my baby because there was not a baby to touch, and yet the dream continued in a way that was bittersweet. The irony of dreams is that anything is possible but nothing is actual. You can best your adversaries or have sex with acquaintances, but when it comes time to touch, the object is air. You wake up feeling cheated and mysterious. But in real life, you have only to see someone you hardly know at the record store to feel elated.

What had motivated the baby dream? I did not wish for a baby, although of course a baby in my belly would have been a very intimate thing, like a best friend in your pocket. And it was definitely true that I could have used a friend. My trails made a complicated design. After one last circuit, I stomped the snow from my Timberlands. There were parts of me I could not feel, so I headed home. Along the way I went through every snowbank because I was the last person on earth and my marks didn't matter. We ruin everything we touch anyway. Why pretend otherwise?

The cats converged on my ankles in the driveway, lifting their legs high and prancing like miniature show horses. They shoved past as I opened the door to the house and followed as I made my way through the living room. I stripped as I moved, leaving my clothes exactly where they fell. The furniture looked suspicious. Furniture of winter is not the same as furniture of summer. Summer furniture looks damp and weak from fatigue, and winter furniture looks hardy but sneaky, as though it has been switching itself about while you were gone. I turned on all the lights and the washing machine and the stove and the radio. Then I changed into my pajamas and built a fire and drew the hood of a night sky on the back of a paper towel.

At nine-thirty, the front door opened, and Jack and Dan came in. I hadn't seen Jack in so long, I thought, though in fact I'd seen him the night before. Behind him Dan was slender and tall and high-haired, tipped like a pencil engaged in the act of writing. When Jack kicked off his boots, his face became almost level with my face and he scuffed in floppy socks over to the fire. He was wearing a red plaid flannel shirt over a shredded wool sweater, and his cheeks were also red, making two circles, and the hair that had come loose from his ponytail was frozen in strips. His eyes surveyed the room. Everything transformed beneath the dismal heft of his regard.

Dan flopped on the couch, and Jack lit a cigarette. His narrowed eyes glowing as he reclined to view me. I didn't move. It was like standing still to let a bee buzz past.

"We passed your tracks," Jack said, leadingly.

I nodded. "Want tea or something?"

Dan grabbed at my leg. "Hold on, Evie. The ones in the parking lot. You really made them?"

"I guess—I mean, yeah."

"That's fucked up," Dan said. "You two are totally fucked up."

"It's a small town, Daniel," Jack said. "A gnat's ass town."

He followed me to the kitchen. He propped his cigarette on the rim of the sink, opened the refrigerator and hunted. I jumped onto the counter. "So you must be feeling better," he said, plucking olives from a jar. He stood by my knees. Beyond the blanche of his hair the tea water bubbled and burst.

"How was rehearsal?" I asked, my eyes wide in a type of trance.

He reached for his cigarette, drawing hard to reignite the dying ember. "We messed with the songs for the play for so long, that by the time we got to Tangerine, those guys were too wasted to rehearse. Dan puked twice and Smokey passed out on the floor," Jack muttered in disgust. Jack did not like people to pass out or vomit. He said it defeated the whole point of getting high. Why waste money and drugs, he would say, when you could lick raw chicken to achieve a similar effect. "I shoved Smokey's pony tail under the drum stand," he said, "so he's in for like, a totally rude awakening."

"I'm glad you came," I told him, which was true; I was glad.

"I came up with a nice riff—want to hear it?" He began to sing a wordless melody, *Da-da da-da da-da dum dum da da-ah da*.

"God, Jack. That's really beautiful."

WE LISTENED TO ELLA sing Cow Cow Boogie, and we stared at the Candle.

> *That cat was raised on local weed*
> *He's what they call a swing half-breed*
> *Singin' his Cow Cow Boogie in the strangest way—*

The Candle looked like a square drinking glass. It was a rectangular mosaic of translucent panes—eggshell white, moon yellow, lapis blue. Each side depicted the same thing, the seashore, with planes of sand, sea, and sky comprising equidistant thirds, and directly in the center, a flying bird. Because the landscape was collapsed, it was hard to tell whether the bird was flying over the beach or over the ocean.

Dan looked inside. "Are you sure that's the original wax?"

"Positive," I said.

"It's the candle that Jesus blessed," Jack said caustically.

Dan respectfully replaced it. "It's *definitely* over the beach," he declared, referring to the bird. He wiped his wire-rimmed glasses with the hem of his shirt. "If it were over the ocean," Dan speculated, "it'd be closer to the line between sand and sea."

"Right," Jack agreed. "If the bird had been positioned at the bottom of the middle instead of at the top, you would think low—small. *Small*, meaning *farther away*, meaning *over the ocean*."

"But it's not," Dan went on. "It's high in the middle, meaning *big* and *near*. It's over the sand."

"Exactly." Jack sucked on a joint as he spoke, his voice constricting with a chestful of smoke. He offered the end of it to Dan. Dan accepted it gingerly.

It didn't seem exact to me. The candle had no converging lines, no infinite distance, and no vanishing point. There were three flat planes and a bird with no apparent diminution in size. Comparatively the bird was huge. And it was on the central plane—the water. Because perspective kind of comes from light hitting a surface, the candle maker was most likely playing with the idea of *inside* light or *emanating* light—the flame.

Dan screwed his face to one side and coughed. "I don't know, Jack. She doesn't seem convinced."

Jack squeezed my shoulders. His cheek on my cheek. "Why not?"

"Just the way it looks. I mean, I guess you can apply laws of perspective to something without perspective. You can do anything you want, but what would be the point? Giotto painted gold rings on the heads of saints—the rings are halos, not sunrises." I pointed to the glass. "There *is* no close or far, or over, or under. There's *on*. And before and behind. Like screens. Or layers."

I was trying to say something about layers and time, about layers meaning many times at once, as compared to perspective meaning *one* time, one shared time or universal time, with one shared or universal light—that being the Heavenly light. I wondered about the Renaissance and religion and God and perspective and how they all got interconnected in meaning, like Coke standing for America. Maybe the search for spirituality is as difficult to explain as the search for freedom, especially when you have to spread it out over billions of people, across hundreds of years, that's why giant tools get used. Maybe perspective is just another tool, an excuse for seeing faraway, for applying time to view. The factual spatial markers of the viewer, or the *eye*, give substance to the theoretical vanishing point, transforming it into a physical locale, connecting mankind to God through the idea of *Heaven*.

"You are very fucking high," Jack said to me, "aren't you?"

"Where did you get that pot? It's pretty trippy."

"From Frankie," Jack said.

"Fat Frankie?" He was always talking about Fat Frankie.

"Yeah, except he's not fat anymore. He lost fifty-five pounds."

"Fifty-five!" Dan said, "That's almost half my body weight."

"He went on that Moonie thing. That thing Denny does."

"The *Scarsdale Diet?*" I said. "That's crazy."

There was a thump at the front of the house. Kate was home. We all called, *Kate!* She secured the door and stomped her feet on the mat and unwrapped her scarf. The exposed part of her hair and lashes were frosted. Behind her through the glass was a complete wall of white, like a down quilt.

"Oh no," she moaned, "not the Candle."

"Katie," Jack said, "who'd you kiss at midnight?"

"No one," she replied. "Yet."

Dan stood, combing back his hair. "What time is it?"

Kate draped her coat over the banister and she checked her watch. "Twenty to twelve."

"Shit. I thought it was like, two in the morning."

"That's because you've been drinking since breakfast," Jack said.

"The roads are really bad. Coco is having people sleep over. I told Denny and Michelle just to come here. Did Mom call?"

"She did," I said. "She's staying in Bridgehampton."

Dan asked if Kate had seen the tracks I'd made by the A&P.

"I didn't see any tracks."

"Maybe they're gone by now," Dan speculated.

Jack peeked to see my face, to see if I was sad, then he held me. Jack was most virile near a hearth fire. If in public he used me—the look of me—to indicate his mannishness, by a fire he needed nothing. He was invincible.

Kate went to get undressed, and I followed. From the corner of her bed, I watched her shadow on the floor beneath the partly opened bathroom door. She seemed quiet. I wondered if someone had hurt her feelings. If she'd been offended, I hoped it had just been by over-bright lighting or a poorly stocked buffet. Possibly they'd had mismatching cocktail napkins. If the cocktail napkins were Halloween leftovers with pictures of grinning pumpkins and arched black cats, that could be depressing. Or Coco might have served pigs in a blanket, with blankets made of Bisquick. Maybe *everyone* had sequined and unseasonable outfits, not just Kate, maybe there was the stench of cheap cologne and music by Journey or Boston.

"How was the party?" I asked.

"Everyone was drunk. Acting like assholes."

I re-tied the string on my sweatpants. It embarrassed me when Kate cursed, not because I objected to profanity, but because she was not particularly good at it. Jack swore so effectively and so constantly that he would exercise restraint for dramatic emphasis. When Kate said the word *asshole*, she pronounced the *A* like in *a-ha* or like when you stick out your tongue at the doctor's office. *AAAA-hhhhh.*

She unpinned her hair. In the mirror her eyes were like plums. It was strange to reconvene there, when earlier she'd been looking forward to the evening, but after it she was depressed. Jack always said the trick to happiness is to expect things to be shitty, then you won't be disappointed. "Just keep a low-level plane of dissatisfaction going," he'd advise.

Dan called up the stairs. "*Happy New Year!*"

"Oh, gosh," Kate said, shaking herself awake. She came halfway to me, and I came as far to her. Our cheeks met like praying hands. "Happy New Year," we said in unison, sending the words out into the universe beyond the petite round of each other's shoulder.

TO CELEBRATE JACK PUT on Oscar Peterson's version of Cole Porter's "In the Still of the Night." It was the snow song, the anthem to the snow. We cuddled on the couch, the four of us, eight legs and knees, facing the fire.

"I have some thoughts," Dan said, "on the psychology of perception. Does anyone mind?"

Kate and I did not, but Jack stipulated provisions.

"No talk of functional neuroses or maladjustments. No dream analyses."

"No, no," Dan said, "I was just thinking about the difference between names and interpretations. For instance, take begonias."

Jack said no. "I hate begonias."

"How about hyacinths?" Dan slurred.

"How about something you can pronounce without spitting."

"Okay, a *rose*. We can both call it *red*, even though I might see coral and you might see pink."

Kate was next to him on the couch, brushing her hair. Her neck was pale and bared. "Do you mean color blindness?"

"Not exactly," he guided gently. Dan was always gentle with Kate. At parties he would dedicate songs to her, or he would write compositions called *Kate 9* or *Kate 16*. "My point is that it's impossible to know that what *I* see matches what *you* see when we say *red*."

"Big deal," Jack said. "Perception is variable. If you perceive a car to be forty feet away when it's really four feet away, and I perceive it to be four feet away, then I'll jump, and you'll get hit. Relative perception doesn't change the position of the car, and it doesn't affect the color of a rose. The rose doesn't care what color you think it is."

"So, physical absolutes exist," Dan said, "but *absolute perception* does not. Some people possess perfect pitch. If other people can't hear pitch absolutely, it doesn't mean the perfection of pitch doesn't exist or is not a possibility."

Jack turned. "What's your point, Daniel?"

"I'm just thinking about the Candle again."

"That's it!" Jack swatted at Dan. "Get rid of that fucking thing!"

"I'm just saying, Evie sees that way, sort of like perfect pitch, like a rare genetic thing. And I get what she means—there is no bird, there never was. The artist was not looking to *prove* a bird."

Kate wanted to know what happened to the rose.

Jack said, "Good point, Kate."

"Art that's intentionally näive is proving that it's not part of the system— it's trustworthy," Dan said. "If Robert Johnson hadn't deviated from the rules, the blues wouldn't have evolved."

"Until deviant art acquires its *own* set of rules, and those rules become new absolutes. Nothing is trustworthy. Besides, we're talking about a stationery store candle. Maybe there was no bird, but, for all we know, there was no artist *either.*"

For a long time we drifted, separately and in a group. Dandelion seeds float like that, like feathery starships. I felt bad for Dan. It was nice of him to defend me, but he should've known better than to argue with Jack.

BY THREE-THIRTY IN the morning a lead curtain had closed down upon the whole house. The snow fit like a form, like a house on the house, or a skin on the house, and inside was bright without lights, snow bright. Kate had gone to sleep with Denny and Michelle, Jack and Dan had gone home, and all things through the living room window were pale cinder. My palms and my cheeks left cool dripping circles on the frost-covered glass as I measured the frailness of the membrane that shielded me from the vast universe. I wondered by what accident of chance I'd been blessed with warm and dry shelter. There were creatures whose only sanctuary was the flat valentine heart of night. Possibly they were magic.

I would look through darkness to find them, with their nestling necks and heavily lidded eyes, huddling in clusters between twigs and rocks, sharing fur and feathers, breathing in shallow puffs to make heat. I could never find them, but when I would return to my little wooden bed, it would be with a renewed humility, with a distilled awareness of my conditional fortune. I would burrow into my blankets over and over, shifting until my thoughts became non-linear, until they became round like a ball or globe, like something drawn together by centrifugal force, something spinning with aspects made present at random or in turn, and I would think, *That was strange, that was nice, that may even have been a dream.*

"You require reassurance," my mother speculated when I told her that sometimes I wake up in the night.

I didn't disagree. My mother seldom fawns on me. When she does, she does so excessively and briefly, like a toddler mothering a baby doll, and it seems cruel to interfere. But in fact reassurance is not a requirement of mine. And if it were, I wouldn't look for it in darkness. Darkness is just one particular blind or veil in an inexhaustible sequence of blinds and veils. Beyond the gorged metropolis of any night is a new day again—and beyond that, night to follow. If you look, you can see them, stacked like panels one behind the other. If you listen, you can hear them, moving in tempo. And you think about your part to play being so very small.

The phone rang. I lifted the receiver and walked with it from the desk to the front door, pulling until the cord could stretch no further. I stepped out into the snow, my bare legs vanishing to the knee. Was I clear from the sky, was I a speck, a stain, a spot to spoil the white—tiny, so tiny—the eye of a needle, the head of a pin, a nick in the arctic void, aimed like a magnetic compass through the inaugural waste to the place I knew Rourke lay. Or—did I not appear, was I incapable of being seen, was I nothing to no one, and my intuition, my failure. Was I wrong to feel manifest, wrong to feel seeable. Wrong to feel like a giant just to know he was alive.

"Hi." Jack said.

I said hi.

"They're still there," he informed me, meaning the tracks. "Do you know what you made?"

I said no. He said he didn't think so.

"A fleur-de-lis," he said. "It's practically perfect. Just one part at the top was fucked up, but I fixed it."

I thanked him. On prairies there are creatures like weasels, and they live in packs. One stands sentry while the others sleep. The one waits, scrawny and long, perched on hind legs, reading the landscape with coalified eyes, scouting for predators. Its generosity is not without incentive. It gets to run first.

I WIPED A STREAK FROM DENNY'S FACE. IT WAS SMUDGED BLUE BECAUSE HIS clock was weeping. The assignment was to render one object from several advantages—I'd chosen an onion. Denny picked a clock. Miss Lilias Starr from Baton Rouge had handed out a mimeographed list of considerations. And the list had that smell.

> *External—Superficiality! Command.*
> *Surface—Tenderness! Durability! Watertight?*
> *Skeleton—Concretization. Uprightness vs. Decline!*
> *Positive and Negative Space—Yin/Yang.*
> *Center—Viscera/Gut/Breadbasket.*
> *Mood—Disposition/Habits/Dreams and Regrets.*

"Actually," Denny said, "the *viscera* are weeping. The face is cheerful. The face is the evil extrinsic manifestation of humor and regrets. I was going to do ticking for external manifestation, like there's no clock at all, just the sound of ticking, but I'm saving ticking for *Skeleton*. I have this idea for *bone tick*."

"That's gruesome," Alicia Ross said. Alicia was doing a bird's nest.

"Clocks *are* gruesome," Denny said with a shiver. He pulled his denim jacket tighter. Two buttons were on his breast pocket—*No Nukes* and *Rocky Horror Picture Show*. "It's so cold in here, I wished I'd picked a space heater."

Miss Starr flitted like a fairy about us, materializing at our elbows in aromatic bursts. She smelled like bergamot and eucalyptus, guava and blue gum. Her hair was the color of Granny Smith apples. Everyone said I was lucky because I'd been to her studio, and she'd been to my barn, and she insisted I call her Lilias. Her studio was a potting shed behind a cottage off of Springs Fireplace Road, near the Pollock-Krasner House. "It has no plumbing," she explained when I visited, "so I pee in a bottle. But isn't the light divine?"

She appeared at the counter near Denny and me, coddling a still life she'd painted—a bowl of flowers, very accomplished, velvety and Dutch. It reminded me of a painting my dad and I had seen at the Met. "I think the artist's name was Brueghel," I said.

She flicked her hair back behind her long goosey neck. "Oh, Eveline," she cooed, "do you really think so?"

When she left, Denny whispered, "Brown nose."

MR. MCGINTEE SAUNTERED IN. "Hello, hello."

Directly after was Rourke. He was all that I saw and all that I could see, and it was strange, as if the door had opened and water flooded through. He came and there was simply nothing else. He was wearing a camel hair dress jacket with a crewneck sweater underneath that was like aerated cream. His hair was windswept, his skin olive brown. I returned to my work, dipping my head. Why did his name sound Irish when he looked Mediterranean, like the type of person who vacations on yachts. Sometimes my mother spoke of the Black Irish; maybe he was that kind of Irish. His eyes settled on my face. I didn't look, but I could feel the way they settled. I bit at the top of my turtle-neck, hiding my lips and chin. I wrote to myself.

> *He is here and I am here, and his eyes the hue of carbon, they are eyes like animal eyes. His hair is silk that drifts from the kingdom of his face, drifting as though there is wind, only there is no wind.*

I breathed an expulsory breath, a cleansing breath, telling myself, *God, Jack is so much better than he is.* I hated myself for ever thinking of him and ever writing his name and for memorizing his face and also for knowing the smell of him, his sweat. Earlier that week, I'd seen him three times in one day. The first time there were people, so he ignored me and I ignored him and we ignored each other. The second time our bodies defied our minds. The second time we were alone. I felt myself come to a stretching stand and leave the year-book office exactly as he loitered by my doorway, hunting through pockets for elusive items, quarters or keys. Later that afternoon, I was in the main office delivering college recommendation requests, and he passed by. He leaned on the door frame and smiled at the flank of thoroughly enamored secretaries, saying, "Any of you ladies plan on answering that phone?"

Mr. McGintee was remarking on Miss Starr's still-life. "It's *nice.*"

"Eveline says it looks Flemish, like a Brueghel. Would you agree?"

He smiled vaguely. "Absolutely!"

Rourke moved to greet Alicia Ross, and together they looked ravishing and dark like Spaniards or Arabs conferring. He would speak and she would respond, briskly and surely, with the charismatic self-confidence of a well-bred someone. Alicia had attended Spence in Manhattan until tenth grade, but she transferred out when her dad came to their summer house to recuperate from heart surgery. Mrs. Ross didn't want Alicia to graduate from East Hampton High School, but Alicia didn't care. She adored her father.

Alicia would imitate her Mom. *You'll never get into an Ivy League! You'll lose all fashion sense! You'll marry a dentist!*

"What's wrong with dentists?" Denny asked.

"I guess she thinks they're kind of, *dentisty,*" Alicia shrugged.

I loved Alicia. If she was over-animated and uncommonly direct, within her resided a colossal humanity. When she wore hats, she wore them with pious flair, like black church ladies. And she always remembered things I said.

"How's your cousin?" she'd ask.

"Which one, the one who's converting?"

"No, not the physicist, the potter."

Unfortunately, Alicia was always talking about her father's famous clients; he was an entertainment lawyer. You had to steer your way through dialogue.

"Parker and I saw one when we were skiing," she stated on one occasion. We'd been speaking of bobcats.

"Can you hand me the glue," I requested.

"Sure!" Alicia reached for the bucket. "We were in Aspen and—"

"What do you think of this?" I lifted my decoupage.

"You need a wider margin," she suggested. "Anyway, he's even—"

"Wider? Are you sure?"

Alicia crammed in her sentence. "He's even more gorgeous in person, if you can imagine."

"Who is this we're talking about?" I asked.

"Parker!"

"Parker who?"

"Parker Stevenson, silly. From *The Hardy Boys*."

MISS STARR EXPLAINED TO the class that the family who had donated money for the drama program had insisted that portions of it go to the art and music departments. We were being invited to submit ideas for backdrops and costumes for the production at Guild Hall. I wasn't really paying attention. Neither was Alicia. She tugged twice on the lapel of Rourke's jacket, saying something that made him smile. Then she spun on her stool, and her straight black hair bobbed serenely about her face, which was not an oval and not a rectangle but something in between, a rowboat maybe. I wondered how they knew each other when she was not even in drama.

Cathy Benjamin asked, "When are the drawings due?"

"You're the experts," Mr. McGintee said, "you tell us. A week? Three days? I'm guessing here." He waved a half-erect index finger in an arc around the room. "Any suggestions?"

"August," Denny answered, and everyone laughed.

Mr. McGintee laughed too, falsely, expertly, starting generously, withdrawing rapidly. And an uncanny quiet descended, as quiets sometimes do when you hear a trivial ringing. I lowered my head, engrossing myself in my task. I was about to be called on. Sometimes you just know. "Miss Auerbach," McGintee said, "your thoughts?"

I didn't look up. "Is *Our Town* supposed to have scenery?" In Kate's playbook, I'd read something about no scenery.

Mr. McGintee laughed again, this time as though something was actually funny. "Bravo! If only our actors were as familiar with the script. Isn't that right, Mr. Rourke?"

Rourke was still next to Alicia. He stepped forward, his body soaking emphatically through space like an inky spill. He located without effort the precise center of the room.

"The script calls for no scenery," he said, looking at me, me looking at him, "that's true." His voice was mossy and opaque; it had this lastingness, this abidingness. "But I think that the more people who get involved the better the experience will be for everyone. I think we can get away with some limited design without compromising the integrity of the play."

No one moved when he spoke, not even Miss Starr. Everyone just stared with idle faces, like they were getting something good off the look of him. I bit a tag of flesh on the inside of my cheek. When he was talking, I wanted him to stop, very badly I wanted that. I continued with my onion, with the silky feel of it. I'd penciled a luxurious arc that tapered to a flush and narrow run, with feathery stuff at the end. It was madness to think I knew him when I did not. I inclined my head to view my drawing.

"How about, like, a village green?" Dave Meese asked.

I touched the actual onion. Its barrier was no more than a dried membrane, papery brown and tearable. It was ironic that something so potent could have such a fragile shell.

"A chapel," I heard myself say.

McGintee said, "What's that Eveline?"

Denny answered for me. "She said, 'a chapel.' "

"Wonderful! A chapel. And Dave, yes—a village green."

Miss Starr encouraged the rest of the class to see what they could come up with, and people turned to their tables. She was a fan of spontaneity. Frequently in the middle of class she would call out a challenge. *Two minutes— low tide! Ten seconds—a toe!*

AT LAST HE CAME, and when he came, the room died in the wake of his steps. He touched down at the bench on my left, and I was concealed from the world and the world was concealed from me. And things became clear. He reached for a piece of paper and moved the sheet to my belly. I was fascinated by the size of his arm and the whiteness of my hand. A certain energy assailed me, as though insects were crawling from his skin to mine. He lifted the rendering of my onion, raising it just an inch from the table, tilting it.

"What is it?" he said.

"Well, it's not an onion," I said, and he smiled. "It's the *feel* of an onion." It was not at all difficult to draw with him closing in, with the line of him grazing the line of me, with the sunlight beating down upon the snow in the courtyard, and the light, which repeated through the studio, drenching the two of us, making things chalk and silver. I soared beneath the umbrella of his protectorship, thinking of nothing more menacing than color—in particular of white.

I traveled back to a place I'd once visited, a town in winter—Amherst. At the home of Emily Dickinson, the floors squeaked like slowly stabbed things, and through the ruffled purling windows day was sterling and without mercy. White can be scary if white is all you see. After lunch, Dad and Marilyn bought a Portuguese rosary from an antique store in a barn near a stone bridge. I waited on the stairs of a clapboard church beneath trees with no leaves.

Rourke's arm moved minimally, signaling for me to stop. I formed two more lines. We studied the paper. It was unifying to share a visual object with him. Usually we looked at each other. I imagined what it would be like for us to have a child, the way we would observe it, separately and sometimes together. The steeple of my church extended at a gross and peculiar angle, tipping forward like an antler or horn, and the main body of the building was low like a plank. Rourke took the paper from me, and he returned my onion.

"I'd like to take this," he said, meaning the chapel. He spoke softly. No one could hear but me.

He had not moved, not physically, but he was receding. I felt him abandon the solace conceived by our nearness. He had things to do. I thought that he was brave. I wished that I were brave. But I was not. I was left to measure the range of my own frontiers, palpating my own insides the way mimes feel pretend walls. I discovered a plaintive vacancy there. I felt every hole and hollow because he had filled them so perfectly.

He was waiting for an answer.

My eyes focused keenly on nothing in particular—a name carved in the counter, *Winn*, a date that followed, `76. I wondered where was Winn. Four years was a long time to be gone.

"You can take it," I said. It was just a thing, a sign, a disclosure, the consummation of action and influence, the result of something foremost and leading, the result of him. What he actually took away was far more precious, infinitely so.

HE CAME THROUGH THE DOOR OF THE DARKROOM AS I WAS LAYING OUT prints to dry. Betsy Callaghan and Jan Schecter were developing in the back. My drawing was in his hand.

"Okay," he said as he returned it to me.

"Okay," I repeated, taking it from him.

There was the sound of the girls. *"Don't you dare!"*

And the other girl squealing back, *"Ha! Too late."*

Rourke and I were face to face, not quite face to face, since I came only as high as his shoulders. If I were to lie against him, my cheek would fit into the recess beneath his breastplate.

I did not raise my head, just my eyes. "Is that it?"

He nodded. "That's it."

REVEREND OLCOTT EXITED THE rectory, his belly jiggling ever so slightly as he crossed the driveway. He was dressed as usual in casual black, no silk, no sash.

"Hello there, Eveline," he said, "long time no see."

I'd been leaning on a tree, regarding the church spire through the rolled up tube of my sketch. "I've been so busy. You know—school and the yearbook and everything."

He raised a comforting hand. "Any word on college yet?"

"NYU, probably."

The Reverend came from Wisconsin. I could not recall the name of the town, but it must have been a nice town if everyone in it was like him. He was a clean scrubbed man of restless intelligence and limitless energy—Powell always said that the Reverend has so much bounce as to make you think privately of fleas. If Kate and I or Jack and I happened to be feeding the ducks in the morning, we'd see him jogging past, or, if you stopped by the church to use the bathroom or get a drink of water you might see him painting. Everyone said he was the best Cajun cook on the East End.

I gestured with my sketch. "I'm designing a chapel. For the drama club."

He jerked his neck toward the church. "C'mon. Let's have a look."

The mammoth white door fastened behind him with a tidy click, and the room we entered was stark and still. I didn't know how it feels inside an egg, but I could imagine. We moved past the altar in the direction of the pews. I sat and the Reverend sat and he examined my sketch.

"Yes," he nodded, "I see."

With a low stroke of one hand, he referred to the body of the church, which was nothing compared to the steeple. "The congregation is minimized," he said, "so the architecture becomes part of the landscape, part of nature."

My eyes ventured to his face. His glasses bridged the base of his nose and his head was tucked into his neck, adjusting to the near distance of the sheet of paper.

"But the steeple, the *reaching* to God—to Godliness—is immense. Very symbolic, muscular, like a fist thrust into the air." He tapped the drawing twice and returned it to me. "Very nice."

I considered his remarks. Usually I could trace my thinking back to my own head. It was strange to have communicated something that I believed but didn't know I knew how to relate.

"It's the striving that intrigues you, the theoretical endeavor," he proposed, "*abstraction*." Reverend Olcott cleared his throat. "Do you know it's been thirty years since I joined the church? January, 1951. In that time, I have encountered as many allegiant worshippers who lack true compassion as," he paused to search for a word, "*individualists* who possess a pious reverence for life."

He pointed to the paper, now in my hands. "I especially like the easy lines, the quickness of hand, the conservation of voice. Spontaneity is too frequently mistaken for immaturity. We are spontaneous when we are at our genuine best—childlike as opposed to childish. Standards of goodness and propriety are necessary, of course. They are guideposts for those who stray. But ideally, decency resides in the heart, undiminished from birth." He continued "One sometimes wonders whether purity of heart is sufficient."

"It does confuse me," I said. "The whole idea of God as a man." The Reverend looked toward the altar. I hoped he was not offended. "The beard and the robes. Seven days to create the earth."

For a while we waited. I gathered he was thinking what to say. Probably he wanted to choose his words carefully. It did seem like a risky and unofficial way to discuss God, sitting in the first pew with our legs stretched out.

"Some prefer to draw inspiration from the story of Jesus rather than from that of a *personal* God." His tone was circumspect. "We can be certain that a man named Jesus existed and that he preached—at great personal sacrifice and without material compensation—the virtues of faith and forgiveness. And from that ancient narrative, we continue to extract messages pertaining to the sacredness of devotion, and we follow its prescriptions for living peaceably. In fact," he added as he gestured to my drawing, "Such a proposal is very much in keeping with your notion of ideological enterprise, the expenditure of spiritual energy in working toward actual understanding. That's the reaching part," he said. "Do you see?"

I thought I did. I thought he was telling me it was okay to be confused. I thought he was alluding to how he himself had come to terms with confusion. After all, if I struggled with the idea of a physical God, then surely people in the field contemplated such things as well.

"It's like, Heaven is not necessarily an actual destination," I said, "but a conceptual place of peace."

He said nothing, which was okay. I understood that he could not. It seemed like the right time for the conversation to end, so I stood and he stood. He encouraged me to sit for a while and think.

"Oh, no," I said. "It's hard for me to sit and think. I have to move and think, or sit and do. It's just one of those things." I held up my sketch. "But thank you very much."

Reverend Olcott and I parted and waved, and I thought again of eggs, of light glowing through them. I thought of uncolored glass, of mosaic and overlap. Maybe I could use texture instead of color and line. Maybe I could use pieces of vanilla canvas to make a collage. I walked to Guild Hall to see if anyone was there. Maybe I could shine a light through the back of a flat to make it glow like an incubated egg. I was thinking back to the candle in my house, of light emanating from an interior, of a decidedly reduced perspective.

BY THE CURL OF THE BREEZE, I COULD TELL NICO HAD ARRIVED. HIS BOOK landed on his desk with a drifting *whumpf*, and he straddled his seat, peeling my hands from my face, prying them apart like shutters.

"Happy Valentine's Day," he said. His hands smelled like powder.

I blinked and shook my head. "Is that today?"

"*Is that today?*" he said, dropping my hands in mock disgust.

I sat up tall and stretched. "I'm just a little—"

"Out of it." Nico kicked his left hand up in a wave to Mike Stern. He spoke to me, but his eyes darted professionally. *Professionally* because to some people popularity is a business. "You gonna get a rose in homeroom today? Or is your boyfriend anti-flowers?"

I lowered my head. "He's anti-flowers."

Somebody smacked Nico as they passed. His desk knocked into mine. "Watch it. Evie's napping." He tousled my hair. "Poor kid."

Mr. Shepard entered. I propped myself on one arm and flapped open my notebook. I set my pen on its point, and, as he began to talk, the instrument began to move, transcribing every utterance and random eruption. I created lines, I practiced lines, I located the microscopic electromagnetic pathways between the roots of all sound and the receivers in my brain. I extended those passages down into my hand and onto the notebook, making the paper the point of convergence. By that exercise I kept awake—if only fractionally.

> *Louis Napoleon, son of Louis Bonaparte, King of Holland—a locker slams and another, hey Farrell, wait up you prick—nephew of Napoleon Bonaparte, is elected Emperor by universal suffrage. In 1853 he marries Eugenie de Montijo. By the way, Montijo is not a new Oldsmobile—moans and yawns, desks scraping, erasers whizzing and bouncing—The Second Empire becomes one of the most productive monarchies in France's history, sustaining itself— whooping howls from English 10 next door—propaganda—a squeaky film cart arrives at the open door, did you order A/V Mr. Shepard—no, I did not—whining, c'mon Shep, let's have a flick.*

I started to drift, so I wrote my name, over and over. *Eveline Aster Auerbach.* I didn't know what it was supposed to mean, my name, how it promised to define me.

"It should rhyme with *mine* or *fine*: *Ev-e-line*," Jack would say.

He loved the way Maman used to say *E-vleen*, but she was French and we were not, and nothing is more annoying than when people insert European pronunciations into everyday talk. One of the things Americans do best is mispronounce things they know nothing about. It's a confession of sorts. It's like saying, we may be stupid, but we're not pretentious.

I wrote the letter *A* over and over, one cursive *A* leading to the next, charging forth like a locomotive, stark and emphatic, the way screams are discharged—*AAAAAAAAAA*. Just as the row neared the margin, my wrist dropped sharply to produce a single vertical line, then it retraced that line to the top, unfolding in a curve to the right, making a bubble and collapsing at last in a bar to the finish: *R*. I finished it off—*o-u-r-k-e*. It was true that I was tired, because when I looked at his name, at the precarious way I'd written it, jittery and uncertain like in letters from immigrants to home, I began to cry.

Stephen gestured to me, shaking one corner of a test paper. The class was going over the exam. I pulled mine from beneath my notebook. Stephen got a hundred. I got an eighty-nine, which was depressing since I hadn't even studied. Being slightly better than average at schoolwork is like being a good soldier or a talented receptionist. I covered my face with my hands until all that remained were glowing strips, insinuations of fingers. I wondered about the phrase, *Water seeks its own level.* It starts out with the idea of atmospheric pressure but then gets extrapolated to imply that there's some scientific inevitability to negative human behavior, that there's no point trying to improve certain people, that life has its losers.

The class laughed in unison. The noise broke out in a jolly crack—*Oh-ho-ho*—causing me to jump and to feel truly separate. Three minutes remained. I tore a corner from a page in my notebook.

> *J—I think I am shrinking. Someone told me that today is Valentine's Day. I am sad because I have no gift for you. I'm sorry. I'm so tired. I love you, promise. E.*

AT THE BELL WE rushed the doorway, and to get through we took miniature steps. The door was congested like a waist. It was like winnowing through an hourglass. But in the packed corridor, we turned anonymous. I crossed perpendicular to the tide and entered the library.

Mr. O'Donnell was at the counter, performing the sort of grim rituals librarians perform with index cards and oak drawers and stumpy pencils. Those rubber stamps with columns of rotating numbers. "Hello, Miss Auerbach. What will it be today? Hugo, Camus, Cervantes? I can't recall, have you read *Don Quixote?*"

"Do you have a book of poetry by Emily Dickinson?"

He paused somberly, toying with the tightly twirled tip of his mustache. One true thing about librarians is that no matter how seriously they are engaged in their work, they are always glad to be interrupted when the theme is books. They consider all queries scrupulously, no matter how simple the search or how behind on time either of you may be. They savor excursions into literature and love to have their knowledge tested. They lie in wait; they will not be rushed.

"Let's see," he said as he puttered out, taking to the aisles with a trifling waddle, inching to a halt at the stack near the windows, "poetry. *D, D.* Well, here's Baudelaire, Byron, Davies, Drayton. No, no that's misfiled. You see what happens when one sorts poetry helter-skelter. Let's pull that out and replace it as so, and here we are, Dickinson, Emily."

He handed me the book, and I thanked him. Behind him, the halls were empty. "Run along. I'll sign you out. It's against policy, of course, but I'll make an exception since it's Valentine's Day. One must never interfere with young love. Bad luck, you know."

"Thank you, Mr. O'Donnell. I'll return it before lunch."

I stopped in the art studio for colored paper and scissors—later in study hall I would make cut-out hearts to stuff inside the envelope. By the time I got to homeroom, I had just enough time to copy half of a poem on the bottom of my note to Jack.

> *It's all I have to bring to-day.*
> *This, and my heart beside,*
> *This and my heart, and all the fields,*
> *And all the meadows wide.*   E. Dickinson, c. 1858

AFTER THE ANNOUNCEMENTS, MRS. Kennedy passed out roses wrapped in paper like shiny green wands, strained shut and dirt red. They looked like living headaches. Karen Drapier got one and Missy Burke and so did Warren Baxter. "Mind if I keep it?" Mrs. Kennedy asked when Warren said just to throw his in the garbage.

Jack was not waiting as usual at the door of my English class, so I went to his locker and crammed the package I'd made through the top slot. When still he had not materialized by lunch, I wondered if he had taken off. I vaguely recalled him saying something about fifty dollars and a homeopathic dentist in Connecticut. In sixth period calculus, my seat felt slippery and severe as I observed the advance of the clock hands—three, four, seven minutes, and he did not come.

"All right, people," Mrs. Oliphant called, "let's go." She launched the door from its propped station in sync with the articulate prong of the late bell. The door whooshed, decelerating and depressurizing, winding down like an exhausted electronic thing. Just as it was about to click shut, an arm caught it—Jack's. He was wearing a new sweater and jeans that were clean. Dan was behind him, looking handsome as well in a blue blazer, despite unwashed hair shaped in a flat jaunty spray on the left from the pressure of his pillow.

"Glad you could make it, fellows," the teacher said.

"Glad to be here," Jack said.

He deposited an envelope on my desk and sat behind me, his feet punching squeakily into the gap between the base of my seat and the attached book rack. I played with the pouch he'd left, making lazy orbits with one finger. It confused me to see him in school. It's confusing to greet your privacy when access to it is prohibited. It's like going home for lunch when you have to leave again. Mrs. Oliphant made a slanting series of numbers on the board, which joined together into the shape of a melting torpedo. I unraveled the packing string that bound my gift from Jack, and it eased its way open like a dilating thing. Nestled within imperfectly plied sheets of crepe paper was a dried flower, of a kind I'd never seen, with elegant petals that faded in hue from tip to base—violet, lavender, white. Mustard anthers had fallen into the folds of paper, staining its crevices. On a second sheet was an exquisite and meticulous drawing of the same blossom, shivery and crisp. And there were words.

> *For the girl. I picked this last summer, it's a Camas. I slept in a meadow full of them on a mountain in Wyoming. This flower thrives when closest to the clouds, just like you.*
> *I love you, Jack.*

A shred of graph paper landed on my desk. It was a scrawled response to my Valentine's note:

> *You are small because you forget to eat. You're too obsessed with your space needle set design. Dan and I are cutting out at 2:30, so we can finish the music for that asinine play. How about something red for dinner—J*
> *P.S. Your eyes look bruised.*

I TOSSED MY HEAD into the air, and it seemed to careen indefinitely back. My shoulders too, thrust forever up, higher and higher, like a rabid stalk speedily departing the rightful range of its form. The atmosphere was murky and cold, gripping and moorish, though I could not be sure about that. As the blackened halls of my mind grew cavernous, with the stony vaults doubling, trebling, out and up and back, I lost all sense of position and place. I labored in vain to stem the epidemic nothingness, but I could not fathom any known beginning—*I could not fathom my beginning.* The farther back I hurtled, the more numerous the roads that lay about me, entrances in a flickering starry crest, puffing and dragging like smoke from throats, luring me, admonishing me, telling me that nothing is original, that everything—*everything*—is invention.

"It's me," a voice was saying. "Please, please. Baby, baby."

I awoke in pitch dark. Denny was shaking me. Behind his shoulders, I recognized the bare yellow bulb of the darkroom. I wondered who had moved the ceiling fixture to the wall.

"I'm going to lift you honey, okay? I'm going to lift. Ready, here we go." I felt his arms digging under my back, and, as he straightened his knees to raise my body, the bulb disappeared upward in a fluid arc.

He eased me onto the stool. It was not good to sit. My head throbbed. I reached to touch the place that hurt, and that hurt worse. Denny moved my hand away, and with gentle fingers he measured the knot, which had seemed to me to be about the size of a lime.

"I can't tell if it's bleeding, I think it's bleeding," Denny said.

"It's like a lime," I asked, "isn't it?"

"Okay," he said, searching nervously around the unoccupied darkroom for someone to consult, someone other than me. "I've got to get you out of here." He wagged his hand in front of his nose. "This air is poison. I keep telling you—*Solvents kill.*"

Denny ducked beneath one of my armpits, and he lifted me. Denny was strong. When he hugged you, it was like entering a whole new room. Once he heaved Nico into the air and smashed his head three times against the lockers—*boom, boom, boom*—saying, "You filthy runt—you're lucky I don't toss you under a fucking car." I didn't see it, I just heard about it, not from Denny but from Lisa Tobias. Denny probably didn't mention it because he was a gentleman, and it had to do with me. On the same day, L.B. Strickland got two broken fingers and a dislocated shoulder.

We stopped at the main office. Denny leaned me against the door frame while he ran in.

"Can we help you, Mr. Marshall?" one of the secretaries asked as he hustled past. She stared contemptuously over the top of her glasses. Her tongue curled odiously against her teeth; it was the color of beaten yolks.

"Just getting an ice pack, Mrs. Miller." He went through the side door of the unattended infirmary and came out almost instantly, blue plastic bag in hand. "No need to exert yourself on behalf of an injured student. Here, honey," he said to me, handing off the pack, sweeping up my body, glancing back over his shoulder and shooting a look at the women inside. "God forbid they should burn a few calories."

In the car he talked incessantly but lovingly, the way some dogs bark. "You shouldn't have been in there alone. What if I hadn't come? What if you tried to get up and then fell again? You're lucky you don't have a concussion. And the chemicals! Haven't you heard that every egg you'll ever have is in you already? You could do some damage."

My head was on his leg with the ice wedged between his belly and my skull. I drifted comfortably as he spoke, inhaling the detergent scent of his corduroys. He was explaining the phrase, *mad as a hatter. Something, something,* he was saying, *and licking mercury.* As we turned into my driveway, he tried to rouse me. "Time to get up."

"Please keep driving," I begged him.

"I knew you'd say that. But I have to go."

I opened my eyes and studied the scar on his chin. It was glossy and impermeable to hair, like enameled skin, and it made the shape of a division sign with extra dots on top and bottom or a hieroglyph of a squashed sun. He'd slipped on the jetty at Georgica Beach and had to get fifteen stitches. I drove sixty miles an hour to Southampton Hospital with the hazards on while he plugged up his chin with a three-pack of tube socks. He recorded his recovery for a biology report—the action of the phagocytes, capillaries, epithelial cells, collagen, and so on. We learned that a scar differs from normal skin due to the alignment of protein fibers.

"Isn't the body incredible?" he speculated one afternoon as we were photographing. He had me document the maturation phase. "A scar is like a warning. Reminding you not to let the same thing happen twice."

Denny was good in science, but you had to be careful not to act impressed or say, *You ought to be a doctor!* Though all his test scores had been nearly perfect, he refused to consider a career in medicine. "I just spent eighteen years pretending to be straight," he said the day we drove to the post office and mailed his application to Fashion Institute of Technology. "Medical school would kill me." He acted like he was happy that day, but I knew he was not.

"Do you have a date?" I asked.

"I do," he said with a single nod. "And you are not invited."

"A Valentine's date?"

"Yes," he said, "a Valentine's date."

I stirred and the upholstery squeaked. After lifting me to sit, he bounded around to the passenger side to help me out. I tried to recall the last time I had as much energy. It seemed like such a long time ago that it must have been never.

"There, there," he said, hugging and releasing me in one motion. He pointed me toward the house and gave me a tiny shove. I hit the hedges, missing the path entirely. "Oh, you're breaking my heart," he moaned as I stumbled along to the porch. "Sneak in back. In *back*," he directed, throwing a loud whisper over the top of the car. He waved his arm in frustration when I reached the steps. "Too late. You'll never sleep now."

In the living room Kate was stretched across the couch, phone in hand. It occurred to me to go back out, but Denny was already gone. He tapped his horn before taking off down Osborne to Cedar. I shut the storm door. I felt like I was entering a box, drawing over the lid.

"Gotta go," Kate said to the other party, Coco probably. "Evie's home." She sat upright. On the shoulder of her sweater was one of the school roses. "I got it anonymously," she said, coming to show me. "It's from *Harrison*."

The vessels in my temples clogged, like maybe the blood from my lump got sucked back and doled out evenly behind my eyes. I felt the veins grow with each beat of my heart. I wondered was it possible for them to rupture. The zipper from my coat got caught in my scarf. I said, "Shit."

"I'll do it," she sighed, coming over. I raised my chin and within seconds she'd wiggled the zipper to the base. Some girls are just good at things.

I dropped the coat and made my way to the bathroom where I ran the water and pretended to pee. Possibly Kate was right. I had no idea of Rourke, what he felt. In the mirror I examined the irregular terrain of my face, the pyramidic zones of shadow and light. I thought how handsome Jack looked in calculus. Maybe there was another girl he liked, one with bruiseless eyes, like Nina Spear, who rode horses, or Joss Mathers, who had signed his cast and given him a blow job two days before he and I had met. I thought of Denny's date in Springs and of Kate and her rose and how everything was bursting forth from dormancy. Everyone was falling in love, in real and active love. I felt trussed to my own axis, like some dead meat spinning.

Kate called through the bathroom door. "You hungry?"

I splashed cold water on my wound and mussed my hair in back to hide the gooey spot. Flakes of blood stuck to my fingers, rehydrating and staining the towel in scarlet dots. In the medicine cabinet was an old compact with powder clinging in a deranged ring to its outer edge. I pried off sharp chunks and dragged them on my face.

"Not really," I called. "Jack's bringing food."

"Maybe he wants to be alone with you. For Valentine's."

I smoothed in the make-up. "I doubt it."

When I came out, Kate was making coffee—laying out cups and spoons, filling a pitcher with milk.

I cleared my throat, saying tentatively, "Did you say something?"

"To Jack? About what?"

"No, I mean, you know—about the flower."

She regarded me with curiosity. "Are you wearing make-up?"

"Why? Do I look funny?"

"Not at all, you look pretty. You always look pretty."

I leaned up to turn on the light. It was early for lights, but I wanted to move the day along. I wanted to get to night.

"At rehearsal," Kate began, "Harrison said, *Nice rose*." She started peeling an apple over the trash. "And you know when you can tell someone is thinking something? Well, he was definitely thinking something. I could tell." She finished with the apple, went to the counter, and cut it, offering me some.

I said no thanks.

Kate continued. "So, *I* said, 'I wish I had someone to thank, but unfortunately, there was no name on the card.' You know, I kind of hinted around to see if he would say anything."

Black bubbles were rising from the coffee pot, and she moved to turn off the heat. I felt embarrassed—for her, and also for Rourke. Kate could be very coquettish. I rested my head in the basin of my arms. My chin touched the table; the glass was cold.

"And *he* said, 'I doubt whoever sent it will stay anonymous for long.' "

"Then what?" I asked.

"And then, well, that's it." She handed me a hot mug.

"That's it?"

"Well, Michelle had a flower, so did Ellie, but he only mentioned mine."

I took a sip of coffee. It was really good. I felt better already. It was nice, actually, spending time with Kate.

THE FRONT DOOR SLAMMED and Jack stormed in. He dumped two pizza boxes on the table and snapped apart the stapled lid of the top one, flicking it into the air. Inside, the pie was shaped like a heart.

Kate said, "Neat."

He gestured to the pies with great annoyance as he wiped his nose with his sleeve. "All they had to do was cut the crusts to make two lousy hearts, and they wanted an extra buck per pie. Fucking proletariat morons."

"Was it crowded? They were probably busy," Kate said.

Jack chucked his coat on the floor in the hall. "No, it was empty. They just knew it was for her," he said, referring to me, "so they gave me a hard time." He hopped onto the counter. With his sneaker, he opened the base cabinet door and rested his feet on its rim. "Save the second pie. For Irene."

He shot his hand through his hair and examined the room. Kate whistled cheerfully, immune to his sullen influence. Her body grazed his as she slid three unmatching glasses from the plastic goblet rack over his head. I considered what was between them, what they felt, what they blocked. There's always something between people.

Jack scratched absently at his jaw and glowered in my direction. "You haven't slept yet, have you?"

I shook my head. "Not yet."

"Oh!" Kate interrupted, thrusting her shoulder in his direction. "I almost forgot. Notice anything? Like my rose?"

The color drained from Jack's eyes as he contemplated her with extreme disinterest. "I know about your rose."

"What do you mean, *You know*? How do you know?"

Jack capitulated, plunging his arm to his lap. "Because Dan sent it. I've had to hear about it for, like, weeks"

"Dan?" Kate writhed slightly and set her coffee down. She padded out, saying *Dan,* and then *Dan* again. Moments later her bedroom door slammed, and there was the distant sound of sobbing.

"What the hell's wrong with Dan?" Jack demanded. He leapt off the counter and moved to the table, and began plucking mushrooms from the top pie. I stretched the skin of my face in circles with both hands. I wondered what to do. It felt a little perverse to be in my position. But Jack was contemplating me, and the longer I remained silent, the greater the opportunity for him to construe that silence as evasion. It was amazing, the work his mind could do. He let the pizza lid float to a close. Stamped in red ink on the cover was a mustached guy in a chef's hat holding a steaming pizza. He looked happy. I wondered about that, about his happiness. Was he really happy, or was he just trying to convince me that he was happy so I'd think that the pizza tasted better. It was a little insulting, actually.

Jack raised my coffee cup. "*Caffeine*? Are you *trying* to kill yourself?" The mug smacked the table and coffee looped over the lip. "Dennis called me."

I said oh.

"Were you planning to tell me what happened?"

"You just walked in."

"Well, did you faint, or what?"

"I guess I—I fell. Or fainted." I wasn't sure what happened.

He was behind my chair. "Stay still," he urged, then he tilted my head to examine it. "Christ, Evie, there's blood on it. Get the first aid kit."

"It's upstairs in the bathroom."

"You better go. If I go, I'll find Kate and smack her."

I headed up slowly. Some people get bloody noses, others sleep-walk. Marilyn can get the hiccups for three days straight, and Dad falls asleep in strange places—I happen to faint. I've fainted at the Guggenheim and at Woolworth's on 23rd Street and in an IHOP parking lot in Cape Canaveral. Whenever Dr. Scott checks my blood pressure, he says, "Eighty over fifty. It's a wonder you're alive."

It was somewhat contradictory for Jack to get so upset over blood and caffeine, considering the abuses he leveled against himself. I wasn't sure what he wanted. Kate either, or, for that matter, myself. When we were young, it seemed as if there was no wilderness between needs and ends, no work to do or interests to protect. There was order without the business of keeping order. When people talk about *precious youth*, they're basically referring to the time before you had to connive to get what you want.

I nudged Kate's door. She was curled up in the corner of the bed, crying. Her face was splotchy and dented, like soft fruit. I played with the beveled glass doorknob, jiggling it in its socket.

"You don't understand," she said, her chest heaving as she spoke.

If she meant I didn't know what it felt like to be in love, and in love with Rourke, she was wrong. But if she meant that I didn't understand the risk and ruin of invention, she was right. She'd gone too far into self-deception. If she did love him, it was a love that conveniently bypassed natural law.

"He's a man," I said, "you know, with stuff on his mind."

"You can say *sex*," she blurted. "I'm not a fucking retard."

I felt light-headed, so I moved to her bed. I looked to the spot in which I had just been standing. I tried to imagine what it was like to talk to me. Was it hard or easy. Jack had said the blood was fresh. Maybe it was running down my back like a mane or tail.

"You think you know everything," she told me. "Well, you don't."

Kate was alluding to sex. I supposed she felt pressure. I supposed she felt it was time. Probably she felt that to venture further into virginity would be to attach unwanted magnitude to that condition. Probably she hoped to resolve that, just as some people need to get their driver's license at sixteen, though they have nowhere to go. It's a perilous business, devising to be taken—the flouncing and cuing, the skittish surrender of reason. Sex demands equality because sex involves the will, someone's will, preferably one's own.

"Maybe I don't know everything," I said as I moved to get the first aid box from the bathroom. "But I do know one thing—he's not crying right now. He's not crying over the valentine you didn't send."

I DREAMT I WAS A PAPER DOLL. I WAS ONE IN A ROW OF PAPER DOLL CUTOUTS sitting on a swing set. We wore triangular lime green dresses, and we had shoulder-length flip hairdos, like from the 1960s. There was singing, melodious and modern. In school I tried to draw the dream, but it was not possible. Beyond the neat doll bodies, there had lain a sleepy hint of magic, a steamy curtain, a foggy aqua essence, something astral and sublime that continued to insinuate itself upon me for the remainder of the day, like an ocular echo.

After school I rummaged through the record albums, listening to all the bossa nova—Jobim, Gilberto, Gil, Getz—the voices were very delicate and de-emphasized, like the feel of my dream. I stripped to my long johns, leaving my clothes in a pile near the hearth, and I sat, closing my eyes to reconstitute the overall imagery as I'd perceived it in sleep—its elusive vitality, its lightness and lift, its civic femininity. There was this way my mother used to walk through Manhattan when I was little, tossing her arms and kicking her legs just like the girls in the songs "Georgie Girl" and "Windy."

The figures on the swings had been serene and insurgent, separate but connected—it would not have been possible to extract one without collapsing the whole. I realized I shouldn't have tried to *draw* the dream but to *cut* it, so I got a stack of giant green paper from the basement and some sewing scissors and began to work.

By the time I heard the rain, it must have been six. Frozen drops were making this glorious spreading sound on the roof, like nickels on a tent. I realized it was raining when I found myself thinking of water. I was thinking of water converting to ice in clouds. I would like to make a film of it—a time-lapse film like you see in science class of a flower blooming or a bean plant sprouting—to dramatize a metaphor of *becoming*, to remind people that what falls to their feet is the product of its own miraculous history.

I once proposed a reenactment of the water cycle for a science fair. I would stand baby daisies in astroturf at the base of a tank near a tiny lake. Sprinkling water would land on the flowers, causing them to grow, which would be accomplished by discreetly placed fishing wire. Under the lake would be a hidden can of sterno or Bunsen burner to simulate evaporation. The plan was to reconceive the majesty of rain, to restore through art what had been long lost through living.

Nick Kraft, the earth science teacher, said, "*No way*. Do not try to make rain. Vapor extraction is a nightmare." He recommended a tidal wave or a volcano. "Tragedy is more fun anyway," Nick told me. "You buy some glue and plastic doodads at the 5 & 10 and you create a theater of disaster."

I was not surprised. In school, the study of the earth is the study of maps and catastrophe, as though the only possible points of interest to teenagers are border wars and biblical devastation. History is the history of battle, language is the study of English, and science is an excuse to play with acid and cut frogs.

If you are waiting for some creative digression into the rhetoric of math or the zoology of conquest, you will be waiting a long time.

I spread my legs wide as possible and folded another sheet of paper in rectangular strips. I'd been having trouble with the hairstyles. They weren't flipping properly. In my dream the hair had been weightless, curling up and in, like tails with party kinks. I often dreamt of hair but never of happy hair or bouncing hair.

The room darkened freakishly; the sky turned to ash. A hard wind discharged against the picture window in erratic gusts and there was an itinerant commotion—the sound of people running through rain, of voices caught in pockets. The front door blew open with a slam, and Kate burst through, her body huddled against the water. Tim Storey followed, urging her in, swatting her in, going, *C'mon, c'mon*. Tim stomped his feet and shook his head like a two-legged dog. It was funny to think of him that way, as a transient biped, as though he were standing upright with difficulty, as though he would have been better served on all fours. He charged directly to the fire. I drew my papers protectively into the pocket of my legs.

The door did not close. It was braced by a single hand—Rourke's. In one enormous stride, he moved from the cement porch to the pale plank floor. When he passed through the door frame, he had to lower his head. His eyes found mine easily, as if he had expected me to be exactly where I was.

"Hey," he said, and I replied, "Hey."

He dried his feet and smiled shyly, and I saw the edge of his perfect teeth and the dimple on the right side of his face, which was a deep furrow like a pen puncture. I returned to my work but continued to regard him from beneath the hood of my head. He unzipped his soaking jacket, and there he was, in my tiny house. It was like having a constellation down from the sky.

"It was raining too hard for me to walk," Kate explained. "Now it's raining too hard for them to drive. You can put your coat there," she told Rourke, referring to the couch back, then she turned on the desk lamp. The incandescence blanched the firelight, and I flinched. "Sorry," she said, smiling and snapping her head in a neck curtsy. *Curtsy* is an awful word. Jack had declared a two hundred year ban on it. Two hundred, in case cryogenics takes off.

"Evie hates lights," Kate said, "and, honestly, she has so many vision problems because of it."

Rourke scrutinized my mother's bookshelves, the exhausted textbooks and frayed novels, the thumbtacked newspaper clippings and the loose nudes on cocktail napkins. How small the house seemed with him in it, how steeped with color and congested with effects. It was like a feast or a carnival, the ceiling seemed to swag. His eyes lingered on a white wooden sailboat I'd built in my dad's shop when I was five, and he lifted it—feeling the canvas triangle crisp with paint, running one finger across the name painted on the block bottom. *Eveline*. It was nice that he looked for me there, no one had ever looked for me there.

Kate invited her guests to the kitchen. Tim hopped right off the hearth, but Rourke remained, continuing to scan the shelves in silence. When she called him once again, he moved to join them, first turning off the desk lamp that Kate had put on. His hand lingering on the switch, his back to me.

I looked for new music. I'd lost interest in the bossa nova. The woman Rourke awakened in me was not gifted with delicacy or cause; she was vigorous and without culture. She came in an atomic rush, possessing nothing more than instinct and courage. Van Morrison seemed right. The album cover was gray like my impression of the quarterlit hail was gray, and the first song on side two was gray as well.

> *This is a song about,*
> *Your wavelength and my wavelength, baby.*
> *You turn me on when you get me on your wavelength—*

I knelt at the window by the stereo, extending my arm through. The drops marked my wrist, turning it pink. Probably one line of precipitation could slice your wrist open, if it kept falling over and over in a row, like a sewing machine. Rourke's jacket was across the room, catching the light and making a tranquil gloss. I resisted as long as I could, and when I could not anymore, I crawled to the couch and up the side. My hand, still blushed from the stroke of the rain, caressed the leather. How strange was compulsion, how strange to see my hand moving so surely even as my thoughts did glorious battle. I raised one finger to the light. It had captured a frail globe, a lone bead of water, purest at the rim and murkiest at the pendant dome. I rotated my hand to rescue the pearl, then I deposited it gently on the palm of my opposite hand. It was like a ladybug. I watched the molecules vanish into the net of my skin while in the kitchen they chatted capably, as though they'd been brought together by choice, not chance.

"Actually," Rourke was saying, "I took a costume design course in college."

"You're kidding!" Kate giggled.

Tim said, "Hey, why not? It was probably an easy *A*."

"Not quite. I missed so many classes, I almost failed."

"Oh, shit," Tim groaned sympathetically. "There goes the GPA."

"I asked the teacher if there was anything I could do to bring up the grade. 'As a matter of fact, Mr. Rourke,' she said, 'there is. I'll give you the weekend to make a wedding dress.'"

There was an explosion of laughter. "The *bitch*," Tim said.

"What did you do?" Kate asked.

"I made a wedding dress."

"And did your grade go up?"

"I got an *A*," Rourke said, "and several marriage proposals."

They laughed again and then moved into a discussion of politics and sports. Rourke talked about President Carter and the Soviet Union and

Afghanistan and the boycott of the Winter Olympics. Coming from his voice, with its authoritative underside and its stately cadence, worldly things did not seem vulgar or petrifying. It intrigued me, the way he excelled socially, the way he spoke that language but also mine. If I was sorry to not know more about current events, I was consoled by the fact that I'd read every novel in the house and that I could mold a finch from clay and also recount in detail the aroma of a half-dead oak leaf. But possibly that all counted for nothing.

One by one, I burned my cutout attempts. The dolls made a contorted lattice on the logs, leaping up eerily to puppet-like existence, contracting down to pitiful cinders. It was like a breath—like breathing life *into*, like sucking it out again. There was a place in the middle where they looked best, a place past the mirage of perfection, prior to the corruption of form. The place of my dream.

A single sheet of paper remained. I folded it, then cut without penciling, my body reaching immodestly for each new inch, going by sense of feeling, the most important sense to cultivate. And as I went I kept thinking, *It's not the chime of the bell, it's the echo of the chime.*

To make the inner openings around the bodies and swings, I used a blade, unfocusing my eyes, steering through resistant folds, guiding my wrist, forearm, and shoulder in perfunctory pulses. Just as I made the final incision, and the curious remains dropped to the floor, the glow of the firelight darkened.

"What are you making?" he wanted to know.

He spoke with care, as though aware in advance of the difficulties he might face. He wanted me to know he regretted using words on me so soon after using words on them and that *these* words were different words, and that he knew how not to lie. His caution was not inappropriate. I felt I'd been lied to, which is weird, but I did.

A fragment of light split the floor, a fracture between the shadows of his legs. It vanished as he squatted, his knees coming to the height of my shoulders, not twelve inches away. He made a band of heat, a barrier where none had been. He allowed me to examine him, letting my eyes go very slowly over. In his willingness to be searched and to be seen, in his conscious quietude on my behalf, I perceived his dedication and resolve—I had the feeling he would never leave. I had the feeling of being a cat to catch. Once Powell taught me how to catch cats. We were at the tracks, crouching to lure a lost kitten. "Build trust," Powell instructed, hardly moving his lips. "Gesture slowly."

Rourke's forearms ventured off his legs. They reached into my vicinity then paused. When I did not recoil, they came farther. He took the paper, and I let him.

"I had a dream," I said, speaking because he willed me to. "I was a cutout. On a swing."

From each end of the chain, he grasped a doll's hand, a fist really—there were no fingers—and, gently, he pulled. The hair was perfect. He smiled. "Which one are you?"

I stared widely. "Which side is the front?"

"This side," he said. The side facing him.

I pointed to the third from the right. "This is me."

Dishes clattered in the kitchen. I startled, but to reassure me he did not move. He just reassigned his weight to the opposite leg. He seemed disinclined to give my dolls back. Maybe he was going to take them away, like he took the chapel. But no, he released them—reluctantly. There was a single second during which we each held one end of the dolls, and, in that second, I felt a riveting and arduous bliss.

"No more hail," he said, looking out the window. Then he stood, penetrating faraway space. Though I was sitting, I felt I might topple. My hand grabbed the floor.

"I'll see you soon," he pledged confidentially as his arms entered the sleeves of his jacket.

"Yes," I said, pledging too. "Soon."

"WHAT WERE YOU TWO talking about?" Kate asked. The headlights scanned her face through the window as Rourke's car backed onto the street, and implications of raindrops slithered across her cheeks, elongated, then in rushing clusters, skulking left to right like legions of obedient insects. I was thinking of an old detective movie, *The Big Sleep* or *The Maltese Falcon*. Kate and I had come to inhabit a menacing realm of extremes, shadows and light, desire and aversion, faith and betrayal, wins and losses, and, in that realm of spades, we were liars, each of us. "Nothing," I said. "The rain."

Kate hoped I was friendly, at least.

I told her I thought that I was.

She fell back on the couch. "I can't believe he was actually here."

"Neither can I," I said, agreeing. It felt good to agree with Kate. It had been a long time.

6.

At six in the morning I lay awake, obsessed with the idea of what a sneaky game chess is. On Thompson Street, in my father's neighborhood, there are chess shops where players sit face to face, inert and imperturbable, insouciantly grazing knees and sharing breath. Yet, in the chess section of the newspaper, you read of cornering and abducting, lunging and capturing. The combination of physical inertia and mental vigor is weird, like the glacial way reptiles hunt.

Opaque olive casements separated my bedroom just negligibly from the backyard. In summer my room was like the outside of a terrarium, with leaves bearing down—robust and spectacular leaves, living, stalking leaves that threatened to fracture the glass and suffocate me. That's when I would move to the barn. Winters were cold in my room but tolerable. In winter things turn skeletal and brown; the earth clings to its occupants. Air moves and sounds whistle. Brown things are simply sleeping things, and you can't fault a thing for that, for conceding to nature with such humility as to willingly shrivel.

I taped my cut-outs to the glass. Rourke had held them thirteen hours before. I liked the idea of many figures extracted from a solitary plane, of that plane meaning time, of those figures meaning uniformity of principle through design. I would make more—Victorians and flappers, suffragettes and ladies with afros. Nuns.

At eight-thirty the phone rang. I rushed to the living room, sliding in my socks to stop the second ring so no one would wake up. I wanted to be ready first, before all the initial lack, the colliding needs and pop-up hair, the talk of nightmares over cold cereal. The cats clustered at my ankles, sticking to my feet like a crazy beard, like from one of those make-a-face magnet shaving games. "Hello?"

"It's me," Denny said. "Did I wake you?"

I whispered, "No."

"Good," he said, whispering too. "I stopped at Guild Hall on the way back from Woolco last night to get out of the hail. Did you see the hail?"

"I did. It was beautiful."

"Well, it practically cracked my windshield. Anyway, rehearsal was over, so the place was empty except for Richie—the lighting guy, you know Richie—and Paul Z and Jason Mulford. They told me the scenery had just arrived, and I went to check it. The flats were completely wet, so I got those guys to help me stand everything up. There was a tiny bit of damage—don't get upset—it's nothing we can't fix. I'm picking up Dave at ten. Feel like coming?"

"Sure," I said, "I'll take my bike over."

"Meet you around ten-thirty," he said.

I left right away. I wanted to be outside. I wanted to be cold. I stopped at Dreesen's to buy a bag of raisin bread, then I went to the nature trail. The ducks must have been hungry because they got out of the water and came to me, climbing rocks and waddling briskly—it's awful for a thing to waddle briskly. They ate all that I had and then they left. Ducks can be scary. Water does not penetrate feathers and beaks are weapons. Their heads look like helmets. Jack disliked water fowl. He did not feel obliged to relate to creatures with liquid feces. "Give me another piece," he would urge when we went there, and he would squeeze the Wonder Bread into pellets to chuck.

I rode very incredibly fast down Main Street, and right before the offices of the *East Hampton Star,* I leaned sweepingly into the vacant oncoming lane and bounced onto the sidewalk in front of the brick theater, where I came to a skidding halt.

Guild Hall is a community center. Sometimes plays are held there, sometimes art shows or classes, sometimes lectures or films. Unlike the VFW in town and Ashawagh Hall in Springs, local people didn't use it too much. It was kind of a luxury that the drama club was having its play there since the high school auditorium didn't even have a real curtain. In the gallery to the left of the entrance, two ladies were hanging art for an upcoming show. They wore headbands on gray-blonde hair with growing-out bangs and those wool cardigans with the floral design around the neck and shoulders that look like champion horse wreaths.

The room was white and entirely without detail, somewhat like a habitat, and the radio played a plonky kind of jazz. There was an open ladder and skipping circles of masking tape on the floor. It reminded me of Sweden—the light, I guess. The light seemed northern and superior. I'd never been to Sweden, but some things you just know. I waved as I passed. One woman smiled, the other just turned.

The theater was empty—cast call wasn't until noon; I knew from Kate's schedule on the refrigerator. From the top of the theater the sets looked okay and not so very damaged at all. We called them *the chapel* and *the village green*, but they were just monochrome collages of geometric shapes—one was a huge vertical diamond attached to a horizontal polygon in ivory, like the throat of a bird, and the other was a trapezoid in smokey rust, like fox fur, because Dave Meese decided that in the village it was autumn.

At the end of the far left aisle, there was an archway leading backstage. I went through and ran into Rourke.

We collided in the boxy shaft between two doorways. He retreated, so did I, each just a step. Scarcely two feet of air divided us—I had to tilt my head to see his face. Burgundy drapes cloaked the door behind him, and the creamy glow from a safety bulb gave the vestibule the appearance of a tasteful coffin. I tried to locate us in time. We seemed timeless to my eyes.

"I came to fix the flats," I said.

Rourke shoved a hand in his pocket, debilitating himself, neutralizing something. I'd seen him do it before. In the record store.

"Sorry they got messed up," he said. "I should've stayed last night."

"It was raining pretty bad—I guess," I said.

"Yeah," he said, "I guess."

I didn't mind my work getting damaged; it's the nature of art to yield. When you're an artist, you possess a drive, you clear yourself of it, you relinquish the outcome. Someone else takes it and marks a new beginning. You can't get crazy about things. Susan at the laundry next to Dad's house gets crazy. Once Chihuahua Man draped the shirts she'd ironed for him over his forearm. Chihuahua Man has four Chihuahuas and nothing else—no family, no car, no phone. His dogs run loose, crapping up the sidewalks, and all the old ladies with buckets yell and throw bleach. That day, Susan raised the hinged countertop that sequestered her from the rest of the world, and she ran out to the street. I'd never seen her whole legs before. "Take the hanger! Take the hanger!" She certainly was within her rights to yell, since it's rude to demean someone else's labor, but, for all she knew, he was going to take the shirts home and let the dogs sleep on them. Sometimes the best you can do is your small part, perfectly.

For months after, it was the talk of the neighborhood—*What could Chihuahua Man have been doing with those nice shirts?* "I don't get it," Tony Abbruscato kept saying. "He don't even own leashes."

Rourke asked how long did I think it would take.

"I don't know," I said. It was hard to think, actually, with him standing there. "I haven't seen them yet."

"Let's go," he said, leading me back through the stage door, holding it for me. At the light board he paused to survey the bank of switches and levers. There was a unanimous crack and the stage was illuminated. A sultry pressure cosseted the back of my neck as I crossed to the rear, him behind me—and the sound of his footsteps.

I loosened a bent shingle from the chapel, just going back and forth. "The glue will have to dry before I can paint. It might take a few hours," I said. "Will I be in your way?"

His breath, my ear. "You won't be in my way."

In his shadow everything felt right. If it was wrong to be close to him, I didn't care. I didn't care if we were seen, and I didn't care by whom. It was a feeling of being outside the world, like he was outside and I was outside, and I had been waiting and he had been waiting. And by providing me with what I'd been seeking, he proved not only that I had *been* seeking but that I'd been *correct* to seek. I was grateful to be thus confirmed. I felt his grasp of me. I'd never felt anyone's grasp before. That was sorrowful, but the sorrow did not move me. I simply saw the precariousness of home, of friends, of life.

"I'll be back," he said. I felt myself list. I felt him tend as well, then stop, then straighten. Him whispering, "That okay with you?"

When he left, I emptied my knapsack and tubes of glue and paint spilled onto the floor. Denny was late as usual, and for some time I walked. Walking on stage is the same as walking in life, only the lights make you a star. When you reach the end of the stage, you sort of have to fold back into yourself, into the zone of your familiars. In movies, characters ramble, using space without modesty or restraint. That's why people in America make movies, and people in England make theatre—America is a wasteland, but Britain is an island or anyway, a series of islands, so they need to stake space mentally which does not exist actually. Maybe that's why they are civilized to a point of madness. I stretched out on the floor and closed my eyes to the brightness. I touched my ribcage and I drifted, and I think I slept; I think I dreamt of molecules, of intricately detailed diagrams of molecules, and when I woke, I woke to light pressure on my chest, like a cat's paw.

"A peace offering." It was Denny. He was wearing the purple pimp hat that Alicia Ross had made for him. He looked like a dyed mushroom leaning over. I raised my head and saw a flower on me, a lily. "Don't ask what took so long," he said, tossing off his coat and launching anyway into an explanation.

The lily was exquisite. Six petals burst from a tubular casing, proud and electrifying like fireworks inscribing the sky. I touched one and it was bumpy, with a lone blaze of yellow crimping it down the center. Symmetry is weird—two halves of a dog's head, the obliques of a fish, the eyes of a hawk. I wondered about the purpose to the cleft of nature. There's always some purpose. Probing boldly into the atmosphere, despite its comic frailty, was a lettuce-green stamen that concluded its reach with a three-chambered penile tip of blistered orange. This was girdled by a choir of six pistils—rusty, hovering commas. The fragrance was combative: a gluish, maudlin aroma. Lilies are bullish about their capacity to best decay, to alter utmost conditions. It was true what my mother said about flowers hiding the stench of the dead. Maybe I could draw the smell.

"And then," Denny concluded, "we couldn't find green tape." He unscrewed three coffees from a paper deli bag, handing one softening cup to me. "I finally tried Vetault's. Thank God Jen Miller was working because I bummed the tape from her. And the flower."

I sat up and popped the lid off my cup.

"The tuna macaroni's yours. And the Chocodile. The chips are for Dave and the Tab's for me. I'm losing ten pounds by Wednesday."

"What's Wednesday?" Dave asked, joining us, dropping his green snorkel coat on the pile Denny and I'd started. "Hey Evie," Dave said, nodding to me.

"Day after Tuesday," Denny said. He took off his hat and set free a mop of black hair. Denny had gorgeous hair. His cheekbones were high under his eyes and his teeth were perfect. Everyone said he looked like Elvis, which depressed him. "They don't mean Memphis Elvis or Elvis at Sun Records," he'd complain. "They mean Elvis in Hawaii. 'Caught in a Trap' Elvis. Fat sweaty Elvis. Elvis on dope."

From the figureless murk of the theater came the springy gong of a seat bottom folding up and smacking its frame. I squinted to see Rourke heading up the aisle to the lobby. I wondered how long he'd been there. It occurred to me that he hadn't left at all.

WHILE THE GLUE DRIED, we watched from the audience. Rourke dictated cues to Richie, who was backstage at the lighting board, and to Paul Z, who was operating the spot. First the lights would blacken, then they'd rise to a uniform faintness. Then Peter Reeves would come to deliver his monologue as he arranged furniture.

The name of the town is Grover's Corners.

Peter had the part of the Stage Manager. The Stage Manager remained on the periphery during the play, acquainted with both performers and audience but allied to neither, proving that loneliness is the price you pay for omniscience. Peter was a good actor. Denny said Rourke helped him get into NYU Drama. Peter and Denny were going to get an apartment together in the city, and they said I could be their roommate if I wanted.

"Good job," Rourke said, "Let's go to the flashback."

Kate and Tim came out, and Tim chased Peter off stage. There was an awkward pause. Rourke filled it. "Whenever you're ready."

Tim began. "Can I carry your books home, Emily?"

"Why, uh, thank you. It isn't far."

The two moved stiffly across the stage. Tim was lousy. Kate wasn't exactly great, but she wished so strenuously to please that she semi-succeeded. It was like real life—she could be exceptionally sweet if she wanted. But she could also turn cruel. My mother always used Shakespeare to caution her.

Lilies that fester smell far worse than weeds.

Rourke stood near me, at the end of my aisle. He froze dully as he watched, one hand gripping his jaw. I could see his body through his sweater. I could see his shoulders pressing down, his chest poised on a hip. He appeared ready to spring. He said something to Richie. The lights changed. The actors faltered and stared out. "Go on," Rourke said.

"He seems pissed," Denny whispered.

"They're not stopping on their marks," I said. "They're out of sync with the lights. They keep delivering lines in shadows."

Mr. McGintee and Toby Parker, the music teacher, came in and slipped into two seats. They did not remove their coats.

"Look who's pretending to earn paychecks," Denny said. "This is the first time I've seen them in weeks."

Kate and Tim began again, and the lights tried to follow them—once, twice, flashing all the way up. Richie cursed, and Rourke bolted, jogging to the front and vaulting fluently onto the stage, taking everyone by surprise.

Denny said, "Holy shit!"

Rourke startled when he faced the performers, as if surprised to find himself there—in the center, in the light. He gripped his temples with two fingers, sucked in one cheek, then exhaled. He faced Kate and smiled an introductory smile, then he took a step, a meaningful step, a transforming step. Though there was no frame, I knew he'd crossed a threshold. He dug his hands into his pockets and inclined his chest when she spoke, listening closely as he shepherded her down a country lane. As the two moved through shadow and glare, I became more aware of the conversation than I would have otherwise. I heard the promise of consequence. The lights helped link courtship and tragedy. You get the feeling that because Emily marries George, she dies.

Rourke withdrew abruptly, turning to Tim. "Got it?"

Tim nodded and they shook hands, and everyone clapped, except me, and Denny, who whistled, and McGintee, who yelled, "*Bravo!*"

He jumped down and took to the aisle. A shock of hair fell forward. He ran a hand through it and his eyes passed over mine. "Okay," he called out. "Try it again, guys."

I couldn't stay. I squeezed past Dave and Denny and went backstage. Rourke's voice trailed my steps, creeping like fingers of vapor, clawing at each room I passed, begging me not to go. I went as far as I could from the front, all the way to the last dressing room. I could still hear him so I squatted in the corner and wrote on my arm with a pen I found there.

Sorry for my eyes, sorry to have seen you so.

When the door opened, it was Denny, coming and kneeling behind me. He caressed the long and incompliant muscles of my neck.

"You know what I was thinking," he said, very, very tenderly. "I was thinking that maybe you should go get some sleep. Kate will be here for a while. I'll drive you, then I'll come back to finish with Dave."

"I have my bike."

"I'll put it in the trunk. I'll drop you and come back."

He helped me to a stand, and when I stood he carefully rolled down my sleeve to cover the writing on my arm. He led me through the auditorium, and he retrieved my stuff. Rourke was busy so I didn't say goodbye. Denny loaded my bike into his car, and he took me home, where I slept straight through to Sunday morning, except for one brief exchange with Jack.

"Actually," Jack said, "I sat with you for three hours."

W HEN WE GOT TO THE DRESSING ROOM, KATE TOLD ME TO STAY. MICHELLE Sui and Adrienne Parker were there, hunched over a cracked console, somberly applying makeup. The mirror was fingerprinty. Uncapped tubes and jars were everywhere. Clothes and shoes and stockings had been thrown all over. Two gray wigs rested freakishly on Styrofoam heads—the wigs were skewed, making me think of zombies or monsters. I said I'd wait up front.

"You sure?" Adrienne said, her lips not moving a millimeter. She stroked each eyelid over and over in succession with turquoise shadow until the glaze was thick and round like bakery cookies. She did not seem at all terrified by the mannequin heads.

"Yeah, sure. I'm sure." I waved. "Good luck."

Kate lingered. She leaned across the doorway, one arm swinging. Behind her, boys dressed as villagers had a karate match.

"You're gonna be great," I said, stepping back, and back again.

"Evie. Thanks for practicing my lines with me."

"Oh. It was fun, you know, I guess."

My words sounded insincere though they were not. I wished she hadn't thanked me. Sometimes it's better to suppress gratitude. Sometimes it puts the person you are thanking into a tiny crisis of cognizance. I reminded myself to say nothing the next time I found myself overwhelmed with appreciation.

"See you," she said, and I waved.

At the top of the dim auditorium was a case of programs. I pried apart the lid and took a copy. The smell was inky. I walked to the ninth row from the stage on the right, draped my coat over my shoulders, and snuggled into the third seat over. In the booklet I found the paragraph devoted to Rourke. He'd acted professionally as a teenager, he earned a B.F.A. in drama from UCLA in 1978, he acted in Los Angeles for a year and a half before moving back East. That was it. Yet the epigrammatic brief contained more information than I wanted to know. It was awful to think what a minor part of his history East Hampton represented when it was all I knew of him.

California—I'd discerned no evidence of that place in him, which proved that people can see only as far as the eyes can see and that no one can ever know your story unless you broadcast it, which is not always seemly. I wondered if his work on *Our Town* would amount to a sentence in his next bio or just a clause, and when he wrote it, would he remember me. More than likely it would not appear. And like some sharp pain once preoccupying but since resolved, I would be disrecalled. In a few hours we would be divested of common topics and shared episodes. We would have no reason to talk again. I tried to devise a notable thing to say. *Good luck!* Or, *It's been nice.* Neither sounded particularly right.

There was a rush of cold. It did not come in a single draft but in a multiplicity of gusts, scrupulous and exacting. If the feeling had been a sound, it would have been the sound of bird wings flapping or guns discharging. It was a perfectly enunciated cold. And a fragrance—favorable, alien. Rourke took the seat alongside mine. I did not close the program; I did not care if he noticed the page. We sat for several minutes, mute and unmoving, the staring ahead way you sit when you go to the movies with someone you know very well and you're waiting for the picture to begin, but you don't feel like talking. Between the simmering frontiers of stage and lobby, in the circle we occupied, time tarried momentarily, as though there was nothing of great relevance to mark or chronicle. I had one knee propped on the back of the seat in front of me, and I was low, with my head coming only so high as his shoulder. He slouched a little too, but he was too big to do so with conviction. The effect was that he looked weary, which was perhaps the case. I thought of the way Jack slouched. No one could slouch quite so well as Jack.

I sighed in my mind, thinking, *Los Angeles,* as if things suddenly made sense, though actually they did not. I could not imagine Rourke spending five and a half years in the artificial pink glow, touring by bus the locked deco gates of stucco mansions, hanging out on the prairie-like boulevards beneath the looming and incongruous Hollywood sign. My father and Marilyn visit her sister Elise in Venice Beach every Easter. According to Dad, the water in L.A. is totally weird. When you dry yourself, the towel gets soaked, but you still have water on you. "I have to use Marilyn's blow dryer," he always tells me.

I wondered if Rourke had ever noticed the repelling attributes of Californian water. His seemed like the type of body that water would cling to for an especially long time, in beads that glittered like jewels. Maybe that was the scent I'd noticed, prismatic water clinging to him, the aroma of a man who happened to have showered recently. Jack always smelled like wet wool.

I felt a forward lurching. I thought he was transmitting his goodbye. I wished I could do or say something to make him stay, but I could do no more than give myself over to the dubious graces of fortune, which as a feeling was unhappily familiar. I wondered what did it mean when I'd been fine before he came, but then he came and then he was leaving and I was not fine.

Rourke did not rise. I waited, but he did not rise. And like so many of the things he did, this gave me confidence. Just when I believed that nothing short of contrivance would make him stay, he stayed. Despite my silence, he stayed. He stayed because there was a confluence of need between us. In staying, he reminded me that I am not usual and he is not usual, and that together we fall outside the common dictates of circumstance. He rested his forearms on the back of the seat in front of him, his head on his wrists. His tie hung perpendicular to his body, his dress shirt stretched across his back. Through the taut fabric, I could see his shoulder blades protruding.

"How are you?" I asked.

The words left my mouth, going as far as they could, then pivoting back, going from willowy to firm, rehardening like wax, like wax melting and cooling—losing shape, changing shape, keeping shape. I'd never heard that voice before. It was a voice of invitation and daring, deep and devoid of inflection. It was the voice of a woman. Sometimes in movies when enemies meet, they greet each other with deference and civility, acknowledging affiliations more profound than the competition itself, acknowledging a parity, an evenness of match. At the end of *The Hustler*, Minnesota Fats and Fast Eddie say goodbye, and it's sad, sadder even than when Eddie's girlfriend dies because life is full of twists and tenderness where you do not ever think to find it.

Rourke tilted his head to his right and he regarded me. His face was magnificent. It was square from forehead to jaw and graded mildly to the chin. His skin was clear and thick, drawn securely across a commanding crib of bones. His eyes were black, I confirmed. I searched for what made them so. Eyes can be *called* black, but I didn't think eyes could actually *be* black. Rourke's were a reverberant black, a blackness of conviction, as if they had forfeited subordinate hues by decision, as if they were black by will. They were the eyes of someone who reads the world in terms of opposition, who refuses to tolerate the nonsense hybrids of subtlety and allusion.

And yet there was light. I could see where they were susceptible. I could see blind pools where the light hit and bounced back, flickering like white ladies. Quick as it came, the light was gone. It was replaced by a cataract of grave, grave insights. His pain was vivid once grasped—having seen it, I could see nothing else. I suspected such a lucid hurt to have been of the worst sort, something localized and noxious, viperous like stings. I wished to help him. I had the feeling I'd been put there to help him. I understood that feeling to be durable and true, and confidential to me. In a flood I felt the dependability of my own devotion, which as a feeling is a miracle when it comes. Surely he knew. That was why I'd been sitting there and why he'd found me and why our legs—our calves and our thighs—leaned in and leaned upon and did not retract in modesty one from the other.

"Looking forward to the end of this," he replied, and he smiled an ingenious smile, with one side of his mouth rising slightly higher than the other. In the natureless dusk of the theater, he shamelessly memorized my face. I memorized his as well.

Light burst out and away like an accordion fan as the lobby door opened and closed. The house lights went up, we discerned a milling gurgle, and Rourke stood. He walked to the basin of the auditorium, his legs striking the ground positively, then he disappeared into the vestibule where we had collided a week earlier. I found myself thinking, *There's so much to do*. Though, in fact, there was nothing to do.

I thought I might go to the lobby. In the lobby people were protected by their measure from a trifling wasteland. They were sheltered from the frigid March night by the walls of the theater. I wanted to join them. I wanted to know the joy of being one among many, of possessing a form that corresponds to other forms. I wanted to mingle, to rove in a herd, to be unified by the democracy of design.

When I stood to go, near the corridor to stage left into which a keyboard had been placed, a bubble of light purred to life. Dan appeared, music under his arm. Jack stepped next from the tombish obscurity of the corridor, grim and hunched and scowling. He looked kind of like *Nosferatu*. I was surprised to see him, though of course I should not have been.

"Hey, Evie," Dan said quietly, taking a seat at the bench, adjusting the light, turning things on, testing keys.

Jack wouldn't look at me, he'd obviously seen me with Rourke. He plied the brown felt keyboard cover with painstaking precision, pulling and folding, pulling and folding, reminding me of my crime, challenging my conscience to profit from his misery. Beneath the stage drapery, someone said, *Shush!* and the lobby doors swung apart. People charged down, snatching seats. Was I mad to have deceived myself into collegiality? I had nothing in common with these people, or with anyone.

All I recalled of the play was intermission. Jack and Dan stayed bent over the keyboard, toying like alchemists. The music discharged from the corner as if from a void, radiating like steam from a crevice in the earth, taking everyone by surprise. The first piece was lush with nuance, busy with conversing chords—Dan's. Jack's was less sophisticated, leaving nothing to chance. Its complexity came from layering, from a nagging superimposition of the central refrain, which had been written in a minor key, evoking heavy-heartedness. Despite the tortured prophesies of the song, people were enticed back from the lobby. They stood in creature-like awe with their criss-cross peanut butter cookies and warping paper mugs of cider. I felt pride for Jack and, also, I felt a sickening, forward-moving guilt. A guilt that would not soon end. I didn't know how to resolve the difference between wanting something you cannot have and having something you cannot want, and I resented that it was my time to learn it. No one else seemed to be learning what I was learning. No one else seemed to be learning much of anything.

And his song. In my heart, it rang and rang again. He is my hero, I told myself, with all his messages and abilities.

When the curtain call came, the audience stood, and Jack and Dan played again, and I went to find Kate. Backstage, kids scrambled to sign programs and solidify romances. Parents obstructed staircases and dressing room doors, kissing greased faces, bestowing obligatory bouquets. Joey Miller pushed a towering stack of chairs past me, and Richie adjusted the lamps behind the chapel. At the lighting panel, I came across the stage manager, the *actual* stage manager—Peggy Graves. Her large body was doubled over an orange crate filled with an old scrim, and the box was crammed behind a pulley bolted to the floor. I offered to help. She eased her massive head back and peered through the slits that were her eyes. Her pretty face was coated in pancake powder and sweat and her gray hair was slick around the temples. She wore bright pink lipstick and a silk scarf printed with Monet's *Water Lilies*.

"I'm Eveline," I said. "I made the chapel."

Peggy raised herself with difficulty and rested her palms on the small of her back. Her breathing was labored. She shot a gust of air to her forehead. "I've known you since you were this high," she said resolutely beneath the din, and with difficulty she gestured to her hip. "Peg Graves," she told me, reminding me of the part I already knew, which was her name. "From Spindrift."

Spindrift was a theater group my mother joined when we first moved to East Hampton. "It only *sounds* like a mental institution," Mom used to joke. I felt bad that Peggy had not said hello to me previously. Maybe she assumed I would be rude. I hoped I did not appear to be rude. I repeated my offer of help. "No lifting for you. You need to make babies some day," she stated with a wink. As she maneuvered the crate again, I wondered if it was true that lifting can keep you from having babies. I'd never heard that before. "Tell Irene Peg Graves sends regards. Tell her I said you're the spit of her."

I journeyed again with an ever-increasing sense of melancholy. The evening's incidents congealed in my brain to form something that was the size and shape of a star, and inside, it churned and scraped—Kate thanking me, Rourke and Los Angeles and the flickering in his eyes, Jack like a vampire, and that song, the lonesome winded stage manager, the mention of my mother, the memory of me as a little girl. I had a troubling sense, a visionary sense. I felt once removed, disembodied. I felt I was holding hands with myself, guiding my shell through an evening previously lived.

At the crowded door of the girl's dressing room, I was made desperate by the sight of Rourke's back. The shape of him possessed precisely the clarity that everything else lacked. It alone belonged to the future, yet it did not belong to me. I could not touch it though I wanted to touch it and to take shelter there. I wanted to go there and be an angel, his angel.

I squeezed past Adrienne Parker's grandmother and stopped alongside Rourke, who was standing with his thick arms folded thickly and all the talking drifted down to nothing I guess because I'd come so far in out of nowhere.

"Congratulations," I said to everyone, telling Kate that she was great.

In her lap was a stack of small square papers, which were direction notes. Every note he'd written to her was in a shoebox at the bottom of her closet. Sometimes I would go there when she was not home. I knew all his letters, the tall, stiff way he formed them—the loop at the top of his *T*s. Adrienne and Michelle had notes too. I wondered if they kept theirs and if so, where.

My shoulder secretly on his shoulder, secret, secret, both of us holding very still.

Kate asked me for her car keys. I'd driven because she'd said she was too nervous to drive. At home her hands shook so much that water spilled over the edge of her glass. I tossed the keys to her. She wasn't prepared, so the chain bounced off the heels of her hands, popping back in the direction of my face. Rourke reached and snatched it, inches from my eyes. He leaned and handed them to Kate. "Aren't you going to the cast party?" she asked me. "Everyone's going, even Jack, even Mr. Rourke, isn't that right—*Harrison*?"

"Only going if *she's* going," he said of me, and they all giggled like he was joking. Then he turned, brushing slowly by me—onto me—his body flat and hard against mine, his head bowing down, his face looking to my face. *It's a treacherous world,* his eyes seemed to say. His eyes did not deny the treachery. "Time to give notes to the men," he said. "Wish me luck."

I staggered up the theater aisle toward Dan's father, Dr. Lewis, and his wife, Micah. Also Jim Peterson, the sax player from Dr. Lewis' band, and Toby Parker, the music teacher who played bass. Smokey Cologne was on the left, still in his seat. And Troy Resnick, Kathy Hanfling, Joss Mathers, Nina Spear, Dave Meese. All waiting for Jack and Dan to break down the keyboard.

Dr. Lewis hugged me. "Fabulous sets! Where's Irene?"

"A lecture, I think. She's coming tomorrow. To the matinee."

"What's she teaching this semester," Jim inquired, "poetry?"

"Short stories."

He nodded and they all nodded, saying to say hi.

Micah caressed my cheek with one finger. Her wrist bangles clattered like distant porch chimes. "Coming to Daniel's party, Eveline?"

"Of course she is," Dr. Lewis said.

Smokey stood, which meant Jack was there. Smokey crammed his hands into the pockets of his tattered herringbone coat and shook his purple hair from his face to little practical effect. I could make out the knurled rim of the fuchsia scar that skulked across his forehead like spilled wine. I wasn't sure if it was a birthmark or a burn. Beneath Smokey's bangs, his eyes were grainy tags, chronically claret and watery, making it appear as though he'd reached you by way of channel. "Smokey is one strange dude," Jack would always say, "but a great fucking drummer."

Jack swung an open hand to Smokey in greeting. The blond of him was fantastically bright. "Marvin," Jack said. "What's up?"

"Nice job, men," Dr. Lewis launched a new round of applause. "Glad to know my gear is being put to good use." His hand rested on Jack's arm. Discreetly he asked, "Did your parents come?"

"He didn't even tell them about it," Dan informed his father, and we all headed for the door in a funny bundle.

ON THE BRICK PATH that led from the doors to the street, we dispersed. Dan climbed into Smokey's black Nova, and Jack and I headed east on Main Street. The world had hardened since I'd seen it last, turning geologic, turning to fossils and ore. Jack unfolded his collar and pulled his Chinese Red Army cap to his eyes. I tucked my hands into my sleeves then linked the arms of my jacket. He offered his gloves to me, telling me to take them. As he wriggled one onto my left hand, the other slipped from under his arm and fell to the ground. We knocked shoulders gracelessly as we bent to retrieve it.

"What a load of shit!" he proclaimed. "What a criminal waste."

"I don't know, Jack. Your song was pretty."

"That's hardly an endorsement for the play. The acting sucked."

"People have to start somewhere. You weren't born a musician."

"The difference is I've been playing every day since I was four. This is like handing out thirty guitars to people who've never played before, who'll never play again, and trying to get something coherent in three months."

"At least it's not football."

"Now *there's* a comparison. It's *exactly* like football. Half-assed recreation, a distraction for the kiddies. It's about deceiving taxpayers into thinking local juveniles are being kept off the streets."

I tried to remember my point. I wasn't entirely sure I had one. "Well, Kate worked hard, and—"

"And *you* worked hard," he said, though I hadn't even considered myself. "That shit was a waste of your time—it was *prostitution*. Your church will be in the trash on Monday."

I hadn't considered that—the trash. I said, "You know what I mean."

"I know what you mean, *Ev-e-line*." Jack stretched my name to fill three syllables. He faced me. "Do *you* know what you mean?" His blue eyes were bleached and even, making a handsome strike through his face like the cross-bar of the letter *T*. "Listen to yourself."

Kids from the play closed in on us from behind. Jack slipped into the garden of the Huntting Inn, and I followed. He sat on an enormous rock, took a joint from his pocket, and lit it. Our eyes met above the embers. I wished to be drained; I wanted him to drain me.

"The whole thing got me down. The whole fucking night." Jack was referring to Rourke, though he would not introduce that name to our dialogue. He would not risk making it more real than he guessed it to be, real as it was. I kicked the ground. He kicked the ground as well, setting a piece of ice to fly. "You're headed down a bad road, Evie. I won't be able to see you through this."

THE WOODEN PORCH OF the Lewis house creaked under our paltry weight. It was a moldy cedar-shake colonial on Pantigo Road, held together primarily by its odor—a gluey composite of curry and candle drippings. Micah refused to live there, choosing instead to remain at their apartment on West End Avenue and Eighty-second. She visited East Hampton rarely, almost exclusively in summer. "The heat burns off the negative ions," she once told me.

Inside was a bungling sequence of rooms lined with instruments, dubious art, obsolete electronics, stacks of flaking scores, and mountains of damp books. Inside, you never knew exactly where you were or how to get out. The wainscoted hallways were papered in framed photographs of Dan's father with greats such as Oscar Peterson, John Coltrane, Dexter Gordon, and Sonny Rollins. Dr. Lewis was also a professor of music theory at Juilliard, which he called his *day gig*. He and the band traveled to places like Newport, Hamburg, Edinburgh, Paris, and Sao Paolo. When in town, they would sit around discussing the evolution of jazz, debating East and West Coast signatures, lamenting the loss of quality clubs and declining musical interest among young people. My mother would sometimes be with them. She and Dr. Lewis had dated when Dan and I were in grade school, the winter before she met Powell. This was a big deal to Jack, who was obsessed with the idea of Dan and me as siblings and his coming to live with us and Mom and Dr. Lewis in one big jazzy, literary house with everyone being cared for by Bitsy. Bitsy was the house-keeper from the Philippines. She wore ill-fitting sweatsocks and threw down paper plates of muddy lasagna and yelled uniquely when Dan put his feet on the table. After yelling, she would squish his cheeks together and slap the side of his head. Bitsy was seventy-one and an avid golfer.

Jack joined Dan and Smokey in the living room, hastening to the piano, greeting the allegiant instrument, bowing over, his powdery white hair splay-ing in a fan. There was a guitar on the couch. I wished he would have selected the guitar instead. He was less sure of himself on guitar, and his vulnerability plus his refusal to relent was beautiful. I wished he would be beautiful.

Denny and Kate were at the base of the stairs, laughing. Kate's face was flushed. Probably they'd been drinking. Denny snatched me and reeled me in, squeezing like toothpaste. The smell of Chablis mixed with the smell of his deodorant depressed me. It was lousy to think of him standing at the bureau in his room, considering the evening and deciding to reinforce himself with antiperspirant. Lousy because there was no one for him where we were. No one good.

A flurry at the front door was followed by shouting and whistling. Dr. Lewis, Micah, Lilias Starr, Mr. McGintee, Mrs. Kennedy, Toby Parker, and Jim Harrison were there—Rourke too, stomping in, depositing ounces of mid-night cold as he moved through the foyer. McGintee unraveled his scarf and complimented everyone he met.

"Terrific job! Top shelf! Top shelf all the way! And that meeting house," he said, coming up with the others and giving me a wink. "The sets were the finest we've ever had."

"Thank you, thank you," Denny said, patting me on the back, taking my hand around to pat himself on the back. He thrust mine into the crowd. It stuck out like a little clock arm. "Your hand is like ice! Are you anemic? I think she's anemic."

"You do look pale, Eveline," Lilias said.

Rourke reached for my hand, collecting it as though taking up a baby, baby homeless something. The accuracy and detail of my hand in his was striking. My bones felt like bird bones or cat bones, like crayons or small pencils. I demurred with a smile, not at him, but at the space between us. Not a smile, but a vague flickering. It was nice for a moment to have a friend, sad to have to lose him.

I burrowed my hand into the pocket of my jeans and withdrew to the liv-ing room, where Jack was leafing through a songbook. He appeared wafer-thin, wraithlike, there and not there. I wondered whether we were alive or whether we were dead. Was it possible that we'd been killed on the way over, that our forms had forged on by force of habit? Denny said how cold I was. *Anemic* was the word he used, and anemia had to do with bloodlessness. Didn't everything seem corrupted by vitality? My body moved about the perimeter of the grand piano, landing light in the patrician bend. People were surrounding Jack to listen. And so he was alive; only I was dead.

Dr. Lewis joined Jack on the bench. A cigarette hung precariously from the corner of his mouth as he slapped his legs and swiveled his head on his stubbly bohemian neck. And banging, there was banging—Smokey, whipping the lid of the piano with the heel of his hands. And Jack's fingers hitting the keys, *thump-thump, thump-thump-thump*. And him singing.

> *I wonder who's gonna be your sweet man when I'm gone?*
> *I wonder who you're gonna have to love you.*

In his singing there was a whole new weight, a masculine weight. He'd never really been hurt by me before; that night was the first. At least I'd given him *something*, even if only a passport into sorrow. When the last chord came, he jammed the piano one final time—*bwomp!* And he smiled mordantly into the crowd, his bright eyes latching onto no one and nothing—no, not onto me. His rejection was correct, and the sensation was not disagreeable. If in life there is flow, a current or a course, I had the feeling I'd found it. I discharged my belly from the instrument's anchoring might, my hand drifting from its surface, my body faintly following.

At the western edge of the room, a wall of windows extended from floor to ceiling. The frayed drapes bubbled and cooed like peacefully grieving things. I moved behind them to the furthermost window, the top half of which was open. Pantigo Road lay ahead. The oily gloss of the street suggested that it was raining. I saw no drops, but I could taste the rain. I could feel the rain. I could behold the changes it generated. There were no passing cars. Soon there would be cars. Wheels on wet pavement make a very particular going-home sound, serene and conclusive. I wondered what Marilyn was doing. Maybe she was making tea, scooping stray leaves from a wrinkled paper sack with *Golden Assam* stamped in withering red. Maybe she and Dad were reading. If she was looking out the window at the rain, perhaps she was thinking of me, with her hair, whisking up.

"I'm leaving," Rourke said, his voice coming from within my mind.

I was not surprised, lots of things were in there—him too. My eyes didn't leave the street. I was in some unattended place, some dangerously unattended place, someplace without propriety. Beyond me, season and century thundered tumultuously. His dark margin lay to my left. He was outside, on the porch, leaning against the scaffold of my window. I could not see him. I did not need to see him. I could feel him, the nearness of his flesh, the way you can close your eyes and feel a hand above your skin, the way you can be blind but feel the rain. He emitted something electrical, and I responded, electrically—the cadence of his blood, I trailed its avenue, and the scent of him, the scent that captivated me, it was the scent of his blood, the blood of a man, different from mine, and did it taste different too.

"I want you to know," he said, between the blunt and bottomward strokes of his pulse, "that I think you're very talented." Quieter, down an octave. "I believe—you'll go far."

A car passed. I traced its lights eastward. It was a curious thing to mention talent. A naked thing, an intimate thing. He spoke the exact opposite thought from Jack's, as if he knew it would be the most effective gateway. He wanted to persuade me of something. I might have told him not to bother trying. Though I could not name the choice, it had been made the first time I saw him. My preference for him was absolute—*feral*, the type of choice animals make. Hadn't that desire been so easily conceived? Jack was mistaken about the capacity of conscience to move humanity. It's only natural will that inspires us to action. Love, hatred, hunger, indigence—the things that find no home in logic. What I felt for Rourke was a partiality that situated, defined, and animated me.

He would not leave until he made some gesture to mark the bond between us. In the house he tried to hold my hand. I'd pulled away. Perhaps I'd offended him. Perhaps I should have said I was sorry, only I was not sorry. If I'd hurt him, I felt I'd done well to hurt him. He moved, his shadow changing radically from a lean vertical strip visible only from the corner of my eye to a carbon shield that canceled out the horizon, like a door swinging decidedly shut. His mouth landed on my cheek, my right cheek, the one farthest from him. With his jaw he pressed my face into the hard pocket of his inclined chest, and my breath crept down the tendons of his neck like thick verona cane. Beneath the fine membrane of his lips lay the complete and threatening remainder of his body. I could feel the way he held himself in check. Just when he might have retreated, he lingered, noticing perhaps as I did the way the pulp of his mouth had been shaped by God to fit the triangular hollow beneath my cheekbone. When he did withdraw, the skin of his lips and the skin of my face adhered slightly, resisting separation. Then he hovered inches away. You hear people say they feel weak in the knees. What they actually mean to say is that something caught in the small of the back has broken loose, and, like a line of thoroughbreds from a block of gates, it circles the arc of the hips, charges into the tops of the thighs, and lands at last in the knees. The knees are not the place where the feeling originates but where it concludes, setting you off balance.

"I have to go," he said, apologetically.

I wondered when we'd reached a place of apologies. "Yes," I said. "Go."

Rourke leapt from the porch. He seemed dauntless, satisfied with himself, and also with me. Evidently I'd pleased him. He reached his car—a cameo-white 1967 GTO with a parchment interior that looked to me like a tank full of moonglow. I knew the year because I'd heard him describe it to Denny. Rourke opened the door, and his body vanished. I wished to vanish also. I could not. I was not free. I was bound to the things that professed to designate me—parents, friends, school, culture, country. How had I arrived in that position, the position of their influence, when these things referred to something other than what I felt myself to be, when that influence was not actual? I was no prisoner, and yet when faced with an occasion for determination, I was not to follow the lead of my will but to endure in tedious familiarity, remaining accountable to totems of the past. What is freedom when you're too beholden to act spontaneously, and desire that is absolute but untimely, and self-respect when you must ignore the soul's conviction? Is obligation truly a virtue when in your heart you feel not a shred of devotion?

But knowing this did not bring him back and knowing did not move me. Only he could have brought himself back, only he might have moved me. And that is just slavery of another kind—and that was something to consider, something he was considering and I was considering as well.

I listened to the push of his car in reverse—a steady, hard push. Taillights coming back. I nestled into the glow, and then he cut out to the right, in the direction of Amagansett, possibly, or Montauk. The road remained empty, not one car succeeded Rourke's. I thought of his solitary drive, of the scenic rows of trees that would be grazed by his lights and the patchy heat that would pass through the dashboard vent onto his face, leaving his feet and chest cold. And the abounding maritime silence that would dilate in the night once he switched off his engine, I imagined it, and also the number of strides he would take on the short run into his house. Beneath the blankets, his body would lie without my body, and that was an improvident waste.

And so I was to go back, go back and face Jack and Kate, my parents, school on Monday. I was to gather away the monster I'd become, and, in the meantime, count on him for nothing. He had acquainted me with the next place, but he would not take me there. I felt slightly doubtful, the way caterpillars must feel in the instant they are awakened to become butterflies.

That was the promise I'd made to Rourke—to fly.

The piano was unattended. I moved to the kitchen at the rear of the house, where I came upon Jack and his friends, an androgynous, invertebrate puddle of flannel and denim, entrenched in a sooty cloud of pot smoke. It was that homegrown pot Troy kept in a garbage bag in the tire well of the Vista Cruiser. I could tell because my throat closed, and because Jack's mood was harrowing. He was slumped so low in a ladderback chair that his head met the middle rung. One foot jutted belligerently across the dining table, and he was rubbing the gummy label from a beer bottle with a bruised and nail-bitten thumb. Nothing depressed him more than Troy's homegrown pot.

"*Here* she is," Denny said cheerfully, to fill the hush I'd inspired.

"Where have *you* been?" Kate demanded.

Jack said nothing, and the rest of his friends said nothing. They looked kind of happy actually. Happy that Jack was mad at me. They thought I was no good for Jack, that his love for me was by my design entirely.

One time Trish Lawton called me a calculating bitch.

"Who's Trish Lawton?" I asked Jack.

"Troy's sister's friend from Michigan. From Flint."

"Hasn't she met Trish?" Dan inquired mildly.

Jack said, "I guess not, no. Pretty sure she hasn't."

If it was my sexuality they distrusted, they weren't mistaken. But if it was Jack's capacity for manipulation they were blind to, his hunger for intellectual ascendance and moral leverage, his aptitude for dealing abuse, he was more friendless than I.

"I'm gonna go," I announced.

Denny threw his arms up and we kissed goodnight. I was sorry for the thought about his deodorant. It smelled good to me actually, once it wasn't going so strong.

"Evie!" Jack thrust back his chair, standing before the legs were square, so it marched and threatened to topple. He stormed up behind me and tossed his coat over his shoulders. One limp sleeve touched my back skimmingly. He waited while I fished through Kate's bag for her car keys, then dropped them behind the radiator. She'd look for them, give up and walk home. I'd come back with her to find them tomorrow.

The screen door slammed behind us, hitting twice. I left and Jack followed. He was free to do so. He was lucky to be in love with me and not Rourke. His feet punched the porch steps as he descended, and when our bodies were aligned, he zipped his jacket and handed me his gloves again. The cold was not the same tranquil cold as when we left the theater but a bracing chill that entered my head like rods of glass, giving it new architecture. Jack and I walked as we'd always walked, on the streets we knew so perfectly well, and as we did, the drama of the evening began to dwindle into distant nonsense. How many walks had we amassed in our time—without purpose or prospect. I wondered about all our vagrant mobility. I wondered whether we hadn't achieved something near to perfect.

At my house I washed and put on long underwear and socks, and I felt more like myself again, whatever that was. I joined him on the floor. He was picking threads from the torn knee of his jeans.

"I know what's happening," he said into his hands.

I didn't bother to ask what he meant. If I forced him to put his thoughts to words, they would appear to lack foundation and that would be unfair. He could only say, *I saw you two sitting together, not talking* or *I saw him take your hand after Denny offered it to the crowd.* I could defend myself against any accusation, but that was a lawyerly way to waste time, assailing an argument's logic rather than conceding to its probable essence. Something *was* happening, it was true.

"I'm very upset," he said.

I was also upset. "I don't want to lose you."

"You're not losing me," he said. "You're forsaking me."

Forsaking implied choice. I had no choice. I could not prevent the blood from leaving my veins when I saw Rourke, from seeping out to the mantle of my skin and staining it crimson. I was servile, though I didn't say that, exactly. I said, "I love you."

Jack tilted his head far back and for a long time remained silent. He was heartless to retain his grief, to inflict me with the knowledge that I was the cause of his torment, not the remedy. The thin ridge of his extended neck rent up like a mole tunnel from his chest to his head. His existence seemed so tenuous, his figure so fragile. He was just one body, leading one life. Beneath his skin lay a skull, a calcified skeleton with yawning eye sockets. For purposes unknown I had been entrusted with the care of his soul, and so it was the most vile type of treason for me to have enriched his self-loathing. My head reeled. A terrible premonition seized me. "I think I'm crazy," I said.

He exhaled. "You're not crazy."

"Sometimes I feel myself falling, then I see it, as if the falling thing is not me anymore. When I reach, my hands catch nothing."

Three lines filled the middle of his forehead. For some time, he remained quiet. When at last he reached for me, I folded into his arms, happy to give him the thing that I lacked—the object of his desire. I wondered if he felt happy when I said I loved him. I wondered if he was relieved that I did not say different things or worse, nothing at all. Through his sweater I assessed his breathing. I knew it by heart. It was shallow, like water you can hardly wade in, and unsynchronized, as if he could not match with the atmosphere.

"Such gentle breaths," I whispered, patting his chest with my palm. A pain clenched my abdomen. I hoped maybe the hurting thing inside would rupture and I would go to the hospital and everyone would send cards and lucky trumpet daffodils and Rourke would move back to the somewhere else he came from minutes before my release, proving that destiny works just as well in reverse.

"You're shivering," I heard him say. *Jack* say, I heard *Jack* say. I had to remind myself. There was all this slipping inside.

He took the comforter from my bed and wrapped it about my shoulders, then his, making us a nest. Jack stroked my hair and I kissed him, a thousand times I kissed him. And we listened reverently to the night—to the chronic buzz of the refrigerator, to the occasional lurch and jerk of the boiler, to the dainty tink of the metallic numbers on my digital clock, flapping scrupulously. At three-thirty, he said that he should go home.

"Not yet," I said, "please." I couldn't be alone, not yet.

8.

I KNEW WHAT TO DO. I WOULD RENOUNCE MY FEELINGS. I WOULD PLEAT gracefully in, filling my own remotest reserve, harboring snugly in the tapered pit of my sightless, mindless self. I would lessen and lessen. I would regard the dispossession of Rourke as a gesture of life's perfect impermanence. I would resume early loyalties. My longingness would recede in hue and diminish and convert, going from a landscape of brilliant welts to a dilute and heavenly affliction.

My days began and ended the same as anyone's—with light, with dark. The difference was that I stripped mine of the routine that generally divided the middle. I forfeited the comfort of habit. I wandered unpredictably, leaving school early or staying late. I began to accept offers. If Lisa Tobias or Will Steck or Rocky Santiago asked if I needed a ride home, I said okay. When Alicia Ross invited me to O'Malley's for Sara Eden's birthday dinner, I brought balloons. When my mother invited me to watch Francis Holland do his Dylan Thomas impersonation at the college, I accepted. When Denny needed me to drive with him and his mother to her pulmonologist in Stony Brook, I did. And when Dad was building frames for my final watercolors, Jack and I went into the city to help.

Though everyone was grateful for the congenial way I was acting, I did not enjoy doing the things I kept agreeing to do. My aim was to avoid Rourke until April. Kate said April was the last class. In science fiction movies, women in suit dresses and men in skinny ties stand at plate glass windows, waiting for the invading things, ants or birds or pods, to finish whatever they're doing, breeding or eating, and to leave. Home for me was a place infected with risk.

All time became my time, regulated by an inner mechanism, infinitely superior to the clock. I understood time; clocks only measured it. I would simply rise to leave one place and move to the next. I did not need to know that it was Tuesday or Thursday afternoon to detect his occupancy in the building. I could feel the changes he rendered—in the halls, in the rooms, in a track that drew in the school like a belt. The floors and walls retreated to accommodate his presence, warping slightly the center of everything. My ear could perceive curious gaps of silence punctuated by razor-sharp flashes of sound. When I sensed that he had engaged with whatever it was that he had come to engage with, I knew I could safely leave. Weeks went by this way.

"I'M TOTALLY CONFUSED BY this new schedule," Jack grumbled. He came into the yearbook office and hopped onto Marty's desk.

"You always seem to find me," I said.

"Yeah, well, I don't want to make a profession out of it," he complained. "What do you do in here, anyway?"

I shrugged. "Make lists. Sort."

"Sounds pressing," he said. "C'mon, let's go."

"A few more minutes."

He reached for Kate's flute case. "What's this doing here?"

"Kate asked me to take it home for her."

"What's the matter," Jack asked, "did she sprain her wrist?"

"She has drama. She didn't want to carry it there."

He opened the box. Inside was a peculiar bed of opaque sapphire fabric, that crushed velvety stuff. The knuckles of his right hand were badly scraped. Skin flapped over in certain parts and was missing entirely in others. The blood looked parched but not old. He peered inside the joints of the flute, then pieced it together obligingly, the way mothers brush newborn hair. When he blew into it, it cooed sweetly.

He paused. "I was accepted at Berklee," he said.

My thumb brushed the edge of a sheet of paper, and he began to play again. I lowered my head to his lap. His skinny thighs felt compact, inelastic. I clicked my jaw against his leg, lazily and repeatedly, and the rim of Marty's desk carved a trench into my chest about four inches beneath my collarbone and parallel to it. Berklee was a music college like Juilliard, only in Boston. Jack could have gone to Juilliard with Dan, which would've been best, especially with me at NYU, but he refused to live in his parents' apartment. "No contest," he'd said. "I'd take up hair dressing to avoid living at home."

We both began to talk at once.

"What did you say?" we asked, simultaneously also.

"Go ahead," I offered.

Jack insisted, "No, you first."

I'd forgotten what I'd intended to say, and he seemed to forget also. His leg started to swing, slow then fast, even and hard, like a carpenter's hammer, with the toe of his suede blue Puma kicking the metal garbage can and the heel bouncing against the side of the desk. In one jolt, he banished the canister into the defenseless center of the room. It pirouetted on its rim in the suspenseful manner of a rolling coin. "We're driving up this weekend," he said. "My old man hasn't been there yet."

It would have been a good time to cry, but I didn't really feel like it, and it's not possible to force tears. You wrench up your eyes and think of the tragic things you might truly feel, but nothing comes besides a gooey wetness and a useless, squeezing sensation behind the face.

Jack started again to speak, his words got lost in a change in pressure, a nearly inaudible sound that passed just as it appeared, like the light nick of a record skipping.

I raised my chin and cocked my head. "Let's go."

"Excellent," he said, somewhat surprised, "cool."

KATE COULD MAKE ME nauseous. I was reading one night in the living room, and she came in and answered the phone and started talking very loud. When

I tried to get up, I fell back down in a queasy cyclone of confusion. My stomach pitched. I lowered my head to my knees. My abdomen was splitting into halves. Not halves. Halves means equal. Portions.

My mother's hand touched my neck. "Let's get you to bed."

She tucked the edges of my blanket around me, trimming the perimeter of my body. Probably I resembled one of those homicide outlines, marked indelibly in the position of my collapse. My mother sat, and I was consoled by the meek depression made by her body in the mattress. I drew her hand between my palm and cheek. I had the feeling I might sleep. There was a chemical coming in, dripping in, either seeking my cells or being produced by them. I remember feeling microscopic pulses of something, diminutive gates opening.

"When was the last time you ate?" It was my mother, asking.

My eyes opened—how much time had passed? It seemed like she'd been sitting only seconds, yet it had been long enough for me to dream a dream. Something about lost passports and missing luggage and foreign customs officials in a single-story room near the tarmac. Me late for a flight home, me flying alone, and seats on the plane that were sideways. Also I was standing, looking out of the warped bullet nose of a jet that was flying through the space between buildings, diving through rivers.

"Be right back," my mother said. She took back her hand and ascended the steps to the kitchen. A ruthless dusk replaced her, hitting quick, like a jail cell shutting. The time was five forty-five. Not as bad as five-fifteen, which itself was not as bad as four-fifteen. Four-fifteen is the worst.

Kate popped in, her hair rippling like a flag. "Sick *again*?" she said, and I pulled the quilt over my face. "Well, excuse *me*!" she shouted.

SLEEP WAS NOT POSSIBLE. The three aspirin I took each night before bed did nothing to outstep the disease in me—the malignancy of night and lust and loneliness. I would shift from side to side and back to face until eventually all that I'd struggled to subdue during the day would erupt into the authorless dark, with spontaneous confessions and reversed denials flooding the keen and disparaging silence of my room. Behind my eyes I'd find him, like an object through bright water, a shivering richness. In glistening clarity we would convene—no, *reconvene*—in some substitute district, some alternate age, with his not speaking and my not speaking and around us everything being white walls. In those false regions, at his false side, I found my first peace, my only happiness. Yes, that is true, that is right. That is exactly true, and it still breaks my heart to say so.

Me looking for the lamp, me fumbling to find it, turning it on, dropping back to bed in stark light, saying in a voice that was pure and harrowing and uncontestably my own, *Oh God, Rourke*. But there was no God, there was no Rourke, there was only me. And three degrees beyond me, the vast and terrifying reign of illusion.

It was then that I began to write. I did not think of myself as a writer. I did not think of writing to be read. I wrote to clear my mind and perhaps to sleep. I tried to write the way I draw. Maybe it's possible to write the way you drive if you happen to be a racer. To draw, I form a feeling—there is some unrelatedness to make related, either me to it or it to me, or it to something else. It's like looking at a level surface and perceiving some captivating excurvature, and so you touch it. It's like exploring that prominence by lifting it from its source and introducing it to a new flatness, a flatness of your own making. The way I wrote was the same, starting always with the evenness of my heart and the conspicuousness of him upon it.

I composed a list. One column for all the times I'd seen him, another for each time I'd heard him mentioned. Nargis would have called this a *table*. I liked the idea of a table, of providing a frame for runaway numbers or dodgy ideas, like cages stacked in pet stores for hamsters. Peripheral details such as conversation, clothes, and weather were subsequently introduced. I used a code for names, which was dumb since the list was in my room in my handwriting, and there were not enough characters in my life to outwit a motivated intruder. For Rourke's name, I substituted the letter *S*, which followed *R* in the alphabet. Kate was *B*, which preceded *C* for Catherine, and Jack was *G*, the last letter of Fleming.

> *On the night of the play S. and I sat next to each other in the dark. He has eyes that are black. I know black is all color, but his black is no color. The smell beneath his shirt was good and I wondered who gets to touch him. Is there anyone who touches him? I spoke and my voice was strange. G. saw us—S. kissed me on the cheek through a window at Dan's. He said I'm talented, which made me feel strange. I wanted to go with him, he wanted it too only I didn't go, though there was a beautiful rain—G. and I sat all night like we were waiting for something. He said my chapel would be garbage by Monday—B. & Denny came home at 3:00 and we made vanilla pudding and the four of us ate it hot even though the pot bottom cooked off and there were Teflon flakes inside—Today B. made me sick. She was on the phone, saying over and over how in love she is. Mom measured my temperature at one hundred and two and put me to bed with a bowl of tomato soup which tasted like scalding ketchup water. Mom's hand felt bony. She says Powell will be home for Easter and that she'll cook lamb though she won't and anyway I can't eat lamb. Is it possible to be annoyed so much that you catch a fever?—It's still raining. It's been raining since last Saturday. Even after five days it's a beautiful rain—*

On paper the entire matter seemed illusory and formless—seventeen encounters in six months. I thought to burn the document, but I couldn't. I was prohibited by the idea of my leaning like a very crooked someone over the fireplace to light the four corners of my notebook and watch my own handwriting melt and warp, stretch and shrink and shrivel into a mound of ash that could be blown to oblivion in one gust. Anyway, I liked the compact and illegible blocks of handwriting. The dense and inky look of the pages was official and purposefully slanted, textured to the touch, like the original Constitution.

And something else—it's good to have a record to refer to when you cannot confide in friends. My friends were not untrustworthy, but I didn't ever want to discuss something that was hardly real as though it were indeed very real, thus tricking friends into authenticating me and Rourke. As soon as someone expresses a view about you in real time and space, and brings you into their universe, you are validated and substantiated and stamped, somewhat like a postmark.

9

SOMEONE CALLED MY NAME FROM THE PAY PHONE BOOTH. "HEY EVELINE."

I moved to the alcove across the hall from the main office and peeked around the edge of the wall. Ray Trent was in the rear of the cubby, picking through a handful of change. He wore a black turtleneck and blue jeans and his blond hair was feathered back. The girls said he looked like Tom Petty. Under his arm was a liver-brown phone book. It seemed urbane, the need to make calls from school. I wondered was my number inside.

"Did I scare you?" he smiled. "I didn't mean to scare you."

"No, I just, no—you didn't."

"Feel like going to an Islanders game?"

I hesitated, though I kind of like hockey.

"Nassau County too far to go?" He lined up dimes on the phone.

"Nassau's okay," I said, "It's just—"

"That's a nice sweater."

"Thanks, it's Kate's."

"I'm sure it's nicer on you," he said, then he told me to think about the game. "You don't have to let me know until Monday." Ray held up one finger. Into the phone he said, "Hey man, it's me."

I waved and began to withdraw. He covered the mouthpiece with his hand. "What are you doing Sunday?"

Jack would be in Boston with his dad. I said, "Nothing."

"Ever been to the St. Patrick's Day Parade in Montauk?"

"No," I said. I hadn't.

"Great," he said. "I'll pick you up at nine."

AT EIGHT FIFTY-FIVE there was a knock. Mom answered the door. Steam was rising from her coffee mug, fanning her face. "Hi, Ray," she said. They'd met before—the first time was the Junior Prom.

"Happy St. Paddy's, Irene," Ray kissed her cheek.

My mother raised her cup. "I made coffee. Want some?"

"A quick cup, sure." He stepped into the house and followed Mom to the kitchen. The screen door tagged lightly against its frame. I had no idea why I'd said yes to the parade when I'd successfully said no to the hockey game, except to say that the invitation had taken me by surprise, coming at the end of a conversation the way it did. Though I knew Ray well, I was nervous to be with him. I felt hyper-conscious of being female, like I was widening some circle I had no intention of widening. Once you've experienced the very private feeling of being a woman to the person you're in love with, being that woman in general feels gross. Being a woman is always indelicate and extreme, like you're operating heavy machinery. Regardless of size or shape, every woman knows the feeling of being a stack of roving flesh. Sometimes all you have accomplished by the end of the day is to have maneuvered yourself through space without grave incident. You antagonize fellow women, transfix children, and offend the elderly. You resign yourself to men and their tireless desires— in school you endure pokes and pranks and pilfered caresses, and in the super- market you tolerate the guy who follows you down aisles. Men in passing cars stare. At home, an amorous friend is waiting. Phone messages line the desk.

"Have anything warmer?" Ray felt my coat. "It's cold out there."

My mother reached deep into the closet. "Take this, Eveline."

"Cool jacket!" Ray said.

"United States Navy," Mom informed him as she put it on me and cuffed the sleeves at my wrists. The coat was black and plain with a blunt collar and a zip pocket on the left breast. It went straight to the tops of my thighs. If Jack had been there, he would've said, "Put that fucking thing away." The coat had belonged to Arlo Strickley. Arlo was from Tennessee; he was Powell's friend from the Navy.

Once during a stop-over in Montauk, Arlo got leave and came over, rag- ing drunk. Jack and I happened to be home alone. Arlo cried when he saw me. "Carolyn'd be just about your age now, Evie," he bawled. Carolyn was his daughter.

"Where is she?" Jack demanded testily. He did not like people to cry. "Is she dead?"

"No," Arlo sobbed. "She's in Far Rockaway." Arlo then launched into the maudlin story of his luckless life—three failed marriages, two episodes of financial ruin, the loss of his parents in a charter bus accident outside of Roanoke, and a sinus infection that had plagued him for seventeen years.

Jack tried to piece together elusive details. "Hold on, Arlo," he'd say, "are you talking about *Gloria* or *Louise?* We're still in '74, right? Isn't Louise with the Cuban chef? Are we still in Santa Clara, or not?"

"Did I say Louise?" Arlo belched. "I meant *Lois.*"

When finally he was done, he stumbled to a stand and began to divest himself of his jacket, tearing his arms from the sleeves and turning them inside out as he did. "You hang on to this," he insisted. "Carolyn probably wouldn't want it." When I said that I couldn't, he blindly passed it over, missing me entirely. *"Evie, please."*

It was no use explaining the story of the coat to Ray. One fact of life is that it's hard to explain old things to new people. "That coat will keep you good and warm," my mother assured me as we stepped into the frost-beaten yard. I turned at the door and kissed her goodbye. Her fingers arrived uncer- tainly at the spot on her face where my lips had lain. She seemed surprised. "Bye-bye!" she said.

Ray tapped the horn of his Mustang as he backed out. She waved through the hedges. "Your mom's pretty. She looks like Julie Christie."

"Thanks," I said, and to warm up I pushed my feet to the floorboard. Lots of people said that. We rolled like mercury onto Route 27, heading east. The car was clean and lush. I wondered if *lush* was right. Maybe lush means drunk.

If lush means drunk and lush also means luxurious, that is strange. Ray pushed in an Allman Brothers cassette and the world streaked past, like a banner of khaki ribbons. To drive in morning is to feel winged; it's to feel like part of the universe. Like your journey is unbroken in terms of all things forgoing. Like today is yesterday. Like you're wearing the clothes from the night before.

Last Sunday morning, the sunshine felt like rain.

THE VILLAGE OF MONTAUK had the appearance of being deflated and horizontal, like something dropped from the sky. As we descended into town, I had a sense of belonging. There was no place in the world I'd rather be.

"You like pancakes?" Ray asked.

"Not really."

"Eggs?"

"Not eggs." Chickens inside.

He parked halfway up Main Street, and we met at the trunk. "I know what you need," he said, waving to cars going by. "Coffee."

"Coffee would be good."

John's Pancake House was packed and congested with sausagey smoke and smells. We unbuttoned our coats at the door, and all eyes turned to us. Ray nodded a few hellos, and several lapsed conversations tentatively restarted. "Must be your hair," he whispered. We squished through to a table in the far corner, and I picked the seat facing the wall. Ray collected the dirty dishes and carried the pile to the counter, where he greeted someone he called *Captain.*

"What do you want, Eveline?" Ray called back to me.

"Why she'll have the pancakes, of course," the Captain said, as if Ray was missing the obvious. He tucked his neck into his chest and bellowed, "Stack of blueberry! And you, Raymond?"

"Sorry about that," Ray said when he returned. "I ordered eggs so you can have the toast."

"It's okay. Maybe they'll like me better if I eat the pancakes."

A harried waitress appeared like a wall over our checkerboard table. She wiped it roughly and deposited two worn mugs of coffee with cheap spoons sticking out. She withdrew a mass of napkins from her apron and plopped it between us. Her hair was carroty orange, and, beneath her beige polyester-blend polo shirt, her breasts looked square. I felt bad about her working versus my not working. Probably it wouldn't have mattered to her that I bus tables in summer since the moment was not summer. Frequently things only matter to people in the moment.

"Busy, Deirdre?" Ray asked.

She blew out some air. "It's just me today."

"Guess you're buying tonight," Ray joked, and she walked away, telling him not to hold his breath.

He tore the tops off of two sugars. I took the packets from his hand and tipped them at an angle above his cup. We watched the boxy grains cascade and disappear—not disappear, *change*.

"I can't say I've ever gotten a reception like that," Ray said, reaching over to smooth down my hair, which evidently was messy from my hat. "It reminds me of the Bob Seger song." He leaned in and began to sing.

> *When you walk into a restaurant*
> *Strung out from the road—*

And I added,

> *And you feel the eyes upon you*
> *As you're shaking off the cold—*

"You have a really nice voice," he said.

"It's an easy song for me to sing." Jack always liked me to sing that song. He would make me sing it over and over. In the ashtray, the crumpled sugar packet papers struggled to unwind.

"You in chorus?" Ray asked.

"No. I'm not so good at singing in that style. That chorusy style."

"With the parts that are supposed to come together."

"But they never do."

"And the shitty songs they give you," Ray added heatedly. "When my sister was in chorus, she had to sing the theme from *Oklahoma!*"

"I quit with 'Eleanor Rigby.' "

"*Eleanor Rigby*," Ray said. "Jesus. It's depressing enough when the Beatles do it. If they picked better music, they'd get better singers, real performances. They could do fundraisers, whatever—hospitals, weddings. Then at least you're *really singing*, which would help with college, and basically, boredom. The problem with these teachers is they have no business sense."

Deirdre was back with hot plates, and so Ray and I leaned back, the partly reluctant way you do when your food arrives and you've been leaning in having a good time. I was surprised to be having a good time, leaning in like that. Being in Montauk was like being on vacation in America, maybe Cape May or Nantucket or Colonial Williamsburg. Nothing looked the same as it did at home, though nothing was very different either, except there were no phones to answer, and you weren't sure where your next meal was coming from.

"I'm glad you came," he said, trading his toast for pancakes off my stack.

"Me, too," I said. It was true, I was glad.

"IT'S CALLED MASSACRE VALLEY," Ray said. "The last battle site of the Montaukett Indians. Fort Hill is there and behind us is Montauk Manor."

Mike Reynolds tapped the keg that was set up in the back of his van. Two sleepy German shepherds were inside on scraps of carpet. "Across the street is Fort Pond," Mike said, "and above it—"

"America," I said, and together they said, "Right."

The mist was sober and ample. I didn't really see America, but I could squint and pretend I did. What would it be like to head blindly into it, to be thoroughly migratory? Would it be easy to vanish, or hard? I hadn't even begun, and yet the instinct was in me to start over.

Mike handed out foamy cups of beer, and we toasted and behind us was the sound of bees. Not bees, motorcycles. Mike walked excitedly to the row they made when they parked, his stickish legs taking succinct steps. Ray followed, excitedly too. It was nice, the way they got excited to see people.

There were three bikers—Ralph LaSusa, a fish counter for the National Marine Service, and Will and Janey from England, glaziers who'd lost their factory outside London in a fire. They took the insurance money and moved to America. Will sounded well-educated despite his mottled beard, and Janey was a tall, chesty blonde with a pie-shaped face. Ralph was lame. His left shoe had one of those shoe-shaped blocks on it.

"How about a ride, Eveline?" Will offered. "Before I grapple with that keg." People with motorcycles always assume that everyone without one wants a ride. I said sure. "Be a love, Janey, lend us a helmet." He snapped his fingers.

"Lend a *helmet?*" Janey repeated liltingly. She cocked her head. "What, so *she* can ride with *you?*" The leather of her jacket hugged her strenuously, emphasizing the breadth of her hips and the roll of her buckled belly. I thought I'd never seen a woman so confident.

"S'right," he responded.

"You think I'll allow you to nick up that face," she asked, referring to me, "or those legs? I think not, Sir." She threw one beefy arm around my shoulders. "*I'll* take her out." Janey thrust her hand at his chest, and Will grinned sheepishly. He surrendered his helmet, seeming to cherish her all the more for such minor victories.

"Suit yourself," he said. "More beer for me."

I followed Janey to her bike, wondering what we looked like, two women leaving together. I had the feeling we looked like something.

Janey's motorcycle was shimmering and crimson. "What kind is it?"

"A Ducati," she said. "It's the only thing I carried over from home— besides Will." She offered her own helmet to me and she kept her husband's, which I took to be a display of biker etiquette. The helmet wobbled on my head like a globe of ice cream on the tip of a pin. "Don't you have any gloves?"

"Just one," I said. I'd lost the other. Maybe at breakfast.

She started the engine with two powerful thrusts of her right leg. "Don't be nervous. Will's reckless, but I'm not." I climbed on. "How about you?"

I looked to locate the foot pegs and wriggled into the seat, wrapping my arms around her luxurious waist. "About half."

"Half-reckless," she laughed. "Yes, I can see that." Janey flexed her wrist, and we took off peaceably. The drive down cliffside made a corkscrew, and we leaned so far into it that there was very little space between my ankle and the ground. "Go with me," she commanded. We dipped lower, maybe forty-five degrees off the road. Angels must have seen us, drilling into the earth, wending our way, rotating in and rotating around without intersecting our own line, screwing conchoidally, like a shell. We emerged alongside the parade, which was just beginning, and then cut behind the backs of the crowd onto some street, Elroy or South Elroy or something similar, heading north toward Gosman's. Janey opened up the engine, and the bike accelerated in shifts, winding out to the full capacity of each gear. It felt good to do that, it felt like purging yourself of pent-up feelings. I didn't even know I'd had pent-up feelings until I experienced the sensation of purging them—they peeled off, one, then another, clapping down against the asphalt behind us. It's true what people say about the way bikes vibrate between your legs. Janey's hip bones met the pale backs of my forearms, and my clenched hands burrowed into the pillow of her middle. I wondered what it's like to love a woman. And I wondered—*Is it nice, like this?*

SHE DOWNSHIFTED AT THE entrance to the wharf, and the air slackened as we coasted into a spot near Salivar's. Charter fishing boats lined the pier, making an iron queue. Not iron, maybe steel, or fiberglass. I didn't really know my boat materials. I reminded myself to ask Dad. She hit the kickstand, and I removed my helmet, reacquainting myself with the planet's peculiar stillness. I pretended I was on Mars. I let everything be new and Mars-like. It's leveling and humbling to travel by motorcycle, to suffer the cost of time travel. You feel cocky like you've earned every inch of distance covered.

Janey kicked out her legs as we walked, and she drew a vivid breath. It was as if she might begin to sing a song. "Will's good enough," she said, "good enough."

I shoved my hands into my jeans pockets. They *were* frozen.

"Are you in love, Eveline?" she asked.

I said that I was.

"Not with Ray though."

"No, not with Ray."

The ships squeaked resignedly against the wooden pier, making me wonder if the dock was moving beneath us. I did not like ships to squeak or docks to move. Probably that particular dock could not move. It was too big. Then again, the boats were also big.

Janey seemed unperturbed by the aches and grunts. "I am in love," she proclaimed. "With Martin. He lives in Devon, in England." *Ma-tin*, she said, without the *R*. The first syllable sounded sympathetic, maternal, almost bored. The —*tin* barely escaped the pinkish zone of her mouth. It was crisp and close, making it easy to imagine his honey brown eyes and honey brown hair, and the two of them tumbling happily and normally, having happy normal sex. At the end of Gosman's was water. She turned a quarter-turn, eastward, toward her home, toward him. "I come here to look," she said, "you understand." Her mannish resilience fell away as she conjured her loss. Magically, it animated her, just as toys dance to life behind closed doors. She appeared younger, healthier, prettier, there was a breakableness that she revealed, that she'd been *longing* to reveal. I wondered about that, about her tenderer aspects, how closely they resided. I wondered as well how she had recognized in me a pitiful equal. *Will's good enough*, she'd said, reminding me of the savage enormity of the world and the interminable length of life. I did not possess equal gifts. I would wither in such compromise. "And yours?" Janey asked. Her face was serene, immune to the stiff bite of the wind. Her words were crisp, her eyes so wide. "Where does he live?"

I did not think of Rourke as mine, though I supposed he was. Martin was not Janey's, not really, but probably no one loved him more. She reserved the best of herself for him—her essence. That's no easy task. That's like a work of art. She slept with her husband, but, in giving her flesh, she gave nothing of consequence. I wondered if Will knew. I wondered if he knew but didn't care, and if she despised him for that. Or if secretly he despised himself.

"I'm not really sure where he lives."

"Ah," she responded, seeming to absorb in full the meaning of pretty much everything. "It's not an easy one then, is it?"

I shook my head. "No. It isn't."

"Find out where he lives," Janey solemnly advised, "so you'll know which way to face when you lose him."

WE RETURNED TO THE weasely and gaunt pitch of bagpipes. As a sound it was ironic, solitary but allegiant. Notes shot like silken missiles into clouds of ore. Will folded Janey into his arms, and I handed my helmet to Ralph, then drifted, with Mike's dogs following. I came upon a child suspended on his father's shoulders, waving a pennant. Painted onto each of his cheeks were waxy kelly clovers. He was Irish. I am Irish, too, and German, though these things are like dreams dreamt. I have no known predecessors—none other than my parents, who speak nothing of their respective heritages. Though in my cells these nations exert their influence, on the surface I feel only the worldly crush of all that my parents have forsaken. Parades just make me feel the loss of link more acutely. Beneath the boy and me, a raggedy stream of bodies and floats slithered down East Lake Drive. I could discern brows and skulls, an untidy and inglorious mass limping through the flinty landscape. Together we endured the sorry, sorry sound of sprinkled handclapping.

There was a piercing whistle, and Mike's dogs bolted past me on their way back to the van, where Ray was waiting. I turned and waved. Directly behind me, a few feet from where I stood, was Rourke.

How mysterious to see him, mysterious and gothic, with the noses of the motorcycles poking over the face of the bluff like gargoyles and the scrambling strands of our hair reaching for the heavens like evangelical arms. The muddy platform on which we stood choked off into a walkway, or ropeway like between two bluffs, like something precarious that is the only available avenue. I felt the planet creaking by degrees—it had revolved sixteen times since I'd seen him last, and though I'd mourned the time lost, by the look in his eyes I could say for certain that none had been.

There was a red car behind him. A guy appeared, a wiry guy with a handsome haggard face who looked like he was from Brooklyn originally. He wore a white and green baseball shirt that read *Katie O'T*—O'Toole's maybe. The last letters fell beneath his unzipped sweatshirt. He placed a bottle of Beck's in Rourke's hand, and he gestured with his head toward Ray.

"Better watch out," he warned me, "your boyfriend's gettin' nervous."

I didn't bother to say Ray wasn't my boyfriend. They knew that. I just said, "Hi, I'm Eveline."

"I know who you are," he said, raising himself onto the hood of his car. His accent was concentrated and compressed and familiar to me. He took a tight suck off his beer and minimized his eyes. He extended the bottle in my direction. I stepped forward to him, took a mouthful and handed it back.

"This is Rob," Rourke said unceremoniously, as though stating the obvious, the way a wildlife guide might say, "This is a lion." He looked down and kicked at the sandy ground. "Cirillo."

"Where are you from?" I asked Rob. "Brooklyn?"

"Brooklyn," he said with a grimace. "Jersey." He flipped his chewing gum between his teeth. "I'm visiting this guy. He lives across the street." Rob turned to Rourke. "She doesn't know that?"

Rourke twisted the cap off the bottle he held. "Guess not."

"Oh," Rob said, "and I figured you were a smart girl."

"Guess you figured wrong," I said as Rourke's forearm jerked to his chest. I flinched, and he paused, chillingly. His fingers snapped the bottle cap, firing it through the open car window.

"Guess I did," Rob said, "figure wrong."

Rourke's anger was new to me. It was not corrosive and sullen like Jack's, but measured and mature, volatile but sophisticated, huge and accustomed to hugeness. It moved through him like a network of incendiary things. And it had a public quality—it seemed to involve everyone, everywhere. I didn't know Rob well, but clearly he was nervous. I looked to him for an explanation, and he looked to me, withholding one. I was glad Rourke had such a friend. I would've given anything for a friend like that.

"Let's go," Rourke said.

Rob slipped instantly from the freshly waxed hood, popping the latch of the driver's door. There was an emblem on red fender, an especially fitting emblem—the chrome head of a running cougar. Rob unrolled his window before getting in. He slammed his door and laid his elbow on the ledge. "See you around," he proposed with a cautious wink.

Rourke got in on the other side. In his lap, his hands were loosely cupped.

"See you," I said, walking off before they pulled out, thinking, it was nice of Rob to let me go first.

BY THE TIME WE got to The Tattler, I'd lost the spirit of the day. Everything seemed painful and foreign. People were acting assertive in themselves and amongst themselves, as if they were the only people, and their society was self-contained and thoroughly impermeable to the basic axioms of the beyond.

"Let's hit Surfside," Ray said. "It'll be more mellow."

"I'm sorry," I said, "I think I better go home. Sorry."

"Don't worry about it. I'm just glad you came."

"Can you give me a ride to the train?"

"I'll drive you straight home," he insisted. "I'm totally sober."

"The train goes right to my house. I like the train."

"Don't be a stranger to Montauk," Mike said as I kissed his freckled cheek. Then I kissed Will and Ralph and his girlfriend Claudia from Ecuador. Claudia had hair like wine. There was a word for the color that my mother often used—*vinaceous*.

Will patted my shoulder. "Take it easy there, Evie."

"Don't worry Will," Mike joked, "she'll take it easy *everywhere*."

Janey purred in my ear. "I saw you with your beau."

"Oh," I said, "not the skinny guy."

"I know which was him," she snapped amiably, "I'm not blind." She held me. I did not like to leave her. "Now, now, give a hug, there's a girl. And don't ever forget Martin."

On the platform, Ray checked his watch. "Six minutes." Montauk was nearly dark. I wondered did Montauk get dark first in all of America because it's so far east.

"Almost," Ray said. "The New England coastline is further than we are. I think the most eastern spot is in Maine."

"Still," I said, "coming almost first in nightfall."

"And in dawn," Ray said.

"Yes," I said, "almost first in dawn. That's pretty big."

"You'll have to visit again. When it's less chaotic."

By *chaotic* Ray was not referring to the parade but to Rourke. Though they hadn't spoken, it would have been impossible for anyone to overlook the chaos of Rourke. If he had been a drawing, he would have been a scribbled hive or an inky twister approaching at a treacherous incline from the corner of an otherwise unpopulated page.

A uniformed man approached unsteadily from the engine car, drunk or exhausted. We moved to meet him. He looked somewhat like Oz, not the Magnificent Oz, but the roadside fortune teller in the beginning of the film.

"And what can I do for you young revelers?"

"How much for one, to East Hampton?"

"Why now that depends on whether or not you're Irish."

Ray said, "Isn't everyone Irish on St. Patrick's Day?"

The conductor mounted a set of steps to the last car. "You've a fine head, son. No charge!" He scanned the empty platform and cried out, *All aboard!* Silence filled the wake. "Looks like you're the only passenger, young lady," he said. "Either you're a rebel or you know something no one else does."

"A rebel," Ray said admiringly.

The trainman told Ray to check again. "This one has a secret."

Ray gave me a kiss, and I climbed up. "Come again," he said.

"I will," I promised, knowing I would not, anyway, not to see him, which was an eerie knowledge. Life is full of such eerie knowledges. The train rocked back, readying itself, then jolted forward, and I waved. I took my seat and thought how I'd never yet said goodbye to Rourke, and, despite the odds against seeing him again, there was always another time. It was sort of risky, sort of like gambling. One day I would miscalculate, and there would be no next time. I looked through the scraped window at America's nearly first night sky, thinking, *Once Janey boarded a plane bound for the States.*

CARS WERE PARKED ASKEW all down my street, like porcupine needles. Through the front window of my house, I could see heads and faces lit by candles and hurricane lanterns softened by the grisardy gauze of smoke.

Inside was Jim Peterson, Francis Holland, Big John, and Tee Nolan, a disc jockey from WRCN. Joanne Clymes was singing "Tangled Up In Blue" into a wooden spoon. They waved as I passed into the kitchen.

Lowie and her boyfriend David Hill were at the table, and Mom was helping Joanne's fiancé Lewis get a refill from a pitcher of beer. Lewis was disabled. He referred to himself as a crippled dwarf or a twisted midget. "Anything but *small man*," he'd say. "Small is relative."

When they saw me, they all shouted. "*Evie!*"

"Kate called," Lowie said. "It snowed ten inches in Montreal. She can't fly out until Tuesday. She says the baby lifted its head."

"How was Montauk?" Mom asked.

"Okay," I said. There was food on the counter. "Who cooked?"

"I did." David stood. "Let me fix something for you."

David was a cook at the American Hotel in Sag Harbor. Occasionally, on a night off, he and Lowie would stop by with something good like roasted lamb chops with rosemary sauce and Yukon gold potatoes au gratin and brussel sprouts sauteed in fresh ginger.

"I'd cook at your house, Evie," he would say, as we unloaded pans and trays from his car, "but your mother's got no knives, no spices, no pots, and no silverware. The few dishes she does have are cracked, and half the time she is surrounded by a starving multitude. I'm not a rich man!" David was a fastidious and temperamental talent. He was in constant competition with other cooks. Once we attended a bake-off he'd entered at the Bridgehampton Baptist Church. He took us around to the tables of his competitors. "Try one of those biscuits," he'd whisper through a public smile. "See how it flakes. Grip it tight and it flakes. Go ahead, grip it. Too much buttermilk!"

"The zucchini bread has walnuts," he told me, "That okay?"

"Walnuts are fine."

"I bet you haven't eaten all day."

"I had breakfast. At John's."

"I know John's," Lewis said. He was standing by a chair waiting for a boost. "I used to tutor near Rushmeyers'."

"Let me get you a phone book," Mom said to him.

"The chair's fine, Irene."

Lowie asked how was the parade.

"It was okay. I went on a motorcycle ride."

"In Montauk?" Mom cried out. "With whom?"

"A girl I met." David handed me my plate.

"Does she have a name?"

I said Janey.

Lowie said, "Janey *what?*"

I shrugged.

"You didn't get a last name? Did Ray know her?"

"What if you got into an accident?" Lewis asked.

"We might not have known until it was too late," David said.

Lowie said, "Who would've given the hospital your blood type?"

"*I* don't even know her blood type," my mother said.

"How is that possible, Irene?" Lowie reprimanded. "You're her mother."

IN THE SANCTITY OF my room, I lay in bed, and the fluid of my body compressed like I was horizontal and half-full, like I was a lowering reservoir. I had some paper so I drew a tornado. The hard part of drawing a tornado is the frenzy of contradictory motion—lightness and leadness, something to strike and stroke you, something there and not there, heavy and heaving and cruel and oscillating, ancient and sweetly imaginary as ether. All around it, in helical type I wrote,

> *Sometimes in sleep he appears—as atmosphere, as terrain, as a motivating sense of place. If it is me who sees, it is not me who moves. I am simply somewhere, and simply I see. What I see is tranquil. All the world moving like the hand that marks the hour. When I awaken, the memory of him is clear. Though I lie unmoving, trying to keep him there, he vanishes. My already seeing eyes burn out from within, searing through the skin like two scorched medallions.*

There was music—sweet, slow clapping, a harmonica, a guitar. I opened my bedroom door. Through the crowd I saw my mother on the Eskimo dogsled chair, low to the ground, her elbows on bent knees. Jack was next to her on the enamel blue hearth. The room got quiet but for her harmonica and the squeak of Jack's fingers moving great distances along his guitar strings. He began to sing, and his voice was pure and in his purity was pain. Music amounts to a confession that you can be hurt that much.

> *Jesus met the woman at the well*
> *Jesus met the woman at the well*
> *And He told her everything she'd ever done.*

Soon Mom stopped playing and joined in.

> *She said, Jesus, Jesus, ain't got no husband*
> *And You don't know everything I've ever done.*

At the end came applause, and my mother hugged Jack, and he smiled. He loved her, everyone did, and she loved him with a special love she reserved for things so flawed. Jack especially admired the way she played harmonica. "The only thing my mother can play," he'd say, "is bridge." On the night before he left for Outward Bound in 1979, the same summer Maman died, only before it happened, my mother loaned him her best harmonica. The kind with a button on the side so you could change keys.

Jack revolved it reverently in his hands. "I can't take this, Rene."

"Sure you can," she said, "I insist."

Jack thanked her and inquired as to whether she knew that Ben Franklin had invented an instrument called an *armonica*, an upright glass harmonica. Jack adored Ben Franklin.

"Yes, Jack," my mother said, "Franklin was a wizard."

HE CLIMBED IN BED next to me, both of us facing the wall. Jack was in front, and he reached back and raised my hand over his waist. I was happy he was home. I'd missed him. The uncomplicated way things could be.

"I want to take off," he suggested. "To where they'll never find us. Let's go to Italy. We'll hang out in olive groves and drink Chianti."

It would not be good with Jack in Italy. "How about North?"

He lifted his head. "North? To where?"

"Someplace with ghosts. Someplace white and cold. Norway."

"Norway has no ghosts," he said dejectedly, going back down.

"It does, Jack. They're silvery and tall and they have capes with shredded edges like icicles."

And we were quiet; we stayed for hours, quavering wholly, wholly clear, drawing off love and affection from one to the other, my face nuzzling into his baby fine hair, his back pressing into my chest. If I am left with the regret of having been so blinded by the new fierceness of life in me that I neglected to *see* him—substantially lighter, wasted and debased following a weekend with his father at a college, enclouded by the view of a life of vulgar specificity in which he could not endure—I am grateful to God that I have in my heart, like a jewel or a coin, that solitary piece of his nearness, the warmth of his body, the heat of his voice as he sang along to the music ongoing in the living room, his clean, firm hands holding mine, calming me, comforting me, passing off his remaining shreds of courage. Passing off generously, passing off like he knew. I moved on in my mind that night; I had received the imprint of his release.

The unusual thing about quiet is that when you seek it, it is almost impossible to achieve. When you strive for quiet, you become impatient, and impatience is itself a noiseless noise. You can block every superficial sound, but, with each new layer extinguished, a next rises up, finer and more entrapping, until you arrive at last in the infinite attitude of your own riotous mind. Inside is where all the memories last like wells, and the unspoken wishes like golden buds, and the pain that you keep, lingering and implicit, staying inside, nesting inside, articulating, articulating, through to the day you die.

Debris from the previous night was still on the counter when I got back from school—leprechaun hats and empty whiskey bottles and David's ham, covered in flies. I didn't think flies came in the cold. I thought flies were warmish bugs. One by one, I killed them, then I cleaned the kitchen, quietly as possible. Though it wasn't ready, I turned off the coffee and the pulping bubbles got swallowed back through the triangular mouth of the pot.

In the living room I sat by the dumb white ash that had once been wood, and before that trees and before that other things, people and moss and tall hares. My eyes stared into the soot, the way eyes sometimes do, numb when you are nothing to no one. And in the shower I washed until I could no longer bear the hiss of the water. When I turned the knobs to stop it, it stopped, and I was glad for the simplicity of that enterprise. Strawberry light seeped through the strawberry drape, which was pretty but sad—sad to be unattended in prettiness. I pulled the curtain carefully, and carefully my body went white. I could see it change in the mirror. I could see myself turn exceedingly still. I watched my head cock. I watched myself listen, though I did not think to listen. I could see myself, approximating, calculating, knowing something before I knew it, which was scary, like applying math to true space and time, and impossible, like using geometry to stop meteors.

I climbed out of the tub and moved to the staircase, where I could hear the throaty purr and crack of a new fire. Jack had just left, my mother was teaching, Kate was in Montreal. I leaned against the door and grabbed my jeans, wrenching them up around my wet hips, tugging one side up then the other. I pulled a t-shirt over my head and started down the stairs. As I walked my legs went dead, so I went slow, then slower, because, just because—it was as if I'd never before felt the plush of the carpet, the arid pocked walls, the wormy surface of the banister. The upper floor retreated above and behind in backward drunken jerks as I descended.

He was at the hearth, his hand against the mantle, his head hanging. The flames blistered and dilated and spread spaciously from one flank of the brick cavity to the other before plunging upward into the colorless chill of the chimney. He turned, and his eyes accidentally assessed me. I shoved my shirt into my jeans and zipped them. He stepped around the table to my right. I moved left, taking his spot at the hearth. I shook the water from my hair.

The fire jumped irritably, keeping rhythm, keeping speed, carping and stuttering before hurling itself into an empire of glorious nothingness—if you have dreamt a dream at night of flying, that is what you have dreamt. Rourke's mouth in the firelight appeared swollen as if stung by bees. I longed to kiss it. I hoped I would not die longing that way. His features stiffened as I surveyed them; his eyes retired unfeelingly. He could be cruel. By cruel I did not mean seeking pleasure from causing pain, though that may have been so, by cruel I meant a refusal to be moved by the effect he had upon others.

He reached to pry something from his back pocket, and he tossed it on the coffee table—my glove, the one I'd lost in Montauk. He said nothing. But anyway, I understood. He'd seen me at breakfast with Ray. It was strange, the way the glove hit the table with a knock instead of a slap. I wondered was it frozen.

He crossed the room to leave, and the door closed after him with a punitive click. I looked at the glove. Usually I don't look at my gloves, usually I feel them. It lay very still, palm uppermost, fingers serene, as though caught in a gesture of divine meditation. Not in any gesture, but in *my* gesture because the glove possessed the shape of my hand. Though it was compelling to think of myself in terms of such things as absence and presence, evacuation and ingression, me and not me—I was drawn more to themes of Rourke. I could not help but view the glove as his, insofar as it had fallen into his custody, insofar as in his trust it had achieved dynamic new meaning. The glove was not a lost garment, nor was it some lurid emblem of indiscretion and insolence, it was a just way of speaking. I thought he was telling me he could not be provoked. Asking me.

I turned down all the lights and moved to the window, letting the fire languish. I left off that night with thoughts of princes and honor, of falcons and gloved wrists and golden chalices and light ascending, of victory and nobility and hieroglyphs of hooded birds. I left off thinking that something must have hurt him very much for him to have traveled so far.

He was kissing me, and I was wondering about all this stuff, such as school and Kate and where sod is farmed and how to spell *ankh* and how I'd never seen a single episode of *Saturday Night Live* or *Eight is Enough*. Our lips pressed lifelessly. I'd never noticed the lifeless quality to Jack's kisses. It occurred to me that they'd always been that way, like kissing the heel of bread, if in fact there was bread that tasted like Blistex.

Kate was at the base of the stairs. Her hair was in a series of elaborate pigtails, and she was wearing vanilla silk pajamas. She pressed her hands onto the screen door, talking through to us.

"Coco just called. There's a party tonight at Mark Ashby's house."

"And there are rings around Saturn," Jack said. "That doesn't mean we're going."

As usual, we got high, and for a change, we played dice, the three of us sitting on the kitchen floor, listening to *Let's Cha Cha with Puente* with the volume raised to ten. "What's your favorite?" Jack shouted as he jiggled the dice interminably, "Cha Cha Fiesta," "Lindo Cha Cha," or "Let's Cha Cha?"

"Cha Cha Mungo," Kate yelled back. "Hurry up and roll."

This made them laugh, and they laughed and, as they did, I could see into their heads. I could see Kate's teeth and Jack's teeth, base-to-base archways, like propped apart coon traps. Teeth ought to be clandestine, like spies meeting down dark alleys. Jack stuck his head in the refrigerator because he became asthmatic, and Kate smacked the oven door repeatedly with the back of her head saying *Ouch* every time. Her silk shirt caught the light the way pearls do, the way pearls in light look like milk on fire.

I tried to remember the funny thing, the first funny thing. If I found it, it might be like a pass or key. My mind toiled, working back until everything outside had turned as soundless as inside which was like a sudden inward rush of air, or a backward explosion, or, an inside-out explosion, or you might say, an implosion. They were looking at me, looking with dog-looking-at-rabbit eyes. *If the pendulum is nailed to the wall, the clock should continue to swing,* I wanted to say, though I wasn't sure what I meant by that, and, besides, my mouth was awfully dry.

I switched up to a chair, and with a pen I found I played a sullen game, which was taking one finger and skittering it around the center of the pen, making a windmill on the table. Then I drew on the bottom of my sneaker, trailing the rubber passageways until I got frustrated. It is not a good maze, a sneaker maze, but a brainless one. I felt enervated, which is the opposite of energized, which is odd.

Jack shut the door to the bathroom. The tame arc of his pee made a bright bursting sound. Before the toilet completed its flush, he joined me at the table. Kate remained on the floor, pinching a wooly strand of her hair. *Palomino, fallow, ringdove*—those were her colors in names. Her shoulders sloped downwards. She asked if I felt like splitting a can of spinach. I did not. Then she said something else that I didn't hear.

There was a matchbook Jack found on the floor, and he folded and unfolded it while Kate scraped at the grout under the sink with a giant safety pin. I did not like to think of that pin, the giant tear in the giant object it proposed to mend. It bothered me, so did the macerated matchbook, so did everything. It was like I was standing in the center of a cube that was collapsing—*phoom, phoom, phoom*. I was feeling three sides down—one more coming. I was feeling an end feeling.

"I'm going for a walk."

Jack said, "Where to?"

I said, "The tracks."

In the living room, we stirred inexpertly. Kate knelt to pet the cat. It regarded me with that questioning look cats make when they pull back their ears. Cats are insane—with the whiskers and the tail. Anyway, it's insane that we live with them, with the way they are so shrewd and they shed fur as a sign of anxiety.

Jack offered me his Dartmouth sweatshirt—Elizabeth had given it to him. It slid past my head and hips to my thighs, and it smelled of puberty. Did I need to weep? Possibly I needed to weep. Possibly there were docile tears within, little waters waiting, ornamental drops like globes of yarn that bowl across cottage floors, taking thorough turns, paving tracks of turquoise and caramel. Near the base of my throat was a virtuous circle, a perfect *O*, not an excavated place, a burgeoning one. Though signs of my damage lay everywhere—things stricken, things remaindered, broken heads of flowers and smoking empires—I knew I had no gift for violence. I knew as well that they were not entirely innocent. They knew it too; I could tell by the way they hung their heads. Kate padded up the stairs.

"See you, Kate," I said, wishing all of a sudden that I could make her happy, knowing I could not, grieving because it was right to grieve. Baby birds annihilate the only world known. The treasure is flight.

"'Night, Katie," Jack murmured.

The pallid light from the landing broke through the bars as he gripped them, slitting his features, and her feet paused on two separate steps, causing me to wonder if they could ever fall in love with each other, which would have been a divine type of providence. The door creaked when I opened it, and the cat bolted. I plunged down the porch steps and was rushed by the night. It carried me the way the wind carries a hat.

Our house was shielded from the railroad by a barrier of gnarled vines on the south side of the driveway, which did nothing to keep the train from shaking the house or to block the beacons that stalked the dark, flooding and filling the rooms before fading petulantly away. At the end of the driveway on the other side of Osborne is a street lamp. Bright light cascaded in an inverted cone from the bulb to a spacious pool at the base. Jack was already at the far outer rim of that light, on the tracks to the west. I wondered was he moving very fast, or was I going very slow. One of us was out of time.

I kept my eye on him as I walked the length of rail between us, watching the whole way the patchwork of his limbs, lunar white and scarcely fastened, ready as ever to tumble up into stellar obscurity. I sat, and my hands stroked the rail. It was blistered somewhat from the load of the train, but better for the blisters, better for the inference of its own lastingness.

I asked Jack where the rails run to and why.

He reached with desiccated fingertips to fold the cuff of his pants. His jaw was lightly bearded and red, and it drew his concave cheeks down. His hair spilled forward, teasing the dual arenas of his eyes. "They run the train's distance. Because the train needs them."

His voice was so near that it might well have originated in my own head, and it reminded me—mostly that I had to be reminded. And me, did I remind him, or anyone, of anything? I felt sad and looked at him sadly.

"No," I said, "they run their *own* distance. They run because they have to. It is the thing that they are."

He poked at the tar with a stick, his chest low by his feet.

"Jack," I said, regretting for his sake the sound of my voice. Its sheerness, its vicinity—its *disappearing* vicinity. He did not lift his head but rotated it obligingly, leaning to rest his chin on the back of my hand. His face came into the ring of lamplight. His eyes were there—blue, a very inconspicuous blue, a blue so refined as to be devoid of value. His skin was warm; I recognized its temperature.

There was a flicker. Jack did not move exactly, but his figure conveyed new poise. He seemed to settle and turn stable exactly as he shut down against me, leaving me to wonder if I'd ever even seen him, ever even known him. Has he saved himself, I wondered, for this day? The idea surprised me, that he'd saved himself.

I became mindful of my sacrifice, of the ugliness of my enterprise. I imagined the places he would go, the people he would meet. I thought of his music, of me listening anonymously and in vain for my residence in his songs, of his offering to others the words that had once gone from his lips to my ears. I thought back on the dreams we'd shared. How our lives had not been actual—we'd never once felt actual. We'd never once taken for granted our place or our liberty. Though it could be a consolation to no one, I would regret the loss of him for the rest of my life. Almost as great as that personal regret would be the inevitable public impression that I'd loved him less than I'd been loved by him. This was not so; I'd loved him truly. I began to cry, and the stars, the hundreds and thousands of stars, joined into one gaseous avenue that draped over his head like a cowl.

"Did you ever think how dumb it is to cherish the stars," Jack said. "Most of them have extinguished by the time the light reaches us."

"Oh my God," I said, "Jack."

"Love is like starlight. Just a signal, a flare, diminishing in brilliance from the point of origin, dead by the time you get it."

"I'm so sorry."

"I fucked up," he said lifelessly. "Not you."

I lowered my head between my knees, and for a long time we sat. It would be one of the last times sitting, so we were careful not to hurry. When at last he stood, I stood as well, and at the street we parted. He walked to the corner, his figure bouncing down and away like a ball shooting out of reach.

I DID NOT WANT to go back to the house. The house seemed earthy and loamish, like damp dirt, like dirt that you die in, like nutirent-rich dirt that eats you, which is weird but true, I guess, because, just because.

I stumbled down the driveway as if drugged, kicking gravel, wasting time. Outside was dark, a flat, generous dark, with night taking hold in pockets and strips, here and there, patches and pools like warm spots in the ocean. The air was powdery and soft, making outside into another inside, like an auxiliary room, like an evening previously lived, an evening when the trees reached to plead with angels, an evening before you were born, in a place you never lived, when there was dancing and a veranda. I lifted my ear to the sky and listened for the wail of the train. Sometimes you can hear it, even if it's not there—sonorous and low, riveting and heroic, dejected and alone.

I began to spin. When I was little I would spin through rain. I would stand beneath the bursts and clots of water that came from the serrated, splay-mouthed gutters of my dad's apartment building. My closed umbrella would skip and stutter along the fractured cement like it was a cane, and I would stretch my pockets to catch the drops. They came to me out of the whole world because I loved them best. Skinny strings of hair would cling to my face and stick in my mouth as I spun into brick walls, colliding and twirling, full and alone.

I rolled along the row of privet that divided the front and side lawns from the driveway. At the farthest end, I spun off, singing the words to a song I'd never heard, humming and singing something about *trees, trees, trees and lights out*. When I came to a stop, there was a sound—mournful and clear, righteous and alone. I wished I knew enough about music to name the note. I perceived in it a calling, a cry to life. It was Rourke. He said, "Hi."

"Hi." I swayed slightly. "I didn't see your car."

I glanced over my shoulder. It was definitely there. Right on the street in the grass near the top of the driveway. I could see the white of the hood and roof coming in pieces through the leaves. It looked like a horse, like it was chewing grass, waiting.

Twigs were on my sweatshirt—no, Jack's sweatshirt. I brushed them off. I hadn't thought of Rourke all night. That wasn't true. I hadn't hardly thought of him. He was against the side of the barn near the forsythia. I moved to join him. His thick legs were crossed and skylight spilled against them, though his face remained shaded by something, a cloud maybe. I looked to see. Oh, the peak of the roof. How lovely, how apt, a *V*-shaped prow like the hull of a ship jutting into the oceanic sky, piercing the vast and gently oscillating universe—Rourke. I pulled at the forsythia. Forsythia is a pioneer: first to bloom, first to wither. Every year it flowers without my notice. Every year I vow to catch it next time.

"I just came back from Jersey. I was driving by."

I said, "Oh."

If there was something else to say, I could not think of it. Maybe I should have asked about driving past my house when it wasn't on his way, or how long he'd been in Jersey and when he was going back, or how much older was he than I, and did he love me too. Love as a word is weedy and imprecise unless you feel it, and then it is the only possible word. It's the lucky heir of a filtering into one of all its attendant emotions—terror and joy, hope and despair, and fascination that is supernatural and abiding. If you had to feel each of those things individually you would not last one day. I wondered if he was still angry. He did not seem angry.

"Forsythia," I said, opening my hands to show him all the petals. "Always blooms without me."

I nudged the torn flowers in my hand. I was sorry for what I'd done. I could not refasten the petals to the stem, I could only cast them off, and I did, watching them spin down like lemony propellers. It was true that I was still a little high. You know that leaning kind of reasoning, like a glass on one side and all the contents tipped against an edge.

I was walking, he was also walking, and when we walked sometimes our hands would touch. At the garage we stopped. His face was close to mine, and his eyes. To stand before him was to stand before a body of natural consequence, an orchid, a stallion, something maverick and elemental, something too exquisite to last and so you feel strange pain. His drive issued forth, aqueous and imperative. I tore a splinter of cedar from a shingle. I wondered if he knew about Jack and me. Probably—he seemed to know everything. If he were normal and I were normal, I might have solicited his sympathetic regard and allowed myself to be persuaded by it. But it was not tenderness I wanted, and it was not tenderness he would have expressed, only self-interest. Maybe all tenderness is self-interest anyway. Maybe Rourke is just more honest than anyone else.

He looked at me, into the realm about me, like he was comparing me to surrounding things, to the trees, to the dark, like he was seeing me as he would have had me seen, as he would have had me see myself, and then he smiled, coldly, professionally, expressing himself in his heat and his prime, making my grief over losing Jack into the nothing it surely was. I twisted the knob near my waist and entered my bedroom, half-hoping he would follow. We stood with difficulty on opposing sides of that threshold. Behind my back, my little room, a jewel box—at the end of the driveway, his car, grazing.

I closed my door. I rested my forehead against it, with my palms caressing. It was not a door, but a dead tree. I'm sorry, I said, apologizing for its dismemberment on my behalf. Maybe Jack knew certain things, and Kate and my mother knew certain things, but only Rourke knew the madness of my ambition and the innocence of my desire. Only he knew the fluent pain that hovered within me, fluttering like diaphanous wings.

A long time passed before I heard his footsteps and the muffled thump of his car door and the churn of the engine, and, when finally he had gone, I spent the remainder of my night in cardinal desolation, comforted only by the knowledge that his was spent in the same way.

12.

OUTSIDE THE AIR WAS SILVER, AND ALL THE GREENS WERE SAINTLY GREENS. I walked lightly, collecting dew like jewels as I crossed the rim of each lawn, the spring ground depressing like foam beneath my feet. When I arrived at school, I could not think of why to enter, so I waited on the football field for the bells to ring.

Mr. Shepard did not request a late pass. He was discussing the Advanced Placement exam, telling the class what was the lowest possible score we could get and still earn college credit for the course. As I cut past him, Nico cleared his throat very loudly and Stephen Auchard raised one eyebrow because I was late. I took my seat and looked past the sky blue cinderblock walls into the courtyard garden that no one ever used. Denny once tried to organize a garden club. He had the idea to grow produce for the cafeteria and flowers for the art class to draw. Science students could study mulching and gases and insects, and shop students could make benches. He wanted to call it *IGA*, for Integrated Garden Alliance. Denny hoped one day it would be a model for public schools across America.

"They didn't even look at my blueprints," he told Mom and me after his presentation to the school board. "They said there's no money in the budget for courtyard maintenance. I said, 'Well, that's the whole bonus of a club—*free* maintenance.' Like, duh." He shrugged. "I didn't even get to tell them about the poetry teas."

The garden wasn't a garden. *They* didn't want it to be. It was some mind control thing, some remedy for the psychosis of confinement, like a mural or indoor waterfall. They did not want us to notice that we were not being trained or inspired, we were being held in custody until it could be proven to at least sixty-five percent of some dubious national standard that our ingenuity had been thoroughly assimilated into the tastes of a comatose generation. Then you're ready for college. *You have to go to college. This is America. In Russia, they don't even have tampons.* And yet how often had I heard my mother complain, "I'm not teaching Shakespeare. I'm teaching phonics."

In fact, we would have crippled the job market and drained social services if our dependency had not been extended. That is the truth behind college for every American, even the dumb.

Nico had been accepted to the University of Vermont.

"Cool," Jack said. "Is he going to major in Physical Molestation?"

"Actually, he's on the payroll," Denny said, "they're going to study him in biology lab."

THERE ARE PEOPLE ON staff at high schools to feed the college machine. Agonizingly mild, pink-faced men like Mr. McGintee help students *evaluate qualities* and *calculate options*. Ladies with dry hair and degrees-in-progress, like Lydia Kilty, let you know whether or not you have the *right stuff*. At seminars in emptied guidance rooms, cultish recruitment officers draw looping arrows on glossy easels with bizarre-smelling Vis-à-Vis markers, while you sit in a cataleptic stupor, tracing dust pyramids in the air and making planes out of pamphlets until the sales pitch slithers to a suspicious semi-halt.

You are roused in the midst of a damp handshake, and you wonder, "Good God, have I just been initiated?"

If you take time off after high school, you are a pariah. Former friends ignore you on the streets, and their parents freak out like you are a dope addict. Parents cannot really be blamed for their paranoia, when all they ever hear about are tests and essays, scores and tours and fees. At money management assemblies, they are reassured that what they cannot provide through scholarship, savings, second mortgages, and home equity loans, the government will generously supplement with low-interest credit.

"What a racket," my father said when he read the brochures. "Jimmy the Onion never had it so good."

One thing they make sure to teach in high school is how to drive. Well-meaning people such as Mr. O'Donnell, the librarian, and Kathleen Provost, the animal hospital receptionist, believe that driver's education contributes to public safety. They don't see that to accommodate third and fourth drivers, families need more insurance, more gas, and more automobiles. Or that teens enroll just to get lower insurance rates, or that insurance companies give those rates because insuring teens is good business—otherwise companies wouldn't bother to do it, no matter how many lives might be saved. The fact is, when you give cars to people with no responsibilities, no destinations, and no privacy, they will most likely use them for things other than driving.

Two weeks after Troy had won the coveted "Driving Ace" award in high school, he and Jack got so stoned off homegrown pot in their shampoo bottle bong that Troy drove the Vista Cruiser home from Indian Wells beach in reverse.

Sometimes you hear of town planners bringing in one species to lower the population of another, and then the town is overrun by the predator. Sometimes you interfere with nature, and its ferocity emerges in new ways, in perverse extremes of attitude or number. Sometimes it happens quickly; other times, you cannot see the effects until it's too late. Sometimes you can't help but feel you are part of a giant out-of-control science experiment. *Out-of-control* because no one in charge ever seems to consider consequence or aftermath.

Jack and I once stopped at a state park in Pennsylvania where there were so many flies the benches seemed to move and so many caterpillars that under our feet there was crunching. We were on our way to the Ben Franklin Museum. We asked the man what was going on. *The* man because there was only one. He was in a body net.

"They brought in the flies to kill the caterpillars," he explained, "figuring the birds would eat the flies. But these are the wrong kind of fly. These are the foul-tasting, non-caterpillar-consuming kind of fly."

Dad said that when they introduced rabbits to Australia, the rabbits had no natural predators, so they evolved into a new crazy kind of rabbit. They decided to poison the rabbits, only the poison was the wrong poison, and all the rabbits died an exceptionally cruel death. "I can't even think about it," he shuddered. My dad loves animals.

If you ask him, "Who are *They?*" he'll say, "*They*. Those college bastards." According to my mom, "*They* are the ones who killed Kennedy." Jack would say, "*They* are the pharmaceutical companies."

Mr. Shepard had finished the lesson. I heard the notebooks flapping shut. Too bad about the courtyard. The grass looked nice. I would like to run out and fall and soak into the earth the same way you run down a hill and drop into snow and get buried to your shoulders. My face would protrude from the tips of the blades like a pale embossment or bas-relief, like a cameo or a mask. I would sleep, peaceably anchored, listening in my dreams to the ecstatic trill of the sparrows. And with the heat of the sun on my front and the magnetic calm of the earth against my back, I would think, *Once we were children, once we wanted to run like the wind because we were the wind.*

MISS PANETTA SIGHED HARD. "Are you really going to rule out (A)?"

Jodie Palumbo sank in her chair.

"The answer is in the reading, Miss Palumbo."

On the lapel of the teacher's raisin-blue blazer was a gold brooch in the shape of an enormous contour. I wasn't sure if it was supposed to be the letter *C* or a partial moon or just a confusing shape, a scythe or a crook. She repeated the question, enunciating peevishly.

"The most common way for a new species to form is—*what?*"

Arms shot up, sleeves lightly whipping.

"No thank you. Miss Palumbo is going to impress us with the truth."

Jodie stirred in her chair, her chin glued to the palm of her hand.

"Find the first paragraph," the teacher directed as she turned to erase the board. Jodie flipped lethargically through her book, picking a random place and reading lamely. "According to Mendel's theory of—"

"Not there, Jodie," Lynn McMasters whispered. Lynn was sitting next to her. "Page 227."

Everyone started laughing, except Ryan Healy who took advantage of the commotion to talk to Billy Martinson. "We went to Tick Pete's last night." Tick Pete sold beer from the back of an old shut-up diner in Amagansett. Tick slept behind the counter on a cot and watched TV, living off Slim Jims and Trix, Jack claimed, though Dan swore he once saw Tick Pete eating Chinese take-out from Lyons.

"We still have half a case left," Ryan told Billy. "Meet us at Sammi's Beach before Donkey Basketball."

Ms. Panetta shuffled some papers on her counter and shot a glance at the clock. "I—think—we—should—call—it—a—day."

KELLY KAY CRUMB WAS at the wheel; the rest of us were crammed in back. She was telling the story of how her bra strap had been pulled while she was at her locker, and, when she went to the main office to report the incident, Vice Principal Martin said there was nothing he could do unless she knew who'd done it. "I mean, have you ever heard of such a stupid thing?" Kelly Kay asked. "Can you imagine the police telling you they can't follow up on a crime because they don't know the offender? The least he could've done was thank me for letting him know what's going on in his hallways. I mean, I wouldn't care so much," she confided, "but they unlatched the clasp."

"I didn't think they put clasps on training bras," L.B. said.

She glared into the rear-view. "Shut up!" The car swerved.

"Caution, darling," Linda warned as she reached to steady the wheel. Linda was the driving instructor from Massapequa. Her hair was the color of a cartoon oil slick. It was a jet blue haystack that remained in one unit even with the windows open. "When I was a kid, they used to give wedgies," she reminisced, as her fingers poked her hair and vanished to the third knuckle. "Now, that was something to bitch about."

I settled against the door and closed my eyes, and L.B. put his arm around me. "Come on," he said, "buck up." When he was finished lifting my spirits, his arm stayed in place.

MY LOCKER CLOSED, AND all down the hall they slammed shut in succession, clacking like dominoes. Inside I'd found three bundles of paper. The first was from Denny.

> *Guess what. This is so unbelievably stupid you will die. Today in chemistry The Walrus was substitute and Vincent and Nico took one of Stephen Auchard's chess pieces, a horse, and they drilled a hole in its face and attached the bottom of the horse onto a gas hose and lit its mouth and fire shot out and burned Marty Koch's legal pad. All I kept thinking was, I am so glad Evie is not here to see this. You would have been disgusted. Here's a drawing—*

The second was from Kate:

> *Do not show this note to anyone under penalty of death. I thought essay was spelled SA. I kept thinking what in God's name is an SA? Do you and Denny want to go dancing at Mellowmouth or does Teen Night depress you? Michelle and Tim are going and they asked me to go so you have to come only you have to promise not to dance and leave me alone. Mr. Myers keeps scratching his back against the edge of the door and his eyes go foggy. Don't forget the Spring Concert Saturday. C.C. P.S. Let's go to Buckets for Chocodiles later. P.S.A. News bulletin: Kip and Tony G?!? P.S.A.A. Check out Lisa's elephant ankles!!!!*

The third was from Jack. The third I couldn't open.

AT LUNCH I RESTED my head because my body felt poisoned. There was an acidic feeling in my eyes and my tissues felt toxic, but I didn't want to go home. At least people in the cafeteria spoke to me, and even if I didn't speak back, I was glad for the company. I could make out the forms, coming and going like drifting islands, jostling the table and that was like being shaken to sleep. Each person peered carefully, as though trying to secure in me some capricious pattern, as though I were kaleidoscopic. *Knock, knock. Anybody home?* I could not materialize. I could not say hello. I kept lapsing, lapsing, receding like a once discrete entity into its constitutional whole, like a gem to its mine, a drop to its sea.

I asked myself, "Is love always this awful? This awful and absolute?"

I WAS MAKING UP lab reports in the bio room, and I heard music, piano music. It was Dan, playing "I Get A Kick Out of You."

I knew it was Dan because no one else in school was good enough except Jack and Dan played piano differently than Jack. Jack steadied the keys and smoothed them, hunching fretfully as though they might bark or bite or turn on him. But Dan played with exuberance.

I crossed the hall to the choral studio. He brightened when he saw me. He slid on the bench as his right hand tapped out melodies and his left tested rhythms, one leading to another—"The Shadow of Your Smile" to "Rhapsody in Blue" to "Stormy Weather" to "Summertime." I sat on the lowermost carpeted choral step and listened, still clutching my dirty scalpel. It had been submerged in formaldehyde; it had poked through bobbing corpses to locate the aurora pink tissue of a fetal pig, my very own pig. I knew which pig was mine because around the right eye was a gray wheel, cracked here and there at the outer edge like a pineapple ring. As Dan played, I was thinking that jazz works the way the mind does—something occurs to you and you think it, or, in the case of jazz, you play it. Jazz gives me the sense of air conditioning. It's brisk and thin, an easy refuge. Dan had probably heard the news from Jack about our break-up. It was nice of him to play for me regardless. Would I miss Dan, I wondered, or just the time we'd shared, the original meaning of me? I would miss him, I thought, definitely miss him.

GYM WAS LAST. I considered skipping, but I didn't want to be anywhere else. Wherever I was depressed me, but wherever I was not depressed me also, sometimes even more. In the locker room girls laughed as they changed. Girls have a giggling way of bending forward when they laugh. Boys present their chests proudly to the city of God. I covered my nose and mouth with my shirt to block the stench of girl feet and girl perspiration and locker aluminum that is the smell of the flavor of blood. It's strange to think that blood tastes like the smell of metal—does it have metal in it? The fabric crossed my face to cover my ears, but still I could hear the bending laughter and the squeaks of sneakers slapping the ground and the flatulent squirts from near empty bottles of body lotion. Later there would be water—toilets retching, sinks spewing. My lock would not open. I yanked the round base but nothing happened. I tried the combination again, concentrating fiercely on the spinning black dial, the midget numbers, the ricey lines of uneven length, short then long, alternating like the sunrays of a child's drawing. My forehead grazed the damp bones of my hand. I could feel my body weave back into a writhing meadow of sound, which was strange—*into sound*—tumbling and victorious sound, with all that I saw and all that I could not see vanishing equally, though that could not have been so. Probably things had remained in place; probably it was my ability to perceive that had failed me.

Caroline Boylan was offering her hand. I guessed I'd fainted. She wasn't wearing a shirt or bra, so I couldn't help but notice that her breasts were like cabinet knobs. In eleventh grade, the *$10,000 Pyramid* had chosen her to play in its national teen tournament, making her into a lesser sort of celebrity. As I lay there, the memory of her on television returned to me vividly, her giving clues to her partner from Appleton, Wisconsin for "Things That Have Sauce." *Pizza, spaghetti, spaghetti, pizza, pizza, pizza.*

"Thanks," I said, coming up to sit. "I'm all right."

The crowd disbanded in the sulky mistrustful way crowds disband, like they haven't quite gotten their money's worth. I made my way onto the bench beneath the wall of lockers and lowered my head and squeezed the muscles in my thighs to send blood back up because that was what Aunt Lowie and Dr. Scott said to do whenever I fainted—either that or lower my head, which I did as well.

"You okay?" Someone must have told Coach because it was her voice I heard, and when I lifted my head, it was the myriad surfaces of her body that came into complex focus through a weird mist of puckered stars. Her dimpled knees and distended belly were well known to me and that was comforting. Perhaps she was not grotesque but straightforward about the inescapable fact of herself. Perhaps I had abused the privilege of her candor. I wondered what it was that she expected from us. She seemed to expect something. "Need the nurse?" she asked.

The nurse would just give me a place to rest. It's impossible to rest when everything smells like the sweet of Band-Aids, and when the kidney pan she puts near your mouth is riddled with those crazy black finger smudges, and there are depressing posters about alcohol abuse and car wrecks, and you have to wait for an appropriate amount of time to pass before you can leave, hoping nobody you know comes in for some really gross and graphic problem. Before you leave, you have to thank the nurse like she actually did something to heal you.

"Can I just stay with you?"

Coach gazed widely, blankly. She nodded once, and her oaky button eyes folded back into the confectionery flab of her face. "Let's go out to the tennis courts." She did not help me up, but she did get me a cup of cold water and a bag of salted cashews from her desk while I pulled on my shorts and sneakers. Together and alone, we crossed the deserted gymnasium, which was a queer sort of distinction.

The cyclone fence around the courts was cloaked in pine green tarps with those cut-out flaps—I sat and rested and waited for things to end, things such as the day and the tired way I felt. It helps to have an end in sight and to promise yourself to go no further, saying—*that's it*—very firmly. Six-thirty in the evening seemed right as an end to whatever it was that I was feeling, though I fully expected to be challenged on that.

The sun beat against my lids, creating geometry underneath, wandering and upraised like swimming Braille. The balls smacked the rackets and the spongy ground to create a succession of hollow pops. *Cluck-pop, cluck-pop.* In the cavern of my room, in the merciless clarity of the previous evening, my eyes had trailed the ceiling in just such an exchange, *cluck-pop, cluck-pop,* arcing back and forth, loosening the paint, reanimating it, making it newly viscous, causing it to melt down on me as I waited for dawn. After Rourke left, I was stricken with an incompetent longing, a clumsy physical loneliness. I was not clever with that lonely feeling, with its drift and wicked magnitude. I caressed my own body, seeking heat, seeking restitution, seeking rewards withheld, and in my heart I felt sin. I felt I had transgressed. It was not me I wanted but him, and that was a sorrowful offense, sorrowful because I was an animal and he was an animal, and yet we lay separately in the gaping obscurity of one anonymous night on earth.

I DID NOT CHANGE from my gym shorts after school or bother to get my books. I just walked from the court, cutting through the side yard to the street, stopping when I noticed the GTO in the front lot, parked a little crookedly. I immediately re-entered the building. I navigated the crammed halls quickly by minimizing myself—everyone else had grown so much bigger during the day. In the crowded lobby, I found Rourke talking to Mr. Parker, the music teacher. They shook hands amiably, saying *Good luck* and *Take care,* and when Mr. Parker slipped into the auditorium where the janitors were setting up for the spring concert, Rourke cut through the pack to where I stood.

He said hi. I said hi. He seemed younger, or just tired like me. There were lines beneath his eyes. "How are you today," he asked. "You all right?"

"I'm okay," I said, and together we walked, him behind me. I was aware of my thighs, the bareness of them, the way the muscles were smooth, the way I knew he was looking.

"I have to pick up a check," he said. "I'll meet you at the car."

I sat on the front steps and watched everyone leave. *The* car, he'd said, not *my* car. As the last yellow bus chugged around the bend leading from the school lot to Long Lane, a set of dressy feet appeared on the sidewalk before me. The shoes were loafers with tassels and pock marks and ruffled tongues cut low to the toes. It was Mr. Shepard, finishing bus duty.

"*Miss* Auerbach," he said definitively, as though he'd come upon me in the thick of the jungle. *The* jungle, because in my mind there's only one. Though of course I'm mistaken about that. *The* car, *the* jungle. One symptom of exhaustion must be that you start to obsess on articles.

I blocked the sun from my eyes and looked up, just looking.

He smiled tightly, and his chin gathered into his neck in that skeptical way that older men have, which they use on you when no one else is looking, and which is actually a patronizing manner of flirting. Skepticism suggests they know more than you do, and a superior intelligence is the only seductive power that remains to them, or so they think. Lowie once dated an alligator handler who was very handsome at forty-five. And most firemen are sexy, no matter how old, as are men who work on water, like Powell. In general older men can be attractive as long as they use their accumulated experience to bully things other than you, such as reptiles, fire, and the sea.

"Late to come, late to leave," he remarked as he started for the lobby. "Your timing is off today." At the main entrance, he encountered Rourke, who was on his way out. Rourke drew in his chest and swept his arm like an awning to hold the door from inside. Shepard looked from Rourke and back to me, figuring, figuring darkly.

Rourke came down the steps. "Let's go."

It was easy to obey him, so few things were easy. Nothing was attached to that obedience. It was as though the moment he spoke was the first moment, and each new moment was again a new moment, with nothing adding up, no attitudes or ideas. In the car, we sat for several minutes, and the leather was warm. Traces of him were everywhere—the confidential fragrance that had incubated beneath the roof, the microscopic shed of skin, the fingerprints on the Madrid vinyl dash. I felt an uneasy resolution—like everything finally right, yet nothing very. He had his last check; I had six more weeks of school. When I considered his keys, the slick conviction of his hand as it forced them into the ignition, I felt a manic envy of the vehicle, of its prominence in his life. I squeezed into the gap between the bucket seat and the door, and the car bolted from its spot. As he swerved left from the lot onto the main driveway, the car leaned mightily against its two right wheels, against my side, and I heard a giant swish of wind—my door, flying open.

Rubbery tentacles of air whipped at my chest, suctioning me, summoning me. My hair scrambled for my face, and my knees pulled as if inside the caps there was heavy metal and somewhere outside there were magnets. I began to slide and I thought, *My God, I am going to die. I am going to plunge through air and crash down and fracture and unravel across the asphalt, pink over black, a death uniquely befitting a butcher of baby pigs.*

The whole thing took so long, the seconds ticking and unticking, the space transforming telescopically between the status of my body and that of the ground, until at last it came, not the fall, but Rourke's hand, slap-curling like a whip around my ribs.

I thought to break his grip, to continue my fall—I'd been so very tired lately. But he would not relent. Though I didn't know if he loved me, I knew at least that he would not allow himself to be defeated in action, not ever. My right arm reached left, my fist clutched his sleeve, the car straightened, and my door slammed shut. I collapsed in a fetal ball against him, and he held me, shifting over the bridge of my ribs. We were breathing, both of us breathing, our living chests rising, falling, and rising—calibrated. I did not move and Rourke did not move as we made our way to my street, at which point each muscle of his hand eased individually, coming loose one at a time exactly as my body peeled itself from the electrifying shelter of his.

The screen door shot open like a slap. Kate leapt from the front porch and skipped across the slate walkway. She leaned on the passenger window, looking in. "This is a funny surprise," she said with an inquisitive frown.

I popped the door, shoving her a little and slipping past, then I proceeded to the garage entrance and into my bedroom, where I stripped before the mirror, strictly and with care. I examined my naked body to see what it was that I felt, when what I felt was ever mortal, ever viable and real. I felt a rush and a sweat. I felt inspirited and curiously inclined to forgive. In the glass, I looked like a girl, and I looked like a woman and in my eyes was a consecrated knowledge. I could perceive hills and hearths, existing and elapsed and the cherished ones to come. I could see my every home because through my modest figure wisdom pushed like a river, touching universally with a labor that was clarified and lithe.

The outline of his hand had absorbed into my ribs like a spill to a towel. It was pink, and I could trace the flourishing bruise, which would soon turn yellow-green like a certain class of algae.

I sat to think because suddenly there were so many things to think about. A few chance seconds had intervened to resolve months of allusion, and that was a serious reminder about the brevity of time and the fugitive constitution of life. A door opened, and I nearly fell. In those moments, I confessed a willingness to die, and he confessed an unwillingness to let me. I wondered if death is always so proximate, if life and its loss are like two opposing states— life as suspension, death as the reverse—a dissolution of structure, an absence of presence. Reverend Olcott says Hell is a place outside the presence of God. Maybe Hell is just a wall come down. Maybe Hell is only loneliness.

That was probably the part Jack went out of his way to confront—the lucid ease of loneliness, each time telling himself that an end could be simple and near, simpler and nearer than living and its requisite effort, when no one hears the things you say, when everyone has their own ideas of you, when everything you want is impossible to achieve, and inside every day you're dying anyhow. I thought I understood. If I'd melted through the divide, if I'd passed from one side to the other, it would have been better to leave Rourke then, at the moment his body had confessed a pure need for my body, than to prevail and endure the inevitable anguish of the inevitable loss of him.

Jack had felt the same, only for me. On the tracks the night before, he said, *I fucked up*. By that he meant that he'd waited too long. That our time had gone by. Love is like starlight, he said. By that he meant it has its time, and *its* time is not necessarily *your* time. You have to be big, I think, or old or brave or rich, or something other than what I knew myself to be, to make love's time your own.

KATE RAN IN, BREATHLESS. Something about Harrison and Friday night, something about going out, two of his friends in town. I covered my chest with a blanket, hugging myself.

"Will you come?" she said. "He said to ask."

Beneath the blanket my fingers jammed the welt he'd made. The pain radiated in an imperfect circle, and it was good. I liked very much that he had caused it.

"He's outside waiting," Kate urged. "He leaves Monday."

She didn't want me to go because she wanted my company. She didn't want me to go because he'd asked. She wanted me to go because she was afraid to go alone. She had reason to be afraid. It would have frightened me too, to be her, to be beautiful but deaf and blind to incentive, to have the world venture no farther than my immaculate facade, dispensing with my soul, my womb, and my empire, everywhere, everywhere, lying to me.

"Please."

I knew what he was doing. He was reminding me that I am a woman. That I am alive, and so, forgivable. That I should not hate myself for my failings when it is those failings that make me desirable. That I stand on one side of the wall and not the other. That nature does not favor those who would resist its hour and its course.

"Okay," I said. "I'll go."

13

THE ROW OF BUDDING WILDFLOWERS RAN LIKE MARCHING MICE ALONGSIDE the southern base of the barn. Delphiniums and phlox come first, then irises and astibles. Tiger lilies rise belatedly. It's usually not until July by the time they ascend and promptly collapse, their overlong necks buckling beneath the heft of their blossoms. There's a lesson in that, I'm not sure what, but I like tiger lilies least.

I rubbed the pigment into my hands and admired my painting. The canvas was just five inches square, depicting a few celery green shoots with tea violet tips, little baby *V*s ascending. *V* as a shape is piercing and effective—the head of an arrow or blade, a plow or a beak, the tip of a plant that creaks up through soil, the cooperative formation of migratory birds and schools of diligent fish.

Hello! My mother approached with two glasses. She handed one to me and I sniffed inside—it was just tea. "As soon as I grade those papers," she began as she sat, "I'll start back here. David can get us six inkberrys from his cousin Greg. Greg works at Agway. Do you know Greg? We'll put them between the house and the barn, then move the hollies to the far side of the driveway. What do you think?"

I said it sounded good.

At thirty-seven, my mother's skin was unwrinkled except for a fine spray of creases about her eyes. She'd had the enviable fortune of exacting revenge on the aesthetic standards of her adolescence. In the 1950s, she was considered scrawny and bookish, but in the 60s and 70s, she was graceful and slender and politically connected, sexy in fashions that would have embarrassed shapelier women, like wide link belts and paisley A-line dresses and bodysuits with twin bear-ear cut-outs around the abdomen. Even poverty became her. It enhanced the atmosphere of liberty and luck you felt in her company. When she entered a room, people stood, recalling like a crisis the hopes they had.

"What a gorgeous day!" she exclaimed, as though it was the first she'd ever lived. The sun was low and the sky was candy orange, the color of those spongy Easter treats. Not Duck Peeps, but the melony ones shaped like peanuts. Why are they shaped like peanuts when they don't taste like peanuts? It's a strange falsification. Jack and I placed some on the tracks once to see if they would widen or reduplicate, but instead they disappeared, possibly sticking to the wheels. "I hope at least we slowed the fucker down," Jack had said as we watched the last train car vanish around the bend.

"Looking forward to the Talkhouse tonight?" my mother asked. "Kate's excitement is infectious. You'll have to say hi to Kevin, if he's working—I think he's working. Is it Friday? Yes, he's working." She drank some tea. "Can you believe I was married at your age?"

Her observation was strictly scientific, making the fact that I was the product of that union into something only slightly more than extraneous. I didn't answer. I just pressed my palms into my eyes. Maybe if I pressed hard I could erase myself.

"What's wrong?" she asked. "Is this about Jack?"

"Jack?" I said, somewhat surprised. "It's not Jack, it's Kate."

"*Kate!* What about Kate?"

"We're just not clicking."

"What do you mean *not clicking?*"

"It's like—we're going at different speeds," I said, striving for clarity, though to hear myself, I didn't sound very clear. "We're not close anymore, you know, spatially." I amended that. "Not *spatially*—I don't know." I elaborated with my hands. "She's not moving."

Unfortunately, my mother thought she understood. Things were always better between us when she did not have the faintest idea what I was talking about. "The first thing you need to do," she said, "is to get over the idea of personal growth as measurable by speed and distance."

I looked at the clouds and bit my lip.

"Linearity is a male notion," she proceeded to counsel my neck and chin. "Progress is not necessarily linear. You can't think in terms of you girls having been shot from the same pistol. You come from entirely different guns. One has bullets, the other has—"

"A flag," I said.

"*Exactly,*" she said. "A flag."

I counted slowly to ten, then stood. I began to gather the paintbrushes that I'd strewn on the grass. It was difficult to see them in the twilight, and I felt bad about that, about them feeling lost.

"That's so pretty," she said of my painting. "Is it for me?"

"It's my final for art, but you can have it when I get it back."

She stood and hugged me, and she whistled as she returned to the house. She seemed satisfied about having been there for me.

KATE'S DOOR WOULD NOT open.

"Watch the ironing board!" she called.

I squeaked through the gap and discovered her in the dark, testing shoes of various heights. The light from a candle flirted against her, throwing her body into horizontal relief upon the wall, creating a smoky contorted bridge. From the foot of her bed, I watched as she dressed. It was like a ritual she had, and a ritual I had. It was like Kate's being in a show and me watching a show, both of us keeping the power of opposing positions. I'd never known anyone to dress the way Kate did—usually I just threw on jeans like my mom.

I wondered if being loyal means being honest or being kind. If there had been a cohesive truth to tell Kate about Rourke and me, it would have felt cruel to relate it, and yet it did not exactly feel kind to say nothing and to watch as she employed her best strategies to win—win something. She wasn't even sure what.

"What do you think," she inquired. "Collar up or collar down?"

"Down," I replied, "I guess."

"You *guess*, or you're *sure*?"

"I'm sure."

"Sure *down*, or sure *up*?"

Neither was very good actually. "Up."

"Ugh," she said, ripping off the shirt. "What is *wrong* with you?"

Maybe she was right and Mom was right. Maybe something *was* wrong with me. Kate did not seem bothered in the least by the fact that everything between us had changed. That, though the intimacy had slipped away, we forged ahead, relying on habit in the absence of devotion. Maybe such breaches are obligatory, like, in the biological sense. Maybe it would not do for girls to evolve beyond pubescent attachments, to become more than allegiant, to exceed basic constancy. Few men could match such standards, and then no babies would be born.

"Can you at least try to be friendly tonight," she said.

I promised to try, though I doubted sincerely that my will would have any bearing on the evening. I was so convinced of the meaninglessness of the will in relation to the night that I wasn't even planning on participating very actively. When ghosts escort people through time, there is a rule against interaction. It can be perilous to modify destiny. Everyone is just supposed to float on the periphery in pajamas and chains, thinking thoughts. Life is random and strange. People always believe their choices are singular and circumspect when really they are trifling. Despite the odds, we had all strayed anyway into the night—Kate and me and Rourke and however many others, our fates assigned and histories synchronized. It had been resolved.

"Go take aspirin," Kate said, so I did.

In the kitchen there was a cabinet alongside the oven where the liquor was kept. I didn't realize it was my destination until I found myself filling a coffee mug with brown stuff—Jim Beam. No one would notice the loss of alcohol, except Jack, and he wouldn't be coming by so much anymore. It was amusing, actually, the idea of his visiting sometime in the future and right away going, "Hey, who polished off all the whiskey?" Jack was amusing, unlike most everyone else.

My arm reached to the shelf where the medicine and spices were kept. The unopened spices had been a wedding present to my parents, which made the jars and the contents older than me. I did not ever like to touch them. It was as if they knew me, or *measured* me, as if they contained not herbs but my life—my secrets and stories—and if you wanted you could make a potion. My hand plucked the aspirin bottle from a vast field of caps. I popped the lid and shook a few pills out, thinking how medicine and spices are similar since both are concentrates. Savory, Cumin, Marjoram, and Mace are totally weird substances that probably even the greatest chefs don't know how to use.

"*Ev-ie!*" Kate shouted.

When I passed back through the living room, Mom was talking on the telephone to Lowie. Her vitality was being expressed in voice, and the voice was going through a perforated plastic barrier, getting trapped, getting transformed, getting sucked along miles of cable to a Bridgehampton basement then back up through wire and plastic into the kitchen, into the ear of her sister. Maybe not first to the basement, maybe first to a switching station. I couldn't recall about switching stations. Maybe they went out with teletype and cablegrams. I'd have to check with my dad.

"Tell me about it," Mom said. "I had to submit forty-six pages!"

My mother is talented on the phone. She always sounds so connected. I never even feel that connected in person. I wondered if the connectedness she finds there is real or imaginary, fact or anti-fact. Feelings are real when you feel them, but where is *There*? *There* is probably where *They* live.

I looked up the stairs. Kate's head was hanging out of her door, music was sweeping past—David Bowie's *Rebel Rebel*. "What are you wearing?"

"Why? Do you want to borrow something?"

"No," she said. "I want to know what you're wearing."

I swallowed the aspirin with a gulp of liquor. Aspirin or aspirins. It could be like deer or fish. I began to choke.

Kate looked concerned. "Are you okay?"

My mother held her palm over the receiver. "Do you need water?"

I waved. "I'm okay." I waved more. "I guess I'm wearing jeans."

"*No jeans*," she said. The blow dryer came on, and she was gone.

IN MY CLOSET I had just one okay dress. *Okay*, meaning not for holidays and funerals. I'd bought it at a thrift shop in the city on Greenwich Avenue near Charles Street. I got it from the closet, re-filled my mug with whiskey, and went back upstairs to shower, this time avoiding Kate. I took in the radio and locked the doors. I did not want to be influenced by her monstrous good cheer. Not monstrous. What was the word my mother had used—*Infectious*.

I sat on the bathroom sink, taking several swigs. Pieces were repositioning inside, jockeying about, here and there. I figured I might as well drink whiskey because—just because. Kate was out there singing and dancing—*shuffle-shuffle-skid, skid-shuffle*—bouncing around like a balloon. I considered opening a window, leaning on the sill, waving as she whooshed out—a neatly knotted, thoroughly effaced sphere, tumbling up to master the meaning of true height. "So long," I would call to her with a salute. "Farewell."

The liquor started to move easily, going down my throat instead of up my sinuses. I wiped my chin with the back of my hand, and I hiccuped, saying *Shit!* because that is the thing to say when you get the hiccups. To get rid of them, I employed a method invented by my mother, which is to close your eyes, point a finger at your forehead, and gradually move it in to touch a pretend spot. Maybe it was not invented by my mother. Maybe she'd only heard of it. Maybe she only made it sound like her own.

"The principle," she would explain academically, "is to concentrate electrical energy above the neck, thereby depriving the diaphragm of the means required to spasm."

I wasn't too clear on the mechanics, but anyway it worked. I closed my eyes and my finger journeyed to a hypothetical spot, which was a pinwheel, slowly blowing, silver and aluminum blue, a millimeter higher than my skin—*tick-tick-tick*. My forehead could sense the erotic nearness of my finger. *Erotic* because there was fighting back. The patterned arcade of my fingertip rotated in minuscule circles in the inverse direction of the wheel—*tock-tock-tock*.

When I opened my eyes, the hiccups were gone. Too bad Kate wasn't with me. If Kate were there, she'd be sitting beneath me on the edge of the tub with me resting my feet on her knees. Maybe she'd say something funny, and we'd laugh. When I tried to think of the funny thing Kate might say, my mind drew a blank. When I tried to think of a funny thing Kate had ever said, my mind still drew a blank.

I unzipped my jeans, peeling them slowly back on two sides like flaps of a tent. In the medicine cabinet mirror I looked for the woman he saw. If I looked with his eyes, I could see her. It was good to trust Rourke's vision, even if it was not good to trust him. He had no preconception of me, no idea at all beyond the fact that we fit.

"Fit," I proclaimed to myself, "is everything." Fit and timing.

Rourke would never call me feral, and I would never have to explain to him the enigmatic orthodoxy of loyalty or the hidden selfishness of virtue or the irrelevance of expectations in relation to the night—*a* night, *that* night. I spun in a smooth circle with airplane arms that were buoyant and lax, proving air to be a type of gel. I did not need to lie to elicit his desire. I was a package in his eyes, a cowgirl in May, a jaguar, and a soul to cleave, a nasty nasty something, I could not think of what. I leaned into the mirror, close and closer, observing my olive green eyes through half-closed lids. My eyes were blue plus yellow, more yellow than blue, which as a realization had come late in terms of being an artist, and I was depressed about that and also about the oblong way I looked if you were kissing me. Jack had neglected ever to mention that. Oh Jack, I thought, with an unripened sort of sorrow. As an early sorrow it grieved me, and grief made me thirsty, so I raised my mug.

"To Jack," I said, "my very special regret."

My mother's voice arrived suddenly, casting brightly off the walls of Kate's room, obliging and bee-sweet, mixing with Kate's voice, which itself tinkled and chimed and passed like avian needles through the seams of caulk in the door frame.

Mom rapped on the door. "Goodnight, Evie. Have a good time."

"Okay," I said, waving to the wall. "Bye."

In the shower it was hard to distinguish what I was feeling, something vague, something clear, something crooked but also straight, like a beach blanket in the wind. I was thinking a word—*Martinique*, which I did not see as a place but as soft and tarnished gold like rosettes behind elegant door knobs. Alcohol crept through my veins and it pooled and it swirled. It inched up the bony path of my spine to my brain like a worm, with one lead segment working to advance and the remainder depressing itself consecutively, squishing up into a plump line behind the first.

"Here's David Essex," the deejay said, and I left the tub feeling peaceful, disburdened, feeling like nothing. The song gushed from the radio onto the floor and over to my feet, boiling up my legs like liquid rubber. *Shoop*.

> *Rock on! Oh, my soul!*

I moved from side to side in cinched waves, and I felt the coming muscles. Maybe not muscles, maybe nerves, or nerves in muscles. Mopping made me feel them too. The band of my underwear cut into the dulcet swell of my belly, which looked tantalizing and indefensible, like Haviland eggshell. Its delicate yield was my own and that was a very private wealth, a very lonesome knowledge, like carrying a lot of cash in your pocket through a pitch and populated alley.

> *Hey, shout summertime blues,*
> *Jump up an' down in the blue suede shoes.*

I found a lipstick the color of brown shoes and applied some with one finger. It's strange that no one ever names patience as a characteristic of wild animals. I felt patient that way, the wild animal way. When the song ended, I was sad. It's one of those songs that should never end.

I inched a pair of stockings over my legs. Then shoes, then the dress. The dress had cost three dollars, and, if anyone asked, I would say exactly that. It was clingy and plain and no longer than a skirted bathing suit, with long sleeves and a crew collar and darts at the breasts. The fabric was a complicated green of uncertain relation—not trees, not grass—turtles maybe. I reached back and tugged the long zipper up in portions. The girl in the thrift shop said for a fact the dress is a de la Renta, circa '66 or circa '73, and for a fact it was worn to Studio 54, possibly by Bianca Jagger. I did not bother to ask how she had managed to establish such facts since, if the facts were not facts but fictions, they were affable fictions with the effect of contributing positively to my overall state-of-mind and undoubtedly to hers. When I tried it on, she peeked into the bathroom. Her pumpkin hair formed a cone on her head, like one of those Halloween corn candies. I wondered if could she receive signals.

"I'll be your mirror," she said, as there was none. Softly adding, "Oh, my, it's *celestial*."

FROM THE TOP OF the stairs I heard voices. I wondered how long they'd been waiting—I had no sense of public time. I drained my cup and started down. I wished I'd been born to a better staircase, to a sophisticated flight of sloping marble with a wrought iron rail. I wished I could alight into a portrait-lined receiving hall, barren but for a gilded mirror, a grandfather clock, and an inlaid table adorned by a wax-sealed envelope. And a chair, a solitary chair.

As I rounded the corner into the kitchen, I saw Rourke and Rourke saw me. There was a change in his face. It did not liven or lift so much as it latched squarely on. By the rigor in his eyes, he tried to guide me. I labored to sustain my way.

In the recess to the left, sitting at the table, was his friend from the parade, the one who looked like a bookie or a short-order cook, and another guy, and Kate, in yellow. Kate said, "This is Rob and this is Mark. These guys went to UCLA together."

Mark was well-dressed and collegiate, and Rob was the same as the first time we'd met—shifty, like he was looking for a fight.

"I'm sorry," Mark apologized, and he stood. "I didn't catch your name."

"That's because no one said it," I replied. "I'm Eveline."

I set my cup on the peak of undone dishes. I felt capable and ready, loose in the limbs, tight in the trunk. If I were to play ball right then, I would not miss one catch. Rourke was at the counter, leaning against the part I always sat on, leaning massively. His waist was solid and inviting like a safe place to encamp. I wanted to feel it. I needed to feel it, though it belonged to him and what belonged to him was not mine. I turned out, knocking back twice against the sink edge. My sleeve brushed his and I was mindful of the impact, of the way we had reduced the room to silence. The spectacle of us commanded unanimous attention, which had to do with things concrete and thermal, with matter and motion and radiant energy. Despite the unspeakable will of the flesh, he would not seize the arm that dared to graze his own, nor would I move to join our hips. Besides, his hips were higher—they would not meet mine but press into my belly instead, which was a staggering realization.

I looked up and the guys at the table turned away, flinching a little like I was swinging a sharp object. I bit my tongue in a fine line between my front teeth. "Are we going?"

"Impatient?" Rourke said quietly.

"Hardly," I answered, thinking of big cats. "Just the opposite."

"WE WERE RIPPING DOWN the Bruckner at four in the morning," Rob said as I slid over to the place behind the driver's seat. "We passed some cops, but they didn't budge. Two seconds later, Bobby G. cracks up."

"No shit," Mark said. "How fast was he going?"

"Like forty when he hit. He flew up like a friggin' ragdoll."

"Harrison said he destroyed his spine," Mark said.

"Yeah, his legs, too. One leg. He got busted up pretty bad."

"I'll take the hump," Mark offered as Rob began to climb in back.

Rob ignored him, continuing over, coming next to me.

Behind us, Rourke paused on the driveway—I knew because my body was keeping his body in range, tracking it. "Better put that in here," I heard him tell Kate. The car bounced twice as he tossed her pocketbook into the trunk, then he shut it again.

"Anything you need to put in the trunk, Countess?" Rob asked me.

"Yeah," I said, "a corpse."

"That's pretty funny," he said. "A corpse."

Mark squeezed in next to Rob, and Kate won by default the seat up front. There were sounds—a door, another door, a cassette, the engine, the mincing snitch of leather against vinyl. In the rearview mirror, Rourke's impression consulted with mine. Our images floated spotlessly, clinically, like we were co-conspirators, like we were passing in a crowd, like we were synchronized. I closed my eyes to retain the look. It was like saving a fallen leaf.

"I can't remember," Mark said as we headed for Amagansett, "the last time I had a tetanus shot."

"I practically get one a year," Rob stated, adding something about a flooring nail that recently went through his fist.

"You're an idiot," Mark said. "You only need one, like, every ten years." He shifted and Rob shifted in turn, coming closer to me. "You have enough room, Eveline?" Mark leaned forward and asked.

I said that I did. I put my feet on the top of a gym bag that was on the floor, and my thighs came up. My palms made nervous circles, rubbing lightly. I felt uneasy about having so many people embroiled in the business of my destiny. I wondered if they felt uneasy too. I wondered if they felt at all peculiar, like parts or materials.

Rob folded a piece of gum into his mouth then flicked the pack in my direction. I took a stick and watched as he sucked his cheek to his molars. The oblique flare of the street lights plunged rhythmically across his jaw. His eyes were obscured by the blind of the roof. "What's up with that Porsche, anyway?" he asked.

"I'm working on it," Mark said. His fingers plowed through his hair, which made it seem as though he was being deceptive. Maybe he was not being deceptive, maybe he only seemed it. Some people are unfortunate that way. "I should have it by the end of this month."

"Good, because it's been, like, three years already and I'm sick of hearing about it."

Next came talk of a '68 Challenger and various engine options—a 426 hemi, a 440 with a six pack, a 383 magnum. Cars and guns and liquor share terminology, which is indicative of—of something, I wasn't sure what. According to Rob, the two biggest sports upsets were the Mets against Baltimore in the '69 Series and *something, something, Sonny Liston.* Next came talk of classic fights—Marciano KO's Louis, Robinson beats Basilio, Jersey Joe gives bad count, Frazier wins Olympic Gold in '64, Rumble in the Jungle, Thriller in Manila—and some obscure questions Rob had for Rourke about

Sam Langford's blindness and Stanley Ketchel's murder. I just stared out the window, letting everything that was said turn flat and foreign and otherworldly, like the sound of baseball when I was little. On Sundays when I was little, my dad would listen to baseball while Marilyn ironed shirts and sheets with starch from a block. The smell was the smell of mortal rubber, of creatures vulcanized, of monkeys lightly singed. I would become hypnotized by the incessant sports commentary and the excruciating *pfsst, pfsst* of steam as we waited for the moment when I would be returned to my mother's for the week. Usually the moment came at four.

I leaned onto Rob's shoulder, and he leaned back, giving me a little more. It was nice, him knowing I needed a little more.

THE STEPHEN TALKHOUSE IS named after a Montaukett Indian who walked all over Long Island. According to legend, Talkhouse could walk to Brooklyn and back in a day.

"His true name was Pharaoh," Powell told us once when we were fishing for fluke in Shinnecock Bay. Actually, Powell was fishing, and Jack and Denny and I were watching, tying knots and spearing sand eels, and hanging quietly over the side, hoping to spot doormats. "Or *Faro*, with an *F*," he speculated as he cut the engine, and we drifted into the shallows. Powell liked *skinny* water. He said it gave fish the chance to ambush the bait. And also, fluke like the structure of low water—branches, rocks, angles, ripples.

"Not much was recorded back then, and what *was* recorded was not too *carefully* recorded, seeing as how we were experts in our language and they were not. The discrepancy suited us fine, since our language is the language of the law. The only time we adopted their ways is when it came time to buy *their* land. A couple blankets and a dog for several thousand acres. We liked the sound of that."

Powell cast out, hipping smoothly up into one shoulder, the hook touching down like the soft cluck of a tongue. In his wallet is an Indian Status Card. Though he has Nanticoke blood on his mother's side, on his father's he's white, so he's careful not to shy away from the fact that the crimes of his paternal ancestors have afforded him advantages for which many of his mother's are ineligible. "Plumbing, for starters," he always says.

The Nanticokes were tidewater people who believed all things possess a unique spirit. I know because I wrote about the tribe for seventh grade social studies. I'd interviewed Powell's sister Esme on the phone from her home in Salamanca. She's married to Jim, an Iroquois. Coach Red Peters gave me a *B* for improper sourcing—which he spelled *soreing*. When my mother found out about the grade, she lost her temper.

"The purpose of the assignment, *Mrs.* Ruane," said Mrs. Schmidt, the middle school principal, "was encyclopedia use."

"The purpose of an encyclopedia, *Miss* Schmidt," my mother said, looking down, since she refused to sit, "is to assist those who have limited access to reputable information. Encyclopedias are hugely reductive. Their scope is confined to the perspective of the publisher. At their very best, they are supplemental, not primary references, which is exactly how Eveline has been instructed to use them."

Mrs. Schmidt's hands were shaking.

"And might I add," my mother said, "that I consider that gym teacher to be about as qualified to teach academics as *he* would consider *me* qualified to teach football. If you intend to continue to promote white supremacy, I suggest that you go out and try to find one or two whites who are, in fact, supreme."

The next day Coach Peters sent a note home of apology, saying that my grade on the paper had been changed to an *A*. Mom sent a note back. *Your lesson has proven invaluable. Let the B stand.*

TWO GUYS SLUMPED LIKE vultures on the wooden ramp that led to the Talkhouse. I wondered would I have a problem getting in—Kate was eighteen, but I had six months to go. Rob placed his hand on my lower back and escorted me up the ramp. Rourke came next, then Kate and Mark, lagging behind.

"What are the damages?" Rob asked.

"Five bucks a head," one bouncer said. The lump in his neck journeyed unevenly, like a lame elevator.

Rob opened his wallet, and the second bouncer leaned to get a better view of me. Rob blocked him.

"Relax, man," the guy told Rob, and then he said, "Hey, Scorpio!"

I peered over Rob's shoulder.

"It's me." He swatted his chest. "The hitchhiker."

"Oh," I said, "Biff. Hi."

He seemed happy to see me. Hardly anyone ever seemed happy to see me. Three people squeezed past, paid the cover, and went in. Sounds of the bar swelled out in a dull ruff, then came night silence.

"I didn't recognize you," he said. "You know, with the legs. You look great."

"How's rugby?"

"I just got back from San Diego. I played all winter. Where's your friend?" I pointed behind me and called Kate.

"Oh my God!" she shrieked. "Biff! I can't believe it."

A crowd on the sidewalk was waiting; Rob returned to his wallet. Biff waved his hand, and the second guy opened the door to motion us through. Biff winked. "See you later."

INSIDE WAS WOODSY AND damp with the moldy stench of saturated alcohol. We entered in single file, inching through a yeasty shaft. The ceiling bowed and the floor buckled and breathing walls urged us inward. People lined the bar and also the partition by the tables.

Rob muttered into the back of my ear, "Nice going, Countess."

"Don't thank me. Kate's the friendly one."

"She might be friendly," he said, as we paused to let someone with drinks pass, "but she'd never get five through the door."

I did not like to get in for free. It appeared as though the hitchhiker was repaying a favor. Probably he had not done so with foresight or malice, but by letting us in, he staked a piece of me, and the piece he staked belonged to the men I'd come with—or so they thought. But Biff had been to my house to visit my mother, and he thought that left him beholden to protect me. The free entry was not a favor but a signal, a warning, a message between men. It's all very tiring, keeping track of men—the posturing and the egos, the private worlds of their private minds. In public they feign leniency and affect simplicity, but in private what they really want you to know is how they feel so very damaged.

I turned back to Rourke. He was watching me, watching as I walked, but as soon as my eyes found his, he looked away.

I waved to Mom's friend Kevin, who waved back from behind the bar, and I kept moving in, my body caressing unfamiliar bodies, the curves of me conforming to the curves of them. I'd lost the sensation of being connected to Rourke, and that loss dispossessed me of motive and prudence. I forgot who I was and what I was doing and what was the point of everything anyhow. I had the idea of walking through to the rear exit and then out. It would have been funny to go without telling anyone except for the part about no car.

My mood was lapsing; I could feel it lapsing.

Rob touched me from behind. He handed me a Beck's and gestured with his chin to a vacant corner booth. Together we cut around, and when I inched along the seat on my knees to the farthest side, he followed, then Kate, and last Rourke. Mark swung a chair to the outside of the table and straddled it, scanning the room. Rob arranged the clutter left by previous occupants, building a meticulous forest of plastic, paper, and glass, and Kate whispered to Rourke. He inclined his head obligingly to listen, and, like a knife through their necks, the bar sliced the air with a tranquil quality that I kind of liked.

"So, Monday's the big day," Mark said.

"Monday's it," Rourke said. When he spoke, his voice promised to effect change, like when a rudder moves, a ship turns. I wondered was he happy when he talked or not happy. He seemed not very happy.

"Too bad. We could have all been out here this summer."

"We still *can* be, Mark," Rob said. "We'll just stay at your parents' house— for free." Mark laughed. Rob nudged me. I was peeling the foil from the neck of my beer bottle. "You know what they say about people who do that?"

"What's that?" I asked.

"That they're sexually frustrated." He winked and took a swig.

"I haven't found that to be true," I told him. "But I'm willing to take your word for it."

"*Ha!*" Mark said. "She got you!"

Kate stretched to reach Rourke's ear. Next to her, he seemed lighter, easier, approachable—a boy, a brother, a son, a friend. It pained me to see him so at ease; he was never at ease with me. I felt afflicted as if by dozens of stinging things. A slender lock of hair fell by his face, skimming with caution the lashes of his right eye, and I smiled despite my epic disgust, because it was impossible not to admire the handsome look of him. Kate said he was nice. Maybe that was true, maybe to her and to all the world he was.

Hips shimmied across the dance floor at the height of my eyes. The hips belonged to normal people having normal fun. I wished I were one of those normal people and that my hips were happy hips. It was no good with Rourke being hurt by me and me being hurt by him. It would have been better to leave, or to leave but stay. That's the appeal of drugs, leaving but staying. I was glad I didn't have any. Sometimes you'll see some girl slooped up against a wall, half-unconscious. Basically she felt the way I did, only she had drugs. I looked around for Mick Jagger. He'd been to the Talkhouse. That would be good, I thought, to see Mick Jagger—you know, like, not a totally wasted night.

Mark got up. "I'm gonna take a walk," he said. "Be right back."

The table felt strange without him, and I felt strange, unbearably strange, awkward, like I had lost an ally, lonely like I couldn't bear the missing witness. I felt they were staring at me—Rourke and Rob and Kate. I stood, I don't know why I stood, but once I stood, I had no choice but to follow.

Mark was at the jukebox. "I was afraid you wouldn't come."

I looked down into the meadow of luminous tags.

"Pick some songs for me."

My finger floated above the glass. "M-5," I said. "A-7."

He put in the quarters, pushed the buttons, then faced out. I stayed facing in. "That's some dress," he said, his lips hardly moving. He was watching the dancers, not really watching.

"It cost three dollars," I confided.

"That works out to about a dollar an inch," he said. "Next time I see you, why don't you try to find a *two* dollar dress." He turned now, studying, looking for just so long as he thought I could bear. Though no more than a foot away, in the darkness I could see gun metal eyes and sandy straight hair and an acrylic quality to his entire person, like if you scratched his skin the scratch would remain. "Better yet, I'll find you one for *free*."

I looked away. To the table.

"He can't see," Mark said. "Don't worry."

"I'm not worried."

"You *want* him to see."

Actually, I didn't want that.

"If you're uncomfortable, let's go back."

"No," I said. "I don't want to go back."

There was a post behind the jukebox, and that's where I went. The wood pushed between my shoulder blades. Mark propped his arm alongside my

neck to make a barricade between me and—everything. "Why are you here?"
I didn't know why he was there. It seemed there was a reason.

"In East Hampton? My parents have a house here."

"That's not what I mean."

"You mean—tonight."

"Yes. Tonight."

"To see you," he said. "To *find* you."

The jukebox whirred to a start. It was "Bernadette." I held his sleeve.
"Oh," I said, "listen." Then me adding his name, "*Mark.*"

> *Bernadette*
> *People are searching for, the kind of love that we possessed.*

"Do you know the singer's name?"

"Levi Stubbs," he said.

"I can see him," I said. "Can you see him?" The sweat, the indigo skin, the
hands clutching fistfuls of nothing. Maybe I could see him because I knew
about rage. Maybe not, maybe I knew nothing of rage beyond the fact that it
was coming. "The false ending. The way he screams her name. *Bern—a—dette.*
I'll never be loved like that."

He shook his drink, looking into it, looking at me. "I doubt that."

That is when I first saw the eyes. They were more than gray, they were
speckled like the underside of fish. I eased the glass from his hands, and I
swallowed some of what was inside, coughing up a little cranberry.

"Would you like one?" he asked.

"No thanks," I said. "Do you mind if I just share yours?"

Mark leaned to my face. "Dance with me," he said.

He took me to the center of the blackened floor, so black it seemed to be
the loam of a pit. Before drawing me into his arms, he said something else, I
wasn't sure what, but I nodded in any event and laid my head impassively upon
his arm. I held him, grateful that he had given me shelter. Being in a bar is
somewhat like being homeless, if you do not like your friends. You wander and
linger and land wherever there's room and heat, sometimes getting in trouble,
sometimes not.

> *Tell me somethin' good, tell me that you love me, yeah.*

Mark was very good, better than Denny. Maybe it just *felt* better to dance
with Mark than with Denny. It felt kind of like sex, like, there was this place
it hit inside that was good. He wrapped one hand around my waist, bracing my
back, and our hips affixed, bone to pelvic bone. We oscillated, bending and rising in controlled, compact arcs, our torsos hanging slightly back. My arms
dangled loosely. There was resistance in my abdomen and a rip up my thighs,
and our long shadows trespassed against the tables and transfixed the crowd,

restoring Rourke's customarily heavy countenance. I was glad. It had not been good to see him act happy, when I knew for certain he was not.

BY THE TIME WE returned, Rourke had taken Mark's chair and turned it to face away from the dance floor. Kate had moved closer to Rob, who was halfway finished with a burger. There was the broad smell of onions.

Mark gestured to the floor. "How about you, Kate?"

She waved her hand dismissively. "*Please*, no."

"Thank God," Mark said, collapsing. "She wore me out."

"What's the matter? Need a *bed*?" Rob said derisively, not meaning Mark, but me and Mark.

Mark ignored the comment. He reached for Rob's plate, lifted the corner of the bread, and said, "Brave man." Mark was obviously not the type of person who would waste time allowing innuendo and sarcasm to be at cross purposes with determination. I'd never thought of sarcasm as a waste of time, but it's true—it is. I didn't know Mark well, except to say he was fast. He'd reached me quickly, quicker than anyone. I'd hardly noticed him coming.

I set one knee on the outer edge of the banquette, and my thighs pressed into the rim of the table. Mark offered his glass, and I accepted, shaking out some ice and laying it on my neck. My stomach swelled in tandem with my chest, causing my belly to punch out into a little box.

Rourke leaned back in his chair and stared into the middle distance. I thought I knew what he felt. I thought he felt what I'd felt the day I saw him in the gym, when his legs surrounded me and the lip of his underwear was visible beneath his shorts. Rourke was wet that day and there was a sweet smell. When I'd wanted to leave, I couldn't move. I raised Mark's glass to my lips and emptied it, celebrating, oh, I don't know, the engine of me.

"There's a hole in your stockings," Kate said.

I raised my dress to see—the dress didn't have far to go. Kate was right. I took the stirrer from Mark's glass and inserted it into the hole, then I jerked my wrist. The crossed edge of the plastic stick scratched my leg and the nylon, which shredded into darkness like a limited web.

Kate said, "*Evie!*" and Mark said, "Shit," and Rob muttered something that I didn't hear, and they all laughed—except Rourke, who managed to express gross disinterest. I didn't care what they thought or what anyone thought. I was just the shameless thing they'd made of me—a woman, a fiend, my own lowest form. There was a trippingness to it that I liked, a capability I'd been missing. Why remain polite but powerless, in love but a beggar?

"I want to go," I said. "I want to get out of here."

"YOU TAKE THE FRONT," Rourke said to Mark over the roof of the car. He propped the driver's seat forward and gestured for me to get in behind him. I squeezed past his arm.

"No complaints from me," Mark said. "It's cramped as hell back there."

We sped back through the fog. We were going so fast I wondered would we crash and disintegrate into mist. Fog is just a cloud nesting on the ground. When you die in it, your blood and bones vanish automatically to divergent worlds. When you go, there is no trace. Kate was on the other side of Rob, and I was wishing it was winter. In winter you can scrape ice on the inside of your window. I wanted to scrape ice. I wanted my window to be coated in that shattery type of window frost. I breathed onto the glass and with my finger spelled out my name—*Eveline*. I wondered, was I still me when I did not feel like me? Was I still the girl my mother bore, the girl Jack loved? Jack—I thought an unthinkable thought, something about his mercy.

"She looks like that chick from one of those L.A. noir movies," Rob was saying. "Shit, who is it? Beautiful redhead, green eyes."

"Natalie Wood," Mark guessed, "Susan Heyward, Arlene Dahl."

Rob said, *nah*, each time, *nah*.

The car thrust to a laborious and inexact stop at the intersection by the East Hampton post office, and the placid mechanical hum and puckered clicks from the street light slit the air. Rourke looked to the left, into the dead May night, his face lit by a bloody electric haze. Though he was in profile, I could see his eyes, I could see his fear, and in it, the place where I resided. But if he wanted to leave me free, he could hardly object to the application of my freedom.

"Rita Hayworth!" Mark said.

"That's it, Rita Hayworth." And Rob's voice came again, breaking through to Rourke, saying soft, under his breath, "Green light."

At the end, we said goodnight very politely and, very politely the guys thanked us, and Kate and I thanked them as well. Rourke helped me out on the driver's side. In the slender murk produced by our bodies, his hair touched my hair and his hand held my hand. As I turned to walk away, he reached once for me in the darkness, catching me easily by the dress, catching my waist, and with the other hand taking my thigh, grabbing it, reaching through the run in my stockings, clutching up into obscurity.

14.

THE ROCKS IN THE LOT WERE HOT. I STRAGGLED MY HANDS AROUND MY BARE feet, gathering up a wreath of burning sediment as the families of graduating seniors emptied out of cars, sheepish in uncommon splendor, like milling clans at the origin of a parade. There is something spent about the families of teenagers. There is the look of exhausted loyalties. It's only right that we tire and differentiate, leave and adapt. Grow overbig in someone else's space.

"Hey, Evie," people kept saying, and I kept saying, "Hey."

Above us the wilting American flag carved cherry lanes through the ultra-marine skies. Not skies, *sky*. There is just one. Sometimes you wish for more. You dream of cloisters of alabaster and veils of vapor and umbrellas of blue to retreat beneath. You hope someday to evanesce and reconstitute. For you, there is one sky in reserve, one extra vault of heaven to claim as your own.

Sara Eden joined me on the curb. Her skin was brown like friar's robes, her teeth small and white. Daisies were stamped onto her skirt, daisies were in her hat. Alicia made the hat for her. Her eyes sloped at the furthest edges, like the opened wings of a tropical bird. "What are you *doing*?"

I looked down. My shoes were filled with gravel.

"Oh," I said, straightening. "I'm sorry."

"Don't apologize to me. They're your shoes."

She pulled back her braids incompletely on the side nearest me in the dis-arming way that some girls have, and she took one of my shoes to wipe the dust. I observed the work of her forearm. I listened to the tinkling fuss of her bracelets. Though I had not felt sad before, with Sara there I felt sad. She was going to Georgetown, and D.C. is one of those places you go to and never come back from. She handed me my shoe.

"So what did you decide? Are you coming to the party?"

I'd already said no, to Alicia and to her. Though I'd known for weeks, it seemed sad, suddenly, with her leaving for Washington.

"You should get out," Sara said. "Alicia will be sad."

I put on my shoes and stood. A car engine quit alongside us.

Sara waved. "That's my cousin. Marika."

"What a pretty name," I said. "*Marika*—like a spice."

"So what do you think? Five?"

Sure, I said, five is fine.

FOR FIFTEEN DAYS, I'D remained in place, not leaving my house, moving only to touch the things I knew he'd touched—the door frame, the bookshelves, the couch, the paper dolls and the sailboat I'd made, the section of the kitchen counter on which he'd sat. If possible, I would hold them—to the light, to my breast, to my temple—seeing what intuition and exchanges of oils might achieve. I kept my schoolbooks on a windowsill in my mother's bedroom upstairs, where I labored to observe beyond the greening leaves the street he'd traveled. There was a chair, petite and black with a round mauve seat. It was not a comfortable chair, but it was there that I stayed every day until dark, except for brief hours at school, briefer hours in bed.

Everyone was good to me and kind, everyone, deferring, always deferring. I would have answered their questions if I thought I would be heard. They seemed afraid for me, but how could they be afraid for me when they did not know me. They did not know that my path had been decided. My path was unknown to them, and when I moved it was as if through a paraffin corridor in which they were embalmed figures. In my eyes they were rigid with the posture of antiquity.

When anyone asked what I was doing, I would just say, *studying*.

If no one answered the ringing phone before I got to it, I would lift the receiver and drop it. It was always just someone calling, just a person, not Rourke. He would come, not call.

FROM A QUILTED, SEQUINED sack, Kate withdrew a tangle of bobby pins. She secured her graduation cap, tilting her head into the light at funny mannequin angles and contemplating space beyond the cafeteria window. An impeccable razor line separated the two halves of her hair. How long ago had the strands at the bottom been by the scalp? Maybe the ones on bottom were there last time Maman cooked veal for dinner. I'd never thought of the length of hair as a measure of time. It's sickening actually, the way hair sprouts from pores, squeezing up like famished worms even after a body is dead.

"Still in a black mood?" Kate asked.

On my hand I was drawing a cup. I had no idea why a cup. I was trying not to watch the last circus of my peers. A red construction paper sign on one of the doors had been changed from *Pick up gowns here* to *Pick up girls here*. Paulie Schaeffer and Mike Stern were wrestling by the kitchen, Dana Anderson was applying clear polish to a run in her stockings, and Regina Morris was crying because her school ring had dropped behind a radiator— janitors were on the way. Marty was sharing an orange soda with his girlfriend, Ali Rose. In his gown Marty looked like the nebbish cousin of a vampire. Others milled wistfully—Kiki Hauser and Min Kessler and Adam Sargent and Sam Kern and Lynn Hyne—each borne down with memories, each preparing to step experimentally into the half-light of a new life, each ready to go public with the selves shyly tended.

Cameras were flashing—*zic-zhing, zic-zhing. "Have a great summer! See you next life!"*

Jack appeared. I didn't see from where. He thrust his gown at Kate. "Fix this piece of shit. The snap's busted."

"I can't believe you broke it already," she said.

"The snap sucks. All snaps suck. Snaps are for fags," Jack said.

As Kate hunted for a safety pin, he faced me. It was like meeting a puppy I'd given away—I found myself searching for signs of neglect. Wine-colored sacs hugged the undersides of his eyes, attaching like nesting cocoons, like bloody slings. His t-shirt said, *It's cool to love Jesus.* I was surprised to see him there. I had not expected to see him there.

"How are you?" he wanted to know.

"I'm okay." I extracted a strand of hair from the corner of his mouth. "How about you? You okay?"

"Me? Oh yeah, sure. I'm okay."

HE'D COME BEFORE DAWN, just hours before graduation. I was sleeping lightly. I heard the barn door creak. He climbed the ladder, and from halfway up he tossed a bottle of liquor onto the bed. I could feel it hit the mattress; I could hear the cramped slosh of fluid. It sounded one-third empty.

"What time is it?" I asked.

He told me, "Night."

His legs swung off the ledge of the loft. I had the idea he might jump, though he would not have gone far. If I could have taken his pain, I would have because my love for him was as yet undiminished. You hear of paralyzed people who send signals to sleeping limbs.

"I could cut my wrists," he said, "put a bullet through my skull. If I thought I could reach you. But nothing can reach you."

I guided his head to the basin of my lap. I brushed back his hair, and unraveled the many knots. The light was still tarnished and indefinite, so I unraveled by feel alone. If I was cruel, I did not feel cruel. I felt new. I'd met the darker side of life; I'd met its animal. The animal came to me because it knew me. Jack understood what I'd become. I could tell by the wonder and the disgust in his eyes.

"Everytime I see a flower," he said as he wept, "it's your favorite."

KATE FANNED THE AIR as she fastened his robe. "You reek of alcohol."

Jack lifted his chin. "Awesome."

"Where's your cap?" she asked as we started off to find our places.

"Daniel!" he bellowed. Dan's head popped out from the crowd. Jack clapped once, going, "Chuck it." Dan snapped his wrist, and the hat came gliding over from line *L-Z* to line *A-K* like a square Frisbee.

From where we stood, we could hear the band begin to play. Once we were told to do so, we all squeezed forward through the halls in two lines. Andie Anderson and Brett Lawler were the first to reach the auditorium doors. They stopped, and we all stopped in succession. Andie's legs were jiggling beneath her gown—you could see her knees poking like horse noses running a race in tandem. At the first note of "Pomp and Circumstance," Andie and Brett received the signal to *Go*, while every next person was held by the shoulders for a count of two then released with a solemn press to the small of the back. Inside was inky and stifling, lurid and obscene, like the meeting of some secret society. Parents filled the seats, and teachers papered the walls, craning their necks and fanning themselves with programs, bearing witness to our barren indoctrination, giving us over, who knows to what. The sad truth is there is no original future.

From my chair on the platform, I had an unobstructed view of Denny's mother, Elaine, who was weeping. The shank of doughy flesh under her arm wagged as she leaned down to hunt through her pocketbook for a tissue. I considered the saline content of her tears. Were they very, very salty or very, very sweet?

During his valedictory speech, Stephen Auchard fiddled with his notes at the podium, rolling and unrolling the corners as everyone listened to sanitary rhetoric regarding promises and responsibilities while thinking primarily of the rewards of lunch. He could not say what he really thought, whatever it was that that may have been, if in fact it was even known to him. But he had not been singled out for the inventiveness of his sentiments. He'd been chosen as the one most brilliantly weaned of idiosyncrasy. Stephen returned to the seat next to mine, and I bumped against him, giving him a small thumbs up. Poor guy. One day we would meet again, one day when I required surgery and he would be the surgeon, though it was hard to imagine what part of me might need to be cut.

Principal Laughlin beamed and shook my hand like he meant it when he presented my diploma. On it, my name had been carefully written in veering script: *Eveline Aster Auerbach*. People shouted that name exactly as I read it, which was a dizzying sort of merger, people I knew and others I did not know, all clapping loudly. Clapping is bizarre. Powell says in certain places people do not do it. In certain places they call out in repetitive hoots, going, *loo loo loo*.

Afterwards, my parents were in the lobby. It was strange to see them there, representing me. From a distance they seemed credible, semi-sociable, and nicely dressed, making it hard to tell strictly by the look of them that they didn't know me. They were standing with Coco's parents, discussing college acceptances as though they'd played some part in the process, as though they'd helped with applications or offered money. Mr. and Mrs. Hale had visited ten schools with Coco.

"COCO'S GOING TO AMHERST," Denny had said, "did you hear?"

I had heard; Kate had told me twice.

He pulled his chair closer to mine. He'd come to see me by the window. He came every day. He would keep me company, bringing food and presents, these rocks he'd painted, portraits in gouache. I had eleven. They were propped against the screen. Alicia, Sara, Kate, Stephen Auchard, Lilias Starr, Mom and Powell and Denny's mother—all on one rock, Eddie from the record store, Marty Koch with the new yearbook, Coach Slater, the logo Denny had designed for Atomic Tangerine, and Elvis Presley.

"Which is your favorite?" he asked.

I pointed to Elvis.

"I happen to like Coach Slater. I mean, I know she's not your favorite person, but the workmanship is by far the best. Do you know she sat for three hours? Did I tell you that?"

He reached into the pocket of his windbreaker and removed the latest. There wasn't much room left. I'd have to start a second row.

"Your father mailed me a photo," he said as he placed it in front of me. On the irregular saucer-sized rock was an exact replica of Chihuahua Man. He was wearing a starched yellow dress shirt and all four dog heads were floating around him like alter egos. "I used a toothbrush to finish the fur," Denny said. "I cut off all but ten bristles then I melted back the toothbrush wall with a blow-torch."

I thanked him and together we looked out the window. Lots of visitors would do that, come and join me in my gaze. I wondered what they thought we were looking for.

"I almost forgot," he said quietly. "Jodi got off the wait-list at B.C., so her dad must've made a donation. And L.B. Strickland decided on Tufts for pre-med—can you imagine him as your *doctor*? It terrifies me to think of these people with jobs and checking accounts. They'll reverse the progress of the entire preceding generation!"

I pressed my Chihuahua rock against my cheek. It was warm. He must have had it on the dashboard in his car. It *was* strange how much things had changed since we'd started high school. Hardly anyone we knew was liberated, not the way my mother and Denny's mother and their friends had been—free from consensus and imitation. No one wore clothes made from scratch anymore or marched in Washington or went to the record store for musical advice. I'd heard Eddie hadn't received an inquiry in the *Ask Eddie* box for three months. Now people mostly just read *Rolling Stone*. Even feminism had become a joke—a woman picking up the check on a date or having to carry her own heavy bags or standing on a bus while men sit. It was as if there'd been a shifting of invisible walls, some cyclic reply or conservative revival to which we all belonged, even if we disagreed, simply by virtue of the season of our existence. If Denny and I represented one extreme, and Coco and Jodi and L.B. represented the opposite extreme, we were anyway relatives of the hour. Society is like an equilibrium or an arrangement.

"Have you ever seen something magnified through an electron microscope. Something that looks like tubes?" I asked.

"Yes," Denny said, "bark."

"Once I saw something," I said, "possibly bark. I can't remember. It was a gnarled mass of tunnels."

"A network," he said. "Fabric is a network. It has arteries."

"The entire universe might be that way, like everything has a position or place in order, or else systems collapse. The way it is with cells or planets or organs of the body."

"Like art," he said. "Like positive and negative space."

"Maybe order is always order—for plasma and stars, for harmony and tribes. Maybe there are formulas that apply. Like episodes of opposition staying in ratio to ones of correspondence. Like building a ship, when tension and slack are both needed for the sake of function. And if there *is* universal order, maybe people are subject to its laws—not just in terms of existence, but behavior. It could be that cultural movements are not just conscious, but things having to do with order and space. And things come when it's time. Like intellectualism. It rises, it falls, it gets replaced by—"

"Stupidity," he said.

"Yeah, kind of."

"You mean like a three-quarters, one-quarter thing," Denny said.

"Well, just think. One-hundred percent of people acting any one way at any one time is probably really bad. Everyone at once would be like Fascism. If you think about it, maybe it's not even mechanically possible to have acts of heroism without acts of cowardice, or revolution without tyranny, or—"

"Poetry without heartbreak," Denny said, reaching to kiss me. "Don't worry, Evie, he'll be back."

And I don't know, I just started to cry.

"EVELINE IS GOING TO New York University," my mother told Coco's parents, "to study film. Or journalism."

I stood a little behind them. Coco was there too, with shiny coral lips, sipping cola obediently from a clear plastic glass.

My father looked confused. "What happened to art?"

I certainly did not wish my parents any harm; however, I didn't know why I should have wished them well either, beyond the obvious fact that they were nice people. I didn't even think I had anything good to inherit. The dictionary says a parent is any animal, organism, or plant in relation to its offspring, and so of course, in that explicit regard, I was their child. Yet they'd set my soul adrift, tending to themselves with the urgency due me, believing me capable because they needed me to be, never guessing that their facile faith in my strength would not make it fact, or that I might grow dangerously weary of sufficiency. Maman had seen through my mask of adequacy. She'd loved without hope for profit the girl she'd found, but Maman was dead. Rourke had not insisted upon my competence. He had not even seemed to notice it. There was something else in me he'd wanted, something small and discrete—the frailty in me, and my frailty adored him.

My father tugged his jacket cuffs. His hands were brown and beautifully proportioned. My hands were the same, which made me sad, sad to be faced with my DNA, like everything is predetermined, them to me, me to the next.

"Thanks for coming," I said, and they said that I was very welcome.

Sometimes a day is a symbolic day, and you behave symbolically. Sometimes you search inside for a feeling, and, finding none, you remember that no feeling is frequently the most possible feeling.

AT SPRING CLOSE HOUSE for graduation lunch, it was me, Mom, Dad, Marilyn, and Kate and her brother Laurent and Simone with their baby, Jean-Claude. Jean-Claude was cute except for his head coming together at the temples like he'd been plucked out with cob tongs. Laurent also had a head shaped like a guitar or corset, which led to more distressing thoughts of genetic foreordination. I looked out the window. The highway was hot-washed in venom yellow light. I felt a juvenile loneliness, a shark-like, piscine, adolescent loneliness that cannot see past itself, a self-loathing and self-pity, a skulking, circular suspicion that the world is not mine to inherit. I listened dutifully as they spoke, laughed when they laughed, raised my glass as such moments presented themselves, all the while marking time, all the while feeling particularly unactual. I was sorry for the way everyone thought my life was my own, for how confused they were without knowing it, for the way they really did seem to like me, asking did my fish still have bones, saying how pretty I looked. I wished I could give something back. But all that they wanted from me was all that they *needed* from me, and that is a treacherous path to travel—and a treacherous one to *consent* to travel, in the sense of foregoing all things sought for the self. That is to say, being what just others want you to be.

After appetizers, Dad neatened the table, scraping crumbs with the flat of a knife. Jean-Claude gnawed his mother's necklace, sticking it with a dripping fist into his mouth. When the strand snapped, everyone dove and hunted on their knees for scattered pearls, which was a strange and spirited sort of family happening.

Marilyn brushed her skirt and sat again. "So when do you leave?"

Laurent deposited a handful of beads into the ashtray. "In an hour or two. We hope the baby will sleep before we stop for dinner."

"Are you completely packed, Catherine?" Simone asked.

"Except for what I'll pick up in August."

My lips hung over the rim of my drinking glass, which smelled the dusty way water smells if you stop to let it. A smell like a long thin tedium, like the listlessness of an elderly neighbor's kitchen, with its cracked linoleum and spilled prescriptions and over-painted cabinets that do not sufficiently shut. Like the knowledge of passing things.

"What was that man saying to you?" my mother whispered audibly to my father when he returned from paying the check.

"Which man was that?" Dad wanted to know.

"The tall one with the fish tie."

"Fish tie," he pondered, looking around. "I think I would have remembered a fish tie."

BACK AT HOME, KATE flitted in loose circles, hands bent at the wrists like they were loaded with weights at the fingertips. I sat on a wicker hamper stuffed with her fabric scraps and sewing notions and waited while she zipped and tied the last of her luggage. As she moved, there was the scent of roses, little bits here and there, clacking like castanets in an atomic cove about our heads, and beneath me the basket bent and squeaked with that slightly bending wicker sound. I wondered about Kate, how she would do. I wondered whether a femininity so refined is not ominously reliant upon the beneficence of circumstance. I guess she would do fine. Lots of women are out there, doing fine.

"Isn't this pretty?" she said of her dress. "It's chambray."

She finished packing, and we took a drive. Darts of sun pierced the trees along Three Mile Harbor Road, breaking up the retiring darkness with tiny pools of apricot. We made a left onto Flaggy Hole and another halfway down, by Michael's Restaurant. The ballfields of Maidstone Park were vacant and the bay beach was empty too, despite the early summer heat. She parked near the fishing station, by the channel.

"Careful," she said to me. "A broken bottle."

We lay in the stony sand, near the saffron grass, and we watched the boats return to harbor. The water was twinkling and distinguished, reminding me of gin. In the theater you make water by waving bolts of silk from one end of the stage to the other.

Kate began to cry. "I keep thinking about Harrison."

Her tears were peculiar tears that congealed in her eyes like pudding. I tried to forget what a simple creature she was, and we were. Maybe I would take her hand and lay it on my neck, make her say his name again, have her feel my throat convulse. Feel the acid echo, the disease in me.

"Here," I said, stretching my shirt to wipe her eyes. Above us the birds soared triumphantly, arcing, diving, chasing each last swoop. Bellies and backs. White, white, they spun, black.

"I'm sorry," she apologized, "for ruining our last afternoon."

I rested my head on her middle. Her babies would come from there. How sad, not to know them. "Don't be sorry. Don't ever be sorry."

SARA ASKED IF I was okay. I said that I was. If I said it uncertainly, it was only because the armrest was pressing into my spine. I was facing her, not the street—I could not bear to face the street. The street was like a strip or a plank shooting off into nothing. There's this cartoon where the main character drops black vinyl circles on the ground behind him for his pursuer to fall into. It's a terrifying concept—circles being holes, and strange to explain, but in fact that was exactly how I was doing.

"I'm sorry I missed Kate," she said. "Was it hard to say goodbye?"

"Not really. The baby was crying."

There were no more places to park by Alicia's, so we drove to Apaquogue Road and walked back. The Ross house was shaped like a sideways barn, only it was a mansion. On the left was a screened terrace, and on the right, the driveway cut back towards a gardener's cottage. The cottage bordered a pool that was the gray-blue color of goslings, and the walkway was lined with paper bags filled with sand and burning candles.

"Look at this tree," I said, pointing up as we passed it. "It's purple."

"Is it a maple?"

"Yes," I told her, "a Japanese maple."

Though we could see guests gathered on the lawn behind the house, we went through the main entrance. The porch was gracious and white with pink geraniums. Sara put her pocketbook in the front hall closet and she handed a graduation gift for Alicia to a uniformed woman. I offered my wildflowers.

The woman said, "*Si, si, gracias.*"

"*Gracias*, Consuela," Sara said, introducing me in Spanish.

Consuela replied in English, "Yes, hello. Yes hello, yes this way."

We were escorted through an impeccable hallway and down two stone steps into a living room with an ivory carpet and furniture that was snowy and low as if it had settled in a frost. Wide backless maple stairs went up to our right, and, on the far wall, French doors faced the eastern end of a crowded brick terrace. Consuela led us through the formal dining room, which was attached by a sky-lit butler's pantry to an enormous kitchen. Here, the doors to the patio were open. Consuela put my flowers in a vase and set them on the kitchen table. She made a fuss over how beautiful they were. Her eyes twinkled at me; I remember that, her eyes twinkling.

Sara and I made our way out, pausing for hellos and minor introductions. People I knew looked different in ties and skirts and freshly ironed clothes. Past the terrace where the grass began and a reggae band played, was a fountain with a statue.

"Go save us a spot," Sara said. "I'll get some food and drinks."

Above the concrete ring of the fountain was a canopy of willow, with leaves dancing down like necklaces to snatch. I remained still, taking time to relent. I raised my head and closed my eyes, laboring to disremember the historic proportions of the day—the parents and the diploma, Kate's departure, the meager synopsis of a meager me.

It did not take long for me to give in to the lavish setting—the celestial gardens and the lurking servers, the smell of grilled beef, the diamond chinks of genuine glass. My back straightened; my head found center; my eyes dumbed down. Feeling heartened, feeling toned, feeling finally more than meek, I took my place in that robust utopia. I imitated the want of humility of my hosts, and in my mind I became *guest*—someone beautiful, someone chosen. I felt better than I had in some time. If gladness had been a possibility, I could almost have been glad.

At the edge of the packed terrace I saw Mark, Rourke's friend from the Talkhouse. He was moving away from Alicia as though swimming with necessity. I didn't think why he was there. I didn't have time—he was a graphic reminder of Rourke, and that filled me with a barbarian sort of hope. I reached to the fountain, running my fingers through the tiny waters.

He came down, saying, "Eveline."

"What are you doing here?" I asked.

"This is my house," he said, and he smiled. He was handsome. Anyway, the world would find him so. By the dark of the night we'd met, with Rourke there, I hadn't really noticed. "Alicia's my sister."

I recalled Alicia in art class the day last winter when Rourke came in. The way she was laughing and touching his jacket.

"Mind if I sit?" Mark asked. The fountain surged brightly, the way fountains sometimes do. Through the curvilinear gap formed by our bodies, I trailed the crystal swill of water. "I asked Alicia and Sara to make sure that you came. They told me you didn't leave your room."

Strange that my name had been mentioned there. Was it in the hallway or on the stairs or by the pool, or in the butler's pantry? I considered asking. I had the feeling I could ask him anything.

"Is that true that you didn't want to leave your room?"

"Not *my* room," I said. "My mother's room."

"Oh, your mother's room," he repeated, and he nodded.

FOR A LONG TIME he spoke. He'd attended UCLA then he'd gone to Harvard for his MBA. Crew was his sport. He'd biked across Nova Scotia and golfed in Scotland. He'd been hired by a Wall Street firm to do something—something about four in the morning and activity in Japan. In July, he was moving into his own apartment on West Sixtieth Street, twenty-five stories up with a terrace overlooking the river.

"The trick to marinating bluefish," he said, "is milk. Kills the fishy flavor."

The tone of his voice was flat and hypnotic, artificial and intensely sure, pungent and dry as the magenta inside of certain flowers. He spoke without allowing his vocal cords to vibrate excessively, which required great control, and the sound took me away. I felt favorably impaired. I felt this faraway feeling, this night and dead feeling. There was this nightmare I'd once had about a woman with sarcophagus eyes. In the dream we were on a covered porch, on a farm, and a dirt driveway sloped downhill, and there were cars but no people. She whispered onto the back of my neck, and I felt the moving bones of her chin on my shoulder. I saw the hairs on my forearms rise.

I looked up. Mark was staring, ardently. I perceived the ignition of his desire. I wasn't sure what to do about that. Probably it was too late to do anything. My will for Rourke, for all things indirectly related to him, surely only made matters worse.

"If you need a shot of culture this summer, visit me in Manhattan," he whispered as the sun began to set, its lethal phosphorescence slinking unevenly off, like the thin straps of a dress from a woman's shoulders. "We'll hit the Met. Get some lunch. Have you ever eaten at the Stanhope?"

I didn't reply. I didn't have to. He preferred my indifference. He was luring me through to the weakness of my own heart, to the region I was poorest, promising to care for me there. I was not offended. I liked that he was cunning and agreeable and so obviously without ethics. He aroused me—perversely.

"So, Kate leaves today. Alicia told me."

"She left already."

"Canada, is that right?"

"Her brother lives there."

"And in September, she's going to McGill."

I nodded once. "McGill."

"Montreal is beautiful. You'd love it there," he stated with certainty—certain that I'd never been, certain of the things I'd love. "The old city is an island in the St. Lawrence named after Mount Royal, the mountain at its center. The French say, *Mont Ray-al*. In America, we say *Mon-tree-all*, which, of course, is misleading as to meaning."

Sara stepped off the patio, moving toward us. I wondered how Mark had gotten her to stay away so long. He stood to greet her. They called out, and their voices coupled warmly, turning festive, turning buoyant, ruffling like doves emancipated. Obviously, they'd known each other for years. I was the only one who knew no one and knew nothing, which was miserable and eremitic, as if I'd been raised in a convent or hothouse. Mark relieved her of glasses and napkins, and he extracted from the crook of her forearm a saucer of olives. Their mindfulness seemed to extend no further than that doorway at dusk. I wondered why they were not in love, when they were beautiful together, when the world they inhabited was legitimate with manageable particulars. They would have had a normal love, a placid high, a confiding union felt to the core, not the panic I'd known with Rourke, not the desperation I knew when he was gone. Mark spoke lightly, amiably, though the pressure from his mind to mine was serious and unceasing; from that port, he encouraged me to drift. With him I could tend out and tend apart, like an astronaut tethered to a mother ship. He could make me insusceptible. His was an exceptional power—he was blessed, he had no doubt.

Sara keeps keys. They were talking about things to keep.

"Nonsense," Mark teased, "keys. I keep *cars*."

"Oh, well, *cars*," she shrugged. "Naturally."

Mark turned to me. "And you, Eveline?"

I had no collections, none that I could recall except of course the rock portrait one, which technically Denny had started, so it probably didn't count. I was not terribly interested in keys, though I agreed that they are collectible, with the way they clink and cleverly hang.

"And," Mark prompted, "what about cars?"

"I don't know much about cars."

Sara laughed, *Ha!*

"Not so fast," Mark said. "She hasn't seen my latest."

"It *is* pretty," Sara conceded. "Actually, Evie, you might like it."

"It's so nice, the previous owner didn't want to sell it to me," Mark explained. "It took me two years, but he finally gave in to a little persuasion." *Persuasion* is the type of word only certain people can use. I'd never persuaded anyone of anything. He took my hand and pulled me to my feet. "Sara, do you mind if I kidnap your date?"

"Not at all," she said. "Have fun."

I went with him to the rear of the property. As we descended the mild grade to the stuccoed gardener's cottage, I noticed people staring, which was correct—the story beginning to unfold between Mark and me was questionable, surely that was clear to eyes everywhere.

"This is my place," he said, drawing a hand over the cottage wall. "These are my roses. And this," he announced as we stepped in front of an open garage door, "is my car."

It was breathtaking. It was a sleek, black Porsche with an elliptical body and scripted chrome lettering that flickered and repeated. I came and I touched it, bending prudently, as if to pet a sleeping animal.

"1967," he said, leading me deeper into the impeccable garage, popping the door handle, taking me by the elbow, helping me to sit. My legs drew up involuntarily, and when he shut the door, it made a solid seal like the lid of a coffin. On the inside, I breathed fast but also deep—beneath my navel. I could see my belly going in and out beneath my shirt. The leather interior was the color of coffee ice cream. It was supple and medicinal, and I melded somewhat into it. The glove box was at my knees. I was thinking, *Once it held gloves*.

Mark joined me, bringing himself behind the wheel. It felt wrong to be close, but I was not responsible for my loneliness nor for his desire to violate it. People had been speaking to me for weeks, and except for Denny, only Mark had gotten through. I waited for him to refer to Rourke; it was exactly the right time to refer to Rourke. If he didn't, it made him into a type of warrior for me.

"So," he said, "NYU."

"Yes," I said, feeling something sinking. "It's strange."

He started the engine. "Not strange, Eveline. Fate."

THE REST UNTIL THE end was fast. Frequently there is more time to think than there are things to think about. Frequently you sit around and contemplate the most trifling details. Other times it feels you live your life in a minute. Not in the sense of things racing past, though there is that, but in the sense of a twist, like a Mobius strip, in the sense of dimension out of hand, and time out of hand. I did not anticipate such an immediate response to my indiscretion. Maybe that's a lie. Maybe I did. Maybe that's what I mean by Mobius strip. Like events happening and time happening and these things are separate. Maybe they are always separate. Maybe I mean *obviously* separate.

The Porsche coasted past Georgica Beach, but then Mark hit the brakes and popped the car into reverse. We swung into the parking lot. Many cars were there, one of which happened to be Rob's red Cougar and another of which was Rourke's. As we raced past, I saw that though the GTO was clean, though the ghost of my name was still etched on the little window in back.

Let's go back, I said, I thought I said, but Mark killed the engine anyway, and we coasted like an arrowhead into the heart of the lot.

Three figures appeared—a guy in a New Jersey Fire Department jacket and two women in sundresses.

Mark left the car and met them at the crest of sand, kissing the girls and shaking hands with the man, pumping over and over until their palms swung down like evacuated trapeze ropes. Mark secured an object in the distance. I saw his face stiffen minutely.

Through the quivering planes of induline twilight came Rourke, contour and profile, a silhouette ascending the slope of sand from the west side of the ocean, breathing forth with the runaway grace of a gaunt hound. He passed Mark and moved directly to the car, which was not even as tall as his waist. He stopped at my door. The others drifted up behind him.

Eveline, I heard Mark say. This is Lorraine, and this is Anna, and this is Anna's husband, Joey, Joey Cirillo—Rob's brother. Mark pointed loosely from me to Rourke, from Rourke to me, and with an uncharacteristic trace of sarcasm or maybe pity, he said, and, of course, you two know each other.

Rourke looked at me. I could see the vision of my compromise absorbing backward into his skin. His left hand entered the pocket of his Levis and his brown leather jacket hung like armor from his shoulders, dividing him in two at the waist. His hands had steered the white cotton of his shirt along the plateau of his abdomen. I suffered to conceive of his solitude, to think if his thoughts were lonely thoughts. The wind blew back his hair and his body blocked the sky—no, *skies*. The one over him and me, and the other one.

There were things happening—more talking.

What brings you out here? Mark asked.

Harrison dragged us, Joey said. We had lunch in Montauk and a day at the beach. The girls went shopping in East Hampton. We just passed by your house. Looks like you're having a party.

For my sister, Mark said. Why don't you come by?

How about it girls, you up for it?

Yeah sure. That'd be nice.

Heads! A voice. Rob's. A football appeared from the direction of the water, boring cylindrically up to us. Next came Rob.

Rourke stepped twice to catch it, bringing him nearer to me. I could almost reach him.

Look at the new toy, Rob said. And the car's nice too.

He clapped once for the ball. I observed Rourke's arm as he threw it—the lengthening, the retracting, the feverish white of his shirt gleaming like the inside of oysters onto skin that was dark.

Let's go girls, Rob said, let's go. C'mon Harrison. Now.

See you in a few, Joey said.

Mark said, see you in five.

Rourke said later, I did not know to who, maybe to me.

PROBABLY ALL THREE CARS arrived at the same time. Probably when Mark and I went straight through the crowd down the driveway to the garage, Rob and Rourke went to park on the street, and we were separated. I was thinking about picking a place where I could wait. A warm place—I'd begun to shiver.

We did not discuss what to do. Mark led me to the screened-in porch on the side of the house where the roof was low and flat like a tarp. Through the walls the night moved like gentle water. People were lounging on rattan sofas, smoking in corners, and there was music. He chose it because I could easily be found. He knew I would not go to where I could not easily be found. And so I began to perceive the scope of his project—it involved a win, not simply a win, an eventual win, a strategic win.

Alicia knelt at my chair. Is she okay?

She's fine, Mark said. It was colder than I anticipated. I was driving with the top down. It was foolish of me. I'll get some cognac.

Is that true, Evie? Alicia asked. Are you just cold?

My eyes found Mark's. Yes, I said, true.

Mark, she said, I could kill you.

Kill me, please, Alicia dear, he said, smiling, winking at me. Then slower, to me. Not smiling, mouthing the words again. *Kill me.*

Honestly Evie, he's been talking about this for weeks. He drove us out of our minds to get you here and the car here, then he goes and gives you pneumonia. Not smart, Mark.

Sara gave me her sweater, pulling it off, one side, the other. There was an extra hole in her left ear, in it was a diamond that flared in the light. Like a miniature exploding thing, greatly reduced. I'll take her home, she said.

I felt myself stiffen. Mark said no. She prefers to stay. For cognac.

He left the room and Sara retired thoughtfully to the eastern wall to check on the status of the night, her gauzy slacks undulating.

When Rourke came, he filled the doorway to the main living room, blocking the light except for a luminous band that etched the perimeter of his body, giving him the aspect of hanging forward. There was a precision about him. I didn't need to guess his purpose. I felt surrounded; I felt myself at his center. There were special bones beneath my waist that sheltered a canal of flesh. I could feel the flesh, feel the bones. Strange that I could feel them.

Sara said hello to him. *Hello.*

I wondered what she felt to see his eyes. Did she feel what I felt. Did she feel an anthem in her heart. Did she see the beautiful lines of his face. Did she think if she could not hold him she would die. Was she sorry for everything she'd ever done?

I turned back, looking for him, but he was gone.

Mark gave me a glass. *This is for you.* His voice originating from elsewhere. It was detached. I tried to think what it means when the voice detaches, what the myth is. The myth is something fierce, probably something to do with lizard kings and cock's eggs and cats that get snorted from nostrils.

As the tumbler filled my hand, I dropped it. It smacked the tabletop and there was a fanning slosh of liquid. Someone crammed a newspaper against the side of the table to catch the widening stream.

Sara pulled back the throw rug. I gathered fragments.

Mark shouting. *Consuela!*

Blood on my palm mixed with the liquor along the slice. Consuela took me through the crowd to the bathroom, and she left me. The door clicking shut, the dark tile.

In the mirror my face was pale like feathers or froth. I could see my likeness and also his likeness swelling like smoke to encircle my own. I did not think where he'd come from, nor did I think as he lifted me onto the counter and patted my palm with the cloth I'd been given. He kissed me through the sting. The kiss was penetrating and inquisitive, with each of us trying to capture all that could be captured and all that could be perceived and regained— the lifetimes of loss we'd endured, the influences of a demand that is eternal and stark, and presently, miraculously, in hand.

I need to get out of here. For a couple days.

With my mouth I could feel him speak. His voice was like eerie underwater vibrations, like the inky scuffs and thuds you hear in a submarine.

I thought I could leave you. I can't leave you. Do you understand?

Yes, I said, I understand.

All right, he said, let's go.

THERE WAS A PLACE near a pond where the trees divided to accommodate the belly of the moon. It was there that we stopped. The moon was like a body fallen to earth, a stellar wreck and a cameo, and the light it secreted was teeming, plentiful waste, the color of the ribbons of a shepherd. Rourke eased the car forward to where the issue was widest, and he jerked the brake to park. Beyond the windshield day was just a whisper still, making gentle gains on the night, coming and retreating in pulses like the pull and the push of his sweet, edible breath, unraveling like the lead string off a tightly wound spool. How did it feel to be him, to take custody of something very small? When his arms wrapped around me, did he feel a knifelike contraction, a stabbing sensation in the flesh above his groin?

By his hands, I was carefully considered, as if it was not me he wanted, but something I possessed. I could feel the burden of his eyes upon me, a hunter's eyes, keen and suspicious, scanning as if looking at something unlost, as if I were the keeper of some conclusion that he had intuited but of which he retained no factual knowledge. The pressure of my skin on his own, the two adhering.

"Say it," he said, the words clawing the margin of his throat. "No one."

"No one," I said, repeating. I swore, giving my word because I could, because it was true, because if in his arms I was a woman, beyond them I was nothing. I loved him with pain and with something beyond pain, with a barren meter and chiming ache that pealed not in the heart but in the desert dry alongside. And I felt afraid, and to shore myself, I swallowed each breath that dared depart from him—the remains he could not hope to hold became mine to keep, to reserve long after he had gone and I had gone and we had burned and after our dying ashes descended, floating for no one, sinking, twirling, and sinking.

FOUR

MONTAUK

He is an American boy and I am an American girl.
People see us coming, they say—Wow.

SUMMER 1980

I.

It was that preliminary azure cool, with everything coming full around, sanctified and unobstructed, clear as the whistles birds make or the piercing cry of crickets. The ground ascended like a platform into the day, and across it we shot, passing through the last remaining darkness, which was like driving into gaslight clouds or calcified foam. Revolution, revolution, one highway, the next, rolling south, rolling west, with the sun ascending to his left and the ellipse of the planet beneath. Nothing preceded that moment; we were no more than the eye could see, the look of us amounting to the entirety of our story. When you study explorers, Magellan maybe, or Cortez, you can follow dotted lines across oceans and continents. The miles and the perils, the forfeiture of lives and hearts, the years lost and monies disbursed are made into tiny trails of dots and arrows. Rourke and I were like two liquids pouring into the same pot at the same speed from the same altitude. We had entered the tempo of our era. I felt defiant and alive, like a criminal in the midst of crime—visionary and dissolute and hyper-removed from the world about me. I felt the soft inside, the soft of him, and a fever to be alive, to live my life.

He said to sleep if I wanted to; I didn't want to.

The long muscle in his forearm contracted as his hand inched right, and the car began to exit. At the base of the off-ramp, a little green Pacer waited to turn. The GTO closed in on it squarely, shoving up and chasing it out of the way. We turned as well, left then right, going up a hump into a Texaco station. His wrist flipped the engine shut, and you could hear the primordial bing, the strange pleas of a morning world still caught in the paralysis of night.

"Better use the bathroom," Rourke said. "It's a long ride."

Our doors closed simultaneously, and Rourke reached for the pump. A white-haired guy in a white windbreaker approached from the office attached to the garage. His name was Al. Anyway *Al* was stitched on his jacket.

"Good morning, there. You're out early."

Rourke said something that I couldn't hear, and Al laughed, "You bet."

I stepped over oil stains and embedded chips of glass and gleaming variations in asphalt, the tiger likenesses and fighter pilots—if you looked you could find them. My head was hanging, and I was watching my legs, my knees and calves, and beneath them the carob dirt unpacking and smoking up as I walked, adhering in a film to my bare feet and ankles. The dented steel door to the toilet creaked mightily. It had a knotted loop of twine for a handle. You were supposed to tack it over an eye hook on the wall for a lock, which was okay since the room had no working light, and the split animated just enough of the filth about me. I rinsed my face and my hair and I wondered what it felt like to wait for me. He'd never been mindful of my needs before. I hoped he would not think less of me for them. Being in love is like leaning on a broken reed. It is to be precariously balanced, to teeter between the vertical and the horizontal. It's like war. It's to demand of one's sensibilities the impossible— to expect paranoia to coexist with faith and chance with design, to enlist suspicion insensibly in certain regards and suppress it blindly in others.

He was inclined against the hood on the driver's side. His arms were folded, and his legs were stretched and crossed upon the oval island that housed the pumps. My stomach felt weak to see him again, the fullness of his shoulders, the divine gesture of his body. When I neared, he looked over, turning because he knew to turn, because of messages sent between the sex of us. Al spoke, and Rourke answered, not taking his eyes off me. I knew what he experienced when he watched me walk, because I felt my body's response. I felt myself become at once everything I was originally and everything he had taken and touched. I felt my skin assume the burden of the sunrise. I felt the luxury of flesh beneath my dress. My lips were chapped and my hair damp and unbrushed, and when I stepped, my foot touched down with the beneficence of angels. In my heart dwelt a primitive kindness. My eyes were large and prone to tears. Mostly what I felt was relieved to live for his regard. I'd never before considered the monumental burden of free will.

"I don't know which is lovelier, young lady," Al said as he handed Rourke his change, "daybreak, or you."

I pressed my belly against the passenger fender; the metal was hot. Rourke smiled, stretching back across the hood to hand me a Coke. I cracked open the can and drank. The sugar was shocking.

"Now, that's no breakfast," Al said as we climbed into the car. "Try Adrienne's—it's a diner up the road."

One of his arms rested on Rourke's window, the other waved in some unseen direction over the roof. His hand was mottled and chapped with the thumb splaying stiffly, and I felt sorry for that. I hoped Al had been in love once. I hoped, at least, that when he was in his prime, he fulfilled it.

Rourke thanked him, and as we turned onto the service road, he asked was I hungry. I told him no not really.

Highways narrowed as we went. The turnpike to the Garden State—through Asbury Park, Ocean Grove, Sea Girt—to numbered routes, single-lane stretches flanked by clay hills with trees and shuttered houses. As we trailed the flight of the boardwalk, a hot wind caressed my face. I wondered if I climbed through the window, would I fall or float. It seemed like the air out there formed a belt, a channel of heat and salt. "This one's for Leanne out in Mountainside," the deejay said, then came "Benny and the Jets."

I was changing. He was driving, and he'd told me to.

I looked through my bag for my suit, and when I found it I put it on, drawing up the bottoms, slipping my dress straps from my shoulders and tying the top piece around. In the side view mirror I could see the elongated hollow at the base of my neck, the downward pools of my collarbone, the rules of my chest, and above that ladder, my face. New lines marked the skin beneath my eyes, preclusive new lines. I tucked my hair behind my ears. Somewhere were my barrettes, in the seat or on the floor.

NO ONE WAS AWAKE when we stopped at my mother's house after Alicia's party. He parked at the head of the driveway, and our feet made even sounds on the gravel as we walked back to the barn, his sounds heavier than my sounds. He accompanied me because it was correct to do so. It would not have been in him to let me go alone.

"I'll take a walk with you," he'd said, and when we met at the nose of the car, he took my hand. Of course we would not encounter resistance. It was not a possibility or even a consideration. My entire life had led to that moment, and I was grateful for the authority I'd been given over myself. On the night of the play I'd waited, and it had been right to wait. He had waited too. That was what he'd been doing—waiting, and he had come back because it was time. And I was ready, not just ready—I'd been *constructed*.

Rourke opened the barn door for me, and he followed me in. He looked around powerfully, sweepingly, assessing everything at once like seeing for the first time something he had studied only in textbooks. As the things he had imagined came to life, these things as I had known them turned dead. I knew I would never again live at home. If I was mistaken, if, in fact, I would be driven back, it would be because I had failed or because I had brought failure upon myself. I would not fail.

He stood with me by my dresser, him leaning on the wall and me opening drawers and us facing each other. I emptied art supplies from a small canvas tool bag, and in it I packed two t-shirts, a pair of jeans, a pair of shorts, a sundress, some underwear and a sweater, one pair of shoes and a bathing suit.

"Anything else you need," he said, "we'll pick it up."

THE CAR GRAVITATED INTO a parking lot, and we stepped out onto the already steaming tar. You could smell the unctuous glue of it. My feet pressed into the longitudinal slats of the ramp that lead to Point Pleasant, and at the top I shaded my eyes from the glare. The boardwalk spilled out like a carpet, like a platform that made you spectator to the sea. I wondered if it extended along the entire coast, and if so, did it dip intermittently—tucking underground, coming back up, like sewing stitches. It wasn't pretty, but it was democratic, with all the people talking, reading, walking, running. There were old people. I never saw old people at the beach in East Hampton.

Close to the edge of the water, he dropped down the two rolled towels he'd carried from the car, and we sat. They were damp still from him spending the day before in Montauk with Rob and Joey. The sand was not like the sand at home. It was flatter and darker. I took off my dress and waded into the ocean, going far, until my feet didn't touch. I looked back at him, at the discipline of his face, at the wrinkled shirt he'd been wearing all through the night, ice-blue and half-open. Behind him the arcades and galleries papered the horizon, antediluvian as the monuments of Egypt—the sky ride and the photo booth, the ferris wheel and the merry-go-round, the signs for strollers and umbrellas for rent. Soon his arms were there circuiting the concave of my back. In that ring I twirled, wrapping myself about him. He carried me farther under, just the two of us, and water, water all around.

Later the sun turned cruel. When I opened my eyes from sleep, my head was faint from the heat; I could hardly raise it. I knew where I was but not how long it had been. People had settled around us in the ebullient glare, hundreds and thousands of people. There was a common whirr, a public rustle, and, alongside me in the sand, the impression left by the weight of his body. Exactly when I wished for him to reappear, he did, coming from the direction of the water like a spread cape or carbon overlay. His body drowned the light and drowned the noise, and moisture traveled from his skin, and cold. I wondered at his size. I had no concept of his size. He was tall, I knew. And solid— when you touched him, he did not bounce back. Women stared at him, but men also stared.

Rourke kissed me, filling my mouth with the salt of the sea. He said, "Let's get out of here."

He pulled on his jeans and his sneakers and threw his shirt and the towels over one bare shoulder. I stood, unsteadily at first, but then I went to the water, and I was okay. I hoped it was still June. I believed that it was. In June, all of summer remains. In June, old songs sound new again and nothing bad happens, nothing that cannot be explained away by the heat and the surreal. Only hours had passed since we started, I reminded myself—and *hours* is not so very far in.

The way we walked was smooth, with steps that originated in the pelvic cavity. His arm crossed my back, and his fingers gripped the handle of my hip bone. I felt like I was sitting in a sort of chair. Eyes followed us from forlorn

faces, sullen eyes latching like leeches. We were not trusted; we were not wanted; we were different. If we had not come to belong, we had come to deride,
to get the best of the little that remained to them. Rourke was unmoved by
the faces. He did not seem to think the spectacle prophesied a coming end.
He did not care what anyone thought, not then or ever, because every realm
he occupied related back to his decision to occupy it—because with him,
choice indicated possession. He was not oblivious to the vulgarity, but he
seemed darkly entertained by the middling violence of it. He might have been
telling me something, maybe that in such vulgarity lay truths—what to work
against, what to run from. I didn't ask why we were there, on the boardwalk.
Whatever his business, it wouldn't last long.

I observed the life around me as though through a filter or screen. There
was the Mechanical Gypsy Fortune Teller—*Fawchin Tella*—and the Daytona
Driving Game and the cats—*Three down wins choice, dolls must be flat*. There
were the clanging arcades and the rides that once you died for—the Whip and
the Ski Bob. There were fat ladies in skirted bathing suits and peddlers hawk-
ing baby hats with names in dayglow toothpaste script, racks of flexible sunglasses and *Ten chances to win a red Corvette*. There was Lucky Leo's Frog Bog
and Kohr's Famous Orange Aid and the Midway Steak House and, incredibly,
strains of "My Baby Does the Hanky Panky." And that game with the gun that
shoots water into the clown's mouth with the bell that screeches long and
hard and forever-seeming. Through sudden waves of heat, there would be the
nauseating gum smell of honey-roasted peanuts or the greasy snap of sausage
or the crack of frying zeppole. Parentless children in careening lines of seven
would wave beehives of cotton candy and pick candied apple from their teeth
going, *Let's go to the bumpa cauz*.

Though it was a weekday, there were adults—leather-skinned women
squinched into belly shirts and half-naked guys with chains and nesty chests
and meandering scars beneath their ears. All of them immune, impermeable,
happy, I suppose—the cutting edge of evolution.

WE WALKED TO A pale yellow brick corner building with no marking other
than desaturated red letters at the top that were modern and straight and
missing in part.

C-R-I-T-E-R—

By the width of the discoloration, it looked like two or three letters had
been lost due to a drainpipe dumping directly above them. On the way over,
we saw several guys go in, all carrying gear bags. They each turned to Rourke,
noticing him, then waving to him, though for much of the time we were a far
distance from the entrance, and the boardwalk was not exactly empty. One
stopped short of walking in when he saw us, and he waited at the unmarked
glass door. He was over-built—his head was small and his hands, and his eyes

were indocile. He had red hair and red freckles beneath random bruises, and his ears were knuckled up at the edges. His jaw was enormous on the left. It looked as though it had been broken.

Rourke said, "Looking good, Tommy."

Tommy ignored Rourke and checked me out like it was his right, like I was meat and he was shopping. Though I wasn't afraid with Rourke there, it made me sick to think of those freckled hands.

Rourke pulled a folded envelope from his back pocket, and handed it to Tommy. "Give it to Jimmy."

"Not goin' in?" Tommy mumbled. It sounded like gargling.

"No," Rourke said.

Tommy shook the envelope by one weird ear. "What is it—a *Dear John?*"

Rourke stepped forward twice, coming close to Tommy, dangerously close. He inspected Tommy's jaw, first the bad side, then the good. Tommy stood frozen as a big dog getting sniffed by another big dog. Like it was in his interest to be polite, but he might decide to haul off and bite anyway.

"Not a chance," Rourke said with a smile.

KRISPIE KREME WAS PLAYING The Stones, so he bought two cones, and we sat in the shade of the carousel house to eat them.

Angie, Angie. Remember all those times we cried.

I wasn't hungry and my ice cream began to melt, so I gave what I couldn't finish to Rourke, and for a long time we watched the ride go round. Something about the crackled verdigris, the melancholy pneumatics of the tin ponies, the visible filaments of the clear globe lights, and the muffled flicker of the mirror pendants made me sad. The riderless horses, the gentle billow of air, the exhausted wheeze of the calliope. The posted rules. *Three bells mark the start.*

He pulled me to the space between his arm and his chest. I could feel his heart beat. "What is it?"

"It was such a long time ago," I said, "when I was little."

At the end of day when the light went low and the beach had mostly cleared, we went down, passing on the way a beautiful girl in a tangerine miniskirt and a bikini top leaning in the arch of a curtained door. The sign said *Psychic Readings by Diana.*

She curled a finger at us. "Come, come."

Rourke ignored her, and I felt relieved, though I wasn't exactly sure what I was afraid she might say.

We collected pieces of beach glass from the sand while we walked, jagged peppermint treasures. I gave them to him, and he put them into his shirt pocket, saving them for me, for later, which was nice. Nice to think there would be a later. Back at the car, he kissed me again, and a breeze picked up out of nowhere. A wish, I thought—granted.

IT WAS THE COLOR of silver wheat—sweeping and upright, yet modest in the sense of not drawing too much attention to itself. Some of the houses we'd passed really drew attention to themselves. Three giant rhododendrons nestled against the Victorian porch like mountains of butterflies, like a choir of savage ash, pink with blotched crimson markings. My first thought was that it takes a special talent to manage things so wild. These were tended as a river tends rock, by way of neighboring force. I thought about his parents, what they were like, and Rourke became clearer to me in that minute than in all our minutes combined.

The car idled at the front of the driveway while he emptied the mailbox. He walked back over, sifting through a stack, extracting certain pieces and examining the contents of one in particular before getting in, wedging the pile on the dashboard, and easing the car to a stop at the driveway's end. He turned off the engine, and we sat. And it was nice, and it was strange, because though it was not home, it was as good as home, and in fact, it was better—it interested me more.

A wickety brick path led to a painted wooden gate and through that gate into a backyard that was squarely fenced by yew. There were happy birds. There were bob-whites and cardinals, and there were calls colliding as pleasant scents collide. Rourke reached into the lamp case for a key and unlocked the back door to a ground floor apartment. I followed him into a broad, square living room with doors at the left leading to the backyard and a narrow cherry-wood kitchen beyond them. The walls were beautifully plastered, though there was no art. It would have been nice if there were art. A wide hallway on the right cut back towards the front of the house, in the direction of Essex Street, and there was a low stack of boxes and suitcases along the wall. He left my bag on top then moved to the counter, where he rifled through the remainder of his letters, popping a few apart. I circled the couch back and unlocked the double doors to the yard, splitting them for air.

"I have to make some calls," he said. "You're okay?"

"I'm okay," I told him, and he left, disappearing down the hall.

Right away with him gone a heaviness in me was alleviated, a consciousness regained. When people get awakened from hypnosis on television, there's a dumb blink, an apish inner inquiry as to how long they've been witless and what degradations might have occurred. If it is in a cartoon or comic, there are stars about the eyes.

Outside the day was evolving and halfway lowering, like the curtain on a play you wished would never end—the summertime nothingness, the haunting children's voices, alighting then waning—*what do you want to do? I don't know, what do you want to do?* The scraped knees and three-way secrets, Italian ices and sticky palms, bicycles discarded on cracked and crooked cement, wheels lightly spinning, the buzz of electrical cables, the garbled melody of the Mister Softee truck, the anemic drone of televisions just on, the monotonous lapping of the just evacuated pools, grills smoldering, lanterns lit. From somewhere not far away, one phone was ringing. His voice reverted to me from down the corridor. He sounded happy, but his happiness had a barren ring. I was glad not to be his friend. What he gave to me, he gave to me alone. On my thighs was salt from the beach; I licked my fingers to taste it.

The shower was running, and I undressed and joined him. The sunset passed the bathroom window, making mercury through the mottled glass of the stall. The beams were like melting pedicels or weeping stalks, an electric heraldry, proclaiming the extraordinary—and so it was, the effect of light on his skin brought me joy. And the water, running down his chest. I touched him by his heart with one finger, and the shining water parted.

Rourke stepped out, and I could see that on the face of his hips and around the sides, the muscles were like rigging, like cords and knots. He wrapped one towel around his waist and came back to me with another. I noticed the water drying on his body, and the simplicity of that act over-whelmed me, and I began to cry. When tears came, we did not speak of them, either of us. Oh, the closeness of him, the close and excruciating nearness. Perhaps as a vessel I was too delicate for a love so whole. I felt only half-real, half-right. I felt it was my obligation to focus, and yet I could not thoroughly focus or place him safely in me. Though we'd come far, we had not come far enough. It's strange to have succeeded but to feel anyway as though you've failed. I felt alive, and with that, or because of that, I felt endangered.

He disappeared, then he returned in jeans. Hanging limp over one arm was the strange sight of a dress, rayon red and moody. We'd bought it on the way over; *he'd* bought it. He dried me lightly and held the dress for me to step in. The zipper tugged at the curve of my back, and his hands manipulated the liquid on me, dragging the water down the *V* of my shoulder blades. In the mirror we were enigmatic, my eyes so tragic, my dress so low, and Rourke, a triumph of masculinity. He drew on a ribbed sweater with three buttons at the top, navy blue, and he watched as I combed back my hair with my hands, put on lipstick, and fastened my shoes. I felt no shame before him. Shame was a luxury. We had no time for shame.

EVERYONE STOPPED AND STARED when we walked into Mineo's, some resting their silverware. Waiters made way, flattening their chests and inclining their heads. Rourke escorted me through the crammed space, the broad heat of his palm making a warm impression on the small of my bare back. People were waving from a table. They seemed to be expecting us. Rourke introduced two men and a woman named Lee, who was pretty like a doll. The names of the men were similar, Cliff and Chris, though the look of them was different. Cliff was slight and blond with wire glasses like a geologist, and Chris was big and robust and oleaginous with a mole on his forearm in the shape of a crab. I slid sideways across the bench, leaving a place for Rourke, gripping the table to steady myself. I was not steady. I told myself to copy the others. They seemed more or less sure of distances and weights.

"Where's Rob?" Rourke asked.

"Good question," Cliff said.

Rourke right away left the table to make a phone call. In his absence, the men appraised me stealthily. I felt self-conscious of my breasts beneath the halter top of the dress. Did they know about my thighs as well, the bare way they were touching? Men always seem to know such things.

"I hear you're an artist," Lee said, leaning over. Her eyes were millimeters too big for her head, and when she talked, she talked fast, captivating you with her insecurities. "I wanted to be an artist," she confided. "My parents didn't think it was—not that there's anything—actually, I think they were afraid I'd marry—well, you know. It's just, it takes confidence. You must be confident." Lee picked at the antipasto. "Do you eat meat?" she blurted, adding, "I don't. But there are these stuffed pork chops Chris gets that look so good."

Chris and Lee had matching wedding bands. Etched on the gold were murky bars. "The Parthenon," he said, pointing to the inside of Lee's tiny ring; his would not come off. "See the fluted columns?"

Rourke returned, coming up behind the waiter as he was reciting the list of specials, and when the waiter realized that everyone was looking *behind* him instead of *at* him, he turned halfway and said, "Sorry, Harrison."

Rourke waited for the waiter to move so Cliff could get up and Rourke could slide back in next to me. Like a puzzle. As soon as the waiter started again, Rourke cut him off, saying, "We'll take two swordfish."

Chris collected his menu and Lee's menu and tapped them on the table-top before handing them to the waiter. "Make that four."

And Cliff said, "Five."

"So what happened?" Chris asked Rourke. "Did you get through?"

Rourke said no.

"When did you see him last? In East Hampton?"

"Yeah," Rourke said. I pressed lightly into Rourke, and he lifted my thigh onto the rack of his. I wondered if Rob was missing because he was mad. We'd left Alicia's party without saying goodbye.

"So you went to the beach today," Lee said to me.

"Yes."

"It's pretty different from East Hampton," she said.

"Yes," I said. "It is. Very different."

"Hey, Eveline. Did Harrison tell you that he used to run Skee Ball at Coin Castle?" Cliff asked. "Back when we were kids."

I looked at Rourke. "No, he didn't."

He leaned back and smiled. "Must have slipped my mind."

"That's where he met Rob," Lee said. "How old were you guys, thirteen?"

"Thirteen," Rourke said. "That's right."

"And it was love at first sight," Chris joked.

"Not quite," Cliff said. "Cirillo always tried to hustle him."

Rourke said, "*Tried to* is right."

ROB HUNTED THROUGH HIS pockets for something, withdrawing nothing. He'd come with Lorraine, the redhead from the day before. She said *Hello* and distributed kisses, but he said nothing, not to me or anyone, though his eyes frequently darted to Rourke's. No matter what, I felt better with him there, more alive. Everyone did. You could tell by the way they shifted in their seats, coming up higher and adjusting the bands of their watches. You got the feeling there was nothing going on in the world that he did not already know about and have an opinion on.

He pulled up a chair to the head of the table next to Lorraine. I figured she was his girl. She acted bored like she was. "I had rust comin' out of my pipes," Rob reported with miserable enthusiasm.

"You gotta call," Chris said as two pitchers of wine arrived. I wondered who in Jersey took such calls.

"I *did*," Rob said, leaning far back in his chair. "I go, *I'm supposed to shower in this shit?*" His left shoulder wrenched up. "I go, *What am I, supposed to make coffee outta this crap?* It was like clay."

"They must've been working on a main line," Cliff speculated. "They probably stirred up sediment. Give it a day."

Lorraine rearranged her bag and laid a pack of Larks near her plate. She looked like the kind of girl with brothers, the kind with a knowledge of pistons, lures, and end zones. The frayed tips of her ginger hair reached in a fan of kinky curls as if to capture creatures. Her hair was like underwater hair. "I keep telling him, use bottled."

Rob clicked his tongue. "It's the pipes, not the water."

"Lemme tell you something," Chris informed all of us. "That bottled water thing is *bull*. New York State tap is best. Studies show."

"Lot of good that does us here in Jersey," Rob said.

Chris said, "I'm just saying."

The waiter came over to check on Rob and Lorraine's order. Rob scanned the table and said, "What did you guys get, the swordfish?"

Everybody just said yeah, yeah, swordfish, yeah.

Rob flipped his hand. "G'head, Ronnie, make it two more."

Lee asked Lorraine how was Mark Ross' house in Long Island.

Lorraine swiped her hands and said, "Gorgeous." *Gaw-jus*.

Rob shook his head and shot back a whole glass of wine, going, "That fuckin' guy."

VINNY-O'S WAS THE KIND of place my dad would have called a beer garden. It was boozelogged and corrosive and lit primarily by backwards neon. How we ended up there I wasn't exactly sure, except to say that Rob had to meet somebody, and nobody was very happy about it. I didn't bother to ask about the names—*Mineo's* and V*inny-O's*. I got the feeling it was a Jersey thing.

Lee and Lorraine had gone home. Lorraine didn't feel well, that's what she said, but it was obvious she and Rob were fighting, because she took her car.

"Leave me stranded," Rob called after her taillights. "I don't give a shit."

Lee just had to work in the morning. She was a market analyst on Wall Street. Her job sounded like a big job, in terms of responsibility, kind of like being a surgeon or a bus driver. I was surprised that she'd been out drinking pitchers of sangria with us.

When we got to Vinny-O's, Rourke parked the GTO, and Chris and Lee pulled up behind us in their new Cherokee with Rob and Cliff. The guys got out, and Lee slid behind the wheel. Her head rose inches above its northern arc. "It *is* Monday, right?"

Chris kissed her through the open driver's window. "Yes, honey, it's Monday. Go home."

"Keep an eye on him," she requested of me with a wink.

"Okay," I said, though that seemed like a giant obligation. I watched her pull out and wondered at her husband's iron constitution. I would not have been able to let my wife go like that, tottering off into the night like a lame firefly buzzing sideways into an immeasurable wood. When I turned, only Rourke was there. Chris had already gone inside.

"Let's go," he said, taking my hand. "We'll stay for a little while. Then I'll take them home."

INSIDE PEOPLE TALKED OVER the clatter of pinball and the ching of the bowling game and "Two Tickets to Paradise" by Eddie Money. I headed for the bathroom, which was not only filthy, but rigged. Posted over the toilet were instructions on how to flush; they were yellowed, not necessarily from age.

> *Lift tank top* (crossed out) *top of tank to sink*
> *Pull string, hold or tie to hook by lite and replace*
> *Top. Take out string to exit.*

I looked, but there was no sink and no hook. There *was* a string—but it was wet. Needless to say, the toilet had not been flushed for some time. Voices sifted through the wall from the men's room, low and intermittent. When I came out, Rourke was still near the front door, caught up in conversation with Cliff. I went to the bar and bought myself a beer.

"Bottle or tap?" the bartender asked.

"Tap," I said. It seemed like the thing to say.

The louvers to the bathroom corridor flagged on spent hinges; Rob and Chris came out into the bar. Theirs had been the voices I'd heard. Probably they'd been doing coke. They had that cagey look. Chris breezed past to join Rourke and Cliff, who were by the window, but Rob came to me, tossing his arms slightly out, grinning as though he hadn't seen me for so long.

"Holdin' up the bar, gorgeous?" He landed at my side and shifted in half-circles, like a cat getting ready to lie down. Eventually he settled, lit a cigarette, and examined me. Each of his features looked like it had been broken twice, yet there was something appealing about the urgent way it pieced together, kind of like a skyline.

He took a sip of my beer and grimaced. "What the fuck is that?"

I said I thought it might be Schlitz.

He looked over his shoulder to the bartender. "Hey, Marty." Marty didn't move. His arms were folded across his chest; his eyes fluttered back. "Jesus," Rob mumbled to me, then he shouted, "*Marty!* You alive?"

Marty roused himself and hitched lamely over. "Sure, Robbie. I'm alive. Unless you happen to be a bill collector."

"You're startin' to worry me over here," Rob said. "I seen more blood run through a goal post." He lifted my glass. "Gimme something to rinse the taste of this outta my mouth."

"How about a shot of Red?"

Rob pulled a wad of bills out of his pocket. "Nah, I'll take a screwdriver." *Sh-crew-driva.* "You want something else?" he asked me. "A little brake fluid or some rubbing alcohol?"

I told Marty I'd take Courvoisier if he had it.

"That's a giant leap," Rob said, "from Schlitz on tap."

"That's because you're paying."

We got the drinks and toasted. "So, whaddaya think of Jersey?"

"It's all right," I said.

He said, "First time?"

"Not technically."

"Not technically," he repeated with a smile, and he looked off, as if distracted by something, maybe just something in his head. He bit the inside of his cheek and jiggled the ice in his glass, making a sound like a beaded instrument. I waited and I watched, because that was the thing to do with someone who was complicated and high. I'd had lots of practice with Jack. Frequently, people try to act screwed up, but Jack truly was. Sometimes you hear, *He was as strong as ten men!* Jack was not strong that way; he was screwed up that way.

"So, you and Rourke," Rob said. "I'm surprised."

"Oh, I figured nothing surprises you."

He took a drink, and his eyes skimmed the ceiling, lingering there, returning to me. Rob had the kind of eyes that could care for you but wouldn't. Music started, mournful music. "You like to dance," he said. "Come dance with me." He took me to a place between the rooms next to some tables. His wiry arms held me square and polite, and that made me sad.

> *Sometimes when I'm feelin' lonely and beat,*
> *I drift back in time, and I find my feet, down on Main Street.*

"Remember you and Mark danced at the Talkhouse?"

I remembered.

"I called you Countess," he said.

I asked why.

"Because," he said, "you have *great rank*." Then he turned me, leaning close, whispering, "Be careful."

I felt his words gather at my ear. I felt something surge through his body, something ragged and incongruous, frustrated in its effort to transfer smoothly. I felt a rapid friction, a premature content.

And I felt myself traveling backwards. Rourke had my arm. Though he stood naturally, you could tell he was not happy. He didn't need to posture to intimidate, he just had to be within reasonable range of his object. His fingers closed on my wrist.

"Let's go," he said, taking one step in reverse, pulling me closer, my back to his front, like a hostage.

NEXT TO THE SOUNDS of night, our sounds were negligible; our sounds were assumed into the broad eastern waste—the quick hiss of the cedar plank door, the music that escaped from it, the sugary swish of my clothes and the cool knock of his steps, the eerie strike of plasma in my veins, the maddening echo of Rourke's voice—*Let's go.*

In the car, my dress collected behind the small of my back, and I clutched my wrist where he'd held it, wondering would I get another bruise, like the one he'd made on my ribs that time.

The road we took was not the same as the one we'd taken before. It was a local road, leafy and minish, like a route from a horror film, top-lit and wet, despite the fact that it was neither, the kind of road with half-beasts stalking the margins or cars on the shoulders not really broken down but lying in wait. We made it home in minutes. Once there, I felt safe.

Rourke leaned over and popped my door. "You know where the key is?"

I nodded. "In the box."

"I'll be right back," he said. The car squealed in reverse, swung around, then shot forward. How able he was to exist in the misfortune of night. How afflicted he must have been, by ritual, by rivalry, by things mannish and abstruse, to go back out. Whatever home provided was inadequate compared to the riddling principles that moved him.

I reached for the key, estimating how long it would take him to get to the bar and back, and whether he was going to have to drive those guys. I closed the door behind me but didn't lock it—I didn't feel the need to.

The lights were very bright. I turned them off as soon as I turned them on, remembering a small iron lamp on the bookshelves by the couch. It was shaped like an urn with a parchment shade. I searched for it through the dark, and when it was on, it was softly on. I could see that beneath it there were books, and that behind me was a coffee table with a dish full of the beach glass we'd collected. I went into the kitchen. The appliances were new, and the cabinets had new dishes. On the counter there was still a skinny shred of an envelope flap from the mail he'd opened earlier.

"Be careful," Rob had said, then Rourke stopped him. What was Rob bound to say besides, *Be careful?* I tried to think, using only my head. But I couldn't get past the feeling of being in the exact right place—the feeling that I was where I belonged.

I placed my palms against the bedroom door and pushed slowly. The room was empty except for a bed and a Scandinavian-looking wood table with a milkglass light and a black phone. I took up the telephone cautiously, wondering if perhaps it had no printed number, but it did, and a dial tone. The closet was practically empty, but then, he'd just come back from Montauk and in the hall were six boxes and two suitcases. Like the rest of the apartment, the room smelled like cut wood. Possibly it had just been renovated and his parents were going to rent the place—no, they had no intention of renting it. They'd fixed it for him. To think of that, of him as loved, as the recipient of feelings that were worthy and true—

The car. I heard the car and I ran to meet him. I was at the door when it opened, when he stepped in, his shoulders easing through.

"He okay?" I asked.

Rourke threw down the car keys. "He's all right."

He pulled off his sweater and tossed it on the couch. As he unbuttoned his shirt, his hand moved in practiced jerks. The thoughtful way he cast his gaze into space was lonely.

"I'm sorry," I said. "If I—"

He shook his head, as if to say, forget it. "It's—complicated."

I drew in against his chest. I wondered what it might have been like to hold him as a baby. His skin was soft that way. He might have been wondering the same thing because he touched me was like I was new.

What followed was less a kiss, less an embrace than a precise exchange, a diving in from opposite ends and a rolling, gliding lull at dead center, a clock tower marking midnight, mammals swimming expertly beneath the sea, a gift from God that I hardly merited. I felt myself assimilated. He did not have to say that he loved me, not when I could see the rounder cast to his eyes and feel the puerile softness of his lips and the desperation in his hands, and if I did not know exactly what he was risking to be with me, I could feel when he held me the consequence of his choice. And that was a better knowledge than any other; it was a personal knowledge. No one would ever know what we knew. No one but us. Through the night I was filled with an inexplicable peace, despite the promise of uncertainty—*Us,* how nice it sounded.

WE STOPPED IN RED Bank to see a car. Rob was there already when we arrived, taking a slow walk around a '71 Corvette—yellow. Naturally it made me think of Mark's Porsche, just with the way it was sitting in the driveway like a lost shoe, like a princess slipper. I took a look at the GTO and the Cougar, lying like giant slabs of beef in the street. One day in Jersey, and I would never look at cars the same.

"They didn't do too bad a job on the paint," Rob said to Eddie M. "The problem you're gonna have with the 'Vette is the heat coming through the floor boards."

"Tell him what happened to Jimmy," Rourke said, joining the conversation without ceremony. The two showed no sign of having argued in the bar the night before, if, in fact, it had even been an argument. There was a newspaper at the end of the driveway. I sat on the corner of the lawn, flipping through the pages, taking care not to look too hard. I didn't really want to know anything.

"My wife's at her mother's," Eddie M. informed me, strolling over, gawky like a farm hand. His eyes were electric and clear blue, like a husky's. "Otherwise she'd make coffee."

"Why can't you make it yourself?" Rob called over, in disgust.

"Because I don't know how to work the thing."

"It's a coffee maker, asshole, not a backhoe."

"It doesn't matter," Rourke said. "We're going out."

"Where to, Pat's?"

Rourke said, "Yeah."

"I'll go with you," Rob said. "He owes me fifty bucks."

"Me, too," said Eddie M. "I can't sit around all day waiting for Karen."

After Eddie M. put the Corvette in the garage, we took off in two cars, driving past the weeping willows and cyclone fences and idle flags onto the backstreets, where there were forlorn sidewalks and dwarfish brick buildings and the funereal reflection of ourselves as we proceeded in a loose wave past the plate glass store fronts. At a red light, Rob pulled up alongside us, his window inches from mine. The music from his car was deafening. He was singing. *Be my love—*

"Hey, Contessa!" he shouted before cutting in front of us. "What do you think of Mario Lanza?"

WE FOLLOWED HIS CAR onto a four-lane roadway with a concrete strip up the middle and malls on either side, the kind that makes you depressed about the hopeless state of humanity. Within minutes, we were at Morocco's, a spherical diner like a space station or an automotive air filter. Sunshine cast back mercilessly off the steel and glass facade, and saucers of diesel exhaust from the highway formed a plane of smog to walk through. The men fell into a quiet line, with me in the middle, quiet because I was everything to them; I had prominence in the moment. I made them feel on the outside what they felt on the inside—greedy and deserving and virile. Rob and Eddie M. were thinking how Rourke and I had just had sex. I could feel on my skin the tread of instinct and imagination.

The waitress came to our booth. Rob asked, "Where's Pat?"

"Which Pat's that, doll?" she volleyed in a gravel voice. She was old, but her body was solid. If she were your mother, she'd smack you with the back of her hand, no matter who you thought you were.

"What do you mean, *Which Pat?*"

"It's a big place. We got a lot of Pats—Pat Wolf, Cellar Pat, Patty G., Kitchen Pat."

"*Kitchen Pat?*" Rob repeated incredulously. Eddie M. bit his cuticles and smirked. "What do I look like, a bread salesman?"

"No offense, honey, but I didn't bother to check."

"You new here, or what?" Rob inquired.

"Yeah," she said, "I just started about—sixteen years ago."

"Sixteen years, and you don't know Pat Webb—*Spider* Pat?"

"Night shift," she informed him. "If you wanna talk to someone on night shift, you might wanna come at night. We don't got dorms in back." She lifted her pad to her chest. "What'll yas have?"

Rob ordered a turkey club with fries, Eddie M. got pancakes with sunny-side eggs on top, I asked for a grilled cheese, and Rourke pushed the menu towards the table rim. "Burger, medium rare."

"Coffees?" she inquired, taking up menus.

Rourke said, "Yeah, for everybody."

Rob pushed some quarters to the jukebox at the end of the table. He told Rourke to find something decent.

Eddie M. said, "Find him 'Shadow Dancing'."

"Fuck you, Eddie M."

Eddie M. said, "You jellyfish, you love the Bee Gees."

"You jerk off to Gordon Lightfoot."

"Lightfoot's a genius."

"Genius!" Rob snorted. "Let me ask you something. 'The Wreck of the Edmund Fitzgerald'—*What is that?*" Rourke and I laughed, and Rob stated dryly, "I'm totally serious. What *is* that?"

"Lightfoot's a poet." Eddie M. leaned to me and nodded his head to Rob. "He saw Donna Summer—*Live*."

"That's right. I got no problem with that. I'd like to fuck her," Rob said. "Take out an ad in the fucking *Post*."

Rourke flipped the jukebox pages. He had the inside seat across from mine, so I couldn't help but notice how his forehead was square and his cheekbones were prominent, and his eyes had a black and avaricious clarity. The diner's windows were coated with enormous transparencies to mitigate the view of the highway and to tenderize the inclement glare. The sapphire cellophane light gave the impression of things Mediterranean, of him where he naturally belonged, Southern France, Northern Italy, a village with battered streets along the coast of Spain—with me, in white, by his side.

"Want some?" Rob asked, gesturing to me with the ketchup.

I said no thanks.

Eddie M. popped his eggs. "Seen Tommy?"

Rob looked over to Rourke. Rourke said, "Yesterday."

"At the gym?"

"Outside it."

"I heard he got a fracture."

Rob laughed. "Oh yeah? A *fracture*? Who told you that? Darlene?"

Rourke said, "Who's Darlene?"

Rob said, "Darlene—Cunio's girlfriend. Tommy's popping her."

Rourke looked straight at Rob, then into his food.

"Some fracture," Rob said. "He looks like he got hit by a wrecking ball."

"It's gonna be a long summer," Eddie M. said to Rourke, taking a huge bite and looking at me. "Better not sweat to death."

Rob chucked a napkin at Eddie M. "You know what, Eddie M., shut up. And you're a pig. Wipe the yolk off your mouth, for Chrisssakes."

AFTER WE'D EATEN, WE retreated, each of us picking through the wilty last halves of fries, gazing thoughtfully into the theatrical stillness of the dining room—the sloped backs at the counter, the parties of three and parties of five, the crumbs lining laps and the panty hose nesting about quadrangular ankles, the car salesmen in ersatz ties—broad and resplendent and clipped on—the grandmothers gnawing dewy egg salad, the toddlers shoving Sweet 'n Lows under etched pink booth dividers.

> *Mother, mother. There's far too many of you crying.*
> *Brother, brother, brother, there's far too many of you dying.*

The dessert carousel stood near the door like a phosphorescent obelisk, twirling somniferously. Going around in a demented parade were towering meringues, tilting cakes, mammoth pies and puddings, balloon-perfect jelly-rolls, surreal mousses, and those scary things the menu refers to as *Swan*. A middle-aged couple ambled down the concrete stoop into the asphalt lot. The man was picking his teeth, and the woman had a vested polyester summer suit that was pink. I wondered who they were and how they had slipped from the aerobic consciousness of the world. Across the road was a Beefsteak Charlie's, a Dress Barn, and a Carvel. Also a Fotomat and a giant pet shop and a Chinese restaurant, so very, very far from China. I wondered about the woman who stood there, looking out the window before opening for business at night. Surely there was a woman.

> *C'mon, talk to me, and you can see.*
> *What's goin' on. Oh, what's goin' on.*

I remember feeling transformed. I remember feeling aligned and by that alignment being shoved up into the business at the head of our generation and dismissed from the shallow diversions at the rear. I remember thinking that I was about to be badly used by circumstance, that my needs were about to be made subordinate to the politics and pressures of the time, that I didn't care, that I could not go back. And with this admission came acuteness of being. I felt a lonely fury of connectedness, like a minute in a place you've always feared and suddenly you're there, and you look around and think, *Hey, this is okay, this may even be beautiful.* For those who join you in that moment, you feel true love. You see them as they are and yourself as you are, as products of time and place, participants and pawns, the riches and assets of a spurt in the flight of a species.

Rob's fingers drummed the tabletop. He and Rourke looked at each other. There was something overcast or eclipsed between them, something dark but not newly dark, a darkness already tread upon.

"You headin' out?" Rob asked.

Rourke reached for his wallet. "Yeah, right now."

Rob lifted his hand. "I got it."

"Me, too?" Eddie M. asked.

"No, you bastard," Rob said, "you pay for yourself." Then he reached over and slid my sunglasses from the top of my head. He cleaned them carefully, carefully using the corner of his sweatshirt. "I'm gonna have to teach you how to take care of these things."

"I SPENT A WEEKEND in Jersey once," my mother reminisced as she filled two tea cups with Chablis. "At Princeton. Very memorable."

She handed me a cup. I said, "Thanks."

"Sorry about the glasses. I'll get to these dishes tonight."

"Don't worry about it," I said. "I'll do them."

"It feels like you've been gone for weeks." She joined me at the table. "Susan Parsons moved in."

"*Here?*" I hadn't figured Kate's room would be so quickly filled.

She furrowed her brows. "Not *here*. Into an apartment in town. Above the News Company. On Main Street. You remember Susan? Her brother was in the car accident by the Getty Station."

"Oh, right, Susan. David's friend. The caterer."

"You're thinking of Suzanne—Tarkoff, Doctor Hollenbeck's wife. Susan's the astronomer."

I shook my head. "Sorry."

"So when do you start work?"

"Tomorrow."

"I want you to take Powell's car. It's gotten too dangerous to ride your bike. He's away until September, so it's perfect."

I said that I would.

"I'm going to an opening tonight at Elaine Benson's. For Lilith's husband. He mounts bowling balls on wedges and batons. They look like giant olives on giant cheeses. Very *geometric*. Feel like coming?"

"That would be nice, but I have laundry and stuff."

"Think about it," she said. "It could be fun."

"Okay," I said, and I smiled at her. Though it would have been simple to tell myself that my leaving home would mean nothing to her, I knew better. Maybe it was crazy, but I felt bad to take myself away.

After her, the house was empty. I walked through that emptiness as if through time I'd been given. On the mail table there were two phone messages from Kate and ones from Denny and Sara and one from Dad. There were large envelopes from the NYU Bursar and a single tattered card from Jack, postmarked the day before graduation. It was a vintage photograph of East Hampton, with cows in the middle of Main Street. Huge on the right was the tree we loved, and tiny on the back Jack's writing reeled and lurched to form the shape of an owl. I set it writing-side out on the windowsill by the kitchen sink, then I stepped back to study it. It was like a relief or engraving, a sort of a woodcut or specimen. It did not inspire sadness exactly, but something that moved in the mask of sadness, something slippery and undependable at its core, influenced as it was by the infancy of summer and the recent invincibility of my heart.

In the basement, a pile of damp towels from the weekend had consolidated into a flat disc mound. I ran those through first. The floor was cold and dusty, but anyway I sat, leaning against the jiggling machine, removing one by one from my bag the pieces of clothing I'd worn to Jersey, pressing each to my face, deep and close like an oxygen mask, smelling my sweat and his, soaking in each kiss and the last—especially the last, the one in the driveway with his palm taking the ladder of my neck, drawing me in like a rod.

"You know where to find me," he'd said.

I said yes, then I released myself from his grip, slipping out.

The night that followed was a long one. Through the length of it, I felt many contradictory things—I felt alive, but I felt also and intensely the part of me that was dead. Around me lay the fearful settling waste of matters once liquid and hot, silent now, and still. If I was unattended, I was not lonely. I was kept tranquil through the hours by the memory of the prayerful tenderness in his hands, by the devotion in his eyes, by the glorious opposition between us that could never be lost to me, not even if he was lost to me.

2.

AFTER MY SHIFT, I CHANGED IN THE BATHROOM, PUT ON LIPSTICK, AND HAD dinner and a Beck's out back with the lunch staff, all of us listening to Neil Young and watching the sunset spill out of itself across Napeague stretch, like milk from an overturned cup. It had been a long time since we'd seen each other, and everybody was happy. When I left, I headed east in Powell's steel blue Dodge Charger, whipping around the treacherous curves of Old Montauk Highway, ducking oncoming Jaguars, speeding over peaks, sending my stomach flying. I was not going to die—not then, not that way.

In Montauk, the lamps of the ballpark illuminated the top of the traffic circle, and by instinct I turned, finding Rourke's car there. I parked in the lot next to Trail's End across from the field, and, leaving my shoes, I walked north. There were bleachers between the shoulder of the road and the play area, and I climbed them as his team took the outfield. His stride was long, his head modestly inclined. He didn't acknowledge me, though he knew I was there; they all knew I was there. I leaned forward, pulling my skirt close by my knees.

An old man paced on the rim of the field. "Shout it up out there Montauk, you sound like a bunch of mutes!" He turned to me. "Nice night. Not too many bugs."

Rourke was at first base. He wore a uniform that matched other uniforms. I located him through the cloth. I saw his thighs and knew exactly their strength. I saw the drop of his arms and knew precisely their weight. Buttons were missing from the base of his shirt, and beyond the split was his abdomen, the brownness. He was like one-half of sexuality, one-half of humanity, making me the other, making the thrill of his excellence meaningless without the thrill of my own. To behold him was like beholding a large animal run—you stand in awe of its allegiance to its nature, and you forfeit any idea of claim or possession. In him there was proof of our undomesticated origins and forsaken purposes. When the last batter of the last inning hit a foul that popped past first base, Rourke ran sideways and backwards and leapt to catch it. For a moment he prevailed in air, there was a collective breath, the slap of the ball against the hide of his glove, and cheers. Teammates jogging to home.

He came over and straddled the bench I was on. His face lowered to mine, our foreheads grazed, our hair intertwined.

"I missed you," he said, breathing out.

"I missed you too," I said.

"C'mon," Rourke said, giving me his hand. "Let's take a walk."

And we walked, and it felt out of control to be in love with someone so masculine, like being an amateur with your own supernatural capacities, like flying a guided flight. Both teams had collected informally with friends and families around the second set of bleachers, and, as we passed, Rourke was handed two bottles of beer. Them saying, *Good to have you back, man. Hey, nice catch. Next time you move, let a few weeks pass so we can have the girls to ourselves.*

Rourke opened the bottles and handed me one. At his car he bent to kiss me, me between him and the fender, and beneath my feet grass that was wet. Around us the curious imperative of cricket noise swelled to near crescendo.

"How did you get here?"

I pointed across the street. "Car."

"*Car?*" he said, like that was funny. "Get in. I'll drive you over."

But he did not join me inside right away. First he removed his wet shirt, his shadow increasing mightily against the dashboard. He tossed it into the back seat, telling me to hand him a clean one, which I did, holding it out to the brickish portion of abdomen that obstructed the open window. As we were about to leave, there were two knocks on the trunk. Some guy leaned in. On his kelly-green jersey there were numbers, and a name, *Roger.*

Roger nodded to me politely. "You guys coming to Tattlers?"

"Not tonight," Rourke said. "We're going home."

MY FIRST IMPRESSION WAS that it was cold and black. There were earthy odors and the thrill of encampment. I thought of his winter there and the applications of his privacy. I thought in a wicked flash of the nights we'd missed—an entire year. Unlike certain other things, time does not come back.

"Come in," he said, and I did, all the way, shutting the door.

The room was featureless in the pitch. A cast iron stove materialized at the distant right. He knelt before it, matches in hand. One triangular tip of paper swelled to life within the elliptical swing gate, then the flame progressed down the side before catching entirely and illuminating in a fan the shallow range around him, his upraised hand, his powerful leg, several inches of floor. The kindling caught, brightening more—a couch, a chair, a stretch of old windows above the kitchen fixtures, the two suitcases and six boxes and the stereo he'd taken back from Jersey. I'd helped him load the car.

"I'm going to shower," he said.

There was nothing while he showered, nothing other than the sound of running water and the revolving vanes of firelight tripping erratically. When Rourke reappeared, he was wearing a gray sweater, supple and frayed, and a pair of jeans he loved—I could tell by the holes. He seemed sinless and uncomplicated, like the person he must have been at fourteen and at four, like the one he'd be at forty-five. I knew I was seeing not what he chose to show but what he chose not to conceal, which was different. I saw a purity so unfinished that I could not tell if it was native or a oneness highly evolved, the product of some arduous distillation. Though I was glad for his honesty, it made me sad to think of him hiding parts of himself from those he did not trust, of him having to control how he was seen, of him keeping himself separate. I thought of the weight he surely carried, the enormity of expectations that had been heaped upon him. No matter what happened between us, I told myself, in the end he would be as innocent as I. I told myself that. That and also that we had to hurry.

He was tall until he joined me. He rested his weight on one elbow, moving my head to the great wall of his chest. And he asked me a question, not the first he ever asked, but I accepted it as the first. "Will you spend the night with me?"

I knew what he meant. He meant the whole night through to day—he was inviting me to suffer the transformation in his arms.

IT PASSED PRECISELY, WITH EVERY MINUTE REPRESENTING EXACTLY ONE minute—no less and no more. Each day was again a new day, uncontaminated by design. When morning came, it came as if by surprise. The sun advanced upon my skin, and it advanced upon his, cautiously raising our temperatures, burning off the air to breathe, rousing us with revelations of the masquerade we'd forsaken and the sheerness of the barrier that isolated us from it. And his arms would take me tighter. Our hours lapsed with resiliency and poignancy, with a concentration that seemed to mark them for extinction. Had I been sentenced to death, I could not have interpreted time with a fiercer consciousness—every twilight seemed to be the last, every rain the final rain, every kiss the conclusive aroma of a rose gliding just once past your lips.

The house was an anonymous green and white cottage at the crest of a hill that was shielded from East Lake Drive and nearly parallel to it—number seventy-five Fleming Road. The reminder of Jack was unfortunate, but the number you could calculate quickly—seven plus five is twelve, and one plus two is three, three is a third of nine—nine being good, nine being optimal. Stepping through its door was like stepping into the sea, with all things turning plain and blue and faintly menacing. The wide pine floors and cracked stucco walls were infused with the remains of eclipsed love affairs, the melancholy legacy of peregrine sailors and persevering women, and it was there that I met myself. It was there that I discovered my soul's invention, the feminine genius of me. Had there been time, I would have felt like the fugitive I was. I would have thought about life beyond the summer and acknowledged that an end was imminent and that I needed to prepare. The world sloped against our door like a barren belly—I could feel it—but I was not wise enough to dispose of my contentment for a time in which I would surely find no solace.

If he loved me, love wrought no change in him. He did not speak of such things, and I did not speak of such things, because words are false and promises are false, always only resolving nothing. From the beginning he had been attracted to the savagery in me that matched the savagery in him. I was an American girl; I possessed what he valued most—independence and blind courage. Yet, he allowed me to be frail beside him, and so my soundness unraveled, and I began to unlearn things I had been taught. Often I was afraid—it is impossible to be a woman to that kind of man and not feel afraid—but my fear was a natural fear, a first fear, a fear I would not have exchanged for a wasteland of complacency. It was a living fear; it kept me vigilant through the night. If, in the end, I were to be wounded, it would not be because he wanted to wound me. His battles lay elsewhere, with things of which I was reluctant to conceive—time and obligations, ambition and money. I wished it didn't have to be that way. I wished there were no place in life to go. I wished for his sake that I were older, stronger, better, that I might have sheltered him. My God I loved him.

Sometimes when I lay in the cradle of his arms, he would draw me closer, squeezing as if to concede, concede something. Sometimes when his exhausted weight landed against the station of my breasts, and his hair invaded my parted lips, and all I could hear was silence, a profound eruption of silence, a palisade so sullen and arid that nothing could possibly breach it, I would say, "Rourke."

THE DAYS WERE SIMPLE, numb, and narrow. My impressions collected in platforms, in sheets and layers like rock beneath earth, in generations of chalk and shale, impressed and impacted to form a single impression—that I was happy.

I did not write; I did not draw; I kept no record of conversations or clothes, places passed or inhabited, restaurants, bars, beaches. Each moment that expired was a butterfly escaping; you could watch it, imperial in hue and contour, membranous and sheer and split to maximal thinness, fluttering magically, fluttering rightfully, slipping off in fits to the gaping enormity of liberty and oblivion. The remains of that summer are the merest inflections in light, the minorest deviations in sound. Like whispers through grasslands or heath entwined with dew, in my mind, in my memory, all that is left of those days is an overriding sense of neverness, of allness.

In the mornings, I would sit on the step beneath the chipped and swollen front door, waiting while the incandescence of the sun inched around the cottage, like a beast, to dry the water from my just-showered skin. I would push my heels into the grass and lukewarm dirt, thinking, *God really is everywhere*.

Though the demands of my body for nature had mostly been met by the permeability of the frontiers of our house, by days spent outdoors and evenings working in a roadside restaurant, by expressions of flesh and trials of desire, I found no end to my compulsion for the wild. I existed in a prism of contact, sensation, and wonder. I longed to stay entirely outside. I craved the ground and also the heavens. Wherever I looked, I wanted to lie, though that was not always possible. If, at night, I would have dared to leave his side, I would have entered the velvet stealth, mellow as a phantom, knowing that nothing would ever hurt me there. It was like being hungry for blood and smelling it everywhere around and hearing it drive, everywhere drive, and you do not mind it touching you when you are it and it is you, and the merger is sweet. That summer I felt a dissolve in the casing of my skin. I felt myself connect as pools connect.

And him joining me, coming to the porch with a pot of coffee and a cup for us to share. A divide between opposing houses revealed the gelatin green bay, and through that slender break we would look to the west as sunrays from the east advanced like tentacles around the building to find us. And then him reaching, his hands touching the strings of my hair. And pain. Suddenly something jagged in the lesion he had unclosed, a knowledge of the advance of time, an instinct that luck does not last, a feeling of modesty in regard to the opulence of my circumstances.

"Is it time?" I would ask.

"Yeah," he would say. "I bet you're hungry."

The GTO would barely drop speed before veering to the shoulder at Four Oaks, where we bought breakfast—either there or at Herb's in town. Our doors would pound in unison, and I would walk a little behind, watching the even force of his legs as they hit the street. Sometimes Doreen, the cashier, would wave before we reached the door, and Rourke would toss his arm up. If you didn't know already that she drank Jack Daniels, you could tell by her face. Once at Tipperary, Rourke bought her a drink. She thanked him, and when she lit a cigarette, the hand gripping the match trembled. The bartender brought a rocks glass filled with rust-colored stuff, not bothering to ask what she would like, and she sat back in her chair and sipped like she was comfortable, more comfortable there than at home.

Inside the deli, the floor tiles felt stark under my bare feet, and the air was so cold it seemed to come from my bones. There was the tract of refrigerated cabinets in back, the bouncing thud of the doors. Near the coffeemaker was a platter of collapsed and sorry Danish. I would dig through for a few free of flies while "Piano Man" played on the radio. If people were talking to Rourke, as often they did, I would wait by the creaking novelty rack, spinning it to see the yo-yos and water pistols and bendable sunglasses, and the guys behind the counter would calculate the circumference of my ass.

My eyes would pass over theirs—*Do you honestly think you could do to me the things he does?*

Sometimes he would scan the headlines while we waited for sandwiches, other times he avoided them, in either case enduring concessions, striving to follow his way. I could see him return—to summer, to me—seduced again, despite some sounder verdict of which I remained emphatically unaware. It was as if everyone had been evacuated, but by some miracle of stupidity we remained. He would run a hand through the even jet of his hair, and he would turn to find me, as if I might have vanished.

"Is that it?" he would ask, pulling muffins and peaches from my arms, tossing knots of cash on the counter.

At the beach, we would eat. At the beach he would run several miles and swim several miles, and we would sleep, and if he thought I was getting too much sun, he would lay a shirt on my back—the cotton drizzling down like a parachute, brushing down, brim first. When he stood or walked, women would adjust their glasses and arch the bridges of their ribs. If they lay on their bellies, they would tug the strings of their suits higher around their lifted bottoms and spy him through the fragrant triangles between arms and blankets. Like a being endowed with the paranormal, I would turn and face the sun, feeling it heal the flesh he'd used, feeling myself emancipated. They didn't know what I knew. They didn't know what it is to be an enigma. They knew nothing of unconditional discretion or singleness of heart or femininity, when femininity is madness and uncertainty and vertigo in his arms. Jealousy was not possible; no one could love him better or more. By two o'clock he would pull his jeans over his shorts, fastening them—from behind, the perfect plunge of his back lay exposed, and oh, the way the muscle rolls up on either side of the spine to flank the long hollow. During our procession to the car, everyone would watch solemnly, even children and dogs.

He would knock the front door open with his thigh because his hands would be full, and after shaking the blanket and hanging the towels to dry, we would meet by the side of the bed. The influence of his body would weigh down the inferior mattress nearly to the floor, and for a moment we would sit. Sex in the day can be sad, sad when after you must part. It is to risk in light, to reach for things there and not there, to confess that in fact you are searching. It is affecting to meet your need, devoid of the perversions best suited to darkness. We are made more radiant but also more heartbreaking by the dauntless venture through true time.

Tenderly, we would touch, each striking lightly against the skin of the other, as if sketching something without basis. In day, his face was a reflection of my own, his features flushed with innocence and a reassuring lack of sufficiency. At times, I could not bear the monuments there. I felt sick from the sight of the child I'd been, lost until found in his eyes. And him, a child too. I often thought to say something. It was possible that he wished to talk.

There were two small windows with blue woodwork and, beyond them, long boxes, outside boxes filled with red flowers that turned the room the color of love and hearts. And we would lie, like vines. And I never once felt the way I'd felt with Jack—baffled and agitated, unable to articulate some grave humiliation, some feeling that I'd been wrongly used, despite Jack's maudlin concerns and conceited timidity. Jack did not know how to assign his loneliness; he was like a barrier, a reef you could not swim through. But there was dignity in the violence of Rourke, and grace. There was beauty in our separateness and virtue in its dissolution. There was freedom in faith.

As I'd suspected, Jack had been wrong. Desire is not deviant. To seek physical resolution through intimacy and to achieve it is to rise feeling balanced and confirmed, and not as if things have been unclosed and left unclosed and will remain that way until they are unclosed some more, each time a little wider. After sex with Rourke, the nerves in me would be stilled and the blood in my pelvis repossessed in melting beats by my remainder. Afterwards he did not disgust me with tenderness. Afterwards I said nothing, and he said nothing. Afterwards the look of my underwear on the floor did not depress me.

While I showered and dressed for work, he would make phone calls; I did not know to whom. I did not think where his money came from. I never asked what he did while I worked at night. I never looked through his belongings. The fact that I was eligible for such information meant nothing to me. His discreteness was sacred—inside, way inside, I preferred it. It's hard to explain, except to say that when Jack and I used to walk, we would crash into each other, listlessly, lazily. Rourke and I never crashed into each other, never once. If ever we intersected, it had meaning, new meaning, not mine, not his—*third* meaning.

Every Tuesday was my day off, and every Tuesday was difficult, far more difficult than the one that preceded it. He would get up before me, throw on some clothes, and before leaving the room, he would turn his head incompletely, saying, *See you later*. And when late on a Tuesday evening he returned, I would not go to him; I could not even necessarily move. I would just watch him, overwhelmed by the need to vow something, secure something.

MONTAUK WAS THE VEGAS of my imagination, a dwarfish Vegas, with garish toy-like motels and two-story arcades bright as airfields and tourists in unscrupulous attire. Men in black socks play miniature golf at Puff 'n Putt with beet-skinned ladies in extra large t-shirts, while teenagers secret off to the muddy seclusion of paddle boats. Everyone eats double-dip at first dark when the sidewalks are still tepid under bare feet. Chesty guys from the boroughs named Sisto and Vic who eat three- and four-pound lobsters but never get a drop of lung on their shirts, swat at their kids' heads, and check you out through your sweater, while their wives buy miniature lighthouses and driftwood seagulls and boats inside bottles. Locals you never see but read about in the paper grow pot in their gardens and keep arsenals in their basements, and celebrities hide like game in the cliffs. Steps away from the midget scrub pines of the village is the ocean. Not a tranquil ocean, like the lagoonish satin-lit backdrops of Florida or the Caribbean, but a northern one that coerces you into the confidence of its fury. When you swim at midnight, you waive everything, learning there is no fear worse than the rigor of your delusions. Montauk is not exactly pretty; it is something else entirely.

Sometimes we'd go to The Tattler, or to the Montauket for sunsets. The Dock was the place to get coffee after midnight, black or with Bailey's. At the Dock, the tables would fill up with people Rourke knew from slow pitch or the beach and occasionally with people I knew, like Lisa Tobias or Sam the Dominican waiter from Lobster Roll, and his girlfriend, Lou, from the Surf Shop. The first time Ray Trent and Mike Evans walked in, they were surprised to see me. I introduced them to Rourke, and the three of them sat around until closing, talking about rugby, the start of the Olympic Games in Moscow, and whether or not Ali stood a chance against Holmes in Nevada in October. I left them alone, like leaving three toddlers in a room with toys, and when Rourke pushed back his chair that night to go home, I pushed back mine as well, kissing those guys goodbye. Rourke didn't seem to mind them, not like he had at the St. Patrick's parade.

If Rob was in town, we would go to Gosman's for dinner and wait for an outdoor table even if it took twice as long, because Rob didn't come all the way from Jersey to sit indoors.

"I could sit inside at home," he'd snap at the hostess. "Watchin' *Chips* with my grandmother."

From the cocktail patio near the docks, we would observe the eerie cortege of yachts slinking to berth after a day of lusty immoderation, the strings of spotlights on deck shining into the sable wax of cooperative waters. You couldn't help but wonder what it would be like to be them, with arrowhead jaws and matted hair and wrinkled whites, flesh alive with the stink of coconut oil and vodka. All around the docks is the luxuriant smell of tar and the grasping stench of fish and hostile gulls on pylons that face off at your eyes. When the woman with the microphone would call out—*Cirillo, party of three*, we would leave our daiquiris and go slow, the three of us, like we were somewhere else in the world, somewhere with ochre streets, cobbled and precariously narrowed, where bread is wrapped in paper and wine in wax and string, someplace where it does not hurt to be happy, where there are no necessary ends, where it's not humiliating to end up exactly where you start out.

Rob would wake up first because he didn't sleep well except in his own bed, which was a Sealy Posturepedic. He would knock two times fast, and Rourke would sit, throwing his legs over the side of the mattress, tossing a piece of the knotted sheet over my hips, though he didn't have to do that. It didn't matter if Rob saw me. There was nothing I needed to hide.

"Yeah," Rourke would say, "it's open."

The door would creak open, and Rob would hop up onto the frame to do chin-ups, saying, "C'mon, let's go get some eggs."

In Salivar's, there were fish carcasses of an affecting diamond blueness that befit equally the subterranean depths of seas and saloons. Rob would make fast friends with strangers at the counters, talking about how much weight DeNiro gained for *Raging Bull* and the Islanders winning the Stanley Cup and bizarre marginalia from the papers such as streaking or Texaco making gasoline from corn or the surgical detachment of Siamese twins.

"Leave 'em," was his solution to the hostage crisis. "Who the hell's dumb enough to go to Iran in the first place?"

Rob never sat at the beach. He paced restlessly, talking to everyone. He organized volleyball games with burly guys in True Value towels wrapped high on waists, and he played Kadima with every adolescent, like it was his personal duty. He threw balls to lonely dogs, and he built castles with kids and he always only faced the sun. "Why get a tan on my back? If I'm walkin' away from you, I don't care what you think."

When Rourke wasn't around, it was Rob's hand on my waist or his coat on my shoulders and Rob's voice suggesting we get a cup of coffee or a couple of sandwiches and go do laundry.

"We'll be right back," he told Rourke after a morning out on the Viking Star. Rourke was hosing off bluefish in a plastic tub. Rob ran me across the street to Zorba's Inn, a dilapidated motel that was near Gosman's dock, which looked like a lean-to. He pulled an instamatic from his sweatshirt pocket. "Get a shot of me in front of Zorba's. I'm gonna tell Jimmy Landis this is where Harrison is living."

Sometimes when I was at work they would go over to OTB in Southampton and then to the Woodshed by the Bridgehampton drive-in to see some waitress Rob had a thing for. I met her one night at the carnival in North Sea; her name was Laura Lasser. Laura wore blue eyeliner and stonewashed jeans with an eyelet t-shirt and skinny white skips from Caldor. She was pretty but heavy, which was okay by Rob who frankly liked a big ass.

When Rob took her on the rickety old Ferris Wheel that night, Rourke told him, "Jesus, be careful up there."

Like wayward objects from the sky, the guys would show up at one of the picnic tables behind Lobster Roll, usually around ten, straddling the benches and talking shit about Johnny Rutherford doing 142 miles per hour to win the Indianapolis 500 or Otis Anderson or the Steelers or the Lakers or Evel Knevel's Snake Canyon jump, or just old times in Rob's '68 Challenger or on the Boardwalk with Daisy and Pongo and the Chinaman.

When Rob's friend Bobby G. died in August from complications following the motorcycle accident he'd had in March, Rourke met Rob in the Bronx that Sunday for the service. They showed up in Montauk after midnight with Rob hanging limp off of Rourke's shoulder, both of them wearing navy pinstripe suits. Rourke jerked his head for me to leave the room, but Rob said no. "Don't make her go, Harrison. I don't want her to go."

Rob halfway undressed, and he straddled the arm of the sofa in his sleeveless undershirt and his suit pants, clutching a bottle of Cuervo. Rourke made egg sandwiches, and I watched the topography of Rob's skinny tattooed arm flicker as he folded and unfolded a matchbook from Ruggerio's Funeral Home. It was a beautiful arm, like a junkie's arm. When the deejay on WPLR said, *This is Dana Blue, the request line is open,* Rob waved the bottle left and right, going, "Get me the phone, get me the phone." As if by some supernatural occurrence, he got through to the station, and we three drew together in a memorable trinity, with Rourke holding a plate of eggs and hovering over Rob, and Rob on the sofa, legs apart, knees high, holding the receiver, and me kneeling on the floor with the phone like an offering, all of us still except for the manic push of Rob, the life and guts of him.

"I just lost a friend," he said. "You know what I'm saying—he's dead." Dana Blue must have said sorry and asked what could she do because he thanked her then cleared his throat. "Can you send out 'Knockin' on Heaven's Door' to Bobby G.? Tell him it's from Robbie and the Chinaman."

If they came to pick me up before my shift ended, I would bring them beers and fries, which made Rob happy. Rob liked to get a deal, it was a matter of pride, it made him feel less cheated by life. His was a tough predicament. It's tough when the things that make you proud—family, heritage, home—are the same things that shame you. One reason Rourke meant so much to him was that Rourke was like one foot in and one foot out. And Rourke was conscious of that line. Whenever Rob was around, Rourke tightened up, like trying not to stumble. Sometimes they would talk quietly, and when I'd pass by they'd get even quieter, and Rob would start playing with his lips. The corrugated lines from his cheekbones to his jaw would darken and turn thready like burnt wicks. I'd pick up the empty fries baskets and the beer bottles and wipe down the table, and Rourke would lift his folded arms, giving me room to squeeze under.

Rob would invent some crazy conversation. "So, this girl Rudy got pregnant, she's a Born Again. They're over in Stuyvesant Town."

I always figured it was Mark they were really talking about. Once Alicia came in to see me, and she told me they'd all gone to dinner together at a place in Southampton. I'd wanted to ask her how Mark was doing, like with his new job and his new apartment, but I didn't. I wondered if he had heard I was living with Rourke, and did he know that beneath my belly was a box—that you could cut it away, anyway you could try, and it would be a humming pink box.

LAST TIME I SAW Rob that summer was a Tuesday, near the end—at least it seemed near the end. It's not always easy to separate time from its connotations—as frequently as meaning leaps up, it slips away. Possibly there had been a previous end, another day that I hadn't noticed. After Rourke left that morning, I rode my bike to the beach, stopping first at Whites' for gum and candy. The air was still, and the tide was low, so I placed my towel near the waves, and I opened my book—Fitzgerald's *Tender Is the Night*. Two white-haired babies ran around a sandcastle.

Aja, when all my dime dancin' is through, I run to you.

"You waltzed right past me." It was Rob, bending low for a kiss. "I'm over there playing volleyball."

"What are you doing here? It's Tuesday."

"I told everybody I had jury duty. Come on over."

I shaded my eyes. There were a lot of people. "I'll wait here."

"Come *over*. Don't be shy." He gestured with my book as we walked, slapping it twice in his palm. "Good book," he said. "Nicole Diver, that's you." He spread my towel near his, by the net. "You know you're getting burned." He touched my nose. "Right here."

"Hey, Rob," one of the guys called. "Sometime this century."

"Keep your shorts on," he barked back, then he put his cap on my head, adjusting it until it was low near the bridge of my sunglasses. "Red Sox," he said. "Don't lose it."

My bike just about fit into the trunk of the Cougar, and Rob threaded his tank top through the metal coupling and tied a knot to hold it in. I'd never looked close at his naked chest before; it was narrow like a sewage pipe and the skin was intense and rubbery like dolphin skin, glossy and Vaseline-gray. His nipples lay closer together than normal nipples because there was little girth to his back, so they appeared to be in line with his pelvic bones, which perhaps they were and all nipples were. He had white surgical tape around his wrist. I could not see his tattoo from where I sat because it was on his left bicep and he was driving. It was a lightning bolt through the word "Zeus." At the carnival, Rob told Laura Lasser that Zeus came down to fertilize earth. He peered into her blushing face. "You know what I'm talking about, *to fertilize*, right?"

We dropped off the bike and left a note for Rourke to meet us, then we grabbed some pizza and ate it on the hood of the car. Together we witnessed the mellow defervescence of day. In the waning heat, the village seemed a place of endless possibilities. It was like the abating of a fever, the end of a hot afternoon, like an exhausted sickness. Everyone waved like they knew us.

"That's because they do," Rob said. "Everybody knows you."

ON THE WAY TO Surfside, I was thinking of guilt and of leaping through the lunacy of the soul and if anything is lost forever. I was wondering why I'd been given that summer, which was like fusion and fighting a fight and walking contrary to a current. Maybe life is like being born into a prison that is you, and there comes just one opportunity to escape, one second when everything coalesces into something like perfect timing, and you dash, or you don't. Maybe everyone gets a chance to run, but not everyone does. That summer I had the feeling of being on the outside for the first time, and I was thinking about that, about bravery and fusion and identities that are original, and also about the color of my father's wallet, and whether my mother had even wanted me. If my mother hadn't even wanted me, she must have felt bad about that, you know, like over time, through the years. I was thinking of Rourke and of people who love trees. People who love trees want everything to be made of wood, but that necessitates killing trees, which is confusing. If you love trees, maybe you ought to live in brick. I wanted to ask Rob. I had the feeling Rob would have something to say about letting go of the things you love.

"Today's my birthday," he said as I started out of the car.

"Happy Birthday," I said, coming back to kiss him, leaning far because he was still at the wheel. It was nice that he didn't mind spending it with me.

Surfside was in that peculiar state of restaurant nothingness before the full staff arrives, when the kitchen and bar are the only points of activity and the main room is set but sleepy and unpeopled. My mother used to waitress part-time at Bobby Van's in Bridgehampton, and I'd go in with her until a sitter could pick me up. Between jobs such as polishing spots off silverware or folding napkins, I would eat pan-fried hamburgers and do homework and draw flowers on Guest Check pads. If I was returned before closing, I would get chocolate ice cream in the overbright kitchen then sleep in a booth until my mother was done. She would put her feet up and count cash.

"What are you thinkin' about?" Rob asked. We were in the doorway, white ocean light behind us. Probably we looked cool like thieves or ranchers.

"Nothing," I said. "My mother."

THE BATHROOM WAS FRILLY, like a man's idea of a ladies' room. You could tell a lot from a bar bathroom, for instance what kind of night you were about to have. Through a window the size of a folded newspaper, lace curtains blew outward in equatorial pulses, too soft to rid the room of its synthetic cherry fragrance. When I switched off the ceiling light, the room turned the color of puritan cloaks, livid and blue. I brushed the sand from my skin and washed my hair under the faucet with soap then shook it dry. It'd gotten longer and lighter over the summer; it went straight below my jaw and I had bangs and the color was ash. I removed my bathing suit. Two white triangles marked my breasts and one marked my bottom. Other than that, I was all-over brown. I threw on the khakis and the white halter top I'd taken from the house. My breasts had gotten bigger. I wondered how long had they been that way.

Rob was at the bar. I walked over, and the bartender stopped cutting limes. He said his name was Val. I handed Rob the Red Sox hat and said my name was Evie. Val was a curious name for a man, without obvious origin. Rob and I drank two mint juleps each, and when Val started on a third round, Rob said, "No more for her."

"What's the problem?" Val wanted to know.

"With the Contessa over here? I gotta keep my eye on her," Rob stated matter-of-factly. "She's very loosely wrapped."

LATER WE WENT OUT back. The kitchen was shiny like the paint was still wet, and Brian the cook had black hair that was tipped and tall as if he'd gotten sideways shocked. He nodded in our direction then turned to head through a screen door so covered in gunk that it didn't even bang when it slammed shut. It made a sound like a donkey—*hee haw*. And then—nothing. Val followed Brian, and we followed Val, and the four of us sat on a railroad tie retaining wall. Brian took out a joint and lit it. We passed it around and right away all the things I hadn't noticed at first came to life. It had been a long time since I'd gotten high, not since the night I broke up with Jack. There was the smell of creosote from the retaining wall and the growl of the walk-in alongside us. The insects that packed the amphitheater at our backs sawed noisily, and the uneven clamor from the kitchen escaped like an intrepid perfume—the fluid *thud-thud* swing of the interior dining room door, the repeated *hee haw* of the back one, the waitresses arriving and joking with the crew, the sizzling things on the giant Viking, the clinking racks of last night's glasses exiting the dishwasher, the iron pots smacking. My skin felt sunburned, which is to say cold and warm. Rob arranged my hair, changing the way it crossed the part, and I wondered about Val's name, whether it was Valerie or Valentine.

"*Vallejo*—it's my last name. My first name's Rick," he said. "My grandfather was a bullfighter, *Juan Vallejo*. He got pinned in the ring. The horns came on either side of his chest. He had scars here and here." Val opened his shirt and pointed to the pockets beneath his arms. His body was like his name, sleek and curiosity-inspiring.

The cook stretched up with interlocked fingers before returning to the screen door, where he stood, facing in, away from us. He pulled something long from his pants pocket, a navy bandana, and he folded it and ceremoniously tied it around his head. "You guys feel like eating?" he asked.

Rob said, "Absolutely."

"Let's go wait at the bar," Val suggested.

Montauk Daisies are scrappy low bushes that grow in sand, and out by the road there were several. I saw them when we came. It was early for them to come. Usually they come in September, but it couldn't be September yet. I was thinking about those bushes as we paused on our way through the kitchen to watch some kid garnish key lime pies, and I was still thinking about them when three plates of grilled tuna hit the bar. The tunas were triangles with charcoal stripes, and the vegetables were twigs stacked like teepees. I could see the shape of the living fish in the periphery of the fillet; maybe not— maybe fishes were not triangles but ellipses.

"I'm gonna take a walk," I said.

"What are you talking about?" Rob said, taking a mouthful. "The food just got here."

I didn't know what to say, so I said nothing, which seemed to make him more nervous than me saying something because, instead of arguing, he looked into his plate like it was a far-off horizon.

"Where to?" he asked, chewing, not looking up.

I shrugged. "The bathroom."

"The bathroom," he repeated. "You planning to use it, or are you just going sight-seeing?"

"Sight-seeing."

"At least she's honest," Val said.

"Let me tell you something," Rob said to Val, "I'd rather watch some-body's dog than their girlfriend." He tapped my plate with his knife. "Eat first," he quietly advised. "It's on the house."

IT WAS LATE WHEN I finally made it out to the daisy bushes. I sat in the driver's seat of Rob's car and brushed my hair and put on lipstick and rubbed my feet over and over in the sand on the side of the road. The sand was cold the way sand gets in summer. I tried out Rob's eight-tracks—the Four Seasons, the Stones, the Del Vikings, Stevie Wonder, Frank Sinatra—he had an eight-track so nobody could steal his tapes. The floor was littered with empty Chinese take-out containers and flaccid newspapers, and there was a torn-open box of Wash 'n Drys on the dashboard, which was funny if you knew him because Rob is a fanatic about clean hands.

On the back of a cocktail napkin, I drew a Montauk Daisy and composed a birthday note, which contained the usual sort of birthday message, *Happy returns* and so on, except that at the end, right before my name, I wrote *I love you*. For a long time I stared at the words, positive of meaning and sure of fact but flustered as to why that love was suddenly so emphatic, and I began to cry. In the mirror I beheld my tears. They were pretty tears, little missives and epistles, flags and trumpets, blessings and traces of something; I could not think of what because, at that very moment, Rourke appeared.

He walked onto the restaurant's porch, and my tears disintegrated, everything vanishing upwards.

And I heard myself say, *Oh.*

Rob came next, jutting his chin toward the car. Rourke must have asked where I was. It was nice to think that he had come for me, that his interest in living was active at that moment because of me. If Rourke did not exist, then maybe I would have ended up with someone like Val, who would have been nice to kiss, but that would not be love, that would be something lonely and fascinating, like occupying someone else's house for a night or two, if it happened to be a particularly nice house. I wondered about the gathering climate of bleak inevitability. I wondered whether we were not agents of a human exercise that extended beyond what we could, in our smallness, conceive—and that is somewhat like discovering your plane has no pilot but not caring as you'd rather be dead anyway.

He propped his shoulder against a post as though keeping the building from folding in upon itself, and Rob turned and sat on the rail. I could imagine what Rob was saying, with his back slumped and arms moving, but Rourke I could not read, his language was perfectly oblique, his body organized as usual by the most exquisite economy of action. I thought they might be arguing. Rob got up and walked back in. For a moment or two, Rourke stared out.

I stood and got out of the car, and he waved once, acknowledging that he saw me, that I should come, then he turned to follow Rob. I locked the car and took the path back to the restaurant, walking with an impression I'd forgotten something. I felt for Rob's keys in my hand, making sure they were there. I looked to my shoes. They were there too. Behind me was nothing. Not nothing—Rob's car and many cars and Old Montauk Highway. And daisies. The ocean, far down.

The bar had become crowded, but it was easy to find them. A room changed wholly when Rourke was in it—energy tagged about him in a helix or spiral. They were leaning against the bar, shoulder to shoulder. I squeezed through the pack, and they observed me. Rourke put out his arms, jerked me to his chest, and lifted me onto a stool, his hands cramming up like wings into the foundation of my ribs. He touched my halter top.

"Don't you think this is a little revealing to wear in public?"

"Leave her alone, Harrison," Rob said. "It's my birthday."

"Lucky girl," Rourke told me. "Today's your lucky day."

They played a serious game of pool, which Rob won because he was high on coke. The old ceiling fan above the table barely stirred their hair, and there was a sizeable crowd; when you're high that way, your victories are mesmerizing to observers.

"C'mon," Rob said to Rourke. "Double or nothing."

Rourke handed Rob two twenties and sat on a stool, slipping me up onto his thigh. Roger from the slow pitch team said, "I'm up next."

The next game began, but I did not watch. I was distracted by the feeling of Rourke's thigh between my legs. He was distracted too. I could tell by the death-like tranquility of his hands. Through my stupor, I heard the knock and split of the balls, the slugs of color whizzing across the verdant felt, the thuck-ish gulps of the pockets, the dry prismatics of conversation.

"He's really good," I whispered. "Too bad there's no girl to impress."

"There is," Rourke said. "You."

WE WERE OUTSIDE—MIDNIGHT, a little after. Beyond me was the seawall and behind me, the encroaching and excessively coherent chime of Rob's keys. The sound kicked up irregularly, which was an indication of how Rob was walking. He'd had six shots of tequila. Roger and the guys were taking him to meet Irish girls at a bar called The Place.

"You remember who's driving you?" Rourke asked.

Rob took his time answering, as if relishing the messy power he had, as if he could not be completely perceived, as if his drunkenness concealed him.

"We're going dancing," he slurred as he made his way around the rear of Rourke's car, moving with the neurotic confidence of a heavily armed man. Headlights appeared behind him—a car approached from Montauk. "She loves to dance," he said of me, to me. Only not to me. "Come dance."

Rourke grabbed Rob by the shoulders and lifted him forcefully into the fender just as the car shot past. The rush of wind blew open their jackets. He tried to shake Rourke off. Rourke gripped him tighter, shoving him further.

He said, "I'm all right."

Rourke said, "I know you are."

Rob's gaze unfixed itself from Rourke's chest and trawled upward, its focus continuously adjusting until arriving at Rourke's face. His mouth split into a solemn smile of recognition. His left hand skimmed his hair, and he tossed his head to the sky, and when another car came, the headlights glinted off Rob's teeth, and his eyes looked like dry tobacco rings. He threw his arm around Rourke, falling into him, and for a time they were speechless. Rourke took the keys from Rob's hand.

Roger and his friends jogged down the porch steps. "C'mon, birthday boy, let's go get laid." Rob lurched away with the pack and settled into the front seat of Roger's Camero. Roger was a law student who made three grand a sum-mer waiting tables at Gosman's. He flashed his lights as they pulled away and they all screamed out the windows; going down the street, beeping the horn.

THE DOOR TO HOME closed on the night. I showered while he washed dishes, and when the water turned hotter, I knew he was done. I dressed in a half-slip and one of his sweaters, and I knelt alongside him in the living room, which was chill and inhospitable without a fire. He was deconstructing a camera. I had never seen it before. I didn't know where it had come from or what was broken about it. In the action of his hands I tried to follow the action of his mind. He was studying the blown-out mess like it was potentially animate, like a chess board mid-game. His hand hovered in studious benediction over the parts before settling on the pieces to replace. It was like seeking proof of science, the science of shredding a whole, of exposing the viscera of an object, of probing fragments. I felt sad to see him look at things that way and to doubt himself, his way of seeing whole.

He undressed me before the mirror. We floated in reverse on withered and medicinal silver, our flesh dislodged and distrait, our persons alleviated from time, like figures in an old photograph, like a cowboy and the woman he loved. His chest was a block of copper above me; I was copper too, both of us that way from sun. His head was inclined and his hair in flopping strips, his lips moving down from my neck to my shoulder, his eyes following in the glass the work of his hands, his mind consuming the product of its efforts. In bed he drew me onto his chest, and it was there I remained through to morning.

THE NEXT DAY WAS normal. I showered like normal, and after Rourke picked up Rob at somebody's house on West Lake Drive and they got the Cougar from Surfside, he and Rourke acted normal, whatever normal was for them—broken bones and film trivia, plates of eggs and engine options, sisters in trouble. One thing was different—when Rob got in his car to leave for Jersey, he kissed me and said, *I love you too.*

At the Overlook that afternoon, the saffron flare of the west saturated Rourke's skin. We were on our way to the restaurant, to the Lobster Roll. He was driving me to work, and he stopped there. The car swung off to the right and stopped at the edge of the cliff, where he parked, and together we confronted sundown. I told myself that I would die for him. Maybe I did not mean that, when to die for him would mean to be lost from him. Maybe I meant die *with* him, which was different. Yes, I would die with him. If he were to shift the car into drive and step on the gas and we were to rush from the summit, there would be no bottom to hit, no last or lowest. I believed that with my whole heart, and I knew it like I knew my own name; for us there could be no end so terrible as an emotional end.

The light that warmed his torso kept his hips in symbolic darkness. I collapsed into the shadow of his lap, facing him, tracing my name into the parchment of his abdomen. And he sighed, laying his hand upon my bare back, fingering the straps of my shirt.

4.

My mother turned down the corner of her page then pushed her book to the center of the table. She leaned back on the kitchen chair, and her arms came down beside her. The milk in her coffee pooled to caramel streaks at top. "Feel like going shopping?"

"Shopping?"

"To Gertz. Or to the drug store."

"For what?"

She thought for a moment. "Shampoo. Do you have shampoo?"

"I figured I'd just take some from upstairs."

"Are you sure?"

"Sure, I'm sure."

She nodded. "What did your father say when he called?"

"To let him know if I needed money. For books or whatever."

"Great," she said. She rotated her feet at the ankles and stretched her legs. "I'm glad you won't be far from them. Have you finished packing?"

"Almost."

"Well, try to hurry. Lowie and David will be here at four."

Lowie and David were going to Pennsylvania for Labor Day weekend, so they offered to take my stuff to the dorm. All I really had were art supplies. I draped brushes in fabric and placed charcoals in plastic bags and paints in old coffee and cookie tins with lids that did not exactly fit. I tied pencils into logs with rubber bands. The pencils were not sharpened; I felt bad about that, so I took them apart and sharpened them. Once the cardboard box was full, I looked in. The contents appeared strange—I could remember touching them, using them, each of them, speaking shyly through them, but I could not recall what I had previously needed to say. The girl I'd been seemed very far off, like a cloud, as vaporous, as thin, as impossible to touch. There was a purity that was gone from me, a purity of essence—in its place stood something else, something I did not know to name. Maybe Rourke was right, maybe seeing whole was no longer possible. Maybe now was just pieces.

Mom and I left at the same time, and at the end of the lane she drove off with a merry wave, and I walked east towards town. The two main streets in East Hampton come together in an uncentered sort of cross, like the number four. I was uncomfortable with the idea of a crossroad. The crossroad is where people leave things—offerings and belongings of the dead. It's where your fate finds you. At the intersection of Main and Newtown, there's a traffic light. If you look, you can see a ponderous, otherworldly lilt. At least Montauk had a traffic circle.

I spotted Rourke easily from the far side of Herrick playground; he was like one superior beast in a herd. I walked to the northwest corner of the field and stood far from the crowd next to Mike Sheer, who was in a neck brace. He'd been injured while surfing at Ditch Plains, so he asked Rourke to play for him. Mike screamed, and his face gathered into horizontal rolls of flesh. He glanced quick at me. "How you doing?"

"Okay, thanks."

Rourke was in center field. His hair cleaved from the minerals his skin had secreted, and it spindled against his forehead. His thighs were smut green. He looked younger than he must have been. He looked eighteen; he must have been twenty-five.

In rugby, there is shouting. There is the accumulation of bodies like an unlit pyre, a knotted ring of flesh, cranking by degrees then treading as one before a rapid and unaccountable break—that is called a *maul*. And in the moments preceding penalties and free kicks, there are slack hands on hips and aimless walks and heads tossed to the sky or stretched in jerks to either side or dropped, chins to chests. It's a very certain sport, sometimes seeming not a sport at all but a vain and cryptic brotherhood. At the end come the moving monoliths, the departure from the field, the bloody, bruised threes and fours, the resounding emancipation, like every creature on earth freed at once from its cage. At the end there is the turn on you and the sense of being set upon. There is the back-slapping and hip-slapping and the ritual approach to losers. In a ring about the players is a mass of adrenaline, and you are wise to say *Hello*. There you meet the primal gaze. You see the mental exertion followed by a vague sharpening, a pop in the neck, a click in the skull, a sluggish missile up the spine of the special fluid of memory and a not quite coherent response—*Hey Evie*. They all knew me, not just from Rourke but from school, from the pictures I'd taken, from around.

"See you guys down at Pat's," Mike said to me and Rourke.

Rourke wiped his forehead with the tattered wrist of his shirt, shoving up so the dirt mixed with sweat into a streak. "See you."

The car was on Newtown Lane, facing the village. "You can shower at my mother's," I said. "The house is empty."

He made a U-turn. The mask of his skin was stone.

It was a queer and dreary feeling that came from being with him again in that house; the dimensions of everything had changed. We had become larger and home hideously reduced. We were like giants, colossi, Apollo at Rhodes, and Alice in the Rabbit's house, limbs poking through casements, heads cramming through chimneys.

Behind the upstairs bathroom toilet there was a window. I stared through it while he showered, and though I did not hear the water stop, I did feel him regarding me. It was a bastard regard, an outer view, as if I were not me but a likeness of myself. Drops fell from his lashes to his cheekbones, and there was redness there. I wondered if he had been crying. He drew me to my feet, and one of his hands found my throat while the other slipped behind the satiny bridge of my lower back. I could feel how badly he wanted me, with his chest bearing down and his pelvis rigid, and through the towel, his penis. I could feel the agony of resistance. He caressed my neck over and over. His fingertips flattening the slim muscles and petting the trachea, measuring the fragile cervix, calibrating the breaths, considering the enormity of the burden of me.

WE STOPPED OFF AT a house back in Clearwater. Cars lined both sides of the unlit street, so Rourke swung onto the front lawn. I looked back at the GTO as we walked away; it looked as if it had landed from the sky. Through the windows came the thud of Kashmir—*Da na na na nat. Da na na na nat.* An irregular footpath led to a shredded screen door that snapped open as we arrived, exceedingly past its range. It had no spring, so it cracked against the side of the shingled house. It sounded like gunfire.

Black Pat shoved a boy through the door, saying, "Do it outside."

Rourke pulled me back as the boy flew down to vomit.

"Oh, shit. Sorry about that Harrison," Black Pat said. "I just don't wanna get one of those chain reactions going. Next thing you know it's a big mess of puke to clean."

Rourke said not to worry about it.

"You okay, Evie?" Black Pat asked. I said that I was. We'd taken chemistry together and marching band. I wondered if he considered what I was doing there with Rourke or if he knew. He didn't seem surprised to see me there.

Inside, we hit a wall of smoke and alcohol and about thirty guys. The scuffed sheetrock room was flat gray and overcast and filthy with its own smell which was the smell of shedding skin. Rourke was drawn into the crowd—there were people there whom he knew from somewhere, Jersey or college. I walked towards the back to find him, tugging the hem of my shorts down past the hinge of my thighs and straightening my shirt to conceal my breasts, which were perceptible through the cotton. I should have changed at my mother's when Rourke showered. I should have known better. I should have remembered that men are free, but you are not, that they cannot be held accountable for their reactions to your negligence. Sometimes you're too busy leading your own life to remember theirs.

Plastic cups of beer levitated at various heights, and a bottle of Myers made the rounds. Someone handed me some. *Drink up.* I took the cup and pretended to drink. I felt ill; possibly I would vomit. I didn't want to start one of those chain reaction things.

The dining room was empty except for two bicycles propped beneath a regulation dart board, and around the board on the wall was a ring of hole pokes. On the left was a cramped cube of a kitchen with avocado-colored appliances. A man with red hair and a hulking back stood on the linoleum telling stories, jabbing as he spoke. It was Tommy with the strange ears, from the day on the boardwalk. Rourke was directly opposite, leaning on the counter. Nearby there were two pretty girls, maybe not pretty, maybe they just seemed that way with hair to toss, hair that smelled of florid shampoo, hair he could not help but inhale. The girls were not local. I could tell by the way they were dressed. They were Jersey girls; they'd probably come with Tommy. He seemed like the type who'd have two girls.

Rourke looked different. It was the smile he was using, with his top and bottom teeth meeting and his dimple cutting like fire into his face. He saw me. He saw me hesitate. He beheld me stiffly, inertly, as if staring at a compelling design on the wall. He had two beers—one for him, one for me. I moved on.

Past the bikes, through a slit in the side of a closed door, came an insubstantial flickering. There was music, room music—"Dark Side of the Moon." I pushed the door open enough to see five bodies and a television with the sound turned down. They were doing coke. I walked in anyway; I had nowhere else to go. Paneling warped off the walls and two clay lamps were draped with shredded yellow towels. There were six people, sitting upright, sitting hunched, sitting on the floor, all around a coffee table. I sat too, straddling the arm of a vinyl recliner, my left calf grazing the thigh of the person in it.

"Hey." It was Biff, the hitchhiker. "You hang with a pretty rough crowd."

"Yeah, well how else would I ever get to see you?"

Biff was quick to talk, which I took to mean that he had no drugs. As a rule the one with drugs is not so quick to talk. Across from us, perched on the rim of the couch and focusing on nothing in particular, was a big guy with ruddy skin and tame blond hair that skimmed the shoulders of his Jimmy Buffet concert shirt. Powell had friends with skin like that. Beneath the waistband was white to the knees. "This is Chet," Biff said. "Chet comes up from Florida in the summers. On his boat."

I nodded hello, he nodded too. I wondered was Chet short for Chester, and if so, did that account for his transformation in life from whatever he'd once been to what he'd become.

"Florida is hot," I said.

"Not enough for me," he said, averting his eyes as he drove a heap of powder to the center of a plate and began to chop. The muscle in the zone beneath his right eye shuddered. Sometimes you hear of gentle giants. Despite his questionable choices, he did not frighten me. No one could induce the sick fear I felt with Rourke, the fear and appalling pressure, which was a hideous exertion, like a vacuum sucking the liquor of my heart.

Chet nudged the results in my direction. "Oh," I said, "no thanks." I didn't want to seem ungrateful, so I came closer, kneeling.

His eyes met mine; he wore thick glasses. "Go ahead."

"Actually, I feel a little—dizzy, I guess."

Biff took up the plate. He asked, "You looked out of it at the game." He pinched his nostrils.

Two guys on the periphery, one of them still in a muddy rugby shirt, were talking about weather—forecasters, maps, advancements in accuracy. This led somehow to a heated disquisition of world wars and policy coups, with Biff joining in. Their knowledge impressed me far less than the fact that they could sit even though they were so high. You must just hit a critical point of intoxication, a mortal sort of limit, and your body is in shock and indisposed to motion. I waited until they had done another round before I stood to leave, which was on my part an excruciating gesture of propriety.

"Taking off?" Chet said.

"I guess."

"Come on back," Chet said. "We'll be here."

On my way out, I heard a voice say, *Harrison Rourke.*

He hadn't moved from where I'd left him; he was still in the kitchen, leaning on the counter, holding a Heineken. No one saw that he was disconnected from everything about him, that his smile was a lie, that he hated Heineken. No one saw his eyes fixed on the door I'd just exited. Rob would have seen, but Rob wasn't there.

Rourke looked sexier than ever—it must have been the worlds advancing between us. A trace of sunburn reddened his tan, and his skin glowed meanly. The tousled heaviness of his hair, the conceited set to his jaw. His eyes, narrow and impervious as marbles, tilted ever so slightly down at the outer rims, blaming me—not unjustly—for a deficiency that was his own. And his remaining features, all slightly too prominent, though the fit in general was extraordinary. And the excellence beneath the clothes. Through the layers I processed the data of his shape. I thought how lucky I'd been to fuck him, how vicious would be my physical loss. I became exceedingly conscious of my breasts, of their desirability. I wanted to lay his hands upon them, to have him take them into his mouth. Oh, the way he looked at me.

I moved through a set of sliding doors frosted between the panes from condensation, and I stepped onto a deteriorating deck that faced a wall of scrubby trees. There was a dented sweating keg surrounded by guys, one of them pumping the tap, and on his wrist was a frayed rope bracelet, orange and purple. To the right were voices. To the left, past a cluster of taken chairs, an alcove beneath trees. I went left and leaned on the railing. It was a short drop to the ground. It was not impossible to jump, to run to a main road—Springs Fireplace was nearest, but then I would never see him again. If I waited, I would see him again. I considered going back to Biff and Chet, but it would not have been good. Rourke would not stay passive twice.

WHEN THE SECOND BARTENDER arrived at Surfside on the night of Rob's birthday, Val took Rob and me through the stifling, bustling hub of the kitchen to the walk-in, where all things were dead and chilled. Val removed from his silk shirt pocket a brown glass vial with a baby spoon attached by chain to the cap. He stuffed the spoon full and offered it first to me.

"Ho! Forget about it," Rob said. "She stays clean."

"Jesus," Val said. "No liquor, no coke. What kind of asshole is this friend of yours anyway?"

"Not the kind you want to swap punches with, pretty boy," Rob said, adding. "He fights."

"So what? Everybody fights. What do you mean *fights*?"

"Fights, fights, you know, *bing, bing*," Rob jabbed at a gigantic mayonnaise jar on a shelf. "Light heavyweight. One seventy-eight," Rob said. "Exact." *Eggzact.*

"Professional?"

"Amateur. This would have been his first Olympics."

"Oh shit," Val said. "The boycott. What's he gonna do now?"

"Probably he'll turn. He has a couple offers."

"More money to be made in professional."

"There's money to be made in everything," Rob said. "If you know what I mean."

Later that night we were lying there, Rourke and me; around us things were quiet. The lupine night came through the windows, haggard, sinuous, haunting, hunting. Stepping in steps that were bony and tall like wolf legs.

"Do you fight?" I asked.

He did not seem surprised by the question. He said yes.

"Is that why you have scars?" He had several.

He pointed to his chest above his heart. There was a three-inch line. "That I got when I was thirteen. In a fight over my father. After he died." He pointed to his left arm. "This one on my arm like a star is from a dog. A bull mastiff. See, it puckers."

"This one?" It was on his thigh. I touched it.

"You don't want to know about this one."

"And how come you don't do drugs?"

"Because they involve debts to people not worth repaying. Because they show up in blood and urine." He yanked me up the ladder of his chest by the swell of my ass. He aligned us, naturally, perfectly. In a serious undertone he added, "Because I don't like to paralyze myself. Do you?"

"What did you win? Prizes?"

"Prizes, sure," he told me. "And bets."

SOMEONE HELD MY SHOULDERS—Mark Ross. It made sense to see him, in some miserable, supernatural regard. The night had been filled with bad omens, mongrel cruciforms, carried along like sky mats.

He bent to kiss me. The beginnings of a beard sprouted from his chin. "How *are* you?" he inquired. His concern was diligent, as though I'd survived an ordeal, which possibly I had. I didn't bother to ask what he was doing there. He knew somebody, same as me.

He slipped a hand into his khakis and said, "Tommy's out. Tommy Lydell. He and Harrison—"

"Tommy's the big guy," I said. "From Jersey."

"That's right."

"Did he go to college with you guys too?"

"Tommy? I doubt Tommy made it past eighth grade. I met him in L.A. He came a bunch of times," Mark said, "for fights. We keep in touch. He's actually staying at my house tonight."

"Oh." I said oh. Mark's voice going in and going out.

"This isn't really the place for you."

"I guess I've seen worse."

"No, you haven't. Trust me. The night is young."

I took a step back, and he followed, closing further in, parting a fan of leaves above my head that was obstructing his view. When they flopped back, he snapped off the shoot, twisting crudely, throwing the piece down. I looked at it on the deck. Parrot-green ligaments had sprung from the torn wrist of bark. The leaves stayed poised, dumb to the fact of their ruin.

"Do you know," Mark said, "how beautiful you are?"

I thought to change the subject. I thought to make conversation new. I thought of Rourke's frame of mind and my own. I leaned on the rail. Mark leaned as well, his forearm skimming mine. The stars were far—I pointed.

"Look," I said, "September's coming."

"Actually," he said, "September's here."

AT THE DRIVER'S DOOR, he paused. "Want to drive?"

I looked across the roof, and the metal tags cartwheeled over. We changed places, and our bodies brushed at the front of the car, which was unsettling. Behind the wheel, the view was his view, which was also unsettling.

"Ever driven standard?" he asked.

I pressed back into the seat to stop shivering. "No."

"Take the stick." He covered my hand with his own. I felt the mass of his palm, the way he was saturated with himself, and that was secure, like a bony plate or armature. He jiggled the stick. "Neutral."

I started the engine, and the car came alive. Though I knew the car's specifications—a 400 cubic V-8 engine with 335 horsepower and a 4-barrel Rochester carb—I hadn't until then understood their meaning. It sort of lifted and hovered.

"Step on the clutch," he said, and with him I guided the bar to first, where it nuzzled into a nook. There was no need to ask if I was in gear—nothing feels so right as a perfect fit. "Come off slowly, as you press the accelerator."

The car churned down and pulled forward, making me think of sled dogs. It seemed to want to go faster, farther. He drew down my hand, telling me to hit the clutch again, and I did, and he helped me pop it up into second, and then third.

We went to the ocean. It was where he wanted to go. Indian Wells was closest. He pushed a cassette in the deck. I'll never forget the tape. I will never in my life listen to it again.

"Still cold?" he asked, facing the sea.

I said that I was, and he removed his jacket, edging side to side, shoulders and arms moving about in the limited frame of the car, and he wrapped me in it, rubbing my arms and back. It was a navy blue windbreaker with an emblem on it, possibly a Yankees emblem, though possibly I was wrong. I did not know my teams. I felt the personal fleece, the lining that had been impressed like magic to take his shape, and that was unbearable. I could not bear the idea of his existence so confirmed. There was a blanket in back that smelled of sweat and wilted grass, and when he wrapped it around me, sand from the morning trickled down.

He asked about my family. I said I didn't have one.

"You have a mother," he said. "I've met her."

Strange that he had, strange that he'd kept it to himself. Probably he'd met her with Kate. Maybe Kate had called her *Mom*, saying, *Harrison, this is my Mom*, and maybe Rourke shook my mother's hand and told her what a great girl Kate was, all the while searching in my mother for traces of me.

"Yes," I said, since I had nothing to deny. "A father too."

I didn't know what he was getting at, but I was convinced of my parents' irrelevance regardless. I thought of his house in Spring Lake, his apartment, those giant rhododendrons. And his chest, disfigured in a fight over his dead father. You didn't need to know his parents to *feel* them; they were incorporated into the boy they'd raised. But whatever it was that had attracted him to me was the result of *absence*, not *presence*. The thought of his father made me feel guilty to take my own parents for granted in front of him.

He laid his hand on my thigh, and we did not move, immobilized as we were by the insinuation of sex, by its promise to restore us to conditions of denial, to get us past the business of relating.

"It's not what you might think," I said, though it was too late, really, to speak of myself. "It's like something else, like never having been heard."

Rourke withdrew his hand with excessive caution, as if from a house of cards, and he lifted my face—reverently, like a chalice.

"Something," he said, kissing me, "about you."

His mouth, that mouth, nearing, advancing, seeking in vain to capture what I did not have. I wished I could have helped him. I wished I didn't know so well the frustration he felt. His wrists joined beneath my chin, supporting my head. His thumbs pressed my cheeks.

"Do you know," he said. "What I feel?"

I said yes, yes I did. A kiss was not enough and sex was not enough and living with him was not enough. I knew the irony of having failed despite the extremes of our consummation, that it was not conceivable to reach the place we needed to go. I needed to be born once more through the skin of him. On the lids of his eyes were creases. In them were new lights, raw lights. His knuckle dug into my jawbone, forcing my head sideways, my ear to his lips.

"And you," he said. "You would do anything."

"Anything," I said, beginning to cry.

He seemed shaken by the ease of my admission, by my naturalness and my liberty, by my immunity to whatever it was that obliged him. I thought to wipe my eyes, but I liked looking as I felt, a thing half-dead. He covered my mouth with his palm, and he waited, breathing, driving himself back.

"Then I'll take what you can't give," he said. "Nothing."

The light from a street lamp made a pool of white, turning everything osseous and macabre, making pearls in the air, like a stationary rain. In such light I could see. I could see he was alive, extraordinarily alive, and I could see his will to persevere. I could see that he had left that will, that he needed to return to it. I could see the hatred that followed from that, the rage at his defeat in wanting me. Once he had been a man and free. But then me. And him leaving, him going back, him feeling degenerate. It was the fiend he believed himself to be that expressed itself in the light.

We didn't leave until daybreak. We remained in the car for hours. We were there so long that I was very badly hurt. We had to go until there was no going back, until it was certain that we could not meet again without recalling the degradation of our final night, until all that we'd shared had turned irreclaimable. His eyes never stopped staring. They shed their own color, like casting off black. The malice in his face, the wry malice, the animosity, the challenge to his successor—could he see him? It seemed that he could see him. He seemed to be leaving in me some message or a sign; it seemed he could connect or converse.

IN THE END, THE car was moving, and I was receding, every second becoming less and less, all of space shortening and shriveling. I could feel the car seat collapsed, my body on its side, and, through my mouth, breaths like a felled animal, breaths in a surface pant. I could hear the hydraulic thunder of the engine, like a sound from some distant aftertime, and the fizz of the wind through glass.

I might have felt the plunge from the crest of the highway into Montauk. I might have sensed without seeing, the empty and unprepossessing village. I raised one hand to my window. My hand was heavy like lead reaching into the dead sunrise. And, after that, nothing—not nothing, just not the usual some-things.

I dreamt of a woman from the East, from India. She was crying and on her face were tears that were not tears but burnt braids, burnt black hair attached at the underside to her skin, running in lines to her jaw and hanging beneath. *These have not disappeared*, she said, *since coming to America*. Disappeared is such a beautiful word, I thought—*Appeared, dis-appeared*. Your husband must be sorry, I told her. I could see her husband, sitting.

And then an owl and a tombish tree and, in it, a decrepit eagle. Gray saliva spilled from its beak. The skies were also gray. The owl said to me, *Your mother was luxurious and your father was luxurious*. I asked the eagle what I must be. The eagle said, *Be what you were meant to be*.

Inside a ring of tall stumps—there were beasts to kill. I was given a knife. There was a black tiger, its belly synthetic like an inner tube, and a flock of white monkeys that were not complete monkeys, with tongues that wagged like flags from the nook between their legs.

I was hauling boxes through tides of sand. I was alone, and the terrain was dry and ragged. I passed a figure suspended in the cliffs, red and robed and supported by string, warning me. Ahead of me was the camp, ophidian like a train of lantern lights. From the camp I could be seen, and my march was long, leading me to reflect upon my own worst and weakest qualities.

Through my eyes I saw a figure, several figures melding to one, which is chemistry. The figure was a chemist. I was lifted, levitated. I was immobilized, and there was an imposing wetness on my legs, whales and dead otters, and around my neck, a cuff of clay. No thoughts, no thoughts, just a spectrum of points evacuated, glittering. There were hands, sure and soft and hardly there, hands fascinated by the discrepancy between us, the science that separated us, hands that could not conceal the joy of having me defenseless.

I tried to feel my head; my hand could not find it; it hurt to think where it had gone. I did not move from my back. I could not, so I waited. Slowly and by degrees, questions formed in my mind, not many, only so many as my intellect could tolerate. I felt pressure in my pelvis. I wondered if I needed to pee.

"What happened?" I asked. Maybe not, maybe I tried to ask.

A cup met my lips. "You had a fever," he said. His voice.

My eyes, they opened, and my hand. I tried to stop the light, the sunshine was too much. Rourke raised my shoulders inches from the pillow and shifted me to face away from the window. I was bones in his hands. Beneath the sheets I was naked.

"How long—"

He said two days.

Two days. Yes, I remembered—speaking. "What did I say?"

He moved to where I could see him easily. "You slept." I met his eyes; they had grown small. He'd spent two days alone with his trespass and his lust. Two days to think what it meant to abandon me, betray me. I wondered did he fuck me while I was sleeping.

"What did I say?"

"You apologized," he said, cautious not to tender his voice. "You said you were sorry."

A bath waited. He carried me there. Tepid water was lapping against the rim, reminding me of former waters, water from cups and pools and puddles and from other tubs I have known. The porcelain was abraded but clean the way I'd left it, and on the sink was toothpaste we'd bought one day at the IGA on Main Street. He set me down into the bath, feet first, then his hands on my arms, helping me to sit. I would have refused, but I was not sound, I was not well, and he was not to be denied. He sat too, on the rim of the tub. There were marks on his neck by his collarbone and a crimson scab along his forearm by the dog scar. I wondered had I caused them. I straightened my legs and shivered as he trickled water from his hands onto my head, my back, my chest, and he helped me wash. I looked up, and he looked down and there was an admission in his eyes that matched the feeling of admission in my own. It was unfortunate, all of it. It was not supposed to have ended that way, with him clinging so kindly to the shell of me and our eyes meeting. Had we left each other after the car, we would have had only the worst to sustain us. But the accident of my illness ruined everything. His presence by the bed, the remedial caress of his hands, the way he'd nursed me like a dressless doll through an anxious sleep, the pouring of water, the pouring of water—I couldn't think anymore. My heart was thoroughly, thoroughly broken.

"I thought—I guess I thought you would go someplace close."

He looked at me carefully, so there could be no doubt, and he said, "It won't be close."

FIVE

TROPICS

This is where I falter. This is where I lose myself. This is
where years invert and minutes reverse and ideas
of what was good and right upend.
This is where time is dispersed, thrown down like leaves or stones to be read.

It's difficult to say really what happened.
I know that my heartache was indescribable, the depth of my loneliness
astonishing. I know that I worked very hard, and I never intended to hurt anyone.
I cannot describe a life dispossessed of happiness.
Episodes and events stand out as happy,
though that happiness was the sort of euphoria you feel at a party you throw
for yourself, when you say over and over the fun you're having, but afterwards you're
sick with self-loathing, wistful all the more for having come so close, for
having approximated some rhapsody of being.
What I missed was something lost. What I'd lost was my very self.

Perhaps I was resilient, perhaps if called upon by God,
I might have survived fire or famine. But who is so able as to endure heartbreak.
Heartbreak is a puzzle apart—pieces missing, pieces mutilated. It is severest poverty, a
crippling disproportion between what you need and what you have, between what you
perceive and what you can describe. It is to abide chronically for relief
without possessing the vaguest knowledge of what form that relief might take.
It is to be consumed by the wait, and I was.

I became someone new. She was a mystery.
She was striking like the frayed end of a live wire. She took risks
because in order to drown you must stay close to the degenerate arm of the sea.
I remember her, pleading into the faces of friends for nothing. They could give nothing.
Who did they see when it was not herself that she showed.
What was it they wanted when her lack outweighed her capacity,
her desperation exceeded her gifts, her own competence eluded her.
Though always there are angels—people with the soul capacity to see beyond your
mask, who come forward to say something meaningful to the purity in you.

If she was loved, it's because it's easier to be lovable than to be honest.
If she loved in return, and it's not impossible that she did, it was a thin sort of love,
emaciated and apt to vary,
a love that would not alter his design nor fracture his standing.
Often I regretted the confusion I caused.

If there are rules for finding your way through darkness, I tried to follow them.
I tried to behave my way out of sorrow. I gave away the little I had,
unencumbered by a desire for reciprocation.
I had no reason to lie, no agenda to keep me from listening.
My small assurances were trusted, and if it was ironic that as a source of compassion
I above others was preferred—I, who could grasp nothing—it gave me a numb sort of
gladness that those closest to me improved exceedingly.

And yet that attentiveness was not without flaw; it was limited and erratic,
governed by arbitrary factors like dreams and the seasons, cars and passing shadows.
I would be moved suddenly to sadness. A reflection or a trivial wind, or sunlight
receding menially, collapsed against a street corner like a retired bit of machinery.
Sometimes I would get almost to where I was going, only to turn home again.
There would be some influence, some fragment—
a color or noise, a texture or smell—and I would be detached entirely
from the requirements of time. Oh and blankness then,
and lapses of chilling indifference.
Back home, wherever it was that home happened to be,
I would sit in the gentle coma of my affliction, thinking only of him.

This is not fun. This is the part when my youth escapes me,
when I age, with everything shutting down.
These are years without accident or incident,
when the end of each day is determined before it begins—
there is no possibility of him—none, just as in July there is no snow.

There are people you hear about, miners in Siberia,
people who knead the guts of the earth for poor reward,
people too indigent, too cowed by cold and hunger and lightlessness to strike.
They drink themselves to sleep, and why not? Certain conditions are not to be tolerated,
certain states are so deprived of tenderness that you discover the meaning of hell.
Hell is only loneliness, a place without play for the soul, a place without God. How
could there be God in loneliness when God is presence?

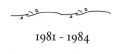

1981 - 1984

I.

YOU CAN'T BRING THAT BIRD IN HERE.

The bird twitches lamely in my scarf. Mark comes at me from the couch, dropping his paper, crossing over.

I don't understand. "It's already here."

"I mean, you can't keep it here. It's full of disease." He ushers me onto the terrace. "Set it free."

I look down 25 floors. I say, "It can't fly."

"It's a bird," he says. "It'll figure it out."

MARK DOESN'T KNOW ABOUT birds. We once saw a documentary about condor eggs stolen from their nests and hatched in captivity at the San Diego Zoo. The narrator said how those eggs are the last, and the risk of them being eaten by predators is very, very great. In the movie, puppet bird-heads nursed chicks through rubber gaskets in incubators, and wildfowl technicians scaled mountains to set fattened chicks in place of the eggs they'd stolen. The camera, the scrupulous, supernatural eye, remained on the baby as it sat blinking and shivering, awaiting the likely rejection of its own mother.

"Why are you crying?" Mark asked. "They're being rescued."

He could not conceive of the depth of the mess. He could not see the calamity of a genetic last chance, of having your offspring stolen because you cannot be depended upon to provide. In his way he tried to help.

"Let's fly to Washington, D.C.," he suggested soon after, "to see the cherry blossoms. And the zoo."

ON THE AIRPLANE THE stewardess catered to us. Her tag said *Jana*. When Jana bent, she bent low. She served us croissants and fruit salad with real silverware and mimosas in real glass, and when we dropped things like sunglasses or sugar cubes, she retrieved them. Jana seemed to think she could get something from us, or anyway, from Mark, like maybe he would leave me on board and take her instead. Humans are remarkable in terms of need. We all have plans like maps in the mind.

"Here ya'll go," Jana said, crooning down cheerfully to hand me aspirin, revealing exquisite cleavage. The color of her eyes saturated off her iris and bled into the white, making a subordinate color, which was spooky. If I had eyes like that, I might have become a stewardess too. They were stewardessy eyes. I took the aspirin and requested two more. It was one of those kinds of headaches.

In our room at the Hay-Adams, there were pictures of cannons and stiff clusters of men in white stockings and small shoes signing documents. Maybe the shoes were not small, maybe that had to do with perspective—what with black being at the end run of white.

I played with the curtains, opening and closing them—White House. No White House. When Mark went for a run, I took a walk and ended up in the lounge. The bartender seemed to think I needed a margarita, and after I finished it, I thought I needed another. There was a stack of cocktail napkins, and I had the urge to draw—not so much to draw as to feel the pen squish into the cushion cube of paper. I drew several intertwining things such as feather lusts and bent brooms, holiday cobs and tatters of burlap.

Eventually Mark rushed in. "Have you been here the whole time? I've been looking all over for you." He talked overloud as if to a dog he'd left tied to a parking meter. Mark doesn't like people to think he is not tending to things. He tipped the bartender then steered me toward the door. "So you've been been drawing!" he said, "Good! Very good." He was always trying to get me to draw.

I left the napkins in an ashtray on our way out.

IN THE EARLY MORNING before the zoo, we went to the cherry blossoms. We were first there, and it was nice to stroll beneath the continuous parasol of flowers with the Washington Monument in the background like a stylus refer- ring to the contradictory infinitude of heaven. Actually *zoo* is incorrect. Zoos are *conservation societies* now, which is why there are pie charts and bar graphs. But visitors who do not want to read about environmental equilibrium can still enjoy the sight of submission. They can still see primal needs mock civility. They can still make secret sense of their own commonplaceness.

Much like zoos, television shows bring us safely to the edge of ourselves, thus alleviating the pressures of civil obedience. We like to witness insolence and audacity because afterwards we feel we have been someplace, done some- thing. Television actors are kind of zoo animals, behaving outlandishly despite the way they're watched. They occupy a dominion, a multitude of dominions—the studio, the camera, the airwaves, the television set, the living room. The America that is depicted and the America that is depicted to, and of course the celebrity they happen to be. The *zoo* of television.

Mark told me the animals have no memory of home. And yet I could see echoes of savagery and pride. I could see first nature. In order to persevere, they have assigned home to a position within. They have stored it, biotically, constitutionally. They are safeguarding it, sharpening its concept over time. By their eyes they say—*We will return.*

There are lessons in the insights of the lost. Look into the eyes of anyone who has suffered diaspora and you will find a home, implicit and original, in pieces no larger than pollen or powder, glinting like specks of starlight through the silk of night. You will wish their home were your home. You will envy their inner richness. You will know irony because you are proportionately homeless and poorer—you have nothing substantial to assist your identity. Home is elusive to you because what you have been endeavoring after is a zone of determination, dignity, self-mastery. Such things cannot be found, only built. To begin, you have to relinquish false knowledge of a false self. You have to let go. You have to allow your learned rendition of reality to turn back to conjecture, allow your life to grow small again, to go to art, like patterns overall in wallpaper when you step backwards, like someone long beloved left at a railway station, growing narrower and shallower as the train pulls away, like a hugeness waning. And when it's far gone, you can actually *see* it.

"There's one there." Mark pointed to a tiger. "*Blanche.*"

She was high in the grass, the fake zoo grass. I saw her eyes and chocolate flame markings. I saw her panting at rest. It seemed to me that she was missing the moonlight. I wondered if she missed the moonlight as much as I miss drunken walls of cattails by the bay and barefoot walks across parking lots coated with the frailest layer of sand, blown like glitter from the palm of a giant hand. Can she hear the thudding bluster of wind against the night the way I can hear the roaring fortress of the sea? Does she too hate her hunger—when her appetite stirs, does a plate appear? The awfulest hunger is the type that is quenched too soon, before it becomes protracted and superior, before it becomes the kind that makes you graceful and clever.

On the way out, we passed a table full of skulls. A zoo worker was speaking to a group of children about primates. I wanted to touch the skulls; they were so shining. Mark said no. He said it would frighten me. But I do not mind bones. They endure; that's why they are called *remains*. People used to perform with bones, minstrels did.

I TURN IN FROM the terrace. The broken bird jerks and trembles. "I'll keep it someplace small," I say. "I won't catch a disease."

Mark sees we have reached an impasse. On certain subjects I cannot be moved. "Let's get Manny," he declares brightly.

Manuel the Super is in his office in the swill-green sub-basement, pouring black wax, which is coffee, from a thermos. He drinks ten cups of Bustelo a day. He is diabetic. When I first said that to Mark, he asked how I had come to know such a thing, and did Manuel confide in me. I said no. I just assumed that anyone so calm who drinks that much coffee is not drinking it for caffeine but for milk and sugar. The next time Mark saw Manny, he asked him directly, and Manny confirmed my guess, only he didn't use the word *diabetic*.

He said, "Technically, yes. I have a *litty touch of the sugar*."

On an otherwise vacant wood-finish formica desk is a miniature TV showing *The Dukes of Hazzard*. While Mark explains about the bird, Manny glides evenly to the cradle of my arms, steaming cup in hand.

"Twisted wing," he surmises, using one pinky to check. His voice dips beneath Mark's, speaking only to me. "Don't worry," he says with a wink. "She's not broken."

There is a cardboard box in a cove behind the service elevator, and when he kicks it out, a thousand keys jounce like sleigh bells against his uniformed navy thigh. Manny builds a bed of rags.

"We'll keep it in the boiler room. I'll tell Frank to lock the cats."

It takes eight days for the bird to heal. Manny constructs a Popsicle-stick splint, and Frank, the Assistant Super, buys it a seed ball. It isn't a very pretty bird, just a sparrow. I call it Windy.

"Technically," Manny says, when we finally release Windy in the courtyard, "we could have freed her sooner." Everything with Manny is always *technically this* and *technically that*.

We watch her skip and flutter. Spring is coming. There are crocuses. It scares me to see them, poking out like little green horns.

"But it was happy," he said. "Maybe it needed a vacation. It's gotta be tough, being a bird like that in a place like this."

WE DRINK STOLICHNAYA AT Cafe Luxembourg, and we lament the decline of America. We blame groups. Blaming groups shows that you yourself are not involved but that you are intellectually connected, especially if the group you blame appeared in Sunday's paper. When I say "we" I do not mean *me*, though I cannot exempt myself insofar as I am present. When a pack of wolves mangles a carcass, it doesn't matter which one's not eating—*that much*.

"You and Mark are so cute," Naomi says in the bathroom. Everything happens in the bathroom. The clock stops. There is a kink in the spin of the world. She comes out of the stall sniffing, pinching her nostrils. "It must be wonderful to be in love."

I don't think I'm in love, I don't know, maybe I am. I smile, sort of. Anyway, I think I smile.

Together we return to the table, me behind her and her ravishing ass ticking like a metronome set high. She hits shoulders, practically, of men in chairs on the way. We sit side by side. Naomi is a model. Sitting next to Naomi is like sitting next to a Kleenex. When you ask a question, she tilts her head and flits her eyes and asks you to repeat yourself, which you don't bother to do, because whatever you asked was already so abridged for her benefit that it does not bear repeating. We order the same meals. That is to say, she copies mine.

"Yeah, that," she simpers on the heels of my order, handing back an unopened menu.

Mark and Richard Spencer switch to Chivas Regal Royal Paisley, and they discuss supply-side economics, the $235 price of Hanson Citation ski boots, fluctuations in the index, and fishing in Argentina, which is the place to go to buy land. Richard is Mark's boss; he is the one with the dent in his head that makes him appear cleaveable. "Mia and I are going in September—why don't you two join us?" Richard says of Argentina, adding discreetly, "Everyone there is white. It's not what you'd think."

Richard's girlfriend's name is not *Mee-a*, but *My-ya*. This you must know without being told. If you cannot intuit this, it confirms your lack of sophistication. Then you will be ostracized and Mark will not make partner at work.

Mia loves September. "All the new fashion!"

Mark looks at me. His eyes wide, his manner encouraging. I'm supposed to reply. His head makes miniature downward jerks as if he's watching me struggle to tap out a dance he's already perfected.

"I've never thought about it that way," I say, slowly, carefully.

September to me is watermelon rinds with motile panes of black ants, and Puerto Rican guys fishing off East Side Drive and monarch butterflies migrating through New Jersey to Mexico and new school books. September is different from January, which is the squeaky bleat of noisemakers, and borrowed sweaters, and luckless romances. April is sitting on the roof at dawn and feeling your way through the house blind. July is cologne that smells like a Saturday night in the Bronx.

Brett snaps a match and lights a clove cigarette. Brett is Mark's best friend. They met in kindergarten at Collegiate. Naomi is Brett's date. Brett only dates models. Brett is sort of a fifty-percent man. He has the testosterone of a whole poured into a half. Not half like left or right, but half like partial or deformed. It can really scare me to look at him and think that half-man way. It's like dragon necks, with all the vitriolic temper of a flaming acid belly shooting up through a constricted passage. Brett is into bonds—Mark says bonds are *the thing*—and when he talks, Brett brays like an old quarterhorse.

"Let's head to Xenon after chow," he says, and a few tables down, a girl cries into her drink. I feel bad about that. I know how she feels.

At the curb I announce that I am not going. The curb is the place for such announcements, especially when everyone is already in the cab. At the curb, when everyone is already in a cab, it's too late for objections. Mark adjusts his gray cashmere overcoat. "What's up?"

"I have some reading to do, you know, for school." I wave lightly into the taxi, into the frosty aggregate of heads. "Goodnight."

Mark sees me to my own cab and pays in advance. It's not that he doesn't trust me with cash, it's his way of controlling outcomes. If ever there are ways to control outcomes, Mark discovers them. "Things happen to you," he always says. "You're like a magnet that way."

Through the plexiglas seat shield, Mark addresses the driver, "Drive safely. Very safely. Keep the change." He kisses me, lingeringly. He wants to come, but it would not look right. It would seem like something it should not. You can always count on Mark to conform, which is good. A girl has to be able to count on something.

The cab pulls out, and I submerge into the duct-taped vinyl seat. It feels good when you're drunk to sink into a taxi seat. It's like settling into a steamy bath or removing tight shoes. I'm happy to be relieved of having to socialize, or more accurately, to appear, somewhat like a logo. There is that flowery smell in the cab, that peculiar taxi smell, lazy and reliable and without obvious origin—not aerosol, not incense, not those little hanging pine trees. Denny says the glass crowns on dashboards contain tinctures and essences—vanilla and vetiver and frankincense—but tonight there is no crown.

The city snakes past, *very safely* past, and I pretend to fly. Sometimes in a taxi you can pretend you are flying. I raise my arms to each side and blur my eyesight like I am swooping, skimming the surface of the planet, absorbing all knowledge, which in fact, is none. At dinner they cataloged the ravages of nature—earthquakes, fires, floods, tornadoes, hurricanes, mudslides, plagues, killer bees. I wondered, why should the earth remain passive as we pave it?

When we creak off Tenth Avenue onto West Sixtieth, Carlo jogs out to the curb and waits. It's like a relay race, and I am the baton passed palm to palm. Carlo is the night doorman. I'm not sure what he does in the days. His children are at school, his wife is at work. Does he sleep past noon, eat cold pork chops, read the *Post*, go to the barber or the bank? When he comes to work, he comes handsomely dressed. Sometimes I see him walking from the subway, in a starched white shirt and a navy blue jacket, a Perry Ellis blazer he bought at Syms. The toes of his good black shoes are woven in a pattern like kitchen chair caning. Invariably there is a storm of aftershave.

Carlo grips the handle and assists me, steering me clear of the vehicle while closing the door forcefully and nodding professionally to the driver. "Thank you, Carlo." The alcohol on my breath vines up about us. I wonder if he pities me. Sometimes you cannot help but pity people you meet.

He whisks me through the entry and gestures to a hideaway by the mailboxes. "There's cleaning." He looks me over and thinks the better of it. "It's too much. No problem. I wait for Mr. Ross."

"No, no. It's okay. I'll take it." He hands it over, and I topple. "Wow," I smile. "Heavy." Mark sends everything out, even jeans get cleaned and pressed. Carlo tries to get the stuff back. There is a minor tussle. "I'm fine," I say, spinning the load behind me and involuntarily going half-round again to face the wall. I right myself. "I need something in here. A nightgown."

He's unconvinced but far too circumspect to confront me on the subject of lingerie. Anyway, Mr. Goldstein is at the curb. Carlo taps the elevator button for me and backs cautiously away. "You sure?"

"Yes," I say, "I'm sure."

"Okay then. Goodnight, dear."

"G'night, Carlo." I lean back as the doors begin to shut. Nice of him to call me *Dear*. I never call anyone that. You have to feel biggish, I think, to call someone *Dear*.

Sandlewood candles line the mahogany console that runs beneath the picture window in the master bedroom, and I light them. Sandlewood is an aphrodisiac, Mark says. Mark says men wear it for potency. I don't particularly like the smell, but at the moment they are the only candles. And electric light seems so explicit and distrustful. There is a mirror he bought for me, a hand-beveled mirror with sterling corner clips from Czechoslovakia. In that mirror I see a reflection of a reflection, something cubist and delusory. A propensity about the borders to transit and rhythm. Me, my face.

"You get more beautiful every day," Mark tells me.

One night I saw myself in another woman, a brunette with dark eye circles and orchid lips. She seemed so luckless, so afflicted, so damaged and indifferent. I could see how a man might want to possess a woman like that. I wondered how she'd made it to that state—breakable with secrets. Did she start out in high school, like me?

I sleep, I wake. I toss, I turn, I brood and flip, and flip, concentrating just to breathe. The ultra-fine texture of my pillow, the detergent smell of the sheets, the genteel tangle of my nightgown. On the bedside table is a bouquet of drying tulips. Every time a petal falls, it cracks when it hits. I think how there is a point at which every person has only six seconds left to live. It is possible to be photographed there, in those seconds, looking normal. Kennedy was photographed there, in the seconds right before he died, and those pictures are harder to look at than the ones of when he was actually dying. I guess we were all naïve before the gunfire. After the gunfire, no one was naïve.

I wonder how long Mark will be. Sometimes you depend upon the sight of yourself in someone else's eyes. Babies bat at toys to confirm their existence; touch proves that they are. Mark is proof. I play with the telephone, dialing, dialing, dropping it, and dialing. The receiver is extra heavy when no one is listening.

ROB CONTRIVES REASONS TO see me. The feeling when he comes is the feeling of a sudden rain. "Hey, lookin' good, doll."

He brings newspaper clippings about the MoMA reopening and Van Gogh at the Met and ones about current events such as artificial hearts and test tube babies. He asks for help filling out his Lotto slips, and he makes plans for all the things we're going to do with the winnings. He teaches me *creative accounting*—game theory and decision theory and magic tricks and hand signals for cheating at cards. How to decipher market data and racing forms and the science behind the daily number. All the tricks behind board-walk games, like pieces of block behind the Cats. "She's quick," he says approvingly to Mark. "*Very* quick. I think she's ready for under/overs."

When he leaves, I stand at the door, and even if I try to smile, the look on his face is aggrieved and blue, like the look of a healthy person leaving a hospital patient alone with their terminal disease. The door *ka-thunks* against the vacuum of the hallway, and I touch myself, feeling for effects. There ought to be effects. Like the swell of food in a previously empty stomach. But there is nothing. Even if the day is a beautiful day, sunny with wind or pluvial but warm, the world is ugly.

"Hold on, let's ask the boss," Mark says into the phone, laying the receiver on his shoulder, asking, "Sushi, baby, or Thai?"

I search for signs of Rob. A pillow he moved. A glass he used. There is a football on the coffee table. He'd rolled it in his hands. He had a new tattoo, a cobra on his right shoulder. Every time the ball spun, the cobra flickered. He was in a tank top, and there was a street film on his skin like he had been riding through the city with the windows open, like maybe outside is hot, like he prob-ably grabbed some pizza at Ray's on Sixth Avenue and a soda and a cherry ice. He talked about construction in Atlantic City, Harrah's and so on, how great it was gonna be, and also the action down at the Criterion. He talked about the Holmes-Cooney TKO, and when Mark said, "Let me tell you something, today's boxers could pummel old timers like Joe Lewis because they're better fed and better trained and all drugged up," Rob didn't bother to argue, or say the things I'd often heard him say, such as, boxing is a measurement of heart and attitude, *first and foremost*. He just said, "Fuck you, Mark."

And the cobra twitched. And I wondered, *Does his sweat taste like metal?* If his sweat tasted like metal that would be good—momentary kind of, and mortal, liberated from accountability.

I descend to the couch, slipping to the floor, squatting. If outside is hot, it must be summer. I do not remember the coming of summer. These seasons collide. I take the football to my belly, clutching it.

"Eveline says sushi," Mark reports into the phone. "We'll meet you down at Japonica at eight."

A KISS AT THE beach, salt on my lips. The sky is slit by a streak of bobbing pen-tacles, a blinding row of asterisks that cascade from the sun to me. I wonder if the sun can blind me.

Mark says no. "It cannot."

He's met some friends by the lifeguard station, The Connellys—Lisa and Tim. The Connellys are architects "talking to the Hilton" in Atlanta. If you ask what is the meaning of that, of "talking to the Hilton," you will be told, *negotiating a major contract*. If you ask, "Doesn't Atlanta have its own archi-tects?" you will be told of the Connellys, "They're hot. They just did Avon."

There is a logic to business, just don't expect to find it. It's actually non-logic, masquerading as logic and it depends upon the fact that you, and people like you, are too stupid or too busy to make inquiries. When considering the convoluted logic of business deals, look for nepotism, cronyism, extortion, insider trading, ordinance evasion, or bulk airline fares.

"We're meeting them at Lobster Roll later."

"No," I say. "Not Lobster Roll."

He stiffens, the hand at his jaw clutching a tiny peak of towel. He pats his face, drying it, and he smiles. "No problem. The Clam Bar."

He goes no further. There is nothing to fix when he finds what he wants in the wreckage of me. Like a missionary, he is called upon to save—saving is atonement for his ascendancy. And like missionaries who marry natives, he is inspired to emancipate deeply, down to the level of the DNA. It does not matter that I feel nothing, say nothing, it matters simply that I am docile. He is mediator and judge. He is resolved and he is apt, and if he suffers from my apathy, he shows no sign of it as he is cunning. There is much at stake in the rescue of me—I cannot begin to guess what.

He comes for a kiss. He says, "I love you." I believe that is true. He truly loves the lie that is me. "I'll tell them there's been a change. You want something for now, an apple, a peach?"

I don't answer. I don't eat fruit anymore. He knows I don't. I can't erase the idea of seeds or pods.

"There's a line at the Doodlebug," he says. "I might be a while. You going to be all right?"

I close my eyes again. In my mind is a place to hide, padded and small like a cell. No one gets in. No one dares to try.

IN MY DREAM, WE were together again. At his sister's house.

"Come in," she said. It was summertime. Her kitchen had hamster-colored counters, and the walls were yellow like walls in Peru. Paned windows went from ceiling to floor, and there was the faint sound of children, like the crackle of fire or the *sotto voce* gurgle of sewer water. A princess phone hung on the wall. Princess phones are better than the other phones, the desk kind with receiver holders like stubby antlers, making the phone into a goat head. There was the picture again, the photo, a woman splattered with blood.

His sister's husband tossed his keys on the counter when he came home, and his hand patted her waist. He called out to the kids, nodding respectfully to me as he passed. My eyes followed him down a corridor. At the end was Rourke. It had been so long since I'd seen him.

He smiled. I smiled too; I was happy.

He was going to take a shower, he asked, "Do you mind?"

I said no, and his sister handed me a letter he'd written. In it he confessed so much. I held it in my hand in a pocket while we walked through a village—Sag Harbor—it was deserted and autumnal with wind that was soft like the soft *S* of a mink or shrouds blowing softly. And as we walked, we decided things, though for me there was nothing to decide.

In the hallway of an apartment on Manhattan's Upper West Side, I attended the future, my future. Rourke was there—visiting. I knew because his feet did not touch ground. One wall was red like grenadine, and he leaned on it, pressing his legs against the opposing side, which was gray or white in shadow. Children chased children, and he and I spoke with affection. There was the feeling that I had withdrawn that affection from a strictly guarded place, like jewels from a box. And I felt honorable that I had kept those feelings safe through the years, and I felt new faith and forward faith that it had in fact been possible, and through his eyes and all things, I felt transported.

The children burrowed in a train under the bridge of his legs, and one stopped, the one that was mine. I knew it was mine by the way Rourke stopped speaking to admire the child. The boy peered up with a curiosity that was riveting. He was like a thoroughbred, spectacular and peculiar in that, with tilted brown eyes like beautiful holes, and with fine skin that was rich and tight like the caramel fur of a tiny mammal. If you wanted to look away, you could not. It was this perceptivity about the boy, this way he seemed clearly to see what we had until then been unable to see, though we had been powerfully seeking. He was so willing to wonder, so lacking shyness and shame, so true-hearted and undeviating and in time with his need that you felt renewed by his purity, and you could not help but consider the meaninglessness of forfeiture and the miserliness of sacrifice.

Two small hands reached to hold the giant leg. And in my dream, Rourke touched him, raising him up.

SAND FILLS THE PLACE in my journal where the pages are stapled. I shake it onto the floorboards of the Porsche, and it hits my bare feet. I didn't bring the book onto the beach, and there is no wind—where did the sand come from, and why do I dream of Rourke's sister when he has no sister and what is the meaning of the photograph with the blood? Why do all the question words begin with *W*?

Alongside the Clam Bar, the Napeague Stretch runs like a creosote river, like a desert highway congested with cars. I don't like highways. Highways uphold the myth of better things lying elsewhere. They entice you to journey on, leading you to believe that everything everywhere, throughout the nation, isn't exactly the same. From the sky, the interstate is a sash of shacks. Once Mark and I flew on a Cessna from Albuquerque to Las Vegas, and for three days I didn't speak. No one should have to see things that way.

The Connellys are laughing with Mark, and I see in terms of rings. The half-dollar ring in the center of their round white metal table where the umbrella fits, the umbrella itself, canopy and shaft, the ring of lobster plates and the ring of beers, which are rings in rings that leave rings when you lift them, and the canvas chairs, which make a ring from above like the white and annular eye of a billiard ball, and the entire surreal protrusion of the covered table that blossoms like a sculpted poodle tail from the silica of an earth that is itself a ring that rings. The real rings are the ones that cannot be seen—the rings in the mind. The interlocking hoops like circus toys. The ones that spin according to motive and incentive—these I do not like to think of.

"I have to get something in the car," I say and I rise. No, I *said* as I *rose*. It happened already. *Now* I am writing, writing this.

> *In my dream we held hands. Rourke's was solid like a rock or fishing weight, something you are compelled to swing and throw but which possesses such a gratifying mass you cannot forsake it. If you were even crazy enough to try, it would leave confirmation of itself in your palm, some dust or bronze, like leaf or foil.*

MRS. ROSS GETS FOUR tickets to see Betty Comden and Adolph Green perform excerpts of their work at Guild Hall in East Hampton. She says, "We'll go to The Palm after the show."

"Great!" Mark says. Mark says great. I do not decline. That would require discussion. It's pointless to discuss anything.

The theater has a smell, musty and untrafficked, making the sojourn to the arena of my former freedoms like a stop at an eyeless pit inside myself, a vestigial track where tissue relics are kept. I don't even know what is the stuff I find, this streaky matter; I cannot guess its necessity, its original port.

Rourke is present and preserved, not antic or surreal like waxworks or taxidermy but simple and clear in my mind. All the places I remember him to have stood are brought undeviatingly into focus, and so too is he, leaning up against the arched backs of the auditorium chairs, soaring through the dome of air that connects ground to stage, walking the rat tail of carpet down the center aisle as if it had been a treadmill to the pirouette of the planet. There are the seats we sat in on the night of that play, the night he told me he was *looking forward to the end,* the night he kissed me, and, though it is not cold, I feel cold, and the way that I loved him and also the blind faith of seventeen. I was never afraid then, though I am always afraid now, which is incorrect and incongruous in terms of actual and expected results since the worst has already happened.

In the bathroom I touch walls. I feel fixtures. The spouts of the sink are icefogged and dewy, and the flat X-knobs do not fit well in my hand. In the room there are places I once touched—walls and stalls and windowsills—that probably have not been cleaned, and that is sad, like I was here in fact, but, in fact, it doesn't matter, like I have ceased somehow but only in portion. To have ceased completely, well that would be something.

I look in the mirror. I think of him back then looking in mirrors—did he think when he looked in September of an actor boxing or a boxer acting, some money to be made and some time on his hands, a few months to escape to a whole new place? Did he see Montauk and think of running, he loved to run, all the running he could do, the hills and rain in winter. And his solitude, he was obliged to his solitude. Then October, then meeting me, then in January, failing the test of fortune—his career delayed. And in spring, in the mirror in his little house on the hill, did he see different things, think different things? Did he think of his fate but accept it, of his waste but endure it? Was he lonely, if he was lonely—

Perhaps he never loved me. But if he never loved me, if he wanted me only for sex and readiness, at least that's better than being with a man who wants you for reasons you cannot fathom. Without the knowledge of why you are desired, you are powerless. At least readiness is power. Many great women of fiction and history have been ready—Juliet, for instance, and Cleopatra. Joan of Arc led France because she was ready. When Rourke left, he lost that, and his loss was another man's gain. Those are the rules. I am sorry for that, for the rules, for the way he surely misses me.

At The Palm we will eat meat, and I will be expected to speak. Not much, maybe just what did I think of the show and is my food okay. "They're going to mention Christmas at the Breakers," Mark told me on the way to town. "Try not to say anything negative about Florida."

From the moment we arrive at the restaurant, Mrs. Richard Ross—Theo—will capture the attention of every decent gentleman as she is breathtaking and ageless with cascading blonde hair and a sea-salted, rosehip-oiled body and cashmere sweaters skimming white skirts narrow to her knees. Over a succession of vodkas, Mr. Ross will tell stories of celebrities and money, because that is what is expected of him, but when he digresses inevitably into tales of his youth, he will address me to the exclusion of others. Unlike the others, I know what it is to have nothing and to lose everything. Unlike the others, I am not imperiled by his nostalgia. He was just a man once, uncultured, unprivileged, a fighter of sorts, very much like Rourke, and I see that, that is to say, I grasp that, and he senses my grasp. He senses what I truly feel—that few things in life are more beautiful than the bareness of a man.

In any event, he is kind and his wife is also kind. It is kind of them to take care of me and to treat me like family when I am not. They are a nice family to have if you have no other. It is nice, and right, to respect your children's choices. When I first started seeing Mark, I sobbed in my sleep in his parents' Manhattan apartment, and everyone rushed to the guest room. Mr. Ross held me and rocked me, saying, "It's okay, sweetheart, it's okay."

A woman in a summer suit comes into the bathroom. I am startled by her features—she is noseless. Her face is spatulate. "What a show!" she says. "You're missing the best part!"

Oh, the show. Yes, the show. I retrace my steps exactly, reduplicating every halt, turn, and swerve. I do not know about reduplicating, perhaps it is enough to duplicate, but it doesn't sound nearly as nice. I'm glad that woman came and surprised me. If Mark had come instead, it would have worried his parents, and that would not have been fair. I do try to be fair. It's good to walk. I like to walk. Movement is blindness, anonymity, ignorance. Suffering requires stillness.

I STOP BY ONE Sunday morning to see my mother. Through the screen door, I hear her. "The apple and the fly are sin and evil," she is saying. "The cucumber and the goldfinch are redemption."

"Well, I need seven letters," Lowie says. "*Symbol of Christian sway*—how about *cypress?*"

"Cypress is longevity," Powell suggests.

"Try crosier," my mother says. "The bishop's staff, the shepherd's crook."

"That fits," Lowie says. "But is it with an *S* or a *Z*?"

I come in and Mom leaps happily. "*Evie!*" Right away I see her face darken. "What happened? Have you been ill?"

Powell kisses me. He squints, and the teardrop ends of his eyes square to form boxes. "She looks good to me, Babe. She looks the same as always."

"She just grew," Lowie insists quietly, drawing me alongside her. "Stand here, honey. Sure you did. Look at this, Irene."

"She has four inches on me," my mother remarks indignantly. "And she's no heavier. She needs ten pounds."

Powell tips his head. "Maybe your mother's right. *Maybe.*"

Mom lectures on the perils of health foods. She is biased against health foods and vitamins. She thinks if you use them, you belong to a giant mind control society. As if consumers of cigarettes, alcohol, sugar, and soda do *not* belong to a giant mind control society.

"Come home for the summer," she suggests. "We'll install a bathroom in the barn. You can work at Lobster Roll again."

It's nice of her to think of me, but sometimes even the nicest plans are backwards and unbearable. Besides Mrs. Ross has a job for me at a gallery in the building on West Broadway where she buys art. The art she buys there is strange, but she claims it will be worth something, and it's true that she knows things. She was an early collector of Warhols and Rauschenbergs. In her latest Hampton collection there are canvases sown with broken plates and electronic read-out signs and photographs of headless babydolls. The entire house was painted white last summer to feature the series.

"It looks like a Yugoslavian burn ward," Mr. Ross complained.

In New York the art is much nicer, though there is no Goya in the living room. One of Mr. Ross's clients has a Goya in the living room. The client has a Fifth Avenue apartment where maids wear black-ruffle French uniforms with sheer aprons like in porno films. I thought those people must have felt very important to buy that painting, to possess something of such historic value, to control its destiny. There is a buzz, sort of, to mix your small fate with the great fate of antiquity. All around the city, all around the world, there is a buzz.

Mark grabbed my waist as I beheld the painting. "Someday we'll have that kind of money. Someday soon."

At the gallery, I'll answer phones, I tell my mother, and file slides and design invitations to openings. New York is nice in summer with no one there. Soho is like Paris in the early morning, wet and cerulean blue. At night I'll go to the movies.

"Or bowling with Dad and Marilyn. Or on one of those walking tours they always take, you know, through Harlem or Brooklyn Heights."

My mother's brow contracts. If she is contemplating my dishonesty, she's also calculating the effort required to engage with it. She decides to let it go, and who can blame her?

I walk back to the Rosses' Georgica house, comforted at least for having been vigorously treated. I'm handled delicately by Mark and his family, as though they are riding horseback with an overfilled glass. Sometimes I find him staring at me the way you might stare at a fish you keep, like he's convinced I don't see him back. How funny it is to be with Mark, the humanitarian, but to be so altered that people who have never worried about you before, not even when you were really in bad shape, suddenly worry.

I TAKE THE LONG way from the Varick Street station to the East Village. A mannerly drizzle makes the city glint amiably, so I go slow, pausing for plaques on brownstones, stopping at the record store on Carmine Street, poking around the chess shop on Thompson. I like the chess shop. Chessmen there are regal and fiendish, like from gory hallucinations you've had.

I buy a knight.

"A replacement?" the man asks.

"Yes," I say. "A replacement."

McSorley's is so packed there's not enough room to choke if you had to. Tony Abruscatto always says that. Whenever a girl walks past the sign shop in tight clothes, Tony goes, "Hey Anton, take a look at this. There's not enough room to choke in there if you had to."

Mark and his crowd are in back, half-sitting, half-standing at their table, calooshing their mugs like Oktoberfest in Germantown. There is the attorney they've all slept with, Marguerite—Margaret, actually—and Richard Spencer's new girlfriend, Rachel, who is not a model but a *former* model. There's a difference. A former model is just as vain as a working model, only a former model is ready to settle down. She is happy to finally be *out of the industry*.

Rachel has eyelashes like the ones my mother draws on faces—flared, sort of, and insincere. Mark's friend Anselm from Berlin and his fiancée, Helene de Zwart, are languishing fashionably, and Mark's unacceptable tie is flapped over his left shoulder as if blown by a powerful wind. Mark has one tie that is unacceptable. I know exactly the kind of night it's going to be. They see me and wave. I unzip my coat.

Richard leaps to his feet and croons loudly; he used to be in a band.

There she was just a-walkin' down the street, singin'
The bar joins in—
Doo wah diddy diddy dum diddy do.

Right off, a couple of guys block my way, asking would I like to stop at their table instead. Mark and Richard bust over, and there is shouting and shoving and miscellaneous intimidation, culminating in a few clapped backs and an upturned chair or two. As our group gets escorted out, Marguerite stands fashionably posed, ankle-deep in sawdust, clutching the milky top to her Chanel Pierrot suit, paying the tab. Marguerite always manages to be fashionable, even in the midst of bar fights. If you're not careful, she will start telling you all about the *Three Bs*—Bendels, Barneys, Bergdorfs—and how she has been engaged four times and how she never wears underpants because they corrupt the clean line of slacks. I guess I'm careful since she never speaks to me, though she stares an awful lot, and once I caught her in Mark's bedroom, poking through my drawers.

The first time we met, she exclaimed to Mark, "*Au naturel!*"

Mark always apologizes for her, which isn't necessary. She's one of those lost women who make you sad, no matter how superior they behave or how scrupulously they dress or what fabulous event they attended the previous evening. There are women who have the opposite effect, of course—high cheekbones and no make-up and blue jeans and a gorgeous eleven-year-old son. All the best women have good skin and gorgeous eleven-year-old sons. Marguerite happens to engender pity.

"That's because she has no ass," Mark says. "Have you ever noticed? It's flat as a notebook!"

Outside on a murky unlit Fifth Street, they straighten their ruffled jackets and calculate what to hit next—Odeon for burgers or Chinatown for dim sum. Anselm pees in a doorway. The shape of the urine on the ground is the exact shape of a lizard—long and peaked from head to toe with two bifold tributaries for limbs, like parallel horizontal strike-throughs, resulting most likely from inconspicuous crimps and cracks in the concrete. At the tip of the tail is a southward kink.

Marguerite takes my hand. "Oooh, how short your nails are! They must be so easy to manage!"

IN SOHO, THE ARCHITECTURE deceives. Tin facades and columnar doorways and pregnant balconies allude to industry though, of course, there is none. Inside the abandoned factories are gutted aseptic rooms, and in this inversion there lies some critique on the lost history of manufacturing that no one wants to think about. Chiseled blondes in Agnes B. mini-skirts and hip Asians in obtuse shoes show transparencies of Jesus and close-ups of genitalia and Elysian landscapes oiled off of overhead projections. At openings, girls with body-painted breasts serve drinks but fail to hold anyone's attention. Faces whoosh at you as though ejected from fireplace bellows. *Such fire! Such rhythm! Where did you get that blouse?!*

During lunch, people in faux tortoiseshell eyewear swarm payphones like flies on fruit, lining up to call their answering machines. They bang in numbers with lightning-fast accuracy, desperate for messages, for recognition, for distinction from among the masses. Yet they have no objection to wearing the same outfit.

I load up on chickpeas and romaine lettuce at Whole Foods and wonder at the incommensurably high number of shoppers of color. Some are like the white shoppers—wise to the hazards of the American agricultural machine. Others seem to be recent immigrants, not yet assimilated into the brain-dead, milk- and sugar-dependent, entitlement-frantic mainstream of American consumerism. I like to think that they shop for organic groceries because they are nostalgic for their respective homes, where fruits are not magically unbruisable and foods are taken in season and overabundance is not a right but an offense. Where fresh herbs are the first line of defense against illness.

Sara Eden has been to Cuba. She says I would love it.

"Don't tell her such things, Sara," Mark said as he uncorked a bottle of Beaujolais Nouveau and filled three glasses. We were at a concert in the park—Rimsky-Korsakov's *Scheherazade*. "You might not realize it, but Castro makes prostitutes of his women."

Sara glowered. "*Most* men make prostitutes of their women, Mark."

Perhaps Cuba is excessively denigrated in America, just as America is excessively denigrated in Cuba and Europe and elsewhere, though Americans are reluctant to admit the possibility of external derision. Of Cuba you hear, *There is no freedom there! Television is state-controlled!* And yet for all the supposed freedom in the United States, there is a confounding deficit of ingenuity in terms of thought and taste. We all want the same stuff, not because it's good or necessary, but because we allow ourselves to be persuaded into believing we can't live without it. If you travel internationally, you will feel shocked by contemptuous talk of America. To hear your countrymen characterized as barbarian shoppers who know nothing of love, food, art, health, and religion, but everything of lawsuits, fast food, and guns, is to experience a national fidelity of which you may not have thought yourself capable. And yet, you're at a loss for a convincing defense. It's difficult to refute the accusation of misapplied liberties when rifles are sanctioned, but public breastfeeding is not.

Mark might not be totally wrong about inequity in Cuba, because Cuba is a dictatorship. But then again, Sara cares about equity and Mark doesn't, and so, if his attack on Cuba is insincere but not completely invalid, her defense is sincere but incomplete. Talk is funny this way, like a volley. Few people are willing to think all the way through to the other side. They take some sort of comfort in positions and extremes.

I leave off dreaming of Cuba as a place of pleasing pigment and undemanding signage. I leave off dreaming of a place where television doesn't pretend *not* to be state-controlled and where supermarkets don't carry pre-decorated cakes. Supermarkets in the United States carry pre-decorated cakes, walls and racks of frosted layer cakes viewable through specially molded plastic flip lids. There are factories where women and children labor without protection and bathroom breaks to make those lids for our cakes, and that place is undoubtedly governed by exactly the sort of despots Americans vilify. It's impossible that all those cakes are purchased and eaten—where do they go when they expire? *Do* they expire? And why do we need so many? Is it cheaper to throw away three than to sell one? Is *shelving* the expensive part? And why do Americans find plenty and its requisite corollary—waste—so reassuring?

If it is blasphemous to dream of living elsewhere, I remind myself that we are a citizenry of refugees, and so it would not be so very un-American to reject one orthodoxy for another in pursuit of more pertinent freedoms.

"Cuba is beautiful, Evie," Sara says fearlessly. Mark stares into the Philharmonic. Was she always so unafraid of him; I can't recall. "It's a world untouched by time. Everybody sings."

On Fridays, he picks me up after lunch and we drive to East Hampton. Other Sonnabend workers stay until six. I never asked for the abbreviated schedule, Mark arranged it that way. It doesn't make me tremendously popular with the staff, though the salespeople are careful to remain friendly in case I can influence Mrs. Ross.

"You're there to build a resumé," Mark says, "not to make friends."

He pulls onto the curb and bounds up to retrieve me because I don't always recognize the car. There's always a different car—he is perpetually testing, borrowing, buying, and trading vehicles. The beloved 356B remains for the most part in East Hampton, except for those special occasions when he needs to make a *dramatic impression*. Whenever I hear that, I think of the first time he showed it to me—and how, yes, I was dramatically impressed.

Whatever car Mark happens to be driving, it is always filled with friends from work or cousins or clients. Or people he met. He and Alicia are always meeting people. The front passenger seat is kept vacant for me, which is a strange distinction.

When Mr. and Mrs. Ross are in Los Angeles or elsewhere, the East Hampton house loads up with chic yuppie strays. Consuela loses dominion of the kitchen to heavy-set debutantes with sweaters wrapped around undulating waists, in open-toed, high-heeled mules intended to slim their legs and feature their Bordeaux-colored toenails. Whenever I offer to help, they say, *Everything is done*. They return to assembling fresh tuna shish kebabs and chugging Chardonnay and discussing diaphragms while they play house to combed-down boys on the patio. There's always this squall of perfumes. And talk of fat content. I never knew until then that cherries could be fattening.

"Sure," Mark's cousin Luce says with a wink. "Everything has a fat content. *Everything*."

Alicia is too busy with her hat-making company to notice the way I'm treated, but Mark is on to them. He misses no opportunity to force them to endure a display of his affection for me. The girls flick mascara-crusted eyes over pink drinks with paper umbrellas that perforate rows of fattening cherries, and they watch us, thinking foul thoughts of what it is I do to make him want me. At the lavish garden table, unsuitably outfitted with crystal, linen, and sterling, Mark defers to my judgment and calls me his *better half* and interrupts any prolonged conversations I might be having with other men, saying, "I worked too hard to catch her, Aaron. I'm not about to lose her."

When we go dancing, he handles me provocatively. If it's suggested that we join the others at the end of the night to go skinny dipping, Mark laughs loud. "Forget it," he'll say, "I'm not sharing."

Despite annual overhauls, the Ross house is essentially the same as the first time I saw it, big and breezy with bound copies of entertainment and fashion magazines in the bookshelves along with the complete works of great authors such as Dickens and Twain and Austen, which are not really books but trompe l'oeil containers for stowing valuables. Classic law texts and journals line the coniferous green walls of Mr. Ross's coniferous green office, but they are of little interest to me as that room is too dismal to visit. Even when Mr. Ross uses it for private phone calls, he drags his armchair out into the hallway. Ironically, it is the only fixed space in an ever-changing décor.

"What the hell happened here?" Mr. Ross demanded of his wife after one particular renovation. He'd just returned from a business trip to Chicago to find vines stenciled and painted on all the walls, connecting room to room. "Are those supposed to be leaves?"

"Blakely calls it Byronic," Mrs. Ross replied matter-of-factly. Blakely is the decorator.

"*Byronic!*" Mr. Ross removed his jacket at the entrance and stepped tentatively into the living room, looking skyward into bogus foliage. "It looks like Pan might skip through!" He loosened his tie. "Now you listen to me, Theo. An East Hampton home is a country home, and a country home should have a country atmosphere. This place looks like a Lily Pulitzer whorehouse!"

Mark won't let Blakely near the cottage. He knows I like it as it is, serene as an attic in Europe, with the lambent tread of light coming everywhere at once like the sweetest footprints of one hundred nursling animals. He turns off the central air and we lie on linen in front of fans and through the parted shutters little things blow in—golden rushes of pollen and random tourmaline butterflies and flower petals like baby bonnets. At night when the moon is high, I see them skate down the stray prongs of light, and I pretend they are fairies, dancing. At night sometimes I tell myself I can be anything, even a cowboy, even a bird.

I TAXI UP PARK Avenue, three bags of shoes at my hip. I've forgotten where the cab is headed. I cannot recall where I'm going, which as a sensation is fantastic like clairvoyance or déjà vu. I cannot recall how I came to be here, in this moment, and in life. It seems to have taken so much firmness of mind, though that is simply not the case. Oh, I know why I'm confused—architecturally, Park Avenue is completely static, and the driver is listening to the soundtrack from *The Music Man*. The day could be any day that has ever occurred in the entire modern era.

> *Seventy-six trombones played the big parade!*

The afternoon is sunless. The clouds lie like bolts of cloth. Like sleeping streaks, like kazoos. Kazoos are maddening, the way you have to hum into them. *Kazoos!* I can't believe I'm thinking of kazoos. I hate kazoos.

The driver leans back. "Gesundheit."

I cover my face. "Thank you."

"Need a Kleenex?" he asks.

"No, no," I assure him. "I'm fine. I have one."

I reach into my pocket, pulling out a tissue for show. I always have tissues now, though I never used to have them. I'm not sure—what does this mean?

TODAY THE ART STUDIO is cavernous. Today if I walked to the back, I would go farther than the wall. My knees graze the edge of the canvas, and my chin rests against my chest. To my right there is a pile of contorted tubes, crooked and coiled from the pressure of my hands. Fresh paint pocks the upside-down breakfast tray I use as my palette, and that paint looks pulpy and alive alongside the stains of old paint, the desiccated brilliance of former days. From a dented El Pico coffee can, I select the black handle of a putty knife.

I make the music louder. Puccini's *Madame Butterfly*. No one is here. It's the Friday before President's Day, a holiday almost. On almost-holidays, there is the general feel of suspense. I don't like suspense. Suspense is the opposite of clairvoyance. It's when something has *already* happened, and you can *feel* it has happened, but you don't know what it is. Clairvoyance is when something has not yet happened but you feel it anyway, and you are intense and powerful in that—you are an *object*. If you are feeling suspenseful, you are a *subject*.

> *Come una mosca prigioniera*
> *l'ali batte il piccolo cuor!*

On the canvas is a female figure, a face and bare shoulders. I call her Julia. When Julia first arrived before Christmas, I examined her as though I'd discovered a dead bird in the house—I tilted my head, wondering where she'd come from and how to get rid of her.

Her body is like living resistance. The muscles of her chest and shoulders are pronounced as she leans to escape the canvas, and yet her face contradicts her body by addressing the foreground. She connects with the observer despite risk, which is the risk of exposing her leap as a leap to nowhere. She admits the possibility of failure exactly as she reveals her intention.

Don Matthews says her story is one of entrapment and emancipation, a discrepancy not unlike that of Jesus on the cross—wood and flesh, bondage and deliverance, defeat and triumph. Jack used to call the crucifix *the perfect corporate logo*. Mr. Matthews is my teacher, a painter from Dublin. He had just participated in a group exhibit in Bellinzona, Italy, but he returned depressed because he did not do well. He took me to dinner at Knickerbocker's on University Place when Mark was away in Brazil, and complained about the success of a Finnish artist who made lighted sculptures out of tea bags.

"I should have known better," Don said over the first of several warm Guinesses, "than to associate with those *mixed media* types."

I did not create Julia. She emerged on her own over the weeks, inching out like a watery-edged silhouette from fog. Although I feel certain that I rendered what I saw, and that in creeping degrees my work was true, she bears no resemblance to the live model used by the class or, for that matter, to the paintings of the others. Sometimes you perceive a secondary figure in primary matter, like the etching of a cube that changes orientation when you blink or the goblet that is so obviously a goblet until it is two faces kissing. Sometimes you get stuck in that subsidiary or subordinate state, and that is stranger still, when you cannot return to the nascent mental image, when there is this blunt unequivocalness about your seeing. Sometimes if your eye and your mind are very fluid, it is possible to imagine backwards and to return to ambiguity.

There is a lesson in her eyes—a clearness of conscience. Like, even when you lose freedom, you can still have faith. And faith is better than hope. Hope is expectation; hope forecasts an end. Faith awaits nothing—every day of constancy is itself a good day.

"I'm sorry," I say. I say the words to Julia that no one ever says to me, and my knife moves. Horizontally, one side, the other, dissecting with new oil the meringue cliffs and downy ponds of paint that have long comprised her image. There is a candle on the studio floor. I stare into it, and a likeness of the flame imprints itself onto my retina. I close my eyes and follow the ghost form as it drifts upon the screen of my lids, evolving from round to square then snapping back into itself like a window shade or a crossbar, doubling, tripling, repeating, repeating, becoming a series of streaks. My hand follows, making and repeating lines, a fifth, a seventh, ten then twelve then crossing over. Bars. Between the olive rungs, I use a lovely rust color paint, making the two tones corrupt, integrate, marry. Yes, marriage—a corruption, a gain, a loss, a twisted sort of balance.

The room blackens; two palms mask my eyes. The hands are scented. "It's too dark in here," Mark says. He hits the light switch. The fluorescents creak and yaw in their casings then surge to life. He always sneaks up on me. Don Matthews calls him the *ferret*. He didn't tell me this directly; I overheard him.

Mark gasps. "Eveline! You ruined her!"

She doesn't seem ruined to me, but relaxed, as if she has satisfied some pressing desire. She adjourns contentedly into paint, defenseless to the very nature of herself, as if only that which made her unique and which gave her substance has the genius to deprive her of continuance. I like how she looks.

"Consider the importance of process," Don once said to me. "Buddhist monks spend days and weeks and months making sand mandalas, grain by grain. Streams of colored sand are dropped through the tapered ends of miniscule funnels to create magnificent patterns that graph the order of the universe. When the monks finish, the sculptures are swept away."

The painting belongs to the time, not to me. And the time, in turn, is in me, a fragment of my existence. If I had not taken that class, Julia would not have materialized—at least not through me. Possibly she would have come to someone else. Possibly the subjects of creativity are like spirits, existent and wandering, in search of vessels. And of course, if she truly did begin in me, then she hadn't vanished at all. She'd simply withdrawn, the way turtles' heads squirm backwards into their shells.

Farewell, I say. In my mind I say it, then my wrist arcs to obscure her entirely. Mark sighs. I wonder what he feels he's lost. It all seems so exclusive to me. As far as I'm concerned, I've rescued her. It would hurt her to hang at home. Or at Brett's. Brett has bought two other things I've painted, two trees. Whenever we go to his house, I avoid his bedroom. If Mark forces me to go in, I touch them, thinking, *Oh baby, poor baby, oh baby.*

DENNY EATS DEEP-DISH apple pie. "Know what my mother calls this?"

I blow air past my teeth making a whistling noise. *Hush.* Over and over. *Hush.* Behind him Bleecker Street veers west-northwest. We are under the awning at Figaro's and it's raining—it falls, disappears, more comes. People huddle in doorways. A man in a saturated white parachute suit and Birkenstocks passes. His toes are black.

"Pandowdy." Denny takes a forkful. "You look unbelievably tired. Do you have mono? I bet you have mono."

I *am* tired. It's exhausting to give up the past as I do, as I have done. I think of mothers of dead children—those little lost lives were so precious, so unfinished, and yet those women are told to move on, get a job, take a trip, *redecorate.* They are told that to forgive and be forgiven they must let go. But treachery of the heart breaks you down. It is exactly like mono, like an auto-immune disease, a disease against the self. My bones ache and my muscles ache, my eyes sting and my chest is sore. I can't breathe. There's this balance I need to maintain that breathing endangers. When you don't let air in, that is symbolic. Nargis says that everything you have ever done and everyone you have ever encountered is written into your respiration.

There is a cloudburst, then a downpour. The rain is torrential rain, a covalent, sticking rain. When it lands in puddles, sometimes it bubbles up and sometimes it plunks straight. The building across the street has scaffolding, and the raindrops cascade like marbles through a maze of planks and pipes like in that game "Mousetrap." Scaffolding is awful. Sometimes I think how nice the city will look when all the construction is done, then I remember.

"A cloudburst is the same thing as a downpour," Denny says.

I disagree. "A cloudburst can *precede* a downpour," I say, "but a downpour cannot *precede* a cloudburst. If they are not interchangeable in terms of sequence, they can't be the same."

He shrugs and re-props his cane on the back of an adjacent chair. An air conditioner fell out of a fifth story window on Christopher Street six months ago and smashed to the ground in front of him. A piece of metal flew into his leg. He had surgery and he won a twenty-four-thousand dollar settlement.

"If I'd been one step forward," he told me, "it would have killed me. It just wasn't my time."

I often wonder about that lost step—about where it originated, if in fact something lost that way can be said to have an origin. Did it come from a badly-timed traffic light at Hudson Street or from a missed appointment earlier in the day or from a prolonged phone call the night before? Denny could talk on the phone for hours. Possibly it was part of a series of steps dating back to his birth or to his conception or further, through the co-destinies of his parents. It's hard to perceive infinity, especially infinity in reverse. As a topic, people wisely avoid it. However, no one can deny that time factors into fate. If Denny *had* been killed by a falling air conditioner, everyone would have said that it was *destiny*. People would have to say that, just to give meaning to something seemingly meaningless. But he didn't die, and so the incident becomes irrelevant and remains largely undiscussed, which is regrettable because of all the remarkable things about life, the most remarkable are near misses.

"Getting any sleep?" he asks.

"Sort of. Not really. A little, I've been dreaming."

"Well—*good!* Dreaming is good. It's brain work."

"Thank you."

Denny tries to help. It's nice of him to try.

"I read somewhere that death row inmates have disproportionately fewer dreams," he says as he pays the check. "And that a majority of them choose Dr Pepper as their last drink. Wouldn't that make a great ad campaign—*The last word in soda—Dr Pepper*."

The weight of the rain lifts; the sun comes. The street dries almost instantly, mechanically, just like in the car wash with those hooded rollers. Denny and I make eye contact through the picturesque vapor, which is awkward, awkward because I want something from him, which feels like asking for money to buy pills. I want him to tell me about where we started, since where he started and where I started is the same. I wonder if he retains the impression of me and of Rourke like keys to a former house.

I ask, "Do you remember me then?"

"Very well," he says. "You were happy."

"YOU NEED SOME REST."

"Rest is all I get," I tell the doctor.

She says, "Obviously, not the right kind."

I didn't even know there *were* different kinds.

Dr. Mitchell replies, "Well, first of all, rest at home is cheating. You still have the phone and bills and mail and shopping and cooking to deal with. You know, cleaning and laundry."

I do not bother to tell her I do nothing. It's too embarrassing.

She prescribes Halcion and a vacation.

"Don't you have a school break coming up in February?"

"Yes," I say, thinking, *Mark has put her up to this.*

JAMAICA IS HOT, HOT like you will need emergency services. It is a lonesome and detestable heat, a broad, blinding heat, like being tied to a post at a crossroad. Like there is no shelter or friend in sight. Like it's just you, left to burn.

There is a thatch-roofed dock at the end of a long wooden ramp, and in the morning I go out to where the world is arranged in bricks of color—white and blue and blue. Like the candle we used to look at in high school, discussing whether the bird was flying on the sea or on the sky. Not *in* the sky, *on* it. It's funny to think about that conversation, about why we kept having it. I guess it was a simultaneous cognizance thing, like all of us coming awake at once to questions of outer vista and inner view. It seems incredible, how much I've lost—the luxury of time and friends and poetic aptitude, the modest opulence of home, where dreams of paradise were so much sweeter.

In the heat I think without reprieve, or maybe it's the medicine, with outside sounds that grow softer and inside ones growing louder. With these thoughts Rourke appears, rhythmically, mathematically, stable like pilings from the bed of a harbor. Naturally, there are feelings—is this soul preservation or the vanity of sorrow returning? I do not mean to go back to grief, it's just that there are memories—days when I did not have to *do* but only to *be*, when I was desired for the little grace I was. I think, *We all lose such days, why should I be any different?*

Mark has helped me to advance, and so I have advanced, despite an aversion to my betterment, to the twoness of it—to the place I must go in attitude versus the knowledge of the self I stow in my heart. But the further I go, the darker the sphere of being becomes, turning increasingly bereft of principle and natural division. It hardly seems just with so many going untended in their despair, but somehow I feel cheated and dispossessed of leverage. Though I'm conscious of the comparative ease of my position, I can't even access it in my head—it's like pushing peas through molasses. Privilege precludes me from complaining about privilege and from reflecting upon it—there are rules about thinking or saying too much about your place if your place is an especially comfortable one. If privileged is not how I feel, it is how I look, and how I look is how I am viewed, and view is everything.

It's irrelevant that I myself possess nothing, that I am more destitute than ever. If I am dependent, if I am subjected to views with which I disagree, if I live a life of compromise, it's a life I've chosen.

My thoughts turn naturally to my parents, grievously to them. To my mother's struggle to sustain us while she attended college and graduate school, though she could have married anyone she wanted, just for financial security. To my father in his Ray Bans and khakis, ready for a drive in his Plymouth to Gaslight City in Lake George or the Danbury Fair in Connecticut, grateful for the inglorious luxury of a two-day vacation and a full tank of gas. In the visor would be maps and brochures to caverns and motel recommendations and a leather pouch filled with change for the tolls. In a cooler would be the lunch he and Marilyn had made when they got up at five.

The first day Mark and I pulled up to the sign shop in the Porsche, Dad came out with Tony. When I introduced my father as an artist, he shook Mark's hand and said, "Actually, son, I'm a sign-painter."

And now me—void of fury, void of purpose, stripped of wisdom, robbed of instinct and every other fine characteristic possessed by the remainder of humanity, oppressed and unoppressed, into infinity and beyond. Not even a sellout—sellout implies that there is some superior identity I've left behind but should not have; it implies a breach of obligation, like when a black actor takes a role as a porter.

Sometimes I blame Rourke for the circumstances in which I find myself; sometimes I hold him accountable for my choices. I blame him because it feels good to make him part of my suffering, inside I feel—*He is with me still.* It's hard, all very hard—the loss of him did interrupt me. It interrupted me.

Mark is coming. I feel the bob and creak of the dock with every step he takes—forty-seven steps. It's time for breakfast. At breakfast, the tables are immaculately set upon a curvaceous concrete lagoon beneath huge bracts of cranberry-red bougainvillea, where middle-aged Teutonic couples who do not touch in the night suck back poached eggs from thick silver spoons like sucking back oysters off of calcified shells, and where the silence is uncanny until the arrival of our party—we are twelve. When we arrive, we create a chaos that is equally preternatural. With us there is turbulent chair-switching and table-shifting and off-menu ordering. There is the flamboyant tying of slipped bikini straps and the indecent cross-table sharing of food and the rummaging through straw beach bags for cameras and aspirin and lotion and sunglasses. Mark puts his arms around me.

"What are you looking at?"

"Home," I say, because as a couple, we are not without our virtues—I always speak the truth when asked, and I never want to hear what he chooses not to tell. If he lies to me, it's because he knows better; I suppose he knows best. He does not mind that in my heart I betray him. He knows I steal because I've been stolen from. He knows it would take forever to replace all that has been taken from me.

OCHO RIOS IS ABOUT an hour's drive from the Half Moon Hotel, and to get there, we rent motorcycles. Brett found six 1978 Triumph Bonnevilles through a British friend in Montego Bay. We take off east down the road—tranquil highlands to the right, tranquil Caribbean to the left. Mark waves the others on and pulls over at a place called Lovely Lynn's. Lovely Lynn's is made of sundry timber and corrugated tin painted in a caustic berberine yellow. A Jamaican man with an elongated head and spooling facial hair observes from an aluminum folding chair as Mark fastidiously applies lotion to my shoulders and lower back.

Lynn opens two tepid bottles of Red Stripe—there is the limp *chzzt, chzzt* of bottlecaps snapping off. Also the sound of birds and the shallow chuck of the sea. By the noise I think there are a lot of birds, and yet I see very few. Possibly they hide in the heat. Possibly the man in the chair knows.

Lynn sets the beers next to piles of small bananas and neat rows of pineapples and coconuts. Coconuts are hairy and mealy brown, which is a trick of nature. Inside they are otherworldly, chalk-like and cloud-like, with liquid that is nourishing and dilute. I know she's Lynn because right away Mark asked, *Are you the famous Lovely Lynn?*

The man asks my birthdate, which I give. He tells me my number. "Eight."

I turn my bottle in my hands. Eight is sort of a champion non-number to me—stacked *O*'s, sideways glasses, segments of an earthworm, bubbles fused.

He stands and moves in. His sleek forearms slip forward across the plywood countertop. "Eight is your number." *Numba.*

Mark takes a swig and makes a gratified sound. Lynn smiles at him. He inquires about her bracelets. Her arms are loaded.

"Fifty-two," she says, dangling her wrists in air. "One for each week."

"Hey, these three are identical," Mark says. "I don't think they count toward the fifty-two. I think they only count as one."

The man continues to stare at me like I did something wrong, like he can spot a liar. "Eight changed your life. Whatever happened to you, happened through eight."

"We started going out when she was eighteen," Mark says, "1981."

"No, not *eighteen*," the man says dismissively. His eyes bore into me. "*Seventeen*—one plus seven."

Mark stiffens. He pays for the beers, then gives the guy ten bucks. "Buy your lady another bracelet."

At a local happy hour club named Bloody Mary's Jerk Pork BBQ, we all dance on a stage that's like a runway between tables, dressed on the sides in milkrose velvet. It looks like a fancy coffin—a catafalque. I remind myself to smile and throw my head back when I laugh and to be pretty. It's hard to remember to be pretty or remember anything when I am thinking that Rourke is looking, that he's coming, though I know he could never find me. No one can find me. It's dark where I am. I wonder—when Rourke gave me up to Mark, did he do so consciously, like laying a baby on the steps of a particular house?

We dance until dark. The Jamaicans like the way Mark and I dance. We dance the way they do. The men press their penises against the women's thrust-back asses, and the whole place is a party. From outside you could see the little shack shaking, going side to side.

Back at the hotel there is the sanitized rendition of Jamaican culture. We begin the evening with a barefoot stroll by the still water's edge and a stop at the bulletin board to sign up for the next day's activities. We will take the glass bottom boat tour at ten, and in the afternoon I will rest by the pool while Mark goes with Richard to work on his swing. I don't know if swing means tennis swing or golf swing. In New York, it means *squash* swing. Then a dinner of prime ribs au jus, followed by rum punches and a calypso show with steel drums and limbo dancing and crab racing. The staff soaks the crabs in beer because that makes the race better. I do not like to watch the crabs, but I watch anyway because there is nothing else but our group. We are no longer twelve. We turned thirteen when we met Alan Hoodless, a businessman from Dallas who joined our group after having sex with Marguerite in the pool. When Alan tells jokes, I sing in my head so I can't hear.

Dudley nods to me as he passes. Dudley is our waiter. His grandmother Edith drinks Blue Mountain coffee every day; that is how she has lived to be ninety-six. Dudley is soft-spoken with prominent cheekbones upcurving beneath his eyes like wizard stripes. I don't know about that, about *wizard* stripes, except to say they seem to be a sign that is magic. His service partner, Horace, clears tables and rectifies silverware, making all things parallel and perpendicular. When he puts down a china cup the act is delicate, though if he wanted he could crush it. They are dignified and regal, huge and handsome, gentle like Rourke. I look at Dudley and his eyes flicker knowingly. I honestly don't know what to do about the nauseating fact of myself.

MARK GIVES ME A box like a pen box only heavy, heavier than a pen. I think heavier. Unless it's a very nice pen. I try to recall the weight of a very nice pen. The hinges on heavy boxes snap like to bite you. Like crocodile jaws.

"Open it," he says.

A ceiling fan over the bed blows the top of our hair, or is it the *tops* of our *hairs*. *Tick tick tick*. Inside the box is a bracelet like a queue of ivy leaves or spades or spearheads connected by parallel links of platinum lined with diamonds and sapphires. My eyes blur over from rum and two Halcions, and it is hard to see, so I lay it out on the starched sheet. It looks like a procession of angelfish, swimming decidedly. Once clasped, the fish will swim nowhere, just in a perpetual ring about my wrist. How sad, my wrist, a universe.

"That was funny today," he is saying, "that woman Lynn and her bracelets. A coincidence. We have so many coincidences."

I touch each link, count each link, each fish, there are eight—oh, *eight*, my number, another coincidence, one to leave unmentioned. It will be my secret, my secret way to wear the bracelet. A memory of the Jamaican, of seventeen.

"You know what that means," Mark asks, "don't you?"

Everyone will say that I'm lucky. They always say that, how lucky I am, how lucky we are. Mark is so generous, so kind, so faithful—*I've never seen him look at another woman!* And it's true. He works hard to keep me, and he must; we are joined by nothing—filament and fiber; it would take very little to set me adrift. He is so nice, they say he is nice, which is true unless you happen to be sleeping with him, in which case he is not nice, with the things he wants to do to you. It doesn't matter to me what he does, and that is worse. When you don't care what a man does, he comes up with new things until you do. I feel bad for him that he cannot get through, that my tolerance is high, that my indifference exposes him for what he is—contemptible in the dark. Perhaps all men would fall under the spell of their perversions if given the chance.

"*Coincidences,*" he says. He speaks of coincidences, and I lie back. Suddenly so sleepy. Feeling him fasten it. "Keep it in a drawer if you want," he says. "Just wear it at night."

HE HAS A FLU. He smells like illness, and the bedroom stinks like a teenage boy room, like semen and budding funk. I wash his tanned back and legs with cool water. His legs are like baseball bats or doll legs. The connection at the hip joint is startlingly clear. I go to the bathroom and flush the aspirin, telling Mark we are out, that I have to go buy some. Without lifting his head he waves. He knows I'm lying. He also knows I'll be back. I have nowhere to go. On the way out, I go back and flush my prescription pills.

Omar is at the front door. "Where you going?"

"For Tylenol. Mark's sick."

"I have Tylenol downstairs. It's too late to walk alone."

"Oh," I say. "He needs other things too. From the pharmacy."

"What pharmacy? No pharmacy's open this late."

"On the East Side. There's an all-night pharmacy."

Omar's right, it's late to walk alone, so I walk with myself, slightly angled into shop glass, going down Broadway to Columbus Circle. I keep my image in the foreground, steering it like a kite in wind. I see my hair swept back and my lips the color of lilacs that are pale. Beneath my eyes the bones make a Slavic *V*. I behold something imposing but tragic, something resistant but capitulating, something like the flag of a poor but proud nation.

On Central Park South there's a building that reminds me of Rio de Janeiro. The Rio in my mind is mythically urban, like a city forged from an idea of a city. In Rio, bossa nova gurgles like fumes about the mocha ankles of women in turbans with white poodles under their arms. All women there are beautiful with poodles under their arms, not only the rich ones—it is in the enchanted constitution of the place. Possibly only the rich ones sip gimlets on curvilinear balconies, while their husbands work in the air-conditioned halls of finance. In Rio, all men work in finance or else they are tennis pros or musicians. And all the key chains in Rio have just one key.

"Good evening, Miss, what can I do for you?" the doorman asks. Doormen in New York are always very helpful. Mostly they are Irish or Hispanic but hardly ever African or Korean or Australian or Egyptian or other things such as Chinese or Italian. Occasionally they are Russian. I don't know why it happens that way.

"Pretty building," I say.

His arm sweeps through air, gesturing at the lobby, which is covered in wallpaper with a raised velvet insignia, a laurel. Laurels are Greek, not Brazilian. Probably the architects were also Greek and not Brazilian. The doorman is not sure about nationalities, but he thinks the building is thirty years old. "Twenty or maybe fifty or forty."

An elderly lady at the elevator cries out, *Help!* The handle of her shopping bag has popped, and the bag has torn in twin lines down and horizontally across, so the piece remaining in her hand looks like a cowbell.

"Pardon me," the doorman says.

He flies to her aid. He bends promptly to gather tangerines and milk and a three-pack of Ivory soap and one of those plaid boxes of English shortbread cookies, while the lady stands there, arms incompetently lifted, cowbell in hand, muttering as though the incident had not happened *to her*, but that she has come upon it. She wears one of those Hapsburg sweaters, cherry red with braided trim, and she is heavily made-up. It's sad about the make-up and the tangerines, sad that she has no one to accompany her to the grocery store in the middle of the night, that everyone she knows is dead or gone. Mostly I'm sad about Rio, of which I obviously know nothing. Mark is always flying to Brazil. He says he would take me, but in one day he is always back in New York, writing reports, delivering reports.

I continue east on Fifty-ninth Street. Probably I look nothing like I do in the mirror. No one ever looks at you as long as you do yourself. Probably I resemble my reflection. I am light-burst, lace and lash and incandescence, a faltering rush and rapid conversion of dead space to moving points, like passing your eyes over a rack of votives in a church. I am immaterial in true time, capable only of leaving the black vacuum briefly filled.

At the Plaza, I head south, though I do not want south when the pharmacy is north. Sometimes you are awake but in a dream. Your body and mind are not detached, yet you behave unpredictably. Your material condition is permeable; messages from elsewhere keep getting through. When people say, *time heals*, they are lying. Time extinguishes hope. New mothers are told to let infants cry at night to learn to sleep alone—*Just a week, and you're free!*

Yes, it takes one week of hysteria for the child to learn it can count on no one. It takes one week of abject misery to break the spirit, to inure it to abandonment and betrayal. Maybe it took longer with me, but by then I was grown. Now I devote myself to Mark's happiness because I can't see very well or perceive very well. If he laughs or if he is happy, then I know things are okay. If he feels cold, I know to take a sweater. It is only right that happiness be treated like any other need—hunger, exhaustion, thirst—factually recognized, functionally resolved.

Rain. Finally, it comes. I want it to rain hard. I want to walk in rain. I hit Madison Avenue and turn uptown as it begins to fall swiftly, and I drink drops. I walk until I am drenched, until there is a feeling in me that is clear, shining like the street, slick like the torpedo slush of a city bus.

SIX

CITATION

I was his Mary. I was the one who invented his manhood in the back of a car.
I was the first thing to be cast off on his secret path to greatness.
Later I would be recollected privately and with pride,
a symbol of his youth, sweet as softball in summer.

FALL 1980 - WINTER 1981

I.

THE FIRST THING I HEARD WAS SOMEONE SAY THE DATE. I THOUGHT I HEARD
October, though that did not seem right. The next was how fortunate I was,
which was funny. I did not feel fortunate.

"You're a lucky young lady. You got a good bump."

It was a woman. My eyes tried to fix her. The lines of her were out of register, like she'd been drawn by broom and her hair was orange, but that may
have been a trick of the light. She was inserting a needle into the top of my
hand. "I'm a nurse," she explained slowly. "My name's Tilly Keller. Do you
remember what happened?"

A pig getting its throat cut. A swirling world like dancing. Faces in a ring.
Dampness.

Did I think I could manage a few questions, Tilly wanted to know. My age
and name she got from my wallet, but there was no insurance card. Did I have
coverage, or did I know what coverage I had, which was just a way of asking
about parents. My feet were bare. I wondered who had my shoes.

A man in greens skidded in fast, like he was dating two girls. "Look who's
decided to join us. I'm Dr. Tollman."

Dr. Tollman felt my head, manipulating it. My hand reached up. There
was gauze and tape in a line above the eye bone. "Minor injury. We'll get some
film anyway, just to be sure, but I have a few fractures ahead of you. I'm more
concerned about your blood pressure—70 over 50. I think you're dehydrated.
I've ordered a bag of fluids."

The nurse adjusted the bed. "Temp's 101.6," she said to him.

The doctor shined a pen light in my eyes, panning it side to side just like in the movies. His nails were pale and even, his eyes clear and green. His hair was sandy and straight. He didn't seem old enough to be a doctor. He seemed like me, like he could have been my brother, if I happened to have a brother who happened to be a doctor. But I didn't and that made me sad though I tried not to cry.

"You're in the E.R. at St. Vincent's," he explained in a succinct almost-whisper, close by my ear. "You passed out big time. On the subway platform. Lucky you didn't hit the tracks. That ever happen to you before?"

I closed my eyes. "I think so," I said, "yes."

"When you get your period? Tilly tells me your underclothes were bloody. Any chance you're pregnant?"

I did not respond, and he slapped the side of his legs twice. "We'll run some blood just in case. You take it easy. Anyone we can call in the meantime?" He waved loosely. "Parents, anyone?"

"I can bring a phone over if you want," the nurse prodded. "There are jacks everywhere."

"Take your time," Tollman said. "We're not throwing you out."

There was a commotion nearby, and he popped to attention, long-necked and perky alert. "I'll be back," he said as he passed through the curtains. Then ducking in again—*Hey Tilly, get some urine on her.* Tilly did not laugh despite the unfortunate choice of words. Nothing is very funny in an emergency room.

When the nurse retired, she adjusted the curtain behind her. In hospitals they protect you with cloth, and they sew you with thread. Certain inventions cannot be improved upon, like hangers and keys. I felt the heat of her recede and the heat of everyone and everything recede.

"Excuse me," I said, "Tilly."

"Yes?" she asked, her face and shoulder coming back.

"I do have someone to call."

DR. MITCHELL SPUN ON her stool. "When did you first become aware of the discomfort?"

I wasn't sure. "I guess I had pink spots. Then blood, last night. A little, then a lot. Kind of erratic, in eruptions."

She wrote illegibly on my brand new chart. I wondered what she was notating. She seemed to be writing more than I was saying. "The pregnancy did not take," she said. "Sometimes a baby just dies."

I did not bother to disagree. She had no way of knowing that mine was not the type of body to be defeated in an endeavor so natural. That my baby died of a broken heart.

"Miscarriages are common. We used to think they were late periods. Pregnancies are detected so early now, we're finding many late periods are actually miscarriages. It doesn't mean you won't ever be able to have a normal pregnancy and a healthy—"

"How far was—it?"

"Judging by the labwork and what you've told me, I'd say ten weeks."

August, the beginning. I wondered what we'd been doing then, what he'd been wearing—did it rain that day. I remembered one rainy day in particular.

After I dressed, we met in her office. On her desk was a latex mold of female genitalia and a laminated flip-book depicting ailments—tumors, warts, cysts. Photographs of her children.

"Do you want me to call Mark in?" she inquired, leaning to lift the phone receiver. "He's welcome to join us."

I thanked her, saying no.

"You'll need a D & C," she stated. "Do you know what that is?"

I said like a vacuum.

She said a vacuum, yes, or a scraping.

"You might still have tissue inside. You don't want tissue inside. You could get an infection. I've made arrangements for tomorrow morning. They can squeeze us in at nine."

I touched my belly as I walked down the hall. A scraping. How absolutely Rourke would be removed. There would be no trace. A little tissue, a little infection, at least that was something to hold onto.

Maybe it would be best, a scraping. Yes, a scraping.

THE FEELING AFTER LEAVING Montauk was the one that persisted, which was the feeling that I wanted to die. I would have killed myself, but then I might never see him again, and true love is devious.

My mother's house was empty when I arrived, but maybe that is all I noticed. Maybe there was more, only I could not notice more. I once met a woman whose infant turned blue. She ran outside for help, forgetting her other child, a three-year old she'd left behind. I thought I understood. I thought I knew what it was to run with a blue infant, to run without thinking, to confront the shock of catastrophe, to forsake things of prior consequence.

There was no optical completeness that day, no visual flow or cohesion; the view transpired erratically, in windows between great gaps like deranged snapshots, night before day and my likeness everywhere at once—me on my knees in the barn, hands cut, and beneath the palms splinters that were deep, me in my room in the middle of mounds of clothes and furniture, standing before a dresser without drawers, which was hideous like a mouth missing teeth. Later there were lamps, two that I was holding, one that was broken, and then, me again, somewhere else entirely, leaning upright against the wall, clutching it, as though I were on one of those gyroscope rides, erect and per-pendicular and holding very hard because real life is centrifugal, because in the middle of everything is nothing.

If I could see only partially, I could hear everything—cars wafting blithely up the street, the pernicious rap of the kitchen clock through a door closed and locked and sealed with pillows at the base, and laughter, impossible laughter,

laughter without origin like plants without roots, like plants hovering magically though the magic is black. I heard the agitated whisk of my breath and voices inside—his and mine and a third that I did not recognize. I spoke to myself as there was no one else to speak to, and the sound of me was truthful. I seemed to mean the things I said. *Be brave*, I kept saying. Over and over I said that. *Be brave*. I had no idea what I meant by brave. Maybe there was something else I needed to be, only I couldn't think of the word for it.

On my bed were messages. Kate had come from Canada with Marie-Helene to get the rest of her stuff—*Where are you? Meet us later!* I did not know anyone named Marie-Helene, why did Kate write that name as though I knew it? Sue from Lobster Roll called twice, the first time asking was I still sick, the second time saying, *We're desperate, please just come answer phones!* Labor Day weekend—I'd missed the entire thing. Rourke must have called to tell them I was sick. The thought of his doing so made me vomit. Not much, just the banana and toast he'd given me before driving me home, which manifested as chunks and spittle on my comforter. There were flakes and they were orange. That seemed like a mistake since I had not eaten anything to flake orange, but then, the body is a mystery.

I pushed at the mess with the back of my hand. He'd held the food, shopped for it and prepared it, and in the machine of me it had switched to waste. If we had not separated, the waste would be food in a food state because I would still be at his house, and he probably would have given me eggs or oatmeal or something long-cooking. Food has its own tempo and era—frequently that is forgotten. You eat it and incorporate it into human time, bringing it to a premature end, and that is some tragedy of abused vitality to think about.

I scooped what had not yet been absorbed onto the phone messages because you cannot save vomit no matter how in love you are, though frankly, the thought did occur to me. The papers attached to each other fearfully, the ink soaking and swirling in the acidy part. On the way into the toilet, the stack flipped, landing in a muffled plock. The bottom note I read backwards. In my mother's handwriting it said, something, something, *taob*, which I knew to be reverse for boat. That was a message from Mark Ross. *Be brave*, I told myself again, that and something else, some question about vultures, about how they feed, that I could not finish. I just kept asking myself, *When they dive, do they—*

AT NYU, I DID not unpack. I kept one suitcase at the bottom of the closet, a few coats hanging. I never missed a class because, in my room, things went too slow. Sometimes you hear people say, *The cast comes off in three weeks*. A timetable for pain is enviable. If only I'd had some mechanical destination. It did not take me long to realize that if I did not sleep or eat, then at least I could feel some physical something.

I wrote a letter to Rourke, four times, ten times, copying, recopying, my words gaining greater distance from their original meaning with each draft until they became just a string of shapes, like operating instructions in another language, Russian or Sanskrit, strokes and little arches, buckled bridges and circles with proud sashes.

I wanted to tell him that there is this absence, this nonattendance. Somewhat like having been skinned, somewhat like skinless invisibility. I did not send the letter. I did not want to trespass.

My roommate, Ellen, was big and agreeable like a barmaid from a Dickens novel, though that could not have been accurate since she was Greek and Jewish, and Dickens never wrote about big Greek Jewish barmaids, not memorably anyway—the whole thing must have been some random iconic conglomerate lodged in my head. Ellen came from a just-built mansion in Rye. Her dad was a surgeon at Einstein in the Bronx, which amused my father immensely since he was a sign painter and Dr. Carnevale was a cardiologist, but their kids wound up in the same goddamned place anyway. I didn't elucidate the differences—in four years, I would be forty thousand dollars in debt and Ellen would be loan-free, settled into an investment condo, a guaranteed job, and the white leather seat of a brand new BMW.

Ellen had the highest personal standards of anyone I'd ever met. She was devoted entirely to her own comfort. Thursdays to Mondays she returned to her family house because it is common knowledge that dormitory washing machines spread disease.

"Be careful," she warned me the first time I used the laundry room. "My cousin Ruth at Tulane found a used condom stuck to the drum."

Instead of a stereo or typewriter, Ellen brought spa supplies to college. She had rolling wooden massage devices and fleecy slippers and velour bathrobes and plush Egyptian towels that practically made endtables when you dropped them. There were vanilla balms for night and peppermint splashes for day and an ever-replenishing supply of homemade brownies and three-percent milk in her *Permafrost* mini-fridge. Air fresheners were everywhere; they seemed to repopulate, little perforated plastic pillars—*Spring Fling!* In the bathroom were plaque picks and callous shavers and orthopedic shower shoes and super-cushiony toilet paper. Her quilt was made of Swiss goose down and beneath the mattress her brother Nick had laid three-quarter inch plywood for lumbar support.

I never heard her mention boys, not once. She was far too cunning to allow sex to endanger her lavish lifestyle. And since I did not infringe upon her sufficiency, we got along well. She treated me with benevolent indifference, and I found it admirable, actually, that she was so extremely disinclined to be idle, inspired as she was to return home without delay. She went to bed at ten, got up at seven, and was in classes or the library all the hours in between. She wasn't unsociable, she simply had no time for anything other than an hour of television every night, "Dallas" or "Knot's Landing." Invariably she shifted the TV set toward my bed so I could see too. Ellen was a busy girl; you couldn't blame her for not noticing.

"YOU OKAY?" SHE ASKED. "You've been sitting for, like, three days." She poked at the desk lamp near my bed, turning it on, and a saffron light swallowed up the brittle pre-dawn blue that had been making the room into a pond with me at the bottom. I was grateful, though I could not quite say. Ellen took an involuntary step back, an instinctive step, thinking quick, in case I was contagious. On her shoulder was a duffle bag. She was on her way home, that meant it was Thursday. I was pretty sure I'd lain down on Tuesday.

"You look bad. Are you feverish?"

Maybe I had a fever, I wasn't sure. There were cramps in my abdomen. Mice squinching through alleys.

"Maybe it's food poisoning. That cafeteria is shameful. I keep telling you not to eat there." She asked did I want her to wake up the R.A.

"No." It would be like a chain with every next person passing off responsibility right through my parents until it got back to me anyway. I waved for her to go. "You'll miss your train."

Ellen blinked. She considered my advice, but some fundamental sense of ethics prevented her from taking it. "I won't be back until Monday. You could be dead by then." She dropped her bag and found a pair of sweats and a shirt and shoes, and she helped me slip the pants over each calf and replace the t-shirt I'd been in with the new one, and when it came time for feet, she knelt on one knee and sucked back her lips with determination, manipulating the shoes, rushing all the while so as not to miss her train but never checking her watch, though surely she thought to do so. The transaction was extraordinary, not because we were strangers, but because the business of helping someone was so obviously new to her. If I regretted having to inconvenience her with problems that were private, I anyway appreciated the change in her aspect as she condescended to assist me. There was a give to her stiffness, a liquefying and an elongating and a flushing in rings at the cheeks like a Mannerist portrait—with the face like cream to its outermost edge, where it touches upon the surrounding murk. Ellen seemed smaller when she was not so confident, and lovely. I thought to tell her, but it would not have come out right.

"Okay, let's get up," she said, taking my elbow.

There was blood on my sheets. I tried to cover it when I stood, but my hand skimmed the blanket ineffectually. She could not have missed it, though she said nothing. Despite my obvious abnormality and her absorbing fear of contagion, she conducted herself graciously, which I decided had to do with good breeding.

There happened to be two available cabs coming down Tenth Street. Ellen hailed both at once with a superhuman whistle and a mighty wave of a mighty arm. She put me in the first.

"You gonna be all right?" she asked.

I managed to say yes, and sorry about your train.

"Don't worry about it. There's another one in fifteen minutes." She handed me a twenty dollar bill. I declined but she insisted, saying it was the least she could do. "If anything happens to you, Eveline, who knows who they'll stick me with."

She got into the car behind mine, and we each waited at the light on the corner, which was an unfavorable climax to an already inauspicious morning. To see someone you know stopped in a taxi is to see one preposterous fragment of their life. They sit, you sit, each awkwardly chauffeured, and you cannot help but be made aware of the queer formality of mature existence, the nonsense of transit and gesture, the absurdity of the construct we make of ourselves.

My eyes shut. To stop the feeling I had of falling sideways off my seat, I made a picture in my head of what it was to be Ellen Carnevale of the ubiquitous E.S.C. monogram, charging up to Grand Central to catch the 7:55 to Rye, popping into Zaro's Bread Basket and ordering with a certainty that was enviable and supreme a chocolate croissant or a toasted raisin bagel and a coffee—no, not a coffee, she would want to nap—a fresh-squeezed juice—before picking up a few magazines to breeze through on the train as she anticipated the luxuries that awaited her at home—Jacuzzis and tuna salad with fresh dill. On Friday night, there would be a movie on Central Avenue and Chinese food with her grandparents. On Saturday, ice skating and a few hours at Saks. It was all very fifties and chaste except for the part about me. No one would have guessed at her association with a hemorrhaging girl. It depressed me to soil her story. I would have liked to make it up to her somehow, to reverse or erase the knowledge she'd received prematurely through her chance relationship with me concerning the dizzying and rancid phenomenon of carnal life.

I opened my eyes in time to see Ellen wave as she flew east across Tenth, and I made the right down Broadway. I knew by the ponderous set of her jaw that she had been making a picture of me as well, a concept of hellish days to come—the squalid uncertainty of modern disease and remedy, the putrid working back to probable cause, the foul business of changing and cleaning a blood-stained sheet, of flipping a mattress in my anemic state, the dismal occupation of a life without guardians, without ethnic net or religious shield, without refuge or resource. How unnecessarily expanded her mind must have been to review a life as luckless as mine. How relieved she surely was not to be me, poor and parentless, desired but defiled by the opposite sex.

The cab left me at University Place by Health Services, which was closed at seven-thirty in the morning since any respectable student illness occurs during business hours. The walk to the Astor Place subway was macabre, with chained storefronts and no place to make a call and cyclones of trash whisking down the Eighth Street corridor, growing huge as they neared and slapping onto me like magnetic newspaper starfish or plastic wrapper leeches. I would have taken a cab, but I wanted to save Ellen's leftover money for later. I must have known things would get worse later.

I recall being very cold except for the part of me that was hot and wet in blasts. I recall the titanic slope of stairs going down to the platform and sitting to rest every time it would resorb into itself to form a concrete precipice. I don't remember actually boarding, but there is an owlish piece of the number 6 train stuck in my head the way a wad of gum gets stuck on your shoe, proof that you connected. The memory is of something dreamy and brackish and ugly and old, like some functional relic you cannot help but hold to light, an antique doorknob maybe, or a hairpin, and guess about its particular history and enduring bravado. Yes, there was the train, its crippled dynamics, the labored jerk and groan of the brakes and the spitting inside-out puff of the doors, the garbled declarations, the porpoise-gray benches, the scattered souls, and my febrile body making conversions, addressing discrepancies in volumes and capacities—grain to ounce, ounce to pound, pound to mile to watt and degree. Who knows where I was headed. I seemed to have had an East Side hospital in mind. Lenox Hill maybe. I was born at Lenox Hill.

THE STREETS OFF FIFTH Avenue in Carnegie Hill were like halls of windows, and the windows like likenesses shimmering onto themselves, pink gold boxes repeating across the stripe of blue-glaze light that marked the center. High above, the clouds were teased apart like hair weeded from a comb. I was tired, so I sat on the stoop of a brownstone waiting for nine to come. Maybe that's not right. Maybe time does not come. Maybe you come to time, or through it. Or maybe you are a wheel and it is a wheel and periodically you line up.

August made sense. Hadn't I felt unwell at the end and in September? In September there was this tenderness, this ache disentombed like being bruised all over. What I'd felt were messages from a baby, weaving and unweaving, half of me and half of Rourke. I would have guessed such a mix would survive, but how could it when its parents could not find cause? How could a baby be strong when there is no one to be strong for, when everyone else is weak? I knew how it must have felt since as a child I also felt that way, and often. And when I understood in depth the disappointment I'd caused, I began to cry.

There are those who would say I did nothing wrong, that nothing was killed, rather something had ceased to live. But that as a distinction was too subtle for me. At the time I did not feel like taking comfort in the difference between a baby and the pioneer beginnings of a baby, especially when the same sort of people who argue against assigning attributes to a zygote tell you, *Don't wear fur*. They will tell you not to shoot a deer because a deer has feelings. That is not to say that people who advocate wearing fur and shooting deer are not equally hypocritical to speak of the sanctity of life. The thing is, maybe a deer has feelings, maybe the origin of a child is in the protoplasm, maybe it's impossible to know either way or to think rationally when it is not really rational to speak of sensation and spirituality, or a lack thereof, in beings other than yourself.

There is proof enough if you seek it, of peculiar transmissions, especially when you take into consideration the fact of consciousness versus the *articulation* of consciousness, like how cows release adrenaline into their flesh as they're slaughtered, which can alter you when you eat it, and how Mozart wrote concertos at four, and how organ transplant recipients can develop the dead donor's habits. No one can say for sure that the grief of wasted life does not enchase the walls of a woman. God knows you see so much sadness out there.

Maybe I had a political right to have sex without the consequence of pregnancy, but I had not been thinking of politics at the time of conception or any time after, so I did not feel particularly entitled to adopt that defense. If it was tempting to intellectualize backwards or to reason polemically, I did not bother as I had only myself to answer to. Maybe such matters cannot be fully comprehended before they happen to you. Maybe it is impractical to assemble opinions in advance when beliefs frequently rise out of the murk of despair like furnishings as you grope through darkness—the back of a chair, the arm of a sofa—things to cling to when you're not steady. Probably you have to have felt the effects of life in you—the peaceful influence, the pinch and the fold, the peculiar siphoning of reserves to know what it is to lose or keep or end it. What I felt was sad and sickeningly sorry, sorry that I had teased a soul into existence, that I had offered myself as sanctuary, when in truth I was no shelter.

Maybe Rourke would have been relieved to learn I was no longer handicapped with a child, my child, his child, that it was gone from me, drained and gone, that my name was intact, my earning and purchasing potential insured. If only he knew, but he would never know. The knowledge was mine. It was the least I could do. If that seemed melodramatic, I didn't really care; honor is frequently theatrical. The very brevity of the baby's existence was sacred to me—fine force and gossamer essence—in its economy was a lesson I needed to learn having to do with windows of opportunity being fantastically small, with powers I had that were hidden. I had not gone gently as I carried. It never occurred to me that I possessed such aptitude for damage.

I did not have to envision an infant to make myself ill, with eyes of a penetrating hue or flesh that smelled faintly of cornstarch or a prattling voice with the rich husk of its father's or dimpled palms that reached in faith for me. I had only to think of what had happened *in fact* to what *in fact* had been. A cluster failing, perishing, ebbing, an exquisite cellular concentration artlessly awaiting the assistance of its life system, its world and its home, seeking sustenance, hormonal or electrical or foodlike in nature, but receiving nothing—nothing consistent, nothing adequate. I had only to think of atrophy in me, and my heart broke again, and worse. Inside my heart felt bad and I cried for him, and I cried for me. But I cried most especially for the soul that had come and gone like a solitary flicker of the tiniest light. When I thought of the fluttering quills of an angel, consecrated and divine, flapping, flapping, slower and slower to sleep, I cried until the water in me dried, then I did not cry again. For years I did not cry.

"DATE OF LAST MENSTRUAL period?"

I did not know.

"Form of birth control?"

None.

The nurse was preparing a needle. She wore a red pin that was a leaning plastic heart. Like a heart blowing. "Did you eat today?"

"It doesn't matter," another nurse said. "She's a private. She's getting Demerol."

"You're Dr. Mitchell's or Dr. Warren's?"

I said, "Mitchell's."

She drew blood, and her head bent. Her hair was dense and coarse like chocolate wisteria, twining like woody vines into a sweeping high twist, and her nose was wide and her skin caramel with acne scars that were blackish by comparison. I thought she was beautiful. I asked her name. She said Lourdes.

"Are you Puerto Rican?"

"I am," she answered as she snapped the rubber tourniquet off my arm. Her eyes drooped lazily. "Open your fist for me, baby."

The syringe filled rib-red and she withdrew the needle, pressing cotton to the hole. I wondered if her life was nice. Probably there were bridal showers and dowager aunts. A mother with hypertension and a cherished dog. "It's a hard decision, honey," she said. "I've had to make it myself."

"I didn't make the decision," I confided. "The baby made it for me."

IN THE OPERATING ROOM I lay with my legs strapped in and spread apart, knees over padded stirrups, blue plastic sheeting over knees, green foam slippers imprinted with smiley faces flipping halfway off my feet, and a needle with a tube shooting out of the back of one hand—a far cry from his arms in the dark. The room was a small New York room of a certain timeless quality, the kind that had belonged to a detective or a talent agent back when men wore hats. I did not know whether there was a window, but I had the impression of high clouds. In the door was a small panel of translucent glass, and through the frost, bodies passed as intimations, globular creatures of indefinite proportion, drifting darkly by like piles on a moving belt. I wondered with indifference about the possibility of fire. I wondered who would untie me. I didn't care who. They dealt with girls like me all the time, and there is asylum in anonymity.

There were strangers in blue scrubs, monitoring and arranging. A faceless nurse and a faceless black man, a nurse maybe as well, tearing plastic corners from sterilized utensil packs, laying instruments on metal rolling trays. Their hands were professional hands, like the hands of casino dealers, making your game their business, making it real, making it hard for you to pretend otherwise. Eyes modestly lowered, eyes that know your truth—you gave yourself away; you are unwanted. You think your story is a different story, only it's not. You bestowed your legacy, he bestowed his, cells meeting and matching, conforming dutifully to code and process, constructing life new again. But not even the magic of fertility is immune to the wasteful ambiguities that rule the realm beyond the shell of you. Time is wrong or money is scarce or dreams are disparate, and so with helping hands you reach into a place no one should ever touch, and you halt the procession of vitality, returning it—no matter what you think *it* is—prematurely to non-existence. And the lesson of you, the lesson you never counted on, is that of a cowardly world.

My baby was a smart baby. It interrupted its own code. Like a nimble phantom, it stepped into me and out. It would not make a murderer of me. That was a gift it gave, though I had none to give back, and I felt sorrow and gratitude. If I could get it a message, if I could say just one thing, I would invite it to stay in me still. I would say that as a home I was not so bad.

The hands moved quickly; there were others behind. It is a sort of war. "Hi, I'm Dr. Burstein. I'm here to help Dr. Mitchell."

Dr. Burstein was tall, too tall for a room so congested. He seemed to teeter. Perhaps he was perfectly upright, and it was me, teetering beneath. I was not sure about that, about *teetering beneath*.

"I'm going to give you something to help you relax," he proposed in a drawl. He lowered himself onto a stool by my right shoulder, spun it slightly, then shot an already filled needle into the top of the IV bag. I knew the feeling in his fingers, the same feeling as squishing water from a pistol—the swift push, the mellow thrust, how odd and omnipotent to do that with a drug, to make such an infinitesimal gesture and narcotize an entire body.

It took a minute, not a minute, several seconds, two dozen seconds, just shy of a pound of seconds was most precise, though it is not correct to measure time as weight. My arm went cold, my wrist and shoulder went cold as the drug dripped in like ignited ice, scrieving through my blood. I could smell it behind my sinuses. I could taste it and smell it. Was it possible to smell it?

My God, I thought. *I am so fucking high.*

There was a noise, a papery slap, then a growing whoosh like crickets. I opened my eyes. I could not recall having closed them. Dr. Burstein was there, watching me with golden eyes that were kindly muffins. I wondered was he gay from the Midwest. If he was gay from the Midwest, I would have liked to be his friend. I had the feeling he treated his friends well. I felt I could breach the divide of his skin, that I could read his heart like cards. Drugs are not without protocol; they beg you to connect; they insist that you touch down. It occurred to me to ask him how much time had passed. He appeared connected to time and reliable that way, as though time charmed him, and he was not afraid. Only I didn't want to pose a question when questions were complicated with the way they were inverted sentences.

"Do people call you Eveline, or do they call you Eve?"

"Evie," I answered, careful and grave. I could not tell if I was speaking very, very loud or very, very soft.

"*Evie*. Isn't that pretty? Can you tell me how you feel, Evie?"

"Yes," I said. "I feel good."

He laughed, and everyone laughed, though I did not think anyone else had heard. The black man turned his face halfway around, and Dr. Mitchell was there. I saw her, which was strange when I had not heard her coming in or greeting anyone. I didn't like that, the absence of an introduction by Dr. Mitchell. I didn't like that as a team they were accustomed to moving without etiquette or fanfare.

"You might feel pressure."

That was the voice of the doctor. The voice did not emanate from her throat but from a horseshoe about her. She was sitting on a stool or standing low at the base of the bed to my right and people were handing things to her from opposite sides, which made me think of astronaut costumes. Whatever those are.

Dr. Burstein patted my arm. His face had not changed. I knew I could follow his face for change. "How you doing?"

"Good," I said.

He said, "Good girl."

It was nice of him to call me *good girl*, nice of them all, really, they were all very kind. It had been a long time since anyone had been that way, that kind way, and I said so, I said, "You are all very kind," and Dr. Mitchell smiled. I thought she smiled. I could not tell through her mask. I heard her say, "You're doing fine."

And so I vanished, glissading backwards. There was an assuasive firing in my back, an impression of melted petals and paraffin-like drops secreted by bees, an impression of crepe evolving outward and smoothed to ultra fineness, smoothed apart and petted apart, with my body flattening and the flat sheets of me becoming the flat face of the table, the floor, the ground, the earth. Like a fragile snow whiting an uneven terrain, I coated the topography about me. Everyone was touched by the remains of me dusting down.

I waltzed through the absorbing wonder of my own sensation, daring to tour regions ordinarily avoided, hunting despite the promise of grief for the wound he'd made, discovering not one speck or stain but an envenomed entirety, a lesion of such insidious fury that it was positively modern, viral and atomic, an infusion really, like daylight showing inside a blown balloon.

"Almost done," the doctor said, and the sound she made became the sound of my mother, permeating and clever and brightly intrusive. Funny to associate Dr. Mitchell with my mother. Both were kind of experts on the periphery.

It occurred to me that I had not warned her to mind where the baby ended and where I began, in case it and I were truly one, and the soul of me was vacuumed up as well, aspirated was the word she preferred. Aspirated means things such as me and things such as it getting sucked into sterile glass and disposed of by technicians in rubber safety attire because I am hazardous, and the insides of me are hazardous which is a terrible truth of maturity that thankfully escapes you as a child. All children should feel clean since they are, unlike grown-ups who are contaminated no matter how frequently they wash. That is the surprise of adult life, that filth is unpreventable. Filth is seeing things and keeping secrets and wandering through doors upon doors every day, only you cannot travel back.

Demerol is helpful. I could not even feel the baby coming out or hear it screaming. Oh, but that was because it was dead already before. I had forgotten, my womb was a coffin.

A burst, then another, above. Fractures in a dopey haze, splints to cleave the shield that was no shield but just the misimpression of one, which made me sad for me, so deeply deeply sad. The hands were finished, the drug was waning, diminishing, and that is chill and sad as well, the whole thing, me and the pitiful conditions of my existence and the premature return of a consciousness that is despicable and a pain of the heart that is acute and a fact, just like blood is a fact of battle. A word was in my head, one awful word tottering madly like a drunken metal egg—*decrescendo*.

"Thank you," I said to Dr. Burstein, averting my eyes though I'd never see him again, because there was shame again and a return to propriety. I would have liked to tell him it was the first time I'd felt free since Rourke. I would have told him that, but he would have known I was lying.

"YOU OKAY TO WALK?"

Mark met me at the nondescript door they admit and release you through. He led me by the elbow past the girls who had not yet gone in, and he took my bag. *Let me get that for you.* In his hand my pocketbook looked like all the other pocketbooks, lilting and suspicious, filled possibly with germy sanitary supplies and other female stuff such as scuffed vinyl photo wallets and half-empty bottles of 7-Up. I wondered how he could bear to see me there. It seemed impossible that he would want to occupy the aspirated place in me, that he was not disgusted by my failure.

No noise as we walked out, no movement, just forlorn staring, which is the correct thing to do when you're waiting for an abortion, friendly conversation and Hollywood magazines being pretty much out of the question. Patients hunched stoically, and boys in Members Only jackets slouched over the armrests of connecting chairs to nap on girlfriends' shoulders, resting deservedly because it is hard work to fuck and be poor.

In my pocket was a tissue filled with Oreos. You get cookies at the end. At the end you lie in vinyl reclining chairs and watch game shows on a television bolted to the ceiling, and you get cookies and Dixie cups of apple juice like in nursery school. One girl was shivering and crying, refusing to eat, but others ate like it was nothing, so they got to go home.

Mark grabbed the tissue before I could throw it away. "What's this?" he inquired. "Are you supposed to eat these?" He placed them in his pocket. "You'll eat them in the car."

He protected me from the anemic flank of abortion protesters on the curb. They shuffled around like those zombies from *Night of the Living Dead*, rattling oak-tag posters with photos of mutilated babies. They all wore those ankle-length down coats, which was strange. It wasn't even cold out. Maybe it was some tactical choice. Probably you can hide stuff under there.

When I was little, I took a trip with my mother and her friends through a storm with water thick as lymph. There was the dieselized rumble of the Greyhound engine, the low glandular singing to Joplin's "Summertime," and the hydraulic push-pull of oversized wipers. There was the stench of cheap beer and costly marijuana and the idea that every basic act was a caper or stunt against society, including bodily functions. Periodically, the driver would pull off the highway and the bus would dump its contents onto the shoulder, and everyone would urinate. At mealtimes they would descend into diners, plunging wickedly into booths, terrifying humorless customers, provoking beefy truckers, and confounding nest-headed waitresses by making substitutions, switching seats, paying with penny rolls, and tipping with love poems and pocket contents—jawbreakers and torn snapshots and half-exhausted root beer lip smackers. It was a duty. They had been deputized, the anti-establishment ideology had passed to the minds of the masses. It had become the function and the pride of the American youth to topple the old guard, to acquaint it with its inequities, to demand without setting a good example that everyone be civil and courteous. Back in the bus someone would inevitably say, *What the fuck is stroganoff anyway?*

The rain in Washington was bad. My mother liked to say how the mud came to my knees, but I did not complain once. The march was for women's rights, she told me, for my rights and for the rights she had not had. She'd had her abortion in an apartment on East 110th Street, she said, shortly after I was born. My parents were too poor for two children. I did not even have a crib, just a dresser drawer. The story, when I heard it, made me sad, not for my mother who recounted it without invitation for sympathy, but for myself since I had been deprived of a sibling. A brother most likely.

That was all I knew, all I had been told. But of course there must have been more. Prior to Roe v. Wade, there was no Demerol or general anesthesia. There were no medics in hygienic disguise before 1973, and the equipment used to penetrate a woman's cervix and scoop her uterus might well have been the same object employed to probe slits in car windows when you lock your keys inside. I once overheard Aunt Lowie say that there was this substance they used to spray in, like a lacquer or an ammonia. Did they give a girl some aspirin? Did they use a flashlight to find their way? Was there whiskey like in movies about men who get gangrenous limbs amputated? Everyone knows about amputating gangrenous limbs. Everyone knows what it looks like to get a bullet through the eye because as subject matter such topics are sanctioned. No one knows about illegal abortions, though everybody knows someone who has had one—aunts. Lots of aunts have had them.

I never asked my mother how she got back downtown to their apartment from 110th Street. Did they have money for a taxi when they had no money for a crib, or did they borrow a car? And who took care of me that night? Not my father's mother, she could not possibly have known, and six months seems a very untimely age to be left with a stranger. Probably I cried. Was my mother repulsed by my cries when she returned or did she reach for me? No, she did not reach for me. Probably I did not cry. Probably even then I retained my tears, probably I'd figured out that tears were not to be tolerated. As a baby, I was very strong—that's what everyone said, though what they meant was that as a baby I wasn't given a choice.

At Union Square, Park Avenue turns into Broadway, which is a trick of the city. From the sky you would see an *S*. Not quite an *S*, not an *S* at all, actually, but the limber coil of a pried-apart paper clip. I had the exhausted feeling that I could not be alone anymore. I'd been staring at dogs lately. Each time thinking, *A dog would be good.*

"Almost home," Mark said.

My dorm was not home. There was no home. I'd lost home. And now I was grown. Being grown means living among strangers; it means experience that kills. I did not say this to Mark. When you are grown, you must not speak foolishly. It is not profitable, not wise.

"Are you going to leave me now?"

"No," he said. "I took the day off."

And in the shelter of his presence, I dared to touch my belly.

2.

IF YOU THINK THERE ARE NO TREES IN NEW YORK CITY, YOU ARE WRONG. There are juvenile trees—trees shaped like lollipops, trees spaced like in collectible railroad towns, and when the wind goes through, it does not blow but hiss. Through the casement windows of the dormitory, you could hear the sound, like the sound of suffering.

In classrooms and lecture halls people stared, fascinated by the sight of the girl he loved. I was despised; I was desired; there was the stain of disgrace about me. People could read on my skin the consequences of something huge and unimaginable. They looked like looking at a recently landed meteor, assessing the dents, counting the holes, feeling for residual heat from the atmospheric friction, gazing up to wonder at the trajectory between planets. Professors cleared their throats, breathing back into elevator walls. At Weinstein on University or at Rubin on Fifth, boys joined me for dinner despite unoccupied tables, laying down cafeteria trays overloaded with pallid macaroni and cheese and blobs of soft-serve ice cream disintegrating into lather and spume on top of paper cups of Coke and rimless plastic bowls of Raisin Bran stacked two high and buns that click vividly when tapped by the butter knife. *Aren't you the girl from the gym?*

For privacy and quiet, I sometimes went to Loeb Student Center on Washington Square near the library where Puerto Rican guys from Kew Gardens showed off their new ties and Korean girls from Bayside wore cheap dress shoes and everybody paid cash for lunch. At Loeb, people would politely let you cut in line. They didn't care. They would sit for hours, waiting in the warmth between classes, ten or twelve at a table, reading the news.

I became obsessed with the news. I read papers everywhere, sometimes twice, snatching up any rag from counters, garbage pails, exercise bikes, asking doormen, "Is this your paper?" Thinking, he's out there, somewhere.

But the boys could be persistent, circling and landing, taking up residence like insects or ravenous animals, and you give in because we're all vermin anyway, and predators, and who can fault a creature for abusing opportunity when it is simply nature driving it? You might as well try to stop night. At basketball games and in coffee shops, they would come. Messages in the mailbox and shy raps at the door and midnight walks through Greenwich Village that are like quiet dreams you have dreamt. The piping squeak of leather and the scent of sugared coffee and stories that make you laugh for a moment, forgetting yourself. Sometimes there is a meandering wind and animated bits of paper milling down gutter tracks and light that sifts through the desiccated mesh of half-remaining leaves onto the streets and the hoods of cars, quivering there, and through the light, the supple skin of his face, the weighty shape of his arms—boys have such nice arms and nice chests, and every one of them is different with different qualities to his proportions. There is a special purpose to boys, to the limited realm about them, to the glorious idiom of their sex. Sometimes you cannot resist—a night or two is not so criminal, not if you leave as he sleeps, and you keep to yourself the lies a girl should never tell, and remember always to take a boy at his word when he says he loves his freedom. Don't they always say they love their freedom?

I HAD TO PAY Mark what I owed him. Five hundred dollars for the private operation and the shot of Demerol, which was worth about four of the five. Lowie once said that a shot of Demerol is like a week in Bermuda.

"Forget about it," Mark said. He preferred to erase the debt, to pick up after Rourke and to own a piece of me, only he didn't push because he was smart. He knew I would never allow him to lessen Rourke or allow anyone to lessen Rourke. If you ever saw Mark's eyes, you would see him figuring, always figuring.

I said, "I'll pay you back anyway."

"Take your time," he said, fast. Mark spoke fast, giving the impression that nothing was new to him, putting you at a rhetorical disadvantage, giving his remarks the illusion of having been born of experience. "The longer it takes, the longer you stick around."

On the night of the presidential election, I got a job. I happened to be out because my roommate had turned off the television. "It doesn't make a damn bit of difference to my life who wins," Ellen said. Her face was obscured by a layer of chamomile face cream, which made her mouth stand out, like the mouth of the Joker from *Batman,* or like Pagliacci. I was sitting on my bed in half-darkness, fully dressed and feeling weirdly ungoverned, kind of solo. "Watch the results with the sound off if you want."

"Actually," I said, "I need to drop off something at the art studio."

PROBABLY I STARTED OUT looking for a coffee shop or some place with a radio. Probably I headed west when I intended south, or east when I intended north, as it was not unlike me to wander, knitting arabesques through the streets for angels to see.

I ended up on Varick below Houston, in the printing district, where I ran into three men at a blackened commercial doorway of a nightclub. Music thrashed against the wall from the backside, pleading like a prisoner. You don't ever think about it, but sound really does get trapped. There's arithmetic behind noise in space, special theorems involving mechanical limits to the containment of volume.

One guy looked south into lower Manhattan. "Where you headed, doll-face?" He had white hair and a crew cut, which had the effect of making his head seem small and thick, like a nickel. "Hate to tell you, but there's nothin' down there."

A second guy said, "Better watch out you don't get chucked in the back'a some van. Why don't you go home?"

The guy with the nickel-head asked where I lived.

"Tenth and Broadway."

"Aureole's on MacDougal, right Phil? She can cab up with Aureole."

Phil was boss—he had a clipboard. Anytime you saw a bouncer with a clipboard, he was boss. He jerked his head. "C'mon inside."

I stepped forward. "Are they looking for help?"

"Ask for Richard," Phil advised. With one bloated, I.D.-braceleted wrist, he yanked the door handle. He waved me past the cashier and a second set of bouncers. "Tell him Phil sent you."

Inside was purple, like a black-light basement or creepy fish tank. The main room was huge and hardly filled. The place must have been some kind of cafeteria during the day because breakfast special menus hung near the ceilings and the disc jockey was set up on a grill and the decorations were vintage neon diner signs. Five or six customers stood at the perimeter of the cement dance floor, shuffling experimentally to "Treat Her Like a Lady." Another fifteen or so hung off the ledge of a mammoth bar like there was nothing happening in the nation of greater consequence than vodka and cocaine.

"Where's Richard?" I asked a girl at the service bar.

She waved a finger over an emaciated tattooed collarbone. "Try the kitchen." The tattoo looked like a banana. "Yugoslavian flag," she explained. "It didn't come out right."

"I think it looks pretty," I said. "Are you Aureole?"

"Frankie," she replied. "Aureole's around somewhere."

The kitchen was vacant except for a guy reclining on a counter reading a folded newspaper. I could just make out the granular sound of election results on his AM radio. "Richard?"

"Nick," he said definitively, looking over, swinging up, extending a hand. Behind him was a calendar with a picture of a pagoda on it. "Richard's in the office. I'll get him." Nick handed me his paper as he passed. It was the *New York Times* crossword puzzle. "Do me a favor. Help me out here."

I answered as many as I could in the minutes it took for him to return. He came from a staircase in the rear of the kitchen with a crate of Heineken on one shoulder. "He'll be right over," Nick said, turning away from me. In his back pocket was an application. "Fill it out while you're waiting. Use my pen."

I marked Thursday through Saturday as my available days and gave the application to the elusive Richard, a towering, sour-looking man in black leather who appeared from nowhere and gave the impression of being very dead or very guilty.

He scanned it impassively. "References?"

"None I feel like listing."

Our eyes met over the sheet; he smiled weakly. I could not imagine him calling the Lobster Roll. Besides there is a trick to getting a job, which is not really needing it and only half-wanting it.

"When can you start?"

"Whenever."

"Thursday," he said. "Terry's off Thursdays. Stick around and have a beer." And without another word he left, just as he'd arrived, mute and sinuous, disintegrating into concrete and neon, nearing his own departure like volume fading down to nothing.

I had a Budweiser and finished the crossword with Nick while we listened to Reagan's acceptance speech. He chucked my empty bottle into a trash can where it smacked and busted. "They'll reinstitute the draft for sure. It'll be war with Russia."

My head was upside down, between my knees.

Nick patted my back. "Lemme get you an ice bucket."

I waved. "I'll be all right."

"I'm taking my wife and kids to Australia," he confided, and he pulled out a long strip of wallet photos. "You can come along if you want. I mean, just to get you started, you know, with friends."

The club filled considerably. Nick returned to work and dropped me off at the deejay booth. A small sign on the glass grill barrier said, *D.J. Jerome*.

"Jim Jerome," he clarified, laying his cigarette on the turntable frame and extending a hand. He sounded like Mr. Rogers. "It's supposed to say *Jim* but they printed it wrong. People keep calling me *Jerry*. What's your name?"

I told him, and he repeated it twice. *Eveline, Eveline*. He said it thoughtfully like he was imagining a place, trying to recall if he'd ever been there, like, *the Cloisters, the Cloisters*. Jim tucked one headphone cup between his ear and shoulder, and his eyes secured some point in the middle distance. Jim engrossed himself in the mix, fingering the album back and forth. Underneath the song that was already playing came "Emotional Rescue." I tried to remember when songs had stopped beginning and ending, when the mix had become so important, when deejays had turned into weavers. The absence of interruption in music was like proof of cohesion in rough and fast times. No one could bear a second of silence. I noticed that Jim wore an amulet.

The mix was extended, so he took me to find Aureole. He knew where to go. She was in the staff bathroom beneath the kitchen stairs, fixing her hair and smoking a joint. It was a swervy bob the color of Darjeeling tea, situated wiggishly over a pair of doe-like violet eyes. On her left cheek was a mole. She looked somewhat like a young Liz Taylor, only freckled and not such an absolute knock-out. I figured she was my age, around twenty.

Jim stepped in, drawing me behind him. "Hi sweetie. This is Eveline."

"Hi, Eveline. Phil told me you want to share a cab."

I shrugged. "I can walk."

"God, no. I'm happy for company."

"You're sharing a cab?" Jim's eyes twinkled. "That is so precious."

We got high with her, real quick, then we went up together, and the place seemed nicer than before. The lights were satiny and the crowd was original and downbeat. Jim played "My Jamaican Guy" for Frankie, whose boyfriend, Charles, was from Negril, and the whole staff stopped working to dance.

"How'd it go?" Phil inquired. He was alone outside. The others were in the kitchen on dinner break. I'd said goodnight to them there.

"Okay I guess. I start Thursday."

He nodded. "Work out okay with Aureole?"

"Yeah," I said. "She's getting her stuff."

Phil's hair was receding, and he was conscious of that and also of the bulk of his wrists, so when he offered a cigarette, I took it. He didn't really deserve a no. We stood for a while—actually, I leaned. Cigarettes make me dizzy.

"So, Reagan won."

"Yeah." Phil flicked his butt to the curb. "The actor."

HEARTBREAK WAS NOT A great club, it was an okay club, kind of a dive actually, but an enduring sort of dive popular among idiosyncratic losers and peripheral celebrities and iffy stock brokers and borderline rock musicians, those haggard, nicotine-types in creased leather and reedy denim who sleep all day but somehow earn livings and are either present-casual drug users or past-heavy drug users. I worked three nights, eleven to four, earning shift plus tips. I did far more dancing than drink-serving, but Richard didn't seem to mind, and, besides, tips were better that way.

The job exempted me from having to socialize at school, and it gave me a reason for insomnia. Instead of getting up after a sleepless night feeling depleted and suicidal, I felt that way after staying out until dawn, which improved my disposition enormously. I got home from work at five, showered, then went to bed at daybreak. Usually I slept until ten—hardly enough time even to dream. And all the deprivation had an interesting effect on my looks. My features hardened, turning older somewhat and inured to new hardship.

The atmosphere at the club was actually pretty wholesome. Dad and Marilyn stopped by sometimes to visit. Like most everyone working there—gentlemanly bouncers, family-minded barbacks, lesbian cowgirl deejays, film-maker waitresses—I was in it for the money. Like everyone else, I had a complicated past that made me indifferent to entanglements and wild times. If only the loneliness there could have alleviated the loneliness in me, if only a nightclub were not such an institute of longing, of darkness plus disclosure, maybe I would have gotten better.

At two-thirty in the morning one Friday in December, Mark came in. I hadn't seen him since the surgery. Every week I mailed a money order for twenty-five dollars, which he always acknowledged with a phone call, and when he called we would speak at length. I didn't have to force myself—I enjoyed talking to him. It was like a window open, small as a needle's eye. But I never called him, not once, no matter how bad I felt or lonely or reckless.

"I can't stay," he reported. "I have a car waiting."

I was holding a freshly loaded tray. "Okay, let me get rid of this."

I crossed the suddenly packed dance floor to deliver drinks and collect money from this guy who frequently came to the club and would only be waited on by me. He wiggled his blubbery ass and sang gleefully as he fished through his pockets over and over for a wallet. "*I'm comin' out. Yeah, ooooh. Ooooh. Evie, I'm cominnnnn!*"

When he finally found it, he pulled it from a pocket he had checked about ten times. It was not good to think where his hands had been, such as shaking his linty dick over a urinal. When people say, *Don't put that money in your mouth,* they basically mean *he* had it. Denny was always telling me to be careful because guys masturbate in bathroom stalls. *And worse.*

He took his drinks and handed me a twenty. "Keep the change," he said, which was six bucks. A good tip, and yet somehow inadequate compensation for having to interact with him at all. One fact of life is that good tippers are often questionable citizens. They tip you for putting up with them. They compensate you.

Three more orders came in, all for big groups. It wasn't fair to blame Mark for the way things had turned crazy, but anyway I did. Nightclubs are places of explicit laws. It takes just one body to transform a benign gathering into an intolerable mob. Maybe I just resented that he was there, that he felt enough time had passed, that he'd waited long enough.

"Who's the suit?" Adrian the busboy shouted. I was waiting for an opening to cross back over the floor.

"Just a guy I know," I shouted back.

Aureole said, "He's cute. Like, totally undone. It looks like he ran here."

It was true. Mark's tie was loose and his jacket unbuttoned and his hair made Caesar bangs on his brow. He'd been drinking.

Adrian leaned forward. "What the fuck's he doing?"

"Is he busing tables?" Aureole asked, leaning as well, squinting. "Oh my God, I think he's busing tables."

Mark was emptying an ashtray into a gray plastic bucket, wiping it with a cocktail napkin. All the tables around him had been cleared, and he was discussing something with some customers.

When I got to him, I said, "What are you doing?"

He said, "I hate to have you touch filth."

"We have a busboy," I informed him.

"Obviously not a competent one. There's shit everywhere."

"Anyway," I said. "What's up?"

"I want to borrow you. For New Year's Eve."

"I'm working New Year's Eve."

"Take off," he declared emphatically. "How much will you make?"

I didn't know, I'd never worked on New Year's before.

"Take a guess—a hundred, a hundred-fifty?"

I shrugged. "I don't know, maybe."

"I'll double it," he proposed. "I'll give you three hundred."

"That's prostitution."

"Not if we don't have sex." He kissed me and ran out.

THE DORM ON NEW YEAR'S EVE HAD A CINEMATIC EMPTINESS THAT CALLED to my mind the evacuated ministries of European war-time movies or the hospital where they put Don Corleone in *The Godfather*.

Anselm from Berlin was on my bed. He and Mark had met at Harvard. His burgundy shirt was unbuttoned beneath his orangutan-orange leather coat, and his chest was bare. Anselm was not so much a man as an international symbol of one, like a dictionary illustration or a figure on a lavatory door. He was a gorgeous unfortunate, one of those people in whom vanity overwhelms sexuality to become a preoccupying sort of project. I found him to be a little tragic overall, a little childishly divided, a little east/west, much like the city he'd come from.

I pulled on my Girbaud jeans and a low-cut peach Fiorruci t-shirt with a lazy ruffled seam. I dressed in front of them because modesty seemed solemn and unnecessary, because sometimes a night has a natural elegance, and you are transported. Sometimes your constitution is strong despite yourself.

I said, "You look good, Anselm."

"That's what he does best," Mark said, his credit card tapping.

We stayed there for hours, with them talking and me dancing, not really listening. It didn't matter what they were talking about. It didn't matter what you said or anyone said in those days. In those days no one was smart enough to take exception, and generally things went faster than expostulation would allow. Generally you encountered walls in the faces of your friends.

"I wonder what the eighties will be like?" Mark asked.

"Decadence," Anselm declared as he toyed with the radio. His trim thighs were parted like fingers making a peace sign. With his right wrist he spun the receiver dial while his body leaned left and his clothes broke open in a soft-cornered diamond. I was not sure if he knew what he was saying, but it sounded good when he said it. In all the gum and whoosh of his German accent, everything he said sounded jurisdictional. "Decadence and free love."

"Decadence is decay," Mark speculated. "How can sex be decay?"

"Rules of sex," Anselm clarified.

Later, the radio played "Candy's Room" and Anselm said, "This is you."

I looked at him, unable to recall how we'd met, how he'd come to know me. Wasn't it through Mark, hadn't hours passed since we'd been introduced? I was careful not to say anything. I knew that in order to come through, I had to conform.

He was behind me. He said, "Forever you are Candy."

Mark was there too. "Make your lipstick darker. It's a holiday."

THERE WERE NO CARS in Soho. We walked down the middle of the street, and Mark greeted everyone—couples huddled, dog walkers, lost and rambling revelers—saying *Hello* and *Happy New Year* with great congeniality because

Mark was congenial. It was hard to despise him for it when affability is a skill of survival.

He took my hand, I took Anselm's, and we walked, united by darkness and dope. If you pried apart the frontiers of yourself, you could feel the newness, the way you can sense a phone about to ring. It truly was the eve of something, something not yours perhaps but fantastic and connected to you nonetheless.

"A decade doesn't hit its stride until a year already in," Mark claimed. "The eighties start tonight!"

"There are no decades, Ross. No years. They are social and psychological constructs," Anselm said as we turned west on Prince. "In China, it is five thousand something." *Sow-sand sum-sing.*

Snowflakes with the wind blinded me, leaving me dependent upon the mercy of my companions. It had been one year ago that I'd seen Rourke in the record store. I told myself to set the thought aside; it was a dead thought. Yet one year ago was so easy to conceive. It was not infinite galactic space or days when dinosaurs lived or the nuclear minutiae of particle physics. One year ago was yet undeparted. If I felt that way, so did he. Wherever he was, he was not happy, not without me.

"You seem happy all of a sudden," Mark said. "I'm glad."

We turned from Prince onto Thompson and raced to where we were going. Melting chunks of snow straked the building's deteriorated stairs, weeping and rushing, shedding outwards in a minor puddle or charging crabwise in a deranged path. On the way up to the fifth floor, I saw curious portions of shoe patterns and smelled the pathetic odor of currently cooking things mixed with years upon years of formerly cooked things packing up the passage like a dam. Each landing was dressed for the season with a paper snowman head and a sorry bit of garland arched like a diabolical eyebrow tacked beneath a feeble hall light. Where the linoleum was peeling away were those little black and white floor tiles, flat but precipitous in perspective like half-revolved cubes that make you lose your balance if you look down into them. It was exactly like the building my father lived in.

"No kidding," Mark said. "Where does he live?"

"On Elizabeth Street. And Spring."

Two apartments on top joined in front to form one large living area. Through strings of clear lights that made *X*'s over the windows, you could look west and south past the meek roof line of the tenement buildings across the way. The floors were glossy white, and glass tube lights with chrome caps, like devices from old science movies or magic kit props, sat on varnished furniture. A red and yellow tapestry was hanging on the wall above a pumpkinish burl sofa. I was not sure about *burl*. Burl was all I could think.

"I see you admire my hook rug," a voice said. The voice was like cellophane melting. I turned to face a man with a shaved head and brown eyes with pupils like leaping fish, arcing over water, frozen in space. He had stylish razor stubble and stylish sunken cheeks. The drooping contour of his hairline was like the shadow of an elegant suspension bridge. He looked—I don't know—Carpathian.

"So, Ross," he said, not even looking at Mark, "this is the girl I've been hearing about." He passed my coat to unseen hands and said, "Well worth the wait." He kissed me. "I am Dara."

When Dara spoke, his words emerged mindfully, as if spaced by slender blocks. He led me by the waist into the gathering, and Mark waved an encouraging farewell. I felt like a social experiment, something along the lines of Eliza Doolittle. We made our way towards the cryptic posterior of the apartment where people gathered handsomely amidst floor-to-ceiling bookshelves and gargantuan file cabinets filled with—files, probably. Dara and I trolleyed up to and away from bands of sultry internationals—Cara from Wales, Soraya from Sao Paulo, Gunter from Vienna. There were Italians, Jordanians, French. Murat from Istanbul was the one who had taken my coat. He remained at Dara's elbow like an assistant or an aide-de-camp. "As an American," Dara said, not apologetically, "you are among the minority."

He attended to me physically but not intellectually because he was practiced as a gentleman, and practiced gentlemen tend to think of women differently than women are accustomed to being thought of. I was not insulted. It's not reasonable to go through life expecting uniformity of perception. Besides, it can be a charm to be held to lesser standards, to be kept unaccountable, to listen until being called upon to reply, to be asked to contribute only the gift of grace—the lips, the ankle, the fragrance of your hair. Such are the marks of worth when you have no others. These were the things I told myself.

Periodically I remembered Mark, periodically I located him, rustling in corners, other heads and his hunched together.

"Money," Dara informed me. "And people say art is dead."

EVENTUALLY I WAS LEFT with Anselm and Christian, a hedge fund analyst from London. Dara had some things to *attend to*, he said, though I suspected he needed a rest from me, little and willing as I was. When he left he patted my cheek and smiled as if I were a puppy he had grown tired of walking.

"Father gave me one piece of excellent advice when I left for New York," Christian was saying as he filled three shot glasses. "He said, 'Take taxis. Your time is too precious to waste.' "

"I hope *Father* gave you an excellent bank account with that excellent advice," Anselm replied.

"A moderate one. Not everyone is born into a dynasty."

Anselm laughed, and Christian laughed, and with admirable consonance the shot glasses clinked, and we dumped tequila down our throats. Their laughter joined other laughter, and all the laughter loudened into a false and raucous eruption, which was galvanizing—like Broadway laughter. I also began to laugh, at them and at me and at the phenomenon of my poverty. I felt a crippling anxiety to get started, to catch up, to figure some gimmick to win. Everyone I met that night was robust and vivacious, already chic, already traveled, already on the course to fame and fortune.

I did not despise them, I could not, not when I had no better place to be, not when I couldn't possibly spend another night alone, cultivating the company of my own American mind. Not when they had extended themselves to me though I was inferior and underfed with substandard shoes and cheap eye make-up and nothing whatsoever to offer besides the inconspicuous skill of being multiply orgasmic. And so, I endured the talk of easy prosperity as though I were on a plane half-listening to flight instructions that I knew would never save me.

> *Advertising was up 25% by the third issue—It split twice in a year and a half—The Moral Morel, maybe you've seen our trucks—She comes to the office with a portable table—My sister sells hats to Barney's.*

"What's the matta?" Anselm inquired. "You seem, like, *depress.*"

"Not enough blow," Christian diagnosed.

"Come," Anselm thickly insisted, and I acquiesced. Why not, who cared—more coke, less coke. I was glad for diversion, for anything that would impel the night to a close so I could get on with the misery of my particular posterity, so I could go home and lie awake and deliberate ad nauseam the deficiency of resource, opportunity, and luck in my life.

In the bathroom Anselm tapped some cocaine from a packet onto the fin-like membrane between his thumb and bony forefinger, the place where you make ballpoint pen puppet faces. He offered it first to me and I accepted a little, just a little, because I'd had a lot already. I'd never had so much and my body was small and my metabolism rapid and my heart still so terribly unsound. The medicine cabinet was full of apothecary bottles from Europe and ones from Kiehl's and almond soap from Bigelow Chemists. There was a horsehair brush. I asked Anselm to brush my hair the way Denny used to.

"Of course," he sputtered in his German accent as if it had been his intention from the start, and he returned the coke to his breast pocket, fingering it down like men finger down sunglasses or theater tickets. Men are beautiful that way, and heartbreaking. He rinsed the brush in steaming water then shook it, which was a precaution I would not have taken for myself, and I thanked him, and he made a noise not unlike a hum. Not a hum, a zoom. *Zoom.*

His touch was gentle. I could feel the strands of my hair separate between hot bristles that glided like burning oil. I hoped Anselm could not see the holes on my skull where the hair grows. I don't like those holes where hair comes out, those poppy seed holes. I closed my eyes as long as I could, which was in fact extremely short.

"Thank you for not asking who Denny is."

He shrugged. "I try to be sensitive."

I liked hiding in there with him. I had no idea what Anselm felt, but I suspected that even though he had money—*a dynasty*, Christian had said—he wanted something he could not get from seductress accountants in unitards and Peter Cox boots. If I knew his pain, if indeed it was pain that he felt, I would have liked to comfort him through it. If his pain involved a girl, it was a French girl, or a Swede, some imperial china blonde in a chinchilla-trimmed jacket, some cognac and three days in Biarritz.

We came out when the music got good. Anselm took me to the living room with its hook rug and burl sofa and silk-screened Bauhaus posters and red lips Bocca loveseat.

"1959," Dara said of the Danish cone chairs as he handed me another drink, which I drank though it was yellow like venom, like a potion of bee parts. "I purchased them in Milan for two million lire." I handed back an empty glass and joined Anselm in the center of the floor. We were first to dance and that was triumphant but lonesome, like being the first of your group to swim.

> *Fire.*
> *The way you walk and talk really sets me off—*

The floor filled fast after us, and right away someone started to bump, then everyone did, bones and bits of flesh tipping bits of flesh and bones and the arms bobbing overhead, a forest of arms, wintry and erect and dispossessed of covering, like limbs attached to bodies wishing to be extracted, like limbs of things buried alive. Something about the bareness plus the unity, something about the insinuation of universal plea or plan made me feel paranoid as to meaning and confused about my participation. As a girl I felt ruined. I felt hideously inverted, as if the liquid livingness of me had exploded out onto all the tasseled Bally shoes and all the camelhair cuffs, and inside me was dry and hard. Every time I met another superior gaze with another cowardly smile, I became evermore insubstantial, evermore gone.

For the first time, I began to understand the graphics of Rourke's hardship, which I saw as a fraction with failure on bottom and time on top. The meaning of the fraction is that it is impossible to carve even a moderate fortune from a society that is locked; the math of the fraction is impermeability divided by your desire to make it permeable. A wish for success by someone outside the inside reach exposes that person as inferior, which is untrue and unfair. This world was no world for a fighter.

Mark appeared like an emissary or ambassador just as I was discovering a whole new low.

"My God," he said, petting my jaw in upstrokes with the back of his hand, like I was catlike, like I was cunning, "I am so in love with you."

MARRAKECH WAS AN AFTER-hours place on East Fifth. I agreed to go, though I felt an entire catalog of self-revulsion—filthy, common, beggarly. I was consumed by a harrowing cerebral pain, which expressed itself internally in a raised sprawl like allergic welts or wheels. I felt this *swelling-in*. There was difficulty breathing and an itchiness at the ankles. I consented because I knew Mark would be more dependable with me than I would be with myself, which was a loathsome truth proving I deserved no better than him anyway. Sometimes you need a little company, and Mark was exactly that, a little company. Sometimes you do what you have to do in order to get by. He grabbed a bottle of Cristal, slid a ten-dollar tip to the bartender, and towed me like a pull toy through the dance floor to a room that was high and low and missing its face like a tunnel or chute, like a mouth agape.

Right away there was a smuffling pop. Mark poured and I drank, thinking how I hate champagne. I hate long roses too, the long-stemmed ones that look like they came off a conveyer belt.

"Don't ever send me roses," I said. I had the feeling he would.

"You don't mean that. What about garden roses? You don't mean garden roses. Garden roses are flawed and divine."

Garden roses, I thought.

"We have them in East Hampton," he continued slowly, his dexterous voice metamorphosing, turning fervid, turning faint, forcing me to lean in order to hear. "They're extraordinary. They're exposed to wind and rain and are made even more exotic by the cruel forces of nature. The petals get burned by the sun in pinholes in the center and in notches at the crest." He sipped from his glass. "If you lift a bud, it's heavy, like a paper marble. You remember," he said, "by the cottage."

"The cottage," I repeated.

"We walked down the path on the way to my car and there was white lattice and on the lattice there were roses. I should have made you stop. Next time you'll stop. You'll see the veins on the petals. Like spun glass. Like the spray of pink on your eyelids."

I dipped my head. He raised it. "Don't lower your head."

IT WAS LONG PAST dawn and cold when we crossed Fifth Street, turned up Third Avenue, and took Lafayette to Tenth. Mark stayed several yards in front, facing back, because he wanted to watch me walk. At my door I did not kiss him. I did not have to. I'd already given up so much more.

He brushed his cheek against mine, keeping it there. "It wasn't so bad, was it?"

I said, not really. The bad part was to come. The bad part was going inside alone, lying alone, waking alone.

He must have known how it would end for me because he did not leave me alone. He left me with an envelope. Beneath my pillow. Inside was three hundred dollars cash.

"LISTEN TO ME, YOU can't get a word in edgewise."

We were at Tavern on the Green. It was Valentine's Day—not Valentine's Day, two days before. He was too clever for Valentine's Day. Though had he asked I would have accepted. I didn't mind being with Mark. Time with him was public time. There was no need to do anything but project outwards from the sphere we occupied. He was not repulsed by my heartache nor impeded by my devotion. He knew Rourke; he knew Rourke's effect. He searched for it in me the way an archeolologist might crawl through caves, seeking out signs of the primitive and the incredible, feeling for gouges, testing for oxides and ochres. When I was with Mark, I could feel Rourke alive.

"Jesus, what did he do to you?" Mark once said after New Year's.

I liked when he said that; it made me feel good. It validated the blind parts of me. Maybe not blind. Blind is wrong. I do not mean *unable to see* but *unable to be seen*, which is different. The thing in my head about blind is the idea of some permanent disability. I thought about what he said over and over when he left that night—*Jesus, what did he do to you*—and erotic thoughts of Rourke became intertwined with erotic thoughts of Mark, and I had to work to keep the two separate, with one being more recent and the other being less. You get desperate sometimes to keep things recent. The effect of the remark was such that I began to wonder whether he had anticipated my response. It was possible that he had given it as a gift, but more along the lines of a degenerate gift, not to please but to test, to measure the profundity of my need, as if by exacting those dimensions he could gain some advantage against Rourke that eluded him in actuality.

In Bernardin, he talked without abeyance, speaking of sailing Swoosey's boat to Anguilla and a '66 Mustang G.T. 350 he was thinking of picking up and a funeral he went to for someone murdered by the Jewish Mafia. I had never heard of a Jewish Mafia. My dad spoke of the Russian Mafia; maybe Mark meant the *Russian* Mafia. Mark's former girlfriend was a journalist in Los Angeles who'd had breast reduction surgery. "Diane wanted to go out every night," he said as he worked through his crème brûlée. "Xenon, 54, Danceteria. And in L.A., you wouldn't know the clubs in L.A., but she burned through them. Very pretty, like Rita Hayworth in *Gilda*—but shallow. Not like you. In all the years I dated her, she never looked at the stars."

"Why did you stay with her?"

"Because everyone wanted her, but only I could get her."

There was a gift—a book on Giotto he'd purchased while we were at the museum that afternoon. "I can't believe you didn't notice it under my coat. I looked like a Bible salesman." I flipped through the pages. "Ever think about going to Italy?"

I looked at him closely. He and Alicia appeared to be unrelated. He was more neutral in color, with skin that was pale and hair without accent or modulation. He wore it long and back off his face. The color of his suit was the color of his eyes, a grief-stricken gray, like sharkhide. Light licked off them, making him appear shrewd, making him seem to work twice, two times, now and the next. His lips were straight and his nose was straight and his hair, and yet for all that directness of line he was extremely obtuse. Everything he said came out as though in code, one character at a time.

"I guess," I said. "Someday."

"*Someday*," he said with a toss of his head. "I'll take you anytime you want."

Mark became attractive when he referred to money. Money meant attractive things to him—freedom and fulfillment—and a girl cannot be blamed for taking a man as he prefers to be found, or for feeling exhausted beneath the heft of her own meager particulars, or for giving way to self-confidence when it makes itself manifest like lightning before your eyes. It is like being hypnotized.

He assisted me as I stood, placing a hand on my low back. I did not flinch. No one could touch the place that was Rourke's. No one could get through.

"What are you thinking of?" he whispered to my neck.

"Hypnosis," I said. "I'm thinking of hypnosis."

Rob wanted to know what I was doing, did I have plans.

"When?" I asked.

He said, "Tonight."

"I'm not doing anything."

"Good. I'll be over at seven."

At seven I found him sitting on the southwest corner of the security desk, sweet-talking Juanita the guard. Under one arm was a Richard Pryor album, and in his hand was a suspicious-looking paper bag.

"Straight up in Bedford," Juanita was saying.

Rob repeated like he didn't hear right, "Up in *Bedford?*"

Juanita's walkie-talkie hissed at her hip. "That's right."

"*Bedford Falls*, like in the movie?"

"Actually, Bedford Hills."

"Oh, *Bedford Hills*. You had me goin' there for a minute." He creaked his neck around in its socket. "Bedford Falls. That'd be something. That'd be like meeting somebody from Mayberry."

I signed Rob in. Beyond him, the doors to the dorm opened onto the street. There was an elastic allure to the April night, which was the science of things being risen. It was like a puppet being pulled to a stand or bread growing large. Had I been in East Hampton, I would've gone out to the beach or the woods.

I asked Juanita if Rob was giving her a hard time.

"Not at all, honey," she said.

"Me?" Rob exclaimed. "She's the one telling me she's from Bedford Falls!" I pulled him off the desk by his sleeve. "I love that movie—*Zuzu's petal*. I get my injection every year." He paused by Juanita's shoulder. "You wanna know something? I've seen that film a dozen times, and I've never made it through *Miracle on 34th Street* once."

We boarded the elevator, and the heavy doors closed. Inside, the light was bright and bad, and you could read the comments that had been scratched into the metal panels with keys and knives. It was the first time I'd seen Rob since summer, and nothing was different. That is to say, though I had changed and he had changed, there was a place we shared that was enduring, a region of memory and fidelity. In that region, we observed the need for caution. In that region was Rourke.

"Ever chew tobacco?" he inquired, both of us standing straight ahead.

I said that I hadn't.

"You're in for a night, then." He shook the paper bag, dangling it like a mouse he'd caught. "*Elephant Butts*. Charlie Cutlass drove it down from Oswego. I ever tell you about Charlie Cutlass?"

"No," I said.

"Sad story. Tell you later, over a good stiff drink. Remind me."

Rob's eyes would not rest long on me. Every day I dealt with the business of my handicap, so I'd become used to it, but it was new to him, and I was sorry for the shock of his seeing me lame. I thought he would kiss me. He couldn't even kiss me.

Rob had come to tell me something or ask me something, and that something had to do with Rourke. Behind every situation is a picture, and I got the picture quickly. It was a mill of conditional facts, a scrolling circle, like daisy blades that loop back onto a center with each truth arcing stoutly then crimping back with humility—Rob stood by Rourke and Rob felt bad for me; I could not speak without seeming to blame Rourke and Rob could not speak without seeming to betray him; I would not compromise their friendship by speaking of feelings, and yet my silence had the very effect I'd hoped to avoid.

We were sitting on the floor by my bed. "Where's your friend tonight?" Rob asked.

"Which friend is that?"

"Which friend," Rob repeated. He spit into a paper cup, the tobacco juice shooting in a streak between his top and bottom teeth.

I stood to flip the album. I was very high from tobacco. I felt like someone was tossing me into the wall, only there was no one, just the wall. Me flying at it. "He's away."

"Sure. Golfing in Palm Beach. Tough life."

"I don't know. I don't like Florida."

"You'd change your tune fast enough. Those people travel in style. Five stars all the way. For breakfast there's oatmeal, fruit cups, trays of bacon, the papers, a swim. Then sun. Later is shopping, tennis, a massage, another swim. You pop a button off your slacks or spill hollandaise on your dinner jacket, and they got a Polish laundry lady and a tailor in the closet of your suite. Waiting, like elves. They come out when you're gone and pick lint."

I came back down, crashing shoulders. "I wouldn't trade places with him."

Rob slapped his thighs. "No way. Who needs margaritas and white sands when we've got everything right here—chewing tobacco, Richard Pryor, a dormitory carpet, and a couple cans of—what is this crap we're drinking?" He looked around for his soda.

"Tab." I'd taken it from Ellen's refrigerator.

He shook his head. "Jesus. *Tab.* I'm happy as a clam."

"Don't forget the girl," I reminded him.

"No," he said. "Who could forget the girl."

This was followed by a hapless interlude, a spasm in the atmosphere like a charley horse, which I handled with inside thoughts of neutral stuff, such as the image of a spoon standing straight in the middle of a cup of coffee. Rob just kept looking around, nodding serially like one of those hard dogs in the rear windows of cars from the boroughs.

"So," he said, "who does this roommate think she is anyway, one of the Gabors?"

THE MAIN THING TO do at Gulf Coast is drink jalapeno martinis. Rob ordered two as he removed his hooded gray sweatshirt. Underneath was a denim vest, and under that, a t-shirt. *Fantini Brothers Construction. If I had my way I'd tear this fucking building down.*

The bartender said, "Seven bucks."

Rob gave him a withering look then paid. "I gotta get you out to Pinky's. None of this three-dollar-and-fifty-cent pepper water. Served by actors. When's your birthday?"

"November."

"Damn. Too far. What's the next holiday?"

"I don't know. Memorial Day?"

"Nah, Easter." *Easta.* "Tell you what. We'll get a couple bunnies and go to Williamsburg. My mother makes up baskets for the Sunday School kids. I'll get her to make you up a basket. With that shredded crap, that nest crap. Girls like that crap. What do you call it?"

I shrugged. "Shredded nest crap."

He eyed me. "You think I'm kiddin'."

"I don't."

"You're gonna back out on me, aren't you? I'll be sittin' there alone with a beer and a bunny basket, and I'll be lucky to leave Pinky's with my nose on straight."

Denny was late as usual. He and Rob had not yet met, but they'd heard about each other. In any case, I prepared them extra. I told Denny that Rob was not a bigot despite the fact that he might look and sound like one, and I told Rob that Denny was *gayish*.

"What's that mean, *gay-ish*?" Rob wanted to know. "Don't he know by now?"

"Yeah, but it's probably better if you don't mention it."

"Oh, yeah, yeah. Sure, I getcha," Rob nodded and pointed.

I wasn't exactly sure what it was he got, and got so vividly, but I figured I ought to let it go.

"Hey'ya, kid, how's curtain-making going?" Rob said the second Denny walked in.

"Just fine, sweetheart," Denny replied. "I'm knitting you a swimsuit for summer." He draped his blue Aquascutum trench coat on the back of a stool. Denny said it was the same coat John Lennon used to have.

He kissed me and sized up Rob's outfit. "What happened? Did you change a few tires on the way over?"

Denny gestured for a new round by snapping his fingers in the air then making a lasso with his left index finger. Denny was a lefty. Every now and then he would fly into a panic. "Do you know that lefties die on average ten years sooner than righties? It's the stress!"

He acted slightly more gay since moving to New York, which may have been belated self-expression, or something more formulated and political, or just a time-saving transmission of preference. I was confused about whether to be glad for him because he was finally able to articulate himself, or concerned that he was losing his individuality and imitating new friends. He had a lot of new friends.

"FIT is filthy with fags," he'd say.

WE WALKED FROM THE West Side Highway across Twelfth Street and up to Stecky's in Chelsea, and at Stecky's we met a waitress named Majesty, who was married to Billy the bartender. Billy had a handlebar moustache.

"How long's that thing?" Rob inquired. "Like before you wax it. You know, after a shower? Is it down to your chin, or what?" He flipped up his hands. "Just curious."

Billy and Majesty lived in Yonkers, which is where Rob grew up before moving to Jersey, so there was plenty to talk about, such as all the streets—Jerome Avenue, Tuckahoe Road, the Grand Concourse, and so on. Rob kept talking about routes and parkways, saying what a *sweet highway* this was, and what a *sweet highway* that was.

"How about the Taconic?" Billy asked. "Ever driven on the Taconic?"

"The Taconic is really sweet," Rob said.

"*Really* sweet," Billy agreed as he began to juggle two bottles of gin.

Rob threw himself back in his chair. "Ho! Jesus, be careful!"

"Take it easy," Billy told him. "I'm not gonna whack you."

Rob rolled back his shoulders to relax. "Sorry about that. I'm just very accident prone. I'm like an accident waiting to happen."

Denny read out the trivia question written in blue wax on the bar mirror. "*Who was the last triple crown winner before Secretariat?*"

"It's a tough one," Billy said. "It's been up all day."

"Call your dad," Denny suggested. "Anton knows everything. We used to call him for papers instead of going to the library."

"Get him on the horn," Rob said. He asked Billy for a phone.

I dialed. Rob nudged me. "I never heard you mention parents. I thought you came from swans."

"You mean storks," I said.

"No, baby, I mean swans."

Dad picked up. "*Hello.*"

"Hi, Dad, it's me."

"Yeah, hi!" he called out excitedly. My father always calls out on the phone, like he's talking into one of those candlestick jobs. It's a wartime habit, like hoarding canned foods. The basement of the shop is full of canned foods. "What's up?" he asked.

"I'm at a bar with Denny and Rob. What's up with you guys?"

"We just got back from dinner. With Ralph Russo. His nephew's got neck cancer."

"Neck cancer?" I said.

"That's no name for a horse," Rob said in my ear.

"First he had the polyps," Dad told me. "They took them out and biopsied them. Now he's gotta get that operation. The hole and the battery-operated thing. The wand. Poor bastard. He just turned thirty."

It didn't feel right to mention the trivia question considering Ralph Russo's nephew, but the whole bar was waiting on the edge of their stools.

Dad didn't even have to think. He just said, "Citation, 1948."

I asked Billy, "Is it Citation?"

Billy said, "Bingo!"

Denny took the phone to say hello, then Rob took a turn, saying, *You've got one hell of a trap brain and one sweetheart of a daughter*. A few more people grabbed the receiver to say congratulations and ask Dad if he had any tips on tomorrow's races. When I finally said goodbye, my father sounded pretty cheerful. I was glad we'd had the chance to talk. "Bye, Dad. Say hi to Marilyn."

"All right then," he called out, "have a good time."

Billy gave us a round of highballs even though the prize was one free drink. "Soliciting recruits is not legal, but I'll let you slide because I was just about to wipe it off the board anyway."

DENNY WANTED TO CALL Jeff. Jeff was Denny's new friend. He wasn't friends anymore with John, which was too bad because I liked John. They'd been together for four years.

"He gave me cooking lessons for Christmas," Denny complained. He stuck out his hand for more change. He'd already used up most of what I'd had, though he hadn't gotten through. I found one last dime in my pocket. "Can you believe it?"

"Cooking's okay," I said. I didn't see anything wrong with cooking. Denny was actually a lousy cook.

Majesty came by and pointed to an *Out of Order* sign taped to the side of the box. "Can't you geniuses read?"

She took us to use the house phone in the shaft-like kitchen, which was tipped and cramped and craven yellow from years of meat grease. Dented bowls were stacked on shelves, and the red ceramic tiles on the floor collapsed in web-like puddles. Above the deep tub sink, a window not wide enough for a dog opened onto the wall of an adjoining building. In the center of the remaining space was a butcher block table. In the center of that, a sloped pond. I asked Denny where the wood in the middle went to.

"Shavings," he said, covering the receiver. "They attach to food."

Majesty came back in with Rob and two ice-cold bottles of Dom Perignon. "Let's *par-ty*!" She tore off her sweater and tied her hair into a knot at the scalp, leaving the kinky remainder to droop over the ledge of her head like a frozen fountain. She kicked her hips left and right to "Magic Carpet Ride," which was playing out front.

While she opened the first bottle, Rob grabbed four hot glasses out of the dishwasher. His face was sober, and Denny's face was also sober—that was to be expected. Sometimes it's not possible to ignore the link between generosity and pathos, and only the most unfeeling of characters will capitalize lightly on the loneliness of others.

"I'm celebrating," she announced, slurping back the first glassful of champagne. "Me and Billy leave for Cozumel on Sunday."

"Yeah, well, don't drink the water down there," Rob said, "or you'll be celebrating on the can."

"Let's *all* make a toast," she said. "One at a time. You next."

Denny was in love, and Rob won big at Belmont.

We drank two times. "How 'bout you, Evie?"

"Trust me," Denny said, "she's got nothing to frolic about."

Rob spit up, and they both laughed.

"You guys!" Majesty said. "You guys are like totally rotten."

Denny grabbed me. "C'mon, honey, let's go dance."

ROB CASED THE PAYPHONE. He laid his palms on the groin of the box, in a Jujitsu style, then he drew the heel of his hand back and pummeled a tender spot on its side. Right away coins came splashing, and we dove to pick them up. Most of them were probably mine.

"Who do you think you are?" Majesty asked. "*The Fonz?*"

"You know, you remind me of Harvey Keitel," Denny said.

"Keitel's short," Rob speculated as we walked on. "Isn't he short?"

Nobody could beat Rob at pinball since he jumped the machine when he smacked the flippers. While he played, we used all the phone change at the jukebox, putting in our favorite songs and everybody's favorite songs. Denny polled the bar, interspersing each request with "American Pie" until Majesty threatened to unplug the machine. "American Pie" was his favorite. He had about a million favorites, but that was his all-time favorite. And Dusty Springfield was his all-time favorite artist.

Denny and I danced. He was big but he wafted when he moved. His Uncle Archer had taught us all the dances from *Saturday Night Fever*. We must have seen the movie fifteen times. "Seventeen," Denny corrected and we dipped. The bar and the liquor bottles drifted obliquely. "I still have the stubs."

Johnny Mathis came on so he started singing. "*Chances are—*"

I'd forgotten how confusing it is to touch a body that is an attractive body to which you are not necessarily attracted, to be near your opposite but not your match. All the things that click on in your head have to click off. My breasts were bearing into his chest, my hands were holding his biceps, and I could feel the package of his penis through his pants, which was a soft feeling and not intimidating, because his body was his own and not something he hoped to share with me. Denny finished up, belting out the end, and then we kissed and bowed and the crowd applauded.

Rob whistled from his tilted-back chair.

"You two are out of Guy Lombardo!" Majesty hollered.

Rob told Denny, "I gotta get you down to the Criterion."

Denny sat and wiped his brow. "What's that?"

"A club down in Jersey, for fighters. What are you, six-one?"

"About, but I'm fat." He squeezed the skin around his watch band. "I need to lose twenty pounds."

"You're not fat. You just need to make muscle. Somebody light on his feet like you would make good money as a sparring partner. A lot of guys are powerful, but they're dead weight. Fighters need to practice moving. So long as you didn't cry or anything."

"Denny wouldn't cry," I said defensively.

"Let me tell you something angel, they *all* cry," Rob said. "Right at weigh-in. You'd be surprised what the thought of a ruptured spleen'll do to a guy."

It was about two in the morning when Denny said he had to go meet Jeff at the White Horse. I felt nervous about losing him. Rob would probably go too. We said goodnight to the people we'd met, and Rob gave Denny his phone number in case he changed his mind about sparring. When Rob wrote, he hung over the table, parallel to it, focusing his might on the task at hand. I knew why Rourke liked him—for his aliveness, his connectedness. If anything bad ever happened to Rob or Denny, it would just about destroy my faith in living. I wondered if they felt the same about me.

AT EMPIRE DINER, WE sat at the counter, and he ordered four meals. I wasn't very hungry, but he said he'd eat whatever I didn't want.

"You believe in God?" he asked.

"I don't know," I said. "I'm not sure."

"My family believes in God. They stop in church every day. The priest comes by the house—dinner, coffee. My grandmother makes him *pasta e fagiole* to take back to the Rectory. I have to go over there to pick up the used Tupperware, and he comes out with a shopping bag. God is like, the house, the street, the neighborhood. It's the way things are. If you've got a problem with that, or any questions, well, you go ahead and become a priest."

He finished off the last of my cheeseburger, buckling the splayed wedge into his mouth. "When I lived in L.A. I heard shit like, *God is what I perceive him to be.* Or, *I have a personal relationship with God.* Or, *I don't believe in God, I believe in an all-powerful, all-loving being.* All-powerful, all-loving being? What is that? Same as God, only no rules!"

The waitress collected our plates. She was pretty in jeans with bad skin and two black braids. Rob stopped her, touching her wrist lightly and picking off the last little remainder of a tuna sandwich.

"Growing boy," he explained with a wink.

She stood there, plates suspended. "Sure you got enough? There's a sprig of parsley here and an orange wheel."

"I'm good. Just bring some coffee and cake. Whatever you got. Your choice." When she took off, he said, "She's cute. Interesting."

She *was* cute and interesting. Waitresses are universally interesting. They are experts in humanity, like taxi drivers. They all obviously have better places to be, except of course the ones who do not, and those are the *really* interesting ones. The best part of being a waitress is that you're part of a culture, and if you ever start to feel degraded, you just have to think of all the people you work with who are equally degraded, and you feel solidarity. Solidarity is a prize. It's a nice feeling that you can only experience if you have endured intolerable conditions. Life is funny about prizes.

"This girl on the radio is saying how she broke her back and the doctors told her she wouldn't walk for a year. While she was in traction she prayed to God to get well so she can pay the mortgage on her new house in Sheepshead Bay. A couple days later, she's walking. *God granted my wish*, she says."

"That's pretty bad."

"Where I come from, you pray for hard times to get better and they do, not because God pays the mortgage, but because the people next door lend you money. When my mother prays, you can hardly hear. It's like a slow leak in the faucet."

The waitress returned with coffee and cake. The cake was shaped like a circle, not tall but flat like a soggy disc.

Rob threw up his hands. "What happened?"

"Pineapple cheesecake," she said. "It gets wilty."

"It looks like you dropped it onto the saucer from midair."

"It happens to be very popular. You got the last two pieces. I can take them back and re-sell them."

"Nah. I'm just giving you a hard time because I like those braids." But as soon as she turned, he stopped me from taking a bite. "Watch it with creams," he warned under his breath, testing the cake then giving reluctant approval. "They go rancid very easy."

He dumped three sugars into his cup and stirred. "My brother Joey dragged a couple kids out of a fire."

"They okay?"

"Dead." Rob sucked back a sip of coffee and gestured to the side of his skull like he was screwing in something invisible. "Joey's all fucked up now," he said. "My father thinks he needs counseling. *Counseling*—I mean, you gotta know my father. Not exactly the therapy type. But Joey can't sleep, can't eat, he sits up all night staring at his kids. He can't go back to work. And I'm listening to this lunatic on the radio, thinking of my brother running into a burning building. Where was God for those kids? And their parents? And my brother? And what about *his* kids? And—"

"Excuse me." It was a guy at a table. Three guys.

Rob looked over his shoulder and instinctively shifted on his stool to block me. Lots of people say, *Over my dead body*. With Rob, it was true. And unlike with Denny, Rob *was* my opposite. I couldn't help but wonder—does my perfume distract him as much as the way he chews his ice distracts me?

"What's up?" Rob said.

"You ice skate?"

"Me?" Rob lifted his cup. "Forget about it. I'm like, the faster, the better. I got an injury though, from a bike. My knee."

The guy said, "Oh yeah?"

Rob said, "Yeah. A crack-up in the Bronx." He twitched his neck to the left, which I knew was another sad thought, this time about Bobby G. Rob loves his friends, and he loves kids. Whenever you pass a baby, he'll strike up a conversation with the parents, bragging about his nephews, showing pictures, bending to the baby. "Hey, little guy, hey, little buddy, what's the name of your horsey? *Cotton*? Very nice." Rob will turn to say, "See how clever? *Cotton*, because it's puffy and white. Very clever." If the baby is a girl, he calls her *Princess*.

"Where's the best place to skate?"

"In April? Sky Rink's about it. Rockefeller's closed now for the season. But anyway, they'd want fifteen bucks."

They thanked him, and Rob noticed the clock. "Shit!" He half-stood and polished off his coffee, going, "Shit, shit, shit." Then he jumped up and looked at the check, threw down some cash, and waved. "C'mon, c'mon. Gotta go see Uncle Tudi."

ROB HAD A TIGHT bouncy walk. He leaned forward as if his torso were connected in a line to his legs, and he walked with purpose, though it was rare that he had one. He pulled me by the wrist down Tenth Avenue into the meat district, past the hookers and queens and the stalled and steamed Impalas. Girls in sheer babydoll dresses and boys like girls in zipper-back shorts and vinyl boots riding up brawny thighs were rods of color against a groveling, nonvascular backdrop. At the loading dock to Falco's Meats, Rob pulled something folded from his back pocket, opened it up, and checked it over.

I took another look at the prostitutes. They were like lost sentinels, flecking the concrete horizon with bioluminescence and treading stiffly, leaning to solicit the occasional passing car just like they do on *Starsky and Hutch*. At first you are not sure they're there, they go so slow, but when you wait they appear, like jubilantly decorative fish caught in a choke of algae, surprising you with their permanence and omnidirectional eyes.

Rob crammed the paper back in his pocket. He was always cramming stuff in his pocket. Then he headed to the door. Remembering himself, he stopped to hold it for me.

"How ya doin', Tommy?" he said to the guy at the counter, then he rushed past like he'd just been there, like he'd forgotten his keys.

Tommy flipped a wilted page of yesterday's news. "Hey Robbie, que paso?" Tommy had dappled facial skin. There's a name for that disease, it's a pigment disease. Alopecia is losing hair, urticaria is hives.

"My uncle leave yet?"

"Nah, he's still out back."

Rob parted a row of foggy plastic strips for me. "You're not gonna get sick are you?"

"Not in front of Uncle Tudi," I said.

Rob said, "All right. That's what I wanted to hear."

Curtains of animals lined two sides of the aisle, and I held my breath as we raced toward a room in back of the warehouse. Though my eyes were trained on the sawdust, I noticed anyway that the pigs had no conspicuous necks, and I experienced a touch of vertigo, like the floor was a piano string, and I could sprong right off. Pig necks are not so noticeable when pigs are standing in a barn or at a fair, but when pigs are pendant and dead, you can see how directly their backs slope into quadrangular heads, boxy like dice. At the end of the bright, bright run was a filthy glass wall and, behind it, hunched torsos sitting. Four middle-aged men with tinted glasses and caps tipped rakishly and long dog faces habituated to a world of flesh for sale were playing cards. Inside the office was the coiled gleam of a space heater and a tar-coated Mr. Coffee machine and a half-eaten Entenmanns cheese strudel. Inside the office you could see the smocks streaked with brown lines, which were stains of blood and guts and marrow where the men had dragged their freezer-swollen fingers dry.

Uncle Tudi was huge. His meticulous street clothes were an expression of superiority—a dress shirt, a sweater, and a quilted corduroy hunting jacket. I would not normally stare, but his massive anatomy coupled with his dizzying confidence was an incredible sight. Like one of those giant pumpkins you see in October at country stores, he was dumpy and impudent, ghastly and peculiar, squat and sideways-tilted. You couldn't help but try to guess his weight— three hundred and seven pounds.

The guys nodded. *How ya doin' kid? Hey Robbie. What's up?*

Uncle Tudi breathed thickly, towing in streams of candied meathouse air. He finessed the cards beneath the bulk of his manicured fingers. Just past the knuckle of his left pinky was a solid gold ring set with a diamond chip. His cologne was a jungle about him. "Who's the lady friend?" he wanted to know.

"This is Eveline," Rob said, jiggling in place, picking an end-slice of cake off the table and eating it.

"What kinda name is that?"

Rob nudged his head at me in the direction of his uncle.

"I don't know," I said. "Just a name I guess."

"I know it's a name. What kinda name? Irish, English, what?"

"I think my mother just made it up."

Tudi creaked back unevenly in his folding chair. "I thought so. I never heard'a that name before. Sounds modern."

"I fold," the guy across from him sighed, laying down his hand and checking his watch.

"Me too," another said.

The one next to Rob threw a ten-dollar bill on top of the pool, and Tudi did too. They showed their hands. The guy had three jacks; Tudi had three tens and a pair of sixes. He scooped his winnings.

"Maybe it's an old-fashioned name, Tudi, like Ernestine or Lily," the guy with the watch speculated. He swept the cards into a pile and shuffled expertly.

Tudi clicked his tongue. "If it was *old-fashion*, we would'a heard it before. Especially you, Tony, you're older than dead dog shit. That's why I figure it's modern. Am I right?" he asked me, peering intensely and expectantly into my face like a seaman gauging a swelling cloud. One eye was millimeters larger than the other.

"Yes, I guess—"

He interrupted me. "Where'd youse meet?"

"Montauk," Rob answered.

Somebody said, "Montauk! She fishes?"

"I ever tell you, Pat," one of the guys said to another, "the transmission in my car has five settings—park, drive, neutral, reverse, and Montauk. I adjust the arm and it goes." His flattened palm cut into the air, *Bzjump*.

Through his teeth, Rob said to his uncle, "At Harrison's place."

"At Harrison's place," Tudi repeated as he organized his money, lining up bills by denomination then folding the packed knot into his shirt pocket. He coughed a little, repeating, "Harrison," then he coughed more, and the room got quiet. He picked up a napkin and held it over his mouth and he stayed still and everybody stayed still. I had the feeling Rob was going to get hit.

Tudi shouted, "What the hell's the matter with you? It's not the board-walk out there, you moron!"

"Which one's Harrison?" Pat murmured. "The fighter?"

The others nodded grimly.

Tudi stood and adjusted his collar. "You got some papers for me?"

Rob said, "Yeah."

"Gentlemen," Tudi stated formally. "If you don't mind."

We followed him to the door, where he just squeaked through. And in the area close beyond, Rob exchanged the contents of his pocket for ten fifties. His uncle perused the sheets. They were photocopies, lined and filled in neatly with numbers in Rob's writing.

"How'd it work out?"

"Good," Rob said, sounding normal again, which is to say, confident. He always sounds confident when referring to numbers. Uncle Tudi must've felt bad about yelling or good about the papers because he slapped Rob tenderly on the cheek then laid a barrel-sized arm around my shoulders.

"Listen," he said to me. "You seem like a nice girl—with a modern name— don't get me wrong—but don't come down here again, understand?" His face was inches from mine; it was like kissing the moon. "I hate to think what Harrison would do if he knew Rob had you here."

I promised I wouldn't come back, and he seemed satisfied.

He jerked his head to me, asking Rob, "She met your mother?"

"Not yet," Rob sputtered. Uncle Tudi shot him a look.

Rob threw up his hands. "*Whaaat?*"

"Lemme tell you something. Rob was raised decent, with manners. But he was a change-of-life baby. That's why he's spoiled." He lifted a finger to Rob but said nothing. Rob also said nothing, then he nodded and kissed his uncle.

I said goodnight, and before we got to the door, Uncle Tudi was waddling to catch us. "Boneless pork," he said breathlessly, handing me a package the size of a shoebox. "It's nice."

"She doesn't have a stove, Uncle."

"Whaddaya mean *no stove?*"

"She lives in a dormitory," Rob backed away, taking me along. "You know. College."

"Next time I see you two," he warned, "it's in daylight!"

WE SPENT WHAT REMAINED of the night on a stoop on Horatio Street. A jaundiced glow from the inside filled a second story window across the way, and we watched it like a movie. Something had come over Rob, something not unfamiliar to me. A constitutional shift, sort of a shut-down. Sometimes he just stopped, like a machine idling.

"How long have we known each other?" I asked.

"One year," he said. "St. Patrick's Day."

"That's a funny anniversary," I said. "Seems like longer."

He lit a cigarette. "Seems like a year."

"I liked you as soon as I saw you," I said.

"Oh yeah?" he said. He jiggled his knee lightly.

"What did you think when you saw me?"

"I thought you were good-looking."

"Is that what you told Rourke?"

"Not in those exact words."

"You don't remember?"

"I remember."

I had the feeling that I owed him an apology. I thought to say sorry. I thought to thank him for coming, for not leaving me alone that night, only I couldn't, not when I would have had to look at him with gratitude in my eyes and let him know he'd failed. He was the closest thing to Rourke, but he was not Rourke.

"How you been?" he wanted to know.

"Good," I said. "I've been good."

"You been all right?"

"Yeah, I've been all right."

I lied because Rob did not need to be burdened with details. He did not need to hear how Rourke stalked the periphery of night, traveling in light and sound, stealthy as a feline in my dreams, mad as a dream cat. How slowly he went in my mind, lingering, presence and pressure, keeping me whole the way your skin keeps your pieces in. You cannot live without skin. You do not think to manufacture it, but you do, stretching it across your frame. Every seven days it is new again. I did not tell the truth because Rob might say, *Try to be happy*. People often say that. But it is impossible to move beyond certain losses. Fire for instance, like Rob was saying, and death. It gets to where you can't even talk to people who haven't suffered as you have. I lied because I didn't want him to know what it means to be sick. All the time sick. I lied because he knew the truth anyway.

"I haven't slept with Mark, you know."

Rob drew in for the last time from his cigarette. "Not yet," he said. "You will."

SEVEN

TREES

It was in the fall of 1915 that I decided not to use any color
until I couldn't get along without it
and I believe it was June before I needed blue.
—Georgia O'Keeffe

SPRING 1984

I.

THE WATER CLUB IS NEAR THE HELIPORT ON THE EAST RIVER, AND IF YOU'RE careful about your seat there you can avoid the sorry sight of dormant helicopters, which look like women with wet hats. That is where Alicia and Jonathan announce their engagement, over dinner, the four of us alone, the Water Club. The announcement is no surprise. Mrs. Ross told us weeks before; she wanted to prepare Mark.

"He's a pansy," Mark said bitterly. "The asthma, the Mercury Zephyr, the backgammon. He's allergic to mesquite. How can anyone be allergic to mesquite?"

"Jonathan treats her well," Mrs. Ross said. "She'll be deprived of nothing."

"Except in the bedroom," Mark mumbled.

His mother smacked him on the shoulder. "Oh, stop it."

Mr. Ross shrugged. He tries to think of the big picture. His children are nice-looking, well-off, and connected, and that's going to have to be enough since he's dying and will soon be dead. He doesn't have the stamina for the minutiae of survival; as far as he's concerned, no one is going to go shoeless.

I know because sometimes he tells me things. Sometimes I come early for dinner—family dinners are on Thursdays—and I meet him at one of the cocktail tables at 21 or in the Oak Room or at Tavern on the Green. Every now and then we eat at Doubles, a club in the Sherry Netherland. He smiles and waves and lays down his cigarette before he stands to greet me. Then he grabs the waiter's sleeve to order me a Tanqueray and tonic, which I accept even if I don't feel like it because one law of being a gentleman is to know a lady's preference, and it's not good manners for her to keep switching on him. When my drink arrives, we eat nuts with brown husks, the kind that resemble pussywillow buds.

Sometimes I find him smoking across the street from his house, on a bench by Central Park. If it's somewhat depressing to see a successful businessman huddled on a bench like a bum, especially when it's one of those broken benches without back slats to connect the exposed cement posts, it's also clever since no one would ever think to look for him there. He's not supposed to smoke because of his health. I never report him. Everyone else reports him and yells at him, and they never seem to do him much good. I just try to take his mind off death for a few minutes.

He's been dying since I met him and for some time before that. But he's been back at work for four years since his heart surgery and he looks pretty good, so he must just talk about dying to make himself feel like he's about to die, which is sad and deep-down-friendless when you stop to think about it.

"The soul seeks equilibrium," my father speculated when I asked why a man who loves his family and his job would smoke and drink in defiance of medical advice. "People who are responsible and successful often act recklessly to counterbalance all that selflessness. If you're ninety percent accountable for others, chances are you'll fill up the remaining ten with unaccountable behaviors."

One day in particular was unseasonably warm, like seventy-five degrees in March, and after putting out his cigarette under the broken bench, Mr. Ross and I walked south toward the park entrance across from The Beresford. It wasn't anything we'd discussed, it was just a spontaneous simultaneous impulse. We climbed to the top of one of those mammoth rocks with sides that look like the flaky Italian pastries Dad loves, the ones shaped like seashells, with all the layers, called *sfogliatelle*.

"Look at that sunset, Mr. Ross." It was beautiful, like we were standing inside a purple pillow. He set his briefcase between his knees and came down carefully to sit. I put my hand out behind him. He was a big man, almost twice my size. Still, I felt compelled to catch him should he lose his footing.

"Those clouds aren't *really* purple," I explained, sitting also. "It's the orange that makes them seem so. Do you think all animals see them that way? They say cats see in dark. And pelicans catch fish you can't imagine are there. It's like, everything is different, in terms of vision and view. There are variations infinitely subtler than color of which people know nothing. Just because you may not be conscious of color changes, it doesn't mean you can't experience the beauty of a sunset. You know, the purple sky feeling. I bet all animals know that feeling. Like a certain vibration."

He might actually have been unwell because he did not speak for several minutes. Usually he was talkative like the rest of his family. He just lifted his face and squinted like Robert Mitchum into the still point of sundown as if firegazing.

"*The vision is for he who will see it and he who has seen it knows what I say*," Mr. Ross cited, adding, "Plotinus, third century A.D. Plotinus spoke of *the flight of the alone to the alone*."

I wasn't exactly sure what he meant, though he'd obviously moved beyond pelicans and cats. *The flight of the alone to the alone*—what a pretty thing to say at the close of a day, and an appropriate thing, possibly the *only* appropriate thing, and I was grateful as ever for his company. It's interesting to think that in order *to* see you must be *willing* to see, and that you can only truly share what you have seen with those who have also seen it or those who are similarly willing. That's why in movies, kids notice monsters—not only because they are *willing* to see them—but because they are supposed to remind you of your own lost willingness.

Probably the best you can hope for in life is to journey as an individual and to share vision with whomever you happen to meet along the way. The irony, of course, is that since you are moved by the vision and not by the sharing, inevitably you part with those to whom you feel most profoundly connected. You journey on as you must, hoping that to those you have truly known you will remain unforgettable. In the minds of the rest you also endure, only less well, forever a curiosity, forever a haunting, ruinous loss. I wondered if Mr. Ross meant to refer to me and him, or to me and Mark, or not to me at all, but to himself and others.

I shivered; he patted my leg.

"C'mon, sweetheart, let's head inside."

WE GIVE CONGRATULATORY KISSES and handshakes. Mark coughs artificially into his napkin. "So," he says, "when's the big day?"

"June," Alicia replies. "The day after my birthday."

"*June!* That's not much of an engagement."

"Jonathan's parents are moving back to London in June. Besides," she injects meaningfully, "Daddy's health."

"He's lasted this long, Alicia," Mark assures her. "He's not going to kick off any time soon."

"You never know. Sylvie's father died at her graduation. At commencement. In the eighth row."

"Alicia," Jonathan chides. "That's hardly dinner conversation."

"If you're so worried about Dad dropping dead," Mark says, "think what the bill for this thing is going to do to him."

"I've already thought of that," Alicia says. "We're going to have it in East Hampton, at the house."

Mark is silenced. Alicia beat him again. She beats him at everything, even golf. She sets her empty champagne glass carefully near her plate. "Need the bathroom, Evie?"

I don't, only I say I do.

"Great, let's go," Alicia says. I follow her as she saunters elegantly away.

"I'm dying for a cigarette," Alicia says before the bathroom door closes. She shoves it shut and pulls her crocheted purse against her belly and bends over it like she might dive in. "Don't say anything to anyone," she implores as she fiddles first with the clasp and then with the matches. "I told Jonathan I quit, which I will, just—after the wedding."

Her hands shake. It's awful seeing her shake. It's like a cartoon character vibrating after an electric shock. Like Wile E. Coyote. "Here," I say, taking the match from her. "Let me help."

She relaxes into the initial surge of nicotine. "Okay, so tell me. What do you think?"

"About what?"

"About Jonathan. Does he *really love* me?"

I think seriously. Real love is tricky. I would say that it's different for everyone, but I'm not sure that's true. It's more like an extremely subtle flavor that some can't even discern. All I can say for sure is that *whatever* he feels, he feels for her alone. "I don't think he loves anyone more."

She shoots smoke through her nose. "Gee, that's diplomatic."

I figure I'd better pee anyway. It looks like we're going to be a while. Through the slit in the stall, I observe her as she completes her cigarette. It takes me a long time to finish. Maybe not. Maybe I just think that. When you pee with someone listening, it seems like so much more than normal comes out.

I rejoin her, and as I wash my hands, she brushes her teeth. She carries toothpaste and a toothbrush in her bag. Also a lipstick, cigarettes, two credit cards, and a folded fifty. Floating on the outer corners of her marble-round eyes are microscopic ruffles, like lines on a lake or faraway birds. Her eyes are set apart, and the surrounding skin is mahogany-tinted like Venetian furniture. From across a room, it looks as though she's forgotten to remove her sunglasses. From across a room, she could frighten you if you were thinking of squirrelly animals. Her nose is dramatic and Romanesque. Her lips are red. Her beauty is elaborate; it could not possibly exhaust itself.

She dries her toothbrush, and with some difficulty she says my name, "*Evie*." She stops and stares at her shoes. I look to see if she's dropped something. "Jonathan is the—you know—"

The paper towel in my hand is wet, and the garbage pail is behind her. I would have to lean past to reach it or go around. I don't want to appear rude. I continue to dry my hands with the damp towel, which has the opposite effect of rewetting them.

"Well, do you think I'm—I mean, I know you—" She leaves off. There is a funny delay, like dropping an egg that doesn't land. "I'm sorry. I've embarrassed you."

"Not at all," I say, which is true.

With the back of a hand, she sweeps at the atmosphere as if fatigued by the noise of herself. "Let's just go back out." Her amethyst earring catches on the neck of her angora sweater as she turns. I unlatch it and fix her collar, and for a moment we stand, face to face. Her hair is parted down the middle and drawn into a thick twist like good bread. She looks like a Spanish princess, like someone who comes with a dowry of Andalusian horses. "I know about Harrison," she says. "About what happened."

I don't feel myself wince, but possibly I do because she jerks forward, as if trying to catch something that has flown from my mouth.

"I don't want you to think that I—I mean, the way Mark tells it, you were practically *kidnapped*. He says that Harrison ruined you. Of course Mark's wrong. I mean, I've known Harrison since I was twelve, since they started at UCLA. I know he would never force anyone to do anything." Softer then, "You two must have been completely in love."

She waits. She wants me to say what it is to be in love, which is like being asked to discuss a murder committed in a prior lifetime. And I can think only of mist. Of driving at night through mist. Of being so entrenched you cannot see past yourself, and you think nothing is there, though everything is there. You simply *see* nothing and *hear* nothing—but inches off is a telephone pole, a startled deer, a sign knocking on its hinges outside a restaurant so leaden, so edgeless, it could be smoke. I think of being powerless to modify the conditions of that failed perception, of reaching to know and reaching to feel, and still perceiving nothing. Of acquiescing, of giving over, of conceding to displacement and stomach-turning distortion, of spinning and spinning, whizzing, inebriated, a spiral in a spiral, and all the world has turned to bowed lines and cambered uplands, and voices are disjoined—no nation, no moment, nowhere, everywhere, nowhere—and of being released. Like that, let go. Suddenly. Flying and you land. With everything turning very, very explicit. And the explicitness is worse than the loss. Explicitness is the worst possible feeling you can feel, worse than darkness, than dampness, than blindness—there is no poetry there. Not *there—here*. I mean *here*.

"My God, listen to me," she says. "I don't mean to be nosy. I just wanted to know what you think. About Jonathan. And me."

The faucet drips behind her. "I, I think you're very passionate—about things. I think Jonathan will give you the security you need to stay that way, the way you are now."

"Is that what Mark does for you?" she asks.

I consider a lie. What good is a lie? A lie will not affect her fate. She's been lied to enough. I will spare her the sensation of being crammed like thread through my vessels to reach the pathetic indentation that once was my heart. It is all lace, like broken glass. When you arrive, there is this sound, the suffocating sound that is the sound of the echo of the fracture—*thuck*. You can go no further. Life from behind urges you on. Like a shoving, angry mob.

She raises a finger to her lips, *Ssshh*, and with those lips she kisses me. I know it's a kiss because I feel the waxy double arc on my cheek, and I am incorporated into a plushy cloud of Chanel and into the society of those whom she adores. It is a fine society. With one finger, her thumb, she wipes lipstick from my face and she breaks into a smile, a gracious smile. Alicia can be quite gracious. She nods twice. There are tears, I see tears, does she cry—it's not necessary to cry.

As we approach the table, the boys stand. "What happened?" Mark asks. "Did some pipes break?"

Jonathan says, "Yeah, did pipes break?"

Alicia takes up her napkin. "Girl talk, gentlemen."

"That's exactly what we're afraid of," Jonathan says. "We're afraid you two might decide to make it a double wedding."

AFTER *TRISTAN UND ISOLDE* we stop at Fellini's for dinner. Mark feels like a plate of fresh spinach pasta with pheasant sauce. The restaurant is practically empty because it is late, and the few remaining waiters leap to life, *Hello, hello, good evening Signor, Signorina.* They seat us in the same place they always seat us—five tables back against the southern windows. The table looks out over West Sixty-eighth Street, which is preternaturally sequestered as if out of a Hopper painting. I don't know what it is that makes us deserving of this particular table, but each time they escort us to it with a smug sort of pride, as though surely they've pleased us immensely.

The waiter recommends a bottle of Aglianico del Vulture, from the Basilicata region, a young wine, 1981—*delicioso.* When it comes, Mark caresses the bottle, approves of the bottle, tastes and nods, thanking the waiter, who pours obsequiously as Mark adjusts his cuff-links, fluted platinum with onyx inserts. A gift from me with the money he provided.

"That fucking soprano gave me an intense headache," he says.

I take up my glass. I imagine it was difficult for him. The rich king versus the dragon slayer, the devotion to the death of the estranged lovers. It didn't help that the king's name was Mark.

"So," he says, drinking then pulling back his lips in a businesslike manner. "Let's talk about what to do after you graduate."

"I haven't thought about it, really."

"Good. I don't want you jumping into anything."

He seems relieved—did he think if I got a job, I would leave him? How could I leave—I have no place to go. I have no friends or resources that are not his. How could I when I have come to value things and have faith in them. Things mean distance between me and everything else. Diamonds mean I don't have to talk to shopgirls with thumbtack eyes and perpetually suntanned cleavage who want to know where I got *those shoes.* Cars mean I don't have to take subways that smell of puke and piss or cabs where drivers ask, *Have you been baptized?*

Sex with Mark means I don't have to wait tables and talk to men who say I look like one of the girls in the Robert Palmer video. And sex with him is perverse. In the absence of desire, it's good to be set upon without expectations of love or affection.

In the end, when I'm overtaken by an abject longing, a longing for something loved and lost, I can get up and walk away and hold that loss without his interference. Each time at the end I am newly bereaved. Every conceivable element of Rourke and me escapes from a safe haven beneath the mask of my consciousness, not in any recognizable sense, not in a language-like pattern or chain, but in the singular opulence of my own gesture and symbol, personal and manifest only to me, impacted, metaphorical, in a princely composite, rather like a solitary Chinese character—there it is, there we are, on the other side of a window shook open, appearing in a flash or flare, like the distantest rupture of starfire, so we are, so we were, a lucent shred in the very, very black—shorn apart, sewn again. And in my throat, his name. And in my eyes, a portrait of myself, a striking likeness. And when I see all that has been laid away in the nerve of me, I feel a familiar sadness, which surely has no purpose, and without tears, I cry. *The life we might have had, the life we might have had.*

No, I will not leave Mark because when I wander through the house at daybreak, heart-sick and soul-sick and repelled by the sight of the bed, by the crooked margin that is mine, which has been infiltrated by him, there is some small consolation in a refrigerator filled with thirty-dollars-per-pound smoked Scottish salmon and organic strawberries and fresh-squeezed orange juice and a mess in the sink that can be left for someone else to clean. In the garage is a car I can drive to anywhere, and in the top dresser drawer is all the cash I could ever need. If being in love is consolation when you are poor, money is consolation when you are not. Life is a trap not because I can't leave Mark, but because there's no reason to.

"The workplace is such a scene," he's saying. "The politics, the bullshit incompetence. I don't want you ending up as the subordinate to some asshole who thinks he can coerce you into—situations."

When the plates are cleared, the waiter brings two glasses of grappa; I don't like grappa; Mark knows I don't. He pulls his chair to mine. He plays with my hair. "You can do anything—photography, painting, drawing. You're so talented. We have to take our time. We'll ask my mother. She'll get your work out there."

THE COKE SNAKES ROUND and round on picture glass, on a picture unattached from the wall. I cannot say what the picture is; I cannot see it; it is covered with soapy clumps. A geometric dog, I think, the one that looks like a cross section of beef cuts. I think it's the Escher. The caviar, like the cognac and the coke, is fine, very special and exceptional—hand-selected Tsar Imperial Beluga. If you want to know about that, about *hand-selected* caviar, you can inquire, but you must endure an exhaustive history of the delicacy—the size of sturgeon, the shape of eggs, the cost per gram, the temperature of the Caspian, the vulgar idiosyncrasies of the Slavs.

So you do not inquire, you do not care to learn or see, and if anyone tells you something, you act like already you know. Here we reside in the future, in the abstract. This is a dream where the sun shines at night and creatures mingle wrongly and seasons are without circumference and all that happens is practical and real and fast. In this place we are voracious and we are clever and we are the victors, which is the same as being the victims because everything here is inversion and irony. No one ever told me about this place; I arrived unprepared. I can't believe I arrived that way.

Swoosey Schicks apologizes to me for shop talk. *Competitor intelligence. Debt-to-equity ratios.*

"It's okay." It's better than most things they discuss—the size of annual bonuses and all the Mexicans "crossing over."

"That's right," Mark says. "It's time she learned a thing or two about the world of finance." Mark decides to teach me the basics of economics. His friends settle into leather armchairs with their chilled vodka and smuggled Montecristos and cashmere pullovers with suede elbow patches, and they listen solemnly beyond moribund undertones of The English Beat and The Psychedelic Furs as he uses the simplest possible terms, which is sexy, and inside he wants very much to be sexy, and so he smiles, frequently, appreciative that I've given him the opportunity.

He's very attractive, really he is, at least, I *think* he is, twinkling isochronally like a movie of himself or a crystal swaying in the starkness of a sunstrike, catching light, losing it, making pyramids that delimit space and time—lunes and kites and cones, the axes and radians and the mathematical eccentricities of the totality of living, secret lines of symmetry and secret lines of revolution and all the occultated lines that enclose and divide.

"Rule of Seventy-Two," Mark instructs as he licks black-light bubbles off a mother-of-pearl spoon, "is the formula used to calculate how long it will take for an investment to double. Divide seventy-two by the interest rate. For instance, seventy-two by eight percent, which gives you nine years."

His eyes are ringed with fatigue from achievement. They are eyes of ash like the cinder of volcanoes. There is a glowering richness to the remains; lives have been lost to form the dust. There are shadows in his eyes, phantoms of the dead, astir, afoot—the poisoned, the stoned, the eviscerated. I don't know why I've never seen him so clearly before—the inclemency in his features, the abrasive cohesion of his skin, like living marble, like he will last forever. And he will. He will prevail. He forges time to fit his will, like bending iron. Timing is everything to him. This is what he knows and what I need to learn.

Maybe I am experiencing dark adaptation, whereby the pupils dilate, the retinas sensitize, and there is a shift in the field of luminosity toward blues and purples. My eyes have at last grown accustomed to conditions of concocted masculinity as though to reduced illumination because as he discusses round lots and odd lots and sinking funds and buying on margin and using capital gains to offset capital losses, his delivery is artfully uninterrupted in flow, gluey smooth as the siphon of a clam, and for the first time I think, *I love him*; anyway, in that moment I do. If I have never said it before, it's because I've never felt it before, and really there is no easier moment to say a difficult thing than when you feel that to some degree it may be true, and, besides, in all likelihood I owe him for the many times he has professed his love for me—also it is only fair to say *I love you* when you mean it and wrong, perhaps, to withhold it.

I lean off my stool, coming to kiss him on the part of his face where the hair is peculiar and fair, fallow, near the jaw if he does not shave. *I love you*, I am about to say, only he is viewing me watchfully; as if through some advantage in position, he noted the change in me before I perceived it myself, as if he'd been observing me stir to life after a severe and protracted sleep.

"I want to marry you," he says, holding my shoulders. "I want you to marry me. Will you marry me?"

I say okay, and the room is reeling.

There is applause and the bright bullish sound of Sinatra followed by champagne pops and high fives and jokes about all the broken hearts Mark will leave behind. This is a surprise—have there been hearts to break? I'm passed from hand to hand and lap to lap, and I am squeezed and kissed by the boys. Alicia is on the phone; she loves me; she has never been happier. "Can you imagine?" she says, her voice so small, so far. "*Sisters!*"

I wonder where she is, where we have reached her. Possibly she's still at Yale, working hard, making hats. She is always making hats. We all wear them—Denny, Sara Eden, Jonathan, even Mark. He is good that way, never forgetting where his loyalties lie.

BRETT KNOCKS ON THE bathroom door. *The cars are waiting*.

The cars will take us to Odeon. We travel in cars. There are so many of us that one is never enough. We have to celebrate the engagement. People are anxious to place themselves in relation to me. Already everyone is acting more, more *something*, I don't even know what.

"Make yourself decent," Brett calls out. "I'm coming in."

The bathroom door opens. Probably I have been in here a long time. At the mirror, he rights his suspenders. I do not see him do so, I hear the elastic snaps. The water comes on, and he combs back his hair. I feel the drops.

"What are you doing?" he asks, his voice like a cough, a croupy cough. "Listening to the neighbors?"

My hand is on the wall. My forehead on my hand. If you rest your forehead on the back of your hand, you'll notice how many protruding and breakable bones your hand has, like a chicken foot. It's a disgusting feeling, the feeling of your own skeleton. "Yes," I say. "Listening to neighbors."

MARK HAS A CONFESSION. He opens the solid fir closet door and reaches into the breast pocket of a quail gray Armani suit. Some people eat quail; I have seen him eat quail. He withdraws a ring box.

"I've been waiting for the right moment."

Yes, I think. A public moment. *Witnesses.*

The ring is a big square diamond, a rare chameleon. Looking into it is like looking into a well of infinite angles. It is like the implement of a wizard. He tilts the box and light hits the jewel top, devising prisms on the wall, a kaleidoscopic arbor or bower. I strain my neck to see, awed like a peasant beholding an act of sorcery. It is not wrong to compare Mark to a magician when he is so clever, when he turns my methods against me, obliterating the natural with equal doses of the artificial. He seduces as he himself was seduced, by what or by whom, I cannot even say. If I don't know, it is because he does not intend for me to know. Like a true master, he leaves nothing to chance. Like a true connoisseur of ruin, he does not destroy me directly but lures me to my own destruction. He hands me champagne.

He bought the diamond first then had the ring made to specification. *Built* is the word he uses, by Ronnie Armeil, a West Coast jeweler who is a client of his father's. Armeil builds for Victoria Principal and Stephanie Powers. There are characteristics. I don't want to know characteristics. Talk of characteristics is code for talk of cost, and I don't want to know cost. I'm sure it cost at least five thousand more than Alicia's, and everyone knows the cost of Alicia's. It's a sanctioned topic of conversation. Mark would never be outdone by Jonathan.

He moves to put it on me. I stop him. He takes hold of my waist. "Sweetheart," he says. "What is it?"

I look into his eyes. I remind myself that I know him. I've always known him, from the first night we met. That is something, something important. I'm not sure what.

"I said yes because every day I think the worst has past. Every day I think I can't feel as bad as I did the day before, and every day I'm wrong. I said yes because he's not coming back."

The ring remains suspended near my finger; I wonder if it can drive off the terrors of the night. I hope that it can. "Now you can put it on," I say. "If you still want to."

HE SENT ONE LETTER, ON YELLOW LEGAL PAPER, CAREFULLY FOLDED. I WILL never forget the way it was folded, four times down, once in half, like a note you get from a friend in high school, like something casual but intensely personal, like something natural to his day. I opened it on an April morning as I cut through Central Park in a taxi cab, past dogwoods in full bloom. Every time I see dogwoods in bloom, I go back to the day of the letter and back again to seventeen. Bare feet and virgin skies and sand on his skin, brown like whiskey, and that day is invariably a good day.

Isn't life amazing—the letter flew to me on an airplane, the plane touched down. In a canvas sack the page was carried, delivered to me by anonymous hands. At the end, his name, at the beginning, my own. My name, tenderly rendered. Clear, perfect—*Eveline*. Proof.

I HAVE ONE PHOTOGRAPH. In it he is young, sixteen maybe, maybe nineteen. I keep it with the letter in a box on Mark's dresser, my box, where my things are kept. I do not fear discovery; discovery would change nothing, not my feelings, not my station or status. If Mark had wanted to take these things away, he would have. He prefers me to have the illusion of privacy. I remove the photograph to touch it, sometimes when I can't help myself. Sometimes when I look for him, I need to find him. First it is strange, like looking at a picture of fire, feeling no heat. Then I fall into the false dimension, then I feel him, warm like flesh and soft.

Rourke faces the water at a moderate angle; the sun sets behind him and the boardwalk stretches south, big as ten football fields. Guys horsing around. Lowly seaside architecture. Rourke. There are no lines in his face yet; his skin is clear, his cheeks are mesmerizing hollows. He is lean and refined, solid and tall, too tall and too separate from the crowd and tragic in his separateness, somewhat self-conscious of it. I want that boy; I want him. I draw my fingertips along the line of his jaw. I want to know him then, kiss him then.

"That's the Criterion," Rob told me the first time I saw the photo. He pointed to the second story of a yellow brick building in back, the one Rourke took me to that day on the boardwalk. "Harrison was like 34-2 at the time." He lifted the wallet closer. "That's Eddie M. in back there, yanking up his pants. Remember Eddie M.? And over by the corner is Tommy Lydell. And that's Chris DeMarco. You had dinner with Chris and his wife, Lee." Rob waited for me to say something. "Take it out," he said. "Go ahead, take it."

I removed the photo, thinking, time is so important, time is everything. It's a mystery, the way time for us was wrong when time is right for so many useless things. When things that should be impossible are in fact possible, but we could not be together. After all, there are flags on the moon.

"You keep it," Rob said, folding his wallet back up. "I got the negative somewhere." He seemed embarrassed. I hoped I had not embarrassed him.

THE REST IS INTANGIBLE. A few conversations in those first few months, like things exhaled and evaporated and so lacking in exactness as to demand breadth of interpretation. The phone rings and you run, you know it's him, you feel it is him, and when he speaks you can imagine him sprawled across his couch, lit by the pulsating lapis light of his stereo, in the glorious aquarium of his underfurnished living room, wherever it might be. You are roused by his loneliness, by the desperate arc to his voice. You recall the eyes that you adore; you want him to be happy, but you want him to tell that you he is not, that like you, he is incapable. Why did you go away, you want to ask, why did you leave, why are you back?

"I dreamed of you last night."

"I dreamed of you too," he says. "You were beautiful."

IN TIME I CAME to grasp the nature of my position among women and to see that, despite what I knew to be the rarity of my bond with Rourke, my feelings of uniqueness were not unlike other women's feelings of uniqueness. At bridal showers, at picnic tables, in dressing rooms and hair salons and kitchen gardens, I listened with compassion—if every woman has made herself available or has given over despite some better knowledge, isn't that the same as faith, and aren't women so faithful? It's unkind to ridicule the way women talk when they're hurt, when the grief they describe is sincere and the return for humanity great. Women talk as a way of addressing the baffling sea at their feet. They talk to name, and in naming, make real. They talk to reclaim the selfhood they've lost. Like men who name flowers and viruses and boulevards, they talk to stake ownership. Such talk creates unity among women as it penalizes by exclusion the men who would misunderstand them. And yet if it's true that talk heals, then ultimately, ironically, talk benefits its targets most.

In 1981 the whole Jersey group came in to attend a holiday art show I was having. It was my second year at school. Denny organized everything with some help from Rob. Chris and Lee bought a charcoal of Madison Avenue rooftops, and Mark bought a diptych of trees. Afterwards we all walked to Patisserie Lanciani in the West Village for coffee and dessert, and on the street was a film of snow like a layer of slag. It was Rob and Lorraine, Denny and Jeff, Chris and Lee, and Cliff and Sugar Lovett, his fiancée from Dallas. Also Mark and me. Halfway through pastries Lorraine ran out because of something Rob said; I didn't hear what. It must have been bad because the men at the table hung their heads and shook them. Lee followed Lorraine, taking their coats to the bench in front, where they sat. Through the glass you could watch them. Lorraine's cuprous hair fanned against the storefront like a corona of hooks and coils. From inside it looked like an octopus or squid sucking up against the side of a tank.

"Fucking guy," Chris said. "What's the matter with you?"

"I don't know how you expect to keep a woman," Mark said.

Rob said, "I don't want a woman to *keep*, just one to fuck."

"Yeah, well," Mark replied, "any woman worth fucking is a woman worth keeping."

"Yeah, well," Rob copied Mark's voice, "*exactly* my point."

I figured I'd better leave. Lorraine and I weren't exactly friends, but it wasn't proper to listen to men discussing her. It felt unprincipled or unsportsmanlike. Sugar never met Lorraine before that night, so she was okay to stay at the table. Besides, Sugar was a debutante. Debutantes almost never sit outside in winter. I joined the girls on the bench. It was cold but pleasant and, in particular, poetic—that is to say, gestural and eloquent and worldly revealing, if you can manage to pick it apart. West Fourth Street is mythically pretty in snow, with the flesh-colored lamplight seeping through awninged branches and everybody with dogs and packages, going slow. Lorraine was relieved that I'd come, though I couldn't say precisely how that relief was communicated.

Lee was striving to boost Lorraine's self-esteem, which we all knew was a futile project since Lorraine's head was junked up with crazy information. By the pool at the Ross house one day when they visited, she saw an article in *Cosmopolitan* called "Keeping Your Man Satisfied—10 Tips to Great Sex." Just as I thought, *what a profitless bit of journalism*, Lorraine tore out the article, folded it, and placed it carefully in the back flap of her datebook. I couldn't help but wonder whether the woman who's afraid that she isn't satisfying her man is being satisfied herself. Is anyone giving *him* tips?

Lorraine kept blowing her nose and shaking her head, saying she lives in constant fear of Rob getting arrested or busted up or worse, but when she asks him things, she's told to mind her own business.

"*Mind your own business?*" Lee repeated indignantly.

Lee could become very indignant. She was not the average Jersey girl, she was going places, you could tell by the impeccable way she dressed. The way she dressed reminded me of Francesco Le Blanc, the teaching assistant in my photography class. Francesco was from Peru, and he worked as a freelance art curator. He did installations at Chase Manhattan on Broadway and Houston, where he was known as *Fran*. "I'm not fashion-flashy," Fran would say in his thick Peruvian accent, "I'm fashion-worshipful!"

"If only he would talk to me," Lorraine sobbed, guilty to have impeached Rob's character. "It's just, he won't even talk to me."

"Don't defend him!" Lee snapped. "His behavior is inexcusable."

I actually thought it was okay for Lorraine to feel guilty since life is complicated, and she and Rob are also complicated, and it is difficult to render into language the dynamics of the heart. Especially when there is snow. When it snows, there is a lowered ceiling on the universe, and all the unmatching things begin to match—such as signs and automobiles. With snow, all loss is like a steel plate against your chest, abdominally compounded and gray—Quaker gray like the world in utero, midmost gray like a color without complement, homogenous and evenly divided gray, like all that you see when your eyes are closed. When there is snow, the trees purr like baby rattles.

After the cafe we walked around the Village in twos and threes, looking into the parlor windows of brownstones, saying how great it would be to live in this house or that house, and just as we were about to turn the corner from Bleecker onto Eleventh, Lorraine stopped me. Behind her was a bird shop. Cats in mistletoe and candy cane collars lay passively beneath huge sleepy tropical birds with fancy crested heads and short, butted bills.

"Thanks a lot for listening over there," she said. "It helped me out, you know. Us girls sticking together."

Something about the skittish look in her eyes and the fine plump hand, like a young mother's hand lying mildly on my wrist, made me see that I hadn't been fair to her. Something about her freckles and those birds made me realize that there's a formula to humanity, which is that all that anyone wants is to be loved, even the ladies at the Department of Motor Vehicles. Maybe access is indirect. Maybe to penetrate you need to keep trying new ports. Lorraine wasn't necessarily angry and hateful. It was just her love of Rob that made her seem that way. In the beginning when they first met, that love had likely been an agreeable love. But along the way it had changed, and she was sad about that. Probably she should have let Rob keep his secrets, since answers only disabled him further in her imagination. Probably it would have been good for her to have quit back at the best time, feeling capable, feeling desired, and to have kept custody of that first love, that ideal.

I could see myself there in her aspect, cinched behind a screen of heartache, obliged for the most minor of charities, blinded and despairing and assigned absolutely to the legend of my own besotted sorrow. I felt a revived collapse of self-respect, if in fact you can revive a collapse. I felt ashamed to think that I'd been holding out hope for something hopeless, and that in so doing, I was contributing to the disintegration of whatever Rourke and I had once shared.

I remember that moment. I remember setting it all to drift like a stick in a river. I remember telling myself, *Just let go*.

"No problem, Lorraine," I said. "I hope things work out for you guys."

THE BOTTOMEST ITEM IN the box is a phone message taken by my roommate, Corrine. Corrine became my roommate in sophomore year when Ellen got an apartment, a hygienic duplex on East Twenty-first Street with a terrace facing northwest to the Empire State Building. Sometimes I go to Ellen's for dinner, sometimes with Mark as she is my one respectable friend, and he is equally respectable and unquestionably clean, and they are both happy for me and happy over the stalwart and prosperous fact of each other. Once Ellen had a cocktail party and asked me to come early to help set up, which I did, and she introduced me to guests as her *best friend from school*, which depressed me. I felt she deserved better.

Corrine was an economics major who danced to the GoGos and Cindy Lauper and Katrina and the Waves in orange shirts with cut-off collars and turquoise leg warmers, and Corrine could do splits and backflips. That's all I know of her since I never slept in the dorm again after freshman year. I only stopped by on busy days or to shower and dress after using the gym if Mark wanted to go out someplace downtown like Il Cantinore or Chantarelle. He kept telling me to *go off of housing for God's sake*.

When Corrine called me at Mark's about the message, I went down to Tenth Street to pick it up even though I knew already what it said. Such things truly matter, you know, paper.

> *12/22/81. 7:50 pm. Harrison Rourke.*
> *Harrison again, 10:30 pm.*
> *HR 1:15 am. He wants to see you, now. Mayflower, Room 112.*

I gripped the note, turning it over—it was torn from one of Corrine's graph books, so there were all these little squares, and it was pale green, accountant's green. On the side there were eleven of those funny little shreds from where the metal binder had been. I kept wondering if Corrine had written while he was on the phone with her, or if she'd written after the calls. For some reason it mattered to me. Instead of going to class, I accidentally went back uptown to Mark's, walking the whole way. Once inside, I stared at the phone and thought hard about calling. I just stared and thought and thought, and one complete day transpired that way, without me leaving the apartment. Tuesday somehow became Friday, and by then it had become too late to call, too anti-natural. Not anti-natural, *unnatural*. Anti-natural means like implements of war in equatorial heat, like part of some calculated decision or supreme design. It's not that I made a decision *not* to call, it just happened that I couldn't decide *to* call, which is different.

"You must be coming back late," Mark said when he arrived home from work Friday night. Mark always left the apartment before me in the morning and returned hours after I did. "Manny told me he hasn't seen you all week."

"I've been staying in," I told him. "Headaches."

A FEW WEEKS AFTER, the phone rang at Mark's. Not so much a ring as a calling. I knew it was Rourke.

I was quick to answer, under my breath, saying hi.

He said, "I've left six messages."

"I'm sorry," I said, slipping the phone around the corner into the hall. That wasn't a lie. I was sorry to ever keep him waiting.

"I'm flying into Boston tomorrow."

"What for?"

"For a fight."

"Oh," I said, "a fight." Him getting hit. Him bleeding. Him being watched with imaginations laying claim. That is what imaginations do with irresistible individuals. They lay claim. "Are *you* fighting?"

"Not me," he said softly. "A friend of mine. Jerry Page. I can get you a plane ticket. You can pick it up at an agency."

I thought of—I don't know what I thought of. Nothing good. Maybe Lorraine, waiting and waiting, loving but being misunderstood; maybe my parents, yes, my parents, how they had loved each other and still loved each other but how that didn't matter, and also of this drawing teacher I had who lived in Hoboken with her cats. She was fifty-five. And Jack. Also Jack.

"I can't. I'm sorry."

When he hung up, I hung up. I sat numbishly, like I'd just heard the news of death. To get out of it, I told myself that I am not some possession that he has lent, that he cannot appear out of nowhere to assert his rights. These are the things I told myself, but the words in my head sounded stilted, like the sound of rote practice, like memorizing a phrase in a foreign language or a phone number when you have no pen. If ever you are talking to yourself and you hear a stranger's voice or a memorizing voice, listen carefully. Sometimes in life, years go by.

"Who was that?" Mark asked. He was wrapped half in a towel at his dresser, holding a glass of wine, looking for collar stays.

I said, "Harrison."

Mark froze. "Harrison? What did *he* want?"

"He wants me to meet him in Boston for the weekend."

The glass Mark was holding slipped from his hand and hit the side of the dresser. He caught it, and though the wine splashed out onto the towel and not the carpet, he sighed with annoyance. The glass cracked. He hates to break glass.

"Don't worry," I said. "I told him I couldn't."

3.

WITH THE SHOWER OFF, I HEAR A BOTTLE POP AND MUSIC. VOICES.

"So what's up with Lorraine?"

"Same old shit."

"*Same old shit*," Mark repeats. "I mean, where is she?"

"She couldn't make it," Rob says.

"What do you mean, *couldn't make it*? Didn't she know we have something to celebrate?"

"She had plans."

"You didn't even tell her, you prick, did you?"

Mark stops talking when I come out and Rob stands. He's dressed like a manager at the movies. His jacket is plaid and his pants are flat at the waist and too short for his legs.

"Congratulations," he says, handing me champagne, kissing me spiritlessly. "Lorraine has a virus. She couldn't make it."

I try to think of what to say, but I'm unable to speak. Rob helps me despite his displeasure, proving what I know—that he loves me. He pulls me close. "So where's this rock I had to hear about?"

AT AREA, I GET stuck dancing with Dara and Murat while Mark and Rob take off to argue. They've been wanting to argue all night. When Mark comes back, he comes back alone, walking past me, going straight to the bar where he orders a drink. Mark swings around and confers gloomily with Miles, who works for the State Department, and his wife, Paige, a pharmaceutical heiress and equestrian. Miles and Paige are up from their estate in Arlington to attend a re-election fundraiser for Reagan. They are very high. They are frequently high, injection-high. If it's hard to notice, that's because they are professional about concealing. Miles has this way of locking down, of stiffening and leaning like plywood against a wall, only there is no wall, and except for an occasional Buddy Holly-type spasm of his left leg that comes so fast and hard you think his knee has buckled backwards, you might believe him to be musing and meditative. Paige adjusts—constantly. She flicks her feathered rabbit-brown hair and reapplies lipstick and tweaks non-existent particles from her over-broad shoulders and straightens the skirt of her dress even if she is wearing pants. When she takes up the fabric on the thigh of her pants to go down stairs, she is the picture of Southern refinement.

We don't call them *drug addicts*, though Paige has been in rehab twice and last month Miles drove his car through their garage door. We say, *They like to party*, I don't know why, since *party* means sharing euphoria, whereas whatever they feel, they conceal. They get giddy off stealth, as if what they crave is not the substance but the subversion.

At least Jack had some ideas about culture and society and the political capacity of mind-expansion. It is sad to think about how the survival of people like Miles and Paige is more secure than the survival of someone like Jack. They're chic; Jack is a junkie.

Around Christmas I ran into Smokey Cologne at Canal Jeans, and he told me that Jack had basically *blipped off the radar*. For a while he had been doing fine—a new band, regular dates at CBGB's and Continental Divide, an album's worth of recorded songs that they were ready to mix—until all of a sudden, Jack pulled out and hit the streets. I told Smokey to call me if he thought I could help. Out of curiosity, I asked him the name of the band.

Smokey said, "Piss Pot."

I approach Mark. I wait politely. He's concentrating on Paige's face as if watching an ant farm. Even he cannot view her in her spasmodic entirety. It's too nerve-wracking; it's like watching in dread as a speeding car veers between lanes on a highway. Mark is saying he wants to protect Paige's interests. Frankly he's worried about unscrupulous operators trying to get their hands on her trust fund and ever-burgeoning pharmaceutical inheritance—*especially now with the whole AIDS thing*. "Ever heard of churning?" he inquires.

Paige shimmies out of time to the music in her raspberry velvet slippers with nautical insignias like gold admiral ropes, re-screwing a diamond earring. "I'm doing it right now, honey," she drawls and Mark laughs tinnily.

"I'm going to the bathroom," I say.

"Fine," Mark says. "Watch yourself with that ring."

ROB IS ALONE BY the back bar, pounding Chivas. An attractive girl is alongside him, lonely in rubber and rope. She is cat-like with liquid mascara and Patricia Field leotards and lace-up Peter Fox boots, like Diana Rigg from the *Avengers*. He doesn't even notice her. I watch from the stairs as he clears two tumblers and signals for a third, then pushes the hair off his forehead like he just received bad news. Rob is particular about touching his hair and about anyone else touching it. If you want to make him mad, just touch his hair. One night we got a flat tire on Route 3 outside Montclair, and he pushed his hair back that same way as cars whooshed past in neon blue-red rocket streaks, making the windows rattle back at the January rain, and he laid his head on the steering wheel.

"Welcome to Montclair," he said. "Birthplace of Yogi Berra."

I go down as if drawn by magnets, as if by something outside myself. I like to see him this way; it is the bond between us. We each admire in the other the tendency to travel great distances and, covertly, we push. Neither wants the other to be hurt but both of us long to behold true audacity, modern heroism. It's like watching a moviestar cowboy. You forget sometimes that beneath the skin the blood is real.

> *Now he's in control, he is my lover.*
> *Nations stand against him he's your brother.*
> *Been a long time, been a long time now, I'll get to you somehow.*

Rob sees me coming. He stands straight, shoving his latest glass to the rear rim of the bar and rolling his head in its socket. "Shit," he says, "you got some fucking legs."

I take his hand. "How you doing? You okay?"

He pulls back to make eye contact. "Who me?"

"You seem upset."

"Really? I don't know. I'm not sleeping much," he says. "That could be it. You know, my back." He bends to pluck something off the floor—a five-dollar bill. "Look at this! Must be my lucky night." He looks around and says, "C'mon, let's split a beer."

WE WALK A FEW blocks to a photographer's party in a loft on Varick Street. Mark and Miles and Paige and Dara and Murat and me and Rob. There's a crowd lined up outside Heartbreak. I wonder how Aureole is doing and also Phil and Adrian and D.J. Jim Jerome and Nick the barback. I haven't spoken to them in a long time. Maybe they don't even work there anymore. Maybe Aureole finally made it to L.A. Maybe Nick is with his family in Australia. That would be great but sad, if they left and I left and we never saw each other again. No one ever warns you in life about fast turnovers like that.

The building we enter has morgue-like light and industrial halls, and the filthy cement smell, like behind the sheetrock is wet concrete, like you can bite the air and eat mortar. We ride up the elevator with fabulous strangers. All of us brushing shoulders and someone giggling.

The music gets louder as we go up, like a temperature rising, and when the doors open we are hit by an enormous blast of sound. The place is packed; there are hundreds of people. We squeeze through to the bedroom, where we find Anselm and Helene and many others. As soon as they are preoccupied, I slip away, following the edge of the room to a hallway, a door, a staircase, the roof. There are other guests up there, dancing and playing children's games. Some are so fucked up I wonder if they will try to fly. When I was a kid, dope fiends were always trying to fly. Nobody tries to fly anymore. There is something to that, I think.

> *Mother says, Take six wondrous city pigeon steps!*
> *Mother May I? Yes! You may.*

In the bedroom, Miles and Paige will take out their alligator skin kit bag full of pills and foil and pipes and rocks of powder. That's their community kit; there's another that you never see. Women will come, women always come to money, mannequin women with six-ounce breasts like tea cups, with washboard abdomens and waxed pubic hair intended to appear to be the ghost of a penis. If you have sex with them, you can shut your eyes and pretend they are boys. I don't even care if Mark is down there, except to say that I'd really like to go home.

Over the roof rail, the cars look like gribble in the streets, lonely like bugs in paths on rotting wood. Lonely because loneliness is a path that usually you walk upon, only suddenly you see it from above.

"Anything out of place?" a voice asks, referring to the view.

Rob. Looking back on him is like looking back and seeing sunlight, a horizon, bright and warm but out of reach. His elbows line up next to mine on the rail, and we stand as though looking off a ship, a strange ship. The music from the loft below is like the pounding of the boat on the water, and our emigré faces press into the nightwind as if seeking relief from some indwelling nausea. Unlike our fellow passengers, we are disappointed with where the ship is headed, yet we assigned ourselves to its course long ago. No asylum ahead can approximate the one we once imagined. Nothing can replace what we've lost.

"I figured you were downstairs," I said, "with the rest of them."

"Me, nah. You know I don't touch dope. And forget about Ecstasy. Look at those free-love lunatics." He gestures to the kids across the roof, skipping in pairs. "They were playing *Duck, Duck, Goose* before—the *normal* way—then all of a sudden a duck holds hands with a goose and that's it—*chaos*."

A boy sees me watching the game, and he charges over. The bounds of his eyes are white as cake flour and his pupils gyrate, soaring periodically, like a blind man's eyes. "I'm Julien."

"Hi," I say. "I'm Eveline."

Julien squeezes my hands like they're clay. "Pretty name for a pretty lady. We're going to mingle. Would you like to come mingle?"

"Thanks, buddy," Rob says, "but she's got a full mingle right here."

Julien resists. I consider Rob's mood and the height of the roof.

"You're very sweet," I say. "I'll be down in a few minutes."

His friends *ooh* and *ahh,* and he walks to meet them at the wired-glass roof hatch. They descend in a line, good ducks and good geese, the abstracted, pearlized silhouettes of their heads snuffling down.

We're alone, Rob and me, just us on the roof. A chimney nearby makes a wide pipe of black smoke, and two planes flicker through the great distance like creeping stars. Between the near and the far is a cove of light, a shawl of light—electricity, covering this city, covering many cities. I wonder where the planes are headed, whether the people sleep. Usually people sleep at night on planes, heads collapsing onto neighbors' shoulders.

Rob says, "Listen," and I sigh. I don't like when people start sentences with *Listen.* No matter what comes next, it's not going to be good.

He finds my eyes. "I'm getting out of here. I don't want to tell you what to do or anything—I know it's not my place—but I think you're better off coming with me."

Rob asks if I understand. I do. He's telling me that things downstairs are bad. But I know that. They were bad already at Area when Mark argued with Rob, and next with a bouncer, and then when he got knocked down the stairs. Rob is saying that my commitment to Mark is for the present nullified—that he is under a prevailing obligation to see me safely home, an obligation to Rourke. I understand that by agreeing to go and by honoring foregoing loyalties, I betray Mark, and in turn condemn myself for my moveable allegiance.

I say okay.

"Okay," he repeats. "Let's do this fast. What's down there, a pocketbook?"

"A sweater."

He nods, calculating. "Okay, fine. A sweater. I'll wait by the elevator. I won't leave alone unless you walk out and tell me you're okay. But I'm warning you, you're gonna have to be pretty fucking convincing." He takes my hand. "Let's go."

GOING DOWN THE ROOF stairs, going back into that party, sickens me. There's this feeling I have like all the people I know have turned. Like on the back of their heads are second faces. Like I am unmoored. Like there is nothing. If not for Rob, I think in fact I would try to fly.

Everyone is dancing to the *Age of Aquarius*—not dancing so much as staggering like zombies or knee-people, like they're about to pass out.

Rob points to the entrance. "I'll be right there."

The door to the bedroom where I left Mark and everyone is open now, split about eighteen inches. Through the rupture I see him, reclining on a chaise in the center of an encampment of people, king of a wax tribe. He shifts when I come. He knows I'll go no farther than the edge of the bed. As I hunt for my sweater, he says, "C'mon, people, let's dance."

Two of the girls flanking him lend arms and aid him to his feet, and he laughs, at himself, I suppose, and the way he thinks he is. He uses them like canes to right himself across the treacherous path to me, where he stops, shaking them off with a burst of manly animation. The girls saunter insolently past as if to imply that he slept with them while I was gone or at least expressed willingness. Obviously they know nothing of his revulsion to disease or of his fear of being cheated on by me in return. How he craves to be appreciated for what he erroneously believes to be sincere, how he would never touch a woman whose attraction to him is defiled by a lust for assets. He figures himself a man of intelligence and ideals. He loathes to be typed as privileged. This is too deep to be done away with; it has to do with his father, whose character was formed at the hand of hardship.

And jealousy—I feel no jealousy where Mark is concerned. There's no block, no feelings that cannot flow; I simply have an emptiness in the place where such things might reside, a basin, a pucker or hole.

The room is clear; his friends are gone. He walks forward, plowing me back into the door frame, writhing, worming. He smiles a false smile. He wants to say something sexy but cannot. The veneer of his skin is colorless as birch, and his upper lip is a band of unsalted sweat. I'm not sure about the unsalted part, that's a guess. I just figure if there's any salt to be had, his tissues will want to keep it. His breath smells bad, like licking steel. His nose runs. I wonder what he's been doing, smoking coke or snorting heroin. Possibly both. Usually I am the excuse he uses to resist the influence of his important friends. I wonder what I've done to keep him from resisting their influence. Probably I should have seen this coming. That's my job, I think, to see things coming.

"Maybe we should go," I say.

He pulls my sweater from my hands.

I reach for it. "I think I'm going."

"I think you're staying." He flings my sweater behind him across the bedroom, and he knocks me between his pelvis and the open door. His hands drive my skirt towards my waist, and he grabs my ass, taking up the flesh and groping it. I see Rob across the dance floor. I see him starting over. Through the leather of his jacket, I can make out fists in the pockets. Mark follows the direction of my eyes, and casting a lethal gaze at Rob, he turns my back outward, exposing me to the crowd. Then he takes a single step back and kicks the door shut.

"*Mark!*" I shout. I'm thinking, *Rob is going to jail. Shit, Rob is going to jail.*

The master bathroom door pops open in the opposite corner, taking both Mark and me by surprise. Dara emerges with Anselm and Helene. Helene sways feverishly to the music, dancing as if alone on earth. It's at the horn part, at its most hallucinatory and cultish.

Let the sun shine! Let the sunshine in! The sun shine in!

Dara assesses the situation quickly. He retrieves my sweater from the floor and dusts it off. Then he helps me to disembark from Mark's arms as though assisting me off a high-speed amusement ride. I don't kid myself into thinking he cares. As far as Dara's concerned, I'm property, and it's my place to acquiesce. But he knows Rob is out there and he's thinking, *For all I know, that barbarian is carrying a gun.*

"Your fiancée is obviously unwell, Ross," Dara states. "You are wise to send her home. Unless, of course," he adds with contempt, "you have a headache also?"

Anselm laughs and Mark laughs and the bedroom door breaks open, with Rob lurching in and Mark lurching out and Anselm squeezing up the middle. Except for Helene, we congeal into a dynamic solid, like one of Michelangelo's slave sculptures. I don't know who has my hand. Someone has it tightly. Oh, it's Rob—I can feel the leather cuff of his jacket.

"Let's walk," Dara insists with a public smile, taking the lead step, and we cross the room as one. "Now, does the future Mrs. Ross have a car, or does she need a taxi?"

"Taxi," Mark answers. At the elevator bay, he reaches for his wallet. The force of his own hand in his breast pocket throws him off balance. He goes back two loose steps. Mark finds two twenties, pinches them ineptly, then thrusts them at me. I join Rob on the elevator; everyone looks at each other like factions facing off. Mark then dumps the remaining contents of his wallet onto the floor and kicks the bills at Rob.

"Here," he says, "go buy yourself a matching outfit."

As the doors begin to creak closed, Mark tosses out an arm again, blocking them. Rob pushes me behind his back, and Dara and Anselm grab Mark's shoulders. There's that irregular thucking that elevator doors do.

"I'd warn you to keep your hands off her," Mark says, "but I won't bother. You've always been too afraid to try."

I LOOK AROUND FOR a cab, but Rob snaps his head to one side, going, "C'mon, we're taking the Cougar."

The ride home passes in withering silence. I consider telling Rob that what he saw was an aberration, that Mark was not himself, but I don't bother. It's beside the point. Mark is beside the point.

Rob glares through the windshield, head somewhat down, eyes somewhat up, as if checking for broken bulbs in the street lamps. He chews furiously— a toothpick, I think. I think it's a toothpick or *was* a toothpick; I don't know since it's trapped inside the coffee and cigarette-stained canyon of his mouth, frayed most likely, frazzled at one end like a paperless cocktail parasol. We take Sixth Avenue all the way up past all the silver towers. During the week, people work in them doing things that are important, such as music and publishing, and when they receive their paychecks on Fridays, their names are typed not handwritten. I'd always been pure to Rob, from the beginning, a palace in his mind. He had erected me and tended to me. I wonder if we'll ever recover, if we can find a way around our disgrace, or if the purity is lost, the purity of definition.

He hits the hazards and comes to my door. He hands Carlo a five-dollar bill and tells him to keep an eye on the car. We go up to the apartment because Rob has to do *something*. Leaving me on the curb is not an option. In both our minds is the meaninglessness of his prudence. Mark has keys, just like me.

I WILL NOT SAY that Mark and I have sex when he eventually comes through the door. I will say that somehow he manages to ejaculate inside me despite the stubborn flaccidness of his penis, and right away he passes out and right away I bathe, allowing gravity and soap and near-boiling water to purge the tapioca clots of stinking ethylized debris he deposited in me. Men make fun of the way women taste and smell. If only women had voices.

4.

I THROW MY LEGS OVER THE SIDE OF THE BED. MY HEAD IS POUNDING, THOUGH I had nothing toxic last night. Mark is on the phone in the living room, I can hear him and see him, and he can see me. He hangs up and comes in carrying juice, and he sits, facing me. His face looks like a shield, like an African war shield. Like giant eyes out of proportion to the chin and lines by the bones going across thick as rulers.

"If you're not too disgusted, I'd like to apologize."

I shrug. "Whatever."

"Not whatever. Don't say *whatever*. I behaved shamefully. I hurt you. Say what you feel."

"It was embarrassing."

"I'm sorry you were embarrassed. What else?"

"It seemed like you were mad at me."

"Not you. Never you." He reaches over, pets back my hair. "I got caught up. One thing led to another. I was drinking gin. You know I can't drink gin." He follows me to the bathroom and watches me wash and dress. "It's not like I was with another woman, for Christ's sake. C'mon, I'm a wreck about this."

This is only a partial lie. Obviously he's a wreck about something. I say, "Just forget it, Mark."

"Oh no," he states with sudden menacing rectitude, "just the opposite. I won't forget it. In fact, I've called everyone. I just got off the phone with Rob. I want you to know, I took all the blame."

I brush my teeth. I wonder if there's a difference between *taking* the blame and *being* to blame. If there's a difference, I'm sure he's referring to it. At the front door, I grab a coat and my knapsack.

"Where you headed?"

"School."

"The gym?"

Mark doesn't like me to go to the gym. He says it's a pick-up scene. If I promise to avoid the basketball courts and the weight room, and just go to the pool and sauna, he'll say that's worse because of the lesbians. Once I said, "What lesbians? I've never noticed any lesbians," and he said, "*That's* precisely the problem."

"The library. I have to finish my papers."

"I thought you finished your papers. Aren't they due Tuesday? You really should have told me. If I'd known, we wouldn't have gone out at all last night." At the elevator, he kisses me on the forehead, speaking into my temple. "I have your graduation present. I spoke to the travel agent this morning. We're going away the day after Alicia's wedding. I wanted to surprise you, but we'll need to have your passport ready. What would you say to Italy—The Amalfi Coast, Rome, Florence, Venice."

Italy, I think as I board the elevator. It's the least he can do.

FROM THE LIBRARY I take a twelve-dollar cab ride to Pinky's. The driver goes up Third Avenue to the Queensboro Bridge because there's an accident on the Williamsburg and the Manhattan is closed for repairs. "Everybody went to the Brooklyn," he says, waving his free hand. "The BQE's a parking lot. We're better off on the Pulaski."

The streets glisten from an evening rain. Outside is very warm, even for May. Through my window I hear the ravishing tick of tires against wet pavement. On public radio, a speaker of European descent discusses intrinsic and extrinsic realities to a Californian crowd. I'm not sure about the Californian part, except to say the sound system has a leafy open-air quality that makes me think of Santa Barbara.

"When we walk," the speaker explains, "our intrinsic reality is, quite simply, that our legs move in a given direction toward a given destination. Extrinsically, however, we are reliant upon the earth beneath our feet. If the earth were as absent in reality as in our perception of reality, our legs would swing in air."

"Relationship is never merely one-sided," he continues. "It possesses a truth separate from that which is easily named or known. Equity can exist, but independent of the *interpretation* of equity, which by nature is variable. Therefore, what we feel intrinsically is, and can only ever be, a partial truth."

The taxi skulks to a stop at Fifty-eighth Street near Alexander's department store before making the turn onto the bridge ramp. Creaking up to consume my entire field of vision is that bizarre mural of globular buttons over Alexander's doorway, like a collection of hemisected eyeballs, like some insane manifestation of things urging me to see.

And so I see.

It has never occurred to me to move beyond the idea of having been abandoned, beyond the position of victim. For years, I've behaved that way, not because I've been victimized, but because inside I must feel it's all that remains to me—one is a victim when one does not triumph. The parts of me that came to life with Rourke were parts I could not have conceived alone. Naturally I believed if the best I could be was *with* him, then *without* him I was nothing. Losing him was like walking very well, then falling. Like a toddler unkindly reverted to infancy.

It should have been enough to love and be loved, but *there was more,* I thought, I must have thought, because at some point everything changed from my simply wanting more of him to my wanting more of something else—some substantive normalcy—all the while denying the egocentricity of my aspirations, all the while disrecalling the universe we'd made. What we made was a sphere revolving, something stellar in orbit, something real and vital, ringing out through the vertical sheet of night, something that perhaps cannot be touched but can surely be perceived and so then cherished—a diamond to the naked eye, Olympian, supreme, celestial—an impenetrable grove of heaven blazing through millions upon millions of magnifications.

The cab is on the lower roadway, cables and girders thoomping past, animating riverish windows and, in them, fervid cities, fiery lights, making each rhomboid like a new page of a cartoon flip book—black jeweled water, black jeweled skies. You hardly discern movement, yet you move.

When he left, I told myself that he wanted someone better, older, prettier. I see that my anguish rendered me insensible. At the time, I forgot that life is strange and long and beautiful, and that something so extraordinary in its success could hardly be ordinary in its failure. I persuaded myself to believe that he did not love me, that he never had; and yet, not once when we were together did I need to tell myself he did. Love is just a word. I forgot that too; I forgot that constancy can be more capably expressed.

I feel shame to recollect the naturalness of his earliest investment, the absence of artifice, the way he knew me when he met me, the way he worked to move us, to eternalize us, despite obstacles of age and position, the way he trusted that I would feel as he felt, the way he was patient and true. Oh, the ghost of him looming, the strain in his muscles at the sight of me.

Since he knew things at the beginning, maybe at the end he knew things too, things I did not sense or refused to sense. That we had achieved enough, that we had moved as far as lightness and clarity would take us. That nothing is more sacred than youth or more hopeful than turning yourself over to one person and saying, *I have this time, it is not a long time, but it is my best time and my best gift, and I give it to you. When I revisit my youth, I revisit you.* No gift is more lasting or pure. Now I know too. I had not been walking on air. Rourke had been there, pressure, earth beneath my feet, always.

EVERYBODY'S WATCHING TELEVISION. ROB is down at the left end of the filmy, decrepit bar, in his usual place, by the telephone. His mood has not improved since last night—the stiff hunch to his back, the shaking leg. He does not smile when he sees me, he just kicks out a stool. I drop my book bag and climb up. Something happens in the game, and the men shout in unison—*Ho, Shit!* Rob's voice joins the chorus. He concentrates on the set, pretending to ignore me, which is a trick men play on the women who matter. Eventually he turns, his eyes wafting toward my lap. My legs are crossed, and with the pants I'm wearing, the crevice between my thighs is particularly revealing. I slide my hands to cover myself.

Rob sneezes and blows his nose hard. "I'm allergic to something in here." He looks over each shoulder. "Must be somebody's cologne." He gestures to my knapsack. "It seems like you've been in school longer than anyone ever— why is that?"

"I don't know."

"You don't, huh?" he says. "Well, when are you done?"

"I have three papers due Tuesday."

"And that's it?"

"And a presentation."

"A presentation, excuse me. What's that, like Darren Stevens?"

"Kind of. Only no witches."

He faces the bar, puts his elbows up, and wipes his nose one more time. "Where's the ring?" he asks, talking into his tissue.

"I left it at home."

"Home," he repeats facetiously. "That's not fair play. Some poor slob might get the idea you're available. Unless of course you weren't *allowed* to wear it. Did he tell you I'm gonna steal it and hock it?"

"He doesn't—"

"*Mrs. Ross.* Tell you the truth, I'd rather you were gonna marry that queer friend of yours. He's actually a good guy."

"Mark's okay."

"Yeah, sure. Okay. Capital *O.*"

"Do you hate him because he's rich?" I ask.

"Do you sleep with him because he's rich?" Rob asks back. "Oh, no, I'm sorry," he taunts, "you sleep with him because you *love* him."

"No, I—"

"*No?* Then why do you sleep with him?"

"I, I'm not sure. He was there—"

"Lots of people were *there. I* was there." He slaps his chest. "How come you never fucked me?" His fingers come together. "I'll tell you why. Because I know the code." He clenches his jaw, leans back, pulls out his wallet, and drops a fresh ten horizontally in the north-south direction of the bar. Rob's wallet is full of cash. Rob's wallet is always full of cash. The bartender draws two tap beers and pushes them to us. Rob says, "Thanks, Pink."

Pinky leaves the money untouched. "How you doing, sweetheart? Long time no see." Pinky's an albino. They call him Pinky because he looks like the inside of a conch. I had a cat like that once, like Pinky, with two different colored eyes, only my cat was deaf. Pinky can hear just fine except for a vague ringing sometimes. He keeps thinking there's a break-in at the pork factory across the street.

"Sorry, Pinky. I've been busy with school."

"She graduates next week," Rob reports. "Top honors, 4.0 average, dean's list. She got a certificate. One of these rolled-up parchment jobs. They made her a *University Scholar.*"

"If she's so smart, what's she doing out here with you?" Pinky cackles as he chugs off, sideways and slow, like a failing tug.

"She must be drawn to the superior quality of this establishment—*wise ass!*" Rob lifts his mug and polishes off a third of the contents in one swallow, then bends in like he's got a secret. "You wanna know what I think? I think you're with him because he doesn't care that you don't love him. Any other guy, any *normal* guy, shit like that matters. But you don't want anything normal because you're holding onto the past. He knows this. That bastard worked your, your—*situation* to his advantage. Just like a crook, he saw an open window, and he climbed in." Rob's eyes strangle down like the lens of a camera to pinholes. "Lemme tell you something about Mark—he don't come through. You know what I mean, *come through?* Principles, ethics, *the code*. He knows the fucking code. He knows it and he ignores it."

"What difference does it make?"

"It makes a difference," Rob says. "Certain things you don't do."

"Rourke left."

"He had no choice."

"He had a choice."

"Don't tell me. I was there." Rob wipes the bar around our mugs with a cocktail napkin. "The only reason Harrison took that job with those kids in the first place was Diane backed out."

"Diane *who?*"

"Diane who," he repeats.

"I'm serious. I've never even heard of her."

"Nobody over there ever mentioned Diane *Gelbart*. A Mr. and Mrs. Gelbart? Do those people open your mail too? Take your calls?"

"Diane. Do you mean Mark's old girlfriend?"

"You *have* heard of her."

"I guess I just forgot."

"I'd like to forget her myself. She's a jinx. All the bad luck started with her. She's insane and overaccustomed to getting what she wants. And what she wanted at the time was—well, you can imagine."

He doesn't have to say. I *can* imagine.

Rob stares into his mug, picturing graphics in the froth. "I'm surprised you two haven't run into each other. She's always flying back and forth from California—like a carrier pigeon. Her parents are very friendly with Mark's parents. They have one of those places in Southampton. Between the ocean and the pond."

"Gin Lane," I say, sounding outside myself.

"Yeah, that's it, Gin Lane. Very swank. She tried to persuade Harrison to live there that winter, but forget about it. He'd rather live in a cold-water shack and have his freedom, if you know what I mean."

I shift on my chair, lifting my ribs roofward and breathing deep. I try to remember what I'd heard about Diane, something about Rita Hayworth and nightclubs and never looking at stars. I think of her beauty, her glamour—surely she's beautiful and glamorous. Probably she visited Rourke's little house in Montauk, telling him it was *quaint*. Maybe the plans he'd had that first New Year's Eve were with her. And during the summer we spent together, Rourke probably went to Gin Lane when I was working at the Lobster Roll, going to play tennis or eat dinner by the poolhouse, and when he left that September, he probably—No, Rob is right. Rourke would rather live in a shack and have his freedom. Rourke had integrity, unlike me. *You know what I mean*, Rob said. Yeah, I know what he means.

Oh, I remember what Mark said. *Everyone wanted her, but only I could get her.* I feel sick to my stomach. I rest my head in my hands.

Rob's hand touches my shoulder. "You okay?"

"It's—hot in here."

"That's because Pinky's a cheap bastard. He hates to put the air on before, like, August. I keep telling him it's gonna kill business, but he has the brilliant philosophy that heat makes people drink more. I go, *Yeah, Einstein, at the bar down the street.*" Rob whistles. "Hey, Pink! Spend a couple dimes and hit the AC! She faints easy!"

Without removing his chin from the saddle of his left hand, Pinky breaks from the television to acknowledge Rob fixedly then heads out from behind the bar to flip the toggle by the front door. The machine in the transom sputters to life deep down in the cheerless dark of its barrel, then it starts to spit through its grubby vents.

"Maybe we should stop right here," he says.

"Maybe you should just tell me what you know."

Rob makes a squeaking noise with the side of his mouth, and he stares at the ceiling. He looks like Reverend Olcott the time we talked about God. Like he has a whole reserve of information but is afraid to release it so fast it floods me. And yet, he knows I want truth, and he wants to be truthful. I see him take a walk through the conversation a couple of times, weighing the dangers of honesty versus the uncommon opportunity for personal gain. He hates Mark. There may not be another chance like this one.

"Okay. So, Diane's two years younger than us. We graduate back in '77, me and Harrison stick around L.A., doing our thing. He fights, I do grad school, Chris DeMarco goes back east to NYU Law, and Mark heads to Harvard, not breaking off with Diane. He prefers to string her along. She knows what's up, so she hooks up with a bad crowd—booze and coke mostly but, like, a lot of coke. Several grams per week is a gentlemanly estimate. UCLA puts her on probation, her parents threaten to cut off the cash and ship her up to some Minnesota rehab—but she just keeps going. Finally she ends up at some party in the Hills where her girlfriend drowns. Very big deal. Mark is worthless, of course. He flies out with her folks for one day—*one day*—the day she makes the declaration to the cops. That's it. Her parents offer to send them on a vacation. A couple weeks in Europe, the Caribbean. He's too busy with school, he claims, he can't spare the time, et cetera, et cetera. Basically, she's a total fucking liability, and he's worried about his reputation. You know, he wants to run for office someday, have a seat on the Exchange, whatever—that's why he hangs around with those addicts from Washington."

"Because they have money?"

"Lots of people have money. They have *connections.* Anyway, Mark backs out; she calls Harrison. She's alone, she's scared, but basically, she's vindictive. Of course Harrison steps in—me, I wouldn't have bothered—and one, two, three, she's clean. Nobody knows what he did to get through, but he got through. In my opinion, she got well out of spite. She has a very strong spiteful streak."

Oh, but I know. Just his eyes alone, looking at you.

"Naturally her parents are grateful. They pull some strings to get him a big shot agent who right off the bat comes through with decent stuff. Bit parts, but decent—commercials, voice-overs, print, extra work in TV, and a couple of movies—but it turns out to be a deal with the Devil. Harrison is like under obligation to look out for Diane and follow through with this agent—Eliot something, from William Morris. Of course, Eliot wants him to quit fighting and behind Harrison's back goes head to head with the trainer out there, Chucho Lopez, Charles Lopez, who happens to be connected himself, and who's counter-pressuring Harrison to get management and start the climb for a title. I don't know if you realize the kind of money that's at stake. Do you realize?"

I shake my head. I have no idea.

"In fighting? Could be millions. Could be many millions. I've been to houses that would make that Gin Lane place look like a trailer. And the owner will be some twenty-two year old kid living with twelve friends, eight Mercedes, and a basketball court off the kitchen. Harrison is smart, he's mature and—" Rob tosses up his hand like it's a lost cause. "Anyway, Eliot gets his tires slashed and other stuff I don't even want to get into, and in the middle of it all, we can't shake Diane. She's showing up at the fights, hanging around the gym. Every day she's at the fucking gym. Once she got her teeth in, she infected everything, like a rabid dog."

"Were you guys planning to stay in L.A.?"

"We had no plan."

"Did he want to turn professional?"

"Yes and no. Yes, because of money. No, because of interference. Let's just say he's got a problem with the concept of management. I could take on some small stuff, but as far as cutting title deals and what have you, I was twenty-three. Just one guy. Obviously I've got access to organizations through my uncle, but signing on independent of Harrison would've meant a break. And I wasn't gonna do that. I'm not interested in repping other fighters. On top of it, with the acting thing a distinct possibility, he's suddenly not so keen on ruining his face. He's been lucky so far. Luck like that doesn't last."

I think about that all the time, his face.

"So," Rob continues, "Summer '79. Diane graduates—her parents want her in New York so they can keep an eye on her. She's not saying nothing, but you can see the writing on the wall—she's gonna stick to Harrison like shit on a shoe. Her folks set up that cozy job on Long Island by making a couple anonymous donations here and there to the playhouse, to the school through some friend on the board, figuring it's East Hampton in winter—if she goes berserk on dope again, nobody is gonna be the wiser. Meanwhile, did anybody think for a second about those kids stuck with that freak? Well, surprise, surprise, she refuses to leave him in California. That's when Harrison decides to go for the Olympics. It's the honorable way out all around. Jimmy Landis, the trainer he's had since he was a kid, was working with two other fighters for the Games, and to top it off, the Olympics is just about the only organization big enough to intimidate Diane. She flips out anyway and goes on a weeklong binge. As it happens, the thing with KCBS opens up—she's some kind of entertainment reporter now—and with a little added incentive from her folks, you know, new house, new car, she jumps on it. The whole thing was too good to pass up, even a cokehead like her could see that. Harrison had the idea to take her spot in the school to help her parents save face and to throw Diane off the scent, so to speak. Make her think he was on board and keep her out of trouble in L.A. while she settled into the job. He figured she'd settle. Nobody else believed it. But he was right. Her parents owe him big time."

Rob breaks to drink some of his beer. I remember Alicia asking about Rourke. *You two must have been completely in love.* She must have been thinking about Rourke wanting to get away from Diane, but wanting to be with me.

"You can see why Mark hates him. Harrison saves the day and looks like a prince, whereas Mark dumps his nightmare on other people, runs for cover and looks like the rat he is. Mark's father almost disowned him over the whole thing, but he had a massive coronary instead. I'd like to say it was related, but I know you love the old man, so I won't talk out of my ass. Let's just say it certainly didn't help matters in terms of Mark being in the spotlight looking like such a dick. Mr. Ross had open-heart surgery, but he can't take a day off because he's afraid of the damage Mark will do. He's counting on you to make Mark a better man. Good fucking luck."

"Were you upset to leave California?" I ask.

"Me, nah—I hit bottom out there. Besides Harrison could fight anywhere. And it got her claws out of him. You know me, I'm very superstitious. Last thing I wanted was her bad blood hanging over his head or *mine.*" He clears his throat. "Long Island turned out to be a good deal. Harrison was looking to focus on the Games, get his mind off—*things.* Jersey was out of the question. The temptation would've been too great to go pro, make some money. Between his talent and my talent, it's like sitting on a gold mine. Once he made the choice to go for the Olympics, he had to relocate. Montauk was perfect, not just because of the kind of shape he got into physically, but mentally, which after L.A. he needed. He needed a *wash.* He was running, biking, swimming over at Gurney's, coming into Brooklyn five, six days a week, training with Jimmy—doing qualifiers, the Eastern Trials, the whole bit. Next thing you know, the Soviets invade Afghanistan, President Carter starts talking boycott in January, and by April, it's official. *Poof,* that's that. No more Olympics."

He takes a minute to reflect. There's an ad on television for Michelob, a weird ad, considering it's for beer.

You're on your way. You're moving up. You can have it all.

"Remember the night in the meat district?" Rob asks. "You asked what I said the first time I saw you."

I look to my lap. "And you didn't tell me."

"And I'm not going to now." He sucks back his cheek again, and his head twitches right. "Something dumb, not too bad, just the kind of thing guys say to each other. Well, it practically got me killed. I was like, *Jesus*." He returns his gaze momentarily to the television. He drags a finger around the top inside of his glass. I wonder what he is thinking about. Possibly just the game.

"Hey, I never told you this," Rob says, perking up, "but if I hadn't been there that day, I think your boyfriend with the Mustang, that blond kid you were with, would've taken a short walk off that cliff. Like joined the parade from top down." He makes a diving motion with his hand.

"Ray Trent. Nice guy."

"Nice *alive* guy," Rob adds. "With nice *operative* legs."

"He wasn't my boyfriend."

"He wasn't a *friend* either. That was clear. To Harrison, anyway. Was he wrong?"

"No, he wasn't wrong."

Rob holds his jaw with one hand and smiles, shaking his head. "That's funny," he says of Rourke. "Fucking guy."

There is something peculiar on my face, something chill. A tear, it's a tear, not running but pendant. Strange, I thought all the tears had dried. Like bouquets of upside-down wedding roses.

"I know what you're thinking," Rob says. "You're thinking, *He left her, he left me; he lied to her, he lied to me.* You're drawing a comparison, only there's no comparison. First off, he was dealing with a hysteric and a cheat. The thing about cheats is they don't just *cheat* you, they make *you* cheat. That's the objective—the failure of your character." His voice deepens. "With you, it was different. You would never do that to someone. You did him a favor. You let go."

That's not what I'm thinking, but it's sweet of him to feel this way and to have been feeling this way all along, sweet to be grateful for my having treated his friend gently and to be proud of me, like I'd preserved something fragile. As if I *hadn't* become hysterical, *hadn't* cheated him, cheated Rourke, cheated Mark and myself. As if I *hadn't* lied. Perhaps a stronger woman, one with her own family and house and car—an entertainment reporter, for instance—would have fought for her rights. Frequently you read about them. Mrs. Ross calls them *go-getters*. "*Go-getters*?!" my mother said in disgust and disbelief when I used the term. "We're *all* go-getters. *Go get* me a cup of coffee! *Go get* the groceries! *Go get* the kids! *Go get* undressed."

The bar phone rings. "Take a number, Pink," Rob says, not even looking. He moves closer to take up the tear.

"Did he love her?"

"He never touched her, if that's what you're asking. Even if she'd been halfway sane, he wouldn't have touched her."

"Because of Mark."

"Because of *the code*. Because Harrison doesn't just *know* the code. He invented it." Rob is so close I can feel the downward stamp of his breath. "He wasn't gonna stay in Montauk that summer, Evie. He was gonna come back to fight. He had the apartment in Spring Lake, dates in Atlantic City. The idea was to take time, stay strong, figure things out. A gym, maybe. We always said we'd open a gym, a chain—Jersey, L.A., Miami, Vegas, the Bronx."

I consider for the first time all that Rob has lost. It's there in his face—a grasping sadness, a lonely frenzy. No one likes to surrender the best place to be. It's like forfeiting riches. It's *exactly* that.

"But that shit wasn't happening, especially once Ross got into the picture. What a fucking judgment lapse. I think about the night we all went out to that place in Amagansett, what Harrison could have been thinking. My guess is he wanted to force his own hand, you know, introduce Mark so he'd have to come for you. And he did. What did he last in Jersey, for like, two *weeks* before turning back?"

"Fifteen days," I say.

"*Fifteen* days," Rob says with a smile. "He trained hard for fourteen of them, sparring every night, wiping out the entire local roster, everybody's going crazy—radio, newspapers, the whole boardwalk is coming to life. On the fourteenth day, he kicks the shit out of Tommy Lydell, who hasn't missed a day in the ring since he was born. Harrison cracks his jaw, right in the second, you could hear the snap through the auditorium, and we had a couple hundred people there, then he lays him out with a body shot—Rourke's impeccable on the inside. We were fucking flying. Next day he says to me, '*Let's take a drive.*' I'll never forget it. '*Let's take a drive. Two cars.*' Okay, I say. We go to East Hampton, we take the girls around, the beach, the town, shopping. Then we go to your house. Me and Harrison. We go in. You're not there. Your mother is—nice lady, by the way, sexy, very unusual. She sits on the back of the little couch there and folds her arms, checking us out. She says to Harrison, 'Eveline hasn't been out of the house for two weeks. Are you the one she's been waiting for?' Harrison just goes, 'Yeah, I'm the one.' "

You have a mother, Rourke said to me, *I've met her.*

"She tells us where she thinks you are, a party, and that some girl from school drove you over. 'Take care of her,' your mother says. 'I intend to,' Harrison tells her. But before we go to find you, I make him stop at the beach to cool off. I figure with the way he's been fighting, he might take lives. And what happens, you pull up with Mark—*in the Porsche.* Thank God Joey had a football in the car, so I could keep Harrison's hands busy." Rob looks at me. "I'll tell you what I was thinking at *that* moment. I was thinking, *Shit, this girl's dangerous.*"

"I never would have—"

"That was obvious. How you felt was obvious. Obvious as how Harrison felt. Obvious as what Mark was doing. The whole situation was painfully fucking clear. But it's unchartered territory, showing need. In the end, it brings you down. Remember I told you—*be careful?*" He points to the counter. "*This* is what I was talking about. This very day. Mark made his decision the first time he laid eyes on you. He cased the situation. He *mastered* the obvious. Here we are. Four years later."

Pinky hands me a half-empty soft pack of tissues. I thank him.

"The rest is history. You come to Jersey, he goes to Montauk. And who could blame him? No sense rushing out to get hammered when you got a, a thing—*a girl*—you know, whatever." He nudges me with his shoulder. "We had a lot of fun that summer, didn't we?" His voice darkens. "But sooner or later, a man's mind turns to money, usually from *some* money to *big* money. He had to get back to training; he settled on the '84 games. What was he supposed to do that would've been better or faster than fighting? Maybe he didn't want you watching him get beat up—it's not pretty stuff. Maybe he thought you should start your own life, school, what have you. Maybe he didn't do the right thing. Maybe he didn't know *what* to do. He just figured you'd be okay. I guess he had more faith in you than he did in himself. That's what I mean by saying he had no choice."

He takes a tissue from me and blows his nose hard. "The part that threw *me* was him going alone. At first I was pissed. You remember, you were there— my birthday, at Surfside. He told me he bought a ticket to Miami, that Jimmy hooked him up with some Cuban coach. Right off with the way he was talking, I knew I wasn't part of the plan. 'We'll meet up later,' he said. 'A couple months.' I wanted to fuckin' kill him." Rob shakes his head. "*Miami.*"

Rob tears open a pack of Halls and tilts it in my direction. I decline. He pops one out, unwraps it, and sets it in his mouth. "Eventually I chalked the whole thing up to misunderstanding—whatever. I mean, no promises were exchanged. I never asked him anything; he never said anything. He's not exactly chatty—as you know." The cough drop flips around between his teeth. I hear it click; I smell eucalyptus. "I let seven months go by, the longest we ever went without talking."

Seven months. April. When he came to see me in my dorm.

"You weren't looking so good," he said, as if reading my mind. "But you were very, I don't know—I thought, *Shit, if she, if she's*—" Rob stammers into a burdensome silence. The virulent type of midgut silence that longs for some means of discharge, some emetic. I'm not surprised by the heaviness; I think I've known all along. Mark told *him* what happened. *He* told Rourke.

"Harrison called. He was coming to New York. He wanted to see you. I said I'd take care of it. There was no listing for you in Manhattan. NYU had a dorm, the one on East Tenth, but no student number—that's because your old roommate got the phone. I tried your mother. I knew the address, but her name is different from yours. Like an idiot, I call Mark, thinking he could get your number through Alicia. Well, he had been *waiting* for that. He told me you didn't want anything to do with Harrison, then he told me why in no uncertain terms. How he paid for an abortion, how you were found practically dead in the street, how he took you to the hospital, how he took you home, how he cleaned up after *that animal*, how he was the only thing standing between you and a nervous breakdown."

I must be in shock because the first thing I think of isn't Rourke. The first thing I think of is Mr. Ross. And the green study upstairs in East Hampton. Mark telling him the story of me in there. A *private* conversation. No wonder they all tiptoed around me. Mark had told them I'd been kidnapped, raped, abandoned. *Found practically dead in the street.* Didn't that imply I'd done it to myself, like with a coat hanger? Next I think of Rourke, how I hurt him, how I owe him the truth. Last is Mark. He robbed me. I would rob him back.

"First of all," I say, "he *loaned* me money. I paid him back."

"Sure, sure. I'm sure he blew it out of proportion. The fact is, you could've called me. You *should've* called me. You gotta understand, men are funny about certain things. You can't have one guy stepping in like that to another guy's— I mean, you know what I mean. I hope Mark didn't convince you to do something you weren't comfortable with. I'm Catholic, and I don't have to tell you how I feel about kids, but I wouldn't go around twisting arms."

"Rob, it was an accident."

"What do you mean, accident?"

"Not an accident, I mean—like, a loss."

"A *loss*," he repeats.

"I don't suppose Mark told you that part."

Rob lays his elbows on the bar and rubs the inside of his eyes with his fingertips. He turns to me, our faces are close, practically grazing. Beneath his eyes are the hard lines of misfortune, they go like pink wires back to his brain. You cannot read him through his eyes. They defy, they oppose. Rob's eyes are not how you see in, but how he sees out. They are the frontpieces of a complex system of risk; if you love him, you know the eyes are not the beginning, they are the end, his end, where messages appear. He's in shock, like me, only my shock is less and his is more. I live with Mark. I belong to a society that is unbenign, to a circle of people who are duplicitous and disposable. Rob's is a world where ties extend beyond blood, where people keep track. I'm sad to see him forced to confront questions of complicity and involvement among friends. It's like he's got rats in the house. But at least now we know. Of all the reckless ways to live—liquor, drugs, fast driving, sex without birth control, gambling with people who can break your legs—the most reckless of all is an absence of influence over your own affairs, a loss of voice.

"What was I supposed to do, Eveline? Everybody knowing his business but him, it wasn't right. If he ever found out that I knew too—bad enough I knew for a week before he showed up. I wanted to tell him in person. As it was, it took me days."

"Three days. It took you three days."

"You remember the night. At Ear Bar."

"I remember."

"I should have—I felt too—"

"Me too, I—I don't know. I don't know."

"And ever since Harrison's father died, it's like he's under this pressure. Everything goes back to that. This went back to that."

"God, Rob. I'm sorry. I'm sorry."

"Ah, it's just bad luck. Bad luck all around. Except for Ross. He scored a triple win—retribution for Diane, a shot at you—which, I mean, he never stood a chance—and Harrison—well, he never fought again. Mark called him an animal, and he believed it."

Rob shakes his head. "You know, it's taken me a while to figure it out, this whole thing. I can't believe I've been so stupid. Harrison left without me twice because he wanted me to stay. He wanted me to look out for you. And I failed—twice."

He goes away in his mind, drifting for a minute, two, then suddenly landing, coming sharply back down, returning like a rock thrown skyward. He drums his hands on the bar and cracks his back to the right. I wondered what he was going to do. He was going to do something.

"Do me a favor," he says to me. "Just think. Think before you act. Think about everything. And remember what I told you the first time—*Be careful.*"

Rob said to think, so i do, though it is difficult to find in myself what happened when my mind has transformed it, remaking it over the years into a thing finally crippled, finally deformed, abbreviated in measure like bones missing from a body, until all that endures is a speed-infused hallucination or violently edited time. I try to think, but the gaps in my story are great.

The first thing is the night in the meat district, the phone call from Rob—*I'll be over at seven*—the delicate way he acted when he saw me. The next is a Sunday, one week later. Rob and Mark showing up at my dorm. They were going to play football. "It's a beautiful day," Mark said, swinging open my closet door, "you should get out."

I can still see them standing there looking at the empty hangers, then down to the ground at my suitcase because I hadn't ever unpacked. Rob turned away, but Mark kneeled and went through like a surgeon, careful not to disrupt the piles that were folded and squared and belted tightly. "This is perfect," Mark said, pulling out something white. He placed it on my shoulders. "C'mon, let's head to Central Park!"

The Cougar was double parked on Tenth Street. We drove down Broadway, and Mark ran into Delion for coffees and sandwiches and a pack of Wrigley's for Rob. Rob combed back his hair with his fingers then threw a lithe muscular arm over the back of the seat. I could feel the electricity behind my neck.

"He's coming back," Rob said, clearing his throat as though he wanted to be very precise. "For a couple days. He'd like to see you. You gonna be okay about this," Rob wanted to know, "or what?"

I said. "I'll be fine."

Rourke had agreed to help a friend on a job in Rahway, in Jersey. The friend was the Chinaman, and the Chinaman needed Rourke because Rourke knew martial arts and could defend himself, and Rahway was dangerous. No one told me any of this direct or outright, I learned in pieces. They must have thought it was the best way to tell me, in pieces. I remember wondering was I still sick.

"What's Rahway?" I asked Rob later. We were sitting in the grass, on the Great Lawn. He said it was a prison.

Next is a marina in Jersey. And sail masts towering disproportionately as if to tear night from the sky and stars like shattered dishware, rabidly strewn. And the hebetudinous bluntness of Pink Floyd in Mark's car, followed by the excruciating clarity of the beyond—the clinking chiming ropes, the welted slap of the water against the wharf, the *flap-flap-flap* of plastic grand-opening flags that draped the raised butts of drydocked boats. Me wondering why those flags were there. I had to walk on my toes, I recall, to keep my heels from sinking into sand, the lot was sand. Lights like flames hung in gravid loops along the restaurant's awning, and more ivied down the banister from the dining deck, still closed for the season.

"Rob ever take you here in summer?" Joey going up, asking Mark.

"Couple of times," Mark saying.

"Nice sunsets, right?"

"Gorgeous. We were here in `79, for the wedding."

"You bet," Rob said. "That bastard Eddie M."

"Yeah, yeah," Joey said. "That's right, Eddie M. He is a bastard."

Mark palmed Lorraine's back. "What do you think Lorraine? Nice place for a wedding."

Lorraine wouldn't hold her breath.

Rob stopped at the landing and faced us. "I've often thought about marriage. But it always ends up being just that—*a thought*." He busted out laughing, and Lorraine gave him a whack.

"Why you gotta say such stupid shit?" Joey wanted to know. He and Rob, walking abreast. "I swear."

We approached a big circular candlelit table in a room to the left of the entrance, and right away Rob excused himself. He had to make the rounds, make a couple calls. He looked at me before he left, and he winked like everything was gonna be okay. I watched him fold into the jacketed arms of men, waiter jackets and owner jackets, white and brown, white like doves and brown like mud, like many white things being overtaken by mud. Then I couldn't see him anymore, but I stayed staring into that spot just in case he might return to fill it.

"Sit down, Eveline, sit down," a voice saying.

It was Lee, the same Lee from the year before, and Chris, her husband. I hadn't seen them since the previous summer, at Mineo's, which was unsettling like everything was unsettling. Voices reached me equally at once in a merging flush like sleeping alongside a waterfall, and the gestures kept turning stone-still, freezing up as executed, like we'd all breathed ether. I remember the harbor, the lights like fairies in tar, and time, a gathering of windows, an accumulation of views, a cluster of active periods, proving each thing, each moment, each thought—living, dead, present, past, forward, and in reverse— to possess qualities that are intra-relative and extra-relative. And the look of life being new again, which is the newness of layering, which is infinity.

"You have your driver," Mark was saying, "your mid-iron, your putter, and your spoon."

"There's also a brassie, a mashie, and a niblick," Brett added.

Brett had come with Mark. I'd never met him before that night. They picked me up at school after eighteen holes in Eastchester, and on the way to Jersey they spoke of recipes for venison and peaches. Open-heart peaches, open-rock peaches, and open-seed. Freestones are the ones from which the pits are easily removed. Mark drummed out the syllables on the dashboard for my edification—*Free-stone*.

"A niblick!" Lee said. "You guys have got to be joking!"

From the moment we arrived, Mark didn't talk to me, he just kept watching, like eventually I was going to drop, and eventually he was going to have to catch me. His mannishness came across as fussy and classically standard, in a chronic state of suspense, like that of a male ballet dancer.

"Lobsters all round," Joey told the waiter. "Three two-pound, lemme see, five three-pound."

When Rob got back, Joey started in on him, like what he was up to and who was he calling. Rob sat and stared, picking sesame seeds off bread sticks. He played with his lips, and he flexed his jaw, making those two dark creases that arced parenthetically from his cheekbones.

Chris said, "What's the matter, Joey, nostalgic for the old times?"

"What about the old times?" Brett inquired, shaking the ice in his glass.

"Fireworks," Lee said.

"Small stuff," Joey said. "Sparklers, bottle rockets."

"Fuck you, *sparklers*." Rob rolled his neck in its socket. "Listen to this, *sparklers*."

"That's right, sparklers." Joey looked around. "I'm a fireman, for Chrissakes."

Rob turned to me. "Strictly big stuff. Rockets and bombs. NASA quality. Nuclear." *Nucular.*

"From running bombs to running fights to running numbers," Chris said.

"And my mother had big hopes for him," Joey said. "Her *baby*."

"Yeah, well, I'm not dead yet."

"*Yet* is right," Chris said. "You don't have a bodyguard anymore."

Rob tilted back his chair. His arms hung straight off his sides and his thighs were apart. "My mother wants me to be an accountant. I go, *Ma, think of me as an accountant with a mobile office.*"

"Very funny," Joey said. "Four years of college, then grad school, and he's standing on street corners. My parents had to take out a second mortgage to pay tuition."

"I don't stand on corners."

"Run slips, whatever. You're in the wheel. You're a spoke."

"I don't run slips either—you know what Joey, you don't know what the fuck I do. *Wheel. Spoke.* Where do you get this shit from—*Baretta?*" Rob's chair slapped down. Lorraine shifted an inch. "First of all, if there *was* a wheel, I'd be at the hub. Number two, I paid back Mom and Pop three times over. And while we're at it, do you think major brokerages recruit guys like me? Harvard Mark and his buddy over here'll each make partner at Goldman in a couple years, but I'd be walled up in some cubicle, crunching numbers, making fifty grand, thinking up scams. You know how easy it is for me to think up scams?" Rob mashed his teeth together. "There's a big difference between a prison-bound entrepreneur and prison-bound clerk."

"True," Chris said, "only one can afford a good lawyer."

"Besides," Rob added, "Lorraine over here is very high maintenance. Very Park Avenue." His hand slipped up from her shoulders into the uncivilized nest of her hair. Her favorite feature was her hair, she emphasized it hugely. It was long and flinty gold like from spray-paint. If Lorraine were a cat, she'd be a calico—pretty but peculiar, and somewhat of a genetic error. Her leather-brown eyes and eyebrows were like dots and arcs on her pale face, and her mouth was broad. She carried a huge pocketbook, which always contained the thing Rob needed most. "Hey Rainy," he'd say, flicking his knuckles into his palm, "got a deck a cards?"

"How come your father can't get Rob a job at some corporation?" Joey asked Mark. "Something honest."

"Honest, *ha*," Rob mocked. "Corporations. Honest. Go back to pissin' on fires, Joey."

"No problem," Mark said convincingly. "My father loves Rob."

Lee leaned over to me. "So, how's everything with you. School?"

"Yeah, how's it going, Eveline?" Chris inquired.

"It's going okay."

"She's all *A*s," Rob said. "Forget about it."

"And it happens to be a very rigid curriculum," Mark added.

Rob said, "It's not like she sits around drawing pictures all day."

I wondered why they felt they had to defend me. I wondered if I seemed dumb.

PAST THE HEADS OF Lee and Chris was a scabrous plastered archway leading to the packed central dining area, and on the far side of that, another archway, another hall, this one to the bathrooms and kitchen. Red-vested waiters flounced into the first room, one on top of the other like out of a musical, each carrying sweltering aluminum platters, and one time through the steam came Rourke. I remember thinking, *How did he get into the back? Did he get there before us, or did he come in through the kitchen?*

The seven months had left him altered, heavier and harder, with more lift to his frame, with greater dispatch. I noticed a mechanical efficiency, a half-human impassivity. It was like having an animal enter the room, and the animal is also a machine, if you can picture the way animals occasionally sim-ulate machines, if you can picture a fascinating confluence of aspiration and design. His skin was dark; he was letting his hair grow. Above his left eye, a whole new scar. I would not have thought it possible for him to be sexier, but he was. If he were a killer, I would not have known whether to run or stay and be killed—I would not have wanted to miss a moment of him.

If it's sad to reflect upon the wrongness of that particular impression, of him as capable of killing, it is germane, I think, to the history of my failure when, in fact, I've never known anyone with such a pervading reverence for body and spirit and for the sanctity of the individual. It's easy to speak in favor of independence but grueling to live a life of emotional economy and physical reserve as Rourke did. His capacity to cause real harm obliged him to exist mindfully. I never knew him to impose or to practice upon. Ironically, it was his sober self-containment, his refusal to equivocate, that threatened and hurt people most. I know because nothing has ever threatened or hurt me more than the moderation of his heart.

I felt conspicuous inside the grasp of his gaze. Before he even reached the table, I remember feeling that he was done, that he'd gotten what he had come for. He'd come to see me, to test and to conclude his desire. To remind himself that I was not very smart and not very pretty. That my eyes were smoldery underneath and my skin was pale like potter's clay. That I did not have a nice haircut like Lee's or nice make-up from Saks or tiny gold hoop earrings. Surely he noticed my five dollar haircut. Five dollars because at Astor Place, Dominic insisted on charging me the men's rate. Probably Rourke guessed that beneath my clothes my underwear had lost its original elasticity and in my pocket was all I possessed—a work/study paycheck for sixty-six dollars. Solvency was an impossibility for me. He must have realized this and thought, "What a loser." That was my feeling. I don't know. Sometimes a feeling is all you get.

"Hey, hey, it's the grifter!" Joey said, rising first to greet him.

The girls rushed Rourke, and the men stood and the waiters came too, gathering around, everyone gathering except me. He kissed the girls and smiled at the others, then he looked in my direction, and nodded, saying, "Hi."

And I said hi, and the rest after that went more slowly. I remember the twist of my shoes against the floor.

Chris squeezed his shoulders. "You ready, or what? Look at this!"

"He's training to go one-on-one with me," Joey said.

"I'd pay big money to see that." Mark reached and shook fixedly with Rourke. "Harrison, you remember Brett."

"Good to see you again," Brett said with a deluge of respect.

Rourke shook hands and moved on. Rob was above me; the two embraced. Rourke's arm locked onto Rob's back, and his face inched out over Rob's shoulder, his black eyes looking through space.

Rob patted him genially. "How you doin', man?"

"I've been good. You?"

Rob pulled back and his head tilted modestly. "Same old shit."

"Oh yeah?"

"I've been following," Rob said, "you know, checking in."

Rourke took the available chair, across from mine. I was between Lee and Rob; he was between Lorraine and Joey. Joey's wife was home with the boys. "I heard," he said. "Jimmy told me. Thanks."

JOEY PROPOSED A TOAST with his lobster, lifting it ceremoniously like a heave offering. "Welcome home to Harrison, the next Light Heavyweight Champion of—"

"The neighborhood," Rourke said, and everyone laughed.

Others took turns toasting him, and the lobster hung there, vertical in the air, wilting groundward at two poles like a defeated daisy. Rourke was uncomfortable, but they didn't care. One sad fact of life is that it's simpler to live vicariously than to live free. They singled him out because he got away, and they hadn't and that reflected badly on them unless he happened to be specially endowed. Often one person's courage to escape mediocrity allows others to bypass the ordeal of experimentation.

He reacted to the flattery as if in response to narrowing roominess. He unobstructed his vision. He continued to read the action of the table while taking in all that constituted the periphery. I followed the cross-section of his metamorphosis—the leathering of the skin as it turned impervious, the shoring up of the under-muscle, and beneath that, the viscera shrinking back. There was the pulse stopping up expertly. There was the steadiness of his body incorporating into the steadiness of the chair and bleeding through to the steady limose chill of the earth. He looked at me—for something, reassurance possibly. I looked away, withholding it. Though I longed to assure him of what he already knew, that nothing had changed, that I loved him all the more the less he tried, I knew already that the end for us would not be good—another confrontation, another loss. I could not bear another loss. I played with my food.

Rob broke into talk about St. Patrick's Day in Montauk, about the parade he and Rourke went to that time, that time they ran into me. It was a message to Rourke and me, a reminder of better days. He had seen the exchange between us.

"Evie gets off a red Ducati driven by this big blonde and walks away like she doesn't even know the girl. She passes off her helmet to a guy with a club foot, and two dogs start following her. Shepherds. And they were playin' that accordion thing, the thing the fire department plays. What is that thing? C'mon, Joey. Help me out here."

Lorraine poked her stirrer through her drink like she had a job to do, which was to perforate the bottom of the glass. "The bagpipes."

"That's it," Rob said. "The bagpipes. I remember thinking, *This is different. Very different.* Right, Harrison?"

Rourke nodded, once. "Very different."

AFTER THAT CAME THE usual figuring who was going in which car. People in Jersey always seem to switch cars mid-night. Lee, Mark, and Chris decided to go in Mark's Saab because Chris was thinking of buying one, then Rourke, Brett, and Joey got in the GTO, leaving me, Rob, and Lorraine for the Cougar. Rob didn't even give me a choice or anyone else a choice, he just said, "C'mon, sweetheart. You take a ride with us. It'll give me an excuse in case Lorraine gets any ideas."

In the car, Lorraine kept putting lotion on her hands, over and over. All three of us were up front, and Rob was singing.

You're just too good to be true,
Can't take my eyes off of you.

It was like a dream we were having—Rob and I were having—a dream that was joined, with his voice coming from someplace beneath the place we could speak of, like it was rising from a single slumber. And I remember having dreamt the same dream on many occasions, not necessarily *of* Rob but of a person who, in fact, as it turned out, happened to *be* Rob. And though that dream came long ago, when I was a child, I suspected I'd only just dreamt it.

Lorraine was singing too and looking at nothing out the front window with his hand on the tight of her thigh, with that one thigh higher because of being on the hump. The perfumey heat of her against my left and the cold of the door on my right and the smell of Jergens and the feeling of connecting over and covering over and someone inside my head and that someone being not a brother but a friend unlike any other friend.

The place where Rob was living was flat and flimsy, and with all of us inside it felt like a Winnebago or the cabin of a boat. We barged in on his roommate Uncle Milty who was lying on the floor watching the Rangers play Edmonton. He leapt to his feet and tucked in his shirt and nodded hellos, and he made a snack platter while Rob went to walk the dog. Rob was the only one who could walk the dog because it was a Doberman he'd rescued from a gas station. Rescued meant *stolen*, but Rob had no problem with that, since the dog was abused and the stinking fuck owed him money.

"You should've told me you were coming," Uncle Milty said from the kitchen. "I would've bought sodas for the girls." He was short, so just his chest and head were visible over the island that divided the two rooms. He loaded up a cutting board with olives and leftover tuna and a couple of tubes of Ritz crackers still in wax paper.

"Damn, Uncle Milty," Joey said. "You're hospitable." He and Chris were on the sofa, checking out the end of the game. Mark too. Brett was using the phone. Rourke was on the arm of the couch, and I was near him. On the arm too, staring at the set.

Lorraine and Lee were going out to wait and did I want to come.

"It may surprise you to know," Mark said, "that some girls can sit and watch a game."

"Is that what you think she's doing?" Rourke said, taking us by surprise.

"Looks that way to me," Mark said.

Rourke said nothing else, he just shook his head.

Rob walked in. "What's wrong with you gavones, you just ate."

"What do you care?" Uncle Milty asked. "It's my food. You last the week on a jar of peanut butter."

"I'm just sayin'," Rob huffed. The dog sniffed at the bare platter. "You coulda saved a couple crackers for the dog, that's all." Rob gave the chain collar a jerk. "C'mon, Cujo, they don't give a shit about you."

AT THE NEXT PLACE I was completely disoriented. I couldn't remember where I was—geographically. I didn't know which way was north. Despite the attentiveness of Rourke—his voice as it petitioned my ears, the tenderness I saw in his eyes—everything felt loaded with intention instead of the random way it once had been. I had the sense of personal motive, which was like standing at the base of an inverted pyramid, with all the invisible tonnage and heft of my own need poised precariously above me.

I ended up sitting with Lorraine and Lee, though I had nothing to say to them and no shared interests and I was obviously only waiting for Rourke, which was pathetic, and surely they pitied me, though there was not much I could do about that.

He was leaning against the bar in a midnight blue cotton bomber jacket, and he was telling a story about golf—I could tell because he simulated a swing, then bent and tossed up an arm, waving flat into the horizon as if to hail an imaginary party onward. His hair swept boyishly about his face. With one hand he righted it then said something to make everyone laugh. To watch him was to feel again what I'd felt exclusively with him—feminine and frail, unearthly light and in love with all men. He was such a flawless ambassador of masculinity that he could not help but remind a girl of her own essential qualities. Sometimes you set yourself aside. You act out two halves, losing the one you truly are. With Jack, I'd always felt we were intrinsically the same, and though there was refuge in that, there was also a forfeiture of individuality. With Rourke, I'd experienced opposition, like the simple reflex of a knee when you knock it—legitimate and artless and completely beyond your personal control.

Mark and Brett were leaving. I remember him bending down. And Brett's waist beside me, bloated and budding and immune to the slimming effect of dark pleats. "We're gonna take off."

And me feeling ashamed, ashamed of his familiarity, that he felt entitled to it, that he felt he'd earned it. I knew what he wanted. He'd been clear. I'd also been clear, or so I thought. It was not impossible that I'd misjudged things, and in the process, that I'd misled him. Often I misjudged things. "Okay," I said. "Goodnight."

Mark reached into his pocket. "My numbers," he insisted, screwing a card into my palm, pushing my hand to my belly. "And some cash." *It's a long walk back to New York.*

Mark passed through the crowd like a mayor, smiling and shaking hands, Brett by his side. I turned the papers in my hand. He'd implied that I was not wanted. That Rourke saw me as a burden, that he'd been standing there saying, *What's with her?* Maybe Mark knew things. I kicked out my chair, grabbed my coat, and ran to the door.

"Where to, Countess?" Rob—stopping me. "This is Jersey."

And then a sensation, lifelike in me still, of Rob's two hands on my waist, of him inducing me back from the door, steering and stepping like a generous partner, delivering me to the haven of Rourke's arms. There is forever the imprint of Rourke's hands on my shoulders, of his mouth on the base of my neck, the mouth I'd waited for, like for proof of God. And the kiss, the first kiss, the first new kiss, and the wonder of the taste, the most incredible taste, like a willowy almond after-flavor. He was tall, so I had to stretch and he had to bend, lifting me a little, I remember that, and the imperfect dark of the room that we occupied, a post-meridian dark, a dark to a subordinate degree, as if in the black is light, just a negligible consignment, a sliver or percent. How we got to that room and how we got out is lost to me; maybe it was the kitchen of the club or the office. It didn't matter. As always with Rourke, there was a detachment from repercussion and aftermath. Aside from some nagging suspicion that the corridors of our history were numbered and circumscribed, it was nice, like home again or anyway as close as you can come, with his breath joining mine, with the beautiful looseness of his hair.

There were words; I do recall the words. He was holding me.

"You feel small," he said. "Are you smaller?"

I think, yes, anguish makes you so.

He looked at his watch; I looked at it too. It was thick stainless steel with a marine-green face, and the silken hairs of his arms were pressed beneath it. It was eleven minutes after four.

"Rob and Lorraine are going to take you back to the city. That okay?"

"It's okay."

He zipped up my coat for me. "I finish on Thursday. When's your last class this week?"

"Thursday night."

"Feel like taking off for a few days? How about Atlantic City?"

"I would like that," I said. I think I said.

"I'll call you." He kissed me on both eyes.

I remember thinking, *He seems so happy*. I wanted to be happy too.

EAR BAR IS ON Spring Street, and by the time I arrived Thursday after class, they were drunk. Rob was near the door, with Eddie M. and Lorraine and Lorraine's friend Tracy Hollis, a dental hygienist. The elastic cast of rum stretched in a girdle about them. One of Eddie M.'s hands was cupped on the base of Tracy's ass. I wondered about his wife, Karen, whether she was over at her mother's. Karen was always over at her mother's. I'd never even met her. "Me neither," Rob liked to say, "except that time at the wedding."

Rob kissed me fast and light, without breaking from his story. He was criticizing Lorraine—something derogatory about bowling.

"First off, she's got her own ball, which is some designer thing like the cosmos, if the cosmos happened to be manufactured by Jordache. The thing weighs about a pound, so she gets it up over her head, see, like this, but she can't insert her fingers all the way because of the nails—so she goes on her toes, and the ball is back here, not too secure, and she starts toward the pins, and I'm sittin' there thinking, if anybody so much as sneezes, she's gonna break her back."

A few stools away was Rourke, flushed and alone and tilting forward off his seat. He wore a ribbed pale gray turtleneck, and there was something onerous about the look of him, something heavy and broken, something of a light gone. He looked exactly like what he was—a drunken Irish boxer. I glanced back at Rob, who was emphatically preoccupied. He wouldn't even look to check. Normally he was always looking to check.

I went to Rourke. Slowly, with a sick feeling, the sickest feeling. He watched me approach, lifting his beer bottle, draining it, then dipping his head slowly, swallowing hard.

He said, "Hey."

I said, "Hey."

His eyes circled my face. He lowered his head and took my hands into his. "How was school? What classes did you have?"

"Sociology. Drawing from Life."

"Drawing, that's right. I asked you on the phone last night. You're working on rooftops—a drawing of rooftops."

"Rooftops, yes."

"Did you bring it with you?"

I said I didn't. Shaking my head, no.

"Oh," he smiled, "too bad." He seemed to wait or prepare or gather something stray. "I said good-bye to Black Jack today—did I tell you about Black Jack yesterday?"

"You didn't."

"One of the inmates we worked with this week. He ran guns through Jersey in the fifties." Rourke struggled for words. "He took the fall for a murder he says he didn't commit. A trooper. No witnesses." He looked at me then beyond, eyes darting around table legs, over floor tiles. "He's been in twenty-six years. His wife remarried. He's never seen his son."

It was a strange story to tell. There was a delicacy to his tone and an honesty to his overture, as if he was entrusting me with something important, as if there was more that he wanted to say, if only he knew that I would have listened. I suppose I should have inquired further into his feelings, but as it happened, the moment of his openness coincided exactly with the moment of my resolve to defend myself against it. I had contented myself for so long with opaqueness that I preferred it. I drew my jacket tighter. It was cold. I looked over my shoulder. The front door was open. Rourke whistled and Rob looked up and in seconds the room turned warm again.

The bartender came by with two shot glasses. "Girlfriend?" he asked, meaning me.

"We spent a summer together once," Rourke said.

"Lucky man."

"Used to be."

One of his hands let go of mine, but the other held tightly. Tighter than before. He lifted a shot glass to my lips, but I declined, so he emptied it himself. Then he emptied the second.

"I took a job," Rourke said, his speech turning lucid, his voice growing hoarse. "A regular job."

"I don't understand," I said. "When?"

"Six hours ago. Out West. Colorado Springs."

That seemed far, farther than the last place he went, wherever that was. Maybe it was just the fact of being told, the fact of the sadness in his eyes, a sadness inwardly compounded. I said, "Oh."

"Training," he said. "Other fighters."

The lineature of his face set in and set back, becoming like a plate inscripted with its own image, becoming like an enchasing of compartments, like the cryptic plateau of a battleship from above. His jaw ticked left to bite back some abhorrent thought. I wondered did he feel clipped or cowardly. I hoped not. That would be bad if he did.

"No more fights?"

"No more fights. A few. A few commitments."

I did not say I felt happy for him since I did not, and he would not have wanted me to lie. What I felt primarily was an acquiescent and moving grievedness like a tiny, tiny cortege passing in the rain or a bird very far in the sky.

"Sorry about Atlantic City. I leave Saturday."

He came forward, his head tapping my head. "You wouldn't want to take a ride cross-country, would you?"

The feel of his drunken breath on my neck was soft, and the smell was fragrant and intoxicating, like honey-wine, like mead. I remember listening into it and hearing things like when you listen to a shell and hear the sea. There was his remorse over returning and leaving, over leaving me again to myself, over things I did not want to fathom. I wondered if he could hear me too, I wondered was I audible—did he hear how I would never become part of the cherished but uninhabitable asylum of his home? How I would sooner move on than allow myself to be aligned with things in his heart that were dead.

Whether or not he was sincere about the drive across country, I answered as if he was because, in fact, he should have been, because, in fact, he wished to be. Sometimes men hate themselves for not being heroes, and they need to know they can be forgiven. Sometimes when you love someone, you need to pass their tests.

"I don't think it would be—for me, you know—such a great idea. It's just too close to—" I left off. "I'm not sure, really, what I'm saying."

Rourke took my hands closer into his lap, and he manipulated them thoughtfully, tracing the veins. With his head bowed, I was free to regard him—exposed and illogical and lame and drunk and sorry. I never loved anyone or anything more than I did him at that very moment, and the only thing that kept me from saying so was the fury inside me. Just like the rest of his friends, I was glad to see him almost gone. What I felt for him was completely unsustainable.

"You don't understand," he slurred, bowing his head and nodding downwards. "You'll never be what I am."

I asked what that was, and he said, "Exactly what you see in front of you. A failure."

"DO YOU REMEMBER," HE asked, "how to drive shift."

His legs were parted and his knees skimmed the dashboard. His head drifted back onto the seat, and he closed his eyes. I started his car, keeping to my side, though I was small. Being next to him was like being a Lilliputian, like stepping with due caution about a slumbering giant—by his size you knew that the setback was only temporary. I read his body through his clothes; I'd forgotten how you could do that. You could do that with anyone, of course, but with Rourke you could hardly do otherwise. I drove him back to Jersey because he'd asked me to, because I loved him, because I trusted no one else, and as I drove I remember feeling no feeling. I remember just moving through the quills of highway light thrown down to make a forest of hollow bones— feather bones because light comes in wings, and walls of light are wings of angels panting while at rest. If I was not clear, that was because there was nothing inside. My heart was a cipher, also my head, and there was nothing to hope for or to anticipate, nothing whatsoever to move me but the familiar drudgery of decline. And the music on the radio, the music like a watcher, like it had intellect, like the box had eyes.

> *Juliet, when we made love you used to cry*
> *You said I love you like the stars above, I'll love you 'til I die*
> *There's a place for us, you know the movie song*
> *When you gonna realize it was just that the time was wrong? Juliet—*

A precise halo of clove-pink light marked out a papered room on the top floor of his house, a room I had not noticed before. From the street I could see the wallpaper, indigo with ropes of yellow rising like blossom ladders to a better place, a place with continual music, music of the spheres, beguiling music, music derived from the choreography of heavenly bodies. In the driveway was a white Oldsmobile; I pulled alongside it. I did not have to wake him. He had been roused instinctively by the sense impression of the streets in Spring Lake, and for some time he had been staring ahead, grim in the grim richness of his thoughts, and this consoled me, ironically.

I accompanied him to the door of his garden apartment. I retrieved the key from the grass when he dropped it, and though I did not help him undress, I laid his clothes on the corner chair. There was the wool turtleneck and the jeans, and his shape, benevolently possessed by each. When I turned, he was striving effortlessly for sleep, curled like a deserted boy on his left side, which was peculiar since I'd known him always to sleep facing up—I used to place my head in the crevice by his shoulder, and my arm would go light upon his chest, my leg curling over his thighs. Possibly he'd slept that way for me, on his back. He was in his underwear. It was true he was bigger since I'd seen him last, but his weight was decisive and controlled. Once Rob told me and Lorraine that when Rourke hits his fighting weight he has to maintain it to the quarter-pound. Rob said, "He sucks the water out of lettuce and spits green."

God, it was awful to see him drunk, to see him give up.

Gently I joined him. Gently I journeyed like a pilgrim to the wall of his back, close enough without touching to reclaim some of the life of which I had been so cruelly dispossessed. Jack used to say that you're not entitled to another person, but I *was* entitled to Rourke. My ownership did not depend on his acknowledgement of it. It existed beyond him; it longed only to apply itself. I knew that I adored him and that I was devoted, and if I felt rage, it was not rage over losing him, it was rage over not being given the chance to care for him when I suspected he needed me most.

I could be forgiven for seeking out memories of Montauk—of being sun-burned, of being in love, of a darkness naturally broken. After passing once more through these halls, I sealed them off like rooms locked from the inside. I would not go back. I would ask no more of life than that it allow me in all fairness to possess the perfect knowledge of these perfect things, no matter that these things are things no longer in hand. I told myself maybe love can be love regardless of the absence of its object—and devotion, devotion—so long as you are very rich in there and willing to be captive to it, and you stow it secretly, like a mad relative in the attic. Maybe there is an invisible way to love him, like a radio frequency. Maybe if I listen at night, I can draw it.

I remember that he stirred, raising himself onto one elbow, making a miniature city of his infolding abdomen like a marketplace—stalls and huts and incommodious walkways—and he drank from the glass of water I'd set by the bed. He was not surprised to see me, which was bittersweet. It was as though I had infringed upon his nights as often as he had upon mine. His arms went around my hips and his fingers slipped through the empty belt loops of my jeans and his head settled into the crease of my thighs. And I touched his hair, though I was afraid to touch it.

From where I sat, I could see the crevice at the base of the door. If I crawled on my belly across the floor, I would see the bathroom through that gap. Once we'd showered there, and I had cried, and he'd been good about that, about not asking questions. Next to the bathroom was a door to an interior staircase, and at the top was the indigo room, empyrean and O-like, a pendant dangling from the neck of Diana. If I climbed those stairs, she would be there, and I would find her, still awake, reading in her robe. Mothers who wait up always read and wear robes. I drew my fingertips across the standing hairs on his jaw and he breathed softly, coming closer.

I wondered when as a man he was proved. Did he become a man and an outsider after the fight over his father, the one that gave him his scar? And would we die without meeting again, or would we meet and smile in the slightly embarrassed manner of former lovers, with all the intervening seasons of regret alive in our eyes? And if I died, would he come to my funeral, and who would call him, and would he grieve—yes, he would grieve; but would he know that if I were given one day, one hour, one minute more to live, I would accept only if I could spend it with him? Is it possible that a baby conceived in July would have been born in April, maybe on a night such as that night? That would have been an unusual biological coincidence, to have been brought together for conception and then again for the would-have-been delivery. *Would-have-been* since, of course, there was no more baby. I wondered if babies come for a reason, and if so, was ours taken away for one?

As I watched the ascension of day, with every ripple of light coming like drops to fill a bucket, I held him, and I persuaded myself to come to terms. The moments were so strangely inscribed, so mixed and contradictory. I felt most gloriously alive just as I prepared to recede from the hazards of sensation. Like some animal gazing out into the wondrous world through the door of its dank cave before bowing off to voluntary sleep, I breathed greedily, assimilating the nearness of him and the realness of him as if each trapped ounce of his vitality could be called upon to sustain me through the dreariness of hibernation. In time, I could go no further than the scuttle of the birds, the chute and helical flare of their shadows like passing bells. I remember arriving at some small place of solace. And in that place I became seized by a whole new sorrow, a loving sorrow. Although once again it was Rourke who was leaving me, this time I would bear the burden of the sacrifice. I was turning him over—to soul corruption, to the inclemency of survival. I would not have accepted compromise where he was concerned. If he were to stay with me, I would have worked every second to keep him true to himself.

I said, "Mark Ross is not going to give up."

Rourke said, "I know." His breath on my wrist.

I left as he slept, the worst and the hardest thing I'd ever done. Possibly he expected me to stay, but I could not withstand the look of loss in his eyes. At daybreak, I walked to the main road, then I hitchhiked as far as the highway, where I hitched again. Few things have the capacity to remind you of your own miserable desolation so much as hitchhiking. Feeling forlorn as I did, and lacking a destination, I might have traveled on as far as the road would have taken me, Albany or Boston or Canada, except that I got a ride directly into the West Village from a Polish guy and a very heavy woman, best friends, they said, who left me safely at the corner of Hudson and Morton.

AT A MEXICAN RESTAURANT on Columbus Avenue, Lee and Chris held a surprise goodbye dinner for Rourke on Friday night. Lee had called me that day from her office on Maiden Lane, near Wall Street.

"I initially planned this for Sunday, since you guys were going to Atlantic City, but I found out he's leaving tomorrow. It's been crazy getting organized."

I came late. By the time I climbed the restaurant's staircase to its balcony and joined the party—there were nine people, including Mark—they were swiping their spoons through dishes of flan and fried ice cream. Rourke looked up quietly and quietly looked away, and everyone else seemed very uncomfortable, whether that initiated with my late arrival or before it was hard to say. I can't imagine it was a good idea to have invited Mark, but probably Lee knew nothing.

"You're here," Lee said with a kiss. "I'm so glad."

She called over the balcony to the waiter for another espresso and an ice water, and she drew out a chair at the table's head, which I dragged to the side, to Rourke's side, so I could not see him, though I could hear him. The sound of his throat was not fully opened. I wondered what he would have preferred me to do or how he would have preferred me to be. I understood he was preferring things to be different.

People attempted to chat mildly, not knowing what to expect. They were even more ignorant of the goings-on between Rourke and me than we were ourselves. I could feel that uncertainty everywhere, mingled with his disappointment, like a critically elevated temperature. And me, I was not without relevance, but it was the ugly relevance of position and presence—*position*, because by coming late I had shown myself to be maverick and ungovernable, and *presence* because, evidently, I had the power to ruin the evening. As Rob would say, *Things were pretty dicey*. Though not much happened, it was without question the ugliest hour of my life.

Cliff raised his café con leche. "Best of luck, Harrison."

"Cheers," everyone said, and within seconds, he stood. He had to get going; he wanted to spend time with his mother. There were hugs and kisses and handshakes and squelching chair-scraping, and when he got to me, the sensation of his lips on my face was the sensation of a burn. I remember wanting nothing more than to leave with him, to go and meet his mother, to help him pack, to have a private goodbye, and that moment of all moments in retrospect lacks opacity—it is most maddeningly vivid to me; it is the last legible need I experienced in years. In a heartbeat, he was gone.

Chris paid the check, and we finished in silence.

Rob said to me, "I'll give you a ride."

I told him no thanks.

"C'mon," he insisted, "I'm taking the Holland. I'll go straight down Ninth Avenue, take Bleecker to Tenth, and then shoot west to Seventh on Ninth Street." *Boom, boom, boom.*

I said I would be okay.

"Would you like to walk a bit?" Mark asked.

"Thanks," I said, "I would. Home just seems like—" I waved one arm.

"Like home," Mark said. "Say no more."

Rob did not take his eyes from me. "You're sure about this, Evie?"

"I am," I said. "I'm sure."

THE NIGHT WAS MAGNIFICENT, as such things go—prime and pale, and we infringed upon it mildly, strolling up one side of Columbus Avenue and down the other, gazing into shop windows.

"You look like an Italian movie star," he said to our reflection. "With your sweater over your shoulders and just the top button done."

I tried to recall if I'd ever told Mark about the way Marilyn and Dad said I was like Monica Vitti. That was the type of guy he was, the kind who makes you think he's gotten hold of your file.

We turned east down Seventy-sixth Street and headed toward Central Park. I remember climbing onto a low wall and holding his shoulder as I walked and when he helped me off, I slid through the shaft of his arms.

"Like an angel," he said, "just descended."

"Fallen, you mean."

"No," he said. "That's *not* what I mean."

And I came down and he kissed me and I let him because my lips were deserving lips wishing to be kissed and my body was a deserving body wishing to be touched and because there is a moment in every life that is the lowest. It is the moment even lower than the lowest you think you can possibly go. It is a cocktail most painstakingly composed of disgrace and virulence and longing unreturned. In that moment you are not you but a monster of you, a creature and a fiend. In that moment you are enticed. Malicious limbless hands call upon you to stalk the cloisters of your own despair, and you do and you feel better in there, crazed and incautious, rotten and free. You feel you have reached the other side, you feel you have passed through the pain, though you have only capitulated to it. In that moment you are lucky you do not have a gun. If you had a gun, you'd shoot yourself.

"This is where I live." We were at the Beresford on Central Park West. "Actually, my parents. I grew up here."

He escorted me through the set of doors facing the Natural History Museum. "Good evening, Mr. Ross," the doorman said.

"Hey, Ralph," Mark said. He shook the doorman's gloved hand warmly. "This is Miss Auerbach."

Ralph walked us to the elevator. I wondered what he was thinking. Men are always thinking things, doormen in particular.

Mark and I went to the sixth floor, and when we stepped out of the car, he moved to the easterly door. It opened onto one of those quintessential New York prewar apartments that is august and sublime. If ever Manhattan could be smelted and poured, it would take the shape of an apartment like that. The difference between it and the house in East Hampton was dramatic—the plaster walls and original detailing, the chain of rooms that were connected by high-ceilinged corridors. A Steinway grand was situated near a bank of windows overlooking Central Park. Naturally, I thought of Jack. Naturally, I wondered where he was and where I was and how we had managed to stray so far. I saw a de Kooning, a Stella, a Diebenkorn, and three Picasso etchings. Mark had bought the Diebenkorn at a gallery in California and had given it to his parents for their twenty-fifth wedding anniversary. In the bedrooms were lithographs by Miro, a charcoal by O'Keefe, a photograph by Weston.

Mark rummaged through the refrigerator. "You didn't eat anything at the restaurant. Let me make you something."

White cabinets towered from floor to ceiling all around in the main cooking area, but there were also cabinets in the hall and that was a sort of larder. The floor was black-and-white square ceramic tile, and near the maid's room, a door with dead bolts led to a service elevator. Garbage was placed there; invisible hands retrieved it. The kettle whistled. Mark transferred the boiling water for tea into a china pot with a crackled creamy glaze and bright baby sprigs of cornflowers kind of melting away on it. When he lifted it to fill my cup, it left a dewy ring on the table that I dried with my sleeve. There was the seedy smell of rye bread toasting.

By the kitchen clock, it was three in the morning. Rourke was packing, or with his mother. No, not with his mother. He was alone, thinking of me.

"Where are your parents?" I asked.

"Milan," he answered. "On vacation. Then they hit Monte Carlo, do a little gambling, and then shoot through Nice over to Cannes for the festival."

TO GET TO WHERE we were going, we had to walk far and as I moved through hallways I could see myself, moving through hallways. One room we passed had window seats and long boxes of pansies. I faltered, it was so pretty.

"Alicia's room," he said. "I wish Yale were farther away—she's too attached to my parents."

Mark's former room was at the end. It was smaller and darker than his sister's but elegantly appointed. There were built-in cherry bookshelves and a cherry roll-top desk and hanging things such as photographs, pennants, diplomas—Collegiate, UCLA, Harvard. The room was nice like one of those funny coin pockets in your Levi's, the perfect place if you happen to have the perfect thing to fit inside.

"You must miss it here."

"Not really. I love my new place. So will you."

I understood that Mark had not taken me to his apartment because there was a chance I would have declined. But the visit to his parents' house felt accidental and edifying, and I did not mind being there; in fact, I felt safe, like deep in the tail of a snake. I felt anonymous and forgotten. He was right, he was always right, anyway, his instincts were—and fortune was with him. These are superior traits in a man when you can find no others.

At the edge of his bed, he kissed me again and he unbuttoned my blouse. It was cotton, a doe-skin color with pearl buttons—I still have it. Next Mark lowered the straps of my bra, thumbing down the lace. "Am I dreaming?" he murmured. "I must be dreaming."

I did not bother to stop him. I did not bother to say no, not when the sun was already rising and he had walked me through the labyrinth of the night, not when he had worked so hard for so long, and he had waited, one year I think he'd waited. And Rourke was no god, no king—he was a solitary, solitary man. If it was true that he wanted me, perhaps it was also true that he needed to forsake me. Perhaps his sacrifice helped him to proceed; there are men like that, men who need loss to exempt them, who feel unconsecrated without forfeiture. In any event—did it really matter, days alone or days with Mark, when his hands had touched Rourke's hands, when his eyes had seen Rourke's eyes and my eyes and the exchanges between them, when his loathing of Rourke was so malicious and so vital as to move him to claim me. When his claiming—

Him kissing my neck, him stepping back to stare. Me not moving. I'd read somewhere that power takes as ingratitude the writhing of its victims. I did not want him to think I was ungrateful.

His hands slipping to my waist and opening my pants, tearing the halves apart and partially down to disclose twin pelvic bones and the low white rule of underwear, and when he followed the line beneath the elastic with one finger, his lips hung apart and he caught his breath, shuddering. Mark steered me back onto the bed and removed the rest of my clothes, though not his own—not for a long time did he remove his own. And I remember that when he tossed my jeans on the floor there was the sound of coins rolling. My money, falling out.

6.

I MEET ROB AT A GARAGE, AND WE ARE CLEAN, VERY CLEAN, BOTH OF US, AND FREE, emotionally. There is a post-war feel, a 1950s feel, and outside is sky, with everything being low, and everything being wide.

I follow him to the back where it smells nice—of incubated diesel and desiccated oil, and beneath one of the cars is Rourke. He rolls out. It has been a long time since I've seen him. I want to touch his face, but I cannot reach. Rob is there and Rob will help, and so I try and so I reach because in fact the ground is not far but near. We touch and things begin to grow—the light and the warmth and my sense of myself—growing from the bottom up, like plants.

It feels provisional or probationary being close. Like being reunited with someone dead, the one you loved. That would be all right, that would be enough, except the rules of the dead are different. I don't know the rules. What will keep him from vanishing again and me from returning abruptly to life? It's as if there is a live wire hidden beneath the floor. No matter how carefully I step, sooner or later I will trip it.

We are in a room, I don't know the room, but it is brightly lit without windows and the door is ajar, like a door of a hotel room. Rourke leans over a suitcase, holding a picture frame—tenderly, he packs it. There is blood on the frame, female blood, and the smell is of cast-iron pans.

He has to go, he says, kissing me, but only for a few hours. He is in the street; I see him from the window. I am parting the curtain; I am waiting, always, because I know he told the truth when he said he'd be back.

I'm not sure about the time passing, if any has passed.

Someone called for you, Mark says. The house is Mark's. Some guy, calling your name—Eveline. From the bedroom, he says, go on in.

The quilt in the bedroom is the amber brown of burned foliage, and on the pillow is a solitary graphic, a flint-gray checkmark. Beneath the covers is a shape, his shape, Rourke's shape, and I go in next to it, I mean go under, he is naked and he brushes back the hair from my face, once, twice. We lie, close and broke apart, known, unknown. Darkness, like a dark hole.

Baby, he says, I missed you baby.

I am wearing a slip with buttons. He unbuttons, expertly. One hand holds me still while the other—he is in me. We lie on our sides, hardly moving. And our hearts, joined in time. I keep rhythm with his pulse, I strive to be an organ to him, sightless, mindless, aptly attached. Is it true, could it be true, is he back, has he come back? I'm sorry, I say, I love you. Saying it, but feeling I am not his mirror, I am not. Whereas once I would have felt myself repeat and return, now I feel a deadness of direction—

Yes, he says, starting faster now to push. I love you too.

My eyes squeeze shut, they will not open, they know not to open. The sight of Mark would kill me. It kills me.

BEFORE MARK AWAKENS I take a pile of cash from the dresser and I get the BMW, going to see Rob at church, just showing up. It's his family church, where he goes every Sunday at nine, by his parents' house, in Rumson. I've been there a few times for a wedding and for Charlie's communion. Charlie is Joey's son. Also for a photography project, so I know the way okay.

I wait on the steps in the drizzle and listen to the end of Mass, at first hiding my face from the water and then thinking, why am I hiding when behind the clouds there is sun, so I look into the sun. The priest is talking about *the Knack*. The Knack is the ability to live in the present, which is something God has and Lucifer wants. I'm not sure about that, about the Knack. Priests can extrapolate a lot. Is he implying that God, or the goodness in people, is satisfied with the gifts of each ordinary moment, and that Lucifer, or the maleficence in people, prefers things lying ahead and behind— like dreams and regrets? It seems like a lot to expect, constant in-the-moment gratitude, but possibly I'm wrong. It's been a while since I've been to church.

Rob dips out with his mother and his father's mother. They are hooked onto him at the elbows. When he sees me, he stops in his tracks, they all do, in a line. The elder Mrs. Cirillo loses her balance. He steadies her. "What happened?" he demands.

"Nothing."

"You okay?"

"I'm okay," I say. "I'm fine."

I kiss the ladies hello. *Bacio*—that's a kiss. Rob's mom is dressed in a union-blue shirtdress with a Peter Pan collar, a zipper-back, and darts beneath the breasts. Nona Cirillo is wearing a pressed housecoat with a black crocheted sweater around her shoulders, and with her free hand she clings to her bag, tight, like somebody might snatch it. She never remembers me, but that's okay since she never remembers anything other than obscure details from her past such as the shoe sizes of dead sisters and the prices of tomatoes from the grocery store the family used to operate on First Avenue.

"You're soaking wet, Eveline," Mrs. Cirillo says, taking out a tissue from her sleeve, wiping my face. "How come you didn't come inside?" She turns to Rob. "How come she didn't come inside?"

Rob looks around. "How did you get here?"

I point to the BMW.

"The 3.0 cs? Whose car is that?"

Mark bought it. For me. For me to use. I don't say that. I say, "Mark's."

"That's a nice car. He never told me about that car." Rob shakes his head, like in queasy disbelief. "Follow me back to the house."

AT VINNY-O'S THEY ADDED a partial wall to make a dining area. Except for a Maximum Occupancy sign and a Heimlich Maneuver sign, it looks the same as it did four years ago. "All they need now," Rob says, "is a chef and a kitchen. A couple customers. Maybe a menu."

He takes over like he owns the place, like he's back at the dining room table of his parents' house. He leans on the bar and grabs the phone and pops off a few calls. There's a bandage on his right palm that hadn't been there the night before when we were at Pinky's. He fingers back the tape and says something to somebody about the under/over being 100/80, so he *lightninged* the over 200, and there he was, 8,200 down, and how he swears he would get the rest next week because he's got something big about to break, bigger than big, which you can get a piece of if you want.

I gesture for money to play the bowling game. He tucks the phone in between his neck and his shoulder, reaches into his front pocket with his good hand, and gives me a fistful of change. I cross the room and drop in a quarter and the lights flash slow. *Left-right, left-right.* They haven't upgraded the design of the game since the sixties. The cartoon boy is wearing pegged-leg pants with two-inch cuffs, and the cartoon girl has teased hair and a headband and a linguini-thin belt around the waist of her dress. I whoosh the disc around and there's that feeling of the metal platter swilling back and forth over a saw-dusty alley. You get this wobbly snap in your wrist, like wagging a weapon through the air. I take it to my belly and shoot it. *Bee-Baw. Tough luck! A split!*

"Not enough force," Rob says, coming up from behind. "You get that from height. Try again." He lifts me. I feel my form in his hands, which is like coming to know your own bones, which is like saying, *These are me and these are mine and you are different.* I draw the disc to the far left and shoot it diagonally right where it slides under one pin, meets two points of the corner and ricochets left, sliding to a standstill right under the second pin—*Chick-ching. Aces! A spare!*

"Nice job," he says, lowering me down, soft and slow, straightening out his pants around his penis.

Through the window beside our table, I see silver sky but nothing else, no markers, no trees or planes or buildings. The silver seems to reel, like cooking silver, like a pot of silver cooking. Sometimes you get no sense of time. For some reason, I have no sense of time. I stack the leftover quarters in front of Rob. He flicks one up and spins it on the tabletop. He blurs his gaze into the twirling coin.

"Sometimes when—in my sleep, I make a mistake and I think Mark is him. You know."

Rob slaps down the coin.

I look up. Our eyes meet. I go on. "Sometimes when I dream of him, there's a woman. A picture of a woman. I can't see her because there's blood on her picture. Burgundy, like movie blood."

Rob nods, small nods, minor nods, his head tilted somewhat right. In the light his hazel eyes are green. Most days they are like cork. "C'mon," he says. "Let's take a ride."

When we leave, he swings the front door open and props it for me to go past, forgetting his bad hand. "Shit," he says, shaking it.

I ask him what happened, and he said nothing glamorous. "I was eating salted peanuts out of a can."

IN SPRING LAKE PEOPLE have the Knack. They wash cars and clip hedges and there is this feeling that the worst is over, that there is nothing going on in the world besides you. We pass a ballgame in the street and Rob brings the car to a crawl, giving advice.

"Hey, who taught you to hold a bat?" he asks. "The vacuum salesman?"

As we approach Rourke's house, I get the sensation of coming home after a war or a long stay in a psychiatric institution. Everything looks the same—the butterfly rhododendrons, the oilish flickering density of the asphalt on the driveway and the tiger faces in the tar that materialize when you pass over, the carbonated green of the garden hose, and the red-infused blueness of the wallpapered corner room upstairs, his mother's room. I wonder if everything looking the same is worse than everything looking changed, since of course nothing is the same; three years have passed since the morning I was last here, the morning I walked out on Rourke, and so the familiar feel of my approach is on the whole painfully incongruous.

A clean figure in khakis and a denim blouse kneels in the front garden, and at the throaty sound of Rob's car, she turns and squints, palm crossing her eyes. The shadow of her salute conceals her face in part; it hovers, fluttering there, like the shadow of a flag. When she stands she is not small or big, but medium—my size, a little bigger.

Rob hesitates before cutting the engine. "Listen," he says, "there's gonna be a fight. I don't know if Mark said anything. I talked to him after you left Pinky's last night."

"What kind of a fight?"

"The come-back kind, with long fucking odds. The kind where Harrison beats the shit out of somebody and we make a lot of money." Rob flips the key. "Frankly, I'm in a bit of a situation."

"When?"

"Soon as I can swing it," he says. "Couple weeks. The reason I mention it is—she's pretty touchy about fights."

"She's not going to mention fights to *me*—is she?"

"Hard to say." He leans to open his door. "She's got, like, ESP."

Rob swings to my side, snap-jangling his keys and stretching his chin out a bit. He helps me to a stand then tosses an arm over my shoulder, bending down into me. "Ready?"

We walk, Rob and me, our footsteps clapping on the criss-cross brick. There is the *thsst-thsst-thsst* of a sprinkler and the *thwock* of a ball and a voice—*Gloria-aaa*. And again, birds. Maybe the same birds as the other times I came, maybe different birds. I've forgotten the lifespan of a bird. Kate once had an African finch that lived for five years, but that is not the right type of bird. Again, the impression that what I experience is not so much sight as sound—an étude, a musical sketch, something that repeats but is ever new. Something aware of its own imperfection.

Rob says hi. She offers her cheek. He kisses it. "This is Eveline."

She plucks off her gardening gloves and extends her hand. "Eveline," she says, "what a beautiful name."

Her skin is the softest I've felt not on a baby. Her smile, her hair, her eyes—it's really very hard. I bite the bottom skin of my lip, inside my mouth where no one can see. Like her son, she projects an aura of radiant health, a health outside the reach of contamination. Her manner of speaking is faintly aristocratic. She married beneath herself, I think—she married for love. Rourke has that kind of beauty, the kind that comes from people in love.

"How are your parents, Rob?" she inquires.

"They're at each other's throats, so they must be okay."

"That's right. It's when they stop scrutinizing each other that you have to worry," she says with regal detachment.

Rob reaches for a cigarette then recalls his hand. I've never seen him so edgy, except the time with Uncle Tudi. "Listen, Mrs. R., I gotta grab some stuff from the basement."

"Help yourself," she says. "When you're finished, I'd like you to carry down some boxes from the attic. They're stacked beneath the street-side window." She turns to me. "I'm giving everything away. You'd be shocked by what accumulates over a lifetime."

"A *lifetime*," Rob chides. "From the look of it you've got at least two more of those to come, Mrs. Rourke."

"Careful, Rob. You're liable to make me suspicious. Eveline and I will be inside. Come find us when you're finished."

He falters as he backs away, nearly tripping over a queue of boxwoods, moonlike and low, thumbed into the ground like upholstery tacks. He straddles it. "You gonna be all right?"

"I won't rough her up, Rob," Mrs. Rourke says. "I promise."

She takes my arm to climb the porch. Each broad step of the five we mount is one upon which he sat or walked, as a child, as an adolescent, and surely, at some point, the outline of my foot fills the melted away outline of his foot. It is sad to think of our hideously divided courses, to think if only I'd known him before the misadventures and misconstruings of maturity. There's some solace, actually, in Romeo and Juliet lying dead in the hush of their tomb, shielded from the engine of circumstance.

The half-glass of the front door is etched and blocked in part by a linen curtain shaped like an hourglass. I pass inside; inside is cool. The corridor walls are papered with frail caramel pinstripes and columns of cyan. Tucked behind the curve in the base of the banister is an oval writing table with a Bakelite telephone and a Lusterware pitcher full of hydrangeas, those fading purplish ones.

"Victorian burr walnut," she says of the desk as she runs her hand across it. "Look at the inlay."

"It's beautiful." In back is a raised compartment, oval also, with slots. "Is this for stationery?" I ask.

"Yes," she says, "that's right. The desk belonged to my mother. Most of my furniture belonged to my mother. The house was my grandmother's."

The kitchen is airy and brightly lit, and what is wood is a pallid milk-ice blue. It is a cook's kitchen, spacious and fully implemented, with inflections of red—the clock, the dishtowels, the moiré swirls in platters, and the teased-up ticks in fabric. I am seated at a table for eating, and in the corner to my right is another for working, which has a cherry-checked vinyl cloth. It is covered with an assortment of split-open cookbooks and textbooks with frayed paper page markers. She puts heat under the kettle and busies herself, withdrawing cups and plates from the china cabinet and a beer glass for Rob.

Although I would not have expected her to be lonely, I'm amazed by how busy she is—the pile of mail, the ringing telephone. The world whirls about her, her world and my world and all the worlds that can be conjectured, but of course, this is a matter of perception, her formidable perception of herself co-mingled with my peculiar perception of what a mother should be or could be—my mother and Rourke's mother, and all mothers at large and in general.

I watch for signs of him. They share an internal richness and a physical conceit, but it is in the subtleties of environment that the bond between them is clearest to me. There is nothing arduous or sentimental about her domes-ticity. Like his masculinity, her femininity is uncontrived. She moves too fast and too well to be false. Her capability is free of the air of compulsion. Her superiority is pragmatic—like her son, she's good because no one else is better. The house is charming, and yet, I don't feel covetous. It's easy to be seduced at the Ross houses, to become desirous of things you don't even want, such as Baccarat dolphins. Instead, I feel pressured uniquely to achieve, to comply with her independence of vision—though I barely know her, I don't want to disappoint. And I feel she has faith in me. I count the minutes before I have to leave, before her influence will be lost. That, too, is familiar.

"This one's on pies." She's talking about cookbooks; she has written three. "I've baked and tasted just about every pie you can imagine—from apple to quince crumb to mince-meat." Mrs. Rourke rests back on the counter, facing me. Her eyes are like the dark of sky between stars, and there is the lightest cover of lotion on her skin, at certain angles I catch it, like pink rising off, like sunshine off the arc of a Persian dome. I'm not sure about Persian domes. I might mean Turkish, or Byzantine. Possibly Byzantine.

"I despise spice pies. Do you despise spice pies?"

"I don't know," I say softly. "I've never tasted one."

Naturally, I think of Maman. If I am reminded of Kate's mother rather than my own; it's not because I loved her more, but because I have a limited inventory of imagery to draw upon as regards the business of the kitchen. The whole thing with Maman was strange. How auspicious for a woman with an abundance of resources to come upon a child with a surplus of lack. How inauspicious to have died in the midst of that. I recall our awareness of the barter—it was like a tutorial, like a sorcery behind the eyes. Next, in an unwelcome leap, I recall the germinating deadness of Maman's home, the picturesque dryness, the claiming back process of nature, the complex science of decay, the scenic rot that wove out as if via high-speed loom, upwards and outwards, embroidering her into a trellis of disease until she was more part of it than not. Her face, trapped there. Lost to me, but what was lost—I don't know, when I don't even know what was gained. I hope at least that I gave her some of what she wanted.

Mrs. Rourke's hand on my shoulder, me feeling it. I feel it.

"Why don't you make a trip to the pantry while I pour the tea. There are cookie tins on the left. We're giving my niece a baby shower tonight. No one will notice if any are missing."

The right side of the slope-ceilinged room is lined with shelves, and to the left is an old meat safe or pie safe, which is where I find the canisters. I lift one with Dutch children dancing. I know they are Dutch by signs of the Dutch—clogs and windmills and tulips, merry yellow hair and red sailboats. I turn to leave; the pantry door has drifted closed. On its back I see what appears to be a ruler embedded in wood, there are so many lines—a growth chart, his. My parents had never measured my growth, not once, though that is nothing to me now. Now I see only Rourke, metamorphosing downward through the years—the diminuendo of his features, the reductive synopsis of his figure back to the fundamental boldness of proportion he surely possessed as a child. I go down, grazing each strike on the way, knowing that, in fact, he was there every time one was carved, arriving at last at the first—twenty-nine inches, not much higher than my knee. I feel heartstricken and regretful, as if flicking in reverse through a photo album of a child I gave away, at once jealous of and beholden to the woman who kept this simple study of him, this careful anthropology.

"This last one is Thanksgiving—1978." She is above me, on the other side of the frame. Through the gap I see the cherry printed dishtowel in her hand. "Six-two. Although he might actually be taller now. He refuses to stand for me anymore."

No, I think, he is six-two exactly.

"Would you like to see the rest of the house?" she inquires kindly, no longer divining. She finds in the gruesome clarity of my eyes what she surmised from the moment we met. She does not look away. Most people look away, unable to bear the sight of him there.

"Yes." I say yes, and we go, leaving the tea untouched.

The tour she gives is not merely a tour of his childhood—where he smashed his head, where he carved his initials, where he took his first steps—but a scholarly sort of assessment, as if we are in professional accord as to the relevance of the obscurest technicalities of our shared passion. Being there with her, Rourke becomes a practical totality, something greater than essence, something graphic and graspable and possessed of its primordial perfection. It's like holding a globe while discussing the sum and substance of the earth.

She leads me to the room I have long admired from the street. It is hers, for writing. An IBM Selectric rests on a table between stuffed barrister bookshelves, and there is a withery chintz chair with a cashmere blanket folded over one arm. Photographs of Rourke are everywhere—him upside down at two, him swinging a bat skillfully at eleven, his muscles already standing out, him brown at the beach, hugging her, by a palm tree.

"Hawaii," she says. "We went for Christmas once. When he was still at UCLA."

There are old black-and-white photos, the square kind with scalloped edges, and bleached ones, in color, of a man—her husband. There is the boy on his father's knee in green, green grass, the two emerging from underwater in a pool, two faces the same, the infant tucked in the crease of his father's arm. I turn away.

I go to the window. I look down onto the place from which I've so often looked up. I don't want her to go back through my eyes, not with the way my eyes tend to see. I feel protective but oppressed in that protectiveness, as if my need to shelter her from pain is futile and mislaid, meaningful only to me. Possibly I feel overwhelmed because I have mastered such a loss—of love, of potential—because despite her husband's death, she is more fortunate than I—she at least had a child. The simple fact of Rourke's aliveness does not console me. I struggle everyday with the consequences of my loss. If I'm wrong, I'm not ashamed, not before her.

Her fingers stutter tristfully over the photos. "Remarkable, isn't it—nostalgia. I can't bring myself to remove them."

On the far side of a bathroom passage is a narrow room with a small bed, a round table piled with books, a lamp with a heliotrope-blue shade, a marble-topped chiffonier.

"For so long we had nothing," she explains. "My husband and I eloped. My mother refused to help us—financially—though she was certainly capable. My grandmother gave this place to us, and we had Harrison. Of course my mother fell in love with him and had an immediate change of heart. Every week new furniture would arrive, or silverware, or china. Bill's colleagues would visit and accuse him of accepting graft." On a shelf with iron brackets, there are three tea cups, not of a kind. "Trinkets," she says, lifting one, tilting it. "Things I find in the garden—thimbles and tags—rocks Harrison gave me when he was a boy. Beach glass. He was forever giving me beach glass."

I follow her to the end of the hall. This I have seen; in dreams he stands at the end of a hall such as this. Her left arm lengthens against the door and she pushes it, flattening back, allowing me to pass.

I do not see portions or fragments, I see an entirety, like looking at a shoebox diorama. There are trophies and ribbons and fight posters from the Olympic Stadium in L.A., the Municipal Stadium in Philadelphia, and Madison Square Garden—Palomino vs. Muniz, Jersey Joe Walcott vs. Rocky Marciano, Ali vs. Frazier, and many, many others printed crudely on tangerine construction paper fading at the borders with data in weird foreign type, and also ones from the Criterion—Harrison Rourke vs. Little Tommy Lydell, vs. Johnny Amato, vs. Piggy Harding, vs. Chester Honey Walker.

To the right is a dresser, a mirror, the keeper of his image, the bank of his appearances; I stand before it. It is not neutral. It is eloquent in its energy, it undulates between fields, it conjures what has vanished. I see him, contemplating the twinness of self—the real and the reflected—coming up prematurely against the riddle of being in this tiny vault. I see me, at seventeen, hardly anything really, negligible and slight and unable to help him comprehend the mysteries of duality, the secret of the egg—that what appears not to exist in fact *does* exist, that no single phenomenon represents reality, that the antithesis is the complement, not the negation, that serenity lies in the balance between halves, in the communion between center and circumference.

In an instant we are gone. The mirror stands alone, non-reflective, a murky break in the wall, a mark of dangerous separation, a door, a portal, a passage for those who fear center, who might be lured by the decoy of appearance. Of course he feared center, the radii of a wheel meet at center—center is the point of intersection for all the things you have ever known and loved, for all the things that move you, make you, uphold you. God is at center—she is there, heartbroken. If I had not just felt for myself the futility of my desire to protect her, I might never have guessed at the feelings of inequity that hold Rourke. If I had not just felt envious of the brief intimacy she had attained, which I had also attained, but which had been far far briefer, I might never have understood the fury in him.

I turn from the mirror. If I lived with it, I would cover it.

"HE WAS BORN HERE," she says, looking at the bed. The bed is a double bed, perfectly made, as if she expects him home this very evening, which I understand. On the bedpost is an autographed glove—Ray Mancini's. I sit and lift the glove, holding it in my lap. Boxing gloves are strange to hold, like rolls of leather paper.

"My husband was a detective assigned to lower Manhattan, to the 1st Precinct. He raced home, but Harrison was already halfway out." She gestures with a short toss of the head to the memorabilia. "Some of these belonged to Bill. He was a fighter in Ireland, in Belfast. I don't know how much you know."

"Only that he died."

"Fifteen years ago April." She lowers her eyes then raises them. The charm of her midnight eyes is accentuated by black bangs and prominent cheekbones. The remainder of her shoulder-length hair is pulled into a twist. I wonder about her ancestry. She is beautiful in the locked-off, genetically undiluted way of a Senegalese or a Norwegian. Perhaps she is Russian. "I gave this room to Harrison after he got into a knife fight. The doctor said he fought because he needed space. As if it's not in his blood." She laughs and she tours the room, adjusting like a museum proprietor, as though these artifacts now belong rightfully to her, as though if asked she could relate the day and hour each was installed in her life. "After Bill died, it was like having a bull in the house. My sister suggested acting. For years I shuttled Harrison to and from New York for commercials, auditions, lessons. The idea was that if he was making money with his face, he would have some incentive to keep it presentable. Well, he loved acting, but he didn't stop fighting. He just became more selective about it."

There is a leonine purity to her voice as she speaks of her son, as she visits the place her devotion is kept. In her voice there are alchemies and energies, pourings-out and pourings-in, proof upon proof that the strength of his bones came from the strength of her own, and the strength of his character comes from hers still, continually, by her good grace. I try to recall the legend of Isis—the shorn hair, the blackness of mourning, the dead husband. Isn't it the husband of Isis who becomes a tree? Isn't it he whose floating coffin catches in river weeds and causes them to become a huge tree by the supreme vitality of his body escaping?

She says, "They would bet, you know."

I did not know. Maybe I did. Maybe he told me. Yes, he told me. Yes. Rob told me too. *There's gonna be a fight. The come-back kind.*

"He and Rob made a fortune before I found out and threatened to have them arrested. Those were trying times. Thankfully, they met a Chinese gentleman who taught them martial arts and introduced them to a trainer from the Criterion, Jimmy Landis. "

"I've heard of them."

"Despite my reservations, Harrison turned into a fine fighter. I don't know whether his father would have been proud or horrified." She looks up from his desk. "Have you ever seen him fight?"

I shake my head, no.

There is a flicker, a smile, instantly disintegrating.

"Naturally, everyone wanted him to turn professional. Naturally, I wanted him to go to college, and since his father would have wanted it as well, he consented. The boys were accepted to UCLA, which was the best of both worlds—they would be together, Harrison could pursue his interest in acting, and L.A is full of gyms." Mrs. Rourke sits alongside me on the bed. The slats of the wood blinds stutter lightly. "Rob majored in economics and went on for a second degree—he has an uncanny competence for numbers. Harrison did some acting and some fighting, mostly fighting. He wanted to get through the Olympics and then use the credential to get investors to develop an athletic club, a succession of clubs. Somehow, it fell apart. Even before the boycott, it fell apart. I don't know why. When Rob got his master's degree, we all flew to California. Rob had a black eye—completely hemorrhaged, swollen shut. He was lucky his cheekbone hadn't been broken. I knew of course that Harrison had done it. I felt awful for Mr. and Mrs. Cirillo. Their whole family was there. Carmen's parents had flown from Bologna. I took Rob aside. I said, 'Robert, your eye.' 'Don't you worry about it, Mrs. R.,' he assured me, 'It was my fault. I said something stupid.' 'What could you *possibly* have said to deserve this?' I asked. And he said, *'The wrong thing.'* Do you know, I still wonder what the *wrong thing* could have been?"

I POUR THE REBOILED water; she lays cookies on the plates. Rob makes the last of several trips to the attic. There is the machine gun stomping of footsteps. She likes the noise; it's been a long time. We lift our steaming cups, eyes connecting above china.

"I'm glad you came," she says. "I hope it won't be the last time."

I wonder about a world left to her and me. In such a world, it would not be the last time. Her eyes search my face. She reaches across the table, touching my hair. Her hand makes me warm.

"It's longer now. It used to be very short."

"I'm sorry," I say. "I don't understand."

"There's a picture he carries. You're in a gymnasium."

ON OUR WAY DOWN the porch steps, she calls out for us to wait. She returns with a letter for Rourke, asking Rob to mail it. Rob is farther than I am, so I reach, taking it in my hands. The paper is thin, fragile. It is a wonder she does not take greater care.

"Goodbye," we say, grasping hands.

I feel something pass over. Courage coming in, and confidence, soundness and health and fortune. If you think it's impossible to feel worse than the worst you've ever felt, you're wrong. Worse than barren, worse than numb, worse than solitude and despair, is to possess one particle of hope, to feel the feel of fate brushing so close you think you will die.

Rob honks twice, and we back out and drive away. He pulls up at the first mailbox.

"Not this one," I tell him, "the next."

He leans on the accelerator and smiles.

"How did his father die?"

Rob's head dips into his neck, and he reaches to smack down his visor. We must have turned west. The sun, going down.

"He was murdered. By the brother of a guy he killed. He was on duty, he threw a punch and killed a guy. A fluke. A robbery on Chambers Street. The kid's brother came down from Detroit to settle. He got killed too—Billy Rourke's partner shot him. In the face. It was bad. It was a fucking mess."

"How old were you?"

"Thirteen. We were thirteen."

THAT NIGHT WE ARE AT A PARTY. I CANNOT LOOK AT THE PEOPLE, ALL THE people are like stand-up pigs, like pigs in suits. The eyes are dead and round in faces that are not real faces but compilations of parts—teeth and noses and millions of hairs blown and combed and lips that liberate opinions through tangles of smoke, sideways disclosures about mentions in *Variety* and the luminescence of diamonds. I stay by my seat. I know it is mine because there is a card with my name. The card is the color of spoiled cream or curdled cream, and the ink is a sort of ochre.

Behind my upholstered dining chair is a wall that is a window and through the diaphanous barrier the city churns, catastrophe and chance, bits and bits in unison beneath one vascular radiance, one arc or bridge or monotone rainbow that astronauts can detect from space. We are high up, but we cannot escape the violence of the streets; it clings like ivy to the walls that protect us. We content ourselves not to see—it is not the fact of indigence that distresses us, just the spectacle. A red light windmills across the treetops of Central Park, swiping the towers as an ambulance delivers a body to the aid of strangers. Red lights are a sign. They refer to a person and to pain, possibly to death. Every night is the worst night of someone's life. It's easy to forget that.

It is time to turn, so I turn. Arms come together like branches of a star over the center of the table. Jeweled fingers and gold-cuffed wrists grip clear tulips. Candlelight inhabits the champagne, making effervescent caramel.

"Hear, hear," they say and we drink—to Mark, his promotion, his engagement. His success.

There is epic meaning in the erect and stately circle we form, in the alliance of ready arms, in the fists clutching brittle glass. It is a ritual aside, a communal departure, a cooperative meditation, a type of prayer. We step out of time because we have vanquished it. We are superior to the things of which we speak. I think of valorous knights and courageous kings, of fugitive powers expired, notable deeds forgotten, great heroes disrecalled. Yes, it's true, congratulations are in order—quickly.

Mark claims the ensuing interlude. "A second toast," he says, his voice fashioning tenderness. "To Eveline." He gestures to me, and they gesture to me, and I bow to straighten my perfect dress, which hangs against me perfectly. In the glimmering moon of my china plate, I discover a watery likeness of my face. Mindful of the way I hang my head, I right myself to confront the sea of eyes. "May the rest of our lives be as happy as these three years have been."

"*Salud*," they murmur kindly, though they are not kind. To them I begin with Mark. He is my origin and objective. To them I am what I appear to be. They go to lengths to keep me in the prison of their view.

"Hurry up and drink," Alicia says. "Dinner in twenty minutes."

Bodies cleave from the table, forming genial clusters. There is no opening. I wait for an opening, which is like waiting to be picked for a team. "Three years," a voice thunders from behind my back. I know the voice. It belongs to Mark's friend, his friend Brett. "A long time. A damn long time."

I'm uncertain whether this is true. Sometimes a year is lavish and profuse, riotous as a gale. Sometimes it goes breath by breath by breath, in tiny, tiny sighs. Minutes can be critical, decades without meaning or contour, and so I might say, but he is done with me. My reticence is proof to him of my stupidity. To him I am useless unless seen. He scans the crowd hoping we've been noticed. He feels manly when he stands with me, just as some people feel learned when they carry books. His gaze returns to my body, pouring over.

I am intrepid in this regard. I probe his as well, careful not to conceal my disappointment. His eyes are mean and his skin prematurely wrinkled, and the shock of brittle hair that marks the center of his skull is girdled by hairless prongs. His nails are manicured, and beneath his cashmere turtleneck his breasts droop. The proposition he makes with his eyes is stealthy and simple— money and power for sex. I wonder by what error of nature has he come to feel so virile. And yet his audacity is not without weight. Brett is a man of business, of wealth and renown. No opportunity is to be left unexplored, no friend is so dear that he cannot be betrayed. Maybe I will take him with me into the kitchen. In the kitchen, appliances gleam harshly, sending back warped ideas of yourself. In the light I will let him touch me—he would like that, to touch me. His greedy fingers will knead my flesh, cramming into scars—scars are everywhere, no matter where you touch, you cannot miss.

"Yes," I will say to Brett, through the kitchenish glare. Kitchens are always bright, like car tunnels. "Three years is a very long time."

MY GLASS IS EMPTY. I twirl it by its stem like a baton, sorry for the delicacy of the marks I make. They are specific and very small, like baby bridges. I think of fossils, fishy and particular, weary cadavers in khaki rock—proving, proving something.

Brett and I are joined by Swoosey Schicks, whose name sounds like a drunk with castanets. They discuss treasury bonds and cycling in Bali and the price of Brett's 14-carat-gold octagon Rolex—$1,950. Across the room Mark begins to dance with Amy, a redhead who appeared in *Amadeus*. Or *A Passage to India*. I always get those movies mixed up. Amy wears a green satin blouse. Redheads like green; they think it becomes them.

"Uh oh," Brett says. "Things are beginning to get interesting."

I excuse myself, leaving. I do not go unnoticed. There is a tinny, zincy pressure—all eyes on me. I go to the bathroom. I always go to the bathroom. It is the one place to hide. Men want to know what women do in bathrooms. They *hide*.

I sit on the edge of the bathtub. It is a good tub, a round-edged, pre-war New York tub. I don't need to pee, but anyway I lift my dress and lower my stockings to my knees. The division is strange, black to white—I don't know why we blacken our legs. I touch the division over and over, jumping the line, my finger popping—*nylon to skin, skin to nylon.* From the elastic of my bra, I remove a pen, and on my thigh I draw some fossils, not just any fossils but rose fossils, which are petrified rose remains. Last time I saw my dad we ate *gelato* and he told me that rose fossils have been found dating back 32 million years. He gave me a newspaper article. Also I write of time, of whether it is long or short, and then my name. And a word, *vinca*, which is short for *vincapervinca*, which is Latin, I think, for periwinkle. Periwinkle is an herb and an ivy and a snail, all of which share the color that is the color of my dress—light purple blue pink. Snails are not lucky for much, but they're lucky for their color. My dad—I haven't seen him in a long time. *Gelato* means summer.

Behind the shower curtain above the tub is a tall window set deep in a tiled rectangular cubby the size of two ice blocks stacked. It looks onto a sheet of brick, which is the neighboring building. Outside is music from an adjacent apartment. It's not an old song, but old is the way it feels because it comes from a time when music had no picture, when music used to say who you were instead of how to look, and life was a dream you dreamt streaking by like you're staring out of a speeding vehicle. Nights were dark back then, nights were mother of coal.

I climb into the tub. I push the shampoo bottles to one side of the sill and crank the window open. Some dust blows in, a little ash.

> *Do you say your prayers little darlin',*
> *Do you go to bed at night*
> *Prayin' that tomorrow, everything will be alright.*

The song curls in the airshaft between buildings before getting drawn back through the duct into vastness. I follow its route. Sometimes you see a balloon going that way, bobbing in jerks against nothing, and that is mysterious and that is beautiful, and always will be, forever throughout eternity, even when the earth is reduced in the end to shredded metal and desert. A balloon yanked up like a toy retracted by God makes you nostalgic, and nostalgia is human and humane and hopeful despite the frequently gory conditions of reality. It is seeing the child you once were and conceding that more are coming—you are not the last.

Quiet now. Not quiet but the whimper and rumor of voices skulking through the fissure between door and floor like irreversible rodents. I try to think though thinking without thought to resolution is a waste—the dividend is the same as multiplying by zero.

At the sink I wash the ink from my hands. I touch near my eyes. Eyes are truly glass. Within them the soul appears, inexact and enigmatic, rippling like a likeness on a lake. I unravel a strip of toilet paper to wipe my footprints from the bottom of the tub. It's not that I am neat, it's just that I have so much time to kill.

MARK'S BODY APPROACHES MINE. His hands tow across my skin like damp mitts or squirrels. I feel without feeling, which is nothing, which is easy, like sterile mechanics, like being sensorial with your palms when washing your face. I am thankful he does not insist upon cognizance. There are certain things a girl cannot tolerate.

There is a place to go, a place no one can access. When I am there I do not think of a man, nothing so practical as a man. If I long for a man, it is for an abstract of a man, the way a native shore is a coastline when viewed from the deck of a ship. I go to a barrier; I do not know what it blocks, but I move to it, journeying, further and deeper, to reach the place where—I don't know, just a place.

"You okay?" Mark asks. He always asks. If only he would not ask, I might like him better.

"I'm okay," I say as I stand to leave, "just thirsty."

This is not a lie. The thirst is supreme, as though inside I have shriveled. I stand at the refrigerator, drinking everything, one container at a time, moving left to right so I can keep track of those that I have emptied. I am afraid to raise an empty container as if it is full, the way your hand flies up, deceived.

Against the bedroom window is the Hudson River. It is shallow like a decal or a holiday transparency. I can't see past the glass, only in it. I see my arms and face, white from blue moonlight or blue from white moonlight. My arms look like dead arms, clipped to my shoulders by pins, dangling. I stare into indigo deadness as my image detaches from my silhouette, stepping away.

She touches her cheek. My arm remains hanging. She pivots, winding one-quarter around, though I am still. Her hands draw behind her back and rest airily on the rise beneath it, which is square, which is round, she is a girl. I know this girl, I think. She may be the one I once was. In my throat I taste the extract of her desire, in the slope of my waist to the billow of my hip I see the same petition for seduction. She is driven. I was driven.

I wish to speak, to say something. But things that are legible to the senses are often captive to language, such as the dizzying faraway feeling you get from the way daylight pools on the kitchen floor, mesmerizing you in the midst of sudden misfortune, making you think of the frailty of life—and the beauty. Or the shimmery persistence of a perfume that lingers in the air, filling you with longing when you pass through. Possibly it is the fragrance a teacher wore, or your mother. No words can describe what it means to lose someone you love, or tell what it is to grieve.

And loneliness. I should say something of loneliness. The panic, the sweeping hysteria that comes not when you are without others, but when you are without yourself, adrift. I should describe the filthy province of mind, the blighted district inside, the place so crowded you cannot raise the lids of your eyes. Your shoulders are drawn and your head has fallen and your chest is bruised by the constant assault of your heart. No air, no air, nothing but your own sticky breath, panting wet and sticky. I want to convey the burden of despair, the ruin of compromise. *Be brave*, I should say, the way brave used to be—desperate to live and to love. I want her to prepare for the curse of perseverance. She may not know about resiliency. That she will last.

My belly still hums from coming—that is electricity I think. I wonder—can she see me. I hope she cannot see me. I don't want her to know that sex here is loveless, that here I achieve a goal, an end, like reaching for a ring. But no—she sees nothing. She recedes, losing edge, losing center. She slips back to the chamber of my heart where I reserve like liquor the essence of her—and of him. Secretly I keep us, a rustling quilt of madness unfolding like pealing chapel bells that go gradually softer and farther, twining in and twining around, extending beneath and beyond anything anyone can perceive. I cannot say that I loved him—it wouldn't be right. I can say that I've watched myself die, and that I've seen my lips form his name with my final breath.

8.

I USED TO BE TELEPATHIC. I USED TO KNOW THINGS BEFORE THEY HAPPENED. It's like feeling wind when there is no wind or hearing an echo that has no source. Of course, sometimes you suspect something will happen, and so you wait, but nothing does. That's because fortune has intervened to *prevent* connections, to demonstrate its might, to prove we are free only within its boundaries.

There are those who attempt to manipulate fate. There are those who gamble for purposes of self-deception. They are stranded on their paths but want to feel otherwise. They want to feel the thrill of determination. They circumscribe the conditions of chance. They create a reality in which there is nothing but the game. This sort of risk is not for the faint of heart. Afterwards comes the disintegration of fiction and re-entry into fact and the grit required to endure the misery of the impact. This is Rob.

There are those who leave nothing to chance. They will not be seduced. They connive and hoard to distend the aggregate of what they are, all the while straining down the world to something small, like a stone to clench. The refusal to be enticed is a means of control, a way to guarantee they are not violated, a way to exploit the business about them. It is a matter of filtration, of preprocessing, of determining truth before it determines you. Mark.

There are those who risk to ascertain that they have nothing, that they need nothing. They are open to prospect and blind to hazard because they've been hurt, which is just another way of saying *informed*. They are bodies moving through space, inviolate and impermeable. Life is an ocean against them. They are full on the inside; nothing beyond can speak on their behalf. They require no nominal validation. They are owners of themselves. That is Rourke. At one time, it was me too.

I don't know whether life is pre-decided. Perhaps it can be better conceived as a series of hallways, growing wider or narrower, depending upon your receptivity to chance. The trick is to stand always at the crest of fate, to become proficient at response. Never get stuck thinking small, thinking slow, thinking any one state a finality; otherwise, life inverts and reverses and turns stagnant—the hallways narrow. This is an abuse of the gift of mobility.

I think of nomads. If nomads had not conceded to forces outside their control, they would not have survived. Unpremeditated accident in the form of weather and predators and migration of food sources guided action. They persevered by staying open to change. It wasn't until we started to cultivate and civilize and reduce all conceivable risk that we turned hard to the missives of nature, making ourselves susceptible instead to new things, social things, things entirely beyond our natural grasp.

When I lost Rourke, I shut down entirely to chance. I intuited nothing, risked nothing. I left the table. Once out, you do not get invited back. You have to charm your way, muscle your way.

I LOOK LIKE A whore. At home I tried several outfits, but no matter what I chose, I looked like a whore anyway. On the way downtown everyone stares at the whorish way I'm dressed. The problem is, I don't know how to be. I don't know whether to be the girl I was, the one who came alive through his eyes, or the other one, the one I've become, proof of the mistake he made in leaving me. Anyway, the girl—I'm afraid to go back. That's why I look like a whore. Sex is a type of armor.

I take four concrete flights up to a loft north of Chinatown on Lafayette near Cleveland Place. A letter-board at the head of the stairs lists classes and events. Fridays at four is NYPD Combat Tai'ji. Today's guest is boxer and Olympic trainer Harrison Rourke.

Twenty-two guys sit in a semi-circle listening to a Chinese man in a canvas robe and loose pants—Mr. Xinwu, I guess. The Chinaman. Right away I find Rourke, the way a magnet finds north. His large back is there among all the other large backs, his cotton jacket taut across it, wrinkled at the arms same as the rest; still, I would know his back anywhere. My mother used to say she could pick me out of a line of a hundred girls in matching snowsuits facing away from her. I never believed her. I feel bad about that.

The room is lined with trophies and banners with Chinese lettering. To my right there are framed quotes and photographs of masters—Yang Chengfu, Zheng Maqing, Ben Lo, Wang Shujin. There is a huge parchment paper document and lines without attribution.

> *Those who master others are strong;*
> *Those who master themselves have true power.*

"Remember, direction of power," Mr. Xinwu admonishes as he demonstrates drills—silk-reeling, push hands, sparring gong. His body pivots and makes face-forward shapes like a slow clock. "Power moves legs, arms, hands. Body makes root in earth for *qi* power. Root prevents fighter from getting thrown down. Meaning is the same as good wife—keeps man straight in unbalanced time." Everyone laughs, then gravely he adds, "Root is more lethal than gun."

Mr. Xinwu nods to Rourke, and Rourke joins him, standing like a house up-rising. He sets his feet shoulder-width apart, bending at the knees and tucking the hips. He hollows his chest and raises his back like the hood of a cobra. When he turns in profile, I feel something go through me—heat and something else, something strange, something new—frustration. Other than desire, what I feel principally is disentitled to him, disqualified from possessing something that is essentially my own. Incredibly, I feel cheated. I did not expect to feel cheated. Next, I feel the sick lie of myself, tripled in sickness by my reaction. The idea of being alone with him is terrifying. I step back twice, thinking to leave. Maybe it is my high shoes, but I stumble. There is no chair. I lean firmly against the wall in case I faint.

"All fighters must understand root," Xinwu is saying, his eyes flickering at me. "Body must possess knowledge of root before moving to strike, sweep, throw, choke. This is why every beginner starts high—starts crane, goes down to tiger, maybe snake. Lower down, the better the *qi* sinks to Tan Tien. Better legs, better balance, better *root*. Snake is very difficult—dangerous unless fighter is very strong."

Rourke demonstrates all three, going almost to the floor, one knee bent, one leg straight.

"Mr. Rourke strong snake!" Again laughter; Xinwu laughs also. "Tai'ji is very important for Western boxer. Boxer stands too much upright, a stand-up body gets taken down. Nothing hurts like a body hitting ground. *But* special to boxer—*incorporation of pain*. Of all fighters, only boxers can function under extreme physical stress."

Xinwu readies himself. Rourke also readies himself. They incline their heads and chests ceremoniously. "When my friend was a small boy, he was making street fights," Xinwu relates haltingly as they begin formally to spar. "When he came to me, he was big mess—very brave, very lacking skill." Rourke snaps a kick, which Xinwu blocks with incredible economy of action. "I say, 'Mr. Rourke, first relax muscles to use muscles.' "

They break, moving again, like sculptures painstakingly positioned and repositioned. They stop, they turn. They go lightning fast, then dead slow, and when they move, they move through a bladder of air in sequence you can count—*one, two—three—four, five*. There is a queer fidelity to the sounds they create. There are no peaks to the tops or drops to the bottoms, there are no hisses or hums. It's beautiful, really—Rourke towering over his friend, and yet he is no match. Xinwu anticipates every next move almost as if he can read the objective of Rourke's muscles.

"Recently my friend returned—still very brave, now very skillful, still big mess. I say, 'Mr. Rourke, first control emotion to control body. First find *silence*.' " Mr. Xinwu moves in and finishes to the body. Rourke's body is hard, like brick. Anyway, it gives, giving brick. He folds in and down and goes gracefully to the floor. I suppose there are tender points, like hinges. Even giant buildings can collapse. Even the planet snaps. "There is a Chinese saying," Mr. Xinwu tells the room. "*Ten thousand things come from quietness*."

Xinwu releases Rourke, and Rourke stands. Everyone applauds. I think back to the first time I saw him in school and the first time I saw him on stage and all the times I've seen him. It is easy to imagine him as an actor—even the policemen are spellbound. And yet, as always, there is something offensive to me about his being watched. Maybe just the unkingly supposition that he would seek validation there, worthiness there.

Xinwu nods to Rourke, excusing him, and Rourke passes through to me.

I AM IN THE hall; that is where we meet. His hands locate my waist like picking a flower at a positively right place on the stem—yes, a hinge. I snap off the floor as he lifts me, and we kiss. His face has changed. There are lines and small recesses and definition like code writing in the most infinitesimal muscles like splinters or needles. I hold him—just breathing. Holding him is like clinging to structure when everything around you has been leveled to refuse and dust. He is striking. I know that, I've always known that, and yet his qualities are new to me, to the moment—his refined darkness, the softness of his lips, the docile eyes looking down.

"I thought I saw you today," he says. He shrugs. "You know, not you." He lifts me once more, then he remembers, then he returns me, stepping back.

"Rob said you'd be here."

"Yeah," he says. He nods. "Rob."

Mr. Xinwu uses volunteers to demonstrate various martial arts methods—Karate, Aikido, Jeet Kune Do. He talks about throwing an opponent's balance without causing harm, about love for that which is protected rather than hatred for the adversary. And Rourke, his breath. I hear him breathe.

"How is it," I ask. "Where you are?" Adding, "In the West."

"It's all right. Have you ever been out there?"

I nod, clumsily. Clumsy to admit that I've been to his particular part of the world without him, clumsy to invoke Mark even by inference. "To New Mexico. And Nevada. Colorado."

Rourke's eyes stir, yielding a degree of their luster, and his weight shifts. I have lost him; he is lost to me. I can read his intent before it is manifest. I am like Mr. Xinwu. A master. Would it help Rourke to know that I looked for him everywhere—every restaurant, every bar, every street. I tried so hard to see him that sometimes I did see him, only it was not him. He would understand. Didn't he just say, *I thought I saw you. Not you.*

We turn, and we stare into the main room, watching the cops drift into pairs. One of each set turns his back to the wall, and the other faces him. "Remember, wall-men," Xinwu is saying, "neutralize pushes. No hooking. Keep control. Confrontation is inevitable. People resort to violence if they do not master non-violence. The only separation between you and a man in jail is control. For police, control is a special obligation."

"Is this what you taught at that prison?" I ask.

"More or less. More respect. Less combat."

"Do you still do it?"

"When I can. Xinwu does it full time."

"And boxing? How does boxing fit in?"

"Boxing takes control," Rourke replies solemnly.

"As opposed to regular fighting. Street fighting."

"In regular fighting you have to overpower your opponent or outwit him. There's no shared weight or class. No opposing moral forces. It's a match of intention. How much something means to you versus how much it means to the other person. You could lose everything."

Everything, yes. A wife, a son, your life. "When did you get here?"

"About an hour ago," he says. "I took a cab from JFK. Rob will drive me down to the shore." Rourke looks away stiffly. "I'd better head back in," he says. "Are you gonna—I mean, did you want to stick around?"

"I guess I—should—you know, get going."

The staircase is tight, like a matchbox staircase, economical and fireproof gray. I start down, gripping the rail. He's there, near me, leaning. Over the harp of bars we kiss.

"Goodbye," he says courteously. I have never been the victim of his courtesy before. He hands it off like a bomb. "It was nice to see you."

Three steps down, I turn. His elbows are on the rail. He is bending and his jacket splits and I can see inside to where it is beautiful. I don't just see that it is beautiful, I feel that it is beautiful. I know that I have so much at stake. That I have only seconds. That I am there, at the crest of my destiny. I am about to say, *Rourke*.

"Tell Mark I said hello," Rourke says, stripping the towel from his neck, shaking it at his side, looping it back over his shoulders. "And, by the way, congratulations."

ON THE R TRAIN, a man with two big boxes on a wheeled cart asks, *Are you okay?* He hands me a pamphlet. I wonder what he is carrying in those two big boxes, two televisions maybe, or two of those small dormitory refrigerators. I open the pamphlet.

> *Sin mars, wrecks, ruins. Sin brings pain and misery.*
> *The wages of sin is death. Jesus saves.*
> *Jesus grants eternal life.*
> *Romans 6:23*

I return the brochure and thank him. I get off at the next stop. I don't know. I don't think I can bear the reward of eternal life.

THE GTO SKIDS UP as we exit the building. It moves alongside us, plowing into the asphalt like a grounded meteor. My first thought is that I haven't seen the car for so long. Seeing the car is different from seeing him. It's as if there has been no car since, and his car is the only car. It was the place where you kept your clothes and heard your music and ate and slept and had sex; it was a car when you needed to move. Since then there have only been vehicles.

Mark leans to the roof, and his foot slips off the curb. "Harrison! What are you doing here?"

"Visiting," Rourke replies. "Get in."

"Thanks. My car's right there." Mark points to the garage.

"And mine's right here." Rourke leans to pop the door. "Get in."

Mark bites his lip. "Let me tell the garage to repark it." He jogs across the street—not fast, not slow, but calculated, like arithmetic. It kills him to leave me at the door of Rourke's idling car, but he has to pretend at least to trust I'll be there when he returns.

Rourke's arm rests on the seat back. He stares down its length to where I stand. My body is conspicuous implicitly through the dress I wear. The eggshell silk reveals my every limb and division. It was a gift from Mark. Tonight I look like a whore, same as this afternoon, only tonight I look like Mark's whore, and that's different. Earlier Rourke rejected me because he could, because I was giving him the choice. Now there is no choice. I'm with Mark. That's the code.

A simmering gust of wind hits my hips. I stand into it and the dress impresses deeply. With him there I feel like something soaring or airborne, something capable of sustained flight. Over and over in my head is the sound of his voice. There are places on his neck that vibrate when he speaks; I know those places, stretched like the membranes of baby drums. I bend to the door and pull the chrome lever and knock the front seat forward with my knee. I climb back and sink into the upholstery as if sinking—

Mark surfaces and cuts back over the street. He looks handless and foot-less like an anonymous figure on a street sign. Rourke observes him, his eyes like an assassin's eyes. Around us is mostly silence. In that inaudible fusillade, things are made known to me, things such as my own strengths and failings.

Mark shuts the door. "Cirillo told me you just bought a jeep out in Colorado. How do you like it?"

"It's all right," Rourke says, shoving the stick into first.

"When did you get in?" Mark asks.

"This afternoon."

At the traffic light on the corner, Mark says, "So, where to?"

Rourke turns south on Ninth Avenue. "Around."

After that, there is no more chatter, no more pretense of friendship. Nothing good, nothing good at all.

AT BROOME STREET BAR, we take a table—Mark and me with our backs to the wall and Rourke facing us like an interview. Rourke draws his chin into his neck and drops his head to the left, and a girl appears as if in response to a silent whistle. What an obligation to be him, to possess such formidable pow-ers of seduction, such dread competence.

"I'll take a Beck's. Bring one for her as well."

"Hold on. Do you even *want* a beer?" Mark asks, laying his elbow on the table and pointing lazily to the waitress, to me, to the waitress. "Actually, she'll have wine. What kinds do you have?"

"What kinds of what?" the waitress replies.

"Wine. What kinds of wine."

She furrows her brow. Then with confidence, she says, "House!"

"House," Mark repeats. "Would that be Chablis, Chardonnay, Pinot Grigio, or something you people express in the basement?"

"Don't worry about it," I say. "Whatever you have is okay."

"No, go check," Rourke instructs. "Check very carefully. Make sure it's wet and cold and intoxicating. And make sure it's in a glass."

"Tell you what," Mark snaps. "Bring the most expensive bottle you can find. And a Stoli. Double. Rocks." As soon as she returns with the drinks, he tells her, "Gimme another Stoli."

I check his glass. It's true. It's already empty.

MARK DUMPS VODKA AFTER vodka down his throat, and Patti keeps my wine glass filled. Her name is Patti; I know, because at one point Rourke asked. He turned his head insinuatively into the tonnage of his own shoulder, just as a boa caresses its own mean, and the meaty spume of his voice plastered her neck as she bent to exchange glassware. He said, "What's your name?"

And she reddened, fast and strange, like a flower infused with artificial color. Beneath her wispy black hair, she demurred. "Patti."

Patti with an *i*, not a *y*, I am certain, because she is a particular type of Patti, more contemptible than the other sort. I don't hate her, I hate the way Rourke admires her, the way she is pretty and hard-working and uncompromised. I used to be that way too, uncompromised at Heartbreak and, prior to that, uncompromised at Lobster Roll, and pretty when I paid my own way and possessed a very, very firmness of will. I too used to demure. One must demure when there are no walls, when one is pretty with hair that wisps, and alone. One must take care not to let things get through. Now I am at liberty to be immodest and indecent and indiscreet because I am inaccessible and there are frontiers about me. I belong to Mark—to circle and to legion—like a cadet belongs to the military. I am a recruit, a conscript, an instrument, a dependent. I cannot be hurt; I have an army. Like most disciples, I was chosen because nothing confines me, because I can travel, because I can go where no one I know or have ever known will go, because the place I must go is closed to them as they can never come, only new people. I was chosen because, unlike Rourke, I am without character.

I wonder how many glasses I've had. Eleven, I think.

Rourke says not quite. "More like three."

I don't argue, he is the sober one. He hasn't been drinking his drinks. He just keeps ordering more rounds and exchanging full bottles for new full bottles. I don't mind being poisoned. I deserve, and Mark deserves it. Together we are *deserving*.

"Be right back," Mark says studiously to the tabletop as though taking an exam. He is exceedingly drunk. When he talks, his tongue protrudes, making me think of Venus flytraps. Denny says flytraps have throat hairs that are stimulated by movement, and that's why they eat only living things. The movement is important because they get just *six* meals per lifetime. "Can you imagine," Denny once speculated, "wasting one of the six on a twig or a rock or something?"

Mark stumbles to a stand and staggers into the shoulders of the crowd. He is gone, and I look at Rourke exclusively. It's been a long time since I've seen him exclusively. Every day we'd spent apart is annexed to the architecture of his face. I see a troubled edifice, a misshapen sort of mask. I think to say something, everything; I remind myself to wait.

"It's so strange," I say, "to see you again. Do you feel strange?"

"Little bit." His words slip like pebbles across ice, shooting off and away as they are dropped. His eyes are adamantine, like diamonds, black diamonds. Diamonds are coal before they are diamonds, which is miraculous, which is earth magic, like cyclones and fish who hibernate in dry lake beds. My diamond is a big diamond. Everyone stares at it, though it is nothing compared to his eyes. He leans across, and the glasses make way, parting like a sea. There is a song, I hear it. I think I do.

> *With her killer graces and her secret places that no boy can fill.*
> *With her soft French cream standin' in that doorway like a dream.*

He presses into me, knocking forward, his hands locking down my shoulders. My arm tears, a little, a worm's-length. A sound—*Oh*—shooting out, like air propelled. I bite down, accidentally drawing blood from my lip, and we kiss, and the red seeps in. The taste of him is sweet. Strange that sweetness is the quality I remember and that it has not changed. Strange for sweetness to be the hallmark of a kiss. He pulls back, an inch, less, the thickness of a slice of paper. No, that is not right. Paper does not come in slices, pizza does.

"Is that how you kiss him," he says, foully, like I am foul.

Maybe it's the alcohol or maybe just the blood, the flavor of blood stitched to the perfume of his saliva, but I feel something animal. I think to hit him or to kill him. I think, if I held a knife, some instrument of absolute shape, some perfection of point, would it be easy to employ? Would it make his body turn purple like the capes of queens? I think of the virile final feel, the passage of his influence, the disintegrating fury of his hands and his heart, the spasmodic summary of his breaths, the denouement of his ingratiating smell. His throat, turning peculiar, turning limp and storm-bent, hot as he collapses into me like a dying gargantuan thing, like an anvil plowing.

I have to get away, so I stand and get away.

I move as if upon a belt through a series of belts, unsynchronized and of variable speeds. Mark glides past me in the opposite direction, looking flat and passing, stapled to the face of the crowd, like we live on a space station. I don't know why a space station. The floor heaves through a slough of saloonish greens and browns and skipping lights, little flecks skipping against blackness like circus flashlights. In the bathroom I decide to vomit. Alicia says it is easy, which it is. The liquor shoots out, *plop, plop,* and then a barrage of plops, and, okay, I feel better. I wipe icy paper towels on my face and my neck. I drink some water.

At the bar, I ask for a lemon wedge, and I stand there, leaning, and I eat it. Mark and Rourke are toasting; I cannot imagine to what. Living in a world with men is like being in the center of a ring with hands spinning you in a circle. It's like being spun, three-quarters one way, one-half the other, one full time back around. Wherever you land, there's another set of hands. Men like you to believe they are dangerous when frequently they are not. They cannot be truly dangerous when there are so many things they want that they won't talk about. When secretly you want a thing, you make mistakes.

I thank the bartender for the lemon.

He gives me one and says, "Anytime, sweetheart."

I'm not a sweetheart, I've never been a sweetheart, but it's nice of him to call me one and to remind me that things don't always have to be that way. Someday maybe I will be someone's sweetheart and that someone will take me to Great Adventure on a Saturday in June and camping in Vermont and will buy me running shoes for Christmas. I return to the table and wonder what would have to change before I could become a sweetheart. Something big in me would have to change, I think. The whole thing seems unlikely.

Mark signs the receipt and replaces his American Express card in his wallet. "So. Harri-son. Who do you—plan to, you know." Mark works his way up to a stand and jabs loosely at the air. "Whatever."

"Spar with?" Rourke says. "Whoever's around."

"Oh yeah? Who?"

"There's a kid from Ghana who's pretty good."

"You only have—what do you have?"

"Eight days." Rourke holds open the door to the street and helps Mark through.

"Eight days." Mark nods and steps through then stops. "Eight days? You better do *something*. What happened to the old guy—Jimmy Landis? The one you used to train with."

"He's in Florida."

"Well, I like to say, everyone is replaceable."

"Not everyone," Rourke says.

AT SIXTIETH STREET, ROURKE stops far enough away from the entrance that none of the neighbors will see Mark, who is passed out in the front. Rourke folds down his seat, then he helps me out, offering his hand, which I accept, which is sad. Sad to hold, sadder to let go. He leans on the rear fender, quietly regarding the quiet street, and I lean too, gripping the trunk because the muscles of my legs are not reliable. In Rourke's face is a light. It brightens, it dims. I don't know where the light is coming from, west I think. I look for the river. I don't see the river, though it's not far. That's because we're in the street. There is no river when you're in the street. When you go up, the river is everywhere. It slaps the glass. And I have dreams, river dreams. In the west, where the river should be, a crane points out. Like an ominous projectile. At the tip a signal flashes, hemorrhaging red into the valley of night. That is the light on Rourke's face. There is hissing from the sewer, and blasts of night smoke skulk around our ankles. He looks extraordinary in that tawdry light, like a child evolved beyond his years, like a child prostitute, with insolent features and supple skin and eyes that are shameless. All child prostitutes have a particular look, like they are related despite disparate origins, like they are of a single nationality. Like they are not slavish. Like they have the power to absolve you. Only they can acquit you of the crimes of subjugation you wish to commit.

There are things I know. I know he spoke to Rob, to his mother, but I say nothing, and he says nothing, both of us standing there, caught, black angels in our throats. "So," I say, "eight days." I try to speak without slurring, and I hear myself trying, and I hear myself slurring, but I don't care how I sound, which is a strange thing to feel at a strange time, but I do feel that way.

"Next Saturday."

His arms are folded largely against his chest. I look in wonder; I think of them clenched, the muscle contracted and me inside them, him inside me. It's been three years. How many women have there been. All I can see is the volatile mechanics of his sex, him fucking other women. Though I suppose one would be bad enough. Actually, one would be worse. One gives me an indication of how *he* feels. I hold the fender, dizzily.

"Well," I say, my head swinging a bit. "Good luck in the fight."

Him not moving. "You'll be there."

"I—"

"You'll be there," he repeats. "He'll make sure of it."

"I don't think—" I wave one hand.

"He won't let you miss it. He's betting I get killed."

Carlo comes out to help the Morrisseys unload luggage and sleeping children from their car. The kids are two and four with matching bear slippers. *Ssshh,* the mother saying, *ssshh.* I can't hear that from where we stand, I can see it. Her lips pursed, *ssshh.* Carlo looks over and notices me and notices Mark and gestures; he'll be right over.

"And if I refuse?"

"You won't. Rob needs you."

"Rob needs money. I have no money."

Rourke shrugs. "You *pull* money."

"And you?"

"Me? I pull a crowd. I fight and go home. I'm like you. I'm helping a friend. I don't care who wins."

Carlo's footsteps. He is jogging over and waving apologetically. Together he and Rourke hoist Mark from the front seat, and when they stand, Mark sags down, out at the knees and in at the chest, like a scarecrow. "Got him, sir!" Carlo declares, and Rourke ducks, leaving the two to shuffle off into the overbright lobby. I wonder briefly if Carlo took the spare keys, if he intends to take Mark upstairs. I suppose I should go check. I would prefer to find the river. And to face it, the way Indians did. And to jump. Not for the purpose of drowning but for the elegant sensation of floating away, the picturesque light-ness. I wonder if Rourke would like to find the water with me.

I turn to him, tipping in, taking hold of his shirt. The front of me on the front of him, my face by his chest. I breathe in. I draw upon everything avail-able to me, every ounce of conscience and intuition, and I study him. I feel for the remains of other women—memories of breasts, of legs, of quivering throats in his hands, of swollen lips in his lips, of the smell of them, and the taste. I should be able to feel his memories, the chain that they make. With a man, you feel always a chain, *his* chain; it's not bad, it's part of the law of being male, it's his basis of being. I touch him. I touch the same man I touched the first time I touched him, only now there is no openness, nothing is open. That's because I closed it. And in feeling for them, I find only myself, attached like the deformed skin on a wound.

He looks back, unflinchingly. I don't mind. I don't mind to lose a little grace when by his eyes I possess so much. Surely this night was not without design, surely it will result in the shifting of a pin or the righting of a needle somewhere very far away.

I let go. I step back, not really staggering. Feeling suddenly sober. And the light, the face. Red, white. Red, white.

"You're wrong, Harrison," I say. "I *do* care who wins."

IN THE MORNING MARK rolls off the couch. Immediately he speaks. Everyone says it's good to speak, but frequently those who do are no better off than those who don't.

"*What the fuck was that?*" he says, rubbing his head. The floor pounds when his feet hit. I feel embarrassed. It's embarrassing to have someone outside be angry about events in your life. Teenagers feel embarrassed this way.

I check my watch. Rourke is awake. He's dressed at his apartment. And alone, sitting on the corner of his bed, thinking, not talking. I dreamt of us on a train, on the outside of a train. I dreamt of riding with him on the outside of trains through concrete tunnels. Our hair blowing.

"What a fucking idiot," Mark says. "Showing up like that."

He goes to the kitchen. Despite his hangover, he looks well. He looks fine like an antique as he has begun prematurely to gray; the new pewter tinge suits his doggish capitalist charm. Any woman would be happy to have him. He punctures a can of tomato juice, fills a glass, and drains it until there's just that weedy pinkish sort of film in a rut going around. He peers at me through the framed passage over the hygienic white counter that separates the kitchen from the dining room. The counter is bare. Mark does not allow things on counters. No fruit, no papers, no vases, no dishrack. Dishracks harbor bacte-ria, he says. That's why there are no dishtowels or sponges, only paper towels. In public restrooms he flushes with his elbow and pulls napkins from the dis-penser before he washes his hand. One for turning the faucet, one for drying.

He lays the glass in the sink and wipes his mouth. "Did he *confide* in you? Did he tell you that he doesn't *care* who wins? That he's just doing Rob a *favor*?" He approaches me, coming around, coming slow.

"Don't be stupid, Evie. There is no fight. There's a scam, a fraud, a hustle. It's pre-arranged. Harrison's taking the fall. That's why he came. To prepare you. It's gonna kill him to have you watch him get beaten. But Rob's in too deep with the wrong people. He has to have a guarantee. A loss is the only way he can guarantee the outcome. He asked me for the money, but I told him I can't risk getting involved. Nothing against these guys," he says. "Believe me, I'll do my part. I'll fill the house. But I have a reputation to uphold. I have you to think about. That's why, after this, that's it. We can't walk into our future dragging this shit behind us."

Mark is in front of me; we're face to face. "He's an animal just like his murderer father. Did you know that his father was a murderer? Of course not. Because he's a liar. He lied to you all along." Mark reaches out quickly, but I don't blink my eyes. He slaps his hand around the back of my neck and folds me into his arms. "I feel bad for you, sweetheart, I really do. He lied about everything."

"Yes," I say. "Yes. I see that now."

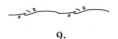

9

THE DAY OF THE FIGHT HE FUCKS ME VERY HARD, LIKE HE KNOWS IT WILL BE the last time. "Shit," Mark says when he is finally done, "you are a sweet taste in the mouth."

THE COUGAR IS DOUBLE-parked outside Astor Place. I toss my bag through the open window onto the front seat.

"You gotta check out this French flick," Rob says, "*Breathless*. There's an American girl with chopped up hair and Jean-Paul Belmondo's cut really tight. Reminds me of the old times. Out in Montauk."

I get in, and we take off. He bounces in his seat as he drives. The night is hot. Rob likes when it's hot. That's because he's a Leo, and Leos are sun kings, and Napoleon was a Leo. On Rob's chest is a new tattoo. Inside the globe of a plankton green sun, it says *Roi de Soleil*. He got it in New Orleans, at Mardi Gras. Mardi Gras tattoos are superior. They bring luck. I switch on the radio.

Cisco Kid was a friend of mine. Cisco Kid was a friend of mine.

The car turns widely, off Houston and onto the Bowery. Outside my window the skies are marbleized blue-black, like out of mythology. Skies like a storm is coming, only no storm is coming. Skies like it's the sixties, like no time has passed since you were a kid. Skies that make you homesick, only there is no home. When we hit Delancey Street, the prostitutes tap the hood of the car. They wave to Rob. *Hey.*

"A case of mistaken identity," he says. "I mean it, baby, I swear."

ROB'S SISTER CHRISTINE SAYS, "Everybody in the pool, and if you don't get into your suit, I'm gonna have you thrown in like that." Christine works the watch counter at Bloomingdales. If you want a watch, go to her. "I'm giving you five minutes, Evie," she warns. "A grace period. Then I'm coming to find you."

The Cirillo house has three doors, one on the porch, one in the middle of the driveway, one in back. The first time I went there, I made the mistake of heading for the front door. "What are you," Rob asked, "the mailman? The last people to go in that way were relatives from Italy." *It-lee.*

The back door by the barbecue leads to the kitchen, which is full of aunts and grandmothers and elderly female neighbors. You can see the ladies through the screen, briefly making contact, like flies against a window. Arms to the elbows appear to hand off trays of peppers and sausages to fry. Stockinged knees prop the door, modest beige lace-up shoes touch down on the red brick step.

Mrs. Cirillo works the grill. "In most families, Eveline," Carmen explains as she flinches into the corrugated charcoal smog to flip a rack of ribs, "this is man's work. But, what happens is, Dom gets to talking and everything burns."

"I'll do it, Ma." Rob grabs at the tongs. "C'mon."

"No, Robert," she says, "you enjoy your company."

I sneak past Christine and go down the driveway, which is wall-to-wall folding tables and chairs beneath criss-crossing strings of tiki lanterns. I enter the house by the side door and go by the living room, where Rob's mother's parents stay in air conditioning and watch golf. Actually it's not the living room. The living room is one room up toward the street, but the living room is dark, dark because it's clean, dark because no one's allowed inside. The room that is used for a living room is only just a bin at the bottom of the stairs, an emptied-out foyer with a television.

Mr. and Mrs. Falconetti pick chicken parmesan off paper plates on TV trays with decrepit hands like mini garden rakes. Mrs. Falconetti is four-foot two with a brushed-back gorilla helmet of blue hair. Everyone is scared of her. Rob says it's because she dresses nice. Whenever she goes out, even in summer, she wears a Burberry's overcoat. Mr. Falconetti is skinny with suspenders and the quakes from Parkinson's. He used to be known as *The Hawk*, back when he was a mob look-out at Idlewild; now he's blind from glaucoma.

"He could have had operations," Rob once explained, "but he didn't want the guys finding out he had such bad eyesight. He never once wore his glasses outside the house. Actually, he never *could* see very well, he just got pegged because of the name. And of course, the nose. Poor bastard."

The Hawk blinks innocently when I kiss him hello, and his wife nods, giving her cheek. With old people, you get the feeling they're present but not present. That's because they've seen a lot, and what they've seen leaves little room for you.

WHEN I CLOSE THE door to the master bedroom, I have to push hard against the carpet shag. There's a plaque hanging by the double-wide dresser. *A mother's heart is miles wide, it helps us when we hurt inside.*

I change into my bathing suit by the window, where the smoke from the barbecue sucks in through eyelet curtains from Sears. Christine has everyone running in the water. From high up, the whirlpool is like an inverted chocolate kiss. Rob's father leans wearily on the upright white pool frame, spraying non-comers randomly with the hose.

"Christine's the ambassador of the pool," Mr. Cirillo calls out. "I'm the artillery."

In the corner of the yard, Joey hovers custodially over his wife, Anna, who sits sideways on a lounge chair feeding the kids. He removes his shirt and approaches the ladder with Charlie. Joey's chest is hard, but his waist is square. Everybody pretends that Rob is no good and Joey is the family man, but Joey's the one they worry about. Rob's lawlessness has a complementary decency, but Joey's righteousness is forced, like he's bored of it, like any day he's gonna snap. There's another brother, in L.A., Anthony, very good-looking. No one mentions Anthony, there are no pictures—except one in Rob's wallet.

"C'mon, Charlie," Joey says, adjusting the band of his shorts, "let's go swamp Aunt Chrissie."

Directly beneath the bedroom window is the back porch and the keg, and Rob filling pitchers. I lean my forehead on the screen to see the long flat plane of his body.

Christine splashes at him. "*Rooooooberrrrt. Get ova here.*" He steps to the side so the water can't reach, casually, not even looking, like he knows the exact measurement from the pool to the keg.

"Forget about it," Joey taunts as he climbs the ladder behind Charlie. "He won't let Evie see him naked."

"Robert hates to get wet," Mrs. Cirillo chides. "He's like a cat."

"In my day a kid never passed up water," Mr. Cirillo remarks. "It's not natural, saying no to water."

"What do I want to get cold for?" Rob says. "It's been a long winter. I'm just starting to heat up again."

I JOIN THE TANGLE of bodies and strollers and pocketbooks in the second blue of night. Second because second follows first and first has already passed. First blue is where the airplanes fly; second drops like a net and surrounds you.

Rob and Joey and Christine's Dominican boyfriend Ray Peña are passing out clear keg cups high to the brim with piña coladas decorated with umbrellas and naked ladies. The plan is to get people in the betting mood.

"Basically, big bets are down," Rob explained on the car ride over, "but ringside is critical. You can rake it in ringside."

Lorraine is there in the driveway with a bunch of girls, cousins probably. Everyone's a cousin. Everyone's either a cousin or they work in the meat or the fish market. All you hear is, *eat the fish—it's fresh*; *eat the beef—it's fresh*. Lorraine lights a cigarette on one of those mosquito coils, and the live ash reddens her French tip manicure. I haven't seen her in a long time. Her hair is straight and she's skinny. She's wearing a sleeveless white blouse and a straight black skirt.

"Lorraine looks pretty," I tell Joey and Ray.

"She's on her way," Joey says. "Chris DeMarco got her a job at the Newark D.A.'s office as a receptionist. Next thing you know, she enrolls at Fordham for law. Now she wears pinstripes," he adds, "even on weekends."

Rob comes over. "Who you guys talking about? *Ironside?*"

I SAY HEY LORRAINE.

"Hey ya, Evie." She kisses me. I kiss her too. "How ya doin'?"

"You look pretty," I say. "Your hair and everything."

"Thanks. Yours too," she says, taking a look around at the back. Touching it. "Jeez, you really went ahead and chopped it off this time. It's almost as short as when we met."

"Yeah, well. Summer's coming."

"I can't believe it. Summer already."

"I hear you're going to Fordham. That's great."

"Yeah," she smiles. "The Upper West Side campus. By your apartment—Mark's, whatever. I saw you one time, you were on the other side of the street. With Mark's sister."

"You should have stopped me."

"I didn't want to bother you. You had a lot of bags."

"It wouldn't have been a bother."

"Next time," she says, and she nods.

"Yeah," I say. "Next time."

"Mark's here?" She looks around. "I didn't see him."

I look around too. "Not yet, I guess."

"He's coming here, or there?"

"Here I think. Or there. Either here or there."

"Big night tonight," she says, turning to face me.

"Yeah, I guess it is."

"You ever seen him fight?"

I shake my head.

"You sit with me. Just in case." Lorraine looks down at her table. "Hey, did you ever meet any of these guys?" she asks. "This is Anne, Kathy, Allegra, Donna—Donna's my cousin. This is Evie," Lorraine tells them. "A friend of Robbie's. A friend of mine."

AT NINE, EVERYBODY MAKES their way to the street, drifting in twos and threes. Nobody gets into cars, they just get ready to get into cars, sitting on hoods, cleaning out glove compartments. Rob pops open the doors to the Cougar and puts in an eight track.

> *My cherie amour, lovely as a summer day,*
> *My cherie amour, distant as the milky way.*

Christine and Ray Peña start dancing in the street, and everyone starts dancing, even Mr. and Mrs. Cirillo. Christine is happy, always happy. She dances, and her body and pool-damp hair swing professionally, like she's under contract to cheer, and all the kids come to watch. They sit on the curb or they take a break from bike-riding, leaning on one leg, mouths relaxed. In the neighborhood, Christine is the one to emulate. She is so defiant in her content, so very outward about having accepted the small circumstances of her small life. And, as with a priest who has actually done some living, there is an element of danger to her decidedly limited aspirations that makes her behavior poetic and especially worth the watch.

Rob takes my arm and draws me close. And we dance too. It's good to dance on the streets in summer, the narrowness and the expanse, the contraposition of your diminutive indigence against the flourish of architecture and the aggregate of humanity, the alliance of your indisputable nothingness with the equally indisputable enormity of existence. The late-blush of the asphalt, the heat bleeding up through your thin shoes.

> *You're the only girl my heart beats for,*
> *How I wish that you were mine.*

Three cars slither up the street in a lights-on procession, and the dancing ends. There is a conversion back to the sweeping contagion of real time—people breaking apart, fixing clothes and hair. Rob's mother steps to the darkened rear window of the first car.

"Late as usual, Tudi. Everything's ice cold."

Uncle Tudi creaks out to kiss her, and over her shoulder, through the inky rounds of his jumbo sunglasses, he eyes me in Rob's arms. His hair is perfect.

He says to Rob, "You ready to head out?"

Rob says, "Yeah, I'm ready. You ready?"

"Yeah, I'm ready, I *been* ready."

"What do you mean you've *been* ready?" Rob releases me. "*I've* been waiting for *you*."

"You wanna stand around and discuss technicalities?"

"Shit no. Let's go."

"All right, then let's go."

AND THEN, ALTHOUGH THE next belongs to the last, the next also belongs to what was to come. What I felt at that moment was a start, an ignition, a disembarkment or a transference of time.

Rob discharges me to Lorraine, who is behind, calling my name. Like the name of a child through an open window—*Eveline*. Ray Peña's powder blue Lincoln pulls up readily, like it's been idling nearby the whole time, and Rob and Joey get in, skirting fast, kind of getting vacuumed down or going fast-motion in reverse. They take off, and when they make a right at the end of the street, I see Rob's forearm hanging out, striking against the door frame. It has a warlike and antagonistic look, a belonging-only-to-him look. It's not usual for him to reveal himself—plotting, scheming, masterminding.

Another car, another ride, this one silent and unscenic, and slow. If there is scenery, it is just a place for my eyes to lie. If there is talk, it is the vacant talk of girls who know. I arrive with Christine and Lorraine at an auditorium somewhere on the Jersey shore. I know it's the shore. I smell the sea. It's a broad blue building with a grand and tame face like the grand tame face of a former picture palace. We drive past twice, looking for a place to park.

"Shit," Lorraine says. "We should have come with your father."

"No way," Christine replies. "He's drunk."

A ticket kiosk in the center of the clamshelled entrance is filled with framed memorabilia from the fifties and sixties of performers like Sammy Kaye at Point Pleasant and Fred Waring in Ocean Grove, and alongside that there is a vintage *Drink Coca-Cola* sign and a Pokerarcade mini-marquee and a poster on a column behind a drilled acrylic panel.

> *For Lease.*
> *Cultural and Religious Events.*
> *John Robin at PhilCo. Mgmt. 201-788-3—*

The last three characters of John Robin's phone number have been scratched off. Someone used a hanger to get underneath the plexiglas. I wonder about John Robin, his adversaries, his offenses. Perhaps he is dead. The sign gives no indication of aliveness. The ink is livid and the paper brittle, and in the whole vicinity of the sign there is mellow wisdom, a knowledge of dead things and dead times, like music in the air. I hear the refrain of nights with distant dates printed on matchbooks and menus.

As Christine pauses to apply lipstick the crisp clip of our steps runs unevenly down. The look of us and of other people coming is immodest and anarchical, oblivious and opportunistic and everywhere at once, like rats shooting through dumpsters. Lorraine winds her new watch. "It's perfect for court," she says. "Thanks, Christine."

"You'll knock 'em dead, Rainy," Christine says, smacking her lips. They are tangerine now, the burgundy tangerine undercolor of orangutans. It amazes me how like Rob she is. Her blunt insensibility is somehow forward-reaching, somehow mature. While I linger on the sill of adaptation, watching and waiting, she is already over and on the other side. She pats my waist. "Don't look so glum. It'll be over before you know it."

Though the once-spacious lobby has been divided, it retains its original height. The high sides of the room's outer walls are still plastered in panels of milk-white wallpaper with a green garden trellis pattern, as if the initial intention was to convey to visitors the idea of listening to music in the conservatory of a fine house. We follow the buckled avenue to the main arena, and the cruel smell of spilled stuff muscles up from carpet to ceiling, filling the lobby like a captive carnivore. At the end, there is a set of doors—no, two sets of double doors. I peer into a mirage of men, hundreds of backs and heads, wavering and ghosted, paraffin apparitions, like skyscrapers half-melting. Past the crowd there is a glow, which is the stadium glow of the preliminary fight. This is the first thing I notice, the location of the glow, which is the location of the ring. The second is that inside is not sloped but level. The third is that the empty balconies are like an old horseshoe made of moon-wax and animal cartilage and beneath them, skirting the walls, are aluminum stands.

The girls cut in through the right. I follow.

Mark is in the center, surrounded by a crowd. Everyone he knows is there—Richard, Brett, Swoosey, Aaron, Marguerite and Alan Hoodless, Miles and Paige, Jonathan and Alicia, cousins and co-workers and guys from the pit whom I've never met. I can tell they are guys from the pit by the pens in their pockets. I get passed through, stepping down from behind. He pulls me from Lorraine; I lose her sleeve.

"Sorry I couldn't make it to the Cirillo's," Mark says, helping me, kissing me. "I was leading the convoy. Twelve cars!"

He passes me to Jonathan and Alicia. Alicia takes my hand, squeezing tightly. Lorraine is about ten feet away now. She smiles as if to say, *Sorry, but what am I gonna do?* She shouldn't feel sorry. I'm used to it. Everyone does what Mark says, no matter what they promise. Everyone believes in the supremacy of money.

The ring is empty now. Like a lunar plane, a space designated for a landing. To prepare myself, I think back to all the times I've seen Rourke at center—a field, a gymnasium, a theater, a classroom, any and every space. I remind myself that nothing I have lived or seen has been random. That I've been made ready.

THERE IS A WAY they tell you to draw trees. A tree should not be a blot on the landscape, divested of obliquity. A tree should express contour, core and *crevasse*. A tree should lift off the paper.

To render contour, you must draw back and draw forward and draw down. To render core, envision center. Center is not the dead point between two edges or the geographic intermediary of what you happen to see but the soul of *O*, the heart of vastness, the umbilicus, the penetralia, the embryonic fleck that encodes the basic order of the nature of a thing, the fixed innerness from which unfixed outerness originates. To render *crevasse*, seek the tree's fortune. Travel in your mind. Conceive of the tree wholly. In every tree there is a carnival of direction—perpendicularity and pendancy, acclivity and transverseness, convexity, and indentation. The tree moves with a spectacular equivalency of energy. It rises with grandeur when it meets with no obstacle; it skews with intent to prevail against adversity; it thickens incrementally, gaining girth with years; it bears down into the floor of the earth with its talons. Like a child, it bruises back in response to cruel occlusion. Like a saint, it drives to the light.

In every tree there is flesh, a system of softness beneath the armature, a velvet refuge, a whisper-sweet sanctuary where potential is stored. There are leaves like weeping icicles and branches like venous chandeliers; there is virid chroma and lurid hue. These are indicators of underside. Underside because often what the eyes cannot see, they will not see. Underside because there is truth and beauty in that, in what is rejected by sight. Underside because in every king there is a boy.

ANTONIO VARGAS HAS GYPSY skin and black hair tied back in rows. He looks like the kind of guy who is good to kids and aging relatives and to the girls who love him. As it turned out, Tommy Lydell backed out at the last minute. When Mark got the call he kicked the coffee table and broke it. After Mark heard Vargas's stats—twenty-two years-old, one-hundred ninety pounds, six-foot even, 25-3 with 20 KO's, and a lefty—he felt good enough to kneel down and check the damage. The leg split, so he had Manny take it to the basement.

"You want me to glue it?" Manny asked, leaning at the door with the table. It looked like he was holding a dead labrador against his chest, legs out. "I have *the clamp!*"

"Throw it out," Mark said. "I'll buy a new one."

Rourke is double-jabbing, steering Vargas backwards around the ring with ambling, edgy grace, his feet hardly touching the canvas. He fights easily, like it's nothing, like he's content, and in a way complete. I don't get the feeling I often get from seeing him in public, there but not there, transcendent to his own performance, his performance transcendent to his reality. There are no messages to me. Usually there are messages. From the first bell, when he walked out to center, he looked at Vargas, lifted his hands, and began to fight. Vargas seemed caught by surprise, by the lack of formality, and I recognized that. I know what it is to be completely unprepared for a being so honest, so instinctive, for behavior so unmitigated by foregoing ideas. I know what it is to face him that way, when it is just you he sees.

In the third round, Rourke gives Vargas a sickening combination—a right to the jaw, followed by a smooth uppercut left, also to the jaw, then a clean right to the indent in the face between nose and cheekbone, and there is shouting, in a roar, like a train popping from a tunnel. And then a bell. And a retreat, to the corners. I keep my eyes on Vargas, watching in spite of the blood. His nose sheds an amber stream from one nostril. The mouth guard gets slipped out, and water goes down his face from the corner man squeezing a sponge. Ice goes on the cheek and the cut man checks the eyes. His head tilts back and people talk to him, giving coarse encouragement.

Rob appears on Vargas's side, about ten feet back from the corner, talking to Vargas's brother. I think it is the brother, by the resemblance. Rob's face floats mat level opposite from where we stand; his hair curls from sweat around his eyes. I suppose it doesn't matter where Rob stands. The men in the ring are the same. Mr. Xinwu spoke of respect between adversaries, and Rourke spoke of *evenness of match*. I feel no animosity toward Vargas. What I feel primarily, is curiosity. His heart, his mind. The bed he sleeps in, the layout of his kitchen. Does his bathroom have white tile; who talks to him through the door? I have the feeling people talk to him through doors, that, like me, he is never alone. No one talks to Rourke that way. Vargas's ice pack falls and hits the edge of the ring, going down, landing most likely on someone's foot and getting kicked beneath for a porter in navy coveralls to sweep up later when the room is empty—still panting, still ringing, the ghosts of us, still here.

Seconds remain. People pull back. Vargas is joined by his brother, who hangs down, one arm linked to the cornerpost. As he speaks to Antonio, both look ahead at Rourke, like viewing a horizon, like speaking of things they see only in the mind. Is Rourke watching; does he see; I hope he sees. I don't look;

I won't look in his corner. Nothing could keep me from going there. The whole room could not keep me from going there.

"Two grand," Swoosey says to Mark, "for every round Harrison lasts after this one."

Mark keeps his eye on Vargas and his brother, and over my head he and Swoosey shake. Not really shake so much as touch hands. "*Four* grand that he won't last this one."

A bell rings. I don't know which—the fifth, the fourth. Vargas shoots over like a junkyard dog. There is a roar of approval as he crosses into Rourke's vicinity. With his right arm and his body, he keeps Rourke in a limited region as his left fist makes contact. Rourke's abdomen, Rourke's face. Vargas goes at him, over and over, five times, ten times, and the swings are not painless; I have to tell myself that they only *look* that way because of the shortness of the thrust. I would like to believe they are painless. Rourke sucks back the force of each shock, trembling thickly like a gong, withstanding and absorbing and losing footing only slightly because he has *root*. I think back to Montauk, to the stoic self-sacrifice, to the almost ghastly oneness, to the tiny preparations required for such a massive exertion. It is awful to see him hit but worse to see him step so expertly into pain, as though returning to his body all the cruelty he fears he has inflicted. When Rourke's right eye turns hard with blood, the blood inside is real, gathered together like sheep, though blood does not come in flocks; that is just how I think of it, as lost and stray.

I let go, admitting only color. The brown lines in his body, the brown lines in the ring, and in the room beyond the ring, the brown sea, the folds, the peaks. There is a warming when my eyes pass over each fighter, a port-wine staining of his silhouette, like a character manifesting out of paint as your eyes cross a canvas, like a painted aura, an energy caught. A creeping dryness, a slow streaking wetness, and a fear, my fear, a fear they will turn permanent.

He can't see. He has to dodge blind. On the next hit, his head knocks back as if following the trail of a jet. For a moment, the long grace of his neck is exposed before the weight of his head rolls back around onto his chest, like a swan getting shot. The back of Antonio Vargas is there, and the referee is there, giving him a standing count. They are all waiting for him to fall, all waiting, all to fall. Vargas trots triumphantly, his people yell, *Ton-y, Ton-y, Ton-io*. If anyone is calling to Rourke he doesn't hear—I don't think he *can* hear—and yet he is standing, he is standing, and though it does not surprise me that he will not go down, I do wonder who it is that he is fighting.

The next moment is impacted. I have the sense of multiple endpoints, of time spilling over like water to define adjoining and previously hidden places. I see Rourke testing those places, *preparing* to test them. The stiff hull of his skin and muscles, superficially hard but on the inside fractured, and through that cleft, the organs being touched by the swirling crossfire of life, and opening more and opening further, opening to all the pain he has incorporated, him allowing himself to feel, which hurts me worse than his blood and blindness.

I gaze without wincing. I see the shame of his emotional exposure, the way he tried to hide. I see the rupture with his mother. The inability to protect and to be protected. I see his father missing. I see his reluctance to claim a space to which he felt by nature disentitled. I see down, all the way down, down into the mat—it's like a well—and I think how good it must feel to go back, to return to the place he was left alone, the place he was marked. I know the feeling. I often go back. To the day, the hour, the minute of losing him.

NO ONE SEES ME. No one sees me retreat to the far reaches of the auditorium. He does not see, though I think he knows, because truly, I tell him. I look back once more, into the ring and into the room, which have breathed out and flattened out into something falsely benevolent, deceptively cool. To my eyes, level, all level, but for him.

He comes off the ropes on the deep left. He seems to stand in glowing water. He tries to right himself. He rises then tips, and his gloved hands jerk toward his ears. I don't know why his hands would move that way. Maybe because of the shouting. Maybe some late and involuntary reaction in defense of his head.

The referee holds one hand back, keeping Vargas in check. Rourke's arms fall halfway down, stopping to float at his waist, and he staggers forward. One step, two steps, walking until every eye in the house is on him. He arrives at center, occupying it despite his confusion. I swear, the ring hangs from his feet. He turns at an angle to face Vargas, as if to say to some acquaintance on the street, *Oh, and by the way*, and out of nowhere, Rourke hauls his right arm back and cracks Vargas across the jaw. Vargas flies, completely stunned. Rourke takes the moment and moves in, starting on the body. Clear and sure. Over and over, a machine.

The last thing is light, a spilling visionary light, summital and white, from where it comes I don't know, possibly my imagination. It is high like the light of great painted battlefields, in which there is no architecture, just the edifice of the body. The light spawns globes about the heads of the fighters like the pre-Renaissance halos of Giotto's saints, like these are men of sacrifice, like they are martyrs, though in fact there is nothing operatic or epic about them. Each is one, each is us. *Us* because we all begin with dreams but end with nothing, nothing more than what we, in our humility, can make of ourselves. And constantly, getting hit. You can tell they are not heroes by the inversion—the light of the ring does not encroach on blackness, the blackness comes upon the ring like a tide, the audience eats away at the stage. I see the black box converging on the white box and, in the middle, men's bodies dancing, and all across, a chasteness of line, a severity of chiaroscuro.

And voices, a hot sea, chaos rising. *Rourke, Rourke, Harri-son, Harri-son.* Voices that make him try. I never made him try.

EIGHT

RIVER

Farewell. You are too dear for the possessing.
—William Shakespeare

Try always, whenever you look at a form, to see the lines in it which
have had power over its past fate and will have power over its futurity.
Those are its awful lines; see that you seize on those, whatever else you miss.
—John Ruskin

JUNE 1984

I.

I'M HOLDING SOMEONE AT THE STATION. IT'S KATE; HER HAIR IS LOOSELY BRAIDED. *I feel the rope of her hair and my hand tucking back strands. Beneath my forearms lie the bones of her back. Her reflection in the soft rectangular windows of the train is melodious, wan; she melts like fire into glass.*

And the station is steady. Through the soles of my feet I feel a heartbeat. This is not ground, I think, this is a beast. My God, the entire time, on the back of a beast. Da dum da dum. In my temples comes the beating.

Hurry, I tell myself, hurry.

I want to run, so I run, and meeting a fence, I climb. The balls of my feet cram into the links, up and up. At the top I leap, I fly. Landing in a trench on the other side, I see sky, everywhere sky, a January morning sky. A stranger hands me a cushion. The word "eulogy" is thickly embroidered.

I'm wet, and the sun is shining. And night comes. Blackish clouds surround the windows of my high school, like the whole world is burning. Oh, I see a classroom. I see desks inside with cards for late-comers. I take my place.

In a castle the air cascades, whipping here and there, perching like darling clusters, like icing roses, and a glorious brume of light seeps through undulating drapes. The curtains go like pinions or fins, platinum white and fine as mantis wings—they move and seem to sing.

We sit in our window seat, receiving them; there are so many. Rourke answers questions, and his voice is tired. I am also tired, though my mind is clear—he is all there is. I sit poised, still as a china doll, pulling straight pins from my wedding gown. And I listen—new ticking—life again.

I GO FIRST TO the mimosa. It does not appear to have grown, and yet it has, which is the remarkable thing about trees. They are secretive about growth. My mother is next—her face in the daylight, how I know it, the fit of her eyes and the color. Like a picture I looked at every day in captivity. We embrace, and I cry, and the tears are a certain type of tears, not of grieving or penitence, but of temperance and of gravity. Each tear is a special tear, a gem or jewel released in a squeeze from the fist of an empress. Each is principal in form because my body is of her body, and the tears I shed express that knowledge.

She is cleaning. In her hand is a spray bottle, also a towel. Tomorrow there will be a party. In the yard, a birthday, a teacher friend from the college, Jann, formerly Jan when he was a she—did I remember Jan, I must remember.

"I do remember. She wore half-glasses."

"Bifocals."

"Exactly, yes, bifocals."

My mother rubs the film from the tabletops—there are all these tables but no chairs—and she tells stories. She is not insensitive, she simply talks around my feelings for my sake. Possibly she has always talked around my feelings for my sake. It occurs to me that I am difficult, that I have always been difficult, especially for her, as we are so very unlike. Possibly she gave more than I knew. Possibly she was kind to love me and to have faith. *Goodnight my Eveline,* she used to say, didn't she used to say that? Didn't she used to smell like lilacs? For some reason I can't recall the words she spoke at bedtime or the way she smelled, like lilacs or not like lilacs.

I give her a kiss. She blushes. She returns to the tables, setting down candles, the kind with plastic nets. I lift one, smelling it. It smells of citronella, of Jack. "There's mail for you in the barn," she says, very quietly. "When you're ready. I put it in a basket and tied it with a pretty blue ribbon."

NEXT DAY I OPEN a box. Boxes, actually. In the barn there are several. I cannot say exactly what it is I am searching for, but where I stop is at a stack of journals, and what I find inside is an account of my past so vivid it is like looking into a narrow tube. It's strange to come upon yourself at the genesis of your own path, when everything was beautiful and new, but then the beautiful newness is gone.

I wonder what it is to age. Aging has less to do with numbers than with shutting down to possibility. It has to do with getting selective about pleasure because you no longer trust life to bestow it at random. It happens when you will not wait for fortune. Aging is hate. Isn't it hate when we refuse to proceed without the protection of position? When we hide behind the singleness of our perspective, rejecting what we know, repudiating what we might become. When we look into another's eyes but refuse to see the story there.

Aging is also hobbies. Once Lowie raised money for the I.R.A., now she collects thimbles. Tony Abruscatto went from being a Division One hurdler to someone obsessed with parking tickets. Tony will run out of a restaurant, leaping over hydrants and trash to put change into a stranger's expired meter if he sees a cop coming up the street. Mark will not tolerate mismatching glassware. If a single glass chips but cannot easily be replaced, he will wrap the eleven leftovers and give them to the superintendent.

"Pretty soon I'm gonna have to buy one of them *breakerfronts*," Manny will say, bagful in hand.

The bluestone at the base of the barn steps is washed in sunlight. The warmth rushes into my bare feet as if from a reversed fall or fountain. It's an old warmth, a same warmth. I remember it as if I never left. To my right is the bed of wildflowers I planted, tangled at the base like siblings sleeping. Shooting first through the thicket is a bone-like cluster of rose vervain that Marilyn and I planted one day when she and Dad visited. We stopped at Miss Amelia's Cottage in Amagansett for an antique fair, and Marilyn bought a starter tray of vervain and two Chinese loveseats that I'd admired. Dad said the seats were probably made in Pittsburgh, but I thought they had belonged to imperial Chinese children. I could see the children sitting, upright and attentive, listening to a tutor, their slippered feet dangling. When Marilyn took them to be re-covered on Grand Street, the upholsterer offered to buy them from her for $1,500. She refused, though they'd cost only $200.

My father said, "We could've bought a new car!"

"They belong to Evie," Marilyn told him, emphatically. "We never would have seen their value."

I go farther into grass, south toward the driveway, beyond which lie the train tracks. There is this sensation, long lost to me, of leaving the house, of staring into sky, this very sky, with nothing before and nothing behind. There was no better place to be than the place I was, despite the little I knew and the little I had.

What I miss, what I possessed, is *immunity*. If modern life can be seen as something high-speed and pathogenic—that is to say, replicating and duplicating and by necessity unoriginal—then childhood by comparison is a period of blessed insusceptibility. Maybe the loss of innocence is part of some practical operation. Maybe there are lessons in its fleeting frailty. Possibly through such sacrifice we remain captivated, bound to the safekeeping of joy when we come upon it. I comb through the flower stems, wondering, am I lost, or do I remain—am I perennial? Have I aged, have I stopped becoming, or do I just prepare?

There are pilgrims who walk and walk, through years and through nations, seeking answers to questions they don't know how to formulate. Is it possible for me to go back to believing in something that I've never seen?

I WALK AT NIGHT in East Hampton. The world tips and turns. I walk a walk of the dead, thinking dead thoughts. Skateboards and scarecrows, tipping cows in Schwenk's field and spitting contests outside Windmill Deli. Tall twilights in November, sitting with everybody on the concrete steps of the

VFW, kicking home through broad shawls of chestnut leaves green with crispy borders, like melting stars or witches' shoes. The circus star antics of boys—flagpole climbing and three to a bike. The heat of the hood of a car in summer, the cupped pop of softballs. Roast beef sandwiches with melted mozzarella from Bucket's deli and vanilla cream sodas and the way you can peel the frosting off a Hostess cupcake, that flatworm ribbon of white down the center. Snoopy cards from Marley's and square wrapping paper packs for the birthday earrings we'd buy each other at Whitmore Gallery. And the train, and the bus, the city people stumbling through the doors on a Friday, weary but ready. I don't know whether or not this is home—whether or not it would have me, whether or not I would be had by it. I know only that I reached a plateau on these streets, some dead end of understanding.

I call my mother from the payphone near White's. A stranger answers. His Manchester accent is swarthy. *Hello?* In back there are the sounds of a party. The one for Jann. I ask for Irene.

"Hang on," he says. There is a portly plastic clunk as the receiver drops. I hear him shout, "Get down and give us twenty!" Then raucous laughter, then unanimous counting. *One, two, thirteen, fifteen, twenty!*

Cheers and more shouting and more counting and the party again, and when no one retrieves the phone, I hang up. The heels of my socks are damp from popped blisters, so I sit on the back step of the pharmacy, tearing away the dead skin. Something blue to consider is the memory of my father flexing the backs of my new school shoes to soften them, bending the patent leather until it became pliable, surely that is a type of love.

BY THE TIME I return to my mother's house, no one remains. A note for me is on the banister. *Went to the Sea Wolf. Meet us there!*

As always when she leaves, she leaves the house unbearably free of her presence. Darkness is broken by the weak-wicked mustard glint of a kerosene lamp, and the room possesses a dubious stillness, as if it has been recently and rapidly evacuated. Glasses are half-full, pillows and sweaters lie about, burning candles lose their sidewalls, weeping down wet with wax, and albums are queued up on the spindle. The sound of Joan Baez seeps through the smog of wine-soaked chicken. I stand in the hallway. I don't feel like going out, but I don't feel like going to bed either. I'm not hungry, and there is no television. I don't want to go into Kate's old room. I don't want to go into my old room. The whole thing feels dangerous, just being there. Going back home is like re-entering a burning building. You evaluate the necessity. You map out a safe course. You decide to go sequentially and in reverse, one room at a time so you don't lose your way—it would be so easy to get lost in there. You wish you had another choice; you do not. There is something you must rescue.

My feet stick as I walk. It must have been a good party. If it is a good party, you cannot walk afterwards without sticking to the floors. *Ha ha,* my father once said on a New Year's visit, *I lost a shoe there in front of the stove.*

I tour the somnolent blue living room, feeling tranquil, feeling numb, in an elegiac sort of trance. Beneath the uppermost stratum of liquor and cigarettes is another fold that is flatter and less fetid. The lower odor is ingrained, like the abiding cabbagey funk of cooked dinners that stretches like nylon across entire floors of New York City apartment buildings. It is confirmation of former days, of lost times. You can read it like reading geologic plates, like searching for fallen cities. The legion of her belongings forms an evidentiary matrix—there are traces in the laminate, faces and voices and artifacts of the heart—reduced down like to salts and minerals, proving presence and endurance of presence. Naturally, that is to say, her own.

And yet, among her possessions there is a love. Like a vessel through granite it channels around the house, aberrant and sheet-like, frozen-in, flattened like a tissue sea. It is a scenic love, a beholdable love, a love that will not reveal the sad origins of its story. I think of myself as a child, small with straight brown hair brushing by my green eyes, waiting stubbornly among these very things for something to appear or to transpire that could not and could never. I come upon the archaeology of my need with delicacy. One must confront one's innocence with caution when it has gotten you nowhere, when it has proven itself fallible, when no more remains, when you discover that you have outspent the purity of your heart.

It is not an easy memory—me, awaiting requital or redress, hoping for someone to take responsibility for loneliness that was my own. I remind myself that, as a child, I endured no more than mild disequilibrium, nothing perilous or vile, that I was loved in a sense, and cared for, and so on, and et cetera, and, just as instantly, I acknowledge that I am brushing off as usual the accountability of my parents, absolving them of inattentiveness because it was benign. I assume responsibility because I am capable. Capable is what I was made to be.

For the first time I recognize something dangerously polemical about this assessment. When I tell myself that it is irrelevant whether love is professed, that what matters is not something public but something desperate and original, which part of me is speaking—the part at peace with my own competence or the part that detests it, the part that longs to be swept away? Am I in pursuit of emotional detachment because I prefer it or because it is what I have known? How curious to have achieved at last the defining sort of love for which I've always longed, something reciprocal that moves the spirit and bears time, and to have lost it. How resourceful to turn a story of achievement into a more familiar one of loss. Such loss is a form of control. It's so much safer to lose outright than to allow something to run its course. It's so much easier to exist on the inside. Have I been working all along to secure my own failure, to collapse the machine that was made of me?

I go back around, one final time. I do not touch the things my mother has chosen to keep; they are not mine. If ever I resented their jurisdiction, that, as a feeling, is very old. Her belongings are without rigor now, without geometry and poise, they simply form the backdrop to my encounter with my mother. If it is painfully evident that I am not present here, that there is no shrine to me, pain is not what I feel. What I feel is close to her, uniquely, as though I move from behind to make her acquaintance, growing taller every step. I feel grave with an understanding of her that is new.

I move to the picture window. I remember when nights were starlit but black. I remember expectation and clear, clear air and footsteps and the fever of his voice. I loved him, I love him, from the very beginning I loved him. I cannot understand how it happened, how it turned to this, when the view is the same view, when the tree does not appear to have grown, when her face is the same face, when once I was a girl.

MMMHM, HUMMING. THE PRESSURE drops and tightness falls from my face, gradually lifting like layers peeling. When the bicycle goes slow, the clicking slows to a sharp staccato. I open and close my mouth, saying *click*, *click*, over and over again, *click*—my tongue tapping against the back of my top teeth and dropping into a pillow of breath. When I want to stop saying it, I can't; it's like a song stuck in my head.

Herrick Playground dangles as if by magic in the redolent air, like a tin marionette against a sheet of whalish, olivine gray. It reminds me of the abandoned World's Fair site off the Long Island Expressway in Queens, only not so sordid. My parents brought me to that Fair in 1964. I remember running through the grass into my mother's outstretched arms. And my father, smiling behind her. And our three figures, pebble-like in the wake of the colossal globe. Besides a brief memory of walking with them beneath a movie marquee in winter, of me with my head against my father's shoulder and the soft bounce of my mother's head alongside, that is all I have of them, the three of us together, my family.

The bike pops onto the curb. It tumbles solid as a billiard ball across the swells in a path that cuts like a fault line through the grass. On the bench near the bike rack is an elderly black man in a baseball cap. In his mouth is an unlit cigar. I wonder what he takes when he leaves the house, probably just the cigar and the hat, maybe a five-dollar bill, some matches.

By the sun, it is nine. Six hours to go.

A young couple in khakis and Lacoste shirts with upturned collars and loafers with inward-sloping soles read the papers while their two children gyrate on the rubber tire swings. I wonder if they have all they ever wished for—it must be nice to have all you ever wished for, if that's even possible. It might be that every time you get one thing you want, another wish pops up automatically, like in that hand-stacking game. Not only do they have matching clothes and haircuts, but they also share height. I do not remember mothers and fathers matching so well previously. Somehow it is a sign of the times. Rourke and I would not have been good at matching. That's probably why we failed and why I was disgraced. It is disgraceful to have failed where lesser people have triumphed. On my womb is a reminder of my insufficiency, an imprint, forever impressed, like a cave painting, like a running horse etched 10,000 years ago.

Sometimes Mark says, "What's wrong?"

I tell him that my uterus aches.

"Still?" he asks. "Is that possible?"

The swings are free. I take one, tucking the chains inside my elbows. My chest slumps down, my shirt bellows out, and the heels of my feet make quarter moons in the dirt, fine arcs like eyes. When I was little I drew a field filled with swing sets on manila nursery paper—pairs and pairs of inverted *V*'s connected at the top by horizontal lines, very big and very small, small implying distance. I must have been four. It is strange to think why I did that, why I would have been experimenting at such an early age with perspective.

"You felt friendless," Jack once explained. "Friendless when you drew it and friendless into the future, as far into the future as your miniature mind could calculate. And it doesn't just represent a fear of future friendlessness— look at the clarity of those lines—it represents determination. *Sensational!*"

I gave the drawing to him. He and Dad framed it, then he hung it near the porthole window across from his bed so it would be the first thing he saw in the mornings. Mornings were hard for Jack.

Cars on the street scissor past the park, low and lateral with menacing ease, with vacant regularity, with bodies inside that are busy on the way to someplace. Everyone is busy on the way to someplace—that is why there is no time. If there were time, everyone would know why all the prettiest and the saddest things are called *blue*. In blue skies and blue music, blue is a sort of opposite.

The slide is across from me. It swells and recedes as I swing. Slides are deceptive—all that climbing for a shot back to no place. No place is the place you land, the place where there is a ghastly hush. At least when you swing, there is no ground to gain, you learn to linger, to be airborne, you are like a final chord suspended. If nothing comes next, nothing comes full, weighted, exquisite. I lean back, making my body straight, swinging and hanging upside down. I wish my hair could drag on the ground. Sometimes I dream it can.

A little boy chases a ball, and his father catches him, flipping him over his shoulder. The boy squeals. It has been a long time since I've squealed or heard a squeal. Squeals are unfakeable, like the catcalls of peacocks. The old black man rolls the ball back to the child, a redhead in overalls. It is a striped beach ball so big that the boy can't see beyond when he holds it. I know what it is to hold that ball, to crane my neck but still not perceive my steps, to feel unreliably the path before me, to read the world in terms of hot and unabashed colors, to inhale the sweet ambrosia of melting plastic.

"Goodbye, sir," I say as I collect my bike.

The man on the bench nods. "Good day, young lady."

I take my leave, slowly clicking away.

Last night I dreamt a dream of the sea. I dreamt of water all around, tossing and rocking a house, my house—not a known house. It was a dream of Jack. We were in the house, and the water was high, and he sang a song. The sound of the song was plaintive, not words but humming, like from a bassoon, and the house rocked as he sang. Rocking gently, like a boat. And we rolled, gently also, like babies in a cradle. Like oils in the shallowest, most trifling light. I rolled, and he rolled especially, and his singing was beautiful.

2.

THE LAST TIME I SAW HIM WAS ON BROADWAY, NORTH OF HOUSTON. IT WAS dark and it was cold, and Mark and I were walking. In the middle of the street, out in front of the car wash, a junkie was blocking traffic. There's a deli right there—anyway, there used to be a deli, by now it may be gone—and the gaseous tea-pink light it produced made the street into a theater. In the vortex of this enormous auditorium was a hunched body—Jack's.

"How disgusting," Mark yelled above the carhorns.

Jack. Deathlike and emaciated and stalled in a choke of municipal chaos. Mark was right, it *was* disgusting. I could see the venom through the new sheerness of Jack's skin, like contagion or secretions, like a million insects crawling.

"C'mon, let's go." Mark tried to steer me away.

Would he come to me, would he know my voice? Yes, he would know my voice. There was a way I used to say his name; if I used it, he would come. If I tried to lead him from traffic, to a storefront, to a doorway, to some place of relative safety, would he let me? Yes, he would let me.

But Mark didn't know Jack or anything about Jack, and it would be bad if I ran out onto Broadway and reached for Jack's hand and Mark shouted not to touch the stinking filth of it. I would not want Jack to feel filthy or stinking in my eyes. If there was trouble and the police came, Jack would be the one taken into custody, not Mark. Never had I wished so desperately for a friend, for Rourke or Rob or Denny, for someone who trusted me. Usually you think of a friend as someone *you* trust. I'd never thought before of a friend as some-one who trusts you. I regretted ever having taken that for granted.

Mark got me onto the curb. "You really are an angel. The way you worry about people. And birds."

Jack is so small, I thought as we walked to the corner. Perhaps it wasn't fair to think that way when his version of manhood resisted dimension. You had only to look into his eyes to locate the power of him. But I had not seen his eyes, only the lids. Later, if there was to be a later, there would be shaking and profane rocking, a triangle to navigate on a city street that would seem to him to span for miles—a stoop, a fire hydrant, the bumper of a car, and after that, a feeble search through some garbage cans, for what, not for food, he would not want food, a little leftover wine, maybe, in a precipitately trashed bottle. Later, in the ruthless and overbright going up of day, there would be for him a dilating consciousness more odious than ever I had encountered as it labored like a half-chewed animal against retreat, against revocation, against the withdrawal of the pacific state he had found in his high.

Before turning west onto Houston Street, I looked back. I saw Jack bend lovingly into his addiction as debris from the street whisked like a symphony around him. The seat of his jeans was black. I wondered if he smelled like vomit. Probably he smelled like vomit. It occurred to me that I was fascinated by the look of him because the look of him was the look of me—we were no different; we had ended up exactly the same, friendless and physically ravaged. Shot up with fluid. Whatever deficits had drawn us together in the beginning continued to bind us.

"These junkies are totally desensitized," Mark informed me, throwing a shearlinged arm about my waist and tugging me. "You or I would end up dead, but that guy can drink out of a puddle and be back on the street tomorrow."

IT'S STRANGE SOMETIMES, THE way stories interlock, like those monkeys connecting by the elbow. Never did I imagine that the lives of Rourke and Jack would conform again in terms of theme or episode, and in fact, they did not. Their narratives synchronized momentarily, coupled as they were by my fragile perceiving and my peripheral involvement, and that is what makes their stories my story, and life itself an astonishing labyrinth, if you dare to think that way. When you share your story with the stories of others, you are very kind or very crazy. There is a fine line between compassion and madness.

There were modulations to their respective manhoods that were similar from the start—the use of the body as a site of confrontation, as a canvas to express, to make seeable some misery they felt otherwise obliged to keep concealed, and of course, the negligent courage. Each sought to pervert a natural gift—Jack by silencing his voice, Rourke by defacing his form. Each possessed enormous confidence, yet felt himself socially lame and utterly alone.

It did not occur to me during the fight to think of Jack on the street, though I might well have—the drug making Jack's skin a wall and Rourke's skin also being a wall. Vargas beat at Rourke from the outside to weaken the underlying flesh, just as the heroin masticated the vitality of Jack, beating him to a finer degree with each next strike of Jack's own heart. Every time Vargas made contact with Rourke, it was like the pounding of a child's body with a club or pole, no matter that Rourke was strong and had made himself hard—to me his flesh was tender when all I'd ever done was touch it tenderly. Jack's paper-white skin impregnated with poison, him wrestling witlessly with that dank intruder, no matter that he had assisted its entry.

It somehow escaped me as I watched Rourke disfigure himself that I had once felt similarly revolted, that the degenerate offering of a consciousness I adored was nauseatingly familiar, that I was only too acquainted with the hysterical futility of wanting to stop a process—unknown and inassimilable to me—that can only be left to run its repulsive course. In both instances I was sickened by the masochistic composure, by the wakeless rapture, by the look of *basic achievement*. How could a man as clear as Rourke ignore the gross arithmetic of cruelty, how could a man so physically disciplined allow the consequence of his efforts to be defiled? And Jack, raping his treasured reason, making himself stupid.

But me—I loved them both, and by both I was loved. What was it that I wanted so badly I needed it twice?

ANDY'S PLACE IS AN all-night diner two empty blocks south of where the fight had been. Whether or not I was lucky to have made it there alive, to be off the untenanted streets, lucky is what I felt. Outside the wind had turned wild. My clothes were whipping as if I was on a speedboat. The whole time walking I thought I could hear my name, near and faraway, recognizable but not, as though the sea itself were calling. *Evie! Eveline! Ev-e-line!*

Inside Andy's Place things went well, so well I worried there might be a message in that, and I suppose there was. It had a clean glass foyer with a clean working payphone and a laminated list of numbers for car service companies to Manhattan posted on the wall by one of those new toy grabbing games. I got through on the first try to Monroe Limo and was told by a polite dispatcher that it would be about fifteen minutes. I figured I should wait in back in case anyone came looking. I informed the waitress that a car was coming, then I ordered some toast. I was a waitress once too. I didn't want her thinking I had bad manners. She had her elbow on the counter in front of the pass-through to the kitchen.

She said, "White or rye?"

"Uh, rye."

"Jelly?"

"No jelly," Those little cups with the pushed-in corners depress me. I pointed to the bathroom. "I'll go wash up, you know, and stuff."

"G'head," she told me, glancing knowledgeably over her shoulder to the street. "I'll knock when the cab's here."

CARLOS WASN'T ON DUTY, Al was. Al gave me forty dollars to cover the ride, plus seven dollars tip. I'd planned to keep the driver waiting while I went up to get cash, but Al pulled out his wallet. Mark would give him an extra twenty for the courtesy, so I said fine.

I got upstairs at 2:00 A.M. I know the time because the first thing I did was pack the Argentine alarm clock Dad and Marilyn gave me for Christmas. *Argentine* because that was the word engraved on the gift box. Whenever I pack, I start with the most important item and work my way down in case I run out of time. I had no idea why the clock—maybe the honest, bright numbers or the effort they'd surely put into choosing it, debating its virtues versus the virtues of all other clocks. For some reason they settled on this particular one, and, truly, I loved it. It was my first time loving a clock. It's sad, actually. I must have felt that was all I needed to be on my way in life—that clock. I removed it from the suitcase and placed it in my jacket pocket, the baby beat against my belly.

After that I packed my books. Last of all, clothes. I lined up four suitcases and a knapsack by the door, then I arranged them in size order, then I reversed the order, then I stacked them so they would consume the least amount of floor space, then I stared at them, all the while considering where to go and how to get there. I took the clock out. I knew I had to go, and go quickly, I could see the time tick by, and I could hear it, and feel it, rapping against my palms, light as a necklace flicking, and yet those little arms seemed so hopelessly thin. No matter where I went, he would follow, and anyone who tried to help would be dragged into a mess, that being my mess, plus a whole new mess, a mess of Mark's making.

It was a relief when the phone rang. I didn't expect the phone. I expected the door. "I got the number from Rene," Dan Lewis said.

For a while he was quiet and I was quiet. It was 2:47. The wind was kicking up like crazy, like it wanted something out of me. Pieces of the street were making it up twenty-five floors, and I remember thinking, *I guess tonight is the night*. And, *Of course tonight is the night*.

"They found him in the woods. An hour ago. At my grandfather's farm."

I'd been to the Lewis farm. Once during a February break when Dan's grandparents were in Florida. There was a blizzard, and we got caught in Saugerties with no food and no phone. I remember Jack informing us over a candlelit dinner of canned beans and roasted marshmallows that a wood pussy is a skunk. I remember that he and Dan argued, as usual, about changing the name of the band.

"How about *The Void*," Jack had suggested.

Dan shook his head. "Sounds like emptying your bladder."

"Not *to* void, dumb ass, *the* void."

"Oh," said Dan, "as in space, as in illimitable distance."

"Exactly," Jack said. "As in the gap between your fucking ears."

DAN CLEARED HIS THROAT, though I had not forgotten him. "How are you doing?" he asked. "Are you okay?"

I don't know, I don't know if I'm okay. I said, "Are you okay?"

"I'm okay," he said.

"How did they know, you know, where to look?"

"I guess he wasn't showing up in the place he usually stayed. One of his friends—whatever—called Manhattan information for Fleming and got Elizabeth, and his family started inquiring. My grandfather had called me from Florida just the day before to say that his tenant had reported a missing gun. He described it to me because he has lots of guns. I knew exactly which one he meant. I just said, 'Yeah, I know it. That's the gun Jack loves.' So I told Elizabeth, and the local cops started searching the property yesterday morning. They went through the night in case he was still alive. Thirty-six hours."

I leaned over the suitcases, crushing my stomach into the handle. I stayed hanging, thinking of boots through leaves. Dogs. Most likely they used dogs. I was thinking of Jack's body. The freckle in the center of his lower lip.

"Mr. Fleming drove up today to identify him."

"How long—was he—Jack—there?"

"One detective said three or four days. Another said maybe less, that he was, you know, thin to begin with."

"His family?"

"Nervous. They're worried about the memorial service. They're afraid there's not much anyone can say. His mother is hoping that we'll speak. You and me. Troy."

An enormous gust rattled the living room windows in the apartment. Dan heard it. He said, "It's windy tonight. Dark like November. Your birthday's in November."

"Funny," I said. "Funny you would remember."

"Who could forget the necklace in the refrigerator box?" he said. And that was sweet, sweet that he said that and not inappropriate. It's not inappropriate at such times to trawl the heart for accidental luster, to speak of forfeited jewels, to allude to matter abandoned to eras and elements. Such things really do coalesce, forming little treasures.

"Take it easy, Evie. Tell your boyfriend I'm sorry to call so late."

"Don't worry about it, Dan. He's not even home."

SOMETIMES YOU HEAR SOMEONE say, *It was like seeing a ghost*. By that they mean that they have endured a penetration of the present by an agent of the past; they have experienced a destabilization. They call the sensation *ghost* because the occasion enkindles curiosity and fear and touches upon the twin marvels of space and time. If Kate had been there before me, I might have tried to reach right through her.

Her voice comes through—plainly. "Hi, it's me."

"It sounds like you're in the next room," I say.

She speaks of films and books and art, and of college graduation. She plans to teach English Literature in France. Her words are not careful. She does not hide her thinking. I'm happy, at least, for that, for careless conversation. No one talks freely anymore, everything is brevity and impact. There's no more time for error, which is sad. Charm comes out of error.

"Have you been painting?" she asks.

"Not much. A little."

In my mind is a picture of a day. We were in ninth grade, in marching band. It was before her mother died, before Jack. The parade started at the library and ended at the Windmill, where there were speeches. All the kids in uniforms were fooling around, poking each other and stealing hats, but Kate and I sat on the curb by the Methodist Church. Billy Robbins came and sat with us. He laid his trombone in the grass near the tulips. Billy had brown eyes and for the fifth grade fitness test he did 250 sit-ups.

Besides that, nothing else. Kate talks, but I can't hear. There is this feeling of insolvency, like everything I once valued is gone. All the things that I believed were important, all the friends I thought I could not live without. Except Denny, who is asleep on the couch on top of my feet. I feel a deeply personal handicap, like my wings have been broken. I can feel broken wings, which is strange, since, of course, I have none. Maybe it's my clothes. Maybe it's because Kate has never seen these clothes. Maybe my body feels they are fake. Maybe my body is mistaken and my *former* clothes were fake. And the phone, the feel of the phone. I wonder am I speaking too loudly.

"Not at all," Kate says. "You sound fine."

On Saturday, she leaves for France, for Grasse. It must feel nice to move away, to possess genetic immunity, to take shelter in your ethnicity, sort of like doubling back on a sewing machine and overstitching. But I don't envy her. I would not want to go to live in France, not when I'm an American. Not when the story of America is as yet unfolding. For me there is no security other than entrepreneurial security, cowboy security. The security of infinite possibility.

"My aunt is in Grasse," Kate says. "Where perfumes are made."

"I'm sorry you'll miss the memorial."

"I'm sorry. Sorry about Jack."

There is a pause. I do not try to fill it. Perhaps *she* will fill it. Perhaps she'll say she remembers a time, some time. The time Mom and Jack were trying to catch a rat. The time Jack came over with Steve Schumacher's goat, or when Jack hid chocolates around the house on Valentine's Day, or the time with the heart-shaped pizzas. Or when we played spies around the Maidstone Golf course, or tape-recorded skits using a haunted house sound effects record, or walked like ducks at the pond, following the imprints of the webbed footsteps. She and I walked, not Jack. Jack watched, throwing pebbles.

"Good luck in France," I say.

"Thanks. Good luck to you, too, in—whatever."

We hang up, me going down first. I don't mean to be rude. It's just there is nothing to keep me from going down first, nothing that makes me think— *slow*. I wonder if Kate, and the part of me she once possessed, will turn dead again. Yes, I think, dead. It just has that resonance to me, the goodbye.

A GIRL WAVERS AT THE END OF MY AISLE. IT'S HARD WHEN YOU'RE A GIRL TO imagine yourself to be the way other girls are. Sometimes they look so breathtaking and soft. Not soft like how they feel when you touch them, but soft like they look when they hurt. She has burgundy hair pulled back at her shoulders and large breasts like she would be lovely to hold in winter. There is something irresistible and wintry about her. Her eyes are bright and small and blue, and her mascara is sooty and smeared. She wears a straight cotton skirt with long and broad downward multi-colored stripes and a camisole beneath a fringed orange jacket that is fastened around her hips with a vintage white plastic belt. She looks like Dusty Springfield, except for the part about not being blonde, and also the tattoos.

"Eveline?"

"Yes," I say. "Hi."

She offers her hand. "I'm Jewel. You know my cousin. Dan."

"Oh sure. Dan is—my friend."

"You used to go out with Jack."

"That's right, I did. I've never met you, have I?"

She shakes her head. "I was abroad at the time, in London."

"Oh."

"You used to live by the train—"

"Yes. By the train." I wonder what she's saying. She seems to be saying something. I take up my sweater from the seat alongside mine, inviting her to sit. I was saving the place for Denny, but he's late, as usual. Jewel folds down as if the string that had been holding her just got clipped, and straight away she begins to sob. Her knees and my knees line up. She smells gentle, like she looks. She smells like drugstore cologne, the kind you get when you turn ten. It's funny, I can hardly make out her sobs, they're getting mixed among the sobs of all the other people. It's one of those kinds of funerals, the communal sobbing kind.

Despite the sounds of grieving, the warm marine afterlight of day is beautiful beneath the tents in the Fleming's backyard. I feel as though I am an occupant of a lunar egg that is landing with care. I don't know about the meaning of an egg landing, except to say that if such an egg ever were to come, it would be a philanthropic egg, an altruistic egg, an egg bearing good tidings.

People have begun to creep up politely on the outer side of each aisle, brushing against the white hydrangeas, which means there are no chairs left, and almost two hundred guests have come. I know because I signed for the chairs when they arrived that morning.

"ONE SEVENTY-FIVE, RIGHT?" the driver double-checked before letting his men unload. Actually the driver was not a driver. It was Billy Martinson from high school. From European History class. Nico Gerardi's friend. Billy told me he'd dropped out of SUNY Oswego after one year and had gotten into the party rental business—*the delivery aspect of it*. Billy had clocked more deliveries than any other party trucker in the Hamptons, whatever that meant. Probably it meant that he was a menace on the local highways.

"The secret to success," he informed me, "is the ability to be in two places at once."

"One seventy-five, that's right," Mrs. Fleming confirmed, tying her robe tighter. She kept making her robe tighter and tighter all morning, though it wasn't even slipping open.

One seventy-five sounded like a hell of a lot to Mr. Fleming, who appeared from the kitchen, Bloody Mary in hand, complete with celery stalk stirrer. When his wife reminded him that it's a Friday afternoon and that colleges are out for summer, she sounded stretched and wilty, like she would not have been able to withstand an objection from him should he choose to make one. He ended up saying nothing, which had less to do with the fact that he agreed with her than that Billy and I were there, staring at him, profoundly.

The service would most definitely be crowded, not only for the reasons Mrs. Fleming had mentioned but because Jack had messages. He may have ruined his friendships, but his messages were intact. She drew a strand of parched white hair behind her right ear and made her robe tighter. She looked old, older even than when the truck had pulled in. It was the nearness of her husband that made her so. I did not suppose or surmise this, I *knew* it. Mr. Fleming with that Bloody Mary, looking exactly like Mark.

"This way," I said, and the men followed me around the west side of the house. Three tents covered the backyard. Three because the yard was irregularly shaped.

Billy examined the tautness of ropes and the fixedness of stakes. "Who did these—Party Animals or Monumental Tental Rental?"

"Monumental, I think."

He shook his head. "You should have called us," he said, and he handed me a card. "Next time."

I'd arrived at the Flemings' at about nine-thirty that morning. I'd been thinking about going over all week, only I hadn't. I just kept driving by the house, making sure things appeared normal, that lights came on at night and cars moved around in day. When my mother found out what I was doing, she told me to knock on their damn door. She told me this is no time for *bullshit city manners*.

"I don't want to impose," I said.

"Kindness is not an imposition."

"Maybe they need space."

"They don't need space," my mother said. "They need someone to answer the phone."

I was pretty sure the Flemings didn't like anyone using their phone. Jack always said how his mother would bleach it every time someone touched it.

"There is no one better equipped than you to make sure the family is holding up—especially that woman—and to see to it that Jack is properly represented. You are a diplomat. A diplomat of the dead."

"Mom's right," said Powell, who had flown home from Anchorage for the service. "Imagine you had died first. Jack would be sitting right there where you are, telling us what and what not to do—what music to play, what clothes to wear, what stories to tell."

"Do you really think he'd be sitting, Babe?" Mom asked. "I imagine he'd be *lying*."

Powell nodded as he considered that. "True. Lying and crying."

"And being a tremendous pain in the ass," Mom added.

"You're right, Irene. He wouldn't be worth shit."

Though I could not exactly imagine the Flemings giving me a warm welcome, I trusted my mother's opinion. She'd been to hundreds of funerals. She was always quick to volunteer in cases of crisis. If anyone tried to discourage her from attending a service, she'd say, "There's nothing worse than poor turn-out at a funeral. I certainly hope you're not alone on the day you bury one of your people."

When the chairs were set—in curves not lines, no lines for Jack—I came in from the yard and found his mother sitting in the living room, dressed at last. She was wearing a taupe pants suit and on her lap lay a closed book, an album of some kind. Though she said nothing, there were two cups on the table and a plate of those triangular sandwiches without crusts. I figured I was supposed to join her.

She transferred the book to my lap as though passing a clipboard in a doctor's office, without fanfare or emotion. It was a photo collection of Jack's life, which she had assembled from family events—weddings, graduation parties, birthdays—and which she intended to display at the memorial. I didn't have to look hard or long to see that Jack was miserable in every shot, despite the fact that he had successfully bastardized all his dress-up clothes—there were Boy Scout badges super-glued onto his wide-lapeled polyester suit and flames painted onto his one silk tie and Wacky Packs varnished onto his good shoes. I could not see the shoes in the photos, but I knew they were there. The shoes were legendary. Denny had borrowed them for the Senior Banquet even though they were two sizes too small, and when we danced, he moved like magic, not missing a single step.

I held the book close to my face, squinting.

"Is something the matter?" she asked me in her normal deflated sort of monotone, not looking up from the book.

"I forgot my glasses," I said, lying.

"Glasses. You're awfully young for glasses."

I squinted that way for the better part of an hour because I didn't want to leave her alone with the wretchedness of memories on the day of the funeral. After the funeral it was going to have to be every man for himself, which is an unfortunate law of life. And, besides, Rita the housekeeper had made a pot of coffee, and though I'd often walked past the Fleming couch, I'd never sat on it, and it was quite comfortable, actually. Mrs. Fleming didn't seem worried in the least about me holding a cup of coffee and eating sandwiches while flipping through the cumbersome album during all my heavy-hearted nose blowing, despite the enormous potential for catastrophic spills, which led me to wonder whether Jack had not made more of her cleanliness neurosis than she deserved. *Heavy-hearted* because I missed him more than ever. I thought he would have liked to be there. I thought it was something we could have gotten through very well together—not the funeral that is, but coffee with his mother. I was sorry we were too young ever to have tried.

"Mrs. Fleming, do you mind if I open the drapes?"

She struggled with the suggestion as though she were having some sort of cognitive lapse, as though a word or term I'd used was foreign to her. Since she didn't specifically object, I stood and drew back the curtains on each window, jerking apart the creaky pieceworks behind the valences. "It's so pretty out today," I said. Pipes of sunshine rammed in and down at varying angles like they'd been waiting. The dreariness the room had known scurried back like insects to crevices in a log when you roll it off the familiar bogginess of surrounding dirt. "Isn't it pretty?"

Pretty as a word might not have been an appropriate choice for most funeral days; however, I used it with authority. The day was mine, I suddenly felt, and even if it wasn't, I was going to take it. In old film noir movies, the detective takes on someone else's problem, and in the process solves his own. He works backward through the crime while moving forward in his mind to crack his own riddle. In such narratives the crime is a metaphor, and the riddle is a metaphor, and though I'd never thought about it, beginning at the end is also a metaphor. The way it goes is this—*The story starts when I enter it.*

Mrs. Fleming blinked as though stunned by the flare of oncoming headlights.

"Are you okay?" I asked. "Is that okay? The light?"

She looked up, wide-eyed and stony. It seemed she had forgotten who I was. She did not seem flustered or disturbed by her disorientation; as a matter of fact, she appeared to have made her way back to safety. This is nothing new, I thought, and here lies the riddle of her chill—she is incalculably depressed. Of course Jack would have wanted to save her. Of course he would have tried. And, of course, his every effort would have been undermined. Yes, of course, this is where he got lost. How sad. In his little boy mind, he was her failure. This was true of Rourke too, except that Jack felt a disgust—his father was no hero. And the riddle of Jack was the riddle of us. Him not wanting to smother me as his father had his mother but doing it anyway. Holding me, teaching me. Him coming whole to my need with his need, and in the end, him leaving as he came, pain carried as if in a suitcase, because I'd done nothing to relieve his burden.

"Look at this," Mrs. Fleming says, tapping a page we've passed at least twice before. I open my eyes wide.

It's a picture of the two of them, Jack as a baby. In it his hair is white and hers is white, albuminous white, like the ball of an eye. They look lovely, mother and son, and hopeful with the new bond between them. He is no more than twenty pounds with his symphony-shell ribs poking over his diaper and his ankles like twigs. And the searingness of his eyes, as though they'd been branded onto his face, as though he'd been awakened already to the nonsense of inequity. I could read the light about him. A hero, yes. With such eyes one might have conquered the world. Tenderly, her lips. Tenderly, his temple.

"Never side with your husband over your children," she confides in a hiss, like scolding a cat. I turn to find her staring. There is something positively eerie about the vacancy in her eyes, the individual helplessness, the inability to invest in anything beyond the sphere of her unhappiness. Looking at her, I feel the way others must feel when they look at me. "They'll tell you to do that. Never do that."

We are interrupted by a crash from the floor above. My hand jerks, and coffee spills narrowly onto the saucer. I'd presumed we were alone. Mr. Fleming shouts, "*Susan! Where did you put my cufflinks?*"

More unnerving to me than the sound was her having mentioned him *before* the sound, her detecting him before he became detectable. Just as I was beginning to pity her obliviousness, I found that she was enormously aware—of her husband. I felt deceived, as Jack must have felt. I thought of my mother telling me to go check on *that woman*.

"I didn't put them anywhere," she replied, walking to the banister. "They're on your dresser."

She waited in case he was going to yell some more, then she returned to me with a joyless smile. "Jack loathed him. I loathe him too. I stayed married because it was the thing to do. *Their* college, *their* future," she says. "What would I have done? Forty years old, with two children. Who would have hired *me?* Loved *me?*" She takes back the book. "At least my son had the courage to go. His father will cling until the bitter end. Unless I kill him first. I'd like to kill him first."

A PROCESSION OF SOMBER guests passes the belongings Elizabeth and I had arranged on the garden wall before the service. There's the stuffed mouse I'd made, the harmonica my mother had given him, his drawings, his skateboard, his surfboard, his Hobie sailboat, his books, and his mother's photo album.

Jewel is still next to me; I haven't forgotten.

"Did you love him, Jewel?" I had the feeling she loved him.

She hunts through her tapestry purse and nods.

"From when?"

"1980," she whispers, withdrawing a tissue. "Dan and I saw him at the Lennon vigil. Jack hardly recognized us. He hadn't seen me in years, but Dan, well—Jack was very high. We took him back to my parents' apartment on West End Avenue—by Dan's dad's apartment—and we hid him in my room. He didn't eat or talk for two days. The third morning he was gone. I didn't hear from him again until he showed up at my apartment at Yale that February. He was in bad shape again, so I cleaned him up and drove him back to Boston. That summer we got a room together in the East Village. In September, he dropped out of Berklee and came with me to New Haven."

"For a while it was okay. We'd go to concerts and movies, and I would borrow books for him from the library. I bought him a guitar," she says, sighing awfully. "I guess he got bored. He put a band together in the city and started to go down. His bass player was on Fourteenth Street and Avenue A. Jack started out staying with him, but then he would disappear for days at a time. His family intervened. It was excruciating he said. All of them in Elizabeth's living room on First and Seventy-seventh with a therapist and these pickled kitchen cabinets. They apologized. But he said they only assumed blame because they'd been *coached* to assume blame. That they hadn't changed, that they'd just replaced their authoritarian ideas with someone else's authoritarian ideas, that they didn't genuinely care, they were afraid of AIDS and the homosexual connotations they'd have to face if ever he'd contracted it. According to his family, Jack sabotaged the whole thing," Jewel says. "If only they could have seen how upset he was. He kept saying, *They're programmed, they're programmed.*"

"They cut him off. They asked us to do the same. There's this rehab place in Minnesota. It all seemed so impossible, but—it's not like I knew what to do. Last time I saw him was Christmas, six months ago. I had a sweater for him. He didn't want the sweater, he wanted a hundred dollars. I said I couldn't do that, I didn't have a hundred dollars. He was like, 'Fine, forget it.' A month ago, I got a call about the guitar. He'd sold it. My number in Connecticut was scratched onto the back, and the guy Jack sold it to had been arrested. The cops figured it had been stolen."

I hand her a new tissue; she's used her last. People keep coming by to kiss me and say hi, or just pat my shoulder. I put my arm around Jewel.

"He never called you, did he?" she asks, her sad soul swimming. "No, I don't suppose he would have." She looks to her lap. "There was a book. He carried it everywhere; it was black. When he slept I would read it. Songs, poems, pressed flowers. Letters to you, letters from you. Do you know the book?"

I said, "I do."

There is a murmur of activity in front. "I'd better get back to my family," Jewel says. "I just wanted to—to say, sorry."

"Don't be sorry. I betrayed him. You never betrayed him."

"No, Eveline, you didn't betray him. The rest of us did."

FATHER MICHAEL MCQUAIL OF Braintree, Massachusetts, begins the eulogy by admitting that he has never met Jack, that he has come as a favor to his friend

Cecilia Hanover, Jack's maternal grandmother, who is too infirm to have traveled from Boston to attend the service. "Although I am a priest," he says, gently bending the microphone out of range, then stepping away from the podium altogether, "I have not been invited to speak in a religious capacity."

He stands before us in a sort of informal traveling priest outfit—black slacks and a short-sleeved black shirt and a handsome stainless steel watch. His arms are tanned and healthy. I heard him talking to Reverend Olcott about running—their *other* mutual interest. Father Michael runs in the Boston Marathon every year.

"I understand that Jack was a plain-speaking boy, and I'm a plain-speaking man, so I won't bother to carry on about a life unnecessarily lost or precious gifts wasted. I will just say that what this individual did to himself and to his family and friends was a crime. Now on some other occasion we might have a leisurely discussion as to whether or not suicide constitutes an *ethical* crime or a *religious* crime, but judging by the pain I see in the faces before me, I don't think that anyone will disagree that it is a *civic* crime. His death *cost* you, all of you."

Father Michael has a speech impediment—he speaks quickly, in a nasal kind of bark. Before one sentence is completed, the next begins its tumble from his mouth. He gives the impression of being smart and sincere and in a bit of a fervor. He places his left hand in his pocket and he walks, thinking as he goes.

"But you know about your own pain. Let's discuss instead what is a mystery. Let's discuss feelings that are at risk of festering if left buried. Let's speak of the idea to which each of you is inwardly clinging, *That those who fail were failed.* You want to know, is it outside the realm of possibilities that somewhere along the way this boy had been the victim of a crime of a magnitude equal to the one he committed? Not some gross act, but a fine crime, a subtle crime, a crime of *omission.*"

A new round of crying begins. It takes minutes for the crowd to settle down. "I didn't travel seven hours to make anyone feel worse than they do already. I came because you would be assembled as a body just once, because I saw Jack's memorial as a moment best applied to frank review. If anyone is too distraught to listen, they are welcome to take a walk around the block. It's a beautiful day." Father Michael lifts the long stem of a rose from the fence alongside him and inhales. He waits but no one leaves.

"I don't have to have known Jack to know that he was difficult. Mrs. Hanover, his grandmother, whom the boy is said to have resembled, is difficult. Ours is a strenuous friendship. Some might ask, *Why bother?* Some might say, *Life is short, don't work so hard.* To me that is tantamount to saying, *Life is short, don't grow so much.* If Mrs. Hanover is acerbic, she is brilliant. If she is self-righteous, she is uncompromising. If she is stubborn, she is trustworthy—if I am made irritable by the fixedness of her opinion, I depend upon the fixedness of her ethics. If she provokes me, she expects to be provoked in kind. If she questions my meaning, it is because, indeed, my meaning needs to be questioned. If my relationship with her were any *less* difficult—if she did not challenge me, did not test me, if she accepted me too easily, at face value, then she would not be a friend, but an acquaintance. If I could not be fully honest with her, I would be no more than a partial self, a concealed self, and my unrevealed remainder—my fears, my aspirations—would rise up in new ways to subvert me. Certainly, at this level of intensity, one cannot have many friends. This is a good thing. Reduced circumstances—social as well as financial—are a natural consequence of truthfulness.

"I don't have to have known Jack to see that he chose his friends carefully. Obviously he chose well. Surely he started out, as all children do, giving what they hope to receive. An unfortunate misconception is that as we age we need to move beyond the perfection of that barter to something more abstruse. I am going to wager that Jack was terrified about making the transition into maturity that you all made with relative ease, that he judged it to be a compromise, and that he tested you—unfairly, no doubt. So you all moved on, relinquishing proximity, retreating to the safe state of acquaintanceship. Terrified by your distance, your politeness—your *cleanliness*, he removed himself in kind, turning disrespectable and filthy. He didn't need narcotics to feel alien, he felt that way already. Narcotics confirmed his feelings and numbed them."

He paces absently in front of the Flemings. Elizabeth is shaking, trilling really, like a cold dog, and Mr. Fleming is slumped with his face in his hands. Jack's mother's head is like stone. She is a bust of herself.

"There are things that cannot be held to common external standards," Father McQuail says, "because they possess an uncommon internal nature. To be kind, to be compassionate, to be a *friend*—if, in fact, it is a friend we want to be—we must struggle to see past outward manifestations in order to arrive at the essence of what we adore."

He rests an elbow on the podium and looks out at us as if memorizing faces. "Being Jack's friends, you people are probably immune to analogies. However, since I speak each week to a far more inclusive assemblage, I've grown accustomed to them, so I beg you to indulge me. If one is a gardener, one cannot treat a rose as one would any other flower. A rose wants coddling, and to be sure, few people have the patience for it—so much of the product, so much of the time, is a wall of thorns.

"Why does God give us the rose bush? To humble us, to better us, to encourage forgiveness and understanding. And for those who show lenient forbearance, the reward is divine. Yet, it occurs to me that the rose is not only the *reward*, but the *acknowledgment* of the success of the sensitivity and the tenacity of our efforts, the proof of the virtue of faith—*The rose singles out the tender*. God has strategically placed the pure in the midst of the perilous to separate out those who can and will strive to reach for an ideal. My suspicion is that once you have been called upon to love this way, once you have proved that you have reach, you will be called upon again.

"I traveled all the way down from Boston to let you know that your experience with Jack was not a failure, it was an *experience*. Jack's is not the only story here; it is a tangential story, a parallel story. In the story of him is the story of you, and similarly, the stories of others. We can't re-write Jack's life. But we can re-double our efforts the next time we meet someone like him. I ask you to be courageous of heart. I ask you to remember that if you were cut in this instance, it was not because you deserved to get cut, or were foolish to get cut, it was because you *risked* getting cut. I ask you not to forsake the willingness to risk."

ELIZABETH LOOKS RAVAGED. HER eyes are swollen and pink and big for their sockets, like thyroid eyes. The pace of her speech is the opposite of Father Michael's. She speaks methodically into the microphone as if she is sedated, though having spent the afternoon with her, I know she is not. She is determined to own up to her part, to sober up to consciousness.

She thanks Father Michael on behalf of her family, then she says, "I'm two years older than Jack, but Jack was ahead of me in everything. School, music, art, ideas. He became a vegetarian when he was ten. That didn't stop the rest of us from eating meat several times a week. I remember sitting at the table, tormenting him with steak. He would stare back with a blank stare, marveling at the spectacle of me being an animal eating an animal, and sure enough, I would start to feel like an animal eating an animal. I would start to feel every cow tendon and taste every cow blood cell, and after dinner I would throw up. I never touched meat again after leaving for college. I can't even stand the smell of it. I've moved from two apartments because of the odor of cooking flesh. I won't let my parents cook it when I visit, or before I visit—and they don't," she says, without forgiveness. "I honestly don't know how Jack coped.

"At nine, he hung a sign he made from a torn sheet out the window to protest the Vietnam War, and, at thirteen, he boycotted toothpaste containing non-essential additives. He used apples and dental floss for months until Dan dragged him to the health food store and introduced him to natural stuff. My parents used to have him play piano at their cocktail parties until the time he said, 'Here's a song I wrote just for you,' and the lyrics were the ingredients of sliced white bread played along to this really bad piano bar tune. In high school—I don't even know why I'm telling you this—I used to hide my feminine hygiene products in a box in a dresser drawer. Once Jack walked in on me going through the box. I screamed for him to get out but he only came further into the room.

" 'Elizabeth,' he said, 'Don't be ashamed. Please. I'm saying this to you because they'll never say it. Don't ever be ashamed to be a woman.' " She begins to cry. "*Please*, he said to me. *Please*.

"Jack loved the blues from the time he was a baby, which was uncanny considering that we never listened to anything but Bobby Vinton and The Carpenters. I used to tell him, *The blues suck*.

"Last night I locked myself in his room. I don't know how many of you have seen his room, but it hasn't changed. Except that now all his things belong to me. I was on his bed crying when I saw his collection of albums on the floor. For the first time I thought to look at them, really look at them, and I did, and I couldn't believe I, I never—there are milk crates full of—"

She bends over the podium like she needs it to support herself. I look away. Although she's standing before a crowd, the moment is private. I feel Jack in the room—no, in the tent—the leaden livingness, the way it used to be. It comes like a miniscule change in humidity. Her father stands to retrieve her. She waves for him to sit.

"—full of rare recordings—78s, 45s, in perfect condition, alphabetized, labeled, exactly the way he left them, because he *loved* them." She continues through her tears. "My first thought was to give them to Dan or Evie because I didn't deserve them. Then I realized that Jack could have sold them when he needed money. But he *refused* to do that. He preferred to shoot himself. He must have known I would receive them. He must have wanted—"

AFTER HELPING ELIZABETH TO her chair, Dan takes her place. Minutes pass before people become quiet again. Dan waits patiently. The more patiently he waits, the more emotional everyone becomes. There is this investment the crowd makes. They think he will help them. He won't. He is too loyal a friend.

"I can't say I lost anything," Dan states simply. "Whatever I lost, I gave up long ago. He got out before I could be hurt by the fact of his absence, so for me, nothing has changed. His absence is his absence, and his presence— the things we did or the music we wrote, that's still a presence, you know, meaningful and ongoing."

Dan tugs the face of his shirt from his chest and adjusts his glasses. He reaches into his pocket and removes a small strip of paper, unfolding it carefully while he talks. "I agree with Father McQuail. I don't think Jack was lonely, therefore got high, therefore killed himself. I think he set out to achieve loneliness because he believed there was something to be gained there. There's a book of his that Elizabeth gave me yesterday, *The Anatomy of Melancholy*, by Robert Burton. Here's a quote Jack had underlined.

> *If adversity hath killed his thousand,*
> *Prosperity hath killed his ten thousand.*

"I've known Jack since we were two. Jack did not stumble unconsciously into adversity. Jack *chose* adversity because he considered himself to be a casualty of prosperity. Unfortunately, drug use is not the kind of thing anyone can control, and loneliness, well, loneliness accrues. I asked my dad how it happened. How Jack went from using drugs sometimes to using them a lot to committing suicide. My father said it's simply a matter of *time in*. Like becoming a musician. Spend more time in than time out and you become an expert."

Dan plays with the paper on the podium. "Jack could scale any building. He liked to walk as the crow flies, and if a house was in his way, he would go straight over it and meet me on the other side. He might come down scraped up, but he would tell me how beautiful the stars were from the rooftop. When I heard he killed himself, the first thing I thought was how he always did like to walk as the crow flies. Next I thought, I hope the stars look good from wherever he is."

TROY RESNICK WIPES HIS nose with his sleeve and leans on the lectern. His hair is short and his skin is clear and he has rimless eyeglasses. He looks healthy, actually, and almost handsome.

"Yeah," he says, looking dauntlessly around the room. "I got kicked out of school in North Carolina, and in sophomore year of high school I got shipped to my grandparents' house way the hell out in the woods of Springs, so it wasn't a great beginning in East Hampton, to say the least. My first day at school totally sucked, until last period in physics—this skinny white-haired kid with a deep voice in the back of the room asked the teacher to explain why ten pounds of feathers isn't lighter than ten pounds of lead. The teacher laughed out loud so the class laughed too, for quite a long time, because we were stupid. The kid got no help from anyone, but he didn't give a shit, he just kept it up like he was talking to the President at a news conference. 'But sir. How do you account for motility?' the kid asked. I should just say *Jack* since that's who I'm talking about, and why stick with riddles. 'The fact that lead does not move easily.'

"The teacher, Bertrand—we used to call him *Birdman*—kept trying to ignore Jack and get started on whatever inanity he had prepared for the day— paper airplanes and rubber bands, magnets and what have you. 'What about packaging and perception?' Jack said. 'Ten pounds of feathers would be comparatively huge. If packaging and perception are irrelevant, how do you account for the success of the advertising industry?'

" 'Jesus,' I said to myself, 'This kid's gonna get tossed out on his ass.' But Birdman didn't have the guts. It ended up taking Jack ten minutes to prove the teacher had no respect for kids, no sense of humor, no, like, spontaneous information to share, *and* no guts. I don't think a single person in that room believed a thing the teacher said for the rest of the year."

Troy picks a spot on the floor in front of the podium and points thoughtfully to his head. "I'm not exactly with it the way Jack used to be, so I ended up thinking about that day a lot. I came to the conclusion that the question was not about lead or feathers, which anyone knows the answer to. The question was about questions. Jack wanted to see if the teacher could be trusted with the weird things kids think, and the answer was *no*. Birdman could have said, *Interesting point, let's discuss that*, or whatever, but instead he laughed. And by laughing he lost us, even if we didn't act it right away. But eventually we did because nobody likes to be chicken in front of a guy like Jack who puts himself out for a cause, especially when he's right. Birdman turned out to be an asshole, and the same goes for whoever hired him. Part of being a teacher is being able to deal with kids. Kids know who's in it for the time off and the pension plan. The message I got from Jack was that people shouldn't drift through life just absently thinking somebody somewhere is in control because usually, that is just not the case. I mean, pull back the curtain and nine times out of ten there's some midget with a microphone.

"The one good thing about that day was me moving my desk next to Jack's. And that's it, the worst day became the best. Whether or not it was his best day too, I don't know. My guess is, no. Like Liz was saying, I was always several paces behind Jack in terms of ideas and bravery plus the fact that he was ahead of his time."

Troy rubs his face under his glasses like he has a migraine. "I'm thinking I'll go ahead and become a teacher or a counselor, because I like kids better than most adults do, and Jack trusted me. That's what I'm thinking. The preacher was right about the rose thing. Jack would have liked that preacher."

FROM THE FRONT, I can see most everyone. Mr. and Mrs. Fleming are on my left, next to Elizabeth and Dan and Smokey Cologne, who is wearing a shark-skin suit. The suit is briny green like a cartoon ocean. Smokey is being patted on the shoulders from behind by Dr. Lewis. Smokey maintained the closest contact with Jack until the end, and there are things he has in his head, things he will not share. He was the last among us to see Jack. When he arrived, I ran to meet him in the Flemings' driveway. Smokey held me and I held him. I never figured we were close friends, but those moments consoled me. It was as if we alone understood what was lost. Smokey happened to be a little crazy, like me. He was the kind of friend who would bleed for you. Holding Smokey, I thought of Rourke and Rob and Bobby G., and of course, Jack, and hoping in my heart that all had been done that could be done but nonetheless fearing otherwise—I started to cry.

Alongside Dr. Lewis is Micah, with the other guy from the band, Jim Peterson, and our old music teacher, Toby Parker. Dan's babysitter Bitsy is wearing turquoise beads the size of golf balls. Dad and Marilyn are back on the left by the screened porch with Denny and his boyfriend, Lance, and Denny's mother. Marilyn's hair is parted on the side and combed straight, her special style for special occasions. And behind them, all the people standing—Laura Lipton, Jack's piano teacher, with Miles, the television dog, retired now. Mom's people take up two and a half rows on the right—Lowie and David, Joanne and Lewis, Francis and Nargis. Powell is there too, but separate. He is standing at the end of the aisle in case he has to catch me. Yesterday when I asked Francis whether there was any advice he'd received as an actor on how to speak in public, he told me to bend my knees and speak from the belly.

I see teachers—Mr. McGintee and Principal Laughlin and tons of people from high school—Alice Lee, Min Kessler, Gwen Akers, Marty Koch. Ray

Trent and Mike Reynolds are there, so is Dave Meese, who probably still owes Jack fifty dollars. Rocky Santiago and his wife, Laurie, who swam with dolphins on their honeymoon, are next to Lizbeth Bennett from the movies who is standing with Rick Ruddle, the Outward Bound counselor from Portland. I never met Rick, but I know him from hiking pictures. Funerals are bizarre because Dino, one of the brothers from the pizza place who was always antagonizing Jack, is sitting next to Jack's cousin, Monroe Fortesque. Monroe had attended Phillips Andover Academy, then Princeton. Jack called him "The Preppy Hangman." I am horrified on Jack's behalf to see Monroe there, all muggy and serious. Even though Monroe is Jack's relative, he is one of those types of relatives you never imagine when you are conceiving your own funeral. If Jack had thought in advance about The Preppy Hangman being invited, he probably would have looked down the barrel of the gun and said, "Jesus, it's enough to make a guy want to think about living."

Alicia is there too, standing in back. I smile at her, then I adjust the microphone so I can be heard. Mine is not the kind of voice that goes far. I want my voice to go far.

"THE GRAND TETONS ARE in Northwest Wyoming. The highest peak there is 13,766 feet. I've never been to the Grand Tetons, but I know the average annual temperature at night and the average rainfall in May because Jack wrote it on the leg of my jeans for me to memorize. He drew the seven continents on the inside of my bathroom mirror so I could study them while brushing my teeth. I've never been to Yosemite either, but I know about the granite domes and sequoia groves, and also the boreal forests of Wrangell-St. Elias in Alaska and the live volcanoes at Lake Clark in Anchorage and the prehistoric rock carvings at the Petrified National Park. On the Continental Divide in West Glacier, Montana, there are ancient Blackfoot hunting grounds and Jack buried a picture of us there, and also a fork I had as a baby. He said it would bring us closer to the heart of the earth. One place I have been is the Franklin Institute Museum in Philadelphia. Jack and I went three times. I can give you directions, but you probably won't ask. I've never even heard anyone mention Ben Franklin since Jack, which is weird, when you think about it.

"Elvis Presley's 'One Night With You' was originally recorded in 1956 as 'One Night of Sin,' by Smiley Lewis, the best rhythm and blues man New Orleans has ever seen. Jack never forgave Elvis for not giving Lewis credit. If you dared to suggest that it wasn't Elvis' fault, that in general he helped to popularize black music, Jack would say, '*Bullshit*. He should have done it as a B-side.' Besides Dave Brubek's 'Take Five,' *Trois Gymnopedies* 'Number 2' was Jack's favorite piece to play on piano. It was written by Eric Satie in 1888 as an accompaniment to athletes. Jack's favorite year in music history was 1959. In 1959, Miles Davis recorded 'Kind of Blue' with Bill Evans, and Oscar Peterson did a version of Cole Porter's 'In the Still of the Night,' which we would listen to whenever there was snow. If you happen to find a copy of that song, listen to it when there is snow and you will know a place in Jack's head that is a particularly nice place.

"I can draw sixty-two species of wildflower from memory. Jack used to quiz me, and I would get points for speed. I've worked since I was sixteen, first in a restaurant and then in an art gallery, but the only money I feel I've ever really earned has come from flower drawings. I've sold six so far, two last week, on Tuesday. They say Tuesday is the day he died. I thought of Jack that day, how proud he would be, how the money was like *our* money. I keep wondering if I was thinking of him at the moment he was sitting with that gun, maybe thinking of me. The mind is strange, with the ways it can communicate.

"I can identify every snake and name every cloud. Jack's favorite cloud was cirrus because cirrus clouds are far, and he liked to look far. 'Look Evie,' he would say, 'They're like horse's tails!' He wanted them to be my favorite too. I agreed with him as often as I could, but not in the case of clouds. I preferred stratus. Stratus are the brooding ones, low like anguish, like neglected boxcars in the rain, like crying in your favorite hiding place—like Jack.

"Turgenev wrote of nihilism in *Fathers and Sons* in 1862. Jack did not teach me that; my mother taught Jack, and I happened to be in the room. He was complaining about morality, how it's a hollow construct, how the only possible reform is revolutionary reform. 'Go read Turgenev,' she told him, 'then talk to me.' And he did. Possibly she meant to show Jack that he was thinking like the great thinkers, possibly she meant to show him that his thoughts were not necessarily original. She felt it was his duty to go further. She always spoke to him very fast like it was a race, like she had to hurry, like Jack needed to get out of his head as quickly as possible.

"This is all very hard for my mother. Like the rest of us, I'm sure she wishes Jack would have called when he was in despair. Unlike the rest of us, she has to live with the knowledge that she could have done something about it. She would have thrown herself on him, like he was on fire."

There is crying, ongoing crying like a faucet running. Under the tent the air is hot. I bend my knees and tighten my belly. "Those were the easy things," I say. "There are other things. Not so easy."

"JACK BELIEVED THAT SOCIETY places too much value on the sanctity of individual human life, though it conveniently tolerates famine and war and other atrocities, such as racial eradication, environmental destruction, capital punishment, species extinction, and other crazy stuff, such as fattening veal and geese in cages. 'It's so stupid,' he would say. 'Suicide is intolerable but genocide is not. Why are the principles that govern the individual more strict than the principles that govern the masses? Because there's *profit* in bending the rules for the masses and none in bending for individuals.'

"It's hard to say whether Jack really planned to die this way all along or if he adopted a pro-suicide position early on because he thought anti-suicide talk was condescending. He rejected the theory that desperate people would be so moved by over-simplified rhetoric that they would reassess their reduced circumstances and discover the previously elusive beauty of living.

"He said that if the mass psychology behind killing is blame—it's always *someone else's fault* if you have to kill them—the mass psychology behind *not killing* is blamelessness. 'Everyone fears indictment,' he'd say. 'The motive behind prevention is the avoidance of humiliation. Think of the humiliation a single death causes a single family. Imagine a city with the highest suicide rate. Imagine the decline in property value. Imagine the crippling cost of *programs*.'

"His body was his alone, he said. He said that by the time he found himself in trouble, any feelings of entitlement others might have would not be real reflections of real relations. They would be fake or residual. 'If love isn't getting through,' he would say, 'it's not real. If we're not sharing it, it's not love. It's fanaticism. It's pentecostal. *The gift of tongues*.'

"It all used to make sense. But, really, only Jack made sense. Because despite his having prepared me, I am bereaved. Despite our separation, I've lost a piece of myself. Despite the fact that I was devoted—and I'm confident of the measure of that devotion—I feel I've behaved recklessly. I can't say if he did the right thing or wrong thing, or if me moving on with my life was right or wrong. Or if words like that should even be applied. Jack always said not to be afraid of words, but it's so complicated. I mean, we're not talking about Jack's *one* life, we're talking about as many as are here today. It's like talking about weaving. It's like an infinite weaving machine. It's inconceivable that between us all we failed to give him cause. The only thing I *can* say is that today is worse than yesterday. When I found out, I was like, 'Oh. Jack killed himself.' But every day I feel more guilty and more betrayed. Guilty because every choice I made from the moment I met him seems to have played a hand in his sacrifice. Betrayed because he promised I wouldn't feel this way, that I *couldn't*. I feel like I'm sinking, like there's nothing to hold. I keep thinking, *Did he leave me nothing to hold?*

"If I have to give up my right to sorrow in order to respect his right to die, I'll never recover. If I absolve him of this crime, he stays a child—an invalid, a freak, a victim. If I don't hold him accountable for his refusal to find a solution, *a living solution*, I make a choice, as if I am godly. But I'm not godly. He has to share the burden of blame. It's the only way I can remember him as he was to me—courageous and idealistic and handsome, with the bluest eyes."

Powell is straight ahead, looking at me with wonder and concentration, staring evenly, attentively, as he stares perhaps at the sea.

"I wasn't sure I would come up. I kept trying to think of what he would have wanted, for me to talk or for me to not talk. If you had it all figured out that he wanted you to do one thing, it usually turned out that he wanted the other. Or possibly he just wanted to argue."

People laugh, though I didn't intend to be funny.

"I thought of trying to reach him. I used to be able to reach him. I don't mean like calling up a spirit or anything, I mean the difference between *saying* that you're thinking and *really* thinking—it's like combining everything outwardly known and everything inwardly known and letting it shuffle together like cards. And then in a way, things really *do* appear. Elizabeth could reach him. Maybe you noticed the change in the room when she was up here. She spoke from a place beneath speaking, from kind of like a tunnel. And when she went down she was brave, and all we'd forgotten of Jack became clear—*he became clear*—and we reclaimed him, not only from our idea of him but from his idea of himself. The way he was good, the way she's always known that he loved her, the way she loved him too. The way he felt himself beyond repair but held out hope for her.

"I spent this morning with Mrs. Fleming, talking and looking at pictures. Jack was clear then too. But his mom was also clear. I found myself wishing that I'd spoken to her sooner, that I hadn't depended upon him to arbitrate, that I'd questioned his version of things when the time was mine. I saw that his view was not entirely accurate, not entirely fair. I saw he had a job to do, which was to forgive. Jack could be very unforgiving, and that, above anything, led to this. It was then that I decided to speak, not even worrying what he would have wanted. Just making his job my job, because that's what friends must do.

"So, here is the last thing. I was thinking today about how not everyone who does what Jack did lives as he did in the end. Many suicides are committed by supposedly normal citizens—parents, scholars, doctors, bankers, movie stars—who take pills or drink too much or drive too fast. You have to question the discrepancy between their accomplishments and their behavior. You have to wonder what face did they show, what lies did they live, what passed for love that was not love at all. You pity their need to please in the extreme and ask yourself whether social success is sometimes not just a means of encrypting the darker corridors. I think that when a false face is adored, it breaks the wearer doubly—in their hearts they are not known, and the love they receive is untrustworthy—it has the engine of intention. The disguise is a challenge. The wearer asks, who dares to meet me, find me?

"Jack hid nothing. Everyone acts like his honesty came automatically, like he had it and we didn't, which is a cop-out when you think about it. It was the product of labor, not just his, but his mother's. He was never made to be something he was not. He was never forced to conform to the rules that bound her. She admired his will, and she identified with it, and if she made an error in setting the bar for truth too high, in concealing in his ideals her own need for freedom, we might do well to remember that it was the boy she raised whom we loved. It's all very American really, when you think about it, like how this country was formed, with oppressed people insisting that their children live freely, that in their every action is the grasp for liberty. That should have been enough to save him. The fact that it didn't speaks poorly of our time and of the terrible pressures we face to conform. If there is no longer a place for the individual, then what are we, who are we?

"All she ever wanted was for him to find his way. You know, so few of us ever get to find our way."

I stand a little straighter. "Think about it. Today we spoke with freedom, the kind of freedom Jack knew every day. Today is a day designed with Jack in mind."

4·

I LEAVE THE CAR WITH THE VALETS AND I CROSS THE LAWN. I MAKE IT NEARLY to the Japanese maple when I hear my name. Alicia is peeking through the vertical window in the foyer. She looks perfect from far away, like the wife in an advertisement for diamonds. As I go to her, I feel the burden of each step, and inside something waning. I look at my shoes. They are nice shoes but somehow inadequate, like they cannot possibly be counted on for support.

The constitution of the house is cool and percolating. Girls with bouquets of Sweet William and in satin A-line shifts surround Alicia, cooing and bucking coyly, like a pack of does. They are pretty in taupe and pink and the hats she made them; the only thing is, you can't tell the difference between them. The taupe of the dresses is the same taupe of Jack's mother's funeral suit. Taupe must be the color. Alicia's cousin Mirelle is wearing the dress that had been made for me.

Alicia's raven black hair is parted in the center, just as she likes it, flat to mid-skull, where cumbrous braids accumulate into a type of turban or hive. Six blood-red roses are enwreathed there. During discussions with the florist, Mrs. Ross had suggested pink or yellow, but Alicia refused. My opinion was solicited. I said simply that Alicia is an artist, and Mrs. Ross, always an adoring mother and art enthusiast, was satisfied with that. I'm glad now about the red; Alicia looks beautiful. Her neck is bound in a choker of freshwater pearls, at least ten strands thick, ascending from collarbone to jaw. Her beaded gown is fitted at the bodice, cresting at the hips. The beads catch light, making motion. With her high forehead and hollow cheeks and enravishing stillness, she looks like a black-figure silhouette on an Etruscan tomb painting.

Tears fill her eyes. "This feels unbelievably bad," she says. "Doesn't it feel unbelievably bad?"

I scrape a square of glitter from her cheek. What has she been glittering? Menus maybe or gifts for the kids. She's that way. It's unfortunate that Jack's suicide has touched her wedding, but that is life and she is part of the living. Marriage of all things has to withstand its share of troublesome associations. Anyway, there's nothing I can do. She seems to think I can do something.

"What you said yesterday, about freedom—"

Her eyes. I think for some reason of Don Matthews, my college art teacher. His herringbone jacket flapping slightly as he walks, his kingly ignorance of blood and sports, his teacherly integrity and square jaw and lively Irish baritone. I think of Alicia's sensibilities and abilities, how I hope they will carry her through to self-discovery. You never know, actually. I withdraw from my pocketbook a piece of onyx onto which I'd carved a flower.

"For you," I say. "For luck."

She clings to me tightly. In her dress she feels stiff, like underneath is corrugated stuff, like a hurricane could not raise her. Maybe that's the point. In a gown the bride cannot get away. She belongs to man, to family, to community.

Like a hot air balloon moored by sand and ropes. "I wish you would stay for the reception," Alicia says.

Mrs. Ross taps us apart. "That's enough girls. Evie, dear, go sit."

JONATHAN'S BROTHER EVAN MEETS me at the base of the center aisle. Evan wanted to play guitar during the service and sing "Turn, Turn, Turn." Mr. Ross said no. He'd have enough on his mind without having to worry about a god-damned minstrel.

"Sorry about your friend," Evan murmurs as we walk, him leading me, grand and slow. In the middle of the section on the left is Rob. Next to him, Rourke. I see the two backs, Rourke's back especially. Like standing water, still but live, like underneath is so much. Beneath my skin, my body becomes desirous, though I mourn, truly I mourn. Jack was right to call me feral. I force down the life of me, like snapping a whip at a beast. I think of Elizabeth eating meat and Jack staring. I tell myself, *Jack is staring*.

Evan delivers me to the second row, to a padded white folding chair behind Mark's grandparents, who are so small I have to lean to kiss them. I am conscious, completely, of Rourke and Rob, mute and upright, eight rows behind me, observing the feline arc of my spine. The string quartet begins Mozart's "Minuet in G," and Cousin Sam and Sam's second wife, Abby, who is seven months pregnant, join me. Abby is in teal. A teal net hangs off her teal hat. I wonder why she didn't wear taupe. Abby and Sam own a baby furniture company on the Upper West Side. One of her gloved hands touches my arm. "Richard told us last night at the rehearsal dinner. Are you okay?"

Richard is Mr. Ross, Mark's father. "Yes," I say. "Thank you."

Sam leans over. I see the map of his goatee, the grand plan of it. "We're both terribly sorry."

MR. ROSS MADE THE announcement at 1770 House the night before. He explained to family and bridal party members that a friend of mine and Alicia's had died, and that due to my relationship with the deceased, it would not have been appropriate for me to participate in a wedding one day after the funeral. I did not hear the announcement; I was at my mother's house. Mr. Ross told me what he'd said at the wedding-breakfast when I came to finish the place cards. By the time I arrived, Mark had already gone to play tennis with Swoosey, and the bridesmaids were lined up with the stylists. I opened the shoebox of cards I'd started two weeks earlier and added all the table numbers. Mr. Ross waited patiently. As soon as I wrapped up the calligraphy pens, he said, "Let's get the hell out of here."

Mrs. Ross suggested I stay. "She's had a rough week, Richard. I think she might like to be included in the styling session. I don't know what we could do with your hair, Evie, but perhaps you want your nails and make-up done?"

"Don't be conniving, Theo. She has no intention of staying past the ceremony this afternoon."

"You never know. She might change her mind."

"We've been through this a dozen times. She's leaving after the ceremony. Besides, she has no patience for such nonsense."

As we strolled past the fountain and the newly erected tents, I was relieved to think that the tents were not the same tents used by the Flemings. Had the events been separated by more than one day, it might have been possible, or *probable*, and how strange might that have been. All those sedimentary tears caught in the canvas, entangled in the lines, dripping down and around the wedding party, absorbing. I wondered if tents are like taupe, if tents are *in*.

When I stopped by the cottage to collect a dress and a pair of shoes for the ceremony, Mr. Ross waited in the hallway. Though the cottage was in fact their house, he and his wife had always afforded us the strictest privacy. In the three years I'd lived with Mark, they'd never stopped by without an invitation, although Alicia walked in all the time.

My suitcases were stacked alongside the closets like rounded chocolate blocks. I hadn't seen them since I'd packed after the fight. I ended up leaving them behind when I received word of Jack, just taping a note to the top and leaving for Penn Station.

> *Took a train to my mother's. A friend died. Eveline.*

Mark brought the luggage when he drove out on Thursday. He assumed it was for Italy, he told me. He planned to leave directly from East Hampton on Monday morning. A car was coming.

I touched the tower of cases. The sight brought back memories of the fight, of Rourke being beaten, of him beating back, of the screams of the crowd dimming onto the desolate boulevard, of my run to the Greek diner and the cab ride home along the monotonous highway, of packing, of Dan's phone call, of the silver clock, and the mad wind. These elements formed a solitary imprint, no detail could be minused without collapsing the whole. Just as a lifeboat, dampness, and fog together are synonymous with *shipwreck* in the mind of a survivor, and flames, smoke, and heat mean *fire*, the suitcases looked like *Jack is dead*.

"You okay?" Mr. Ross called up.

I called back that I was. "Want something to drink?" I asked from the landing. "A glass of ice water?" At breakfast he'd had just three coffees.

He was lighting a cigarette. "I'm fine."

I jogged down the steps, and he held the door for me, both of us returning to the morning heat. On the western bank of the pool, he raised the back of a chaise lounge and set my dress upon it, then we headed to the back of the property in the opposite direction of the caterers, florists, and landscapers. We walked lingeringly, with him making inquiries into the memorial service, with me describing the things I'd heard and said, with both of us breathing deeply, taking our time. Walking with him that way reminded me of walking on the docks in Montauk with Janey, the motorcycle girl. Like there was something we shared. Some language or confidence.

"I hope you don't mind my having said anything last night," Mr. Ross said, "but Mark has had a solid week to inform people. You were up front and timely, and your choice is honorable. Considering your friendship with our own children, Theo and I would be fools to want it any other way." He extinguished his cigarette against a fence post. "I'm not happy that he waited until the last minute. Not happy at all."

"He was hoping I'd change my mind."

"He wasn't hoping. He was *entrapping*."

The BMW Mark had given me sat on the front lawn, balmy and adorable, lanolin green like peppermint foil or chewing gum. Mr. Ross attached my dress to the hook above the rear passenger door and thoughtfully scooped up the bottom, laying it across the seat. He took both my shoulders and he kissed me on the forehead. I could smell the stale nicotine on his breath, and I felt a swelling up of the heart. I recalled my own words from the funeral about Jack never having been forced to become something he didn't want to be, about seemingly perfect people.

"We're kindred spirits, you and I," Mr. Ross said. "Poets."

In the stark mallow of early day, it became painfully clear to me that he was thinning. Originally I attributed the change to a new haircut and new eyeglasses, but in the light I faced the possibility that he was sick again. I hoped someone was paying attention. I couldn't bear to lose one more person. That's why it was a tremendous relief to me that Denny had settled down. After Jeff and before Lance, things had gotten dicey, as Rob put it. One night Rob had to get Denny out of a bad situation over on Gansevoort Street, and afterwards Rob said it was a good thing he took a gun.

"Yes, Mr. Ross," I said. "Poets."

I twisted the sideview mirror and observed his return to the house. As he neared the porch, Alicia and her girlfriends rushed to the window like he was a celebrity and they were his fans. They called him, knocking and laughing through the glass. He waved in feigned annoyance as he mounted the steps, and when he opened the door they engulfed him. I learned an important lesson as I watched Richard Ross rededicate himself to the monster kinetics of family life, allowing himself to be beloved despite the quiet concessions of his heart and mind. Yes, I thought, that's right, a poet.

MARK HAD SHOWN UP at my mother's house at seven o'clock Friday night, one hour before the rehearsal dinner. I'd just returned from Jack's funeral. We all had—Mom and Powell, my father and Marilyn, Denny and Lance, Dan, Troy, and Jewel, Dr. Lewis and Micah, and several of my mother's friends.

Mark had met most everyone over the years but never all at once and never with them so sober and well dressed. Usually when he visited, he would get this look of unfolding shock as though viewing a particularly revolting striptease. But like a politician suddenly recognizing the voting power of a handicapped constituency, he walked in and worked the room, shaking hands and offering condolences.

"Thank you for being there for Evie," he said to groups and individuals. "My grandparents flew in from the coast for my sister's wedding, and I had to pick them up at JFK. I would've sent a car but my grandfather's ninety, and my grandmother has Crohn's disease."

In the kitchen, Mark sat at the round glass table, in the chair nearest the stove, the place he'd sat the night we met four years ago. As it happened, I was standing where I'd stood then, against the counter in front of the sink. Like falling dominoes, the days dropped down. And I was returned to a time in which things had been mainly opposite. That is to say, knowing what you want but having no means of achieving it, versus having means without knowledge.

"Do we *have* to sit in here?" Mark wanted to know.

Looking in his eyes I could see things I'd missed when first we'd met—the undisclosed designs, the skimmingness about the mind. Before I could go further, I was visited by a second memory—one of Rourke—in the same room on that same night, and me, brave like crazy in the stone sex of adolescence. As usual, the simple memory of him was so positive and tactile as to eradicate all current impressions. I felt that familiar crippling sorrow—what I'd lost and what I'd become—and I became dead again to Mark, to his qualities.

Sensing crisis, Mark softened. Jesus, he knew me well. "You're going to break my father's heart if you don't come to this dinner tonight. And I don't even want to think about tomorrow."

I called upon the only authority I possessed—artistic instinct. I forced my mind to meet my eye. I relied on my fluency in the grammar of gesture, and I established an interior to the scene, to *my* scene, and I entered it. I viewed what lay about me as color and light and dimension. The kitchen, so full with prior meaning, so over-spirited with friends and family that I barely even *looked* at anything in there, became something purely physical, a set or stage, a cell or receptacle, something with volume and capacity, something into which Mark and I had been placed.

He was frozen forward. He had taken on the look of a pawn or puppet, only not innocuous. I transposed his interpretation of the situation, like positive and negative space. I could see that his promise to shelter me was based upon the premise of my homelessness. But if I were truly homeless, why did he seek to displace me? What did I possess that he wished to take away?

My feet were bare. And the coldness I felt was the coldness that had been, and for the first time in years I set my feet into ground, all points touching. I pushed through the weakness of my inner legs, using gravity to connect. So often we go about resisting gravity. It is part of the hunger for immortality. The coldness of the floor was not the coldness he brought to the room. These coldnesses were not interchangeable, and this discrepancy was what I needed to name; it was the paintable thing. What he'd drawn in was a top sheath or cowl, condemnatory and cadaverous. In order to be, it required something to die. But the cold that existed beneath me was not bleak or disparaging, it was rich and prismatic and superior to striving. It was the chill of the earth that had nourished me. If it was not my home—through my home it could be accessed. In my head was a quote she used to say, my mother, my *mother* used to say. T. S. Eliot, I think.

> *The ways deep and the weather sharp.*
> *The very dead of winter.*

I walked myself through the years. I knew that I had attended college and that I had a job. Mark and I shared an apartment on West Sixtieth Street, and there was a car for me to drive. Although I liked that car, and I liked that apartment, thinking of them was somewhat like thinking of objects whose value is best understood in terms of an accumulation, like logs. By that I did not mean an accumulation of assets or capital, though surely there was that. In the bank I had $16,000. Any time I paid for something during my time with Mark—school books, Christmas gifts, clothes—the money reappeared in my account. I was referring instead to the technical aspects of a pile, to the hostility of a mass, to its refusal to be teased apart.

I tried to think of Saturdays, any Saturday—*last* Saturday. I had some fractional memory of him on the grenade green leather couch, phone in one hand, channel changer in the other, and between him and the window, a sleepy reef of dust coiling like the spilled milk of the cosmos. Him pulling me down to join him. And the Saturday places—restaurants, nightclubs, benefits, Nantucket, the Vineyard, Connecticut, Vermont, Cape Cod, East Hampton. Balding men, spidery women, the superfluous sounds of sex. Mark's sex was silent. It was stealthy and habitual—meaning like a habit, meaning like some dark routine, something wheeling and periodic. Like he was addicted to the feeling of getting his money's worth.

I see me there with him, imprisoned equally by the impregnability of position in a world purged of sincerity and rife with conceit. Like him and every member of his society, I was just another creaturely thing, defined outwardly by my appearance and inwardly by my paranoia and melancholy, by the ungainliness of my aspirations and the ugliness of my satire. I was rendered most precise not by what I possessed, but by what I had not yet attained. I was left with an obscene sense of having participated in one long masquerade.

Mark was reminding me of my obligations to his sister and to his parents. "They have to supercede," he said, "any conceivable obligation you might have had to this, this—"

"Jack."

He was right. My obligations to Alicia and to Mr. and Mrs. Ross *did* supercede my obligation to Jack. They were living and he was not. I had agreed to be a member of the wedding party. However, these obligations did *not* supercede my obligation to myself. I considered the toll of my innocence and my ignorance. Though I'd renounced everything—home and Jack and Rourke, the habits of my heart remained shockingly same. I may have been passive, but obviously beneath my passivity was agency. My life was never once his versus mine, it was one of my creations versus another. I had the instinct that I should venture no further, that I needed time. The coincidence of Jack's death afforded me exactly that. Jack would not have minded. He would have insisted. Part of me wondered if he had not arranged the entire thing.

"I'm sorry, Mark. I just can't."

WHEN HE LEFT EVERYONE said nice things. *What a straight shooter! He's not so bad! I can't believe it, I always thought he was kind of an asshole!*

Except for my mother, who from a place midway up the stairs brought conversation to a self-conscious halt when wearily she stated, "If you'll all excuse me, I'm going to bed."

Then she turned up and she went, and when she went she went as if there were marbles in her shoes, as if she dare not move as usually she moves, as if she feared shooting off to someplace terribly faraway.

"Hey, Mom," I said, going over. "I love you."

JONATHAN AND MARK APPEAR from behind the ivied trellis. They are joined by the groomsmen who previously have been ushers. Mark looks like a teenager, all dressed up for dinner with his parents, or a movie star in his tuxedo, a lonely movie star, jilted or fallen. I don't know about that—a *jilted* movie star.

Mark winks. I smile. Poor Mark, with Rourke looming directly behind me. Rourke. I hear the sound of running water. I force it back, the noise. I cling to consciousness, I will not go away. I am in the room, I am here. I paint the room, draw the room. Transpose the story, invert the story—stay, stay. I fix my dress, flattening the thin cross of ribbon that binds the bodice. Oh, I'm in gray, I see, dove gray, like a dove, a bound dove. He likes me in gray, though I did not intend to make him like me. I did not intend to think of Rourke that way again or to seek to inhabit foreign places or to live any more of my life by delirium and in absentia. Such living leads to loss. Such living is cruel to those who need you truly. Boys can die, and girls. When the service commences, I listen carefully. I never want to forget how close I'd come.

OUTSIDE THE TENT TO the north of the house, guests assemble loosely before forming a line to congratulate the families. Musicians dismantle with professional grace and begin their exodus to the patio near the pool so that the ceremony tent can be reconfigured for dessert and dancing. Dessert and dancing begin after dinner, which is to occur in the dinner tent. The wedding planner and her staff appear in their khakis and white oxfords to move us out with broad smiles and stiff backs and stretched-out arms. Mrs. Ross asks me to escort her parents to the kitchen, where they can rest until the reception.

"Thank you, darling." Mr. Sacci's head goes in circles like it is following the trail of a tightly flying fly. "Please, if you please." He grasps for his wife's hand, and she grasps for his, both of them missing repeatedly. I take one of each and walk them slowly past the altar to the kitchen, to the province of sugar and steam, to Consuela.

Unlike at the funeral, there are children—pluffy tafetta dresses and little man suits, running, swinging, climbing. Jack did not know any children or anyone with children. I suppose in his circle he was the *last* child. After the memorial service, Jack's mother summoned me privately into the house and she gave me a shoe. A baby shoe. High and white with a soft graying lace and scuffs by the heel and toe. If you put the lace in your mouth you would know the taste.

"For you," she said, breathlessly. She had been climbing. One foot remained on the lowest rung of a step ladder and in her hand was a half-key. On the edge of the closet shelf was an opened fire box.

I turned the shoe in my hands. I wondered if it was from Jack. Maybe not. Maybe from her. Either way the message to me was unmistakable. In it I could see the stubborn will to walk.

"Take it," she insisted. "I have two."

"Thank you, Mrs. Fleming," I said, and for a long time she held me. When I got to Denny's car, we waved, both of us, and driving off, we waved again, and then once more, her alone in the driveway.

ROURKE HAS ALREADY SAID congratulations. He is not far from where I stand at the back of the line. His suit is a midnight blue with miniscule white stitches, cut flat to his body. Beneath is a light blue dress shirt—French blue or rose blue. He's laughing with Rob and Denny and Lance. The right side of his face is bruised and inflamed. I can't make out his eye. I wish I could go, but I can't. In one terrifying moment I have a relapse of every fear I've ever had, plus every fear of losing him. It's like Mark's grandparents grasping blind, one hand for the other, all the world being darkness, though there is light.

"Here's Evie! *Evie!*" Alicia beckons me. "She'll tell me the truth." She pulls me to the bridal party side of the line, which is like stepping behind a register at a store. "Is my makeup okay?" she asks loudly, her face hovering by mine. She whispers, "Did you see his eye? They say it's never going to be the same."

Officially I kiss her, then Jonathan, then the three of us coming together. The photographer takes a picture. The kettle clap of the flash. Alicia winks at me then brightens professionally for the next person. I move on to congratulate the others, and finally, Mark.

"It's been a long week," he murmurs as he squeezes me, his penis filling the space between us. "I'll never make it through the reception." Mark releases me. Over his shoulder is Rourke. "We're going to Georgica for photos. Meet me by the limos." As I walk away, he yells for me to stay out of the sun.

ROB TAKES MY HAND, and we cross the garden to the front lawn. We turn the corner by the summer room, standing where Mark can't see, though it doesn't matter since he's stuck in line anyway. Rob raises his green aviator glasses to the peak of his head. His eyes are red-yellow-brown like hard honey, the way it congeals. He adjusts the fallen strap of my dress, then he lifts me.

"You smell like coconut," he says. "Do you smell like coconut?"

My chin rests on his shoulder. "My aunt gave me lotion."

"Oh," he says. "Lotion. Very nice."

I push away, he sets me down. I'm crying, and I don't want to get his suit wet. His suit is cream-colored, a sort of linen ecru, and his shirt is snow white. His tie is the color of irises.

"You look handsome."

He reaches in his pocket for a tissue, and taking up a tiny piece he touches beneath my eyes. "You like the suit? Lorraine picked it out. She's into fashion now, so I gave her a call. We went to Barney's over in Chelsea. You gotta see her rip through ties. It's like a special aptitude, like those autistic kids who know Mozart. We went to the the Russian Tea Room after. She always wanted to go to the Russian Tea Room, so I figured, what the hell?"

"I'm glad."

"She's dating some lawyer now. Did I tell you that? I meant to tell you. Short kid—five-eight. He's got a two-bedroom condo in Jersey City. I go, 'Hey Rainy, any short guy with a two bedroom condo is wife-hunting.' And she goes, 'That's right, Rob. And any guy living with another guy and a rabid dog in a trailer with no job and a penchant for gambling *is not*. It took me ten years, but I finally figured it out.'" Rob laughs. "*Penchant*, she says. *For gambling*."

"She really loves you."

He looks a little bit over my head and sucks one cheek to his teeth. "How you feeling? You all right? You seem shaky. You shaky?"

"I don't know. I guess, a little shaky."

"Suicide." Rob says. "That's rough. Especially since for a while he was everything. But what are you gonna do? You can't change people. Look at my brother. He's dead. Practically. Soon, he'll be dead."

"Anthony?"

"That's right, Anthony, in L.A." Rob mashes his teeth together and articulates over-clearly. He reaches for a cigarette, recalls his hand, and finds a stick of gum instead. "Tony. Toni with an *I*. All any of us ever heard growing up was how handsome he is. Had any girl he wanted, fifteen to fifty. A guy like that gets a complex, know what I'm saying, like, *Who needs a real job?* So Tony takes an excursion through the magical world of porn. Strictly straight stuff. I tried talking to him. I tried everything. But forget about it, the money was too good." Rob adjusts his tie. "That's the reason me and Harrison stayed in L.A. after college. My uncle was ready to go make Anthony ugly, so he can't shame anybody. I'm like, 'Uncle, what are you gonna do, cut his dick off?' I mean, once you start that shit, where do you stop? I asked for a chance. You know, spend some time, hang around, get inside, pry him loose. I offered to stay on at UCLA—at Anderson—my mother always wanted me to get an MBA. My father and my uncle were a little chilly on the plan. They knew how I felt about my brother. That's when Harrison agreed to stick around. Even so, I got too close. I got caught up. That world sucks you in. Sex and cash. Blow clouds your judgment. That's what's up with Mark, by the way. Too much coke. Those guys keep at it all day. It gets to be like popping aspirin."

At the mention of Mark, we both look in the direction of the bridal party. Through the screened walls of the porch, we can see that half the guests are still waiting in line.

Rob turns back and grips the space around his mouth with his finger and thumb. "Long story short, two years later, worst morning of my life—grad school graduation and, like, *Time is up*. My family's flying in and I haven't gotten through to Anthony. All that's happened is *he's* compromised *me*. Remember I told you about cheaters? Their job is the failure of your character. So I'm crashed on the couch in his, whatever, his bungalow, still high from the night before, still high from an *hour* before, and there are scumbags all over the place—girls, guys, what have you. I'm looking into each face—how did these fucking losers ever look okay to me?

"In my mind, deep down, I'm thinking—*praying*—that Tony's gonna walk down the stairs in some sharp suit like it's Easter in the old neighborhood and I'm seven and he's seventeen, and he's gonna say, 'Let's go kid, you got a big day ahead.' Or else my family's gonna pull up, and Joey'll be there all tight with Pop, with my mother in the back seat of the rental car at the end of the driveway, her hands folded on her pocketbook, and my old man'll go, 'Go up and get your brother, boys. Tell Anthony we're going home.'

"But nothing. *Nothing*. By nine o'clock I'm freaking out. I gotta go. I gotta go. My heart is speeding like it's gonna bust, and just when I think I can't take it anymore, the front door opens. There's this shaft of light, and right past it, a shadow—Harrison. He doesn't set foot in the place. It's too contaminated. I don't want him in there either, it's weird. I jump up and go over. I meet him at the doorway. 'Come on,' he said. 'You've done what you can.'

"And I just fucking snap. 'Fuck you, you fucking prick. I'm not leaving.' I go to him, 'You don't know about family because you don't have one. I'd rather be dead than leave my brother.' All of a sudden, *boom*. Harrison hauls back and knocks me out. Full force. Flat. It was like getting hit by a train. Then he looks down and says, 'He's not your brother, I am.' "

I wipe my eyes. I think of Mrs. Rourke. *Do you know I still wonder what 'the wrong thing' could have been?* Was *the wrong thing* the part about Rob taking death for granted, or the part about the brother, or the part about not having family. Possibly all, yes, all.

"Harrison gave me his hand and helped me sit. And I'm there, bleeding and crying on the steps for, shit, it's gotta be, twenty minutes. I know Anthony fucking heard me, *everybody* heard me. All down the street people were coming out of their houses. I swear to God, Evie, he ignored me. 'If he doesn't come down,' I said, 'it's gonna be the last time I see him, man. I fuckin' know it.' 'One time is gonna be the last time,' Harrison said, 'let's just make it today.' "

"He waited until I was ready, then he picked me up and took me to the gym and got me iced and stitched. I couldn't even stand, I was so screwed up. He had the doctor over there make sure my cheekbone wasn't shattered. It was a double fracture—see?" Rob points to the left side of his face.

I've seen it. But I've never touched it. So I touch it, like I'm blind, my fingers flat, going over. "The eye is smaller, isn't it?"

"But the vision's twenty-twenty. That's all I care about. I could've had surgery, but I don't give a shit, except for the sinus problems. I got busted up so many times in hockey anyway. Besides girls are into it. So Harrison takes me to our place in Ventura, gets me fed and cleaned up, and we make it to graduation on time. My family practically shit. My mother starts sobbing and Mrs. Rourke goes white, but you know what?" Rob drags his fingers across his lips, zipping. "They said nothing—*Harrison was with me*."

Rob looks at me. "Sometimes you love somebody and it's like trying to see the top of the building when you're hugging the ground floor. I know you know what I mean."

"Yeah, I know what you mean."

"That's why—I admire you for letting go."

"I'm not sure I did."

"You let go. Picked yourself up. Kept things together. And it would have worked out except for—fate. Harrison was coming back." Rob points at me. "You *knew* it. No matter how things ended up, you let go because you had faith. I had no faith. I wasn't doing Anthony any good by hanging around. I was desperate, I was stealing time. It wasn't even good time. Now my idea of my brother is ruined. Harrison let me go as far as I could handle—he knew I'd never forgive myself otherwise, but as soon as I got in over my head, he pulled me out. Here's the punch line, Harrison *saved* me. No exaggeration. I got off easy with a busted face—my brother's got *the sickness*. Last time I talked to him, he was down to 138. From 190."

"Oh, I'm sorry, Rob."

"Hey, I'm just saying. You gotta keep your world pretty fucking tight if you want to control other people's outcomes. Like Harrison said, '*You've done what you can*.' I think about that a lot. Who can ever do what needs to be done? You do what you can and hope for the best. I couldn't save my brother because he didn't want saving. Harrison saved me because inside I wanted to get the hell out. Biggest lesson of my life—there is no family other than the one you make for yourself. You're alone except for what you build."

"Jack used to say that."

"Well, there you go. Smart kid." Rob nods to Swoosey and Brett, who have joined the guests gathering around us. I glance through the porch again.

The receiving line is almost gone. "But there's math involved, Evie," Rob says. "You're under obligation to build with family. There's something there. A type of truth you can't get elsewhere. An *unusual* truth. And to go through life wanting saving when you actually need saving, those lanes have to be open. Otherwise you've got nobody to track you, and it's like, constant reinvention. New town, new faces. Believe me, it's not easy. Me and Joey, we try. Somewhere along the way it'll be worth it. When we need that wall we'll turn around and it'll be there. That's the building part. Sometimes there's no work involved. You got an automatic fortress. Like Harrison, like—"

"Lorraine."

"Actually, I was thinking of *you*, but yeah, sure, okay, Lorraine."

We walk to where the limos and the people wait, over to where the bride and groom will pass, where the flower petals will fly. Where I thought Rourke might be, but he's not.

"I gotta tell you," Rob says, "I lost it when I found out you left the fight. I figured you'd stay over my parents'. I coulda killed my sister." He points to the top of his hand. There's a crescent burn along the length of his knuckles. "She hit me with an egg pan. '*Self-defense,*' she told my father, as if I would ever set a finger on her, that she-wolf. My mother called your apartment Sunday morning, and Mark said you were *all right*. That's it. No news about a dead friend. Nothing. I grabbed the phone. 'Then lemme talk to her,' I said, and he goes, '*Forget about it.*'"

"I left before he got there. I heard about Jack, and I took a train."

"You sounded pretty upset when you called me Tuesday," Rob says quietly. "You know I would've driven out as soon as I hung up. You only had to say the word. You know that."

"I know."

"I owe you. You saw me through Bobby G. You and Harrison."

"I'm sorry about taking off from the fight."

"I didn't expect you to make it. I didn't quite count on you leaving the premises either. I just figured you'd cut out with Lorraine. But that's another story. I forget, sometimes, who I'm dealing with."

Oh *there's* Rourke. He's on the far side of the Japanese maple with a red-head—Diane Gelbart. Diane's at Table Three with her parents, six away from Table Nine, where Rourke and Rob will be, which are not far apart, as I'd originally thought, but actually back to back, because the caterer plotted the tables in loops. I saw the blueprint this morning. It looked like a drawing of intestines.

Diane's hair is the hue of poppies. In the light it moves in unison, like a song, like a gleaming song, a song made of plastic wrap. Her flower-print black and red wrap-around dress swells angelically, revealing perfect knees. There is an element of the surreal about her. She seems to have been plucked from a photograph in a vintage issue of *Vogue*. Like one of those Horst models, she is all clothes, all posture, huge and hard at work, a giantess. She examines me from behind the wide brim of her hat. I must be of enormous interest to her, as once she was to me. Now I feel nothing—not exactly nothing.

I look to the street. "How is he?"

"Thirty grand richer," Rob says. "So I guess he's fine." Rob kicks at the grass. "I don't have to tell you it was a straight fight. Whatever Mark—"

"No," I said. "You don't." Of course Mark had been wrong. Rob would never set Rourke up for a loss. Any insult to Rourke was an insult to Rob. That's why he had taken it upon himself to settle for injustices against Rourke. That's what the fight was about—settling. It had to be a legitimate purse and a legitimate gamble. Besides, Rourke works for the Olympics. He would never damage the reputation of the organization or the guys he trained. At the Cirillo's barbecue Joey said it was gonna be the best year ever for U.S. fighters. That thanks to Rourke the team had a chance of taking twelve out of twelve golds in L.A. Rob didn't disagree. He just said, "More like ten out of twelve."

Mark was also wrong when he said Rourke lied to me. Rourke never lied to me. He didn't have to. There was nothing a lie could have secured that the truth would not have. The only thing Mark got right was that Rob *did* need to control outcomes. That's why he relied on Mark's hatred of Rourke, Mark's ignorance of true friendship and true love, Mark's idea of Rob as criminal and corrupt. *In the end need brings you down,* Rob had said. Mark's mistake was in thinking Rob needed cash. Rob *never* needed cash. Rob would never even *suggest* he needed cash unless he was trying to scam somebody; it would have been too much of an implication of incompetence.

"There were like six hundred people there," Rob says. "Harrison still has a huge following, and Vargas, everybody loves that kid. Throw Mark and his buddies into it, and forget about it, the shit was flying. It was like duck or get hit. Uncle Tudi fronted for licenses, fees, purses in escrow. The take at the door covered expenses three times over which would've been enough. But milking Mr. Tennis Togs was worth the whole thing. The look on his face when those numbers were read—*Shit.* I can't believe you missed it. Vargas nearly lost his skull in the tenth." Rob enacts it minimally—hissing and closing one eye, stuttering his head back to the right.

"Harrison was down three years, so I had excellent odds. But use your brain, you *know* he's gonna take it—his record, his style, his character. He trains fucking Olympiads. He's in the ring every day. He's got the whole martial arts thing. Add to that the incentive to burn Mark, and, well, let's just say, I kept my mouth shut and made a few bucks."

"Uncle Tudi too."

"Sure. He set the odds. And a couple people I had to take care of. My old man, Ray Peña, Joey, Harrison. You."

"Me?"

"That's right, you. You know what's the matter with you? I finally figured it out. Ninety percent of the time you think smart. Numbers and letters. Regular stuff. The other ten, I swear, you see in pictures or some shit."

There was more to what he feels he owes me. More he isn't saying, such as what gave Harrison *the incentive to burn Mark*.

Vivica comes by with rose petals. Vivica is Anselm's new girlfriend, the fifth since I've known him. I liked the last one best. Carrie. Carrie was a psychology student at Barnard when she and Anselm lived together. When she left him, she turned gay. Maybe *turned* isn't correct, *turned* is just what everyone said. Swoosey Schicks waves to Rob again through the thickening crowd. He taps his watch.

Rob drags his head to one side like he's annoyed. "I got an *hour*," he calls over. "What's wrong with that kid?" he asks me under his breath. "I could make it to Belmont to place the bet *personally* in an hour. Meanwhile, he lost six grand last week. I think he needs *G.A.*"

"Where you going?"

"OTB in Southampton. I got a horse. Feel like taking a drive?"

"Actually, I'm leaving."

Rob furrows his brow. "Where to?"

"My mother's."

"Oh, sure, right. It's not right for you to be out," Rob says, then he laughs one time. *Ha!* "That's gotta be killing Mark, you going AWOL in front of Harrison and Diane at the family wedding. He's one sore fucking loser. You know, I had to take Uncle Tudi to his office to collect for the fight," Rob says indignantly. "Like somebody stole my lunch money. That's a seriously nice office, by the way, with the double paned glass and those carved African heads. What do you call them?"

"Carved African heads, I guess."

"How long has he had that space?"

"A couple weeks."

"Anyhow, I offered to clear all debts in exchange for the Porsche. He said he'd rather send it off a cliff. My uncle told him that could be arranged— *anytime*. Tudi was pissed off because Mark ran a check on the licenses and permits, which I knew he would. Believe me, I dotted every fucking *i*." Rob scans the faces. "Damn. Who am I gonna dance with?"

"You'll find someone."

"Last time you said that, I ended up dancing with Dennis all night. I got, like, three guys' phone numbers."

The bridal party is on its way. I can't see over the heads of people around us, but there's a cheer, which means the line has finally ended.

"I haven't had a chance to say anything to him," I say. "I will tonight."

Rob nods. "We'll stick around."

"No," I say, "but thanks. It has to be me."

I don't want to seem ungrateful, but I'm nervous about the fact of my luggage. And the car coming Monday. It's like Mark *knows* I'll be ready to go. Like he *knows* I'll want to. Like he has a plan.

"If you really want to help me," I say, "just get Rourke out of here."

Rob is quiet. He shoots a glance past me. Mark must be close. "Come back tomorrow," he suggests, "in the morning."

I shake my head. "He'll come. In the middle of the night. When it's too late to object." I step to Rob's ear, whispering. "And I can never sleep with him again. I was just waiting for the fight to be over."

"I suppose I oughta be happy," Rob mutters, real fast. "But to tell you the truth, I got a sick feeling in my gut."

I feel the compression of the major vessel in my arm. Mark draws me away from Rob, neither of them speaking. Rob crosses over to his car, which is next to Rourke's car, both of which, unlike all the other hundreds of cars going in either direction down the street, are simply parked in the neighbor's driveway. He lowers himself slowly into the Cougar. I feel sorry for him. Men hold your doors and pull your chairs and carry your bags when they're too heavy, but they can't protect you from the one thing that scares them most—you and another man. In *The Big Heat*, Vince Stone's girl gets a pot of scalding coffee thrown on her face when he gets jealous of Glenn Ford and later she gets shot. I've seen this look on Rob's face before. Like he wishes he didn't have to get mixed up with dames.

He gets in his car and starts his engine, and it's like thunder.

ALICIA AND JONATHAN CHARGE through a rain of petals. There is a convivial uproar. Everyone hoots and whistles and claps, except me, except Rourke. He is tall and grave across the way, with Diane Gelbart at his side, with her like something boneless and wise to the rules of transformation. His eyes on mine, then they are gone, he is gone with the white of the veil whooshing past, and the black of her hair, the blood of the roses, the heads going down against the storm of lights. The rain of petals, the rattle of applause. And the noise, the heads tucking into the limo. *Whoomph*, the door. The second and third limos pull forward. These are for the bridal party.

"If you still insist on leaving," Mark says, "the driver will take you to your mother's after he leaves us at the beach. I'll have someone pick you up later."

"Where's—the BMW?"

"I had it parked. On the far side of the house. I'd have to have six cars moved to get to either of ours. And the Porsche is stuck behind the tents."

I imagine Brett and Swoosey Schicks drunk in my mother's driveway, hanging out of the car like tuxedoed apes, beeping and swearing, hot to get back to the bridesmaids, to take them on a tour of the poolhouse. Somebody is always taking somebody else on *a tour of the poolhouse*. There are condoms underneath the bench with the floats. That's why they call condoms *floats*. I would have no choice but to concede. They would never leave without me.

"It's okay," I say. "I'll walk."

"No," he states emphatically. "I cannot have you *walk*."

"Denny will drive me."

"Must Alicia lose *all* her guests? Why not just ask my father to take you?"

The limo driver taps on the horn. Mr. and Mrs. Ross are in the front seat, watching through the windshield. Mark waves and smiles brilliantly, giving the thumbs up sign.

"C'mon," he says. "They're waiting."

IT'S NEARLY DARK AT GEORGICA BEACH. I WALK WEST. I HAVE TO GO WEST; I'LL never go east again. My legs press into sand. I feel the topography. I *see* it, the wedge of the earth. I walk on a slope that ends at the ocean floor, the valley of the sea. I walk on a margin. I feel every grain. Every grain is what I should be, what I want to be, one in a million, one in a million million.

A beach party. I cut past, too closely. Two sideways trucks parked back to back. Men in university sweatshirts and women with frayed ponytails huddle around a fire. Beer and smoke. Music.

What perfect weather for a clam bake!

I climb the jetty to the end. I'm not careful. I know every rock. The wind makes gains, and the sea surges. It pounds the shore at a five o'clock angle. Rain is coming and no one knows. I am the only one. They are not like me, the millions. I am distinct. I die of distinction. Clouds come, walking to me like armies, shields very, very raised.

AFTER THE WEDDING THE barn was the only place to go. I felt safe to hear the familiar shotgun snap of the door as it ripped to the side—*chuck chuck*. Safe to think of Jack opening it, to think of Rourke, once standing alongside it, once coming through to wait while I packed.

Inside was so saturated by twilight that it seemed to have been the recipient of an interior rain, with the wood going soft and the walls bowing down, with the sway out and the sway in, with the sense that you are swimming. It was richly shadowed, like a forest. I began to pace. There were places where I would go dark and places where I would appear, the light on me in pieces. The murmuring sound of my feet like a prayer and me in a forest, a forest of ghosts, hanging over like branches. And me a ghost too, the ghost of me.

The walls were covered in holes from my drawings. My mother had taken them down to protect them. Last year, or the year before. My father made a box and together they gave me my own drawings as a gift, which was strange, also strange was me not taking them out, me not looking in, not with Mark there, just thanking them and returning the box to the barn. It was on the dresser; next to it was a pile of mail. I moved to these things—slowly, thickly.

There's mail for you in the barn, my mother had said. The day I'd arrived. *I tied it with a pretty blue ribbon.*

THE ENVELOPE IS CRIMPED and scotched and sadly corrugated, a rumpled plane, graciously embrasured. The rain clouds have not yet rolled out from land to conceal the moon; its light bleeds up from the ocean. The postmark is legible—*New York, New York.* There it is, not quite faded, not quite lost—in one corner, May 28, 1984, in the other, my address, my name, his handwriting.

Eveline Aster Auerbach

The last time he and I will touch the same object, an article with intention and direction, an article in time, with energy passing from him to me—*life*. The seal. The last glue of his saliva, his pattern, his key. Is the package a test, does it dare me to open it, to betray what I know, to assign value to an object not rightfully mine? Do I make permanent what is best left forgotten? Do I separate the object from its source, bringing it into its own era, making it universal, making it art? Do I attend to my trespasses—do I save *it* when I did not save *him*?

The water slaps the jetty, filling in around my feet, soaking the bottom of my jeans. The ocean. Him drifting, him alone. Alone again, alone some more. Hundreds of thousands of miles. Blue frost, blue floes. I honestly don't see the difference—drowning there, or drowning here. One sea, another sea.

I hold my breath. I close my eyes. The flap doesn't open easily. I have to tear it apart. The contents slide into my hand—Jack's black book. It's been so long. The cuts and the scratches, so many more than there had been. It looks like a picture of itself, like something other than the thing that it was. It looks *deepened*. I flip through, going first to the last page, because there are things I know and have always known that cannot be explained, such as the ways of his mind. Two blocks of writing; a letter and a song. And the card: *Eveline*. The song is thirty-eight words alongside notations and dense, uneven bars. The song is mine. The song I will not share.

Jack's letter is written as if the pen never left the paper. Often we would write that way.

> *for the girl in despair*
> *you must be in despair*
> *foreigners always are and you are*
> *a visitor to compromise, a seer, pity me i couldn't*
> *build a life to keep you in it.*
> *beyond experienced time*
> *and lived time there is pure time*
> *together we found it what we found you can find again*
> *every man needs to be a hero, i learned*
> *by your eyes we all want the secret of your eyes*
> *—it's better to love than be loved.*
> *you are the supreme generous and brave like hell*
> *for giving the only gift that matters*
> *the soul the soul transcends this is a fact because here*
> *in the last minutes there is only you.*
> *and so i'll be a bird to find a bird,*
> *since a bird is what you'll be.*
> *you'll know me, i'll say,*
> *there was a girl, there was a life*
> *I used to lead in the grass in the sand through the air beneath the sky*

under the waves through the rain
through the wind, and the wind oh, the wind. I'll say,
you remind me of the wind.
until we meet again, listen for me,
I will sing to you nightly.
—you are so pretty but be pretty when you wanna be.

p.s. this is not a note of why i'm doing this since
you know that every time i cried no one came
only you made me numb, music made me numb and
dope made me numb—but you and music, well,
you have to practice that, play at it night and day
and dope, jesus,
the shitty illiterate company you have to keep—
the one reassuring constant for me has been
the bizarre grandiosity of my despair it is
the closest thing i have to a friend.
a few messages to all the derelicts and the limbless losers,
all the fakers at the funeral—
to my father—nothing, he is Satan in plaid.
to my mother—that's good just like that. To my mother—
to liz—those records are not for you they're for your kids
tell dan take it easy and tell smokey pick up a box i left for him at
Jeff's on 14th street. And tell jewel, i don't know, you'll think of
something good.
tell Rene thanks for going in where no one else would go—
i've done what i had to do tried to make it right can't think of
anything else for what it's worth i loved you i love you don't come i
don't want you here it is not good here.

I reach to the air. Feeling for his remains, the spiraling iris of his body, the fineness of his being like threads to weave night. My hands return to my cheekbones. My bones are barriers, my skin a blanket. The wind draws down. Am I mad—I must be mad. I want to run. I want to run fast and far, the ground spilling beneath. I want to trample the spine of the earth. To move forward to prior points. To arrive at the day he died, at the place his body lay. I will fit his brains back through the hole made by the bullet, careful to maintain as I go one continuous stream of mind. I will lift his remains. I will take him once more into my arms, and I will find a tree. He always loved trees. I will prop him, ever so gently, ever so, and while he rests I will scrub the woods on my hands and knees, marking with my toil the place of his last—

And running more, running again. Like some brilliant animal, I will move and reach by traveling. Arriving at all that was said and done to make me lose as I've lost. Again, running. Until I collapse. Until a wall, there must be a wall.

I CIRCLE THE BLOCK twice checking for Rourke's car. When I'm sure it's not there, and that Rob's car is not there, I ride my bike onto the front lawn, leaning it alongside the porch. I enter the main house from the side, through the laundry room. The dishwasher is churning and cleaned crystal glassware is stacked on the pantry counter. There is the radio, playing opera, not a nice opera. I go directly to Consuela's door. She appears in a raspberry-red terry cloth t-shirt and matching shorts. Her body is placid, her brown eyes alive. In the brown there is hopping, like invisible rabbits. Behind her, a television plays news of Connecticut. On screen is a map of Hartford. Two wildflower drawings I'd made for her look out from over the bed like mournful eyes.

I am breathless and wet. From the ocean. From riding.

She hands me a towel. "You need some water?"

"I'm okay," I say. I thank her. For everything. Quickly. There's not a lot of time. The flowers in the cottage, the careful pressing of my laundry, the foods she knows I'll eat. "It's been very hard."

Her eyes twinkle. Rabbits hopping. "Yes, dangerous for you."

"I hope you can bring your son." Her son is in a village outside of Bogotá, he is five. She left him with her husband, who died one week after she went away. "Alcohol," she confided when we first spoke of it. "When I leaving I begging him not to kill himself. *Take care of the baby,* I say. But anyway, he kill himself. That was with the drinking. Now I talk to my son on the phone but he don't know me," Consuela said. "He calling my sister, *Mommy.*"

"Goodbye, Consuela. I'll miss you."

"I miss you too," she says, as though I'd already gone, which I suppose in a way, I had. "You do what you do," she states, not meaning me, necessarily, but people in general.

"Yes," I agreed. "You do what you do. That's the whole tragedy."

THE MUSIC IN THE dance tent is deadened by the damp of night. People are still there, about thirty of them. Another dozen or so are in and around the pool. I pass unseen.

In the cottage hallway, the bulb is blown, and the doormat is kicked out. I straighten the mat then climb into a nest of cigar smoke. The smell is of many more cigars than Mark could have finished alone—six or seven. I wonder who has been there and whether there was a fight. Possibly there was a fight. Possibly he let people touch my things. I have the feeling he let people touch my things. A chalk-white scuff scars the base of the cherry closet on the landing. I make a note in my mind to have it repaired—then I remember—then I erase the note.

The door is open and gushing around is the maudlin sound of Roxy Music. In the living room I confront the same odious illumination from the tents that fills the hall behind me. I feel I'm equalizing atmospherically with what I've left behind, which is like returning to your seat in a stadium after using the bathroom.

And the background's fading out of focus
Yes the picture's changing every moment
And your destination you don't know it. Avalon.

Mark is on the terrace, specterlike against the artificial radiance in his seven-hundred-dollar tux, leaning back in his chair, legs on the wooden rail. He looks exhausted, but like a movie director surveying the glow of a just-emptied set, like he is the master of his exhaustion. Like he has executed it, earned it. It is his product, proof of his capacities. His hair falls like sand strings around his face, in a line against his cheekbones, making a mark like a crosspiece of skin, a scar. His hair is nice hair, straight except around the edges where it curls now that it's long. It's just hair, I tell myself. His eyes, only eyes.

Remarkably, I feel a failure of nerve.

Though leaving him is something I expected, it's honestly no less traumatic than something unexpected—the grief of losing Rourke, losing Jack, of cherished things passing—Maman and a baby. When I ask myself whether I love Mark, the answer is yes. I love because I have loved. Because we were brought together, because we stayed together, because we are, in dark regions, compatible. Whether or not ours has been a parasitic compatibility, it has been an enduring one, and the sense that he is mine is exceptionally clear.

Mine, not mine—possession has always been hard for me to assess. There are things we feel we must possess; we believe that they define us. And yet there are the things that chance would have us possess, these also define us. The difference between the two is like owning the tree you have purchased for your yard versus owning the bird who comes to nest in it. I don't know which is more true, more real. I know only that the gentler obtainments enter you, they live and die with you. *The soul transcends*, Jack said in his letter. This is so. I do dream of Jack as though he is mine, though of course he is gone and has been gone—lost first, then dead. I dream that we have a secret and we do. The secret is all that we've shared, that we've known, moments only we have seen.

I sit alongside Mark. Together we watch the wedding's uncivilized conclusion—girls in wet dresses shivering by the side of the pool and guys in pink shirts arguing across cocktail tables. The commotion that occurs in front of the balcony could be miles away. In the space around us there is a sick still, curious and taciturn, like the violence of silence after a bomb blast. I want to tell him that I'm sorry. In his mind he owned the tree, in my mind I filled the nest. Maybe I might have changed that. With my will I might have.

"They told me about a girl," Mark says, wiping his jaw with the back of his wrist, thrusting his hand into my space. His hand is brown from sun and the hairs are red like iodine. I know the weight of that hand, the sting of it. "A girl," he laughs. "Some girl."

It doesn't surprise me that he goes back to the night we met. I'd gone there too, the previous evening in my mother's kitchen. He speaks as if responding to my half of that conversation. He speaks with abandoned reluctance, as if tired of feigning ignorance to my position, bored with keeping my state of mind separate from his state of mind, which is, in fact, the state of reality.

"In your cheap thrift store clothes. In that shitty little shack by the train." He gazes into his drink, a full clear glass—vodka. I look for a bottle. I see broken pieces, a toppled chair. "God, you could dance," he says, looking left, searching my face, outstaring me. "I felt like I was fucking you already."

His legs drop off the rail, slapping the deck. He leans onto his knees and liquor splashes on the leg of his pants. He tries to brush it off but it absorbs. Or the *pants* absorb. I'm not sure. "I thought he'd try to kill me that night. When he didn't, I knew I'd won. He didn't want you seeing him for what he is. An animal. I told you—*he's a liar*."

I go to the railing; Mark follows. In the tuxedo he seems smaller, shoe-black and knife-like. Like he is slicing through the haze. It's the lapels, the razor gloss of the lapels. I have the feeling I've taken part in a lock-down. This is how Jack felt his whole life. Like he'd taken part in a lock-down.

"*Bernadette*," Mark hisses cryptically. "Do you remember?"

"On the jukebox."

"You said you would never be loved so much."

"You said you doubted it."

"Do you know why?" Mark asks.

"Because you knew how you felt about me?"

"Because I knew how *he* felt about you."

The last belt of party lights stops down, causing him to look sharp, only in part, like origami unfolding. I see the package creasing outward, I see the underlying business, the pieces of his prison, the constitutional looseness. He laughs. Not really. Not a laugh at all.

"The problem was he knew nothing about you. He thought you were independent. You're too insecure to be independent. He thought you would wait. You're too impatient to wait."

That's funny—*impatient*. I'd been waiting for years. I'd wait forever.

"You don't think you're impatient? Think again. Every time he hesitated, you penalized him. The first night we met. A year later, when he took off the second time. That's why I never wait. I make sure not to. 'Timing is everything to you,' you always tell me. No—timing is everything to *you*. I'm just a fast learner."

I listen closely. Mark is good at talking. His reasoning is specious, but beneath the sophistry there is always a plan. I try to think of the plan. I can't tell—is the plan to win, or simply not to lose?

"I did my part," he says. "Affection, distraction. I led the way. You refused to follow. You stayed faithful in your mind. I let you have your mind. Frankly, the mind is overrated when you have the body. Too bad your loyalty didn't register with him. The only place that counts to a man like that is *this*." He slaps his hand between my legs, stroking upwards to my pubic bone, stopping and jamming in at the wrist. The heel of his palm hits my low belly, and his fingertips shoot up into the flesh of me. Using that axis, he clamps down, pulling. Mark whispers, "He won't forgive you."

I knock the inside of his elbow to break his hold, but he bends away, then returns, tighter and harder, closing the gap between us.

"He knew I'd get to you. He came back that summer to infect you. I infected you back. I gave you more than money. I reversed a history of neglect. I trained you to live on impulse. You want to drive—have a car. You want shoes—buy six pair. You want to paint—don't work. You want food—there's more than you can eat. What are you going to do now? Work in a restaurant? Sell your art at yard sales? Face it. You can't go to him. He can't afford you." Mark's face closes down quick on the right in a sort of spasm. "Go anywhere you like. The world will be empty without me."

He releases me but doesn't move. It's a dare. If I go back, he'll grab me. I stand, we stand, not moving. Three or four inches between us. I can see the broken glass, very near our feet. I bend straight down to pick it up, my body in a line, and he lets me. I get the circular base and use it as a canister for the rest. There are two stems among the shards. Maybe there was a toast, one of those violent toasts. It occurs to me that Mark isn't slurring. That he's perfectly sober. He doesn't even smell like liquor. The drink in his hand is the first.

He grabs a fistful of my hair and jerks me forward. I fall to my knees, swinging the hand with the glass in time, keeping the palm raised. Mark holds my skull, and he shoves my face against his thighs. I reach blindly to the rails, and twisting my hand through the bars, I let go of the glass. You can hear it crack against the brick below.

"Bleeding on the streets," he says. "Destitute." He spits when he talks. Specks of saliva prick the back of my neck. For a second I thought it was the rain. "Without that abortion you would have ended up dead. Like your junkie friend."

The smell of his penis through his pants, like detergent—I pull my face away. "It wasn't an abortion."

"Spare me the revision. If your body hadn't had the sense to dispose of the offending organism, you would've killed it anyway. You wouldn't have gone to him. You *couldn't* have. And though I was happy to pay for an abortion, I never would have raised his offspring. You might have taken it to your mother, she relishes in sub-social behaviors, but you'd just gotten out. You had no intention of going back. And, by the way, you could have called *anyone* from the hospital—Dennis, your aunt, Sara Eden, even asshole Rob. But you were quick. You were devious. You called *me*. You knew it would crush him. You knew I would tell. You knew how I would characterize the loss. I was impressed by the efficiency of your cruelty. I was shocked, actually, by how hard he took it." Mark bends. "He was *crying*."

He waits for a response. I say nothing. I try very hard to say nothing. And it takes everything. To say nothing.

"Didn't I tell you? He came to the apartment. To give me money. He's so *honorable*. The night of that Mexican dinner. The night I took you to my parents' place. I told him, 'I don't need your filthy money.' He said, 'Then give it to her.' I said, 'Trust me. She's not going to need it either.' He tossed it on the table. I tossed it off the balcony."

"You should have just left me in the hospital."

"No. You were too good to pass up. Besides, I liked the way you played— an eye for an eye. *Biblical.*" Mark kneels now too. He takes me down by the hair to his right. Pulling me around, following with his chest, ready to bear down. He loosens his shirt from his pants. "What did I say before, how long has it been—*a week?*"

Oh, that's the part about his not drinking. He comes and kisses me and his tongue in my throat causes me to gag. If I could scream, I would scream, but a scream—

There's a noise. Something hits the cottage. The wall or the door, I don't know, a rock or a brick. Our heads look toward the rail. In my mind is a picture of us that way, Mark and me, grafted like skin from one part of your body to another. Like living onto dead, reluctantly. "If you're thinking it's Harrison," he says in a sort of under-growl, "you're mistaken. He left with Diane. He's probably screwing her brains out right now."

I have a second, one second. I study his eyes, like discs of clay, like there is no man on the other side. I look carefully, carefully, ever-careful not to show lenience or restraint, not to enrage him further with highness or compassion. If he is a monster, I cannot help but wonder whether it was I who made a monster of him. Didn't I stay too far outside? Didn't I stay untouchable? Didn't I console him by turning slavish? Didn't I give him access to places in me that were persuadable—poverty and heartbreak—in order to stay persuaded? Did I drive him mad with control? His temptation, my consent. For me it was like climbing on, like letting go, falling. Sky-diving feels that way. At least I think it must. The plane is what you know; the sky is everything else. When you go, there's no fear. It's proof, grounds for belief—you're alive. I answered to something pre-existing in him and he in me, and so what I threaten by leaving is far deeper than the motive to hurt Rourke. And what I lose, the audacity, the mute witness—I suppose I must learn to live without it.

He peels back my shirt, and I wait patiently, like getting dressed in bandages after an injury. The water-saddled air lands onerously on my open chest, and beneath me the deck is like ice. My jeans—he starts on the buttons, there are five. Though there are five, and he knows there are five, he races through to three, and starts to pull.

I say, "Mark."

He looks up and at an angle, as if I can't be clearly heard, as if he's picking up on an echo. He did not expect this, my speaking. And it's weird, but I actually hear myself that way, *his* way, ringing out, bouncing back. I find my voice, forcing it, steering it center.

"You saved me. I wouldn't have survived without you. You never broke a promise, and you never left my side. I know you feel like you forced me into something. Like I never loved you. You didn't force me, and I do love you. It's true that I have nothing and nowhere to go. Don't you see? That's not why I *should* stay, that's why I *can't* stay. I never want anyone to do that to you."

He pauses. One hand, the hand supporting him, is on the deck—not on the deck, on *my arm*—the other lingers in broken animation on my abdomen. And my arm, I feel his bone on my bone, what bone is the bone in his palm? Is it one, or many? It seems like one, like a curved plate, like a hook-moon in his hand. His eyes are ten inches from mine. The roiled pigment runs down, bleeding out some of the soul behind. I have pierced something, and yet, he's only been stunned, not stopped. Minutes, I have minutes.

I say, "Don't let hurting me be the measure of your manhood."

Mark looks left again, then bleakens, then collapses, rolling off to the side, my side. I do not move. I stay as I've stayed for more than a thousand nights—still, staring up. These I do recall. The pressure on the bed, the lame ghost of his breathing, my ear trained to the toll of his dreams.

"I'm so fucking tired of this place," he says. "You did that to me."

"You were born that way. You're like your father."

"Like my father." He laughs. "That's brilliant."

I go on, ignoring him. "The only difference between you is that he tries to destroy himself and you try to destroy everything else."

"That must be why he hates me."

"He doesn't hate you, Mark. He envies you."

FOR THE REMAINDER, WE lie corpse-like beneath the iron templum of the Ross home, beneath the potent belt of sky defined by them and defined for them, dedicated to the collection of their omens. If I fall for a little longer within the downward projection of that vault, it's all right. I am part of their history.

The light is tarnished now from the overbearingness of clouds, but in the morning a solitary ray will puncture the pallor, making way for a choir of ultramarines—and in relief, there will be no greater beauty than that lone stroke. In the morning comes the pacific drone of the pool filter and the pre-monitory stifle of the summer air and the dry creak of wicker as his mother sits to remove her shoes and lay out her robe before she swims. The mild slap of her arms. After, the faraway tink of her spoon in a cup.

I remove the ring. I hand it to him.

"Sell it," he says, refusing to take it. "You'll need the money."

I rise in degrees, expecting his interference. I make it as far as the balcony, where I linger without fixing my clothes. I notice in spite of my vulnerability that the garden has never appeared more beautiful than at that moment, the moment of my leaving. Maybe once, maybe the first time, which is incredible when you think about it, since all through the middle it's been mine.

"You almost went through with it," Mark says from beneath. My ankles go cold. "Two more days and we'd be in Italy. We would have married there. You would have been set for life. Now you're straight back to nowhere. Cirillo fucked it up. He got in over his head. I should have loaned him the money instead of letting him bring that stupid fuck back—thirty-five grand. Pennies to keep you."

"What would you have gotten?"

"Something pure," he says. "Nothing's pure."

On my way out I leave the ring on the kitchen table. There is a substantial clink. I hear him shout, *You'll be back*.

THE RAIN BEGINS, JUST a dusting at first, like upwards-floating flurries when it snows, or hose water flying up in a fan after it hits the ground. I take my time cutting through the garden, in case he's watching, and when I see my bike, I pass it. It's harder to hide with a bike.

At the street, I run. There is a split in the air and drops fall faster. Beneath the lamplight it looks like jagged tinsel or shredded foil or chains of mercury specking down. The imprint of his touch washes from my throat and his smell from my hair and that is the water penetrating. I tell myself to hurry. The rain will force him out. He will think me likely to change my mind in the rain. At the corner I turn towards the beach, away from town. He'll go to town, to my mother's house. I'll wait under the pavilion for morning.

With the wind as I run and the rain on my face, I don't hear the sound of the tires. I only think *car* when a fortress of light encroaches from behind and my shape materializes phoenix-like on the ground. The drops fall through the light, but not in the black of my body—I am a cut-out of rain. Like one of my paper dolls.

I stop. The car stops. I start and it starts. I think to hide—a yard, a garage. I look right, for a break in the hedges. When I look back, I realize that the light is not narrow, but broad. Like a blockade. The car moves up, flanking me on the left. It is white, square. Not the Porsche. The door opens.

Rourke says, "Eveline."

Eveline—I've never heard my name like that, as though there is some obvious indivisibility between it and me. I take one instant, just one, standing in the water, learning the sound by heart, feeling—I don't know—just *feeling*.

I climb in, fall in, happy to have a friend, in the night, in the cold, and the rain, when I'm sad. A friend who is knowledgeable of my heart. A living friend. It's not the first time I've received his help. Rourke was there when I broke up with Jack, only that night was dry and I was seventeen. Things were different at seventeen. It was the other side, the side before this. We all spend time there. Rourke was there too, only when he was there, I was twelve.

And Jack's book. *My* book. In my arms.

He makes a series of deliberate turns until arriving at a private road. Soaking overgrown branches slap the windshield until that pass-through empties onto a supernatural hollow, onto a transcendent grassy plain like a moor or Scottish lowland. Directly before us is the navy water of Georgica Pond. He puts the GTO into park and reaches into the back seat for a towel, which he uses to dry me. The towel is stained with blood, blood from his eye, which now I can see. It is slit and stitched on top and awfully swollen, hemorrhaged and violet but inside black, like always, with inscrutable lights. The radio is playing "Angie." We heard it that day on the boardwalk.

> *Angie, Angie.*

"You okay?" Rourke asks.

"I'm okay."

"Would you tell me if you weren't?"

He draws the towel down my arms, not touching the book. The towel is warm. Why is the towel warm? Was it on the floor? Sometimes the floor of the GTO—it gets warm.

He says, "I didn't think so."

I ask him how long he was waiting.

"I watched you go in."

"I went in hours ago."

"About an hour and a half."

"I didn't see the car," I say.

"I wasn't in the car. I was on foot."

"By the street?"

"By the balcony. Where you were."

"Did you hear?"

Rourke looks past the steering wheel towards the pond. His profile and his jaw look like a drawing of a profile and a jaw, the lines are that hard. "I heard enough."

"He said you left with—"

"She left with her parents. He knew that." Rourke turns back to me, speaking as if of a long ago time. "It would have taken me seven seconds to scale that wall. *Five.*"

I can see that he's angry, but I know that anger does not involve or implicate me, it does not seek some premeditated gain.

"You did all right on your own," he says. "Better than I would have."

Better than I would have. That's what Mark had been waiting for. For Rourke to come. I can't even think what might have happened. So I don't.

I go onto the console between the seats. My hand reaches for the eye. He does not pull away but breathes into my touch. His normal lid flutters and beneath my fingertips the distended one throbs, as if the eye below is straining to see. The muscles stay steady in his face. Despite the diligence, there is volatility, charged affinity—like music, like science, like particles clinging richly. I hold him like he is a man but also a child, mine, my child, and we kiss and our kiss is the first, still innocent, still soft, like we dip into mystery, like our love is so delicate and alive, so primitive and original, like true love is first love. In his heart there is a girl; she is me. No contract keeps her, she goes with him, she goes alone, precipice to precipice, upon every ledge agreeing again to leap. She is with him, she has been with him, every minute, alongside. No one can know what we know. Just us. Us. If you listen, you can hear it. In the wide wide sound of the rain—*us*.

6.

WE'RE THERE FOR THREE DAYS. THERE ARE NO MESSAGES, NO CALLS. ONE CALL. One call out. I knew because there was no ring, just the sound of him on the hotel phone. *It's a woman*, I thought, *it must be a woman, or a job.* I fell back to sleep thinking, *That's funny—a woman or a job.*

We sleep in day if we sleep at all. In the day I dream of disaster. Lilting towers with blown-out windows and cars shrieking through side streets with everyone trying to get out, though there's nowhere to go. I dream of the place I dreamt of as a child—lonely, burned-out. The place you are not dependent. Home.

DARKNESS JERKS THE STREETS to life like a pullcord starting an engine. At night we walk through Manhattan—up Broadway or across Central Park or down Tenth Avenue into Hell's Kitchen, through scaffold castles, past lapsed construction sites where wet concrete dust is like whale paste and graffiti like hieroglyphs and the plywood ramps rumble and drum when you stomp them. Truckers and cabs snake against curbs looking into a horizon of half-spent neon for girls and fares, and Korean men squat on overturned buckets, peeling vegetables and spitting streams like glue to the gutter. Men pee into phone booths and the trails run back between their legs, swilling up around the soles of their shoes. The look of night in New York is the look of ruin, only with stores that are open for business.

He walks and people make way. He is fierce and exact and his face is a terrifying mass of bruised flesh. I go freely, never thinking of needing his protection or of his needing protection. If there is trouble, I do not doubt the outcome. It's like walking under an umbrella. I never realized before how frequently I am concerned for my own safety, not only physical, but psychological. For three days I claim sanctuary—I can be me, think me, show me. Here we are not strangers. We are not used. We are fearless, we are vermin, we see but are not seen. There is no civilization; nothing civil applies.

"If only there were a way to live in night," I say.

"There is no way," he says. "I tried. After you I tried."

THE SECOND NIGHT WE pass a piano bar on West Forty-fourth Street. Looking through the cabernet windows is like looking into a fish bowl with the way the view through the glass is an oval cut-out sculpted by wood. He asks if I feel like going in, and I do. It's like a place I've been before. I'd like to go back.

In there he holds me, and that is beautiful and loose-seeming. My face finds the crevice between his arm and his chest, and my cheek rests on his blue jacket where there is cologne mixed with his faintest faintest sweat. The ceiling is low. His head seems to touch.

"This one is for all you Johnny Mathis fans," the piano player says, though counting everyone, we are seven. He begins to play *Misty.*

The Ukrainian cocktail waitress leans on the piano; there are smudges in her reflection on the instrument. I know about the Ukraine because I asked and she told me. She has a visa for school and an aunt in Brighton Beach. I wonder whether I will be alone like her someday in a foreign country, living with an aunt and going to school, not necessarily for my subject. Many immigrants go to school not necessarily for their subject. I wonder whether Rourke will come for me at forty, or at forty will I be waiting.

He is looking in my eyes. I hope he feels safe. He should. That is no joke, me protecting him. I would kill to protect him.

WE TURN OFF THE air and open the windows, and the room goes hot, swallowing up the outside, like the walls have teeth. The heat is a heat where you want to break through your own skin, but the thrill of nearness keeps you in because the thrill of nearness is the thrill of difference and breaking through would make us the same when in fact we are not—we are countervailing.

I'm not sure what we're doing there in the hotel. It's like being in a command center in a war movie, one of those steel-fortified tents where the power congregates, studying maps, decoding messages, strategizing, drinking cognac. We have shut ourselves in to accomplish something brainy and strategic. We prepare, but for what?

Later we watch television, and the light that it makes is cool. The screen blinks and flickers strobe-like against the slender sprawl of night. Something happens in the show that makes us laugh. Rourke stands and turns off the set, which is correct. It is not right to laugh together. Seven minutes pass with him facing the window and me facing the clock. At nine to two the arms point up like the arms of a drum majorette, and that's when I go to him, at nine to two, and he holds me, and we hold each other, together washing away the memory of irreverence. Nothing nearer our hearts, nothing.

WHEN HE MOVES I memorize him. He eats well and sleeps well; he's moral in his motions. He is tranquil and orderly. I suppose there is nothing for him to guard against. When he touches things—buttons and keys and combs and me—he touches without false delicacy, as conscious of his strength as of the refinement of his object. I memorize him because there is no completing the picture, nature has exaggerated him evenly, finding in him her harmony.

A girl is crying. In the hall crying, *Luis, Luis*.

I see his face clear, his instinct fly to life. He sits and reaches for his jeans and his shirt, and he steers his arms back through the sleeves like a surgeon getting dressed. He buttons two buttons, moving like a sea is calling, like it is his duty. Through the closed door I hear him speak, a word or two. There is the sound of her sobbing, the sound of their voices, mixing imperfectly down the long length of the hall, rolling like stones out of range. It's some time before he comes back. I open the curtains wide and watch the room go purple as if purple dusk pouring down the building. I decide to dress. I bend to his suitcase where my clothes are kept, next to his clothes, above them and beneath them and accidentally mixed in. There is a pair of jeans and a baby blue t-shirt with a fuzzy kitten face on it and with little glue-on plastic eyes, the kind with pupils that shake. I brush back my hair and I find some lipstick in the pocket of my denim jacket. I lean out to look over West Fifty-eighth Street, thinking, *The world is mine. Why can't the world be mine, when I need no more of it than this?*

When I turn back, I find him, I see him, standing there, watching me, his body filling the door frame. A breeze coils against my back; it is the first since we arrived. And he is standing, watching, as if amazed, as if I amaze him. I will never forget his outline in the doorway of the room.

I WAKE TO THE sound of his breathing. Without opening my eyes I follow the sound like following a loose thread around the feet of furniture, tracing its source. Someone said, *Should my eyes be lost and my hearing remain, my ears could see the sound she makes.* A painter, I think. Degas. I think Degas. By Rourke's breath he is sad. I unbury my face from his arm and slide up until my chin reaches his chest, where I can see from my perch the finest distance between his eyes. Almost he speaks, but no. He lowers his head. I draw myself higher. My forehead, his lips.

"What are you thinking?"

"If we'd had a son," he says. "Would he have been gentle like you."

A COMPOSITE OF SEA pink and frost yellow light swells in through the cumbrous gold drapes, making stark avenues along the edges and down the central split. The room is like a jewel box. Air conditioning feathers out from a vent in the floor, breaking his hair apart. He sits on the edge of the bed with me curled around his back. His skin appears unusually fair. It is the sunshine against the eggplant pigment of his eye. He looks like a genetic rarity—a white wolf or the fragile product of a hothouse, though he is neither white nor fragile. There is a painting—a Caravaggio—of John the Baptist. John is naked and thoughtful—boy and man, object and subject. You feel the burden of promise, the torment that comes from being so opposite. The phenomenon of masculinity, the flush of virility, the anticipation of action, the crisis of uncertainty. He is ready; you are waiting.

"I'm sorry," I say. "About everything."

He moves when I speak, almost unseeably, stirring though he has not drifted. He is here and has been here, with me and present. At the sound of my voice—he pushes into it as if combing his head into a rush of wind. Reaching back with an arm, he finds my waist and pulls me closer. My belly meets his back, my face impresses on his thigh.

"I should never have asked him for help."

Rourke's eyes close. The bulging at the outer corners of the brows is especially pronounced, they appear more deep-set than usual. The bad one is healing. The blood has gone down and twice I saw the inside. I touch it every day, touching the lid like fairy dust, running my fingertips across, dragging over slivers of tissue. I have this idea of bringing the nerves back to life.

"He said I did it to hurt you."

"I know what he said."

"He thinks I used him."

Rourke looks at me, dipping over. I don't have to wonder what it is he sees because I feel myself appear. Like a flare cutting through space, impacting with nothing, erupting nonetheless into a sea of stars. "You had no choice," he says. "*Use* is the thing he exchanges."

In the city of muscles on his chest, there are shapes. Beneath his collarbone, a whale, surfacing. By his abdomen on the left, a flattened swan. The swan's body is a grim puncture at the base of his rib cage. The mangled neck arcs and twists across the trench that divides his torso deeply. I move in, coming in around his naked hipbone, placing my cheek on his thigh. My weight is of no consequence to him, yet I know my impression is deep. I touch his skin, paving pathways, drawing raindrops against glass, against windows, really. I'm sorry he feels guilty, sorry he thought I'd be better off. Somehow it made sense to him that Mark should win. It proved his worst fears—the value of money and lies, the uselessness of strength and character. Maybe now it's different. Maybe I'd come to him to help him. That would be nice, to have come for a reason, to have been sent.

"I'm not sure how far back to go," he says. "How much I should ask."

His throat stretches to the ceiling, his vision going through to Heaven. Is he asking for help—I have the feeling he's asking for help. When he speaks, his manner is steely but not disapproving. It is just that we have come up against something he understands better than I, something he alone has infiltrated, something at the hands of which he has suffered uniquely—me.

"You could have been hurt Saturday night. But you know that." He waits, but not for an answer. "He'll be back. You know that too."

I do. That's why we didn't stop at my mother's after meeting in the rain. Rourke just drove the backroads—Wainscott, Sagaponack, Bridgehampton, crossing north over Montauk Highway and taking the coast of the bay into Southampton, where he cut back south over Route 27, going all the way through Westhampton to Flanders, past the building that is a duck. The thing about the Big Duck is that it's a roosting duck, not a walking duck. It's squat on the bottom, so you can't help but think it must be larger than it seems to be.

"Next time he comes," Rourke says, "I'll kill him." He turns remarkably still. I have seen this before. It is the stillness of necessity. Part of his training, his expertise. "Try to understand, Eveline, it would be so easy."

In a flash, Jack. Us as teenagers, at the movies. Talking about dying—no, not dying—suicide. *It would be so easy, Evie.* And leaping up, leaping forward, Father McQuail. *The rose singles out the tender. The rose is proof of the virtue of faith, the reward for tenacity. I ask you to be courageous of heart.*

I think of the freedom I've had with Rourke, the trust he placed in me, the constancy of—of it all. I consider happiness, and the fact that I have not yet earned it. Rourke is not alone in his guilt; I am also to blame. From the start I've been content to remain more conscious of his effects than his cause, which is like admiring a bridge without acknowledging the land the structure joins. He never once expected more than I could freely give, and yet I abused that. I gave away what he would not take.

I confront the myth of self-determination. Independence has not made me free, nor has it diminished my devotion. In spite of my liberty, I loved him—I love him. I think what it means to love. First, of course, there is the fact of you, then the fact of *loving* them, then somewhere along the way, the basic fact of *them*. This last fact you cannot ignore. What you do with it— accept, adore, deny or suppress—sort of determines everything. There are points of intersection, these divine assignments of the heart that complete you.

"My mother lost one of us to fighting," he explains, very slowly. "I can't let her lose another."

"I understand," I say, because truly, I do.

"I need to get back to work. I need two months to get through the games. I need to know you're going to be all right."

"What about Denny? I could go—"

"Not Denny. Not Rob. Not your mother. For the same reason you didn't want Mark near Jack. They're the ones who'll get hurt. It's the only leverage he has."

Jack. The four letters out of Rourke's mouth are like an incantation—*Jack.* I have the bizarre feeling that Jack might possibly be restored. I get this, like, heart rush and mind rush. I don't know, it's suddenly very confusing. I cover my face with my hands.

Rourke waits, a minute or two, then he draws my hands down. "You said at the funeral you have nothing to hold. That's not true. You do."

The funeral. He was there. *They* were there. Of course they were. Rob saying, *You seem shaky. You shaky?*

"We were in back," he says. "I would have come up, but you were—I didn't want to make you nervous."

I sit up, next to him, both of us sitting. Though of course I am smaller, I take my place—evenly, equally. His skin looks polished, like wood that is smooth. My skin too. It's the sweat.

"What do we do?"

Rourke says, "I thought you could go to Spring Lake."

The phone call. A woman or a job—*his mother*. His mother. The house, the baking, the books, the attic. A policeman's widow. Mark doesn't stand a chance. If *she* called for a restraining order against him, there would be no question. She probably has a gun in the house; she probably knows exactly how to use it.

"When are you coming back?"

"The games end in August. The twelfth. You can come at the end. You and Rob. If you want."

"Does she expect me?"

He nods once, like it's tough. "She's been expecting you."

Yes, I know. Her eyes, vowing to wait. Her vow matching my vow. My vow to him, unbroken since the beginning, proving me true. It's strange to be that way, that true way, and to meet another; we are so few. It's a sort of mad society. I wonder if when you sit in the backyard you can hear the sounds of her typewriter tapping through the window, like a mechanical woodpecker. That would be nice, to spend a summer there. Drawing flowers, listening to typing.

"I'd like to go to your house," I say. "It's a nice house."

One sight I never expected to see is the sight of his tears. The tears are tears of worlds that coalesce, all the things he loves—his father, his mother, me. It must feel nice to be a man and have all the things you love in one place. Even the bad eye, it cries.

THE SHEETS ARE SOFT and dry, like cooking flour when you are little and you dig in, pressing flat planes. Holding him is like unfurling in clouds or swimming in silk or crossing from air to water. He holds my thighs like he is unwilling ever to release them, and though his face is rough I feel no roughness. When he unburies himself, he crawls to me slowly but also quickly, and my torso with him on top feels like the willowy frame of a butterfly, like the crisp cable of its wings if you drew just one line. He braces himself on one elbow, his fingers going down each rib, counting them as though perhaps I've lost one since last he checked. His palm trails the underside of my left breast. He lifts it; it rises into itself. And the other side, the seam of the bra, he traces it. His face drags to center; his hair spills forward in a circle. It goes up, goes down, just for a moment, moving in time with my breath. His fist secures my hips, his knee slips up between my legs, bracing them apart. He raises himself and looks into the gap between our bodies. I look too, at the breadth of his chest tapering into the drum of his waist, at the ornaments in his abdomen, at the watery curvature of me beneath.

Then he stops. And there is nothing. Not nothing—vibrations, energy, life inside. *Da-dum, da-dum.* His heart beat, blood beat. We make one form, one flesh, one frame, one breath, and our hands, my hands, his face, his jaw, his hair, my eyes. For the first time, I can see through to the other side.

He breathes in. He wants something. Forgiveness, but I will not give it. He took care of me as best he could, better than anyone ever. There is a piece of me he preserved, the only piece that mattered.

"The first time I saw you," he says tentatively, as if somehow breaking a promise, "was like seeing a river. It's like you were there but not there, in front of me, but gone. Something that could be touched but not held. I never wanted anything so much in my life."

THE CAR IS BROUGHT to the hotel entrance, and he helps me in. The door closes and also the trunk and those closing sounds join other closing sounds from cabs and luggage going down and in the heat it makes a thick and thumping collage. Inside we sit very near, and we watch the landscape change from peaked and uneven to crouched and identical. There is that colossal cemetery, like a knee-high metropolis, with its skyscraper tombstones and all the unknown dead. We drive beneath furry tails of jet exhaust, letting every car pass. Even schoolbuses outpace us. If he is trying to miss his plane, he won't miss it. Not today. Today we'll say good-bye. Today I feel a way I've never felt. I feel something for which there is no known word. Unless perhaps there's a Hopi term, or a hieroglyph. In a cup on the dashboard are the pieces of beach glass we found. I reach for them, pouring, palm to palm. Glass does not change, not really.

Before checking out, I'd spoken to my parents and then to Mr. Ross. I wanted to call, and Rourke said yes, it would be right to call.

I reached him at his office. His secretary put me through directly, which broke my heart, just a little. I didn't mention Mark, I couldn't. I guess he couldn't either, because, in fact, he didn't.

"And your things, Eveline?" Mr. Ross asked.

"I guess they're still in the cottage."

"What would you like me to do?" he asked.

"Maybe someone can take them to my mother's."

"I'll take them myself," he said. "I'd like to see your mother."

I thanked him. I felt Rourke's hand on my shoulder, staying, waiting.

"Am I overstepping if I ask whether you're all right? I'll keep your confidence, of course," Mr. Ross said. "But I do feel—well, you understand. It's as though you're—"

"I'm all right. I'm fine."

"You're with Harrison?"

"Yes, sir, I am."

"Well, then," he said, and he repeated, "Well, then." He didn't sound sad, but he didn't sound happy, he sounded like he felt what I felt, which was a little of both. "I suppose it was meant to be."

"Yes, I think so," I said, and I thanked him again, from the bottom of my heart, I thanked him. Those were the last words we ever spoke. Six months later he was dead.

MINUTES REMAIN. I DON'T think to fill them. If there are thoughts, they are late as they arise, like practical ideas after they are practical. My mind draws pictures. The house I was born into—a brownstone, an unseen door leading long to an apartment on the left, another door, a couch behind it, a window at a ten o'clock angle, the television my father watches at night, the one she collapses in front of, crying when the President is assassinated. A walk-in closet where he keeps his tools, where there is a window—is there a window, or just the idea of one? North to the kitchen is the bathroom, the tub where I play when I bathe, twirling and sliding, up and down, and past it she walks, walking by, singing. When there is music that means he is gone, my father, gone. There was no music when he was there. Her legs, the door. Another bath, another night. Is she smiling; is she nice; I do not see her; instead, it is me I see. From my eyes, into my eyes, which is strange. I see into the tub, and also I see out, my head dipping back, my body straight to make an arrow, the white of the room, the white of the water, the white of her legs, and me, the feel of me, an angel, to that point immaculate, and to this, immaculate still— aren't we all immaculate? I remember a haunting tune that haunts me still.

> *When you're lost in the rain in Juarez—*

And morning. Morning is cold, mornings always are, my clothes warming on the open oven door, me sitting in front, me wrapped in a blanket while she moves singing still. There is one dress of magenta velvet, one dress she made. It has a tiny trail of flowers on the collar, and the colors, to this day I try to paint the colors. I can't help it, they come to me, dropping down, melting down as if from a block of colored ice that hangs above my head.

In another home, I am five. Five is not three. Three is when you see things and do not know enough to remember. Five is when you see and try to forget. My parents stand together, which means I am sick. A doctor is there. It is the first time my temperature is taken by mouth and there is a discussion about that, and I am embarrassed to be grown. Another Sunday in that same room, my father returns me after the weekend, and they talk in the hall. I am not there, not there, I am someplace in my head and in my heart. A world faraway. I draw and I draw, my face very close to the paper and when I erase, he comes by, my dad, that is. *Not too fast, Evie, you'll tear the paper.*

And other places, other homes, all with the same reeling sense of loneliness and sorrow that I felt until Rourke. How he is connected, I don't know, I may never know. I suppose it is the thing I seek. I suppose it is this seekingness that he answers.

I look up to Rourke; he is driving. "The first time I saw you," I say, "I had a premonition. I knew the waiting was over. I'd found the thing I'd been waiting for, though I didn't even know that I'd been waiting. The next time I saw you, it was the same. And every time after has been the same."

The hand on my hip takes me tighter.

"I don't want to lose you."

"You won't," he says. "You can't."

AT THE TERMINAL, HE gets out. I get out too. The sun beyond the concrete awning is high and hot, though there is wind. There is always wind at JFK, even in the most stygian heat. I tie my sweater around my shoulders, and I go to the curb, leaning on the car. I slide my sunglasses to the crown of my head and I wait—for nothing really. And the feeling of nothing is so profound, so sure, it's like a guarantee.

He draws out his bags from the trunk. There are two, one is a garment bag. The trunk closes, *thoom*. One of his hands holds the luggage straps and with his free arm he reaches for me. When we hold each other I feel it everywhere, low and high. I go closer, and he comes in as well. I remember looking out the window for animals in the night, for creatures keeping warm beneath leaves; I remember being relieved that they could. I hope that we are that way, he and I, that we'll be okay, like nature in nature. I hope that love is a miracle, this love and all love and especially love that is contingent upon nothing, love enriched so wholly by concessions. Rourke looks at me with gratitude, I suppose for my faith. It's nice to see myself in the effect of my ways. *Every man wants the secret of your eyes,* Jack wrote. *It's better to love than be loved.* He kisses me—once, twice, dragging his lips to my cheek, inhaling. And his hair, I touch it. I will miss his hair.

A voice comes, a mechanical voice. Such voices originate from concrete nests where people with wired necks and eyes like terriers watch through walls and envy the things you do. The revolving door. Ten steps to the terminal. My thighs brush one against the other.

He hands me the keys to the car. "You know where you're going?"

"Yeah," I say, touching the GTO—careful, like it's alive. "I know."

"August," Rourke says.

"August," I say, "yes." August.

I go on my toes, and he comes somewhat down—we meet. My lips print against his lips, soft, the stain of my devotion. And then he goes. I follow him through the lens of the terminal glass, watching him fold in and fold away. How meager the bags look, how small the crowd. The bodies and faces are real, and the colors, real, and the stories real, and yet, only he stands out.

THREE PLANES MARK THE horizon. It's roulette to guess which is his. Planes are modern angels, silver-winged and supernatural, righteous and uplifting, carrying away cargo that is precious. I don't like to think of him there, in metal airborne, in machinery overhead, though it is right for him to vanish this way, cutting through the flat dividing lines of time, soaring into a place that is prismatic and imaginary, like the end-glass of a kaleidoscope—the West.

And me. Does he search the paling membrane of the planet from the brightness of his cabin? Does he find me, can he see, do I appear—miniscule, anonymous, indigent? Does he see the way I become? And I forgot to thank him. In August I will thank him—for leaving me rich, for leaving me courageous, a fighter. For leaving me with everything I've ever ever wanted. I land with my feet on the soil of a nation. I am an American girl.

"Oh Jack," I say out the car window, the wide world flying by. "Now that you are gone, I swear to be filled with twice the life."

ACKNOWLEDGEMENTS TO THE FIRST EDITION

ANTHROPOLOGY OF AN AMERICAN GIRL
was edited by Mary Peters and Hillery Hugg,
and also by Daniel Halpern
I am deeply grateful to have been the recipient of their creative care.

THIS BOOK
was printed by Match, Fine Print, New York City.
Lay-out and design by Vernacular Press.
The typeface is Hoefler Text, Hoefler Foundry, New York.

WRITING A BOOK
is really hard to do.
This project could not have been accomplished
without the help of my closest friends.

MY PROFOUND THANKS
to my beautiful children, Vee, Emmanuelle, and Rainier
for their otherwordly patience,
to Deborah, Mary, and Christine
for loyalty, companionship, and good advice always,
to Penelope and Stephen, for their faith in me,
to Leah, Lisa, Marco, Dave and Amy, Sandy, and Jill for encouragement,
to M.D.N. for early inspiration,
a special thanks to my friend Jovan for her generous help,
to Brenna for the proofreading,
to Margaret and Rose and Nina and Z, for kind support,
to Melissa, Kristina, and Daniel for being there during the hardest months,
to my parents, who have always believed I can do anything,
again, to James for his selfless contributions to this project,
and lastly, to my dear friend Francine—Maman—
for taking care of me when I needed it most.

ACKNOWLEDGEMENTS

QUOTES

Page 13	LITTLE GIDDING, T. S. Eliot
Page 41	SOURCE - PUBLIC ADDRESS, Kurt Vonnegut, Jr.
Page 84	EVANGELINE, Henry Wadsworth Longfellow
Page 165	STRANGERS TO OURSELVES, Julie Kristeva
Page 165	SEDUCTION, Jean Baudrillard
Page 169	A VISIT FROM SAINT NICOLAS, Clement Clark Moore
Page 190	THE POEMS OF EMILY DICKINSON, Emily Dickinson
Page 207	OUR TOWN, Thornton Wilder
Page 207	SONNET XCIV, William Shakespeare
Page 345	THE MASS ORNAMENT, Sigfried Kracauer
Page 345	THE MYTH OF SISYPHUS, Albert Camus
Page 423	SOME MEMORIES OF DRAWING, Georgia O'Keefe
Page 494	TAO TE CHING, Lao Tzo
Page 497	ROMANS 6:23, The Bible
Page 519	SONNET XXXI, William Shakespeare
Page 519	THE ELEMENTS OF DRAWING, John Ruskin
Page 542	ANATOMY OF MELANCHOLY, Richard Burton
Page 555	THE JOURNEY OF THE MAGI, T. S. Eliot

FILMS

Page 35	AMADEUS, 1984, Directed by Milos Forman
Page 35	A PASSAGE TO INDIA, 1985, Directed by David Lean
Page 50	THE STING, 1973, Directed by George Roy Hill
Page 51	STAR WARS, 1977, Directed by George Lucas
Page 53	L'AVVENTURA, 1961, Directed by Michelangelo Antonioni
Page 57	GIDGET, 1959, Directed by Paul Wendkos
Page 57	GREASE, 1978, Directed by Randal Kleiser
Page 73	JULES AND JIM, 1962, Directed by François Truffaut
Page 82	MEAN STREETS, 1973, Directed by Martin Scorsese
Page 86	THE AMITYVILLE HORROR, 1979, Directed by Stuart Rosenberg
Page 113	NOTORIOUS, 1946, Directed by Alfred Hitchcock
Page 120	BIG WEDNESDAY, 1978, Directed by John Milius
Page 127	THE SMILING MADAME BEUDET, 1928, Directed by Germaine Dulac
Page 146	ROSEMARY'S BABY, 1968, Directed by Roman Polanski
Page 156	SATURDAY NIGHT FEVER, 1977, Directed by John Badham
Page 180	THE ROCKY HORROR PICTURE SHOW, 1975, Directed by Jim Sharman
Page 202	THE BIG SLEEP, 1946, Directed by Howard Hawks
Page 202	THE MALTESE FALCON, 1941, Directed by John Houston
Page 211	THE HUSTLER, 1961, Directed by Robert Rossen
Page 212	NOSFERATU, 1929, Directed by F.W. Murnau
Page 320	RAGING BULL, 1980, Directed by Martin Scorsese
Page 390	NIGHT OF THE LIVING DEAD, 1968, Directed by George A. Romero
Page 398	THE GODFATHER, 1972, Directed by Francis Ford Coppola
Page 404	GILDA, 1946, Directed by Charles Vidor
Page 406	IT'S A WONDERFUL LIFE, 1947, Directed by Frank Capra
Page 406	MIRACLE ON 34TH STREET, 1947, Directed by George Seaton
Page 505	BREATHLESS, 1961, Directed by Jean-Luc Godard
Page 564	THE BIG HEAT, 1953, Directed by Fritz Lang